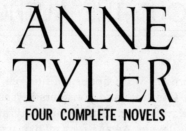

ANNE TYLER

FOUR COMPLETE NOVELS

ABOUT THE AUTHOR

ANNE TYLER was born in Minneapolis, Minnesota, in 1941, but grew up in Raleigh, North Carolina, and considers herself a Southerner. She graduated Phi Beta Kappa from Duke University at age nineteen, and twice won the Anne Flexner Award for creative writing. She has done graduate work in Russian studies at Columbia University and worked for a year as the Russian bibliographer at the Duke University Library.

Miss Tyler has published eleven novels, and her stories have appeared in such magazines as *The New Yorker, The Saturday Evening Post, Redbook, McCall's, Harper's,* and *The Southern Review.* Her most recent novel, *Breathing Lessons,* won the 1989 Pulitzer Prize. She is married to a psychiatrist, Taghi Mohammed Modarressi; she and her husband live in Baltimore, Maryland, with their two children.

ANNE TYLER

FOUR COMPLETE NOVELS

DINNER AT THE HOMESICK RESTAURANT

MORGAN'S PASSING

THE TIN CAN TREE

IF MORNING EVER COMES

WINGS BOOKS
New York

This edition contains the complete and unabridged texts of the original editions. They have been completely reset for this volume.

This omnibus was originally published in separate volumes under the titles:
Dinner at the Homesick Restaurant, copyright © 1982 by ATM, Inc.
Morgan's Passing, copyright © 1980 by Anne Tyler Modarressi
Grateful acknowledgment is made to Warner/Chappell Music, Inc. for permission to reprint an excerpt from the lyrics to "Five Hundred Miles" by Hedy West. © 1964 ATZAL MUSIC, INC. (Renewed). All rights on Behalf of ATZAL MUSIC, INC. Administered by UNICHAPPELL MUSIC, INC. All rights controlled by Unichappell Music, Inc. (Rightsong Music, Publisher). International copyright secured. All rights reserved. Used by permission.
The Tin Can Tree, copyright © 1965 by Anne Modarressi
If Morning Ever Comes, copyright © 1964 by Anne Modarressi
All rights reserved.

This 1990 edition is published by Wings Books, distributed by Outlet Book Company, Inc., a Random House Company, 225 Park Avenue South, New York, New York, 10003 by arrangement with Alfred A. Knopf, Inc.

Printed and bound in the United States of America

Library of Congress Cataloging-in-Publication Data

Tyler, Anne.
    Anne Tyler : four complete novels / by Anne Tyler. — 1990 ed.
        p.   cm.
    Contents: Dinner at the Homesick Restaurant — Morgan's passing —
    The tin can tree — If morning ever comes.
    ISBN 0-517-03204-X
    I. Title.
    PS3570.Y45A6   1990
    813'.54—dc20   90-195
                                                                                    CIP

8 7 6 5 4 3

CONTENTS

DINNER AT THE HOMESICK RESTAURANT

1

MORGAN'S PASSING

225

THE TIN CAN TREE

443

IF MORNING EVER COMES

597

DINNER AT THE HOMESICK RESTAURANT

CONTENTS

1 Something You Should Know 5

2 Teaching the Cat to Yawn 28

3 Destroyed by Love 51

4 Heart Rumors 85

5 The Country Cook 98

6 Beaches on the Moon 125

7 Dr. Tull Is Not a Toy 139

8 This Really Happened 160

9 Apple Apple 191

10 Dinner at the Homesick Restaurant 206

1
SOMETHING YOU SHOULD KNOW

WHILE PEARL TULL was dying, a funny thought occurred to her. It twitched her lips and rustled her breath, and she felt her son lean forward from where he kept watch by her bed. "Get . . ." she told him. "You should have got . . ."

You should have got an extra mother, was what she meant to say, the way we started extra children after the first child fell so ill. Cody, that was; the older boy. Not Ezra here beside her bed but Cody the troublemaker—a difficult baby, born late in her life. They had decided on no more. Then he developed croup. This was in 1931, when croup was something serious. She'd been frantic. Over his crib she had draped a flannel sheet, and she set out skillets, saucepans, buckets full of water that she'd heated on the stove. She lifted the flannel sheet to catch the steam. The baby's breathing was choked and rough, like something pulled through tightly packed gravel. His skin was blazing and his hair was plastered stiffly to his temples. Toward morning, he slept. Pearl's head sagged in the rocking chair and she slept too, fingers still gripping the ivory metal crib rail. Beck was away on business—came home when the worst was over, Cody toddling around again with nothing more than a runny nose and a loose, unalarming cough that Beck didn't even notice. "I want more children," Pearl told him. He acted surprised, though pleased. He reminded her that she hadn't felt she could face another delivery. But "I want some extra," she said, for it had struck her during the croup: if Cody died, what would she have left? This little rented house, fixed up so carefully and pathetically; the nursery with its Mother Goose theme; and Beck, of course, but he was so busy with the Tanner Corporation, away from home more often than not, and even when home always fuming over business: who was on the rise and who was on the skids, who had spread damaging rumors behind his back, what chance he had of being let go now that times were so hard.

"I don't know why I thought just one little boy would suffice," said Pearl.

But it wasn't as simple as she had supposed. The second child was Ezra, so sweet and clumsy it could break your heart. She was more endangered than ever. It would have been best to stop at Cody. She still hadn't learned, though. After Ezra came Jenny, the girl—such fun to dress, to fix her hair in different styles. Girls were a kind of luxury,

Pearl felt. But she couldn't give Jenny up, either. What she had now was not one loss to fear but three. Still, she thought, it had seemed a good idea once upon a time: spare children, like spare tires, or those extra lisle stockings they used to package free with each pair.

"You should have arranged for a second-string mother, Ezra," she said. Or she meant to say. "How shortsighted of you." But evidently she failed to form the words, for she heard him sit back again without comment and turn a page of his magazine.

She had not seen Ezra clearly since the spring of '75, four and a half years ago, when she first started losing her vision. She'd had a little trouble with blurring. She went to the doctor for glasses. It was arteries, he told her; something to do with her arteries. She was eighty-one years old, after all. But he was certain it could be treated. He sent her to a specialist, who sent her to someone else . . . well, to make a long story short, they found they couldn't help her. Something had shriveled away behind her eyes. "I'm falling into disrepair," she told the children. "I've outlived myself." She gave a little laugh. To tell the truth, she hadn't believed it. She had made the appropriate sounds of dismay, then acceptance, then plucky cheer; but inwardly, she'd determined not to allow it. She just wouldn't hear of it, that was all. She had always been a strong-willed woman. Once, when Beck was away on business, she'd walked around with a broken arm for a day and a half till he could come stay with the babies. (It was just after one of his transfers. She was a stranger in town and had no one to turn to.) She didn't even hold with aspirin; didn't hold with depending, requesting. "The doctor says I'm going blind," she told the children, but privately, she'd intended to do no such thing.

Yet every day, her sight had faded. The light, she felt, was somehow thinning and retreating. Her son Ezra, his calm face that she loved to linger on—he grew dim. Even in bright sunshine, now, she had difficulty making out his shape. She could barely discern his silhouette as he came near her—that large, sloping body settling into softness a bit in his middle age. She felt his flannel warmth when he sat next to her on the couch, describing what was on her TV or going through her drawer of snapshots the way she liked to have him do. "What's that you've got, Ezra?" she would ask.

"It seems to be some people on a picnic," he would say.

"Picnic? What kind of picnic?"

"White tablecloth in the grass. Wicker basket. Lady wearing a middy blouse."

"Maybe that's Aunt Bessie."

"I'd recognize your Aunt Bessie, by now."

"Or Cousin Elsa. *She* favored middy blouses, I recall."

Ezra said, "I never knew you had a cousin."

"Oh, I had cousins," she said.

She tipped her head back and recollected cousins, aunts, uncles, a grandpa whose breath had smelled of mothballs. It was peculiar how her memory seemed to be going blind with the rest of her. She didn't so much see their faces as hear their fluid voices, feel the crisp ruching of the ladies' shirtwaists, smell their pomades and lavender water and the sharp-scented bottle of crystals that sickly Cousin Bertha had carried to ward off fainting spells.

"I had cousins aplenty," she told Ezra.

They had thought she would be an old maid. They'd grown tactful— insultingly tactful. Talk of others' weddings and confinements halted when Pearl stepped out on the porch. A college education was offered by Uncle Seward—at Meredith College, right there in Raleigh, so she wouldn't have to leave home. No doubt he feared having to support her forever: a millstone, an orphaned spinster niece tying up his spare bedroom. But she told him she had no use for college. She felt that going to college would be an admission of defeat.

Oh, what was the trouble, exactly? She was not bad-looking. She was small and slender with fair skin and fair, piled hair, but the hair was growing dry as dust and the strain was beginning to show around the curled and mobile corners of her mouth. She'd had suitors in abundance, more than she could name; yet they never lasted, somehow. It seemed there was some magical word that everyone knew but Pearl— those streams of girls, years younger than she, effortlessly tumbling into marriage. Was she too serious? Should she unbend more? Lower herself to giggle like those mindless, silly Winston twins? Uncle Seward, *you* can tell me. But Uncle Seward just puffed on his pipe and suggested a secretarial course.

Then she met Beck Tull. She was thirty years old. He was twenty-four—a salesman with the Tanner Corporation, which sold its farm and garden equipment all over the eastern seaboard and where he would surely, surely rise, a smart young fellow like him. In those days, he was lean and rangy. His black hair waved extravagantly, and his eyes were a brilliant shade of blue that seemed not quite real. Some might say he was . . . well, a little extreme. Flamboyant. Not quite of Pearl's class. And certainly too young for her. She knew there were some thoughts to that effect. But what did she care? She felt reckless and dashing, bursting with possibilities.

She met him at a church—at the Charity Baptist Church, which Pearl was only visiting because her girlfriend Emmaline was a member. Pearl was not a Baptist herself. She was Episcopalian, but truthfully not even that; she thought of herself as a nonbeliever. Still, when she went to the Baptist church and saw Beck Tull standing there, a stranger, glossily shaved and wearing a shiny blue suit, and he asked within two minutes if he might be allowed to call, she related it in some superstitious way to the church itself—as if Beck were her reward for attending with the

Baptists. She did not dare *stop* attending. She became a member, to her family's horror, and was married at Charity Baptist and went to one Baptist church or another, in one town or another, her entire married life, just so her reward would not be snatched away. (Didn't that maybe, it occurred to her, imply some kind of faith after all?)

Courting her, he brought chocolates and flowers and then—more serious—pamphlets describing the products of the Tanner Corporation. He started telling her in detail about his work and his plans for advancement. He paid her compliments that made her uncomfortable till she could get off alone in her room and savor them. She was the most cultured and refined little lady that he had ever known, he said, and the best mannered, and the daintiest. He liked to place her hand in his, palm to palm, and marvel at its tiny size. Despite the reputation of salesmen, he was respectful to a fault and never grabbed at her the way some other men might.

Then he received his transfer, and after that things sped up so; for he wouldn't hear of leaving her behind but must marry her immediately and take her with him. So they had their Baptist wedding—both of them out of breath, Pearl always pictured later—and spent their honeymoon moving to Newport News. She never even got to enjoy her new status among her girlfriends. She didn't have time to show off a single one of her trousseau dresses, or to flash her two gold rings— the narrow wedding band and the engagement ring, set with a pearl, inscribed *To a Pearl among Women.* Everything seemed so unsatisfying.

They moved, and they moved again. For the first six years they had no children and the moves were fairly easy. She'd gaze at each new town with hopeful eyes and think: This may be where I'll have my son. (For pregnancy, now, took on the luster that marriage had once had—it was the treasure that came so easily to everyone but her.) Then Cody was born, and moving seemed much harder. Children had a way of complicating things, she noticed. There were the doctors and the school transcripts and this, that, and the other. Meanwhile she looked around and saw that somehow, without her noticing, she'd been cut off from most of her relatives. Aunts and uncles had died while she'd been too far away to do more than send a sympathy note. The house where she was born was sold to a man from Michigan; cousins married strangers with last names she'd never heard of; even the street names were changed so she'd be lost if she ever went back. And it struck her once, in her forties, that she really had no notion what had become of that grandpa with the mothball breath. He couldn't still be living, could he? Had he died and no one thought to inform her? Or maybe they'd sent the news to an out-of-date address, three or four years behind times. Or she might have heard but simply forgotten, in the rush of some transfer or other. Anything was possible.

Oh, those transfers. Always there was some incentive—a chance of promotion, or richer territory. But it seldom amounted to much. Was it Beck's fault? He claimed it wasn't, but she didn't know; she really didn't know. He claimed that he was haunted by ill-wishers. There were so many petty people in this world, he said. She pursed her lips and studied him. "Why do you look at me that way?" he asked. "What are you thinking? At least," he said, "I provide for you. I've never let my family go hungry." She admitted that, but still she felt a constant itch of anxiety. It seemed her forehead was always tight and puckered. This was not a person she could lean on, she felt—this slangy, loud-voiced salesman peering at his reflection with too much interest when he tied his tie in the mornings, combing his pompadour tall and damp and frilly and then replacing the comb in a shirt pocket full of pencils, pens, ruler, appointment book, and tire gauge, all bearing catchy printed slogans for various firms.

Over his beer in the evening (but he was not a drinking man; don't get her wrong), Beck liked to sing and pull at his face. She didn't know why beer made him tug his skin that way—work it around like a rubber mask, so by bedtime his cheeks had a stretched-out, slackened look. He sang "Nobody Knows the Trouble I've Seen"—his favorite song. Nobody knows but Jesus. She supposed it must be true. What were his private thoughts, inside his spreading face, under the crest of black hair? She didn't have the faintest idea.

One Sunday night in 1944, he said he didn't want to stay married. They were sending him to Norfolk, he said; but he thought it best if he went alone. Pearl felt she was sinking in at the center, like someone given a stomach punch. Yet part of her experienced an alert form of interest, as if this were happening in a story. "Why?" she asked him, calmly enough. He didn't answer. "Beck? Why?" All he did was study his fists. He looked like a young and belligerent schoolboy waiting out a scolding. She made her voice even quieter. It was important to learn the reason. Wouldn't he just tell her what it was? He'd told her, he said. She lowered herself, shaking, into the chair across from him. She looked at his left temple, in which a pulse ticked. He was just passing through some mood, was all. He would change his mind in the morning. "We'll sleep on it," she told him.

But he said, "It's tonight I'm going."

He went to the bedroom for his suitcase, and he took his other suit from the wardrobe. Meanwhile Pearl, desperate for time, asked couldn't they talk this over? Think it through? No need to be hasty, was there? He crossed from bureau to bed, from wardrobe to bed, packing his belongings. There weren't that many. He was done in twenty minutes. He drew in his breath and she thought, Now he'll tell me. But all he said was, "I'm not an irresponsible person. I do plan to send you money."

"And the children," she said, clutching new hope. "You'll want to visit the children."

(He would come with presents for them and she'd be the one to open the door—perfumed, in her Sunday dress, maybe wearing a bit of rouge. She'd always thought false color looked cheap, but she could have been wrong.)

Beck said, "No."

"What?"

"I won't be visiting the children."

She sat down on the bed.

"I don't understand you," she said.

There ought to be a whole separate language, she thought, for words that are truer than other words—for perfect, absolute truth. It was the purest fact of her life: she did not understand him, and she never would.

At the time, they were living in Baltimore, in a row house on Calvert Street. The children were fourteen, eleven, and nine. They were old enough to suspect something wrong, if she didn't take care. She took infinite care. The morning after Beck left she rose and dressed, piled her hair on her head the same as always, and cooked oatmeal for the children's breakfast. Cody and Jenny ate without speaking; Ezra told a long, rambling dream. (He was the only one cheerful in the mornings.) There was some disappointment that the oatmeal lacked raisins. Nobody asked where Beck was. After all, he often left before they woke on a Monday. And there'd been times—many times—when he'd stayed away the whole week. It wasn't so unusual.

When Friday night rolled around, she said he'd been delayed. He'd promised to take them to the Midget Circus, and she told them she would do it instead. Another week passed. She had no close friends, but if she met a chance acquaintance in the grocery store, she remarked that luckily, she wouldn't have to use any meat points today. Her husband was away on business, she said. People nodded, showing no interest. He was almost always away on business. Few had ever met him.

Nights, especially Friday nights, she lay in bed in the dark and listened to the gritty click of heels on the sidewalk. Footsteps would come close and then pass. She would let out her breath. A new set of footsteps approached. Surely *this* was Beck. She knew how hesitantly he would let himself in, expecting the worst—his children's tears, his wife's reproaches. But instead, he'd find everything unchanged. The children would greet him offhandedly. Pearl would peck his cheek and ask if he'd had a good trip. Later, he would thank her for keeping his secret. He would be so easily readmitted, since only the two of them knew he'd left; outsiders would go on believing the Tulls were a happy family. Which they were, in fact. Oh, they'd always been so happy! They'd depended only on each other, because of moving around so much. It had made them very close. He'd be back.

Her Uncle Seward's widow wrote to wish her a happy birthday. (Pearl had forgotten all about it.) Pearl responded immediately, thanking her. *We celebrated at home,* she wrote. *Beck surprised me with the prettiest necklace . . . Say hello to the others,* she added, and she pictured them all in her uncle's parlor; she ached for them, but drew herself up and recalled how they had been so sure no man would marry her. She could never tell them what had happened.

Her old friend Emmaline stopped by, on her way to visit a sister in Philadelphia. Pearl said Beck was out of town; the two of them were in luck; they could talk girl-talk to their hearts' content. She put Emmaline in the double bed with her, instead of in the guest room. They stayed awake half the night gossiping and giggling. Once Pearl almost set a hand on Emmaline's arm and said, "Emmaline. Listen. I feel so horrible, Emmaline." But fortunately, she caught herself. The moment passed. In the morning they overslept, and Pearl had to rush to get the children off to school; so there wasn't much said. "We should do this more often," Emmaline told her as she left, and Pearl said Beck would be sorry he had missed her. "You know he's always liked you," she said. Although actually, Beck used to claim that Emmaline reminded him of a woodchuck.

Easter came, and Jenny had a part in her school's Easter pageant. When the day arrived and Beck was still not home, Jenny cried. Couldn't he *ever* be home? It wasn't his fault, Pearl told her. There was a war on, production speeded up; he couldn't help it if his company needed him more now. They ought to be proud, she said. Jenny dried her tears and told everyone that her daddy had to help with the war effort. The war was so old by now, grinding on; no one was impressed. Still, it made Jenny feel better. Pearl went to the Easter pageant alone, wearing a rakish, visored hat that was patterned after the hats the WACs wore.

When Beck had been gone a month, he sent a note from Norfolk saying he was fine and hoped that she and the kids did not lack for anything. He enclosed a check for fifty dollars. It wasn't nearly enough. Pearl spent a morning pacing the house. First she went over his note in her mind, picking apart his words for underlying meanings. But not much could underlie *right good apartment with hotplate* and *sales manager seems to think well of me.* Then she considered the money. Around lunchtime, she put on her coat and her WACs hat and walked around the corner to Sweeney Bros. Grocery and Fine Produce, where a CASHIER WANTED sign had been yellowing in the window for weeks. They were tickled to death to hire her. The younger Sweeney brother showed her how to work the cash register and said she could start the next morning.

When her children came home from school that day, she told them she was taking a job to fill in time. She needed something to keep her busy, she said, now that they were growing up and going off on their own more.

Two months passed. Three months. Fifty dollars a month from Beck. When the second check arrived, no letter came with it. She tore the envelope apart, thinking it must have got stuck inside, but there wasn't a word. With the third check, though, he wrote that he was moving to Cleveland, where the company planned to open a new branch. He said it was a good sign they'd decided on this transfer—or "invite," he called it. He never called it a transfer; he called it an invite. An invite to this important expansion westward. He began the letter, *Dear Pearl & kids*, but Pearl didn't show it to the children. She folded it neatly and put it with the first letter, in a hosiery box in her bureau, where even that meddlesome Cody wouldn't think to look. In the fourth envelope, again, there was only a check. She saw that he was not in *communication* with her (was how she phrased it), but was merely touching base from time to time. Really, all he was doing was saying, *Please find enclosed.* It didn't occur to her to answer him. Yet she went on saving his letters.

Sometimes she had strange thoughts that surprised her. For instance: At least I have more closet space now. And more drawer space.

At night she dreamed that Beck was new and wonderful again, someone she'd just become acquainted with. He gazed at her adoringly, overturning some unfamiliar center deep inside her. He helped her cross streets, climb steps. His hand cupped her elbow warmly or circled her waist or steadied the small of her back. She felt cherished. When she woke, her only thought was to sink back into her dream. She would keep her eyes shut. Superstitiously, she would play possum, not stirring, trying to persuade the dream that she was still asleep. But it never worked. Finally she would rise, whatever the hour, and go downstairs to make a pot of coffee. Standing at the kitchen window with her cup, watching the sky whiten over the rooftops, she would catch sight of her dark, transparent reflection—her small face and round chin that was taking on a dented look, these past few years; the worried tent of her colorless eyebrows; the pale frazzle of hair that failed to hide the crease across her forehead. That crease was not a wrinkle but a scar, the mark of a childhood accident. Oh, she was not so old! She was not so very old! But then she remembered the accident: she'd been trying to ride a cousin's bicycle, the very first in the family. A "wheel" was what they called it. Trying to ride a wheel. And here it was 1944 and bicycles were everywhere, but so modernized they were hardly the same breed of beast. All three of her children knew how to ride and would, in fact, have had bikes of their own if not for the war. How had she come so far? She had just passed her fiftieth birthday.

There was not a hope of Beck's return. He'd found someone younger, someone glamorous and merry, still capable of bearing children. They were laughing at her—at how she'd always been an old maid, really, always an old maid at heart. How she flinched when he turned to her in the dark, still startled, after all these years, by the concreteness of him—by his scratchy whiskers, salty-smelling skin, weighty body. How she had to have things just perfect, the linens on labeled shelves in the cupboard and the shades pulled evenly in the windows. How she'd never learned to let go, to give in, to float on the current of a day, but must always fuss and pull at stray threads and straighten the corners of things; and worst of all, how she *knew* she did that, knew while she was doing it, but still could not stop herself.

He was never coming back.

It was time to tell the children. She was amazed, in fact, that she'd managed to keep it from them for so long. Had they always been this easy to fool? One good thing about telling them: they would rally around her better. She didn't like to admit it but she was losing control of the boys. Instead of supporting her—taking out the garbage, helping her in various manly and protective ways—they seemed to be running wild; yes, even Ezra. They didn't even do the chores they used to do, let alone take on new ones. Cody in fact was hardly ever home. Ezra was dreamy and forgetful and would like as not walk off in the middle of a task. When she told them what was what, she thought, they'd be horrified at how they'd let her down. They'd ask why she'd hidden it all this time, what she could have been thinking of.

Only she couldn't tell them.

She planned how she would do it: she would gather them around her on the sofa, in the lamplight, some evening after supper. "Children. Dear ones," she would say. "There's something you should know." But she wouldn't be able to continue; she might cry. It was unthinkable to cry in front of the children. Or in front of anyone. Oh, she had her pride! She was not a tranquil woman; she often lost her temper, snapped, slapped the nearest cheek, said things she later regretted—but thank the Lord, she didn't expose her tears. She didn't *allow* any tears. She was Pearl Cody Tull, who'd ridden out of Raleigh triumphant with her new husband and never looked back. Even now, even standing at the kitchen window, all alone, watching her tense and aging face, she didn't cry.

Every morning, then, she went off to Sweeney Bros. She continued to wear her hat, giving the impression that she had merely dropped in and was helping out as a favor, in a pinch. As each customer approached (generally someone she knew, at least by sight), she would give a firm nod and then squint, implying a smile. She rang up the purchases efficiently while a boy named Alexander bagged them. "Thank you, and good day," she said at the end, with another shorthand smile.

She liked to seem crisp and professional. When neighbors showed up, people she knew more closely, she felt she was dying inside but she didn't lose her composure. With them she was even crisper. She had a little rhythm between the key stabbing and the sliding of groceries along the wooden counter; it kept her mind off things. If she allowed herself to think, she started worrying. Summer had arrived and her children were out of school all day. No telling what they might be up to.

At five-thirty she walked home, past crowds of youngsters playing hopscotch or huddled over marble games, past babies set to air in their carriages, women perched on their stoops fanning themselves in the heat. She'd climb her steps and be met at the door with bad news: "Jenny fell down the stairs today and bit her lower lip clean through and had to go to Mrs. Simmons's house for ice and gauze."

"Oh, Jenny, honey!"

It seemed they greeted her with disaster, saved up all their accidents especially for her. She'd want to take off her hat and shoes and fall back onto the sofa; but no, it was "The toilet's stopped up," and "I tore my pants," and "Cody hit Ezra with the orange juice pitcher."

"Can't you just let me be?" she would ask. "Can't you just give me a minute to myself?"

She'd make supper from tins she'd brought home, nothing fancy. She would listen to the radio while she washed dishes. Jenny was supposed to dry but was off playing tag with the boys. Stepping out the back door to heave her dishpan of water into the yard, Pearl paused to watch them—Cody and Jenny dark and quick, high-pitched, overcome with laughter; Ezra pale, a glimmer in the twilight, slower and more wandery in his movements. Sometimes there'd be neighbor children, too, but more often just the three of them. They stuck together, mostly.

She shampooed her hair and rinsed out a slip. Called to Cody to fetch the other two and come inside now.

Nights, she worked on the house. To look at her—an out-of-date kind of woman, frail boned, deep bosomed, as if those pout-fronted gowns of her girlhood had somehow formed her figure—you would never guess it, but Pearl was clever with tools. She patched a crack, glazed a window, replaced two basement stair treads. She mended a lamp switch and painted the kitchen cupboards. Even in the old days, she had done such things; Beck was not very handy. "This whole, entire house is resting on my shoulders," she would tell him, and she meant it as an accusation; but the thought was also reassuring, in a way. She knew that she was competent. From early in their marriage, from the moment she had realized how often they would be moving, she had concentrated on making each house perfect—airtight and rust-proof and waterproof. She dropped the effort of continually meeting new neighbors, and she stopped returning (freshly filled) the cake tins they brought over when she arrived. All she cared about was sealing up the house, as if for a hurricane. She woke nights wondering if the basement were dry, and went down barefoot to make sure. She couldn't enjoy their Sunday outings because the house might have burned to the ground in her absence. (How vividly she could picture their return! There'd be an open space where the house used to stand, and a tattered hole for the basement.) Here in Baltimore, she gathered, she was thought to be unfriendly, even spooky—the witch of Calvert Street. What a notion! She'd known such witches in her childhood; she was nothing like them. All she wanted was to be allowed to get on with what mattered: calk the windows; weatherstrip the door. With tools she was her true self, capable and strong. She felt an indulgent kind of scorn for her children, who had not inherited her skill. Cody lacked the patience, Ezra was inept, Jenny too flighty. It was remarkable, Pearl thought, how people displayed their characters in every little thing they undertook.

Hammering down a loose floorboard, with a bristle of nails in her mouth, she would let time slip away from her. It would get to be ten-thirty or eleven. Her children would be standing in the doorway all sweaty and grass stained, blinking in the sudden brightness. "Heavens! Get to bed," she told them. "I thought I called you in hours ago." But a while after they left she'd start to feel deserted, even though they hadn't been much company. She would lay aside her hammer and rise and walk the house, smoothing her skirt, absently touching her hair where it was falling out of its bun. Up the stairs to the hall, past the little room where Jenny slept, and into her own room, with its buckling cardboard wardrobe streaked to look like wood grain, the bare-topped bureau, the cavernous bed. Then out again and up more stairs to the boys' room, a third-floor dormitory that smelled of heat. The trustful sound of her sons' breathing made her envious. She turned and descended the stairs, all the way down to the kitchen. The back door stood open and the screen door fluttered with moths. Neighboring houses rang with someone's laughter, a few cracked notes from a trumpet, an out-of-tune piano playing "Chattanooga Choo-Choo." She closed the door and locked it and pulled down the paper shade. She climbed the stairs once more and took off her clothing, piece by piece, and put on her nightgown and went to bed.

She dreamed he wore that aftershave that he'd used when they were courting. She hadn't smelled it in years, hadn't given it a thought, but now it came back to her distinctly—something pungent, prickled with spice. A swaggery and self-vaunting scent, she had known even then; but catching wind of it, when he arrived on Uncle Seward's front porch to pick her up, she had felt adventurous. She had flung the door open so widely that it banged against the wall, and he had laughed and said, "Well, now. Hey, now," as she stood there, smiling out at him.

She had heard you could not dream a smell, or recall a smell in its absence; so when she woke she was convinced, for a moment, that Beck had let himself into the house and was seated on the edge of the bed, watching while she slept. But there was no one there.

Dance! Oh, I don't think so, she said inside her head. I'm in charge of this whole affair, you see, and all I'd have to do is turn my back one instant for the party to go to pieces, just fall into little pieces. Whoever it was drew away. Ezra turned a page of his magazine. "Ezra," she said. She felt him grow still. He had this habit—he had always had it—of becoming totally motionless when people spoke to him. It was endearing, but also in some ways a strain, for then whatever she said to him ("I feel a draft," or "The paper boy is late again") was bound to disappoint him, wasn't it? How could she live up to Ezra's expectations? She plucked at her quilt. "If I could just have some water," she told him.

He poured it from the pitcher on the bureau. She heard no ice cubes clinking; they must have melted. Yet it seemed just minutes ago that he'd brought in a whole new supply. He raised her head, rested it on his shoulder, and tipped the glass to her lips. Yes, lukewarm—not that she minded. She drank gratefully, keeping her eyes closed. His shoulder felt steady and comforting. He laid her back down on the pillow.

"Dr. Vincent's coming at ten," he told her.

"What time is it now?"

"Eight-thirty."

"Eight-thirty in the morning?"

"Yes."

"Have you been here all night?" she asked.

"I slept a little."

"Sleep now. I won't be needing you."

"Well, maybe after the doctor comes."

It was important to Pearl that she deceive the doctor. She didn't want to go to the hospital. Her illness was pneumonia, she was almost certain; she guessed it from a past experience. She recognized the way it settled into her back. If Dr. Vincent found out he would send her off to Union Memorial, tent her over with plastic. "Maybe you should cancel the doctor altogether," she told Ezra. "I'm very much improved, I believe."

"Let him decide that."

"Well, I know how my own self feels, Ezra."

"We won't argue about it just now," he said.

He could surprise you, Ezra could. He'd let a person walk all over him but then display, at odd moments, a deep and rock-hard stubbornness. She sighed and smoothed her quilt. It seemed he'd spilled some water on it.

She remembered when Ezra was a child, still in elementary school. "Mother," he had said, "if it turned out that money grew on trees, just for one day and never again, would you let me stay home from school and pick it?"

"No," she told him.

"Why not?"

"Your education is more important."

"Other kids' mothers would let them, I bet."

"Other mothers don't have plans for their children to amount to something."

"But just for one day?"

"Pick it *after* school. Or before. Wake up extra early; set your alarm clock ahead an hour."

"An hour!" he said. "One little hour, for something that happens only once in all the world."

"Ezra, will you let it be? Must you keep at me this way? Why are you so obstinate?" Pearl had asked him.

It only now occurred to her, under her damp quilt, to wonder why she hadn't said yes, he could stay home. If money decided to grow on trees one day, let him pick all he liked! she should have said. What difference would it have made?

Oh, she'd been an angry sort of mother. She'd been continually on edge; she'd felt too burdened, too much alone. And after Beck left, she'd been so preoccupied with paying the rent and juggling the budget and keeping those great, clod-footed children in new shoes. It was she who called the doctor at two a.m. when Jenny got appendicitis; it was she who marched downstairs with a baseball bat the night they heard that scary noise. She'd kept the furnace stoked with coal, confronted the neighborhood bully when Ezra got beaten up, hosed the roof during Mrs. Simmons's chimney fire. And when Cody came home drunk from some girl's birthday party, who had to deal with that? Pearl Tull, who'd never taken anything stronger than a glass of wine at Christmas. She sat him smartly in a kitchen chair, ignored his groans, leaned across the table to him—and couldn't think of a thing to say.

Then Cody graduated from high school, and Ezra was a sophomore, and Jenny was a tall young lady in eighth grade. Beck would not have known them. And they, perhaps, would not have known Beck. They never asked about him. Didn't that show how little importance a father has? The invisible man. The absent presence. Pearl felt a twinge of angry joy. Apparently she had carried this off—made the transition so smoothly that not a single person guessed. It was the greatest triumph of her life. My one true accomplishment, she thought. (What a pity there was no one to whom she could boast of it.) Without noticing, even, she had gradually stopped attending the Baptist church. She stopped referring to Beck in conversation—although still, writing her

Christmas cards to relatives in Raleigh, she remarked that Beck was doing well and sent them his regards.

One night, she threw away his letters. It wasn't a planned decision. She was just cleaning her bureau, was all, and couldn't think of any good reason to save them. She sat by her bedroom wastebasket and dropped in *looks like I will be moving up the ladder* and *little place convenient to the railway station* and *told me I was doing mighty well.* There weren't very many—three or so in the past year. When had she quit ripping open the envelopes with shaking hands and rapidly, greedily scanning the lines? It occurred to her that the man she still mourned, late on sleepless nights, bore no relation whatsoever to the man who sent these tiresome messages. *Ed Ball is retiring in June,* she read with infinite boredom, *and I step into his territory which has the highest per capitta income in Delaware.* It was a great satisfaction to her that he had misspelled *capita.*

Her children grew up and embarked on lives of their own. Her sons started helping out financially, and Pearl was glad to accept. (She had never been ashamed about taking money—from Uncle Seward in the olden days, or from Beck, or now from the boys. Where she came from, a woman *expected* the men to provide.) And when Cody became so successful, he bought the row house she'd been renting all these years and presented her with the deed one Christmas morning. She could have retired from the grocery store right then, but she put it off till her sight began failing. What else would she do with her time? "Empty nest," they called it. Nowadays, that was the term they used. It was funny, in her old age, to look back and see for how short a period her nest had *not* been empty. Relatively speaking, it was nothing— empty far longer than full. So much of herself had been invested in those children; who could believe how briefly they'd been with her?

When she thought of them in their various stages—first clinging to her, then separating and drifting off—she thought of the hall lamp she used to leave on so they wouldn't be scared in the dark. Then later she'd left just the bathroom light on, further down the hall of whatever house they'd been living in; and later still just the downstairs light if one of them was out for the evening. Their growing up amounted, therefore, to a gradual dimming of the light at her bedroom door, as if they took some radiance with them as they moved away from her. She should have planned for it better, she sometimes thought. She should have made a few friends or joined a club. But she wasn't the type. It wouldn't have consoled her.

Last summer, she'd been half-awakened by a hymn on her clock radio—"In the Sweet Bye and Bye," mournfully sung by some popular singer just before Norman Vincent Peale's sermonette. *We shall meet on that beautiful shore* . . . She'd slipped into a dream in which a stranger told her that the beautiful shore was Wrightsville Beach, North Carolina, where she and Beck and the children had once spent a summer vacation. They were meeting on the shore after changing into swimsuits, for the very first swim of their very first day. Beck was handsome and Pearl felt graceful and the children were still very small; they had round, excited, joyous faces and chubby little bodies. She was astounded by their innocence—by her own and Beck's as well. She stretched her arms toward the children, but woke. Later, speaking to Cody on the phone, she happened to mention the dream. Wouldn't it be nice, she said, if heaven were Wrightsville Beach? If, after dying, they'd open their eyes and find themselves back on that warm, sunny sand, everyone young and happy again, those long-ago waves rolling in to shore? But Cody hadn't entered into the spirit of the thing. *Nice?* he had asked. He asked, was that all she thought of heaven? Wrightsville Beach, where as he recalled she had fretted for two solid weeks that she might have left the oven on at home? And had she taken into account, he asked, his own wishes in the matter? Did she suppose that he wanted to spend eternity as a child? "Why, Cody, all I meant was—" she said.

Something was wrong with him. Something was wrong with all of her children. They were so frustrating—attractive, likable people, the three of them, but closed off from her in some perverse way that she couldn't quite put her finger on. And she sensed a kind of trademark flaw in each of their lives. Cody was prone to unreasonable rages; Jenny was so flippant; Ezra hadn't really lived up to his potential. (He ran a restaurant on St. Paul Street—not at all what she had planned for him.) She wondered if her children blamed her for something. Sitting close at family gatherings (with the spouses and offspring slightly apart, nonmembers forever), they tended to recall only poverty and loneliness—toys she couldn't afford for them, parties where they weren't invited. Cody, in particular, referred continually to Pearl's short temper, displaying it against a background of stunned, childish faces so sad and bewildered that Pearl herself hardly recognized them. Honestly, she thought, wasn't there some statute of limitations here? When was he going to absolve her? He was middle-aged. He had no business holding her responsible any more.

And Beck: well, he was still alive, if it mattered. By now he'd be old. She would bet he'd aged poorly. She would bet he wore a toupee, or false teeth too white and regular, or some flowing, youthful hairdo that made him look ridiculous. His ties would be too colorful and his suits too bold a plaid. What had she ever seen in him? She chewed the insides of her lips. Her one mistake: a simple error in judgment. It should not have had such far-reaching effects. You would think that life could be a little more forgiving.

Once or twice a year, even now, his letters arrived. (Though the money had stopped when Jenny turned eighteen—or two months *after* she turned eighteen, which meant he'd lost track of her birthday, Pearl supposed.) It was typical of him that he lacked the taste to make a final exit. He spent too long at his farewells, chatting in the doorway, letting in the cold. He had retired from the Tanner Corporation, he wrote. He remained at his last place of transfer, Richmond, like something washed up from a flood; but evidently he still traveled some. In 1967 he sent her a postcard from the World's Fair in Montreal, and another in '72 from Atlantic City, New Jersey. He seemed spurred into action by various overblown occasions—when man first walked on the moon, for instance (an event of no concern to Pearl, or to any other serious person). *Well!* he wrote. *Looks like we made it.* His enthusiasm seemed flushed, perhaps alcohol induced. She winced and tore the letter into squares.

Later, when her eyes went, she saved her mail for Ezra. She'd hold up an envelope. "Where's this from? I can't quite make it out."

"National Rifle Association."

"Throw it away. What's this?"

"Republican Party."

"Throw it away. And this?"

"Something in longhand, from Richmond."

"Throw it away."

He didn't ask why. None of her children possessed a shred of curiosity.

She dreamed her uncle hitched up Prince and took her to a medal contest, but she had failed to memorize a piece and stood onstage like a dumb thing with everybody whispering. When she woke, she was cross with herself. She should have done "Dat Boy Fritz"; she'd always been good at dialect. And she knew it off by heart still, too. Her memory had not faded in the slightest. She rearranged her pillow, irritably. Her edges felt uneven, was how she put it to herself. She slept again and dreamed the house was on fire. Her skin dried out from the heat and her hair seemed to sizzle in her ears. Jenny rushed upstairs to save her costume jewelry and her footsteps died away all at once, as if she'd fallen into space. "Stop!" Pearl shouted. She opened her eyes. Someone was sitting next to her, in that leather armchair that creaked. "Jenny?" she said.

"It's Ezra, Mother."

Poor Ezra, he must be exhausted. Wasn't it supposed to be the daughter who came and nursed you? She knew she should send him away but she couldn't make herself do it. "I guess you want to get back to that restaurant," she told him.

"No, no."

"You're like a mother hen about that place," she said. She sniffed. Then she said, "Ezra, do you smell smoke?"

"Why do you ask?" he said (cautious as ever).

"I dreamed the house burned down."

"It didn't really."

"Ah."

She waited, holding herself in. Her muscles were so tense, she ached all over. Finally she said, "Ezra?"

"Yes, Mother?"

"Maybe you could just check."

"Check what?"

"The house, of course. Check if it's on fire."

She could tell he didn't want to.

"For my sake," she told him.

"Well, all right."

She heard him rise and shamble out. He must be in his stocking feet; she recognized that shushing sound. He was gone so long that she began to fear the worst. She strained for the roar of the flames but heard only the horns of passing cars, the clock radio's electric murmur, a bicycle bell tinkling beneath the window. Then here he came, heavy and slow on the stairs. Evidently there was no emergency. He settled into his chair again. "Everything's fine," he told her.

"Thank you, Ezra," she said humbly.

"You're welcome."

She heard him pick up his magazine.

"Ezra," she said, "I've had a thought. Did you happen to check the basement?"

"Yes."

"You went clear to the bottom of the steps."

"Yes, Mother."

"I don't much care for how that furnace sounds."

"It's fine," he told her.

It was fine. She resolved to believe him. She soothed herself by wandering, mentally, from one end of the house to the other, cataloguing how well she'd managed. The fireplace flue was shut against the cold. The drains were clear and the faucets were tight and she'd bled the radiators herself—sightless, turning her key back sharply the instant she heard the hiss of water. The gutters were swept and the roof did not leak and the refrigerator hummed in the kitchen. Everything was proceeding according to instructions.

"Ezra," she said.

"Yes, Mother."

"You know that address book in my desk."

"What address book?"

"Pay attention, Ezra. I only have the one. Not the little red book for telephone numbers but the black one, in my stationery drawer."

"Oh, yes."

"I want everybody in it invited to my funeral."

There was a thrumming silence, as if she had said a bad word. Then Ezra said, *"Funeral,* Mother? You're not dying?"

"No, of course not," she assured him. "But someday," she said craftily. "Just in the eventuality, you see . . ."

"Let's not talk about it," he said.

She paused, assembling patience. What did he expect—that she'd go on forever? It was so tiring. But that was Ezra for you. "All I'm saying," she said, "is I'd like those people invited. Are you listening? The people in my address book."

Ezra didn't answer.

"The address book in my stationery drawer."

"Stationery drawer," Ezra echoed.

Good; he'd got it. He flicked a magazine page, said nothing further, but she knew he'd got it.

She thought of how that address book must have aged by now—smelling mousy, turning brittle. It dated back to long before her sight had started dimming. Emmaline was in it, and Emmaline had been dead for twenty years or more. So was Mrs. Simmons dead, down in St. Petersburg, Florida, and Uncle Seward's widow and perhaps his daughter too. Why, everybody in that book was six feet under, she supposed, except for Beck.

She remembered that he took a whole page—one town after another crossed out. She'd kept it up to date because she'd imagined needing to call him in an emergency. What emergency had she had in mind? She couldn't think of any that would be eased in the slightest by his presence. She'd like to see his face when he received an invitation to her funeral. An "invite," he would call it. "Imagine that!" he would say, shocked. "She left me first, after all. Here's this invite to her funeral." She could hear him now.

She laughed.

The doctor came, stamping his feet. "Is it snowing out?" she asked him.

"Snowing? No."

"You were stamping your feet."

"No," he said, "it's just cold." He settled on the edge of her bed. "Feels like my toes are falling off," he told her. "My knee bones say we're going to have a frost tonight."

She waved away the small talk. "Listen here," she said. "Ezra called you over by mistake."

"Is that so."

"I'm really feeling fine. Maybe earlier I was under the weather, but now I'm much improved."

"I see," he said. He took her wrist in his icy, wrinkled fingers. (He was nearly as old as she was, and had all but given up his practice.)

He held it for what seemed to be several minutes. Then he said, "How long has *this* been going on?"

"I don't know what you're talking about."

"Where's the phone?" he asked Ezra.

"Wait! Dr. Vincent! Wait!" Pearl cried.

He had laid down her wrist, but now he set his hand on hers and she felt him leaning over her, breathing pipe tobacco. "Yes?" he said.

"I'm not going to any hospital."

"Of course you're going."

She spoke clearly, maybe a little too loudly, directing her voice toward the ceiling. "Now, I've thought this through," she told him. "I don't want those crank-up beds and professional smells. It would kill me."

"Dear lady—"

"And you know they wouldn't be able to give me penicillin."

"Penicillin, no . . ."

"That's what I took in forty-three."

"Don't tire yourself," the doctor said. "I remember all about it."

Or maybe it was '44. But Beck had not yet left. He'd been away on a business trip, and brought back an archery set for the children. The things he spent his money on! When they were never well off, in the best of times. He took the set on their Sunday drive to a field outside the city—nailed the canvas target to a tree trunk. Oh, he never gave a thought to danger. He was not the type to lie awake nights listing all that could go wrong. Well, anyway. She couldn't say just how it had happened (she was arranging a bouquet of winter grasses at the time, as she no longer partook in sports), but somehow, she got hit. It was Cody who drew the bowstring, but that was incidental; Cody was not the one she had blamed, after the first little flurry. She blamed Beck, who through sheer thoughtlessness if not intention had shot her through the heart; or not the heart exactly but the fleshy part above it, between breast and shoulder. It was the queerest sensation, like being slapped—no sting whatsoever, but a jarring and then a disk of bright blood on her favorite blouse. "Oh!" she said, and she looked down, and went on holding her weeds. Then the pain began. Beck, white faced, pulled the arrow out. Jenny started crying. They drove straight home, forgetting to untack the target from the tree, but by the time they arrived the bleeding had stopped and it appeared there was no real danger. Pearl dressed the wound herself—iodine and gauze. Two days later, she noticed something amiss. The wound was not better but worse, inflamed, and she had a fever. Beck was on another trip, and she had to go to the doctor alone, rushing off breathless and hastily hatted because she wanted to get home again before the children returned from school. In those days, Dr. Vincent was just building up his practice after a tour of duty in the army. She remembered he still had a full head of hair, and he wasn't yet wearing glasses. He gave her a shot of penicillin—a miracle drug he'd first used overseas, he said. Walking home, she felt a tremendous sense of well-being, the way you always do when a doctor has taken upon himself the burden of your illness; but that night, she collapsed. First there was a rash, then chills, then a hazy and swarming landscape. It was Cody who called the ambulance. In the hospital, once the crisis was past, everyone acted stern and reproachful, as if it had been her fault. "You almost died," a nurse told her. But that was nonsense. Of course she wouldn't have died; she had children. When you have children, you're obligated to live. She closed her eyes against the nurse's words. Then two doctors came in and pulled up chairs beside her bed and solemnly, portentously explained about penicillin. She must never, never take it again, and must keep instructions to that effect in her pocketbook at all times. Pearl wasn't paying much heed (she was framing a request to be released, so she could get on home to her children), but she did remember they said, "Once is your limit. Twice will kill you." That impressed her. It was like something in a fairy tale—like a magic potion you could use only once and never again. And here she'd wasted it on such a paltry occurrence: a bow-and-arrow wound. No more miracles! In later years, when penicillin was a household word and her grandchildren took it for every little thing, she would go on and on about it. "Lucky you. Poor me. I'd just better not get an infection, is all I can say, or come down with strep throat or pneumonia."

Pneumonia.

There was a watery, roaring sound in her ears that made it hard to hear her own voice. She had to wait for it to subside before she spoke. "Dr. Vincent," she said.

"I'm here."

His hand was still on hers. It was no longer icy. He had warmed himself on her skin as if she were a stove. She gathered her voice and said, "Tell Ezra I'm staying."

"But—" he said.

"I know what I'm doing."

He was silent.

"Tell him," she said forcefully, "that this is nothing. You understand? I don't want any hospitals. It would kill me, just kill me to hear those loudspeakers paging doctors I have never heard of. This is just a cold. Tell him."

"Well," said Dr. Vincent. He cleared his throat. He removed his hand from her. "Are you sure?" he asked.

"I'm sure."

He seemed to be thinking. He turned away and said to Ezra, "You hear what she says?"

"Yes," said Ezra, closer than Pearl had expected.

"I suggest we call your brother and sister, though."

Pearl felt a stirring of interest.

"But if it's that serious . . ." Ezra said.

"Let's just see what happens," the doctor told him. He laid a palm on Pearl's forehead.

After that, he must have left. The roar came back to her ears and she didn't quite hear him go. She was dwelling on thoughts of Cody and Jenny; it would be lovely to have all her children together. Then suddenly a heavy chill spread across her chest. Why, she thought. Dr. Vincent is going to allow this! Yes, he's really going to allow it. This is it, then!

Surely not.

She'd been preoccupied with death for several years now; but one aspect had never before crossed her mind: dying, you don't get to see how it all turns out. Questions you have asked will go unanswered forever. Will this one of my children settle down? Will that one learn to be happier? Will I ever discover what was meant by such-and-such? All these years, it emerged, she'd been expecting to run into Beck again. How odd; she hadn't realized. She had also supposed that there would be some turning point, a flash of light in which she'd suddenly find out the secret; one day she'd wake up wiser and more contented and accepting. But it hadn't happened. Now it never would. She'd supposed that on her deathbed . . . deathbed! Why, that was this everyday, ordinary Posturepedic, not the ornate brass affair that she had always envisioned. She had supposed that on her deathbed, she would have something final to tell her children when they gathered round. But nothing was final. She didn't have anything to tell them. She felt a kind of shyness; she felt inadequate. She stirred her feet fretfully and searched for a cooler place on the pillow.

"Children," she had said. This was just before Cody left for college, the day she'd burned Beck's letters. She said, "Children, there's something I want to discuss with you."

Cody was talking about a job. He had to find one in order to help with the tuition fees. "I could work in the cafeteria," he was saying, "or maybe off-campus. I don't know which." Then he heard his mother and looked over at her.

"It's about your father," Pearl said.

Jenny said, "I'd choose the cafeteria."

"You know, my darlings," Pearl told them, "how I always say your father's away on business."

"But off-campus they might pay more," said Cody, "and every penny counts."

"At the cafeteria you'd be with your classmates, though," Ezra said.

"Yes, I thought of that."

"All those coeds," Jenny said. "Cheerleaders. Girls in their little white bobby sox."

"Sweater girls," Cody said.

"There's something I want to explain about your father," Pearl told them.

"Choose the cafeteria," Ezra said.

"Children?"

"The cafeteria," they said.

And all three gazed at her coolly, out of gray, unblinking, level eyes exactly like her own.

She dreamed it was her nineteenth birthday and that devilish John Dupree had brought her a tin of chocolates and a burnt-leather ornament for her hair. "Why, John, how cunning! Have a sweet," she told him. In the dream, it puzzled her to know that John Dupree had been dead for sixty-one years. He was killed in the Argonne Forest by the Huns. She remembered paying a visit of condolence to his mother, who, however, was not receiving guests. "It's all been a mistake, apparently," Pearl told John Dupree. And she fastened up her hair with the burnt-leather ornament.

"There's no question," Jenny said. "We have to call an ambulance. What's got into Dr. Vincent? Is he senile?"

"He does all right, for his age," Ezra said. As usual, he seemed to have missed some central point; even Pearl could see that. Jenny sighed, or perhaps just made some impatient rustling sound with her clothes.

"It's lucky you called me," she said. "I come and find everything falling apart."

"Nothing's falling apart."

"And why is she lying flat? She's obviously having trouble breathing. Where's that big green cushion Becky made her?"

Pearl had been skidding through time, for a moment—preparing to go by ambulance to have her arrow wound treated. She was braced for the precarious, tilting trip down the stairs on a stretcher. It was mention of Becky that set her straight. Becky was her grandchild, Jenny's oldest daughter. "Jenny?" she said.

"How are you feeling?" Jenny asked.

"Is Cody here too?"

Apparently not. Jenny leaned over the bed to give her a kiss. Pearl patted Jenny's hair and found it badly cut, choppy to the touch, but for once she didn't scold. (Jenny had lovely thick hair that she tended to ignore, to mistreat, as if looks didn't really matter.) "It was nice of you to come," Pearl told her.

"Well, goodness, I was worried," said Jenny. "You're the only mother we have."

Pearl felt she had come full circle. "You should have got an extra," she said.

"Excuse me?"

She didn't repeat it. She turned her face on the pillow and was overtaken by a sudden jolt of anger. Why hadn't they arranged for an extra? All those years when she was the only one, the sole support, the lone tall tree in the pasture just waiting for the lightning to strike . . . well. She seemed to be losing track of her thoughts. "Did you bring the children?" she said.

"Not this time. I left them with Joe."

Joe? Oh, yes, her husband. "Why isn't Cody here?" Pearl asked.

"Well, you know," said Ezra, "it's always so hard to locate him. . . ."

"We think you should go to the hospital," Jenny told Pearl.

"Oh, thank you, dear, but I don't believe I care to."

"You're not breathing right. Where's that cushion Becky made when she was little? The one with the uplifting motto," Jenny said. *"Sleep, o faithful warrior, upon thy carven pillow."* She gave a little snort of laughter, and Pearl smiled, picturing Jenny's habit of covering her mouth with her hand as if overcome, as if struck absolutely helpless by life's silliness. "Anyhow," Jenny said, pulling herself together. "Ezra, *you* agree with me, don't you?"

"Agree?"

"About the hospital."

"Ah . . ." said Ezra.

There was a pause. You could pluck this single moment out of all time, Pearl thought, and still discover so much about her children— even about Cody, for his very absence was a characteristic, perhaps his main one. And Jenny was so brisk and breezy but . . . oh, you might say somewhat opaque, a reflecting surface flashing your own self back at you, giving no hint of *her* self. And Ezra, mild Ezra: no doubt confusedly tugging at the shock of fair hair that hung over his forehead, considering and reconsidering . . . "Well," he said, "I don't know . . . I mean, maybe if we waited a while . . ."

"But how long? How long can we afford to wait?"

"Oh, maybe just till tonight, or tomorrow. . . ."

"Tomorrow! What if it's, say, pneumonia?"

"Or it could be only a cold, you see."

"Yes, but—"

"And we wouldn't want her to go if it makes her unhappy."

"No, but—"

Pearl listened, smiling. She knew the outcome now. They would deliberate for hours, echoing each other's answers, repeating and re-phrasing questions, evading, retreating, arguing for argument's sake, ultimately going nowhere. "You never did face up to things," she said kindly.

"Mother?"
"You always were duckers and dodgers."
"Dodgers?"
She smiled again, and closed her eyes.

It was such a relief to drift, finally. Why had she spent so long learning how? The traffic sounds—horns and bells and rags of music— flowed around the voices in her room. She kept mislaying her place in time, but it made no difference; all she remembered was equally pleasant. She remembered the feel of wind on summer nights—how it billows through the house and wafts the curtains and smells of tar and roses. How a sleeping baby weighs so heavily on your shoulder, like ripe fruit. What privacy it is to walk in the rain beneath the drip and crackle of your own umbrella. She remembered a country auction she'd attended forty years ago, where they'd offered up an antique brass bed complete with all its bedclothes—sheets and blankets, pillow in a linen case embroidered with forget-me-nots. Two men wheeled it onto the platform, and its ruffled coverlet stirred like a young girl's petticoats. Behind her eyelids, Pearl Tull climbed in and laid her head on the pillow and was borne away to the beach, where three small children ran toward her, laughing, across the sunlit sand.

2
TEACHING THE CAT TO YAWN

WHILE CODY'S father nailed the target to the tree trunk, Cody tested the bow. He drew the string back, laid his cheek against it, and narrowed his eyes at the target. His father was pounding in tacks with his shoe; he hadn't thought to bring a hammer. He looked like a fool, Cody thought. He owned no weekend clothes, as other fathers did, but had driven to this field in his strained-looking brown striped salesman suit, white starched shirt, and navy tie with multicolored squares and circles scattered randomly across it. The only way you could tell this was a Sunday was when he turned, having pounded in the final tack; he didn't have his tie pulled up close to his collar. It hung loose and slightly crooked, like a drunkard's tie. A cockscomb of hair, as black as Cody's but wavy, stood up on his forehead.

"There!" he said, plodding back. He still carried the shoe. He walked lopsided, either smiling at Cody or squinting in the sunlight. It was nowhere near spring yet, but the air felt unseasonably warm and a pale sun poured heat like a liquid over Cody's shoulders. Cody bent and pulled an arrow from a cardboard tube. He laid it against the string. "Wait, now, son," his father said. "You want to do things right, now."

Naturally, this would have to be an educational experience. There were bound to be lectures and criticisms attached. Cody sighed and lowered the bow. His father stooped to put his shoe on squirming his foot in without undoing the laces, the way Cody's mother hated. The heel of his black rayon sock was worn so thin it was translucent. Cody looked off in another direction. He was fourteen years old—too big to be dragged on family outings any more and definitely too big for bows and arrows, unless of course you'd just leave the equipment to him and his friends, alone, and let them horse around or have themselves a contest or shatter windowpanes and streetlights for the hell of it. How did his father come up with these ideas? This was turning out to be even less successful than most. Cody's mother, who was not the slightest bit athletic, picked dried flowers beside a fence. His little sister buttoned her sweater with chapped and bluish hands. His brother, Ezra, eleven years old, chewed a straw and hummed. He was missing his whistle, no doubt—a bamboo pipe, with six finger holes, on which he played tunes almost ceaselessly. He'd smuggled it along but their father had made him leave it in the car.

At this moment, Cody's two best friends were attending a movie: *Air Force*, with John Garfield and Faye Emerson. Cody would have given anything to be with them.

"Now, your left arm goes like this," his father said, positioning him. "You want to keep your wrist from getting stung, you see. And stand up straight. It was archery gave us our notions of proper posture; says so in the instruction book. Used to be that people slouched around any old how, all except the archers. I bet you didn't know that, did you?"

No, he didn't know that. He stood like something made of clay while his father poked him here and prodded him there, molding him into shape. "In the olden days . . ." his father said.

Cody let go of the bowstring. *Thwack.* The arrow hit the edge of the target, more sidewise than endwise, bounced off harmlessly and fell among the tree roots. "Now! What'd you go and do that for?" his father asked him. "Did I tell you to shoot yet? Did I?"

"It slipped," said Cody.

"Slipped!"

"And anyhow, it couldn't have stuck in the target. Not with that hard fat tree trunk behind it."

"It most certainly could have," his father said. "Like always, you just had to jump on in. Impulsive. Had to have it your way. When are you going to start keeping a better rein on yourself?"

Cody's father (who never kept any sort of rein on himself whatsoever, as Cody's mother constantly reminded him) lunged off toward the target, muttering and grabbing fistfuls of weed heads which he then threw away. Seeds and dry hulls spangled the air around him. "Willful boy; never listens. Don't know why I bother."

Cody's mother shaded her eyes and called, "Did he hit it?"

"*No*, he didn't hit it. How could he; I wasn't even through explaining."

"People have been known to hit a target without a person explaining it beforehand," Cody muttered.

"What say?"

"Let Ezra try," Cody's mother suggested.

His father picked up the arrow and jammed it into the bull's-eye, dead center. "Want to tell me it can't stick?" he asked Cody. He pointed to the arrow, which stayed firm. "Look at that: steel-tipped. Of course it sticks. And spongy bark on the tree. I chose that tree. Of course it sticks. You could have lodged it in easy."

"Ha," said Cody, kicking a clod of earth.

"What say, son?"

"Let Ezra try," Pearl called again. "Beck? Let Ezra try."

Ezra was her favorite, her pet. The entire family knew it. Ezra looked embarrassed and switched the straw to the other side of his mouth. Beck waded back to them. "Oh, I don't know, I don't know. I wonder sometimes," he said.

"Ezra? See if you can hit it, honey," Pearl called.

Beck's glance at Cody might have been sympathy, or else disgust. He pulled another arrow from the cardboard tube. "All right, Ezra, come on and try," he said. "Just don't get carried away like Cody here did."

Ezra came over, still nibbling his straw, and accepted the bow from Cody. Well, this would be a laugh. There was no one as clumsy as Ezra. When he took his stance he did it all wrong, he just *looked* all wrong, in some way you couldn't put your finger on. His elbows jutted out, winglike; his floppy yellow hair feathered in his eyes. "Now, wait, now," Beck kept saying. "What's the trouble here?" He moved around realigning Ezra's shoulders, adjusting his grip on the bow. Ezra stayed patient. In fact, he might have had his mind on something else altogether; it seemed his attention had been caught by a cloud formation over to the south. "Oh, well," Beck said finally, giving up. "Let her fly, I guess, Ezra. Ezra?"

Ezra's fingers loosened on the string. The arrow sped in a straight, swift path, no arc to it at all. As if guided by an invisible thread—or worse, by the purest and most natural luck—it split the length of the arrow that Beck had already jammed in and it landed at the center of the bull's-eye, quivering. There was a sharp, caught silence. Then Beck said, "Will you look at that."

"Why, Ezra," Pearl said.

"Ezra," their sister Jenny cried. "Ezra, look what you did! What you went and did to that arrow!"

Ezra took the straw from his mouth. "I'm sorry," he told Beck. (He was so used to breaking things.)

"Sorry?" said Beck.

He seemed to be hunting the proper tone of voice. Then he found it. "Well, son," he said, "this just goes to show that it pays to follow instructions. See there, Cody? See what happens? A bull's-eye. I'll be damned. If you'd listened close like Ezra did, and not gone off half-cocked . . ."

He was moving toward the target as he spoke, oaring through the weeds, and Jenny was running to get there first. Cody couldn't take his turn at shooting, therefore, although he was itching to. He was absolutely obligated to split that second arrow as Ezra had split the first. It was unthinkable not to. What were the odds against it? He felt a springy twanging inside, as if he himself were the bowstring. He bent down and pulled a new arrow from the tube and fitted it to the bow. He drew and aimed at a clump of shrubbery, then at his father's dusty blue Nash, and then at Ezra, who was already wandering off again dreamy as ever. Longingly, Cody focused on Ezra's fair, ruffled head. "Zing. *Wham.* Aagh, you got me!" he said. Imagine the satisfaction. Ezra turned slowly and caught sight of him. "No!" he cried.

"Huh?"

Ezra ran toward him, flapping his arms like an idiot and stammering, "Stop, stop, stop! No! Stop!" Did he really think Cody would shoot him? Cody stared, keeping the bow drawn. Ezra took a flying leap with his arms outstretched like a lover. He caught Cody in a kind of bear hug and slammed him flat on his back. It knocked the wind out of Cody; all he could do was gasp beneath Ezra's warm, bony weight. And meanwhile, what had happened to the arrow? It was minutes before he could struggle to a sitting position, elbowing Ezra off of him. He looked across the field and found his mother leaning on his father's arm, hobbling in his direction with a perfect circle of blood gleaming on the shoulder of her blouse. "Pearl, my God. Oh, Pearl," his father was saying. Cody turned and looked at Ezra, whose face was pale and shocked. "See there?" Cody asked him. "See what you've gone and done?"

"Did *I* do that?"

"Gone and done it to me again," Cody said, and he staggered to his feet and walked away.

On a weekday when his father was out of town, his mother shopping for supper, his brother and sister doing homework in their rooms, Cody took his BB gun and shot a hole in the kitchen window. Then he slipped outdoors and poked a length of fishing line through the hole.

From the kitchen, he pulled the line until the rusty wrench that he'd
tied to the other end was flush against the outside of the glass. He
held it there by anchoring the line beneath a begonia pot. When his
mother returned from shopping, Cody was seated at the kitchen table
coloring a map of Asia.

After their homework was finished, Jenny and Ezra went out back.
Ezra had been showing Jenny, all week, how to hit a softball. (It seemed
her classmates chose her last whenever they had a game.) As soon as
they had walked through, Cody rose and went to the window. He saw
them take their places in the darkening yard, bounded on either side
by the neighbors' hedges. They were a comically short distance apart.
Jenny stood closest to the house and held her bat straight up, gingerly,
as if preparing to club to death some small animal. Ezra tossed her a
gentle pitch. (He was no great player himself.) Jenny took a whizzing
swing, missed, and retrieved the ball from among the trash cans beside
the back door. She threw it in an overhand so stiff and deformed that
Cody wondered why Ezra bothered. Ezra caught it and pitched again.
As the ball arched toward the bat, Cody felt for the fishing line beneath
the begonia pot. He gave a quick tug. The windowpane clattered inward,
breaking in several pieces. Jenny spun around and stared. Ezra's mouth
dropped open. "What was that?" Pearl called from the dining room.

"Just Ezra breaking another window," Cody told her.

One weekend their father didn't come home, and he didn't come
the next weekend either, or the next. Or rather, one morning Cody
woke up and saw that it had been a while since their father was
around. He couldn't say that he had noticed from the start. His mother
offered no excuses. Cody, watchful as a spy, studied her furrowed,
distracted expression and the way that her hands plucked at each other.
It troubled him to realize that he couldn't picture his father's most
recent time with them. Trying to find some scene that would explain
Beck's leaving, he could only come up with *general* scenes, blended
from a dozen repetitions: meals shattered by quarrels, other meals
disrupted when Ezra spilled his milk, drives in the country where his
father lost the way and his mother snapped out pained and exasperated
directions. He thought of once when the Nash's radiator had erupted
in steam and his father, looking helpless, had flung his suit coat over
it. "Oh, honestly," his mother said. But that was way back; it was
years ago, wasn't it? Cody journeyed through the various cubbies and
crannies of the house, hunting up the trappings of his father's "phases"
(as his mother called them). There were the badminton racquets, the
butterfly net, the archery set, the camera with its unwieldy flashgun,
and the shoe box full of foreign stamps still in their glassine envelopes.
But it meant nothing that these objects remained behind. What was
alarming was his father's half of the bureau: an empty sock drawer,

an empty underwear drawer. In the shirt drawer, one unused sports shirt, purchased by the three children for Beck's last birthday, his forty-fourth. And a full assortment of pajamas; but then, he always slept in his underwear. In the wardrobe, just a hanger strung with ties—his oldest, dullest, most frayed and spotted ties—and a pair of shoes so ancient that the toes curled up.

Cody's brother and sister were staggeringly unobservant. They flitted in and out of the house like birds—Ezra playing his whistle, Jenny singing parts of jump-rope songs. Cody had the impression that musical notes filled their heads to overflowing; they left no room for anything serious. *Auntie Sue got dressed in blue,* Jenny sang, *put on shoes and rubbers too. . . .* Her plain, flat voice and heedlessly swinging braids somehow reassured him. After all, what could go so wrong, when she skipped past with her ragged rope? What could go so very wrong?

Then one Saturday she said, "I'm worried about Daddy."

"Why?" Cody asked.

"Cody," she said, in her elderly way, "you can see that he doesn't come home any more. I think he's left us."

"Don't be silly," Cody told her.

She surveyed him for a moment, with a composure that made him uneasy, and when he didn't say any more she turned and went out on the porch. He heard the glider creak as she settled into it. But she didn't start singing. In fact, the house was unusually quiet. The only sound was his mother's heels, clicking back and forth overhead as she put away the laundry. And Ezra wasn't playing his whistle. Cody had no idea where Ezra was.

He went upstairs to his mother's bedroom. She was folding a sheet. "What're you doing?" he asked. She gave him a look. He settled in a ladder-backed chair to watch her work. She was wearing a housedress that he very much disliked, cream colored with deep red streaks across it like paintbrush strokes. The shoulders were shaped by triangular pads that unbuttoned and removed when it was time to wash the dress. Cody had often thought of stealing those pads. With her shoulders broadened, his mother looked powerful and sharp and scary. On her feet were open-toed shoes and short white socks. She traveled rapidly between the laundry basket and the bed, laying out stacks of clothing. There was no stack for his father.

"When is Dad coming home?" he asked.

"Oh," she said, "pretty soon."

She didn't meet his eyes.

Cody looked around him and noticed, for the first time, that there was something pinched and starved about the way this house was decorated. Not a single perfume bottle or china figurine sat upon his mother's bureau. No pictures hung on the walls. Even the bedside tables were completely bare; and in all the drawers in this room, he knew, every object would be aligned and squared precisely—the clothing organized by type and color, whites grading into pastels and then to darks; comb and brush parallel; gloves paired and folded like a row of clenched fists. Who *wouldn't* leave such a place? He straightened, feeling panicky. His mother chose that moment to come over and smooth his hair down. "My," she told him, smiling, "you're getting so big! I can't believe it."

He shrank back in his seat.

"You're getting big enough for me to start relying on," she said.

"I'm only fourteen," Cody told her.

He slipped off the chair and left the room. The bathroom door was closed; he heard the shower running and Ezra singing "Greensleeves." He opened the door just a crack, snaked one arm in, and turned on the hot water in the sink. Then he traveled through the rest of the house, from kitchen to downstairs bathroom to basement, methodically opening every hot water faucet to its fullest. But you couldn't really say his heart was in it.

"Tull?" the man asked.

"Yes."

"Is this the Tull residence?"

"Yes, it is."

"Darryl Peters," the man said, showing a business card.

Cody took a swig of beer and accepted the card. While he was reading it, he sloshed the beer bottle absently to get a good head of suds. He was wearing dungarees and nothing else; it was a blistering day in August. The house, however, was fairly cool—the living room dim, the paper shades pulled all the way down and glowing yellow with the afternoon sun. Mr. Peters looked in wistfully, but remained on the porch with his hat in his hand. He was way overdressed, for August.

"So," said Cody. He nudged the screen door open with his bare foot. Mr. Peters caught hold of it and stepped inside.

"Would your mother be in?" he asked.

"She's taken a job."

"Well, then, your . . . is Ezra Tull your father?"

"He's my brother."

"Brother. Ah."

"*He's* in."

"Well, then," Mr. Peters said.

"I'll go get him."

Cody went upstairs and into Jenny's room. Jenny and Ezra were playing checkers on the floor. Ezra, wearing shorts and a sleeveless undershirt full of holes, stroked his cat, Alicia, and frowned at the board. "Someone to see you," Cody told him.

Ezra looked up. "Who is it?" he asked.

Cody shrugged.

Ezra rose, still hugging the cat. Cody went with him as far as the stairs. He stopped there and leaned over the banister to eavesdrop, grinning. Ezra arrived in the living room. "You want *me?*" Cody heard him ask.

"Ezra Tull?" said Mr. Peters.

"Yes."

"Well, ah . . . maybe there's been a mistake."

"What kind of mistake?"

"I'm from Peaceful Hills Memorial Gardens," Mr. Peters said. "I thought you wished to purchase a resting place."

"Resting place?"

"I thought you filled out this mail-in coupon: Ezra Tull, your signature. *Yes, I would like an eternal home for myself and/or my loved ones. I understand that a sales representative will call.*"

"It wasn't me," said Ezra.

"You didn't fill this out. You're not interested in a plot."

"No, thank you."

"I should have known," said Mr. Peters.

"I'm sorry," Ezra told him.

"Never mind, I can see it's not your doing."

"Maybe when I'm older, or something . . ."

"That's all right, son. Never mind."

Cody climbed to the stuffy, hot third floor, where Lorena Schmidt sat on his bed with her back against the wall. She was new to the neighborhood—a tawny girl with long black hair, one lock of which she was twining around a finger. "Who was that?" she asked Cody.

"A cemetery salesman."

"Ugh."

"He came to see Ezra."

"Who's Ezra?"

"My *brother* Ezra, dummy."

"Well? How should I know?" Lorena said. "You mean that brother downstairs? Blondish kid, good-looking?"

"Good-looking! Ezra?"

"I like his kind of serious face," Lorena said. "And those pale gray eyes."

"*My* eyes are gray."

"Well. Anyhow," Lorena said.

"Besides," said Cody, "he gets fits."

"He does?"

"He'll fool you. He'll look as normal as anyone else and then all of a sudden, splat! He's flat on the floor, foaming at the mouth."

"I don't believe you," Lorena said.

"Some people think he's dangerous. I'm the only one brave enough to go near him, when he gets that way."

"I don't believe a word of it," Lorena said.

She twisted around to the head of Cody's bed and lifted a corner of the window shade. "I see your mother coming," she said.

"What? Where?"

She turned and flashed him a grin. One of her front teeth was chipped, which made her look unstable, lacking in self-control. "I was teasing," she said.

"Oh."

"You ought to've seen your face. Ha! I haven't even met your mother. How would I know if she was coming?"

"You must have met her," Cody said. "She's a cashier now at Sweeney Brothers Grocery. Folks around this neighborhood call her the Sweeney Meanie."

"Well, we do our shopping at Esmond's."

"So would I," said Cody.

"How come she works? Where's your father?"

"Missing in action," he told her.

"Oops, sorry."

He gave a casual wave of his hand and took a swallow of beer. "She runs the cash register," he said. "Look in Sweeney's window, next time you go past. You'll know her right off. Walk in and say, 'Ma'am, this soup can's dented. Can I have a reduction?' 'Soup's soup,' she'll say. 'Full price, please.'"

"Oh, one of those," Lorena said.

"Tight little bun on the back of her head. Mouth like it's holding straight pins. Anybody dawdles, tries to pass the time of day, she'll say, 'Move along, please. Please move along.'"

He was smiling at Lorena as he spoke, but inside he felt a sudden pang. He pictured his mother at the register, with that anxious line like a strand of hair or a faint, fragile dressmaker's seam running across her forehead.

Cody took every blanket and sheet from Ezra's bed and removed the pillow and the mattress. Underneath were four wooden slats, laid across the frame. He lifted them out and stored them in the wardrobe. With great care, he set the mattress back on the frame. He drew a breath and waited. The mattress held. He replaced the bedclothes and he puffed the pillow and laid it delicately at the head. He lugged a pile of magazines from their hiding place in his bureau, opened them, and scattered them on the floor. Then he turned off the light and went to his own bed, across the room.

Ezra padded in barefoot, eating a sandwich. He wore pajama bottoms with a trailing drawstring. "Oh, me," he said, and he sank into bed.

There was a crash. The floor shook, and their mother shrieked and came pounding up the stairs. When she turned on the light, Cody raised his head and stared at her with a sleepy, befuddled expression. She had a hand pressed to her heart. She was taking in gulps of air. Jenny shivered behind her, hugging a worn stuffed rabbit. "Good Lord preserve us," their mother said.

Ezra looked like someone in a bathtub full of cloth. He was having trouble disentangling himself from his sheets. One hand, upraised, still clutched the half-eaten sandwich. "Ezra, honey," Pearl said, but then she said, "Why, Ezra." She was looking at the magazines. They were opened to pictures of women in nightgowns, in bathing suits, in garter belts and black lace brassieres, in bath towels, in useless wisps of transparent drapery, or in nothing whatsoever. "Ezra Tull!" she said.

Ezra worked his way up to peer over the edge of his bed frame.

"Truly, Ezra, I never suspected that you would be such a person," she told him. Then she turned and left the room, taking Jenny with her.

Ezra emerged from his bed, flew through the air, and landed on Cody. He grabbed a handful of hair and started shaking Cody's head. All Cody could say was, "Mmf! Mmf!" because he didn't want their mother to hear. Finally he managed to bite Ezra's knee and Ezra rolled off, panting and sobbing. He must have knocked into something at some earlier point, because his left eye was swelling. It made him look sad. Cody got up and showed him where he'd stashed the slats. They fitted them into place, heaved the mattress back on the frame, and attempted to smooth the blankets. Then Cody turned out the light, and they climbed into their beds and went to sleep.

Sometimes Cody dreamed about his father. He would be stepping through the doorway, wearing one of his salesman suits, bringing the afternoon paper as he always did on Friday. His ordinariness was astounding—his thick strings of hair and the tired, yellowish puffs beneath his eyes. (In waking memories, lately, he was not so real, but had blurred and leveled and lost his details.) "How was your week?" he asked, tediously. Cody's mother answered, "Oh, all right."

In these dreams, Cody was not his present self. He had somehow slid backward and become a toddler again, rushing around on tiny, fat legs, feverishly showing off. "See this? And this? See me somersault? See me pull my wagon?" His smallness colored every act; he was conscious of a desperate need to learn to *manage*, to take charge of his surroundings. Waking in the dark, the first thing he did was stretch his long legs and lift his arms, which were becoming veiny and roped with muscle. He thought of how it would be if his father returned some time in the future, when Cody was a man. "Look at what I've accomplished," Cody would tell him. "Notice where I've got to, how far I've come without you."

Was it something I said? Was it something I did? Was it something I didn't do, that made you go away?

School started, and Cody entered ninth grade. He and his two best friends landed in the same homeroom. Sometimes Pete and Boyd came home with him; they all walked the long way, avoiding the grocery store where Cody's mother worked. Cody had to keep things separate— his friends in one half of his life and his family in the other half. His mother hated for Cody to mix with outsiders. "Why don't you ever have someone over?" she would ask, but she didn't deceive him for a moment. He'd say, "Nah, I don't need anybody," and she would look pleased. "I guess your family's enough for you, isn't it?" she would ask. "Aren't we lucky to have each other?"

He only allowed his friends in the house when his mother was at work, and sometimes for no reason he could name he would lead them through her belongings. He would open her smallest top bureau drawer and show them the real gold brooch that his father had given her when they were courting. "He thinks a lot of her," he would say. "He's given her heaps of stuff. Heaps. There's heaps of other stuff that I just don't happen to have on hand." His friends looked bored. Switching tactics, Cody would show them her ironed handkerchiefs stacked so exactly that they seemed encased by an invisible square box. "I mean," he said, "*your* mothers don't do that, do they? Do they? Women!" he said, and then, musing over some mysterious metal clasp or something that was evidently used to hold up stockings, "Who can understand them? Really: can you figure them out? She likes Ezra best, my dumb brother Ezra. Sissy old Ezra. I mean, if it were Jenny, I could see it—Jenny being a girl and all. But Ezra! Who could like Ezra? Can you give me a single reason why?"

His friends shrugged, idly gazing around the room and jingling the loose change in their pockets.

He hid Ezra's left sneaker, his arithmetic homework, his baseball mitt, his fountain pen, and his favorite sweater. He shut Ezra's cat in the linen cupboard. He took Ezra's bamboo whistle to school and put it in the jacket of Josiah Payson, Ezra's best friend—a wild-eyed boy, the size of a full-grown man, who was thought by some to be feeble-minded. It was typical of Ezra that he loved Josiah with all his heart, and would even have had him to the house if their mother weren't scared of him. Cody stopped by when Ezra's class was at lunch, and he slipped behind the cloakroom partition and stuck the whistle in the pocket of Josiah's enormous black peacoat. After that there was a stretch of Indian summer and Josiah evidently left his jacket where it hung, so the whistle stayed lost for days. Ezra was very upset about it. "Have you seen my whistle?" he asked everybody. For once, Cody didn't have to listen to "Greensleeves" and "The Ash Grove," played on that breathy little pipe, whose range was so limited that for high notes, Ezra had to blow extra hard and split people's eardrums. "You took it," Ezra told Cody. "Didn't you? I know you did."

"What would I want with a stupid toy whistle?" Cody asked.

He was hoping that when it turned up in Josiah Payson's pocket, Ezra would blame Josiah. But it didn't happen that way. Whatever passed between them was settled without any fuss, and the two of them continued to be friends. Once again, a cracked, foggy "Ash Grove" burbled in every corner of the house.

Their mother went on one of her rampages. "Pearl has hit the warpath," Cody told his brother and sister. He always called her Pearl at such times. "Better look out," he said. "She's dumped all Jenny's bureau drawers."

"Oh-oh," Ezra said.

"She's slamming things around and talking to herself."

"*Oh,* boy," Jenny said.

Cody had met the other two on the porch; they'd stayed late at school. He silently opened the door for them, and they crept up the stairs. Each took a great, lunging stride over the step that creaked— although surely their mother would not have heard them. She was making too much noise in the kitchen. Throwing pots through windowpanes, was what it sounded like.

They tiptoed across the hall to Jenny's room. "What a mess!" Ezra breathed. Heaps of clothing covered the floor. Empty drawers had been hurled everywhere. The wardrobe stood open, its hangers stripped, and Jenny's puff-sleeved dresses lay in a heap. Jenny stared from the doorway. "Jen?" Cody asked her. "What did you do?"

"Nothing," Jenny said in a quavery voice.

"Think! Some little thing, something you've forgotten about . . ."

"Nothing. I promise."

"Well, help me get these drawers back in," he said to Ezra.

It was a two-man job. The drawers were oak, cumbersome and inclined to stick. Cody and Ezra grunted as they fitted them into the bureau. Jenny traveled around the room collecting her clothes. Tears had filled her eyes, and she kept dabbing at her nose with one or another rolled pair of socks. "Stop that," Cody told her. "She'll do it all again, if she finds snot on your socks."

He and Ezra gathered slips and hair ribbons, shook out blouses, tried to get the dresses back on their hangers the way they'd been before. Some were hopelessly wrinkled, and those they smoothed as best they could and hid at the rear of the wardrobe. Meanwhile Jenny knelt on the floor, sniffling and folding undershirts.

"I wish we could just go off," Ezra said, "and not come back till it's over."

"It won't be over till she's had her scene," Cody told him. "You know that. There's no way we can get around it."

"I wish Daddy were here."

"Well, he's not, so shut up."

Ezra straightened a sash.

After they'd put everything in order, the three of them sat in a row on Jenny's bed. The sounds from the kitchen were different now— cutlery rattling, glassware clinking. Their mother must be setting the table. Pretty soon she'd serve supper. Cody had such a loaded feeling in his throat, he never wanted to eat again. No doubt the others felt the same; Ezra kept swallowing. Jenny said, "Let's run away from home."

"We don't have anyplace to run to," Cody said.

Their mother came to the foot of the stairs and called them. Her voice was thin, like the sound of a gnat. "Children."

They filed down, dragging their feet. They stopped at the first-floor bathroom and meticulously scrubbed their hands, taking extra pains with the backs. Each one waited for the others. Then they went into the kitchen. Their mother was slicing a brick of Spam. She didn't look at them, but she started speaking the instant they were seated. "It's not enough that I should have to work till five p.m., no; then I come home and find nothing seen to, no chores done, you children off till all hours with disreputable characters in the alleys or wasting your time with school chorus, club meetings; table not set, breakfast dishes not washed, supper not cooked, floors not swept, mail in a heap on the mat . . . and not a sign of any of you. Oh, I know what's going on! I know what you three are up to! Neighborhood savages, that's what you are, mingling with each and all. How am I supposed to deal with this? How am I expected to cope? Useless daughter, great unruly bruising boys . . . *I* know what people are saying. You think my customers aren't glad to tell me? Coming in simpering, 'Well, Mrs. Tull, that oldest boy of yours is certainly growing up. I saw him with a pack of Camels in the street in front of the Barlow girl's house.' And I have to smile and take it. Have to stand there on exhibit while they're all thinking, 'Poor Mrs. Tull, I don't know how she can hold her head up. It's clear she doesn't have the least ability to handle those children; look at how they're disgracing her.' Sticking potatoes on people's exhaust pipes and letting the air out of tires and shooting at streetlights with BB guns and stealing hubcaps and making off with traffic signs and moving Mrs. Correlli's madonna to Sonny Boy Brown's kitchen stoop and hanging around the hydrants with girls no better than tramps, girls in tight sweaters and ankle chains, oh, I hear about it everywhere. . . ."

"But not me, Mama," Jenny said.

"I beg your pardon?"

"I don't do those things."

Well, of course she didn't (only Cody did), but she shouldn't have pointed that out. Now she'd drawn attention to herself. Pearl turned, gathered force, and plunged. "You! I know about you. I couldn't believe my ears. What should I be doing but coming down the church steps Sunday when I see you with that Melanie Miller from your Bible class. 'Oh, Melanie . . .' " She made her voice shrill and prissy, nothing like Jenny's, really. " 'Melanie, I just love your dress. I wish *I* had a dress like that.' Understand," she said, turning to the boys, "this was a cheap little number from Sears. The plaid wasn't matched; there was a ruffle at the hem like a . . . square dance outfit and a bunch of artificial flowers pinned to the waist. A totally inappropriate dress for a nine-year-old, or for anyone. But 'Oh, I wish *I* had that,' your sister says, so everyone thinks, 'Poor Mrs. Tull, she can't even afford a Sears and Roebuck dress with artificial flowers; I don't know how she manages, slaving away at that grocery all day and struggling over her budget at night, cutting here and cutting there, wondering will she scrape by, hoping nobody runs up a doctor bill, praying her children's feet will stop growing . . .'

"And Melanie's mother, well, it's just like opening the door to such a person. First thing you know she'll be walking in here big as life: 'Mrs. Tull, I happen to have the catalogue we ordered Melanie's dress from, if you would care for one for Jenny.' As if I'd want to dress my daughter like an orphan! As if I'd like for her to duplicate some other child! 'No, thank you, Mrs. Miller,' I'll say. 'I may not be able to afford so very much but at least when I do buy, I buy with finished seams. No, Mrs. Miller, you keep your so-called wish book, your quarter-inch hem allowances, smashed felt flowers. . . .' What's wrong with us, I'd like to know? Aren't we good enough for my own blood daughter? Doesn't she feel I'm doing my best, my level best, to provide? Does she have to pick up riffraff? Does she have to bring home scum? We're a family! We used to be so close! What happened to us? Why would she act so disloyal?"

She sat down serenely, as if finished with the subject forever, and reached for a bowl of peas. Jenny's face was streaming with tears, but she wasn't making a sound and Pearl seemed unaware of her. Cody cleared his throat.

"But that was Sunday," he said.

Pearl's serving spoon paused, midway between the bowl and her plate. She looked politely interested. "Yes?" she said.

"This is Wednesday."

"Yes."

"It's Wednesday, dammit; it's three days later. So why bring up something from Sunday?"

Pearl threw the spoon in his face. "You upstart," she said. She rose and slapped him across the cheek. "You wretch, you ugly horror." She grabbed one of Jenny's braids and yanked it so Jenny was pulled off her chair. "Stupid clod," she said to Ezra, and she took the bowl of peas and brought it down on his head. It didn't break, but peas flew everywhere. Ezra cowered, shielding his head with his arms. "Parasites," she told them. "I wish you'd all die, and let me go free. I wish I'd find you dead in your beds."

After that, she went upstairs. The three of them washed the dishes, dried them, and put them away in the cupboards. They wiped the table and countertops and swept the kitchen floor. The sight of any crumb or stain was a relief, a pleasure; they attacked it with Bon Ami. They pulled the shades in the windows and locked the back door. Outside, the neighborhood children were organizing a game of hide-and-seek, but their voices were so faint that they seemed removed in time as well as in space. They were like people from long ago, laughing and calling only in memory, or in one of those eerily lifelike dreams that begin on the edge of sleep.

Shortly before Thanksgiving, a girl named Edith Taber transferred to their school. Cody had been new to so many schools himself, he recognized that defiant tilt of her head when she stepped into his homeroom. She carried a zippered notebook that wasn't the right kind at all, and over her skirt she wore what appeared to be a grown man's shirt, which no one had ever heard of doing. But she had thick black hair and the kind of gypsy look that Cody liked; and he was also drawn by the proud and scornful way she walked alone to her classes— as friendless as Cody was, he thought, or at least, as friendless as he felt inside. So that afternoon he walked a short distance behind her (it turned out she lived just one block north of him), and the next afternoon he caught up and walked beside her. She seemed to welcome his company and talked to him nearly nonstop, every now and then clutching her coat collar tight against her throat in a gesture that struck him as sophisticated. Her brother was in the navy, she said, and had promised to bring her a silk kimono if he made it through the war. And she didn't find that Baltimore was very cosmopolitan, and she thought Miss Saunders, the English teacher, resembled Lana Turner. She said she felt it was really attractive when boys didn't slick their hair back but let it fall over their foreheads, straight, the way Cody did. Cody raked his fingers through his hair and said, well, he didn't know about that; he'd always sort of supposed that girls preferred a little wave or curl or something. She said she just despised for a boy to have curls. They walked the rest of the way without speaking, although from time to time Cody whistled parts of the only tune that came to his mind, which happened to be "The Ash Grove."

He couldn't walk her home on Wednesday because he had to stay late for detention, and the following day was Thanksgiving. There wouldn't be any more school till Monday. All Thursday morning, he hung around the front porch in the damp November chill, gazing northward to Edith's street and then wheeling away and taking midair punches at a cushion from the glider. Finally his mother emerged, rosy from the kitchen, and coaxed him inside. "Cody, honey, you'll freeze to death. Come and shell me some pecans." They were having a meager meal—no turkey—but she'd promised to make a pie for dessert. Already the house smelled different: spicier, more festive. Cody would have stayed on the porch forever, though, if he'd thought there was a chance of seeing Edith.

After dinner they all played Monopoly. Generally, Cody's family didn't allow him in their games; he had this problem with winning. He absolutely insisted on winning any game he played. And he did win too—by sheer fierceness, by caring the most. (Also, he'd been known to cheat.) Sometimes, he would even win when no one else suspected it was a contest. He would eat more peanuts, get his corn shucked the fastest, or finish his page of the comics first. "Go away," his family would say when he approached (nonchalantly shuffling cards or tossing a pair of dice). "You know what we said. Never again!" But this afternoon, they let him play. He tried to hold back, but once he'd bought a hotel on the Boardwalk, things got out of hand. "Oh, my, I should have remembered," his mother said. "What's he doing in this game?" But she was smiling. She wore her blue wool dress and her hair was coming out of its bun, which made her look relaxed. Her token was the flatiron. She skipped right over the Boardwalk, but Ezra was next and he hit it. He didn't have anywhere near enough money. Cody tried to lend him some; he hated it when people just gave up. He liked to get everybody thousands of dollars in debt, struggling to the bitter end. But Ezra said, "No, no, I quit," and backed off, holding up one palm in that old-mannish way he had. So Cody had to go on with just Jenny and his mother, and eventually with just his mother. They played right down to the line, when she landed on the Boardwalk with three dollar bills to her name. As a matter of fact, Cody had a pretty good time.

Then the younger two talked Cody and Pearl into putting on their old skit: "The Mortgage Overdue." "Oh, come on! Please! It wouldn't feel like a holiday without it." Cody and Pearl ended up agreeing to it, even though they were rusty and Cody couldn't remember the dance step that came at the finish. This was something salvaged from his mother's girlhood, the kind of piece performed at amateur recital contests or campfire circles. Pearl played Ivy, the maiden in distress, and Cody was the villain twirling his waxed mustache. *"Ivy, sweet sweet Ivy, lean upon my arm,"* he cajoled her with an evil leer, while Pearl rolled her eyes and shrank into a corner. She could have been an actress, her children thought; she had it letter-perfect, the blushing gaze and the old-fashioned singsong of her responses. At the end the hero came and rescued her. Ezra and Jenny always claimed to be too shy, so Cody had to take the hero's part as well. *"I will pay the money for the mortgage on the farm,"* he told the maiden, and he danced her into the dining room. The dance step came back to him after all, but his mother's tongue got twisted and instead of *wedded life* she said *leaded wife* and collapsed in a heap of giggles. Jenny and Ezra gave them three curtain calls.

That evening, Cody went out to the porch and looked northward some more in the twilight. Ezra came too and sat in the glider, pushing back and forth with the heel of one sneaker. "Want to walk toward Sloop Street?" Cody asked him.

"What's on Sloop Street?"

"Nothing much. This girl I know, Edith Taber."

"Oh, yes. Edith," Ezra said.

"You know who she is?"

"She's got this whistle," Ezra said, "that plays sharps and flats with hardly any extra trouble."

"Edith *Taber?*"

"A recorder."

"You're thinking of someone else," Cody told him.

"Well, maybe so."

Cody was silent a moment, leaning on the porch railing. Ezra creaked companionably in the glider. Then Cody said, "A black-haired girl. Ninth-grader."

"New in town," Ezra agreed.

"When'd you see her?"

"Just yesterday," Ezra said. "I was walking home from school, playing my whistle, and she caught up with me and said she liked it and asked if I wanted to see her recorder. So I went to her house and I saw it."

"To her *house?* Did she know you were my brother?"

"Well, no, I don't think so," Ezra said. "She has a parakeet that burps and says, 'Forgive me.' Her mother served us cookies."

"You met her mother?"

"It would be nice to have a recorder, someday."

"She's too old for you," Cody said.

Ezra looked surprised. "Well, of course," he said. "She's fourteen and a half."

"What would she want with a little sixth-grader?"

"She wanted to show me her whistle," Ezra said.

"Shoot," said Cody.

"Cody? Are we going to walk toward Sloop Street?"

"Nah," said Cody. He kicked a pillar.

"If I asked Mother," Ezra said, "do you think she would get me one of those recorders for Christmas?"

"You dunce," said Cody. "You raving idiot. Do you think she's got money to spare for goddamn *whistles?*"

"Well, no, I guess not," Ezra said.

Then Cody went into the house and locked the door, and when Ezra started pounding on it Cody told their mother it was only Mr. Milledge, having one of his crazy spells.

Monday morning, he looked for Edith on the way to school but he didn't see her. As it turned out, she was tardy. She arrived in homeroom just after the bell. He tried to catch her eye but she didn't glance his way; only gazed fixedly at the teacher all during announcements. And when the first bell rang she walked to class with Sue Meeks and Harriet Smith. Evidently, she was no longer friendless.

By third period, it was clear she was avoiding him. He couldn't even get near her; she had a constant bodyguard. But what had he done wrong? He cornered Barbara Pace—a plump, cheerful redhead who served as a kind of central switchboard for ninth-grade couples. "What's the matter with Edith?" he asked.

"Who?"

"Edith Taber. We were getting along just fine and now she won't speak."

"Oh," she said. She shifted her books. She was wearing a man-sized shirt with the tails out. Come to think of it, so were half the other girls. "Well," she said, "I guess she likes somebody else now."

"Is it my brother?" Cody asked.

"Who's your brother?"

"Ezra. My brother, Ezra."

"*I* didn't know you had a brother," she said, peering at him.

"Well, she liked me well enough last week. What happened?"

"See," she told him patiently, "now she's been to a couple of parties and naturally she's developed new interests. She's got a sort of . . . broader view, and also she didn't realize about your reputation."

"What reputation?"

"Well, you do drink, Cody. And you hung around with that cheap Lorena Schmidt all summer; you smell like a walking cigarette; and you almost got arrested over Halloween."

"Did my brother tell her that?"

"What's this about your brother? Everybody told her. It's not exactly a secret."

"Well, I never claimed to be a saint," Cody said.

"She says you're real good-looking and all but she wants a boy she can respect," said Barbara. "She thinks she might like Francis Elburn now."

"Francis Elburn! That fairy."

"He's really more her type," said Barbara.

"His hair is curly."

"So?"

"Francis Elburn; Jesus Christ."

"There's no need to use profanity," Barbara told him.

Cody walked home alone, long after the others had left, choosing streets where he'd be certain not to run into Edith or her friends. Once he turned down the wrong alley and it struck him that he was still an outsider, unfamiliar with the neighborhood. His classmates had been born and raised here, most of them, and were more comfortable with each other than he could ever hope to be. Look at his two best friends: their parents went to the movies together; their mothers talked on the telephone. *His* mother. . . . He kicked a signpost. What he wouldn't give to have a mother who acted like other mothers! He longed to see her gossiping with a little gang of women in the kitchen, letting them roll her hair up in pincurls, trading beauty secrets, playing cards, losing track of time—"Oh, goodness, look at the clock! And supper not even started; my husband will kill me. Run along, girls." He wished she had some outside connection, something beyond that suffocating house.

And his father: he had uprooted the family continually, tearing them away as soon as they were settled and plunking them someplace new. But where was he now that Cody *wanted* to be uprooted, now that he was saddled with a reputation and desperate to leave and start over? His father had ruined their lives, Cody thought—first in one way and then in another. He thought of tracking him down and arriving on his doorstep: "I'm in trouble; it's all your fault. I've got a bad name, I need to leave town, you'll have to take me in." But that would only be another unknown city, another new school to walk into alone. And there too, probably, his grades would begin to slip and the neighbors would complain and the teachers would start to suspect him first when any little thing went wrong; and then Ezra would follow shortly in his dogged, earnest, devoted way and everybody would say to Cody, "Why can't you be more like your brother?"

He let himself into the house, which smelled of last night's cabbage. It was almost dark and the air seemed thick; he felt he had to labor to move through it. He climbed the stairs wearily. He passed Jenny's room, where she sat doing her homework in a tiny dull circle of yellow from the lamp. Her face was thin and shadowed and she didn't bother greeting him. He climbed on up to his own room and flicked on the light switch. He had set his books on the bureau before he realized

Ezra was there. Asleep, as usual—curled on his bed with a sheaf of homework papers. Oh, Ezra was so slow and dazed; he could sleep anytime. His lips were parted. His cat, Alicia, lay in the crook of his arm, purring and looking self-satisfied.

Cody knelt beside his bed and pulled from beneath it a half-filled bottle of bourbon, an empty gin bottle, five empty beer bottles, a crumpled pack of Camels, and a box of pretzels. He strewed them around Ezra, arranging them just right. He went to the hall storage closet and took out his father's Six-20 Brownie camera. In the doorway of his room he aimed and paused and clicked the shutter. Ezra didn't wake, amazingly enough. (The light from the flashgun was so powerful, you'd see swimming blue globes for minutes after being photographed.) But the cat seemed mildly disturbed. She got to her feet and yawned. What a yawn!—huge and disdainful. It would have made a wonderful picture: deadbeat Ezra and his no-account cat, both with gaping mouths. Cody wondered if she'd do it again. "Yawn," he told her, and he advanced the film for another photo. "Alicia? Yawn." She only smirked and settled down again. He yawned himself, demonstrating, but apparently cats didn't find such things contagious. He lowered the camera and came closer to pat her head, scratch beneath her chin, stroke her throat. Nothing worked. "Yawn, dammit," he said, and he tried to pry her teeth apart by force. She drew up sharply, eyes wide and glaring. Ezra woke.

"Your cat is *retarded*," Cody told him.

"Huh?"

"I can't get her to yawn."

Ezra reached over, matter-of-factly, and circled the cat with his arm. She gave a luxurious yawn and nestled down against him, and Ezra went back to sleep. Cody didn't try for another picture, though. He'd never seen anyone take the fun out of things the way Ezra could.

Cody and Ezra and Jenny went shopping for a Christmas present for their mother. Each of them had saved four weeks' allowance, which meant forty cents apiece, and Cody had a dollar extra that he'd taken from Miss Saunders's center desk drawer. That made two dollars and twenty cents—enough for some winter gloves, Cody suggested. Jenny said gloves were boring and she wanted to buy a diamond ring. "That's really stupid," Cody told her. "Even you ought to know you can't buy a diamond ring for two-twenty."

"I don't mean a real one, I mean glass. Or anything, just so it's pretty and not useful."

They were forced to shop in the stores near home, since they didn't want to spend money on carfare. It was mid-December and crowds of other people were shopping too—plowing past with their arms full of packages, breathing white clouds in the frosty air. Further downtown the department store windows would be as rich and bright as the insides of jewel boxes, and there'd be carols and clanging brass bells and festoons of tinsel on the traffic lights, but in this neighborhood the shops were smaller, darker, decorated with a single wreath on the door or a cardboard Santa Claus carrying a carton of Chesterfield cigarettes. Soldiers on leave straggled by in clumps, looking lost. The shoppers had something grim and determined about them—even those with the gaudiest packages. They seemed likely to mow down anyone in their path. Cody took a pinch of Jenny's coat sleeve so as not to lose her.

"I'm serious," she was saying. "I don't want to get her anything warm. Anything necessary. Anything—"

"Serviceable," Ezra said.

They all grimaced.

"If we bought her a ring, though," Ezra said, "she might feel bad about the wastefulness. She might not really enjoy it."

Cody hated the radiant, grave expression that Ezra wore sometimes; it showed that he realized full well how considerate he was being. "What do *you* want for Christmas?" Cody asked him roughly. "World peace?"

"World what? I'd like a recorder," Ezra said.

They crossed an intersection with a swarm of sailors. "Well," said Cody, "you're not getting one."

"I know that."

"You're getting a cap with turn-down earflaps and a pair of corduroy pants."

"Cody!" said Jenny. "You weren't supposed to tell."

"It doesn't matter," Ezra said.

They separated for a woman who had stopped to fit her child's mittens on. "It used to be," Jenny said, "that we got toys for Christmas, and candy. Remember how nice last Christmas was?"

"This one's going to be nice too," Ezra told her.

"Remember down in Virginia, when Daddy bought us a sled, and Mother said it was silly because it hardly ever snowed but December twenty-sixth we woke up and there was snow all over everything?"

"That was fun," Ezra said.

"We had the only sled in town," Jenny said. "Cody started charging for rides. Daddy showed us how to wax the runners and we pulled it to the top of that hill. . . . What was the name of that hill? It had such a funny—"

Then she stopped short on the sidewalk. Pedestrians jostled all around her. "Why," she said.

Cody and Ezra looked at her.

"He's really not ever coming home again. Is he," she said.

No one answered. After a minute they resumed walking, three abreast, and Cody took a pinch of Ezra's sleeve, too, so they wouldn't drift apart in the crowd.

Cody sorted the mail, setting aside for his mother a couple of envelopes that looked like Christmas cards. He threw away a department store flyer and a letter from his school. He pocketed an envelope with a Cleveland postmark.

He went upstairs to his room and switched on the goose-necked lamp beside his bed. While the lightbulb warmed, he whistled and stared out the window. Then he tested the bulb with his fingers and, finding it hot enough, wrapped the envelope around it and counted slowly to thirty. After that he pried open the flap with ease and pulled out a single sheet of paper and a check.

. . . says they should be producing to capacity by June of '45 . . . his father wrote. *Sorry the enclosed is a little smaller than expected as I have incurred some . . .* It was his usual letter, nothing different. Cody folded it again and slid it back in the envelope, though it hardly seemed worth the effort. Then he heard the front door slam. "Ezra Tull?" Pearl called. Her cloppy high heels started rapidly up the stairs. Cody tucked the envelope into his bureau and shut the drawer. "Ezra!"

"He's not here," Cody said.

She came to stand in the doorway. "Where is he?" she asked. She was out of breath, untidy-looking. Her hat was on crooked and she still wore her coat.

"He went to get the laundry, like you told him to."

"What do you know about this?"

She bore down on him, holding out a stack of snapshots. The one on top was so blurred and gray that Cody had trouble deciphering it. He took the whole collection from her hand. Ah, yes: Ezra lay in a stupor, surrounded by liquor bottles. Cody grinned. He'd forgotten that picture completely.

"What could it mean?" his mother asked. "I take a roll of film to the drugstore and I come back with the shock of my life. I just wanted to get the camera ready for Christmas. I was expecting maybe some scenes from last summer, or Jenny's birthday cake . . . and here I find Ezra like a derelict! A common drunk! Could this be what it looks like? Answer me!"

"He's not as perfect as you think he is," Cody told her.

"But he's never given me a moment's worry."

"He's done a lot that might surprise you."

Pearl sat down on his bed. She was shaking her head, looking stunned. "Oh, Cody, it's such a battle, raising children," she said. "I know you must think I'm difficult. I lose my temper, I carry on like a shrew sometimes, but if you could just realize how . . . helpless I feel!

How scary it is to know that everyone I love depends on me! I'm afraid I'll do something wrong."

She reached up—for the photos, he thought, and he held them out to her; but no, what she wanted was his hand. She took it and pulled him down beside her. Her skin felt hot and dry. "I've probably been too hard on you," she said. "But I look to you for support now, Cody. You're the only person I can turn to; it may be you and I are more alike than you think. Cody, what am I going to do?"

She leaned closer, and Cody drew back. Even her eyes seemed to give off heat. "Uh, well . . ." he said.

"Who took that picture, anyhow? Was it you?"

"Look," he said. "It was a joke."

"Joke?"

"Ezra didn't drink that stuff. I just set some bottles around him."

Her gaze flicked back and forth across his face.

"He's never touched a drop," Cody told her.

"I see," she said. She freed his hand. She said, "Well, all I can say is, that's some joke, young man." Then she stood up and took several steps away from him. "That's some sense of humor you've got," she said.

Cody shrugged.

"Oh, I suppose it must seem very funny, scaring your mother half out of her wits. Letting her babble on like a fool. Slandering your little brother. It must seem hilarious, to someone like you."

"I'm just naturally mean, I guess," Cody said.

"You've been mean since the day you were born," she told him.

After she had walked out, he went to work resealing his father's letter.

Ezra landed on Park Place and Cody said, "Aha! Park Place with one hotel. Fifteen hundred dollars."

"Poor, poor Ezra," Jenny said.

"How'd you do that?" Ezra asked Cody.

"How'd I do what?"

"How'd you get a hotel on Park Place? A minute ago it was mortgaged."

"Oh, I scrimped and saved," Cody said.

"There's something peculiar going on here."

"Mother!" Jenny called. "Cody's cheating again!"

Their mother was stringing the Christmas tree lights. She looked over and said, "Cody."

"What did I do?" Cody asked.

"What did he do, children?"

"He's the banker," Jenny said. "He made us let him keep the bank and the deeds and the houses. Now he's got a hotel on Park Place and all this extra money. It's not fair!"

Pearl set down the box of lights and came over to where they were sitting. She said, "All right, Cody, put it back. Jenny keeps the deeds from now on; Ezra keeps the bank. Is that clear?"

Jenny reached for the deeds. Ezra began collecting the money.

"And I tell you this," Pearl said. "If I hear one more word, Cody Tull, you're out of the game. Forever! Understood?" She bent to help Ezra. "Always cheating, tormenting, causing trouble . . ." She laid the fives beside the ones, the tens beside the fives. "Cody? You hear what I say?"

He heard, but he didn't bother answering. He sat back and smiled, safe and removed, watching her stack the money.

3
DESTROYED BY LOVE

I

SUPPOSEDLY, JENNY TULL was going to be a beauty someday, but the people who told her that were so old they might easily be dead by the time that day arrived, and no one her own age saw much promise in her. At seventeen, she was skinny and severe and studious-looking. Her bones were so sharp, they seemed likely to puncture her skin. She had coarse dark hair that she was always hacking at, much to her mother's disapproval—one week chopping it to a blunt, square shape; the next week cutting bangs that accidentally slanted toward the left; and then, to correct her error, shortening the bangs so drastically that they appeared damaged and painful. While her classmates were wearing (in 1952) bouffant skirts and perky blouses with the collars turned up in the back, Jenny's clothes were hand-me-downs from her mother: limp, skimpy dresses fashionable in the forties, with too much shoulder and not enough skirt. And since her mother despised the sloppiness of loafers, Jenny's shoes were the same kind of sturdy brown oxfords that her brothers wore. Every morning she clomped off to school looking uncomfortable and cross. No wonder hardly anyone bothered to speak to her.

She was about to be, for the very first time, the only child at home. Her brother Cody was away at college. Her brother Ezra had refused to go to college and started instead what his mother openly hoped was a temporary job in Scarlatti's Restaurant, chopping vegetables for salads;

but just as he was advancing to sauces, notice came that he'd been drafted. None of his family could envision it: placid Ezra slogging through Korea, tripping over his bayonet at every opportunity. Surely something would be wrong with him, some weakness of spine or eyesight that would save him. But no, he was found to be in perfect health, and in February was ordered off to a training camp down south. Jenny sat on his bed while he packed. She was touched by the fact that he was taking along his little pearwood recorder, the one he'd bought with his first week's wages. It didn't seem to her that he had a very clear idea of what he was getting into. He moved in his cautious, deliberate way, sorting out what he would send to the basement for storage. Since their mother had plans for renting his room, he couldn't just leave things as they were. Already his brother Cody's bed was freshly made up for a boarder, the blankets tight as drumskins on the narrow mattress, and Cody's sports equipment was packed away in cartons.

She watched Ezra empty a drawer of undershirts, most of them full of holes. (Somehow, he always managed to look like an orphan.) He had grown to be a large-boned man, but his face was still childishly rounded, with the wide eyes, the downy cheeks, the delicate lips of a schoolboy. His hair seemed formed of layers of silk in various shades of yellow and beige. Girls were always after him, Jenny knew, but he was too shy to take advantage of it—or maybe even to be aware of it. He proceeded through life absentmindedly, meditatively, as if considering some complex mathematical puzzle from which he was bound to look up, you would think, as soon as he found the solution. But he never did.

"After I leave," he told Jenny, "will you stop in at Scarlatti's Restaurant from time to time?"

"Stop in and do what?"

"Well, talk with Mrs. Scarlatti, I mean. Just make sure she's all right."

Mrs. Scarlatti had been without a husband for years, if she'd ever had one, and her only son had recently been killed in action. Jenny knew she must be lonely. But she was a bleak and striking woman, so fashionably dressed that it seemed an insult to her particular section of Baltimore. Jenny couldn't imagine holding a conversation with her. Still, anything for Ezra. She nodded.

"And Josiah too," Ezra said.

"Josiah!"

Josiah was even more difficult—downright terrifying, in fact: Ezra's friend Josiah Payson, close to seven feet tall, excitable, and incoherent. It was generally understood that he wasn't quite right in the head. Back in grade school, the other children had teased him, and they had teased Ezra too and asked Jenny why her brother hung out with dummies. "Everybody knows Josiah should be sent away," they told her. "He ought to go to the crazy house; everybody says so."

She said, "Ezra, *I* can't talk to Josiah. I wouldn't understand him."

"Of course you'd understand," said Ezra. "He speaks English, doesn't he?"

"He jibbers, he jabbers, he stutters!"

"You must have only seen him when they're picking on him. The rest of the time he's fine. Oh, if Mother'd let me have him to the house once, you would know. He's fine! He's as bright as you or me, and maybe brighter."

"Well, if you say so," Jenny told him.

But she wasn't convinced.

After Ezra was gone, it occurred to her that he'd only mentioned outsiders. He hadn't said anything about taking care of their mother. Maybe he assumed that Pearl could manage on her own. She could manage very well, it was true, but Ezra's leaving seemed to take something out of her. She delayed the renting of his room. "I know we need the money," she told Jenny, "but I really can't face it right now. It still has his smell. Maybe if I aired it a while . . . It still has his shape in it, know what I mean? I look in and the air feels full of something warm. I think we ought to wait a bit."

So they lived in the house alone. Jenny felt even slighter than usual, overwhelmed by so much empty space. In the afternoons when she came home from school, her mother would still be at work, and Jenny would open the door and hesitantly step inside. Sometimes it seemed there was a startled motion, or a stopping of motion, somewhere deep in the house just as she crossed the threshold. She'd pause then, heart thumping, alert as a deer, but it never turned out to be anything real. She'd close the door behind her and go upstairs to her room, turn on her study lamp, change out of her school clothes. She was an orderly, conscientious girl who always hung things up and took good care of her belongings. She would set her books out neatly on her desk, align her pencils, and adjust the lamp so it shone at the proper angle. Then she'd work her way systematically through her assignments. Her greatest dream was to be a doctor, which meant she'd have to win a scholarship. In three years of high school, she had never received a grade below an A.

At five o'clock she would go downstairs to scrub the potatoes or start the chicken frying—whatever was instructed in her mother's note on the kitchen table. Soon afterward her mother would arrive. "Well! I tell you that old Pendle woman is a trial and a nuisance, just a nuisance, lets me ring up all her groceries and then says, 'Wait now, let me see, why, I don't have near enough money for such a bill as this.' Goes fumbling through her ratty cloth change purse while everyone behind her shifts from foot to foot. . . ." She would tie an apron over her dress and take Jenny's place at the stove. "Honey, hand me the salt, will you? I see there's no mail from the boys. They've forgotten all about us, it seems. It's only you and me now."

It was only the two of them, yes, but there were echoes of the others all around—wicked, funny Cody, peaceful Ezra, setting up a loaded silence as Jenny and her mother seated themselves at the table. "Pour the milk, will you, dear? Help yourself to some beans." Sometimes Jenny imagined that even her father made his absence felt, though she couldn't picture his face and had little recollection of the time before he'd left them. Of course she never mentioned this to her mother. Their talk was small talk, little dibs and dabs of things, safely skating over whatever might lie beneath. "How is that poor Carroll girl, Jenny? Has she lost any weight that you've noticed?"

Jenny knew that, in reality, her mother was a dangerous person—hot breathed and full of rage and unpredictable. The dry, straw texture of her lashes could seem the result of some conflagration, and her pale hair could crackle electrically from its bun and her eyes could get small as hatpins. Which of her children had not felt her stinging slap, with the claw-encased pearl in her engagement ring that could bloody a lip at one flick? Jenny had seen her hurl Cody down a flight of stairs. She'd seen Ezra ducking, elbows raised, warding off an attack. She herself, more than once, had been slammed against a wall, been called "serpent," "cockroach," "hideous little sniveling guttersnipe." But here Pearl sat, decorously inquiring about Julia Carroll's weight problem. Jenny had a faint, tremulous hope that times had changed. Perhaps it was the boys' fault. Maybe she and her mother—intelligent women, after all—could live without such scenes forever. But she never felt entirely secure, and at night, when Pearl had placed a kiss on the center of Jenny's forehead, Jenny went off to bed and dreamed what she had always dreamed: her mother laughed a witch's shrieking laugh; dragged Jenny out of hiding as the Nazis tramped up the stairs; accused her of sins and crimes that had never crossed Jenny's mind. Her mother told her, in an informative and considerate tone of voice, that she was raising Jenny to eat her.

Cody wrote almost never, and what letters he did write were curt and factual. *I won't be coming home for spring vacation. All my grades are fine except French. This new job pays better than the old one did.* Ezra sent a postcard the moment he arrived in camp, and followed that three days later with a letter describing his surroundings. It was longer than several of Cody's put together, but still it didn't tell Jenny what she wanted to know. *There's somebody two blocks down who's from Maryland too I hear but I haven't had a chance to talk to him and I don't think he's from Baltimore anyway but some other place I wouldn't know about so I doubt we'd have much to . . .* What was he saying, exactly? Had he, or had he not, made any friends? If people lived so close together, you'd think they would have talked. Jenny pictured the others ignoring him, or worse: tormenting him and making fun of his incompetence. He simply was not a soldier. But *I have learned right much about my rifle,* he wrote. *Cody would be surprised.* She tried to imagine his long, sensitive fingers cleaning and oiling a gun. She understood that he must be surviving, more or less, but she couldn't figure out how. She thought of him on his belly, in the dust of the rifle range, squeezing a trigger. His gaze was so reflective, how would he hit a target? *They say the whole bunch of us will be joining the Korean Conflict as soon as we are . . .* Why, they'd pick him off like a fly! He'd never do more to defend himself than dodge and shield his head.

I think a lot about Scarlatti's Restaurant and how nice the lettuce smelled when I tore it into the bowl, he wrote—his only mention of homesickness, if that was what it was. Pearl gave a jealous sniff. "As if lettuce had a smell!" Jenny was jealous too; he could have remembered, instead, how he and she used to lie on the floor in front of the Philco on Monday nights, listening to the Cities Service Band of America. What did he see in that restaurant, anyhow? Then a little knob of discomfort started nudging inside her chest. There was something she hadn't done, something unpleasant that she didn't want to do. . . . Check on Mrs. Scarlatti. She wondered if Ezra had really meant for her to keep her promise. He couldn't actually expect that of her, could he? But she supposed he could. He was a literal-minded kind of person.

So she folded Ezra's letter and put it in her pocket. Then she slipped her coat on and walked to St. Paul Street, to a narrow brick building set in a strip of shops and businesses.

Scarlatti's was the neighborhood's one formal elegant eating place. It served only supper, mostly to people from better parts of the city. At this hour—five-thirty or so—it wouldn't even be open. She went to the rear, where she'd been a couple of times with Ezra. She circled two garbage cans overflowing with wilted greens, and she climbed the steps and knocked on the door. Then she cupped a hand to the windowpane and peered in.

Men in dirty aprons were rushing around the kitchen, which was a mass of steam and stainless steel, pot lids clattering, bowls as big as birdbaths heaped with sliced vegetables. No wonder they hadn't heard her. She turned the knob, but the door was locked. And before she could knock any harder, she caught sight of Mrs. Scarlatti. She was slouched in the dining room entranceway, holding a lit cigarette—a white-faced woman in a stark black knife of a dress. Whatever she was saying, Jenny couldn't catch it, but she heard the gravelly, careless sound of her voice. And she saw how Mrs. Scarlatti's black hair was swept completely to the right, like one of those extreme *Vogue* magazine model's, and how she leaned her head to the right as well so that she seemed to be burdened, cruelly misused, bearing up under an exhausting weight that had something to do with men and experience. Imagine Ezra knowing such a person! Imagine him at ease with her, close enough to worry about her. Jenny backed away. She understood, all at once, that her brothers had grown up and gone. Her mental pictures of them were outdated—Ezra playing the bamboo whistle he used to have in grade school. Cody triumphantly rattling his dice over their old Monopoly board. She thought of a faded flannel shirt that Ezra had worn so often, it was like a second skin. She thought of how he would rock back and forth with his hands in his rear pockets when he was lost for something to say, or dig a hole in the ground with his sneaker. And how when Jenny was shattered by one of their mother's rages, he would slip downstairs to the kitchen and fix her a mug of hot milk laced with honey, sprinkled over with cinnamon. He was always so quick to catch his family's moods, and to offer food and drink and unspoken support.

She traveled down the alley and, instead of heading home, took Bushnell Street and then Putnam. It was getting colder; she had to button her coat. Three blocks down Putnam stood a building so weathered and dismal, you'd think it was an abandoned warehouse till you saw the sign: TOM 'N' EDDIE'S BODY SHOP. She had often come here to fetch Ezra home, but she'd only called his name at the drive-in doorway; she had never been inside. Now she stepped into the gloom and looked around her. Tom and Eddie (she assumed) were talking to a man in a business suit; one of them held a clipboard. In the background, Josiah Payson swung a gigantic rubber mallet against the fender of a pickup. Jenny was hit by a piece of memory, a mystifying fragment: Josiah in the school yard, long ago, violently flailing a pipe or a metal bar of some sort, cutting a desperate, whizzing circle in the air and shouting something unintelligible while Ezra stood guard between him and a mob of children. "Everything will be fine; just go away," Ezra was telling the others. But what had happened next? How had it ended? How had it started? She felt confused. Meanwhile Josiah swung his mallet. He was grotesquely tall, as gaunt as the armature for some statue never completed. His cropped black hair bristled all over his head, his skull of a face glistened, and he clenched a set of teeth so ragged and white and crowded, so jumbled together and overlapping, that it seemed he had chewed them up and was preparing to spit them out.

"Josiah," she called timidly.

He stopped to look at her. Or was he looking someplace else? His eyes were dead black—lidless and almost Oriental. It was impossible to tell where they were directed. He heaved the hammer onto a stack of burlap bags and lunged toward her, his face alight with happiness. "Ezra's sister!" he said. "Ezra!"

She smiled and hugged her elbows.

Directly in front of her, he came to a halt and smoothed his stubble of hair. His arms seemed longer than they should have been. "Is Ezra okay?" he asked her.

"He's fine."

"Not wounded or—"

"No."

Ezra was right: Josiah spoke as distinctly as anyone, in a grown man's rumbling voice. But he had trouble finding something to do with his hands, and ended up scraping them together as if trying to rid his palms of dirt or grease, or even of a layer of skin. She was aware of Tom and Eddie glancing over at her curiously, losing track of their conversation. "Come outside," she told Josiah. "I'll let you see his letter."

Outside it was twilight, almost too dark to read, but Josiah took the letter anyway and scanned the lines. There was a crease between his eyebrows as deep as if someone had pressed an ax blade there. She noticed that his coveralls, pathetically well washed, were so short for him that his fallen white socks and hairy shinbones showed. His lips could barely close over that chaos of teeth; his mouth had a bunchy look and his chin was elongated from the effort.

He handed the letter back to her. She had no way of knowing what he had got out of it. "If they'd let me," he said, "I'd have gone with him. Oh, I wouldn't mind going. But they claimed I was too tall."

"Too tall?"

She'd never heard of such a thing.

"So I had to stay behind," he said, "but I didn't want to. I don't want to work in a body shop all my life; I plan to do something different."

"Like what?"

"Oh, I don't know. Find something with Ezra, I guess, once he gets out of the army. Ezra, he would always come to visit me here and look around and say, 'How can you stand it? All the noise,' he'd say. 'We got to find you something different.' But I didn't know where to start hunting, and now Ezra's gone away. It's not the noise that's so bad, but it's hot in summer and cold in winter. My feet get bothered by the cold, get these itchy things all over the toes."

"Chilblains, maybe," Jenny suggested. She felt pleasantly bored; it seemed she had known Josiah forever. She ran a thumb-nail down the crease of Ezra's letter. Josiah gazed either at her or straight through her (it was hard to tell which) and cracked his knuckles.

"Probably what I'll do is work for Ezra," he said, "once Ezra opens his restaurant."

"What are you talking about? Ezra's not opening a restaurant."

"Sure he is."

"Why would he want to do that? As soon as he pulls himself together he's going off to college, studying to be a teacher."

"Who says so?" Josiah asked.

"Well, my mother does. He's got the patience for it, she says. Maybe he'll be a professor, even," Jenny told him. But she wasn't so certain now. "I mean, it's not a lifework, restaurants."

"Why isn't it?"

She couldn't answer.

"Ezra's going to have him a place where people come just like to a family dinner," Josiah said. "He'll cook them one thing special each day and dish it out on their plates and everything will be solid and wholesome, really homelike."

"Ezra told you that?"

"Really just like home."

"Well, I don't know, maybe people go to restaurants to get *away* from home."

"It's going to be famous," Josiah said.

"You have the wrong idea entirely," Jenny told him. "How did you come up with such a crazy notion?"

Then without warning, Josiah went back to being his old self—or her old picture of him. He dropped his head, like a marionette whose strings had snapped. "I got to go," he told her.

"Josiah?"

"Don't want those people yelling at me."

He loped away without saying goodbye. Jenny watched after him as regretfully as if he were Ezra himself. He didn't look back.

Cody wrote that he was being interviewed by several corporations. He wanted a job in business after he finished school. Ezra wrote that he could march twenty miles at a go now without much tiring. It began to seem less incongruous, even perfectly natural, that Ezra should be a soldier. After all, wasn't he an enduring sort, uncomplaining, cheerful in performing his duties? Jenny had worried needlessly. Her mother too seemed to relax somewhat. "Really it's for the best, when you think about it," she said. "A stint in the service is often just the ticket; gives a boy time to get hold of himself. I bet when he comes back, he'll want to go to college. I bet he'll want to teach someplace."

Jenny didn't tell her about his restaurant.

Twice, after her first visit to Josiah, she looked in on him again. She would stop by the body shop after school, and Josiah would come outside a moment to swing his arms and gaze beyond her and speak of Ezra. "Got a letter from him myself, over at the house. Claimed he was marching a lot."

"Twenty miles," Jenny said.

"Some of it uphill."

"He must be in pretty good shape by now."

"He always did like to walk."

The third time she came, it was almost dark. She'd stayed late for chorus. Josiah was just leaving work. He was getting into his jacket, which was made of a large, shaggy plaid in muted shades of navy and maroon. She thought of the jackets that little boys wore in the lower grades of school. "That Tom," Josiah said, jabbing his fists in his pockets. "That Eddie." He strode rapidly down the sidewalk. Jenny had trouble keeping up. "They don't care how they talk to a fellow," he said. "Don't give a thought to what he might feel; feelings just like anyone else. . . ."

She dropped back, deciding that he'd rather be alone, but partway down the block he stopped and turned and waited. "Aren't I a human being?" he asked when she arrived at his side. "Don't I feel bad if someone shouts at me? I wish I were out in the woods someplace, none of these people to bother me. Camping out in a dead, dead quiet with a little private tent from L.L. Bean and an L.L. Bean sleeping bag." He turned and rushed on; Jenny had to run. "I've half a mind to give notice," he said.

"Why don't you, then?"

"My mama needs the money."

"You could find something else."

"Oh, no, it isn't easy."

"Why not?"

He didn't answer. They raced past a discount jewelry store, a bakery, a bank of private apartments with inviting yellow windows. Then he said, "Come and have supper at our house."

"What? Oh, I can't."

"Ezra used to come," he said, "back before he worked in the restaurant and couldn't get away. My mama was always glad to set an extra plate out, always, anytime. But *your* mother didn't often let him; your mother doesn't like me."

"Oh, well. . . ."

"I wish you'd just have supper with us."

She paused. Then she said, "I'd be happy to."

He didn't seem surprised. (Jenny was astonished, herself.) He grunted and continued to tear along. His whisks of black hair stood out around his head. He led her down a side street, then through an alley that Jenny wasn't familiar with.

From the front, his house must have been very much like hers—a brick row house set in a tiny yard. But they approached it from the rear, where a tacked-on, gray frame addition gave it a ramshackle look. The addition turned out to be an unheated pantry with a cracked linoleum floor. Josiah stopped there to work himself free of his jacket, and then he reached for Jenny's coat and hung them both on hooks beside the door. "Mama?" he called. He showed Jenny into the kitchen. "Got company for supper, Mama."

Mrs. Payson stood at the stove—a small, chubby woman dressed in earth tones. She reminded Jenny of some modest brown bird. Her face was round and smooth and shining. She looked up and smiled, and since Josiah failed to make the introduction Jenny said, "I'm Jenny Tull."

"Oh, any kin to Ezra?"

"I'm his sister."

"My, I'm just so fond of that boy," Mrs. Payson said. She lifted the pot from the stove and set it on the table. "When he was called up I cried, did Josiah tell you? I sat right down and cried. Why, he has been like a son to me, always in and out of the house. . . ." She laid three place settings while Josiah poured the milk. "I'll never forget," she said, "back when Josiah's daddy died, Ezra came and sat with us, and fixed us meals, and made us cocoa. I said, 'Ezra, I feel selfish, taking you from your family,' but he said, 'Don't you worry about it, Mrs. Payson.' "

Jenny wondered when that could have been. Ezra had never mentioned Mr. Payson's dying.

Supper was spaghetti and a salad, with chocolate cake for dessert. Jenny ate sparingly, planning to eat again when she got home so her mother wouldn't guess; but Josiah had several helpings of everything. Mrs. Payson kept refilling his plate. "To look at him," she said, "you'd never know he eats so much, would you? Skinny as a fence post. I reckon he's still a growing boy." She laughed, and Josiah grinned bashfully with his eyes cast down—a skeletal, stooped, hunkering man. Jenny had never thought about the fact that Josiah was somebody's son, some woman's greatest treasure. His stubby black lashes were lowered; his prickly head was bent over his plate. He was so certain of being loved, here if no place else. She looked away.

After supper she helped with the dishes, placing each clean plate and glass on open wooden shelves whose edges had grown soft from too many coats of paint. Her mother would be frantic by now, but Jenny lingered over the wiping of each fork. Then Josiah walked her home. "Come back and see us!" Mrs. Payson called from the doorway. "Make sure you're buttoned up!" Jenny thought of . . . was it "Jack and the Beanstalk"? . . . or perhaps some other fairy tale, where the humble widow, honest and warmhearted, lives in a cottage with her son. Everything else—the cold dark of the streets, the picture of her own bustling mother—seemed brittle by comparison, lacking the smoothly rounded completeness of Josiah's life.

They walked up Calvert Street without talking, puffing clouds of steam. They crossed to Jenny's house and climbed the porch steps. "Well," said Jenny, "thank you for inviting me, Josiah."

Josiah made some awkward, jerky motion that she assumed was an effort toward speech. He stumbled closer, enveloped her in a circle of rough plaid, and kissed her on the lips. She had trouble, at first, understanding what was happening. Then she felt a terrible dismay, not so much for herself as for Josiah. Oh, it was sad, he had misread everything; he would be so embarrassed! But how could he have made such an error? Thinking it over (pressed willy-nilly against his whiskery chin, against the knobbiness of his mouth), she saw things suddenly from his viewpoint: their gentle little "romance" (was what he must call it), as seamless as the Widow Payson's fairy tale existence. She longed for it; she wished it were true. She ached, with something like nostalgia, for a contented life with his mother in her snug house, for an innocent, protective marriage. She kissed him back, feeling even through all those layers of wool how he tensed and trembled.

Then light burst out, the front door slammed open, and her mother's voice broke over them. "What? What? What is the meaning of this?"

They leapt apart.

"You piece of trash," Pearl said to Jenny. "You tramp. You trashy thing. So this is what you've been up to! Not so much as notifying me where you are, supper not started, I'm losing my mind with worry—then here I find you! Necking? Necking with a, with a—"

For lack of a word, it seemed, she struck out. She slapped Jenny hard across the cheek. Jenny's eyes filled with tears. Josiah, as if it were he who'd been struck, averted his face sharply and stared away at some distant point. His mouth was working but no sound came forth.

"With a crazy! A dummy! A retarded person. You did it to spite me, didn't you," Pearl told Jenny. "It's your way of making mock of me. All these afternoons that I've been slaving in the grocery store, you were off in some alleyway, weren't you, off with this animal, this gorilla, letting him take his pleasure, just to shame me."

Josiah said, "But-but-but—"

"Just to show me up when I had such great plans for you. Cutting school, no doubt, lying with him in bushes and back seats of cars and maybe this very house, for all I know, while I'm off slaving at Sweeney Brothers—"

"But! But! Aagh!" Josiah shouted, and he sputtered so that Jenny saw white flecks flying in the lamplight. Then he flung out his scarecrow arms and plunged down the steps and disappeared.

She didn't see him again, of course. She chose her routes carefully and never again came near him, never approached any place that he was likely to be found; and she assumed he did the same. It was as if, by mutual agreement, they had split the city between them.

And besides, she had no reason to see him: Ezra's letters stopped.

Ezra appeared in person. One Sunday morning, there he was, sitting in the kitchen when Jenny came down to breakfast. He wore his old civilian clothes that had been packed away in mothballs—jeans and a scruffy blue sweater. They hung on him like something borrowed. It was alarming how much weight he had lost. His hair was unbecomingly short and his face was paler, older, shadowed beneath his eyes. He sat slumped, clamping his hands between his knees, while Pearl scraped a piece of scorched toast into the sink. "Jam or honey, which?" she was asking. "Jenny, look who's here! It's Ezra, safe and sound! Let me pour you more coffee, Ezra." Ezra didn't speak, but he gave Jenny a tired smile.

He'd been discharged, as it turned out. For sleepwalking. He had no memory of sleepwalking, but every night he dreamed the same dream: he was marching through an unchanging terrain of cracked mud flats without a tree or a sprig of grass, with a blank blue bowl of sky overhead. He would set one foot in front of the other and march and march and march. In the morning, his muscles would ache. He'd thought it was from his *waking* marches, till they told him differently. All night, they told him, he roamed the camp, plodding between the rows of cots. Soldiers would stir and sit up and say, "Tull? That you?" and he would leave. He wouldn't answer, wouldn't wake, but simply went someplace else. To some of the soldiers, the youngest ones, his silence was frightening. There were complaints. He was sent to a doctor, who gave him a box of yellow pills. With the pills he still walked, but he would fall down from time to time and just lie where he fell until morning. Once he must have landed on his face; when they roused him, his nose was bloody and they thought it might be broken. It wasn't, but for several days he had purple circles under his eyes. Then they sent him to a chaplain, who asked if Ezra had anything particular on his mind. Was there some trouble back home, perhaps? Woman trouble? Illness in his family? Ezra said no. He told the chaplain things were fine; he couldn't for the life of him think what this was all about. The chaplain asked if he liked the army and Ezra said, well, it wasn't something you would like or dislike; it was something you had to get through, was more to the point. He said the army wasn't his style, exactly—what with the shouting, the noise—but still, he was coming along. He guessed he was doing all right. The chaplain said just to try not to sleepwalk again, in that case; but the very next night Ezra walked directly into town, four and a half miles in his olive-drab underwear with his eyes wide open but flat as windows, and a waitress in a diner had to wake him up and get her brother-in-law to drive him back to camp. The next day they called another doctor in, and the doctor asked him a series of questions and signed some papers and sent him home. "So here I am," Ezra said in a toneless voice. "Discharged."

"But honorably," said his mother.

"Oh, yes."

"The thought! All the while this was going on, you never said a word."

"Well, how could you have helped?" he asked.

The question seemed to age her. She sagged.

After breakfast he went upstairs and fell on his bed and slept through the day, and Jenny had to wake him for supper. Even then he could barely keep his eyes open. He sat groggily swaying, eating almost nothing, nodding off in the middle of a mouthful. Then he went back to bed. Jenny wandered through the house and fidgeted with the cords of window shades. Was this how he was going to be, now? Had he changed forever?

But Monday morning, he was Ezra again. She heard his little pearwood recorder playing "Greensleeves" before she was even dressed. When she came downstairs he was scrambling eggs the way she liked, with cheese and bits of green pepper, while Pearl read the paper. And at breakfast he said, "I guess I'll go get my old job back." Pearl glanced over at him but said nothing. "How come you didn't call on Mrs. Scarlatti?" Ezra asked Jenny. "She wrote and said you never came."

Jenny said, "Oh, well, I meant to. . . ."

She lowered her eyes and held her breath, waiting. Now was when he would mention Josiah. But he didn't. She looked up and found him buttering a piece of toast, and she let out her breath. She was never going to be certain of what Ezra knew, or didn't know.

II

BY THE TIME Jenny reached college, she'd grown to be the beauty that everyone predicted. Or was it only that she'd come into fashion? Her mirror showed the same face, so far as she could tell, but most of her dormitory's phone calls seemed to be for her, and if she hadn't been working her way through school (waiting tables, folding laundry, shelving books in the library stacks), she could have gone out every night. Away from Baltimore, her looks lost a little of their primness. She let her hair grow and she developed a breathless, flyaway air. But she never forgot about medical school. Her future was always clear to her: a straightforward path to a pediatric practice in a medium-sized city, preferably not too far from a coast. (She liked knowing she could get out anytime. Wouldn't midwesterners feel claustrophobic?) Friends teased her about her single-mindedness. Her roommate objected to Jenny's study light, was exasperated by the finicky way she aligned her materials on her desk. In this respect, at least, Jenny hadn't changed.

Meanwhile, her brother Cody had become a success—shot ahead through several different firms, mainly because of his ideas for using the workers' time better; and then branched out on his own to become an efficiency expert. And Ezra still worked for Mrs. Scarlatti, but he had advanced as well. He really ran the kitchen now, while Mrs. Scarlatti played hostess out front. Jenny's mother wrote to say it was a shame, a crime and a shame. *I tell him the longer he piddles about in that woman's restaurant the harder he'll find it to get back on track, you know he always intended to go to college. . . .*

Pearl still clerked at the grocery store but was better dressed, looking less careworn, since Jenny's scholarship and part-time jobs had relieved the last financial strain. Jenny saw her twice a year—at Christmas and just before the start of school each September. She made excuses for the other holidays, and during the summers she worked at a clothing shop in a small town near her college. It wasn't that she didn't want to see her mother. She often thought of her wiry energy, the strength she had shown in raising her children singlehanded, and her unfailing interest in their progress. But whenever Jenny returned, she was dampened almost instantly by the atmosphere of the house—by its lack of light, the cramped feeling of its papered rooms, a certain grim spareness. She almost wondered if she had some kind of allergy. It was like a respiratory ailment; on occasion, she believed she might be smothering. Her head grew stuffy, as it did when she had studied too long without a break. She snapped at people. Even Ezra irritated her, with his calm and his docility.

So she kept her distance, and after missing her family a while began to discard the very thought of them. She grew brisker, busier, more hurried. Ezra's letters—as ponderous as his conversation, just this side of dull—would turn up on the edge of the bathroom sink or crumpled among the bedclothes, where Jenny had laid them aside in midsentence. Her mind just drifted, that was all. And twice, during her first two years in college, Cody stopped to see her while traveling through Pennsylvania on business, and both times she was happy at the prospect (he was so dashing and good-looking, she was proud to show him off), but she felt muffled, gradually, once he'd arrived. It wasn't her fault; it was his. It seemed that everything she said carried, for him, the echo of their mother. She saw him stiffen. She knew exactly what he was thinking. "How are you fixed for money?" he would ask her. "You need a few new dresses?" She would say, "No, thanks, Cody, I'm fine"—really meaning it, needing nothing; but she saw, from his expression, what he had understood her to say: "No, no," in Pearl's thin voice, "never mind me. . . ." She could not straighten his tie, or compliment his suit, or inquire about his present life without setting up that guarded look in his face. It made her feel unjustly accused. Did he really imagine she would be so domineering, or reproachful, or meddlesome? "Look," she tried once. "Let's start over. I didn't intend what you think I intended." But his wary, sidelong glance told her that he suspected even this. There was no way to cut themselves out of the tangle. She let him leave. Back in her dorm room she studied her reflection, her swing of dark hair and her narrow-waisted figure. Then she acted gayer than usual, for a while, and had a sense of having clapped her hands to free them of some thick and clinging dust.

Late in her senior year, she fell in love. She had been in love before, of course—once with an English major who'd grown too possessive, bit by bit; and once with a barrel-necked football star who seemed now, when she looked back, to be a symptom of some temporary insanity. But this was different. This was Harley Baines, a genius, a boy of such intelligence that even his smudged tortoiseshell glasses, pure white skin, and adenoidal voice struck awe in his classmates. He was not outside Jenny's group so much as above it, beyond it—a group in himself. It was rumored that he could have had a Ph.D. at twelve but was kept from it by his parents, who wanted him to enjoy a normal childhood. Next year he'd be at Paulham University, outside Philadelphia, doing advanced research in the field of genetics. Jenny was going to Paulham too; she had just been accepted by its medical school. That was what made her notice Harley Baines. Secure in the center of her own noisy group (which would not be hers much longer, which would soon be scattered by graduation, leaving her defenseless), she looked across the campus and saw Harley Baines passing with his storklike gait, wearing unstylish, pleated flannel trousers and a bulky pullover obviously knitted by his mother. His hair, which could have used a shampoo, was a particularly dense shade of black. She wondered if he knew she was entering Paulham. She wondered if he would care, if he found girls beneath his notice. Was he impervious? Unobtainable? Her friends had to call her name several times, laughing at her bemused expression.

It was the spring of 1957—an unusually late and gradual spring. Professors opened the classroom windows with long, hooked poles, and the smell of lilacs floated in. Jenny wore sleeveless blouses and full skirts and ballerina flats. Harley Baines laid aside his home-knit sweater. Bared, his arms were muscular, thick with black hair. Around his neck he wore a gold or brass disk of some kind. She was dying to know what it was. One day in German class, she asked. He said it was a medal he'd won in a high school science fair, for setting up an experiment on the metabolic rate of white rats. She thought it was a funny thing to go on wearing all this time, but she didn't say so. Instead, she touched the medal lightly with her fingertips. It hung just inside his shirt, and it was almost hot.

She asked him at other times (catching up with him in a corridor, arranging to stand behind him in the cafeteria line) whether he was looking forward to Paulham University, and what sort of housing he would have there, and what he'd heard about Paulham's public transportation system. Offering these questions in an even, noncommittal voice, she felt like one of those circus trainers who take care to present to an animal only the curled-in backs of their hands, showing they pose no threat. She didn't want to alarm him. But Harley didn't act alarmed at all, and answered her courteously, matter-of-factly. (Was that good or bad?) When exams began, she came to him with her genetics notes and asked if he could help her study. They sat outdoors in the grass, in front of the Student Union, on a blue chenille bedspread she'd brought from her room. Their classmates lounged on other bed-spreads all around them—including some of Jenny's friends, who cast her startled, doubtful looks and then glanced quickly past her. She'd been hoping they would stroll over, make Harley a part of the group. But on second thought, she could see that would never happen.

While she framed her queries (acting not so slow-witted as to put him off, but still in need of his assistance), Harley listened and stripped a grass blade. He wore heavy, dressy shoes that seemed out of place on the bedspread. In his probing hands, the grass blade took on the look of a scientific experiment. He answered her levelly, with no question marks after his sentences; he took it for granted that she would un-derstand him. Which she did, in fact, and would have even if she hadn't known her subject ahead of time. His logic proceeded steadily from A to B to C. In his slowness and his thoroughness, he reminded her of Ezra—though otherwise, how different they were! When he finished, he asked if everything was clear now. "Yes, thank you," she said, and he nodded and rose to go. Was that *it?* She rose too, and felt suddenly dizzy—not from standing, she believed, but from love. He had actually managed to bowl her over. She wondered what he would do if she threw her arms around him and collapsed against him, laid her face on his white, white chest, burned her cheek on his scientific medal. Instead she asked, "Will you help me fold the bedspread, please?" He bent to lift one end, and she lifted the other. They advanced. He gave his end to her and then soberly brushed off every wisp of grass, every flower petal and grain of pollen, from his side of the spread. After that he took the spread back again, evidently assuming that she would brush off her side. She looked up into his face. He stepped forward, flipped the spread around him like a hooded cloak, and wrapped her inside its darkness and kissed her. His glasses knocked against her nose. It was an unskillful kiss anyhow, too abrupt, and she couldn't help imagining the picture they made—a blue chenille pillar in the middle of the campus, a twin-sized mummy. She laughed. He dropped the spread and turned on his heel and walked off very fast. A plume of hair bobbed on the back of his head like a rooster's tail.

Jenny returned to her room and took a bath and changed to a ruffled dress. She leaned out her open window, humming. Harley didn't come. Eventually she went to supper, but he wasn't in the cafeteria, either.

The next day, after her last exam, she phoned his dormitory. Some sleepy-sounding, gruff boy answered. "Baines has left for home," he said.

"Home? But we haven't had graduation yet."

"He's not planning to go through with that."

"Oh," said Jenny. She hadn't thought of graduation as "going through" with anything, although it was true you could simply have your diploma mailed out. To people like Harley Baines, she supposed, a degree was unimportant. (While Jenny's family was coming all the way to Summerfield for this event.) She said, "Well, thank you anyhow," and hung up, hoping her voice didn't sound as forlorn to Harley's roommate as it did to her.

That summer, after graduation, she worked again at Molly's Togs in the little town near the college. It had always seemed a pleasant job, but this year she was depressed by the studied casualness of married women's clothes—their Bermuda shorts for golfing and their wide-hipped khaki skirts. She gazed away unhelpfully when her customers asked, "Does it suit me? Do you think it's too youthful?" Next year at this time, she would be at Paulham. She wondered how soon she could start wearing a starched white coat.

In July, a letter arrived from Harley Baines, forwarded from home by her mother. When Jenny returned to her boarding-house after work, she found it on the hall table. She stood looking at it a moment. Then she slipped it into her straw purse and climbed the stairs. She let herself into her room, threw her purse on the bed, and opened the window. She took a square tin from a drawer and fed the two goldfish in the bowl on the bureau. All before opening Harley's letter.

Did she guess, ahead of time, what it would say?

Later, she imagined that she must have.

His handwriting was as small and separate as typing. She would have imagined something more headlong from a genius. He used a colon after the greeting, as if it were a business letter.

18 July, 1957

Dear Jenny:

I unreasonably took offense at what was, in fact, a natural reaction on your part. I must have seemed ridiculous.

What I had intended, before our misunderstanding, was that we might become better acquainted over the summer and then marry in the fall. I still find marriage a viable option. I know this must seem sudden—we haven't exactly had a normal American courtship—but after all, we are neither of us frivolous people.

Bear in mind that we will both be at Paulham next year and could share a single apartment, buy groceries in economy lots, etc. Also, I sense that your finances have been something of a problem, and I would be glad to assume that responsibility.

The above sounds more pragmatic than I'd intended. Actually, I find I love you, and am awaiting your earliest reply.

Sincerely,

Harley Baines

P.S. I know that you're intelligent. You didn't have to make up all those questions about genetics.

The postscript, she thought, was the most affecting part of the letter. It was written in a looser hand, as if impulsively, while the rest seemed copied and perhaps recopied from a rough draft. She read the letter again, and then folded it and set it on her bed. She went over to study her goldfish, who had left too much food floating on the surface of the water. She would have to cut down on their rations. *Dear Harley,* she practiced. *It was such a surprise to . . .* No. He wouldn't care for gushiness. *Dear Harley: I have considered your terms and . . .* What she was trying to say was "Yes." She was pulled only very slightly by the feelings she'd had for him earlier (which now seemed faded and shallow, a schoolgirl crush brought on by senior panic). What appealed to her more was the *angularity* of the situation—the mighty leap into space with someone she hardly knew. Wasn't that what a marriage ought to be? Like one of those movie-style disasters—shipwrecks or earthquakes or enemy prisons—where strangers, trapped in close quarters by circumstance, show their real strengths and weaknesses.

Lately, her life had seemed to be narrowing. She could predict so easily the successive stages of medical school, internship, and residency. She had looked in a mirror, not so long ago, and realized all at once that the clear, fragile skin around her eyes would someday develop lines. She was going to grow old like anyone else.

She took paper from a bureau drawer, sat down on her bed, and uncapped her fountain pen. *Dear Harley:* she wrote. She plucked a microscopic hair from the pen point. She thought a while. Then she wrote, *All right,* and signed her name—the ultimate in no-nonsense communication. Even Harley couldn't find it excessive.

The following evening, just before supper, Jenny arrived in Baltimore. She had burned all her bridges: quit her job, given away her goldfish, and packed everything in her room. It was the most reckless behavior she had ever shown. On the Greyhound bus she sat grandly upright, periodically shrugging off the snoring soldier who drooped against her. When she reached the terminal she hailed a cab, instead of waiting for a city bus, and rode home in style.

No one had been told she was coming, so she was puzzled by the fact that while she was paying off the driver, the front door of her house opened wide and her mother proceeded across the porch and down the steps in a flowing, flowered dress, high-heeled pumps, and a hat whose black net veil was dotted with what looked like beauty spots. Behind her came Ezra in unpressed clothes that were a little too full cut, and last was Cody, dark and handsome and New Yorkish in a fine-textured, fitted gray suit and striped silk tie. For a second, Jenny fancied they were headed for her funeral. This was how they would look—formally dressed and refraining from battle—if Jenny were no longer among them. Then she shook the thought away, and smiled and climbed out of the taxi.

Her mother halted on the sidewalk. "My stars!" she said. "Ezra, when you say family dinner, you *mean* family dinner!" She raised her veil to kiss Jenny's cheek. "Why didn't you tell us you were coming? Ezra, did you plan it this way?"

"I didn't know a thing about it," Ezra said. "I thought of writing you, Jenny, but I didn't think you'd come all this distance just for supper."

"Supper?" Jenny asked.

"It's some idea of Ezra's," Pearl told her. "He found out Cody was passing through, maybe spending the night, and he said, 'I want both of you to get all dressed up—' "

"I am *not* spending the *night*," Cody said. "I'm running on a schedule here, when will you see that? I shouldn't even be staying for supper. I ought to be in Delaware."

"Ezra's got something he wants to say," Pearl said, picking a thread off Jenny's sundress, "some announcement he wants to make, and is taking us to Scarlatti's Restaurant. Though hot as it is, I believe a leaf of lettuce is just about all I could manage. Jenny, honey, you're thin as a stick! And what's in this big suitcase? How long are you planning to stay?"

"Oh, well . . . not long," Jenny said. She felt shy about telling her news. "Maybe I ought to change clothes. I'm not as dressed up as the rest of you."

"No, no, you're fine," Ezra told her. He was rubbing his hands together, the way he always did when he was pleased. "Oh, it's working out so well!" he said. "A real family dinner! It's just like fate."

Cody took Jenny's suitcase inside the house. Meanwhile, her mother fussed: smoothing Jenny's hair, clucking at her bare legs. "No stockings! On a public conveyance." Cody came back and opened the door of a shiny blue car at the curb. He helped Pearl in, cupping her elbow. "What do you think of my car?" he said to Jenny.

"It's very nice. Did you buy it new?"

"How else? A Pontiac. Smell that new-car smell," he said. He walked around to the driver's seat. Jenny and Ezra settled in the rear; Ezra's knobby wrists dangled between his knees.

"Of course, it's not yet paid for," Cody said, pulling into traffic, "but it will be very soon."

"Cody Tull!" his mother said. "You didn't go in debt for this."

"Why not? I'm getting rich, I tell you. Five years from now I can walk into an auto dealer, any dealer—Cadillac—and slap cold cash on the counter and say, 'I'll take three. Or on second thought, make that four.' "

"But not now," said Pearl. "Not yet. You know how I feel about buying on time."

"Time is what I deal with," Cody said. He laughed, and shot through an amber light. "What could be more fitting? Ten years more, you'll be riding in a limousine."

"Why would I want to do that?"

"And Ezra can go to Princeton, if he likes. And I can buy Jenny a clinic all her own. I can pay for her to specialize in every field, one by one."

Now was the moment for Jenny to mention Harley, but she watched the scenery and said nothing.

At Scarlatti's, they were shown to a table in the corner, at the end of the long, brocade-draped dining room. It was early evening, not yet dark. The restaurant was almost empty. Jenny wondered where Mrs. Scarlatti was. She started to ask about her, but Ezra was too busy overseeing their meal. He had ordered ahead, evidently, and now wanted it known that four would be eating instead of three. "We have my sister with us too. It's going to be a real family dinner." The waiter, who seemed fond of Ezra, nodded and went to the kitchen.

Ezra sat back and smiled at the others. Pearl was polishing a fork with her napkin. Cody was still talking about money. "I plan to buy a place in Baltimore County," he said, "in the not-too-distant future. There's no particular reason that I should be based in New York. I always did want land, that rolling Maryland farmland. I might raise horses."

"Horses! Oh, Cody, really, that's just not our style," Pearl said. "What would you want with horses?"

"Mother," Cody said, "anything's our style. Don't you see? There's no limit. Mother, do you know who called for my services last week? The Tanner Corporation."

Pearl set her fork down. Jenny tried to remember where she had heard that name before. It rang just the dimmest bell; it was like some lowly household object that you never look at, and only notice when you return after years of absence. "Tanner?" she asked Cody. "What's that?"

"It's where our father worked."

"Oh, yes."

"Where he still may, for all I know. But, Jenny, you should have seen it. Such a nickel-and-dime operation . . . I mean, not small, good Lord, with that mess of branch offices overlapping and conflicting, but so . . . tacky. Really so easily encompassed. And I was thinking: imagine, just like that, I have them in my power. The Tanner Corporation! The great, almighty Tanner Corporation. That afternoon, I went out and ordered my Pontiac."

"There was never," Pearl said, "the slightest thing tacky about the Tanner Corporation."

Their appetizers arrived on chilled plates, along with a slender, pale green bottle of wine. The waiter poured a sip for Ezra, who tasted it as if it were important. "Good," he said. (It was strange to see him in a position of command.) "Cody? Try this wine."

"Never," said Pearl, "was there anything nickel-and-dime, in the smallest, tiniest way, ever in this world, about the Tanner Corporation."

"Oh, Mother, face it," Cody told her. "It's a trash heap. I'm going to strip it to the bones."

You would think he was speaking of something alive—an animal, some creature that would suffer. Pearl must have thought so, too. She said, "Cody, why must you act toward me in this manner?"

"I'm not acting in any manner."

"Have I ever wronged you, knowingly? Ever done you harm?"

"Please," Ezra said. "Mother? Cody? It's a family dinner! Jenny? Let's have a toast."

Jenny hastily raised her glass. "A toast," she said.

"Mother? A toast."

Pearl's eyes went reluctantly to Ezra's face. "Oh," she said, after a pause. "Thank you, dear, but wine in all this heat would settle on my stomach like a rock."

"It's a toast to *me*, Mother. To my future. A toast," said Ezra, "to the new full partner of Scarlatti's Restaurant."

"Partner? Who would that be?"

"Me, Mother."

Then the double doors to the kitchen opened and in came Mrs. Scarlatti, glamorous as ever, striding on rangy, loose-strung legs and tossing back her asymmetrical hairdo. She must have been waiting for her cue—eavesdropping, in fact. "So!" she said, setting a hand on Ezra's shoulder. "What do you think of my boy here?"

"I don't understand," said Pearl.

"Well, you know he's been my right hand for so long, ever since my son died, really *better* than my son, if the truth be told; poor Billy never cared all that much for the restaurant business. . . ."

Ezra was rising, as if something momentous were about to happen. While Mrs. Scarlatti went on speaking in her rasping, used-up voice—telling his own mother what an angel Ezra was, a sweetie, so gifted, such a respect for food, for decent food served decently, such a "divine" (she said) instinct for seasonings—he pulled his leather billfold from his pocket. He peered into it, looked anxious for a moment, and then said, "Ah!" and held up a ragged dollar bill. "Mrs. Scarlatti," he said, "with this dollar I hereby purchase a partnership in Scarlatti's Restaurant."

"It's yours, dear heart," said Mrs. Scarlatti, taking the money.

"What's going on here?" Pearl asked.

"We signed the papers in my lawyer's office yesterday afternoon," Mrs. Scarlatti said. "Well, it makes good sense, doesn't it? Who would I leave this damn place to when I kick off—my chihuahua? Ezra knows it inside out by now. Ezra, pour me a glass of wine."

"But I thought you were going to college," Pearl told Ezra.

"I was?"

"I thought you were planning to be a teacher! Maybe a professor. I don't understand what's happened. Oh, I know it's none of my affair. I've never been the type to meddle. Only let me tell you this: it's going to look very, very peculiar to people who don't have all the facts. Accepting such a gift! And from a woman, to boot! It's a favor; partnerships don't cost a dollar; you'll be beholden all your life. Ezra, we Tulls depend on ourselves, only on each other. We don't look to the rest of the world for any help whatsoever. How could you lend yourself to this?"

"Mother, I like making meals for people," Ezra said.

"He's a marvel," said Mrs. Scarlatti.

"But the obligation!"

Cody said, "Let him be, Mother."

She swung on him so quickly, it was more like pouncing. "I know you're enjoying this," she said.

"It's his life."

"What do you care about his life? You only want to see us break up, dissolve in the outside world."

"Please," said Ezra.

But Pearl rose and marched toward the door. "You haven't eaten!" Ezra cried. She didn't stop. In her straight-backed posture, Jenny saw the first signs of her mother's old age—her stringy tendons and breakable bones. "Oh, dear," Ezra said, "I wanted this to be such a good meal." He tore off after Pearl. Scattered diners raised their heads, thought a moment, and went back to eating.

That left Cody, Jenny, and Mrs. Scarlatti. Mrs. Scarlatti didn't seem particularly distressed. "Mothers," she said mildly. She tucked the dollar bill inside her black linen bosom.

Cody said, "Well? Does that wrap it up? Because I should have been in Delaware an hour ago. Can I give you a lift, Jenny?"

"I guess I'll walk," Jenny said.

The last she saw of Mrs. Scarlatti, she was standing there all alone, surveying the untouched appetizers with an amused expression on her face.

After Cody had driven off, Jenny walked slowly toward home. She didn't see Pearl or Ezra anywhere ahead of her. It was twilight—a sticky evening, smelling of hot tires. As she floated past shops in her sundress, she began to feel like someone's romantic vision of a young girl. She tried out a daydream of Harley Baines, but it didn't work. What did Jenny know about marriage? Why would she even want to get married? She was only a child; she would always be a child. Her wedding plans seemed makeshift and contrived—a charade. She felt foolish. She tried to remember Harley's kiss but it had vanished altogether, and Harley himself was no more real to her than a little paper man in a mail-order catalogue.

In the candy store, two children argued while their mother pressed a hand to her forehead. Next came the pharmacy and then the fortune-teller's—a smudged plate glass window with MRS. EMMA PARKINS— READINGS AND ADVICE arched in curly gold letters that were flaking around the edges. Handmade signs sat propped on the sill like afterthoughts: STRICTEST CONFIDENCE and NO PAYMENT IF NOT FULLY SATISFIED. In the light from a dusty globe lamp, Mrs. Parkins herself paced the room—a fat, drab old woman with a cardboard fan on a Popsicle stick.

Jenny reached the corner, paused, and then turned. She went back to the fortune-teller's door. Should she knock, or just walk on in? She tried the handle. The door swung open and a little bell above it tinkled. Mrs. Parkins lowered her fan and said, "Do tell! A customer."

Jenny hugged her purse to her chest.

"Keeping warm?" Mrs. Parkins asked her.

"Yes," said Jenny. She thought she smelled cough syrup, the bitter, dark, cherry-flavored kind.

"Why don't you have a seat," Mrs. Parkins said.

There were two armchairs, puffy, facing each other across the little round table that held the lamp. Jenny sat in the chair nearest the door. Mrs. Parkins plucked her dress from the backs of her thighs and settled down with a groan, still gripping her fan. "Radio says the weather ought to break tomorrow," she said, "but I don't know if I can last that long. Seems like every year, the heat just hits me harder."

Yet her hand, when she reached for Jenny's, was cool and dry, with tough little pads at the fingertips. She fanned herself while she studied Jenny's palm. It made her work look commonplace. "Long life, good career line . . ." she murmured, as if riffling through a file. Jenny relaxed.

"I suppose there's something special you want to know about," Mrs. Parkins said.

"Oh, well. . . ."

"No sense beating around the bush."

Jenny said, "Should I get . . . well . . . married?"

"Married," said Mrs. Parkins.

"I mean, I could. I have this chance. I've been asked."

Mrs. Parkins went on scrutinizing Jenny's hand. Then she beckoned for the other one, which she barely glanced at. Then she sat back and fanned herself some more, gazing at the ceiling.

"Married," she said finally. "Well, I tell you. You could, or you could not. If you don't, you *will* get other offers. Surely. But here is my advice: you go ahead and do it."

"What, get married?"

"If you don't, see," Mrs. Parkins said, "you'll run into a lot of heartbreak. Lot of trouble in your romantic life. From various different people. What I mean to say," she said, "if you don't go on and get married, you'll be destroyed by love."

"Oh," Jenny said.

"That'll be two dollars, please."

Searching through her purse, Jenny had an interesting thought. By Ezra's rate of exchange, she could have bought a couple of restaurants for the same amount of money.

She married Harley late in August, in the little Baptist church that the Tulls had attended off and on. Cody gave Jenny away and Ezra was the usher. The guests he ushered in were: Pearl, Mr. and Mrs. Baines, and an aunt on Harley's mother's side. Jenny wore a white eyelet dress and sandals. Harley wore a black suit, white button-down shirt, and snub-nosed, dull black shoes. Jenny looked down at those shoes all during the ceremony. They reminded her of licorice jellybeans.

Pearl did not shed a tear, because, she said, she was so glad things had worked out this way, even though certain people might have informed her sooner. It was a relief to see your daughter handed over safely, she said—a burden off. Mrs. Baines cried steadily, but that was the kind of woman she was. She told Jenny after the wedding that it certainly didn't mean she had anything against the marriage.

Then Harley and Jenny took a train to Paulham University, where they'd rented a small apartment. They had no furniture yet and spent their wedding night on the floor. Jenny was worried about Harley's inexperience. She was certain he'd always been above such things as sex; he wouldn't know what to do, and neither would she, and they would end up failing at something the rest of the world managed without a thought. But actually, Harley knew very well what to do. She suspected he'd researched it. She had an image of Harley at a library desk, comparing the theories of experts, industriously making notes in the proper outline form.

III

"ON OLD OLYMPUS'S torrid top," Jenny told the scenery rushing past her window, "a Finn and German picked some hops."

This was supposed to remind her of the cranial nerves: olfactory, optic, oculomotor. . . . She frowned and checked her textbook. It was 1958—the start of the first weekend in May, but not a weekend she could spare. She was paying a visit to Baltimore when she should have been holed up in Paulham, studying. She had telephoned her mother long-distance. "Could you ask Ezra to meet my train?"

"I thought you had so much work to do."

"I can work down there just as well."

"Are you bringing Harley?"

"No."

"Is anything wrong?"

"Of course not."

"I don't like the sound of this, young lady."

On the telephone, Pearl's voice was dim and staticky, easily dealt with. Jenny had said, "Oh, Mother, really." But now the train was drawing into Baltimore, and the sight of factory smokestacks, soot-blackened bricks, and billboards peeling in the rain—a landscape she associated with home—made her feel less sure of herself. She hoped that Ezra would meet her alone. She rubbed a clean spot on the window and stared out at acres of railroad track, then at the first metal posts flying by, then at slower posts, better defined, and a dark flight of stairs. The train shrieked and jerked to a stop. Jenny closed her book. She stood up, edged past a sleeping woman, and took a small suitcase from the rack overhead.

This station always seemed to be under some kind of construction, she thought. When she arrived at the top of the stairs, she heard the whine of a power tool—an electric drill or saw. The sound was almost lost beneath the high ceiling. Ezra stood waiting, smiling at her, with his hands in his windbreaker pockets. "How was your trip?" he asked.

"Fine."

He took her suitcase. "Harley all right?"

"Oh, yes."

They threaded through a sparse crowd of people in raincoats. "Mother's still at work," Ezra said, "but she ought to be home by the time we get there. And I've put in a call to Cody. I thought we might all have dinner at the restaurant tomorrow night; he's supposed to be passing through."

"How *is* the restaurant?"

Ezra looked unhappy. He guided Jenny through the door, into a dripping mist that felt cool on her skin. "She's not at all well," he said.

Jenny wondered why he called the restaurant "she," as if it were a ship. But then he said, "The treatments are making her worse. She can't keep anything down," and she understood that he must mean Mrs. Scarlatti. Last fall, Mrs. Scarlatti had been hospitalized for a cancer operation—her second, though up until then no one had known of the first. Ezra had taken it very hard. Mournfully trudging down a row of taxis, he said, "She hardly ever complains, but I know she's suffering."

"Are you running the restaurant alone, then?"

"Oh, yes, I've been doing that since November. Everything: the hiring and the firing, bringing in new help as people quit. A restaurant is not all food, you know. Sometimes it seems that food is the least of it. I feel the place is falling apart on me, but Mrs. Scarlatti says not to worry. It always looks like that, she says. Life is a continual shoring up, she says, against one thing and another just eroding and crumbling away. I'm beginning to think she's right."

They had reached his car, a dented gray Chevy. He opened the door for her and heaved her suitcase into the rear, which was already a chaos of *Restaurateur's Weeklys*, soiled clothing, and some kind of tongs or skewers in a Kitchen Korner shopping bag. "Sorry about the mess," he said when he'd slid behind the wheel. He started the engine and backed out of his parking slot. "Have you learned to drive yet?"

"Yes, Harley taught me. Now I drive him everywhere; he likes to be free to think."

They were on Charles Street. The rain was so fine that Ezra hadn't bothered to turn on his windshield wipers, and the glass began to film over. Jenny peered ahead. "Can you see?" she asked Ezra.

He nodded.

"First he wants me to drive," she said, "and then he criticizes every last little thing about how I do it. He's so clever; you don't know how far his cleverness can extend. I mean, it's not just math or genetics he knows all about but the most efficient temperature for cooking pot roast, the best way to organize my kitchen—everything, all charted out in his mind. When I'm driving he says, 'Now, Jennifer, you know full well that three blocks from here is that transit stop where you have to veer left, so what are you doing in the right-hand lane? You ought to plan ahead more,' he says. 'Three blocks!' I say. 'Good grief! I'll get to it when I get to it.' 'Between here and that transit stop,' I tell him, 'anything might happen,' and he says 'Not really. No, not really. In all three intersections there's a left-turn lane, as you'll recall, so you wouldn't have to wait for . . .' Nothing is unplanned, for Harley. You can see the numbered pages leafing over inside his head. There's never a single mistake."

"Well," Ezra said, "I guess it's like a whole different outlook, being a genius."

"It's not as if I hadn't been warned," said Jenny, "but I didn't realize it was a warning. I was too young to read the signals. I thought he was only like me, you know—a *careful* person; I always was careful, but now compared to Harley I don't seem careful at all. I should have guessed when I went to meet his parents before the wedding, and all the books in his room were arranged by height and blocks of color. Alphabetized I could have understood; or separated by subject matter. But this arbitrary, fixed pattern of things, a foot of red, a foot of black, no hardbacks mingling with the paperbacks . . . it's worse than Mother's bureau drawers. It's out of the frying pan, into the fire! The first time Harley kissed me, he had to brush off this bedspread beforehand that we'd been sitting on. Wouldn't you think that might have told me something? Every night now before he goes to sleep he perches on the edge of the bed and brushes off the soles of his feet. These bare white feet, untouched . . . what could have dirtied them? He wears shoes every waking moment and slippers if he takes one step in the night. But no, there he sits, so methodical, so exact, everything in its proper sequence, brush-brush . . . sometimes I think I'll hit him. I'm fascinated, I stand there watching him brush his left foot first, his right foot second, not letting either touch the floor once he's finished with it, and I think 'I'm going to bash your head in for you, Harley.' "

Ezra cleared his throat. "It's the adjustment," he said. "Yes, that's it: adjustment. The first year of marriage. I'm sure that's all it is."

"Well, maybe so," Jenny said.

She wished she hadn't talked so much.

When they reached home, therefore—where their mother had just arrived herself—Jenny said nothing at all about Harley. (Pearl thought Harley was wonderful, admirable—maybe not so easy to hold a conversation with but the perfect person to marry her daughter.) "Now tell me," Pearl said when she'd kissed her. "How come you didn't bring that husband of yours? You haven't had some silly kind of quarrel."

"No, no. It's only my work. The strain of work," Jenny said. "I wanted to come and rest, and Harley couldn't leave his lab."

It was true that the house seemed restful, suddenly. After Ezra left for Scarlatti's, her mother led Jenny to the kitchen and brewed her a cup of tea. One thing Pearl never skimped on was tea. She moved around the room, heating the speckled brown teapot, humming some old, wavery hymn. The damp weather had frizzed her hair into little corkscrews and the steam had turned her cheeks pink; she looked almost pretty. (What kind of a marriage had she had? Something must have gone terribly wrong with it, but Jenny couldn't help imagining it as perfect, all of a piece, her parents permanently joined. That her father had left was only a fluke—some misunderstanding still not cleared up.)

"I thought we'd have a very light supper," said her mother. "Maybe a salad or something."

"That would be fine," Jenny said.

"Something plain and simple."

Plain and simple was just what Jenny needed. She loosened; she was safe at last, in the only place where people knew exactly who she was and loved her anyhow.

So it was all the odder that after supper, touring the house, she felt a flash of pity for Ezra when she looked in upon his room. Still here! she thought, seeing his boyish tartan blanket on the bed, his worn recorder on the windowsill, the stamped metal tray on his bureau heaped with ancient, green-tinged pennies. How can he bear it? she wondered, and she went back down the stairs, shaking her head and marveling.

This was what Jenny had brought with her: a change of clothes, her anatomy textbook, Harley's letter proposing marriage, and his photo in a sterling silver frame. Unpacking, she set the photo firmly on her desk and examined it. She had brought it not for sentimental reasons but because she planned to think Harley over, to sum him up, and she didn't want distance to alter her judgment. She foresaw that she might be so misguided as to miss him. This picture would remind her not to. He was a stiff and stodgy man; you could see it in the thickened line of his jaw and in the opaque, bespectacled gaze he directed at the camera. He disapproved of her reasoning methods—too rushed and haphazard, he said. He didn't like her chattery friends. He thought her clothes lacked style. He criticized her table manners. "Twenty-five chews per bite," he would tell her. "That's my advice. Not only is it more healthful, but you'll find yourself not eating so much." He was obsessed by the fear that she might grow fat. Since Jenny could count every one of her ribs, she wondered if he had a kind of mad spot—if he were insane not through and through, but in one isolated area. It was the uncontrollability he feared, perhaps: he would not like to see Jenny ballooning, the pounds collecting unrestrained; he wouldn't like to see her *getting out of hand*. That must be it. But she did begin to wonder if she might be gaining weight. She started stepping on the scales every morning. She stood in front of the full-length mirror, sucking in her stomach. Was it possible her hips were widening? Out in public, though, she noticed that the fleshy women were the ones who caught Harley's eye—the burgeoning and dimpled ones, blondes, a little blowzy. It was a mystery, really.

Jenny's grades were not very good. She wasn't failing, or anything like that; but neither was she making A's, and her lab work was often slipshod. Sometimes it seemed to her that she'd been hollow, all these years, and was finally caving in on herself. They'd found her out: at heart, there was nothing to her.

Packing for this trip (which Harley saw as a waste of time and money), she had strode across the bedroom to where his photo sat on the bureau. Harley was standing in front of it. "Move, please," she told him. He looked offended and stepped aside. Then, when he saw what she wanted, his face had . . . well, flown open, you might say. His glare had softened, his lips had parted to speak. He was touched. And *she* was touched that *he* was touched. Nothing was ever simple; there were always these complications. But what he said was, "I don't understand you. Your mother has frightened and mistreated you all your life, and now you want to visit her for no apparent reason."

Probably what he was saying was "Please don't go."

You had to be a trained decoder to read the man.

She shook open his letter of proposal. See how he had dated it: *18 July, 1957*—a form that struck her as pretentious, unless of course he happened to be English. She wondered how she could have overlooked the pompous language, the *American courtship* (as if his superior intelligence placed him on a whole separate continent), and most of all, the letter itself, the very fact that it was written, advancing the project of marriage like a corporation merger.

Well, she *had* overlooked it. She'd chosen not to see. She knew she had acted deviously in this whole business—making up her mind to win him, marrying him for practical reasons. She had calculated, was what it was. But she felt the punishment was greater than the crime. It wasn't such a terrible crime. She'd had no idea (would any unmarried person?) what a serious business she was playing with, how long it lasts, how deep it goes. And now look: the joke was on her. Having got what she was after, she found it was she who'd been got. Talk about calculating! He was going to run her life, arrange it perfectly by height and color. He was going to sit in the passenger seat with that censorious expression on his face and dictate every turn she took, and every shift of gears.

Because she knew it would make Ezra happy, she went to visit the restaurant late in the evening. The rain had stopped, but there was still a mist. She felt she was walking underwater, in one of those dreams where a person can breathe as easily as on land. There were only a few other people out—all of them hurrying, locked in themselves, shrouded by raincoats and plastic scarves. Traffic swished by; reflections of the headlights wavered on the streets.

The restaurant's kitchen seemed overcrowded; it was a miracle that an acceptable plate of food could emerge from it. Ezra stood at the stove, supervising the skimming of some broth or soup. A young girl lifted ladles full of steaming liquid and emptied them into a bowl.

"When you're done—" Ezra was saying, and then he said, "Why, hello, Jenny," and came to the door where she waited. Over his jeans he wore a long white apron; he looked like one of the cooks. He took her around to meet the others; sweaty men chopping or straining or stirring. "This is my sister, Jenny," he would say, but then he'd get sidetracked by some detail and stand there discussing food. "Can I offer you something to eat?" he asked finally.

"No, I had supper at home."

"Or maybe a drink from the bar?"

"No, thanks."

"This is our headwaiter, Oakes. And this is Josiah Payson; you remember him."

She looked up and up, into Josiah's face. He was all in white, spotless (how had they found a uniform to fit him?), but his hair still bristled wildly. And it was no easier than ever to see where he was directing his gaze. Not at her; that was certain. He was avoiding her. He seemed completely blind to the sight of her.

"When the Boyces come," Ezra was saying to Oakes, "tell them we have the cream of mussel soup. There's only enough for the two of them; it's waiting on the back burner."

"How are you, Josiah?" Jenny asked.

"Oh, not bad."

"So you work here now."

"I'm the salad chef. Mostly, I cut things up."

His spidery hands twisted in front of him. The crease in his forehead seemed deeper than ever.

"I've thought of you often," Jenny said.

She didn't mean it, at first. But then she understood, with a rush to her head that was something like illness, that she spoke the truth: she had been thinking of him all these years without knowing it. It seemed he had never once left her mind. Even Harley, she saw, was just a reverse kind of Josiah, a Josiah turned inside out: equally alien, black-and-white, incomprehensible to anyone but Jenny.

"Is your mother well?" she asked him.

"She died."

"Died!"

"A long time ago. She went out shopping and she died. I live in my house all alone now."

"I'm sorry," Jenny said.

But still he wouldn't meet her eyes.

Ezra turned from Oakes and asked, "Are you sure I can't get you a snack, Jenny?"

"I have to leave," she told him.

Going home, she wondered why the walk seemed so long. Her feet felt unusually heavy, and there was some old, rusty pain deep inside her chest.

The ash grove, how graceful, Ezra's recorder piped out, *how sweetly 'tis singing* . . . Walking slowly, still webbed in bits of dreams, Jenny found it strange that a pearwood recorder should put forth plums—perfectly round, pure, plummy notes arriving in a spill on her bed. She sat up and thought for a moment. Then she pushed her blankets back and reached for her clothes.

Ezra was playing "Le Godiveau de Poisson" when she left the house.

Down this street, and then that one, and then another that turned out to be a mistake. She had to retrace her path. It was going to be a beautiful day. The sidewalks were still wet, but the sun was rising in a pearly pink sky above the chimneys. She dug her hands in her coat pockets. She met an old man walking a poodle, but no one else, and even he passed soundlessly and vanished.

When she reached the street she wanted, nothing looked familiar and she had to take the alley. She could only find the house from the rear. She recognized that makeshift gray addition behind the kitchen, and the buckling steps that gave beneath her feet, and the wooden door with most of its paint worn off. She looked for a bell to ring but there wasn't one; she had to knock. There was the scraping of furniture somewhere inside the house—chair legs pushing back. Josiah, when he came, was so tall that he darkened the window she peered through.

He opened the door. "Jenny?" he said.

"Hello, Josiah."

He looked around him, as if supposing she had come to see someone else. She noticed his breakfast on the kitchen table: a slice of white bread spread with peanut butter. In the scuffed linoleum and the sink full of dirty dishes, in his tattered jeans and raveling brown sweater, she read neglect and hopelessness. She pulled her coat tighter around her.

"What are you, what are you here for?" he asked.

"I did everything wrong," she told him.

"What are you talking about?"

"You must feel I'm just like the others! Just like the ones you want to escape from, off in the woods with your sleeping bag."

"Oh, no, Jenny," he said. "I would never believe you're like that."

"You wouldn't?"

"Nobody would; you're too pretty."

"But I mean—" she said.

She set a hand on his sleeve. He didn't pull away. Then she stepped closer and slipped her arms around him. She could feel, even through her coat, how thin and bony his rib cage was, and how he warmed his skimpy sweater. She laid her ear against his chest, and he slowly, hesitantly raised his hands to her shoulders. "I should have gone on kissing you," she said. "I should have told my mother, 'Go away. Leave us alone.' I should have stood up for you and not been such a coward."

"No, no," she heard him say. "I don't think about it. I don't think about it."

She drew back and looked up at him.

"I don't talk about it," he said.

"Josiah," she said, "won't you at least tell me it's all right now?"

"Sure," he said. "It's all right, Jenny."

After that, there was really nothing else to discuss. She stood on tiptoe to kiss him goodbye, and she thought he looked directly at her when he smiled and let her go.

"To everybody's good health," Cody said, raising his glass. "To Ezra's food. To Scarlatti's Restaurant."

"To a happy family dinner," Ezra said.

"Oh, well, that too, if you like."

They all drank, even Pearl—or maybe the little sip she took was only make-believe. She was wearing her netted hat and a beige tailored suit so new that it failed to sit back when she did. Jenny was in an ordinary skirt and blouse, but still she felt dressed up. She felt wonderful, in fact—perfectly untroubled. She kept beaming at the others, pleased to have them around her.

But really, were they all here? In Jenny's new mood, her family seemed too small. These three young people and this shrunken mother, she thought, were not enough to sustain the occasion. They could have used several more members—a family clown, for instance; and a genuine black sheep, blacker than Cody; and maybe one of those managerial older sisters who holds a group together by force. As things were, it was Ezra who had to hold them together. He wasn't doing a very good job. He was too absorbed in the food. Right now he was conferring with the waiter, gesturing toward the soup, which had arrived a touch too cool, he said—though to Jenny it seemed fine. And now Pearl was collecting her purse and sliding back her chair. "Powder room," she mouthed to Jenny. Ezra would be all the more upset, once he noticed she'd gone. He liked the family in a group, a cluster, and he hated Pearl's habit of constantly "freshening up" in a restaurant, just as he hated for Cody to smoke his slim cigars between courses. "I wish just once," he was always saying, "we could get through a meal from start to finish," and he would say it again as soon as he discovered Pearl was missing. But now he was telling the waiter, "If Andrew would keep the china hot—"

"He mostly does, I swear it, but the warming oven's broke."

"What's your opinion?" Cody whispered, setting his face close to

Jenny's. "Has Ezra ever slept with Mrs. Scarlatti? Or has he not."

Jenny's mouth dropped open.

"Well?" he asked.

"Cody Tull!"

"Don't tell me it hasn't occurred to you. A lonely rich widow, or whatever she is; nice-looking boy with no prospects . . ."

"That's disgusting," Jenny told him.

"Not at all," Cody said blandly, sitting back. He had a way of surveying people from under half-lowered lids which made him look tolerant and worldly. "There's nothing wrong," he said, "with taking advantage of your luck. And you have to admit Ezra's lucky; *born* lucky. Have you ever noticed what happens when I bring around my girlfriends? They fall all over him. They have ever since we were kids. What do they see in him, anyway? How does he do it? *Is* it luck? You're a woman; what's his secret?"

"Honestly, Cody," Jenny said, "I wish you'd grow out of this."

Ezra finished his conversation with the waiter. "Where's Mother?" he asked. "I turn my back one second and she disappears."

"Powder room," said Cody, lighting a cigar.

"Oh, why does she always do that? More soup is coming, fresh off the stove, piping hot this time."

"Are you having it brought in by barefoot runners?" Cody asked.

Jenny said, "Don't worry, Ezra. I'll go call her."

She made her way between the tables, toward a corridor with an EXIT sign over the archway. But just before the ladies' room, in front of a swinging, leather-covered door, she caught sight of Josiah. He had his white uniform on and was carrying an aqua plastic dishpan full of chicory leaves. "Josiah," she said.

He stopped short and his face lit up. "Hi, Jenny," he said.

They stood smiling at each other, not speaking. She reached out to touch his wrist.

"Oh, no!" her mother cried.

Jenny snatched her hand back and spun around.

"Oh, Jenny. Oh, my God," Pearl said. Her eyes were no longer gray; they were black, and she gripped her shiny black purse. "Well, I understand it all now," she said.

"No, wait," Jenny said. Her heart was beating so fast, it seemed she was vibrating where she stood.

"Visiting for no apparent reason," said Pearl, "and slipping away this morning to meet him like a tramp, some cheap little tramp—"

"Mother, you've got it wrong!" Jenny told her. "It's nothing, don't you see?" She felt she had run out of breath. Gasping for air, she gestured toward Josiah, who merely stood there with his mouth agape. "He just . . . we just met in the hall and . . . it's not that way at all, he's *nothing* to me, don't you see?"

But she had to say this to Pearl's back, hurrying after her through the dining room. Pearl reached their table and said, "Ezra, I cannot stay here."

Ezra stood up. "Mother?"

"I simply cannot," she said. She gathered up her coat and walked away.

"But what happened?" Ezra asked, turning to Jenny. "What's bothering her?"

Cody said, "That lukewarm soup, no doubt," and he rocked back comfortably in his chair with a cigar between his teeth.

"I wish just once," Ezra said, "we could eat a meal from start to finish."

"I don't feel well," Jenny told him.

In fact, her lips were numb. It was a symptom she seemed to remember from before, from some long-forgotten moment, or maybe from a nightmare.

She left her coat behind, and she rushed through the dining room and out to the street. At first, she thought her mother had disappeared. Then she found her, half a block ahead—a militant figure walking briskly. Oh, what if she wouldn't even turn around? Or worse, would turn and lash out, slap, snap, her clawed pearl ring, her knowing face . . . But Jenny ran to catch up with her, anyway. "Mother," she said.

In the light from the liquor store window, she saw her mother reassemble her expression—take on a cool, unperturbed look.

"You've got it all wrong," Jenny told her. "I'm not a tramp! I'm not cheap! Mother, listen to me."

"It doesn't matter," Pearl said politely.

"Of course it matters!"

"You're over twenty-one. If you don't know good from bad by now, there's nothing more I can do about it."

"I felt sorry for him," Jenny said.

They crossed a street and started up the next block.

"He told me his mother had died," Jenny said.

They veered around a gang of teen-aged boys.

"She was all he had—his father's dead too. She was the center of his life."

"Well," said Pearl, "I suppose it can't have been easy for her."

"I don't know how he's going to manage now she's gone."

"I believe I saw her in the grocery once," said Pearl. "A brown-haired woman?"

"Plumpish, sort of."

"Full in the face?"

"Like a wood thrush," Jenny said.

"Oh, Jenny," said her mother, and she gave a little laugh. "The things you come up with, sometimes!"

They passed the candy store, and then the pharmacy. Jenny and her mother fell into step. They passed the fortune-teller's window. The same dusty lamp glowed on the table. Jenny, looking in, thought that Mrs. Parkins had not been much of a prophet. Why, she had even had to listen to the radio for tomorrow's weather! And she should have guessed from the very first instant, from the briefest, most cursory glance, that Jenny was not capable of being destroyed by love.

4
HEART RUMORS

THE FIRST few times that Mrs. Scarlatti stayed in the hospital, Ezra had no trouble getting in to visit her. But the last time was harder. "Relative?" the nurse would ask.

"No, ah, I'm her business partner."

"Sorry, relatives only."

"But she doesn't have any relatives. I'm all she's got. See, she and I own this restaurant together."

"And what's that in the jar?"

"Her soup."

"Soup," said the nurse.

"I make this soup she likes."

"Mrs. Scarlatti isn't keeping things down."

"I know that, but I wanted to give her something."

This would earn him a slantwise glance, before he was led brusquely into Mrs. Scarlatti's room.

In the past, she had chosen to stay in a ward. (She was an extremely social woman.) She'd sit up straight in her dramatic black robe, a batik scarf hiding her hair, and "Sweetie!" she'd say as he entered. For a moment the other women would grow all sly and alert, till they realized how young he was—way too young for Mrs. Scarlatti. But now she had a private room, and the most she could do when he arrived was open her eyes and then wearily close them. He wasn't even sure that he was welcome any more.

He knew that after he left, someone would discard his soup. But this was his special gizzard soup that she had always loved. There were twenty cloves of garlic in it. Mrs. Scarlatti used to claim it settled her stomach, soothed her nerves—changed her whole perception of the day, she said. (However, it wasn't on the restaurant's menu because it was a bit "hearty"—her word—and Scarlatti's Restaurant was very fine and formal. This hurt Ezra's feelings, a little.) When she was well enough to be home, he had often brewed single portions in the restaurant kitchen and carried them upstairs to her apartment. Even in the hospital, those first few times, she could manage a small-sized bowl of it. But now she was beyond that. He only brought the soup out of helplessness; he would have preferred to kneel by her bed and rest his head on her sheets, to take her hands in his and tell her, "Mrs. Scarlatti, come back." But she was such a no-nonsense woman; she would have looked shocked. All he could do was offer this soup.

He sat in a corner of the room in a green vinyl chair with steel arms. It was October and the steam heat had come on; the air felt sharp and dry. Mrs. Scarlatti's bed was cranked upward slightly to help her breathe. From time to time, without opening her eyes, she said, "Oh, God." Then Ezra would ask, "What? What is it?" and she would sigh. (Or maybe that was the radiator.) Ezra never brought anything to read, and he never made conversation with the nurses who squeaked in and out on their rubber soles. He only sat, looking down at his pale, oversized hands, which lay loosely on his knees.

Previously, he had put on weight. He'd been nowhere near fat, but he'd softened and spread in that mild way that fair-haired men often do. Now the weight fell off. Like Mrs. Scarlatti, he was having trouble keeping things down. His large, floppy clothes covered a large, floppy frame that seemed oddly two-dimensional. Wide in front and wide behind, he was flat as paper when viewed from the side. His hair fell forward in a sheaf, like wheat. He didn't bother pushing it back.

He and Mrs. Scarlatti had been through a lot together, he would have said, if asked—but what, exactly? She had had a bad husband (a matter of luck, she made it seem, like a bad bottle of wine) and ditched him; she had lost her only son, Ezra's age, during the Korean War. But both these events she had suffered alone, before her partnership with Ezra began. And Ezra himself: well, he had not actually been through anything yet. He was twenty-five years old and still without wife or children, still living at home with his mother. What he and Mrs. Scarlatti had survived, it appeared, was year after year of standing still. Her life that had slid off somewhere in the past, his that kept delaying its arrival—they'd combined, they held each other up in empty space. Ezra was grateful to Mrs. Scarlatti for rescuing him from an aimless, careless existence and teaching him all she knew; but more than that, for the fact that she depended on him. If not for her, whom would he have? His brother and sister were out in the world; he loved his mother dearly but there was something overemotional about her that kept him eternally wary. By other people's standards, even he and

Mrs. Scarlatti would not have seemed particularly close. He always called her "Mrs. Scarlatti." She called Ezra her boy, her angel, but was otherwise remarkably distant, and asked no questions at all about his life outside the restaurant.

He knew the restaurant would be fully his when she died. She had told him so, just before this last hospital stay. "I don't want it," he had said. She was silent. She must have understood that it was only his manner of speaking. Of course, he didn't *want* it, in the sense of coveting it (he never thought much about money), but what would he do otherwise? Anyway, she had no one else to leave it to. She lifted a hand and let it drop. They didn't mention the subject again.

Once, Ezra persuaded his mother to come and visit too. He liked for the various people in his life to get along, although he knew that would be difficult in his mother's case. She spoke of Mrs. Scarlatti distrustfully, even jealously. "What you see in such a person I can't imagine. She's downright . . . tough, is what she is, in spite of her high-fashion clothes. It looks like her face is not trying. Know what I mean? Like she can't be bothered putting out the effort. Not a bit of lipstick, and those crayony black lines around her eyes . . . and she hardly ever smiles at people."

But now that Mrs. Scarlatti was so sick, his mother kept her thoughts to herself. She dressed carefully for her visit and wore her netted hat, which made Ezra happy. He associated that hat with important family occasions. He was pleased that she'd chosen her Sunday black coat, even though it wasn't as warm as her everyday maroon.

In the hospital, she told Mrs. Scarlatti, "Why, you look the picture of health! No one would ever guess."

This was not true. But it was nice of her to say it.

"After I die," Mrs. Scarlatti said in her grainy voice, "Ezra must move to my apartment."

His mother said, "Now, let's have none of that silly talk."

"Which is silly?" Mrs. Scarlatti asked, but then she was overtaken by exhaustion, and she closed her eyes. Ezra's mother misunderstood. She must have thought she'd asked *what* was silly, a rhetorical question, and she blithely smoothed her skirt around her and said, "Total foolishness, I never heard such rot." Only Ezra grasped Mrs. Scarlatti's meaning. Which was silly, she was asking—her dying, or Ezra's moving? But he didn't bother explaining that to his mother.

Another time, he got special permission from the nurses' office to bring a few men from the restaurant—Todd Duckett, Josiah Payson, and Raymond the sauce maker. He could tell that Mrs. Scarlatti was glad to see them, although it was an awkward visit. The men stood around the outer edges of the room and cleared their throats repeatedly and would not take seats. "Well?" said Mrs. Scarlatti. "Are you still buying everything fresh?" From the inappropriateness of the question (none of them was remotely involved with the purchasing), Ezra realized how out of touch she had grown. But these people, too, were tactful. Todd Duckett gave a mumbled cough and then said, "Yes, ma'am, just how you would've liked it."

"I'm tired now," Mrs. Scarlatti said.

Down the hall lay an emaciated woman in a coma, and an old, old man with a tiny wife who was allowed to sleep on a cot in his room, and a dark-skinned foreigner whose masses of visiting relatives gave the place the look of a gypsy circus. Ezra knew that the comatose woman had cancer, the old man a rare type of blood disease, and the foreigner some cardiac problem—it wasn't clear what. "Heart rumor," he was told by a dusky, exotic child who was surely too young to be visiting hospitals. She was standing outside the foreigner's door, delicately reeling in a yo-yo.

"Heart *murmur*, maybe?"

"No, rumor."

Ezra was starting to feel lonely here and would have liked to make a friend. The nurses were always sending him away while they did something mysterious to Mrs. Scarlatti, and much of any visit he spent leaning dejectedly against the wall outside her room or gazing from the windows of the conservatory at the end of the corridor. But no one seemed approachable. This wing was different from the others— more hushed—and all the people he encountered wore a withdrawn, forbidding look. Only the foreign child spoke to him. "I think he's going to die," she said. But then she went back to her yo-yo. Ezra hung around a while longer, but it was obvious she didn't find him very interesting.

Bibb lettuce, Boston lettuce, chicory, escarole, dripping on the counter in the center of the kitchen. While other restaurants' vegetables were delivered by anonymous, dank, garbage-smelling trucks, Scarlatti's had a man named Mr. Purdy, who shopped personally for them each morning before the sun came up. He brought everything to the kitchen in splintery bushel baskets, along about eight a.m., and Ezra made a point of being there so that he would know what foods he had to deal with that day. Sometimes there were no eggplants, sometimes twice as many as planned. In periods like this—dead November, now—nothing grew locally, and Mr. Purdy had to resort to vegetables raised elsewhere, limp carrots and waxy cucumbers shipped in from out of state. And the tomatoes! They were a crime. "Just look," said Mr. Purdy, picking one up. "Vine-grown, the fellow tells me. Vine-*grown*, yes. I'd like to see them grown on anything else. 'But ripened?' I say. 'However was they ripened?' 'Vine-ripened, too,' fellow assures me. Well, maybe so.

But nowadays, I don't know, all them taste anyhow like they spent six weeks on a windowsill. Like they was *made* of windowsill, or celluloid, or pencil erasers. Well, I tell you, Ezra: I apologize. It breaks my heart to bring you such rubbage as this here; I'd sooner not show up at all."

Mr. Purdy was a pinched and prunish man in overalls, a white shirt, and a shiny black suit coat. He had a narrow face that seemed eternally disapproving, even during the growing season. Only Ezra knew that inwardly, there was something nourishing and generous about him. Mr. Purdy rejoiced in food as much as Ezra did, and for the same reasons—less for eating himself than for serving to others. He had once invited Ezra to his home, a silver-colored trailer out on Ritchie Highway, and given him a meal consisting solely of new asparagus, which both he and Ezra agreed had the haunting taste of oysters. Mrs. Purdy, a smiling, round-faced woman in a wheelchair, had claimed they talked like lunatics, but she finished two large helpings while both men tenderly watched. It was a satisfaction to see how she polished her buttery plate.

"If this restaurant was just mine," Ezra said now, "I wouldn't serve tomatoes in the winter. People would ask for tomatoes and I'd say, 'What can you be thinking of, this is not the season.' I'd give them something better."

"They'd stomp out directly," Mr. Purdy said.

"No, they might surprise you. And I'd put up a blackboard, write on it everyday just two or three good dishes. Of course! In France, they do that all the time. Or I'd offer no choice at all; examine people and say, 'You look a little tired. I'll bring you an oxtail stew.'"

"Mrs. Scarlatti would just die," said Mr. Purdy.

There was a silence. He rubbed his bristly chin, and then corrected himself: "She'd rotate in her grave."

They stood around a while.

"I don't really want a restaurant anyhow," Ezra said.

"Sure," Mr. Purdy said. "I know that."

Then he put his black felt hat on, and thought a moment, and left.

The foreign child slept in the conservatory, her head resting on the stainless steel arm of a chair like the one in Mrs. Scarlatti's room. It made Ezra wince. He wanted to fold his coat and slide it beneath her cheek, but he worried that would wake her. He kept his distance, therefore, and stood at one of the windows gazing down on pedestrians far below. How small and determined their feet looked, emerging from their foreshortened figures! The perseverance of human beings suddenly amazed him.

A woman entered the room—one of the foreigners. She was lighter skinned than the others, but he knew she was foreign because of her slippers, which contrasted with her expensive wool dress. The whole family, he had noticed, changed into slippers as soon as they arrived each morning. They made themselves at home in every possible way—setting out bags of seeds and nuts and spicy-smelling foods, once even brewing a quart of yogurt on the conservatory radiator. The men smoked cigarettes in the hall, and the women murmured together while knitting brightly colored sweaters.

Now the woman approached the child, bent over her, and tucked her hair back. Then she lifted her in her arms and settled in the chair. The child didn't wake. She only nestled closer and sighed. So after all, Ezra could have put his coat beneath her head. He had missed an opportunity. It was like missing a train—or something more important, something that would never come again. There was no explanation for the grief that suddenly filled him.

He decided to start serving his gizzard soup in the restaurant. He had the waiters announce it to patrons when they handed over the menu. "In addition to the soups you see here, we are pleased to offer tonight . . ." One of the waiters had failed to show up and Ezra hired a woman to replace him—strictly against Mrs. Scarlatti's policy. (Waitresses, she said, belonged in truck stops.) The woman did much better than the men with Ezra's soup. "Try our gizzard soup," she would say. "It's really hot and garlicky and it's made with love." Outside it was bitter cold, and the woman was so warm and helpful, more and more people followed her suggestion. Ezra thought that the next time a waiter left, he would hire a second woman, and maybe another after that, and so on.

He experimented the following week with a spiced crab casserole of his own invention, and then with a spinach bisque, and when the waiters complained about all they had to memorize he finally went ahead and bought a blackboard. SPECIALS, he wrote at the top. But in the hospital, when Mrs. Scarlatti asked how things were going, he didn't mention any of this. Instead, he sat forward and clasped his hands tight and said, "Fine. Um . . . fine." If she noticed anything strange in his voice, she didn't comment on it.

Mrs. Scarlatti had always been a lean, dark, slouching woman, with a faintly scornful manner. It was true, as Ezra's mother said, that she gave the impression of not caring what people thought of her. But that had been part of her charm—her sleepy eyes, hardly troubling to stay open, and her indifferent tone of voice. Now, she went too far. Her skin took on the pallid look of stone, and her face began to seem sphinxlike, all flat planes and straight lines. Even her hair was sphinxlike—a short, black wedge, a *clump* of hair, dulled and rough. Sometimes Ezra believed that she was not dying but petrifying. He had trouble remembering her low laugh, her casual arrogance. ("Sweetie," she used to say, ordering him off to some task, trilling languid fingers. "Angel boy . . .") He had never felt more than twelve years old around her, but now he was ancient, her parent or grandparent. He soothed and humored her. Not all she said was quite clear these days. "At least," she whispered once, "I never made myself ridiculous, Ezra, did I?"

"Ridiculous?" he asked.

"With you."

"With me? Of course not."

He was puzzled, and must have shown it; she smiled and rocked her head on the pillow. "Oh, you always were a much-loved child," she told him. It must have been a momentary wandering of the brain. (She hadn't known him as a child.) "You take it all for granted," she said. Maybe she was confusing him with Billy, her son. She turned her face away from him and closed her eyes. He felt suddenly anxious. He was reminded of that time his mother had nearly died, wounded by a misfired arrow—entirely Ezra's fault; Ezra, the family stumbler. "I'm so sorry, I'm sorry, I'm sorry," he had cried, but the apology had never been accepted because his brother had been blamed instead, and his father, who had purchased the archery set. Ezra, his mother's favorite, had got off scot-free. He'd been left unforgiven—not relieved, as you might expect, but forever burdened. "You're mistaken," he said now, and Mrs. Scarlatti's eyelids fluttered into crepe but failed to open. "I wish you'd get me straight. See who I *am*, I'm Ezra," he said, and then (for no logical reason) he bent close and said, "Mrs. Scarlatti. Remember when I left the army? Discharged for sleepwalking? Sent home? Mrs. Scarlatti, I wasn't really all the way asleep. I mean, I knew what I was doing. I didn't *plan* to sleepwalk, but part of me was conscious, and observed what was going on, and could have wakened the rest of me if I'd tried. I had this feeling like watching a dream, where you know you can break it off at any moment. But I didn't; I wanted to go home. I just wanted to leave that army, Mrs. Scarlatti. So I didn't stop myself."

If she had heard (with her only son, Billy, blown to bits in Korea), she would have risen up, sick as she was, and shouted, "Out! Out of my life!" So she must have missed it, for she only rocked her head again and smiled and went on sleeping.

Just after Thanksgiving the woman who'd been in a coma died, and the tiny old man either died or went home, but the foreigner stayed on and his relatives continued to visit. Now that they knew Ezra by sight, they hailed him as he passed. "Come!" they would call, and he would step in, shy and pleased, and stand around for several minutes with his fists locked in his armpits. The sick man was yellow and sunken, hooked to a number of tubes, but he always tried to smile at

Ezra's entrance. Ezra had the impression that he knew no English. The others spoke English according to their ages—the child perfectly, the young adults with a strong, attractive accent, the old ones in ragged segments. Eventually, though, even the most fluent forgot themselves and drifted into their native language—a musical one, with rounded vowels that gave their lips a muscled, pouched, commiserative shape, as if they were perpetually tut-tutting. Ezra loved to listen. When you couldn't understand what people said, he thought, how clearly the links and joints in their relationships stood out! A woman's face lit and bloomed as she turned to a certain man; a barbed sound of pain leapt from the patient and his wife doubled over. The child, when upset, stroked her mother's gold wristwatch band for solace.

Once a young girl in braids sang a song with almost no tune. It wandered from note to note as if by accident. Then a man with a heavy black mustache recited what must have been a poem. He spoke so grandly and unselfconsciously that passersby glanced in, and when he had finished he translated it for Ezra. *"O dead one, why did you die in the springtime? You haven't yet tasted the squash, or the cucumber salad."*

Why, even their poetry touched matters close to Ezra's heart.

By December he had replaced three of the somber-suited waiters with cheery, motherly waitresses, and he'd scrapped the thick beige menus and started listing each day's dishes on the blackboard. This meant, of course, that the cooks all left (none of the dishes were theirs, or even their type), so he did most of the cooking himself, with the help of a woman from New Orleans and a Mexican. These two had recipes of their own as well, some of which Ezra had never tasted before; he was entranced. It was true that the customers seemed surprised, but they adjusted, Ezra thought. Or most of them did.

Now he grew feverish with new ideas, and woke in the night longing to share them with someone. Why not a restaurant full of refrigerators, where people came and chose the food they wanted? They could fix it themselves on a long, long stove lining one wall of the dining room. Or maybe he could install a giant fireplace, with a whole steer turning slowly on a spit. You'd slice what you liked onto your plate and sit around in armchairs eating and talking with the guests at large. Then again, maybe he would start serving only street food. Of course! He'd cook what people felt homesick for—tacos like those from vendors' carts in California, which the Mexican was always pining after; and that wonderful vinegary North Carolina barbecue that Todd Duckett had to have brought by his mother several times a year in cardboard cups. He would call it the Homesick Restaurant. He'd take down the old black and gilt sign . . .

But then he saw the sign, SCARLATTI'S, and he groaned and pressed his fingers to his eyes and turned over in his bed.

"You have a beautiful country," the light-skinned woman said.

"Thank you," said Ezra.

"All that green! And so many birds. Last summer, before my father-in-law fell ill, we were renting a house in New Jersey. The Garden State, they call it. There were roses everywhere. We could sit on the lawn after supper and listen to the nightingales."

"The what?" said Ezra.

"The nightingales."

"Nightingales? In New Jersey?"

"Of course," she said. "Also we liked the shopping. In particular, Korvettes. My husband likes the . . . how do you say? Drip and dry suits."

The sick man moaned and tossed, nearly dislodging a tube that entered the back of his wrist. His wife, an ancient, papery lady, leaned toward him and stroked his hand. She murmured something, and then she turned to the younger woman. Ezra saw that she was crying. She didn't attempt to hide it but wept openly, tears streaming down her cheeks. "Ah," the younger woman said, and she left Ezra's side and bent over the wife. She gathered her up in her arms as she'd gathered the child earlier. Ezra knew he should leave, but he didn't. Instead he turned and gazed out the window, slightly tilting his head and looking nonchalant, as some men do when they have rung a doorbell and are standing on the porch, waiting to be noticed and invited in.

Ezra's sister, Jenny, sat at the desk in her old bedroom, reading a battered textbook. She was strikingly pretty, even in reading glasses and the no-color quilted bathrobe she always left on a closet hook for her visits home. Ezra stopped at her doorway and peered in. "Jenny?" he asked. "What are you doing here?"

"I thought I'd take a breather," she said. She removed her glasses and gave him a blurry, unfocused look.

"It isn't semester break yet, is it?"

"Semester break! Do you think medical students have time for such things?"

"No, well," he said.

But lately she'd been home more often than not, it appeared to him. And she never mentioned Harley, her husband. She hadn't referred to him once all fall, and maybe even all summer. "It's my opinion she's left him," Ezra's mother had said recently. "Oh, don't act so surprised! It must have crossed your mind. Here she suddenly moves to a new address—closer to the school, she claims—and then can't have us to visit, anytime I offer; always too busy or preparing for some quiz, and when I call, you notice, it's never Harley who answers, never once Harley who picks up the phone. Doesn't that strike you as odd? But I'm unable to broach the subject. I mean, she deflects me, if you know what I mean. Somehow I just never . . . *you* could, though. She always did feel closer to you than to me or Cody. Won't you just ask her what's what?''

But now when he lounged in the doorway, trying to find some way to sidle into a conversation, Jenny put her glasses back on and returned to her book. He felt dismissed. ''Um,'' he said. ''How are things in Paulham?''

''Fine,'' she said, eyes scanning the print.

''Harley all right?''

There was a deep, studious silence.

''It doesn't seem we ever get to see him any more,'' Ezra said.

''He's okay,'' Jenny said.

She turned a page.

Ezra waited a while longer, and then he straightened up from the doorway and went downstairs. He found his mother in the kitchen, unpacking groceries. ''Well?'' she asked him.

''Well, what?''

''Did you talk to Jenny?''

''Ah . . .''

She still had her coat on; she thrust her hands in her pockets and faced him squarely, with her bun slipping down the back of her head. ''You promised me,'' she told him. ''You swore you'd talk to her.''

''I didn't swear to, Mother.''

''You took a solemn oath,'' she told him.

''I notice she still wears a ring,'' he said hopefully.

''So what,'' said his mother. She went back to her groceries.

''She wouldn't wear a ring if she and Harley were separated, would she?''

''She would if she wanted to fool us.''

''Well, I don't know, if she wants to fool us maybe we ought to *act* fooled. I don't know.''

''All my life,'' his mother said, ''people have been trying to shut me out. Even my children. Especially my children. If I so much as ask that girl how she's been, she shies away like I'd inquired into the deepest, darkest part of her. Now, why should she be so standoffish?''

Ezra said, ''Maybe she cares more about what *you* think than what outsiders think.''

''Ha,'' said his mother. She lifted a carton of eggs from the grocery bag.

''I'm worried I don't know how to get in touch with people,'' Ezra said.

''Hmm?''

"I'm worried if I come too close, they'll say I'm overstepping. They'll say I'm pushy, or . . . emotional, you know. But if I back off, they might think I don't care. I really, honestly believe I missed some rule that everyone else takes for granted; I must have been absent from school that day. There's this narrow little dividing line I somehow never located."

"Nonsense; I don't know what you're talking about," said his mother, and then she held up an egg. "Will you look at this? Out of one dozen eggs, four are cracked. Two are *smushed.* I can't imagine what Sweeney Brothers is coming to, these days."

Ezra waited a while, but she didn't say any more. Finally, he left.

He tore down the wall between the restaurant kitchen and the dining room, doing most of the work in a single night. He slung a sledgehammer in a steady rhythm, then ripped away at hunks of plaster till a thick white dust had settled over everything. Then he came upon a mass of pipes and electrical wires and he had to call in professionals to finish off the job. The damage was so extensive that he was forced to stay closed for four straight weekdays, losing a good deal of money.

He figured that while he was at it, he might as well redecorate the dining room. He raced around the windows and dragged down the stiff brocade draperies; he peeled up the carpeting and persuaded a brigade of workmen to sand and polish the floorboards.

By the evening of the fourth day, he was so tired that he could feel the hinging of every muscle. Even so, he washed the white from his hair and changed out of his speckled jeans and went to pay a visit to Mrs. Scarlatti. She lay in her usual position, slightly propped, but her expression was alert and she even managed a smile when he entered. "Guess what, angel," she whispered. "Tomorrow they're letting me leave."

"Leave?"

"I asked the doctor, and he's letting me go home."

"Home?"

"As long as I hire a nurse, he says . . . Well, don't just stand there, Ezra. I need for you to see about a nurse. If you'll look in that nightstand . . ."

It was more talking than she'd done in weeks. Ezra felt almost buoyant with new hope; underneath, it seemed, he must have given up on her. But of course, he was also worried about the restaurant. What would she think when she saw it? What would she say to him? "Everything must go back again, just the way it was," he could imagine. "Really, Ezra. Put up that wall this instant, and fetch my carpets and my curtains." He suspected that he had very poor taste, much inferior to Mrs. Scarlatti's. She would say, "Dear heart, how could you be so *chintzy?*"—a favorite word of hers. He wondered if he could keep her from finding out, if he could convince her to stay in her apartment till he had returned things to normal.

He thanked his stars that he hadn't changed the sign that hung outside.

It was Ezra who settled the bill at the business office, the following morning. Then he spoke briefly with her doctor, whom he chanced to meet in the corridor. "This is wonderful about Mrs. Scarlatti," Ezra said. "I really didn't expect it."

"Oh," said the doctor. "Well."

"I was getting sort of discouraged, if you want to know the truth."

"Well," the doctor said again, and he held out his hand so suddenly that it took Ezra a second to respond. After that, the doctor walked off. Ezra felt there was a lot more the man could have said, as a matter of fact.

Mrs. Scarlatti went home by ambulance. Ezra drove behind, catching glimpses of her through the tinted window. She lay on a stretcher, and next to her was another stretcher holding a man in two full leg casts. His wife perched beside him, evidently talking nonstop. Ezra could see the feathers on her hat bob up and down with her words.

Mrs. Scarlatti was let off first. The ambulance men unloaded her while Ezra stood around feeling useless. "Oh, smell that air," said Mrs. Scarlatti. "Isn't it fresh and beautiful." Actually, it was terrible air— wintry and rainy and harsh with soot. "I never told you this, Ezra," she said, as they wheeled her through the building's front entrance, "but I really didn't believe I would see this place again. My little apartment, my restaurant . . ." Then she raised a palm—her old, peremptory gesture, directed toward the ambulance men. They were preparing to guide her stretcher through the right-hand door and up the stairs. "Dear fellow," she said to the nearest one, "could you just open that door on the left and let me take a peek?"

It happened so fast, Ezra didn't have time to protest. The man reached back in a preoccupied way and opened the door to the restaurant. Then he resumed his study of the stairs; there was an angle at the top that was going to pose a problem. Mrs. Scarlatti, meanwhile, turned her face with some effort and gazed through the door.

There was a moment, just a flicker of a second, when Ezra dared to hope that she might approve after all. But looking past her, he realized that was impossible. The restaurant was a warehouse, a barn, a gymnasium—a total catastrophe. Tables and upended chairs huddled in one corner, underneath bald, barren windows. Buckling plank footbridges led across the varnished floor, which had somehow picked up a film of white dust, and the missing kitchen wall was as horrifying as a toothless smile. Only two broad, plaster pillars separated the kitchen from the dining room. Everything was exposed—sinks and garbage cans, the blackened stove, the hanging pots with their tarnished bottoms, a calendar showing a girl in a sheer black nightgown, and a windowsill bearing two dead plants and a Brillo pad and Todd Duckett's asthma inhalant.

"Oh, my God," said Mrs. Scarlatti.

She looked up into his eyes. Her face seemed stripped. "You might at least have waited till I died," she said.

"Oh!" said Ezra. "No, you don't understand; you don't know. It wasn't what you think. It was just . . . I can't explain, I went wild somehow!"

But she raised that palm of hers and sailed up the stairs to her apartment. Even lying flat, she had an air of speed and power.

She didn't refuse to see him again—nothing like that. Every morning he paid her a visit, and was admitted by her day nurse. He sat on the edge of the ladylike chair in the bedroom and reported on bills and health inspections and linen deliveries. Mrs. Scarlatti was unfailingly polite, nodding in all the right places, but she never said much in return. Eventually, she would close her eyes as a sign that the visit was finished. Then Ezra would leave, often jostling her bed by accident or overturning his chair. He had always been a clumsy man, but now was more so than usual. It seemed to him his hands were too big, forever getting in the way. If only he could have done something with them! He would have liked to fix her a meal—a sustaining meal, with a depth of flavors, a complicated meal that would require a whole day of chopping things small, and grinding, and blending. In the kitchen, as nowhere else, Ezra came into his own, like someone crippled on dry land but effortlessly graceful once he takes to water. However, Mrs. Scarlatti still wasn't eating. There was nothing he could offer her.

Or he would have liked to seize her by the shoulders and shout, "Listen! Listen!" But something closed-off about her face kept stopping him. Almost in plain words, she was telling him that she preferred he not do such a thing. So he didn't.

After a visit, he would go downstairs and look in on the restaurant, which at this hour was vacant and echoing. He might check the freezer, or erase the blackboard, and then perhaps just wander a while, touching this and that. The wallpaper in the back hall was too cluttered and he ripped it off the wall. He tore away the ornate gilt sconces beside the telephone. He yanked the old-fashioned silhouettes from the restroom doors. Sometimes he did so much damage that there was barely time to cover it up before opening, but everybody pitched in and it always got done somehow or other. By six o'clock, when the first customers arrived, the food was cooked and the tables were laid and the waitresses were calm and smiling. Everything was smoothed over.

Mrs. Scarlatti died in March, on a bitter, icy afternoon. When the nurse phoned Ezra, he felt a crushing sense of shock. You would think this death was unexpected. He said, "Oh, no," and hung up, and had to call back to ask the proper questions. Had the end been peaceful? Had Mrs. Scarlatti been awake? Had she said any words in particular? Nothing, said the nurse. Really, nothing at all; just slipped away, like. "But she mentioned you this morning," she added. "I almost wondered, you know? It was almost like she sensed it. She said, 'Tell Ezra to change the sign.'"

"Sign?"

" 'It's not Scarlatti's Restaurant any more,' she said. Or something like that. 'It isn't Scarlatti's.' I think that's what she said."

From the pain he felt, Mrs. Scarlatti might as well have reached out from death and slapped him across the face. It made things easier, in a way. He was almost angry; he was almost relieved that she was gone. He noticed how the trees outside sparkled like something newly minted.

He was the one who made the arrangements, working from a list that Mrs. Scarlatti had given him months before. He knew which funeral home to call and which pastor, and which acquaintances she had wanted at the service. A peculiar thing: he thought of phoning the hospital and inviting that foreign family. Of course he didn't, but it was true they would have made wonderful mourners. Certainly they'd have done better than those who did come, and who later stood stiffly around her frozen grave. Ezra, too, was stiff—a sad, tired man in a flapping coat, holding his mother's arm. Something ached behind his eyes. If he had cried, Mrs. Scarlatti would have said, "Jesus, Ezra. For God's sake, sweetie."

After, he was glad to go to the restaurant. It helped to keep busy—stirring and seasoning and tasting, stumbling over the patch in the floor where the center counter had once stood. Later, he circulated among the diners as Mrs. Scarlatti herself used to do. He urged upon them his oyster stew, his artichoke salad, his spinach bisque and his chili-bean soup and his gizzard soup that was made with love.

5
THE COUNTRY COOK

CODY TULL always had a girlfriend, one girl after another, and all the girls were wild about him till they met his brother, Ezra. Something about Ezra just hooked their attention, it seemed. In his presence they took on a bright, sharp, arrested look, as if listening to a sound that others hadn't caught yet. Ezra didn't even notice this. Cody did, of course. He would give an exaggerated sigh, pretending to be amused. Then the girl would collect herself. It was already too late, though; Cody never allowed second chances. He had a talent for mentally withdrawing. An Indian-faced man with smooth black hair, with level, balanced features, he could manage, when he tried, to seem perfectly blank, like a plaster clothing model. Meanwhile, his ragged, dirty, unloved younger self, with failing grades, with a U in deportment, clenched his fists and howled, "Why? Why always Ezra? Why that sissy pale goody-goody Ezra?"

But Ezra just gazed into space from behind his clear gray eyes, from under his shock of soft, fair hair, and went on thinking his private thoughts. You could say this for Ezra: he seemed honestly unaware of the effect he had on women. No one could accuse him of stealing them deliberately. But that made it all the worse, in a way.

Cody half believed that Ezra had some lack—a lack that worked in his favor, that made him immune, that set him apart from ordinary men. There was something almost monkish about him. Women never really managed to penetrate his meditations, although he was unfailingly courteous to them, and considerate. He was likely to contemplate them in silence for an inappropriate length of time, and then ask something completely out of the blue. For instance: "How did you get those little gold circles through your ears?" It was ridiculous—a man reaches the age of twenty-seven without having heard of pierced earrings. However, it must not have seemed ridiculous to the woman he was addressing. She raised a finger to an earlobe in a startled, mesmerized way. She was spellbound. Was it Ezra's unexpectedness? The narrowness of his focus? (He'd passed up her low-cut dress, powdered cleavage, long silky legs.) Or his innocence, perhaps. He was a tourist on a female planet, was what he was saying. But he didn't realize he was saying it, and failed to understand the look she gave him. Or didn't care, if he did understand.

Only one of Cody's girlfriends had not been attracted to his brother. This was a social worker named Carol, or maybe Karen. Upon meeting Ezra, she had fixed him with a cool stare. Later, she had remarked to Cody that she disliked motherly men. "Always feeding, hovering," she said (for she'd met him at his restaurant), "but acting so clumsy and shy, in the end it's *you* that takes care of *them*. Ever notice that?" However, she hardly counted; Cody had so soon afterward lost interest in her.

You might wonder why he went on making these introductions, considering his unfortunate experiences—the earliest dating from the year he turned fourteen, the latest as recent as a month ago. After all, he lived in New York City and his family lived in Baltimore; he didn't really have to bring these women home on weekends. In fact, he often swore that he would stop it. He would meet somebody, marry her, and not mention her even to his mother. But that would mean a lifetime of suspense. He'd keep watching his wife uncomfortably, suspiciously. He'd keep waiting for the inevitable—like Sleeping Beauty's parents, waiting for the needle that was bound to prick her finger in spite of their precautions.

He was thirty years old by now, successful in his business, certainly ready to marry. He considered his New York apartment temporary, a matter of minor convenience; he had recently purchased a farmhouse in Baltimore County with forty acres of land. Weekends, he traded his slim gray suit for corduroys and he roamed his property, making plans. There was a sunny backyard where his wife could have her kitchen garden. There were bedrooms waiting to be stocked with children. He imagined them tumbling out to meet him every Friday afternoon when he came home. He felt rich and lordly. Poor Ezra: all he had was that disorganized restaurant, in the cramped, stunted center of the city.

Once, Cody invited Ezra to hunt rabbits with him in the woods behind the farm. It wasn't a success. First Ezra fell into a yellowjackets' nest. Then he got his rifle wet in the stream. And when they paused on a hilltop for lunch, he whipped out his battered recorder and commenced to tootling "Greensleeves," scaring off all living creatures within a five-mile radius—which may have been his intention. Cody wasn't even talking to him, at the end; Ezra had to chatter on by himself. Cody stalked well ahead of him in total silence, trying to remember why this outing had seemed such a good idea. Ezra sang, "Mister Rabbit." *"Every little soul,"* he sang, blissfully off-key, *"must shine, shine . . ."*

No wonder Cody was a cuticle chewer, a floor pacer, a hair rummager. No wonder, when he slept at night, he ground his teeth so hard that his jaws ached every morning.

Early in the spring of 1960, his sister, Jenny, wrote him a letter. Her divorce was coming through in June, she said—two more months, and then she'd be free to marry Sam Wiley. Cody didn't think much of Wiley, and he flicked this news aside like a gnat and read on. *Though it looks,* she said, *as if Ezra might beat me down the aisle. Her name is Ruth but I don't know any more than that.* Then she said she was seriously considering dropping out of medical school. The complications of her personal life, she said, were using up so much energy that she had none left over for anything else. Also, she had gained three pounds in the last six weeks and was perfectly obese, a whale, living now on lettuce leaves and lemon water. Cody was accustomed to Jenny's crazy diets (she was painfully thin), so he skimmed that part. He finished the letter and folded it.

Ruth?

He opened it again.

. . . as if Ezra might beat me down the aisle, he read. He tried to think
of some other kind of aisle—airplane, supermarket, movie house—but
in the end, he had to believe it: Ezra was getting married. Well, at
least now Cody could keep his own girls. (This gave him, for some
reason, a little twinge of uneasiness.) But Ezra! Married? That walking
accident? Imagine him in a formal wedding—forgetting license, ring,
and responses, losing track of the service while smiling out the window
at a hummingbird. Imagine him in bed with a woman. (Cody snorted.)
He pictured the woman as dark and Biblical, because of her name:
Ruth. Shadowed eyes and creamy skin. Torrents of loose black hair.
Cody had a weakness for black-haired women; he didn't like blondes
at all. He pictured her bare shouldered, in a red satin nightgown, and
he crumpled Jenny's letter roughly and dropped it in the wastebasket.

The next day at work, Ruth's image hung over him. He was doing
a time-and-motion study of a power-drill factory in New Jersey, a
dinosaur of a place. It would take him weeks to sort it out. *Joining
object K to object L: right-hand transport unloaded, search, grasp, transport
loaded . . .* He passed down the assembly line with his clipboard,
attracting hostile glances. Ruth's black hair billowed in the rafters.
Unavoidable delays: 3. Avoidable delays: 9. No doubt her eyes were plum
shaped, slightly tilted. No doubt her hands were heavily ringed, with
long, oval fingernails painted scarlet.

When he returned to his apartment that evening, there was a letter
from Ezra. It was an invitation to his restaurant this coming Saturday
night. *You are cordially invited* was centered on the page like something
engraved—Ezra's idea of a joke. (Or maybe not; maybe he meant it
in earnest.) Oh, Lord, not another one of Ezra's dinners. There would
be toasts and a fumbling, sentimental speech leading up to some weighty
announcement—in this case, his engagement. Cody thought of declining,
but what good would that do? Ezra would be desolate if a single person
was missing. He'd cancel the whole affair and reschedule it for later,
and keep on rescheduling till Cody accepted. Cody might as well go
and be done with it.

Besides, he wouldn't at all mind meeting this Ruth.

Ezra was listening to a customer—or a one-time customer, from the
sound of it. "Used to be," the man was saying, "this place had class.
You follow me?"

Ezra nodded, watching him with such a sympathetic, kindly expression
that Cody wondered if his mind weren't somewhere else altogether.
"Used to be there was fine French cuisine, flamed at the tables and
all," said the man. "And chandeliers. And a hat-check girl. And waiters
in black tie. What happened to your waiters?"

"They put people off," Ezra said. "They seemed to think the customers were taking an exam of some kind, not just ordering a meal. They were uppish."

"I liked your waiters."

"Nowadays our staff is homier," Ezra said, and he gestured toward a passing waitress—a tall, stooped, colorless girl, open mouthed with concentration, fiercely intent upon the coffee mug that she carried in both hands. She inched across the floor, breathing adenoidally. She proceeded directly between Ezra and the customer. Ezra stepped back to give her room.

The customer said, " 'Nettie,' I said, 'you've just got to see Scarlatti's. Don't knock Baltimore,' I tell her, 'till you see Scarlatti's.' Then we come upon it and even the sign's gone. Homesick Restaurant, you call it now. What kind of a name is that? And the decor! Why, it looks like . . . why, a gigantic roadside diner!"

He was right. Cody agreed with him. Dining room walls lined with home preserves, kitchen laid open to the public, unkempt cooks milling around compiling their favorite dishes (health food, street food, foreign food, whatever popped into their heads) . . . Ever since Ezra had inherited this place—from a woman, wouldn't you know—he'd been systematically wrecking it. He was fully capable of serving a single entrée all one evening, bringing it to your table himself as soon as you were seated. Other nights he'd offer more choice, four or five selections chalked up on the blackboard. But still you might not get what you asked for. "The Smithfield ham," you'd say, and up would come the okra stew. "With that cough of yours, I know this will suit you better," Ezra would explain. But even if he'd judged correctly, was that any way to run a restaurant? You order ham, ham is what you get. Otherwise, you might as well eat at home. "You'll go bankrupt in a year," Cody had promised, and Ezra almost did go bankrupt; most of the regular patrons disappeared. Some hung on, though; and others discovered it. There were several older people who ate here every night, sitting alone at their regular tables in the barnlike, plank-floored dining room. They could afford it because the prices weren't written but recited instead by the staff, evidently according to whim, altering with the customer. (Wasn't that illegal?) Ezra worried about what these older people did on Sundays, when he closed. Cody, on the other hand, worried about Ezra's account books, but didn't offer to go over them. He would find a disaster, he was sure—errors and bad debts, if not outright, naive crookery. Better not to know; better not to get involved.

"It's true there've been some changes," Ezra was telling his ex-customer, "but if you'll just try our food, you'll see that we're still a fine restaurant. Tonight it's all one dish—pot roast."

"Pot roast!"

"A really special kind—consoling."

"Pot roast I can get at home," said the man. He clamped a felt hat on his head and walked out.

"Oh, well," Ezra told Cody. "You can't please everybody, I guess."

They made their way to the far corner, where a RESERVED sign sat upon the table that Ezra always chose for family dinners. Jenny and their mother weren't there yet. Jenny, who'd arrived on the afternoon train, had asked her mother's help in shopping for a dress to be married in. Now Ezra worried they'd be late. "Everything's planned for six-thirty," he said. "What's keeping them?"

"Well, no problem if it's only pot roast."

"It's not *only* pot roast," Ezra said. He sat in a chair. His suit had a way of waffling around him, as if purchased for a much larger man. "This is something more. I mean, pot roast is really not the right name; it's more like . . . what you long for when you're sad and everyone's been wearing you down. See, there's this cook, this real country cook, and pot roast is the least of what she does. There's also pan-fried potatoes, black-eyed peas, beaten biscuits genuinely beat on a stump with the back of an ax—"

"Here they come," Cody said.

Jenny and her mother were just walking across the dining room. They carried no parcels, but something made it clear they'd been shopping—perhaps, the frazzled, cross look they shared. Jenny's lipstick was chewed off. Pearl's hat was knocked crooked and her hair was frizzier than ever. "What took you so long?" Ezra asked, jumping up. "We were starting to worry."

"Oh, this Jenny and her notions," said Pearl. "Her size eight figure and no bright colors, no pastels, no gathers or puckers or trim, nothing to make her look fat, so-called . . . Why are there five places set?"

The question took them all off guard. It was true, Cody saw. There were five plates and five crystal wineglasses. "How come?" Pearl asked Ezra.

"Oh . . . I'll get to that in a minute. Have a seat, Mother, over there."

But she kept standing. "Then at last we find just the right thing," she said. "A nice soft gray with a crocheted collar, Jenny all the way. 'It's you,' I tell her. And guess what she does. She has a tantrum in the middle of Hutzler's department store."

"Not a *tantrum*, Mother," Jenny told her. "I merely said—"

"Said, 'It isn't a funeral, Mother; I'm not going into mourning.' You'd think I'd chosen widow's weeds. This was a nice pale gray, very ladylike, very suitable for a second marriage."

"Anthracite," Jenny told Cody.

"Pardon?"

"Anthracite was what the saleslady called it. In other words: coal.

Our mother thinks it suitable to marry me off in a coal-black wedding dress."

"Uh," said Ezra, looking around at the other diners, "maybe we should be seated now."

But Pearl just stood straighter. "And *then*," she told her sons, "then, without the slightest bit of thought, doing it only to spite me, she goes rushing over to the nearest rack and pulls out something white as snow."

"It was cream colored," Jenny said.

"Cream, white—what's the difference? Both are inappropriate, if you're marrying for the second time and the divorce hasn't yet been granted and the man has no steady employment. 'I'll take this one,' she says, and it's not even the proper size, miles too big, had to be left at the store for alterations."

"I happened to like it," Jenny said.

"You were lost in it."

"It made me look thin."

"Maybe you could wear a shawl or something, brown," said her mother. "That might tone it down some."

"I can't wear a shawl in a wedding."

"Why not? Or a little jacket, say a brown linen jacket."

"I look fat in jackets."

"Not in a short one, Chanel-type."

"I hate Chanel."

"Well," said Pearl, "I can see that nothing will satisfy you."

"Mother," Jenny said, "I'm already satisfied. I'm satisfied with my cream-colored dress, just the way it is. I love it. Will you please just get off my back?"

"Did you hear that?" Pearl asked her sons. "Well, I don't have to stand here and take it." And she turned and marched back across the dining room, erect as a little wind-up doll.

Ezra said, "Huh?"

Jenny opened a plastic compact, looked into it, and then snapped it shut, as if merely making certain that she was still there.

"Please, Jenny, won't you go after her?" Ezra said.

"Not on your life."

"*You're* the one she fought with. *I* can't persuade her."

"Oh, Ezra, let's for once just drop it," Cody said. "I don't think I'm up to all this."

"What are you saying? Not have dinner at all?"

"I could only eat lettuce leaves anyhow," Jenny told him.

"But this is important! It was going to be an occasion. Oh, just . . . wait. Wait here a minute, will you?"

Ezra turned and rushed off to the kitchen. From the swarm of assorted cooks at the counter, he plucked a small person in overalls. It was a girl, Cody guessed—a weasel-faced little redhead. She followed Ezra jauntily, almost stiff-legged, wiping her palms on her backside. "I'd like you to meet Ruth," Ezra said.

Cody said, "Ruth?"

"We're getting married in September."

"Oh," said Cody.

Then Jenny said, "Well, congratulations," and kissed Ruth's bony, freckled cheek, and Cody said, "Uh, yes," and shook her hand. There were calluses like pebbles on her palm. "How do," she told him. He thought of the phrase *banty hen*, although he had never seen a banty hen. Or maybe she was more of a rooster. Her brisk, carroty hair was cut so short that it seemed too scant for her skull. Her blue eyes were round as marbles, and her skin was so thin and tight (as if, like her hair, it had been skimped on) that he could see the white cartilage across the bridge of her nose. "So," he said. "Ruth."

"Are you surprised?" Ezra asked him.

"Yes, very surprised."

"I wanted to do it right; I was going to announce it over drinks and then call her in to join the family dinner. But, honey," Ezra said, turning to Ruth, "I guess Mother was overtired. It didn't work out the way I'd planned."

"Shit, that's okay," Ruth told him.

Cody said, "Surely. Certainly. We can always do it later."

Then Jenny started asking about the wedding, and Cody excused himself and said he thought he'd go see how their mother was. Outside in the dark, walking up the street toward home, he had the strangest feeling of loss. It was as if someone had died, or had left him forever— the beautiful, black-haired Ruth of his dreams.

"I knew what that dinner was going to be, tonight," Pearl told Cody. "I'm not so dumb. I knew. He's got himself engaged; he's going to marry the country cook. I knew that anyway but it all came home to me when I walked in the restaurant and saw those five plates and glasses. Well, I acted badly. Very badly. You don't have to tell me, Cody. It was just that I saw those plates and something broke inside of me. I thought, 'Well, all right, if that's how it's got to be, but not tonight, just not tonight, Lord, right on top of buying wedding dress number two for my only daughter.' So then, why, I went and made a scene that caused the dinner to be canceled, exactly as if I'd planned it all ahead of time, which of course I hadn't. You believe me, don't you? I'm not blind. I know when I'm being unreasonable. Sometimes I stand outside my body and just watch it all, totally separate. 'Now, stop,' I say to myself, but it's like I'm . . . elated; I've got to rush on, got to keep going. 'Yes, yes, I'll stop,' I think, 'only let me say this one more thing, just this one more thing. . . .'

"Cody, don't you believe I want you three to be happy? Of course I do. Naturally. Why, I wouldn't hold Ezra back for the world, if he's so set on marrying that girl—though I don't know what he sees in her, she's so scrappy and hoydenish; I think she's from Garrett County or some such place and hardly wears shoes—you ought to see the soles of her feet sometime—but what I want to say is, I've never been one of those mothers who try to keep their sons for themselves. I honestly hope Ezra marries. I truly mean that. I want somebody taking care of him, *especially* him. You can manage on your own but Ezra is so, I don't know, defenseless. . . . Of course I love you all the same amount, every bit the same, but . . . well, Ezra is so *good*. You know? Anyway, now he has this Ruth person and it's changed his whole outlook; watch him sometime when she walks into a room, or swaggers, or whatever you want to call it. He adores her. They get all playful together, like two puppies. Yes, often they remind me of puppies, snuggling down and giggling, or bounding about the kitchen or listening to that hillbilly music that Ruth seems to be so crazy about. But, Cody. Promise not to tell this to anyone. Promise? Cody, sometimes I stand there watching them and I see they believe they're completely special, the first, the only people ever to feel the way they're feeling. They believe they'll live happily ever after, that all the other marriages going on around them—those ordinary, worn-down, flattened-in arrangements—why, those are nothing like what *they'll* have. They'll never settle for so little. And it makes me mad. I can't help it, Cody. I know it's selfish, but I can't help it. I want to ask them, 'Who do you think you are, anyhow? Do you imagine you're unique? Do you really suppose I was always this difficult old woman?'

"Cody, listen. I was special too, once, to someone. I could just reach out and lay a fingertip on his arm while he was talking and he would instantly fall silent and get all confused. I had hopes; I was courted; I had the most beautiful wedding. I had three lovely pregnancies, where every morning I woke up knowing something perfect would happen in nine months, eight months, seven . . . so it seemed I was full of light; it was light and plans that filled me. And then while you children were little, why, I was the center of your worlds! I was everything to you! It was Mother this and Mother that, and 'Where's Mother? Where's she gone to?' and the moment you came in from school, 'Mother? Are you home?' It's not fair, Cody. It's really not fair; now I'm old and I walk along unnoticed, just like anyone else. It strikes me as unjust, Cody. But don't tell the others I said so."

At work that next week, charting the steps by which power drills were fitted into their housings, Cody watched the old, dark Ruth fade from the rafters and hallways, until at last she was completely gone and he forgot why she had moved him so. Now a new Ruth appeared.

Skinny and boyish, overalls flapping around her shinbones, she raced giggling down the assembly line with Ezra hot on her heels. Ezra's hair was tousled. (He was not immune at all, it appeared, but had only been waiting in his stubbornly trustful way for the proper person to arrive.) He caught her in the supervisor's office and they scuffled like . . . yes, like two puppies. A cowlick bounced on the crown of Ruth's head. Her lips were chapped and cracked. Her nails were bitten into tiny pink cushions and there were scrapes and burns across her knuckles, scars from her country cooking.

Cody called his mother and said he'd be down for the weekend. And would Ruth be around, did she think? After all, he said, it was time he got to know his future sister-in-law.

He arrived on Saturday morning bringing flowers, copper-colored roses. He found Ruth and Ezra playing gin on the living room floor. Ruth's reality, after his week of dreaming, struck him like a blow. She seemed clearer, plainer, harder edged than anybody he'd known. She wore jeans and a shirt of some ugly brown plaid. She was so absorbed in her game that she hardly glanced up when Cody walked in. "Ruth," he said, and he held out the flowers. "These are for you."

She looked at them, and then drew a card. "What are they?" she asked.

"Well, roses."

"Roses? This early in the year?"

"Greenhouse roses. I especially ordered copper, to go with your hair."

"You leave my hair out of this," she said.

"Honey, he meant it as a compliment," Ezra told her.

"Oh."

"Certainly," said Cody. "See, it's my way of saying welcome. Welcome to our family, Ruth."

"Oh. Well, thanks."

"Cody, that was awfully nice of you," Ezra said.

"Gin," said Ruth.

Late that afternoon, when it was time to go to the restaurant, Cody walked over with Ruth and Ezra. He'd had a long, immobile day—standing outside other people's lives, mostly—and he needed the exercise.

It had been raining, off and on, and there were puddles on the sidewalk. Ruth strode straight through every one of them, which was fine since her shoes were brown leather combat boots. Cody wondered if her style were deliberate. What would she do, for instance, if he gave her a pair of high-heeled evening sandals? The question began to fascinate him. He became obsessed; he developed an almost physical thirst for the sight of her blunt little feet in silver straps.

There was no explaining his craving for the gigantic watch—black faced and intricately calibrated, capable of withstanding a deep-sea dive—whose stainless steel expansion band hung loose on her wiry wrist.

Ezra had his pearwood recorder. He played it as he walked, serious and absorbed, with his lashes lowered on his cheeks. "Le Godiveau de Poisson," he played. Passersby looked at him and smiled. Ruth hummed along with some notes, fell into her own thoughts at others. Then Ezra put his recorder in the pocket of his shabby lumber jacket, and he and Ruth began discussing the menu. It was good they were serving the rice dish, Ruth said; that always made the Arab family happy. She ran her fingers through her sprouty red hair. Cody, walking on the other side of her, felt her shift of weight when Ezra circled her with one arm and pulled her close.

In the restaurant, she was a whirlwind. Ezra cooked in a dream, tasting and reflecting; the others (losers, all of them, in Cody's opinion) floated around the kitchen vaguely, but Ruth spun and pounced and jabbed at food as if doing battle. She was in charge of a chicken casserole and something that looked like potato cakes. Cody watched her from a corner well out of the way, but still people seemed to keep tripping over him.

"Where did you learn to cook?" he asked Ruth.

"No place," she said.

"Is this chicken some regional thing?"

"Taste," she snapped, and she speared a piece and held it out to him.

"I can't," he said.

"Why not?"

"I feel too full."

In fact, he felt full of *her*. He'd taken her in all day, consumed her. Every spiky movement—slamming of pot lids, toss of head—nourished him. It came to him like a gift, while he was studying her narrow back, that she actually wore an undershirt, one of those knitted singlets he remembered from his childhood. He could make out the seams of it beneath the brown plaid. He filed the information with care, to be treasured once he was alone.

The restaurant opened and customers began to trickle in. The large, beaming hostess seated them all in one area, as if tucking them under her wing.

"Find a table," Ezra told Cody. "I'll bring you some of Ruth's cooking."

"I'm honestly not hungry," Cody said.

"He's *full*," said Ruth, spitting it out.

"Well, what'll you do, then? Isn't this boring for you?"

"No, no, I'm interested," Cody said.

He could look across the counter and into the dining room, where people sat chewing and swallowing and drinking, patting their mouths with napkins, breaking off chunks of bread. He wondered how Ezra could stand to spend his life at this.

When the first real flurry was over, Ruth and Ezra settled at the scrubbed wooden table in the center of the kitchen, and Cody joined them. Ezra ate some of Ruth's chicken casserole. Ruth lit a small brown cigarette and tipped back in her chair to watch him. The cigarette smelled as if it were burning only by accident—like something spilled on the floor of an oven, or stuck to the underside of a saucepan. Cody, seated across from her, drank it in. "Eat, Cody, eat," Ezra urged him. Cody just shook his head, not wanting to lose his chestful of Ruth's smoke.

Meanwhile, the other cooks came and went, some of them sitting also to wolf various odd assortments of food while their kettles simmered untended. Ezra's boyhood friend Josiah appeared, metamorphosed into an efficient grown man in starchy white, and he and Ruth had a talk about peeling the apples for her pie. Cody could not have cared less about her pie, but he was riveted by her offhand, slangy style of speech. She held her cigarette between thumb and index finger, with her elbow propped against her rib cage. She hunkered forward to consider some decision, and beneath her knotted brows her eyes were so pale a blue that he was startled.

They left the restaurant before it closed. Josiah would lock up, Ezra said. They took a roundabout route home, down a quiet, one-way street, to drop Ruth off at the house where she rented a room. When Ezra accompanied her up the front steps, Cody waited on the curb. He watched Ezra kiss her good night—a bumbling, inadequate kiss, Cody judged it; and he felt some satisfaction. Then Ezra rejoined him and galumphed along beside him, big footed and blithe. "Isn't she something?" he asked Cody. "Don't you just love her?"

"Mm."

"But there's so much I need to find out from you! I want to take good care of her, but I don't know how. What about life insurance? Things like that! So much is expected of husbands, Cody. Will you help me figure it out?"

"I'll be glad to," Cody said. He meant it, too. Anything: any little crack that would provide him with an entrance.

Eventually, Ezra subsided, although he continued to give the impression of inwardly bubbling and chortling. From time to time, he hummed a few bars of something underneath his breath. And then when they were almost home—passing houses totally dark, where everyone had long since gone to sleep—what should he do but pull out that damned recorder of his and start piping away. It was embarrassing. It was infuriating: "Le Godiveau de Poisson," once again. Depend on Ezra,

Cody thought, to have as his theme song a recipe for a seafood dish. He walked along in silence, hoping someone would call the police. Or at least, that they'd open a window. "You there! Quiet!" But no one did. It was so typical: Ezra the golden boy, everybody's favorite, tootling down the streets scot-free.

On Sunday morning, Cody presented himself at Ruth's door—or rather, at the door of the faded, doughy lady who owned the house Ruth stayed in. This lady toyed so fearfully with the locket at her throat that Cody felt compelled to take a step backward, proving he was not a knock-and-rob man. He gave her his most gentlemanly smile. "Good morning," he said. "Is Ruth home?"

"Ruth?"

He realized he didn't know Ruth's last name. "I'm Ezra Tull's brother," he said.

"Oh, *Ezra*," she said, and she stood back to let him enter.

He followed her deep into the interior, past a tumult of overstuffed furniture and dusty wax fruit and heaps of magazines. In the kitchen, Ruth slouched at the table spooning up cornflakes and reading a newspaper propped against a cereal box. A pale, pudgy man stood gazing into an open refrigerator. Cody had an impression of inertia and frittered lives. He felt charged with energy. It ought to be so easy to win her away from all this!

"Good morning," he said. Ruth looked up. The pudgy man retreated behind the refrigerator door.

"I hope you're not too far into that cereal," Cody said. "I came to invite you to breakfast."

"What for?" Ruth asked, frowning.

"Well . . . not for any *purpose*. I'm just out walking and I thought you might want to walk with me, stop off for doughnuts and coffee someplace."

"Now?"

"Of course."

"Isn't it raining?"

"Only a little bit."

"No, thanks," she said.

Her eyes dropped back to her newspaper. The landlady slid her locket along its chain with a miniature zipping sound.

"What's going on in the world?" Cody asked.

"What world?" said Ruth.

"The news. What does the newspaper say?"

Ruth raised her eyes, and Cody saw the page she had turned to. "Oh," he said. "The comics."

"No, my horoscope."

"Your horoscope." He looked to the landlady for help. The landlady gazed off toward a cabinet full of jelly glasses. "Well, what . . . um, symbol are you?" Cody asked Ruth.

"Hmm?"

"What astrological symbol?"

"Sign," she corrected him. She sighed and stood up, finally forced to recognize his presence. Snatching her paper from the table, she stalked off toward the parlor. Cody made way for her and then trailed after. Her jeans, he guessed, had been bought at a little boys' clothing store. She had no hips whatsoever. Her sweater was transparent at the elbows.

"I'm Taurus," she said over her shoulder, "but all that's rubbish, anyhow. Total garbage."

"Oh, I agree," Cody said, relieved.

She stopped in the center of the parlor and turned to him. "Look at here," she said, and she jabbed her finger at a line of newsprint. *"Powerful ally will come to your rescue. Accent today on high finance."* She lowered the paper. "I mean, who do they reckon they're dealing with? What kind of business am I supposed to be involved in?"

"Ridiculous," said Cody. He was hypnotized by her eyebrows. They were the color of orange sherbet, and whenever she spoke with any heat the skin around them grew pink, darker than the eyebrows themselves.

"Ignore innuendos from long-time foe," she read, running a finger down the column. "Or listen to this other one: *Clandestine meeting could solve mystery.* Almighty God!" she said, and she tossed the paper into an armchair. "You got to lead quite a life, to get anything out of your horoscope."

"Well, I don't know," Cody said. "Maybe it's truer than you realize."

"Come again?"

"Maybe it's saying you *ought* to lead such a life. Ought to be more adventurous, not just slave away in some restaurant, mope around a gloomy old boarding-house. . . ."

"It's not so gloomy," Ruth said, lifting her chin.

"Well, but—"

"And anyhow, I won't always be here. Me and Ezra, after we marry, we're moving in above the Homesick. Then once we get us some money we plan on a house."

"But still," said Cody, "you won't have anywhere near what those horoscopes are calling for. Why, there's all the outside world! New York, for instance. Ever been to New York?"

She shook her head, watching him narrowly.

"You ought to come; it's springtime there."

"It's springtime here," she said.

"But a different kind."

"I don't see what you're getting at," she told him.

"Well, all I want to say is, Ruth: why settle down so soon, when there's so much you haven't seen yet?"

"Soon?" she said. "I'm pretty near twenty years old. Been rattling around on my own since my sixteenth birthday. Only thing I *want* is to settle down, sooner the better."

"Oh," said Cody.

"Well, have a good walk."

"Oh, yes, walk . . ."

"Don't drown," she told him, callously.

At the door, he turned. He said, "Ruth?"

"What."

"I don't know your last name."

"Spivey," she said.

He thought it was the loveliest sound he had ever heard in his life.

The following weekend, he drove her out to see his farm. "I have seen all the farms I care to," she said, but Ezra said, "Oh, you ought to go, Ruth. It's pretty this time of year." Ezra himself had to stay behind; he was supervising the installation of a new meat locker for the restaurant. Cody had known that before he invited her.

This time he brought her jonquils. She said, "I don't know what I want with *these;* there's a whole mess in back by the walkway."

Cody smiled at her.

He settled her in his Cadillac, which smelled of new leather. She looked unimpressed. Perversely, she was wearing a skirt, on the one occasion when jeans would have been more suitable. Her legs were very white, almost chalky. He had not seen short socks like hers since his schooldays, and her tattered sneakers were as small and stubby as a child's.

On the drive out, he talked about his plans for the farm. "It's where I'd like to live," he said. "Where I want to raise my family. It's a perfect place for children."

"What makes you think so?" she asked. "When I was a kid, all I cared about was getting to the city."

"Yes, but fresh air and home-grown vegetables, and the animals . . . Right now, the man down the road is tending my livestock, but once I move in full-time I'm going to do it all myself."

"*That* I'd like to see," said Ruth. "You ever slopped a hog? Shoveled out a stable?"

"I can learn," he told her.

She shrugged and said no more.

When they reached the farm he showed her around the grounds, where she stared a cow down and gave a clump of hens the evil eye. Then he led her into the house. He'd bought it lock, stock, and barrel— complete with bald plush sofa and kerosene stove in the parlor, rickety kitchen table with its drawerful of rusted flatware, 1958 calendar on the wall advertising Mallardy's oystershell mixture for layers, extra rich in calcium. The man who'd lived here—a widower—had died upstairs in the four-poster bed. Cody had replaced the bedclothes with new ones, sheets and a quilt and down pillows, but that was his only change. "I do plan to fix things up," he told Ruth, "but I'm waiting till I marry. I know my wife might like to have a say in it."

Ruth removed a window lock easily from its crumbling wooden sash. She turned it over and peered at the underside.

"I want a wife very much," said Cody.

She put back the lock. "I hate to be the one to tell you," she said, "but smell that smell? Kind of sweetish smell? You got dry rot here."

"Ruth," he said, "do you dislike me for any reason?"

"Huh?"

"Your attitude. The way you put me off. You don't think much of me, do you?" he said.

She gave him an edgy, skewed look, evasive, and moved over to the stairway. "Oh," she said, "I like you a fair amount."

"You do?"

"But I know your type," she said.

"What type?"

"There were plenty like you in my school," she said. "Oh, sure! Some in every class, on every team—tall and real good-looking, stylish, athletic, witty. *Smooth*-mannered boys that everything always came easy to, that always knew the proper way of doing things, and never dated any but the cheerleader girls, or the homecoming queen, or her maids of honor at the lowest. Passing me in the halls not even knowing who I was, nor guessing I existed. Or making fun of me sometimes, I'm almost certain—laughing at how poor I dressed and mocking my freckly face and my old red hair—"

"Laughing! When have I ever done such a thing?"

"I'm not naming you in particular," she said, "but you sure do put me in mind of a type."

"Ruth. I wouldn't mock you. I think you're perfect," he said. "You're the most beautiful woman I've ever laid eyes on."

"See there?" she asked, and she raised her chin, spun about, and marched down the stairs. She wouldn't answer anything else he said to her, all during the long drive home.

It was a campaign, was what it was—a long and arduous battle campaign, extending through April and all of May. There were moments when he despaired. He'd had too late a start, was out of the running; he'd wasted his time with those unoriginal, obvious brunettes whom he'd thought he was so clever to snare while Ezra, not even trying, had somehow divined the real jewel. Lucky Ezra! His whole life rested on luck, and Cody would probably never manage to figure out how he did it.

Often, after leaving Ruth, Cody would be muttering to himself as he strode away. He would slam a fist in his palm or kick his own car. But at the same time, he had an underlying sense of exhilaration. Yes, he would have to say that he'd never felt more alive, never more eager for each new day. Now he understood why he'd lost interest in Carol or Karen, what's-her-name, the social worker who hadn't found Ezra appealing. She'd made it too easy. What he liked was the competition, the hope of emerging triumphant from a neck-and-neck struggle with Ezra, his oldest enemy. He even liked biding his time, holding himself in check, hiding his feelings from Ruth till the most advantageous moment. (Was *patience* Ezra's secret?) For, of course, this wasn't an open competition. One of the contestants didn't even know he *was* a contestant. "Gosh, Cody," Ezra said, "it's been nice to have you around so much lately." And to Ruth, "Go, go; you'll enjoy it," when Cody invited her anywhere.

Once, baiting Ezra, Cody stole one of Ruth's brown cigarettes and smoked it in the farmhouse. (The scent of burning tar filled his bedroom. If he'd had a telephone, he would have forgotten all his strategies and called her that instant to confess he loved her.) He stubbed out the butt in a plastic ashtray beside his bed. Then later he invited Ezra to look at his new calves, took him upstairs to discuss a leak in the roof, and led him to the nightstand where the ashtray sat. But Ezra just said, "Oh, was Ruth here?" and launched into praise for an herb garden she was planting on top of the restaurant. Cody couldn't believe that anyone would be so blind, so credulous. Also, he would have died for the privilege of having Ruth plant herbs for him. He thought of the yard out back, where he'd always envisioned his wife's kitchen garden. Rosemary! Basil! Lemon balm!

"Why didn't she come to me?" he asked Ezra. "She could always grow her herbs on my farm."

"Oh, well, the closer to home the fresher," said Ezra. "But you're kind to offer, Cody."

Oiling his rifles that night, Cody seriously considered shooting Ezra through the heart.

When he complimented Ruth, she bristled. When he brought her the gifts he'd so craftily chosen (gold chains and crystal flasks of perfume, music boxes, silk flowers, all intended to contrast with the ugly, mottled marble rolling pin that Ezra presented, clumsily wrapped, on her twentieth birthday), she generally lost them right away or left them wherever she happened to be. And when he invited her places, she only came along for the outing. He would take her arm and she'd say, "Jeepers, I'm not some old lady." She would scramble over rocks and through forests in her combat boots, and Cody would follow, bemused and dazzled, literally sick with love. He had lost eight pounds, could not eat—a myth, he'd always thought that was—and hardly slept at night. When he did sleep, he willed himself to dream of Ruth but never did; she was impishly, defiantly absent, and daytimes when they next met he thought he saw something taunting in the look she gave him.

He often found it difficult to keep their conversations going. It struck him sometimes—in the middle of the week, when he was far from Baltimore—that this whole idea was deranged. They would never be anything but strangers. What single interest, even, did they have in common? But every weekend he was staggered, all over again, by her strutting walk, her belligerent chin and endearing scowl. He was moved by her musty, little-boyish smell; he imagined how her small body could nestle into his. Oh, it was Ruth herself they had in common. He would reach out to touch the spurs of her knuckles. She would ruffle and draw back. "What are you doing?" she would ask. He didn't answer.

"I know what you're up to," his mother told him.

"I beg your pardon?"

"I see through you like a sheet of glass."

"Well? What am I up to, then?" he asked. He really did hope to hear; he had reached the stage where he'd angle and connive just to get someone to utter Ruth's name.

"You don't fool me for an instant," said his mother. "Why are you so contrary? You've got no earthly use for that girl. She's not your type in the slightest; she belongs to your brother, Ezra, and she's the only thing in this world he's ever wanted. If you were to win her away, tell me what you'd do with her! You'd drop her flat. You'd say, 'Oh, my goodness, what am I doing with *this* little person?' "

"You don't understand," said Cody.

"This may come as a shock," his mother told him, "but I understand you perfectly. With the rest of the world I might not be so smart, but with my three children, why, not the least little thing escapes me. I know everything you're after. I see everything in your heart, Cody Tull."

"Just like God," Cody said.

"Just like God," she agreed.

Ezra arranged a celebration dinner for the evening before Jenny's wedding—a Friday. But Thursday night, Jenny phoned Cody at his apartment. It was a local call; she said she wasn't ten blocks away, staying at a hotel with Sam Wiley. "We got married yesterday morning," she said, "and now we're on our honeymoon. So there won't be any dinner after all."

"Well, how did all *this* come about?" Cody asked.

"Mother and Sam had a little disagreement."

"I see."

"Mother said . . . and Sam told her . . . and I said, 'Oh, Sam, why not let's just . . .' Only I do feel bad about Ezra. I know how much trouble he's gone to."

"By now, he ought to be used to this," Cody said.

"He was going to serve a suckling pig."

Hadn't Ezra noticed (Cody wondered) that the family as a whole had never yet finished one of his dinners? That they'd fight and stamp off halfway through, or sometimes not even manage to get seated in the first place? Well, of course he must have *noticed*, but was it clear to him as a pattern, a theme? No, perhaps he viewed each dinner as a unit in itself, unconnected to the others. Maybe he never linked them in his mind.

Assuming he was a total idiot.

It was true that once—to celebrate Cody's new business—they had made it all the way to dessert; so if they hadn't ordered dessert you could say they'd completed the meal. But the fact was, they did order dessert, which was left to sag on the plates when their mother accused Cody of deliberately setting up shop as far from home as possible. There was a stiff-backed little quarrel. Conversation fell apart. Cody walked out. So technically, even that meal could not be considered finished. Why did Ezra go on trying?

Why did the rest of them go on showing up, was more to the point.

In fact, they probably saw more of each other than happy families did. It was almost as if what they couldn't get right, they had to keep returning to. (So if they ever did finish a dinner, would they rise and say goodbye forever after?)

Once Jenny had hung up, Cody sat on the couch and leafed through the morning's mail. Something made him feel unsettled. He wondered how Jenny could have married Sam Wiley—a scrawny little artist type, shifty eyed and cocky. He wondered if Ezra would cancel his dinner altogether or merely postpone it till after the honeymoon. He pictured Ruth in the restaurant kitchen, her wrinkled little fingers patting flour on drumsticks. He scanned an ad for life insurance and wondered why no one depended on him—not even enough to require his insurance money if he should happen to die.

He ripped open an envelope marked *AMAZING OFFER!* and found three stationery samples and a glossy order blank. One sample was blue, with *LMR* embossed at the top. Another had a lacy *PAULA*, the *P* entwined with a morning-glory vine, and the third was one of those letters that form their own envelopes when folded. The flap was printed with butterflies and *Mrs. Harold Alexander III, 219 Saint Beulah Boulevard, Dallas, Texas.* He studied that for a moment. Then he took a pen from his shirt pocket, and started writing in an unaccustomed, backhand slant:

Dear Ruth,

Just a line to say hey from all of us. How's the job going? What do you think of Baltimore? Harold says ask if you met a young man yet. He had the funniest dream last night, dreamed he saw you with someone tall, black hair and gray eyes and gray suit. I said well, I certainly hope it's a dream that comes true!

We have all been fine tho Linda was out of school one day last week. A case of "math testitis" it looked like to me, ha ha! She says to send you lots of hugs and kisses. Drop us a line real soon, hear?

Cody felt he had just found the proper tone toward the end; he was sorry to run out of space. He signed the letter *Luv, Sue (Mrs. Harold Alexander III)*, and sealed, stamped, and addressed it. Then he placed it in a business envelope, and wrote a note to his old college roommate in Dallas, asking if he would please drop the enclosed in the nearest mailbox.

That weekend he didn't go home, and his reward was to dream about Ruth. She was waiting for a train that he was traveling on. He saw her on the platform, peering into the windows of each passenger car as it slid by. He was so eager to reach her, to watch her expression ease when she caught sight of him, that he called her name aloud and woke himself up. He heard it echoing in the dark—not her name, after all, but some meaningless sleep sound. For hours after that he tried to burrow back inside the dream, but he had lost it.

The next morning he began another letter, on the sheet headed *PAULA*. In a curlicued script, he wrote:

Dear Ruthie,

You old thing, don't you keep in touch with your friends any more? I told Mama the other day, Mama that Ruth Spivey has forgotten all about us I believe.

Things here are not going too good. I guess you might have heard that me and Norman are separated. I know you liked him, but you had no idea how tiresome he could be, always so slow and quiet, he got on my nerves. Ruthie stay clear of those pale blond thoughtful kind of men, they're a real disappointment. Go for someone dark and interesting who will take you lots of places you've never been. I'm serious, I know what I'm talking about.

Mama sends you greetings and asks do you want her to sew you anything. She's real crippled now with the arthritis in her knees and can only sit in her chair, has plenty of time for sewing.

See ya,

Paula

That letter he mailed from Pennsylvania, when he visited a packing-crate plant the following Tuesday. And on Wednesday, from New York, he sent the blue sheet with *LMR* at the top.

Dear Ruth,
   Had lunch with Donna the other day and she told me you were
going with a real nice fellow. Was kind of hazy on the particulars
but when she said his name was Tull and he came from Baltimore
I knew it must be Cody. Everybody here knows Cody, we all just
love him, he really is a good man at heart and has been misjudged
for years by people who don't understand him. Well, Ruthie, I
guess you're smarter than I gave you credit for, I always thought
you'd settle for one of those dime-a-dozen blond types but now I
see I was wrong.
   I'll be waiting for the details.

                                                    Love,
                                                    Laurie May

"You went too far with that last letter," Ruth told him.
"I don't know what you're talking about."
He was sitting on a kitchen stool, watching her cube meat. He'd
come directly to the restaurant this Saturday—bypassing home, bypassing the farm—hoping to find her altered somehow, mystified,
perhaps tossing him a speculative glance from time to time. Instead,
she seemed cross. She slammed her cleaver on the chopping board.
"Do you realize," she asked, "that I went ahead and answered that
first note? Not wanting someone to worry, I sent it back and said it
wasn't mine, there must be some mistake; went out specially and
bought a stamp to mail it with. And would've sent the second back,
too, only it didn't have a return address. Then the third comes; well,
you went too far."
"I tend to do that," Cody said regretfully.
Ruth slung the cleaver with a thunking sound. Cody was afraid the
others—only Todd Duckett and Josiah, this early—would wonder what
was wrong, but they didn't even look around. Ezra was out front,
chalking up tonight's menu.
"Just what is your *problem?*" Ruth asked him. "Do you have something
against me? You think I'm some Garrett County hick that you don't
want marrying your brother?"
"Of course I don't want you marrying him," Cody said. "I love you."
"Huh?"
This wasn't the moment he had planned, but he rushed on anyway,
as if drunk. "I mean it," he said, "I feel driven. I feel pulled. I have
to have you. You're all I ever think about."
She was staring at him, astonished, with one hand cupped to scoop
the meat cubes into a skillet.
"I guess I'm not saying it right," he told her.
"Saying what? What are you talking about?"

"Ruth. I really, truly love you," he said. "I'm sick over you. I can't even eat. Look at me! I've lost eleven pounds."

He held out his arms, demonstrating. His jacket hung loose at the sides. Lately he'd moved his belt in a notch; his suits no longer fit so smoothly but seemed rumpled, gathered, bunchy.

"It's true you're kind of skinny," Ruth said slowly.

"Even my shoes feel too big."

"What's the matter with you?" she asked.

"You haven't heard a word I said!"

"Over *me*, you said. You must be making fun."

"Ruth, I swear—" he said.

"You're used to New York City girls, models, actresses; you could have anyone."

"It's you I'll have."

She studied him a moment. It began to seem he'd finally broken through; they were having a conversation. Then she said, "We got to get that weight back on you."

He groaned.

"See there?" she asked. "You never eat a thing I offer you."

"I can't," he told her.

"I don't believe you ever once tasted my cooking."

She set the skillet aside and went over to the tall black kettle that was simmering on the stove. "Country vegetable," she said, lifting the lid.

"Really, Ruth . . ."

She filled a small crockery bowl and set it on the table. "Sit down," she said. "Eat. When you've tried it, I'll tell you the secret ingredient."

Steam rose from the bowl, with a smell so deep and spicy that already he felt overfed. He accepted the spoon that she held out. He dipped it in the soup reluctantly and took a sip.

"Well?" she asked.

"It's very good," he said.

In fact, it was delicious, if you cared about such things. He'd never tasted soup so good. There were chunks of fresh vegetables, and the broth was rich and heavy. He took another mouthful. Ruth stood over him, her thumbs hooked into her blue jeans pockets. "Chicken feet," she said.

"Pardon?"

"Chicken feet is the secret ingredient."

He lowered the spoon and looked down into the bowl.

"Eat up," she told him. "Put some meat on your bones."

He dipped the spoon in again.

After that, she brought him a salad made with the herbs she'd grown on the roof and a basketful of rolls she'd baked that afternoon—a recipe from home, she said. Cody ate everything. As long as he ate, she watched him. When she brought him more butter for his rolls, she leaned close over him and he felt the warmth she gave off.

Now two more cooks had arrived and a Chinese boy was sautéing black mushrooms, and Ezra was running a mixer near the sink. Ruth sat down next to Cody, hooking her combat boots on the rung of his chair and hugging her ribs. Cody cut into a huge wedge of pie and gave some thought to food—to its inexplicable, loaded meaning in other people's lives. Couldn't you classify a person, he wondered, purely by examining his attitude toward food? Look at Cody's mother—a nonfeeder, if ever there was one. Even back in his childhood, when they'd depended on her for nourishment . . . why, mention you were hungry and she'd suddenly act rushed and harassed, fretful, out of breath, distracted. He remembered her coming home from work in the evening and tearing irritably around the kitchen. Tins toppled out of the cupboards and fell all over her—pork 'n' beans, Spam, oily tuna fish, peas canned olive-drab. She cooked in her hat, most of the time. She whimpered when she burned things. She burned things you would not imagine it possible to burn and served others half-raw, adding jarring extras of her own design such as crushed pineapple in the mashed potatoes. (Anything, as long as it was a leftover, might as well be dumped in the pan with anything else.) Her only seasonings were salt and pepper. Her only gravy was Campbell's cream of mushroom soup, undiluted. And till Cody was grown, he had assumed that roast beef had to be stringy—not something you sliced, but a leathery dry object which you separated with a fork, one strand from the other, and dropped with a clunk upon your plate.

Though during illness, he remembered, you could count on her to bring liquids. Hot tea: she was good at that. And canned consommé. Thin things, watery things. Then she'd stand in the door with her arms folded while you drank it. He remembered that her expression, when others ate or drank, conveyed a mild distaste. She ate little herself, often toyed with her food; and she implied some criticism of those who acted hungry or over-interested in what they were served. Neediness: she disapproved of neediness in people. Whenever there was a family argument, she most often chose to start it over dinner.

Biting into Ruth's flaky, shattering crust, Cody considered his mother's three children—Jenny, for instance, with her lemon-water and lettuce-leaf diets, never allowing herself a sweet, skipping meals altogether, as if continually bearing in mind that disapproving expression of her mother's. And Cody himself was not much different, when you came right down to it. It seemed that food didn't count, with him; food was something required by others, so that for their sakes—on dates, at business luncheons—he would obligingly order a meal for himself just to keep them company. But all you'd find in his refrigerator was cream for his coffee and limes for his gin and tonics. He never ate breakfast;

he often forgot lunch. Sometimes a gnawing feeling hit his stomach in the afternoon and he sent his secretary out for food. "What kind of food?" she would ask. He would say, "Anything, I don't care." She'd bring a Danish or an eggroll or a liverwurst on rye; it was all the same to him. Half the time, he wouldn't even notice what it was—would take a bite, go on dictating, leave the rest to be disposed of by the cleaning lady. A woman he'd once had dinner with had claimed that this was a sign of some flaw. Watching him dissect his fish but then fail to eat it, noticing how he refused dessert and then benignly, tolerantly waited for her to finish a giant chocolate mousse, she had accused him of . . . what had she called it? Lack of enjoyment. Lack of ability to enjoy himself. He hadn't understood, back then, how she could draw so many implications from a single meal. And still he didn't agree with her.

Yes, only Ezra, he would say, had managed to escape all this. Ezra was so impervious—so thickheaded, really; nothing ever touched him. He ate heartily, whether it was his mother's cooking or his own. He liked anything that was offered him, especially bread—would have to watch his weight as he got older. But above all else, he was a feeder. He would set a dish before you and then stand there with his face expectant, his hands clasped tightly under his chin, his eyes following your fork. There was something tender, almost loving, about his attitude toward people who were eating what he'd cooked them.

Like Ruth, Cody thought.

He asked her for another slice of pie.

Mornings, now, he called her from New York, often getting her landlady out of bed; and Ruth when she answered was still creaky voiced from sleep—or was it from bewilderment, even now? Reluctantly, each time, she warmed to his questions, speaking shortly at first. Yes, she was fine. The restaurant was fine. Dinner last night had gone well. And then (letting her sentences stretch gradually longer, as if giving in to him all over again) she told him that this house was starting to wear her down—creepy boarders padding around in their slippers at all hours, no one ever *going* anywhere, landlady planted eternally in front of her TV. This landlady, a widow, believed that Perry Como's eyebrows quirked upward as they did because he was by nature a bass, and singing such high notes gave him constant pain; she had heard that Arthur Godfrey, too, had been enduring constant pain for years, smiling a courageous smile and wheeling about on his stool because the slightest step would stab him like a knife. Yes, everything, to Mrs. Pauling, was a constant pain; *life* was a constant pain, and Ruth had started looking around her and wondering how she stood this place.

Weekends—Friday and Saturday nights—Ruth tore through the restaurant kitchen slapping haunches of beef and whipping egg whites.

Ezra worked more quietly. Cody sat at the wooden table. Now and then, Ruth would place some new dish in front of him and Cody would eat it dutifully. Every mouthful was a declaration of love. Ruth knew that. She was tense and watchful. She gave him sideways, piercing glances when he forked up one of her dumplings, and he was careful to leave nothing on his plate.

Then on Sunday mornings, yellow summer mornings at her boardinghouse, he rang her doorbell and pulled her close to him when she answered. Anytime he kissed her, he was visited by the curious impression that some other self of hers was still moving through the house behind her, spunky and lighthearted and uncatchable even yet, checking under pot lids, slamming cupboard doors, humming and tossing her head and wiping her hands on her blue jeans.

"I don't understand," Ezra told them.

"Let me start over," said Cody.

Ezra said, "Is this some kind of a joke? Is that what it is? What is it?"

"Ruth and I—" Cody began.

But Ruth said, "Ezra, honey. Listen." She stepped forward. She was wearing the navy suit that Cody had bought her to go away in, and high-heeled shoes with slender straps. Although it was a glaring day in August, her skin had a chilled, dry, powdery look, and her freckles stood out sharply. She said, "Ezra, we surely never planned on this. We never had the least intention, not me or Cody neither one."

Ezra waited, evidently still not comprehending. He was backed against the huge old restaurant stove, as if retreating from their news.

"It just happened, like," said Ruth.

"You don't know what you're saying," said Ezra.

"Ezra, honey—"

"You would never do this. It's not true."

"See, I don't know how it came about but me and Cody . . . and I should've told you sooner but I kept thinking, oh, this is just some . . . I mean, this is silly; he's so sophisticated, he isn't someone for *me*; this is just some . . . daydream, see. . . ."

"There's bound to be an explanation," Ezra said.

"I feel real bad about it, Ezra."

"I'm sure I'll understand in a minute," he said. "Just give me time. Just wait a minute. Let me think it through."

They waited, but he didn't say anything more. He pressed two fingers against his forehead, as if working out some complicated puzzle. After a while, Cody touched Ruth's arm. She said, "Well, Ezra, goodbye, I guess." Then she and Cody left.

In the car, she cried a little—not making any fuss but sniffling quietly and keeping her face turned toward the side window. "Are you all right?" Cody asked.

She nodded.

"You're sure you still want to go on with this."

She nodded again.

They were planning to travel by train—Ruth's idea; she had never set foot on a train—to New York City, where they would be married in a civil ceremony. Ruth's people, she said, were mostly dead or wouldn't much care; so there wasn't any point having the wedding in her hometown. And it went without saying that *Cody's* people . . . well. For the next little bit, they might as well stay in New York. By and by, things would simmer down.

Ruth took off one of her gloves, already gray at the seams, and crumpled it into a ball and blotted both her eyes.

Near Penn Station, Cody found a parking lot that offered weekly rates. It was a good deal of trouble, traveling by train, but worth it for Ruth's sake. She was already perking up. She asked him if he thought there'd be a dining car—an "eating car," she called it. Cody said he imagined so. He accepted the ticket the parking attendant gave him and slid out from behind the steering wheel, grunting a little; lately he'd put on a few pounds around the waist. He took Ruth's suitcase from the trunk. Ruth wasn't used to high heels and she hobbled along unsteadily, every now and then making a loud, scraping sound on the sidewalk. "I hope to get the knack of these things before long," she told Cody.

"You don't have to wear them, you know."

"Oh, I surely *do*," she said.

Cody guided her into the station. The sudden, echoing coolness seemed to stun her into silence. She stood looking around her while Cody went to the ticket window. A lady at the head of the line was arguing about the cost of her fare. A man in a crisp white suit rolled his eyes at Cody, implying exasperation at the wait. Cody pretended not to notice. He turned away as if checking the length of the line behind him, and a plump young woman with a child smiled instantly, fully prepared, and said, "Cody Tull!"

"Um—"

"I'm Jane Lowry. Remember me?"

"Oh, Jane! Jane Lowry! Well, good to see you, how nice to . . . and is this your little girl?"

"Yes; say hello to Mr. Tull, Betsy. Mr. Tull and Mommy used to go to school together."

"So you're married," Cody said, moving forward in line. "Well, what a—"

"Remember the day I came to visit you, uninvited?" she asked. She laughed, and he saw, in the tilt of her head, a flash of the young girl he had known. She had lived on Bushnell Street, he remembered now; she had had the most beautiful hair, which still showed its chips of gold light, although she wore it short now. "I had such a crush on you," she said. "Lord, I made a total fool of myself."

"You played a game of checkers with Ezra," he reminded her.

"Ezra?"

"My brother."

"You had a brother?"

"I certainly did; do. You played checkers with him all afternoon."

"How funny; I thought you only had a sister. What was her name? Jenny. She was so skinny, I envied her for years. Anything she wanted, she could eat and not have it show. What's Jenny doing now?"

"Oh, she's in medical school. And Ezra: he runs a restaurant."

"In those days," said Jane, "my fondest wish was to wake up one morning and find I'd turned into Jenny Tull. But I'd forgotten you had a brother."

Cody opened his mouth to speak, but the man in white had moved away and it was Cody's turn at the window. And by the time he'd bought his tickets, Jane had switched to the other line and was busy buying hers.

He didn't see her again—though he looked for her on the train—but it was odd how she'd plunged him into the past. Swaying on the seat next to Ruth, holding her small, rough hand but finding very little to say to her, he was startled by fragments of buried memories. The scent of chalk in geometry class; the balmy, laden feeling of the last day of school every spring; the crack of a baseball bat on the playground. He found himself in a summer evening at a drive-in hamburger stand, with its blinding lights surrounded by darkness, its hot, salty, greasy smell of French fries, and all his friends horsing around at the curb. He could hear an old girlfriend from years ago, her droning, dissatisfied voice: "You ask me to the movies and I say yes and then you change your mind and ask me bowling instead and I say yes to that but you say wait, let's make it another night, as if anything you can have is something it turns out you don't want. . . ." He heard his mother telling Jenny not to slouch, telling Cody not to swear, asking Ezra why he wouldn't stand up to the neighborhood bully. "I'm trying to get through life as a liquid," Ezra had said, and Cody (trying to get through life as a rock) had laughed; he could hear himself still. "Why aren't cucumbers prickly any more?" he heard Ezra ask. And "Cody? Don't you want to walk to school with me?" He saw Ezra aiming a red-feathered dart, his chapped, childish wrist awkwardly angled; he saw him running for the telephone—"I'll get it! I'll get it!"—hopeful and joyous, years and years younger. He remembered Carol, or was it Karen, reciting Ezra's faults—a *motherly* man, she'd said; what had she said?— and it occurred to him that the reason he had dropped her was, she really hadn't understood Ezra; she hadn't appreciated what he was all about. Then Ruth squeezed his hand and said, "I intend to ride trains forever; it's so much better than the bus. Isn't it, Cody? Cody? Isn't it?" The train rounded a curve with a high, thin, whistling sound that took him by surprise. He honestly believed, for an instant, that what he'd heard was music—a tune piped, a burble of notes, a little scrap of melody floating by on the wind and breaking his heart.

6

BEACHES ON THE MOON

TWICE OR MAYBE three times a year, she goes out to the farm to make sure things are in order. She has her son Ezra drive her there, and she takes along a broom, a dustpan, rags, a grocery bag for trash and a bucket and a box of cleanser. Ezra asks why she can't just keep these supplies in the farmhouse, but she knows they wouldn't be safe. The trespassers would get them. Oh, the trespassers—the small boys and courting couples and the teen-aged gangs. It makes her mad to think of them. As the car turns off the main road, rattling up the rutted driveway, she already sees their litter—the beer cans tossed among the scrubby weeds, the scraps of toilet paper dangling from the bushes. This land has been let go and the vegetation is matted and wild, bristly, scratchy, no shade at all from the blazing sun. There are little spangles of bottle tops embedded in the dirt of the road. And the yard (which is not truly mown but sickled by Jared Peers, once or twice a summer) is flocked with white paper plates and Dixie cups, napkins, sandwich bags, red-striped straws, and those peculiarly long-lived, accordioned worms of paper that the straws were wrapped in.

Ezra parks the car beneath an oak tree. "It's a shame. A disgrace and a shame," Pearl says, stepping out. She wears a seersucker dress that will wash, and her oldest shoes. On her head is a broad-brimmed straw hat. It will keep the dust from her hair—from all but one faded, blondish frizz bordering each temple. "It's a national crime," she says, and she stands looking around her while Ezra unloads her cleaning supplies. The house has two stories. It is a ghostly, rubbed-out gray. The ridgepole sags and the front porch has buckled and many of the windowpanes are broken—more every time she comes.

She remembers when Cody first showed her this place. "Imagine what can be done with it, Mother. Picture the possibilities," he said.

He was planning to marry and raise a family here—provide her with lots of grandchildren. He even kept the livestock on, paying Jared Peers to tend it till Cody moved in.

That was years ago, though, and all that remains of those animals now is a couple of ragged hens gone wild, clucking in the mulberry tree out behind the barn.

She has a key to the warped rear door but it isn't needed. The padlock's missing and the rusted hasp hangs open. "Not again," she says. She turns the knob and enters, warily. (One of these days, she'll surprise someone and get her head blown off for her trouble.) The kitchen smells stale and cold, even in the heat of the day. There's a fly buzzing over the table, a rust spot smearing the back of the sink, a single tatter of cloudy plastic curtain trailing next to the window. The linoleum's worn patternless near the counters.

Ezra follows, burdened with household supplies. He sets them down and stands wiping his face on the sleeve of his work shirt. More than once he's told her he fails to see the use of this: cleaning up only to clean again, the next time they come out. What's the purpose, he wants to know. Why go to all this trouble, what does she have in mind? But he's an obliging man, and when she insists, he says no more. He runs his fingers through his hair, which the sweat has turned a dark, streaked yellow. He tests the kitchen faucet. First it explodes and then it yields a coppery trickle of water.

There are half a dozen empty bottles lying on the floor—Wild Turkey, Old Crow, Southern Comfort. "Look! And look," says Pearl. She nudges a Marlboro pack with her toe. She scrapes at a scorch on the table. She discreetly looks away while Ezra hooks an unmentionable rubber something with the broom handle and drops it into the trash bag.

"Cody," she used to say, "you could hire a man to come and haul this furniture off to the dump. Surely you don't want it for yourself. Cody, there's a Sunday suit in the bedroom closet. There are shoes at the top of the cellar stairs—chunky, muddy old garden shoes. You ought to hire a man to come haul them for you." But Cody paid no attention—he was hardly ever there. He was mostly in New York; and privately, Pearl had expected that that was where he would stay. Which of those girlfriends of his would agree to a life in the country? "You'd just better watch out who you marry," she had told him. "None of your dates that *I've* met would do—those black-haired, flashy, beauty-queen types."

But if only he'd married one of them! If only he'd been satisfied with that! Instead, one afternoon Ezra had come into the kitchen, had stood there looking sick. "What's wrong?" she'd asked. She knew it was something. "Ezra? Why aren't you at work?"

"It's Cody," he said.

"Cody?"

She clutched at her chest, picturing him dead—her most difficult, most distant child, and now she would never have the answer to him.

But Ezra said, "He's gone off to get married."

"Oh, married," she said, and she dropped her hand. "Well? Who to?"

"To Ruth," he said.

"*Your* Ruth?"

"My Ruth."

"Oh, sweetheart," she said.

Not that she hadn't had some inkling. She had seen it coming for weeks, she believed, though she hadn't exactly seen marriage—more likely a fling, a flirtation, another of Cody's teases. Should she have hinted to Ezra? He wouldn't have listened. He was so gullible, and so much in love. Ruth was the center of his world, for some reason. And anyway, who would have thought that Cody would let it get so serious? "He's just doing it to be mean, sweetheart," she told Ezra. She was right, too, as she'd been right the other times she'd said it—oh, those other times! Those inconsequential spats, those childhood quarrels, arguments, practical jokes! "Cody, stop it this instant," she used to tell him. "You don't think I don't see what you're up to? Let your poor brother alone. Ezra, pay no mind. He's only being mean." Back then, Ezra had listened and nodded, hoping to believe her; he had doted on his older brother. But now he said, "What does it matter why he did it? He did it, that's all. He stole her away."

"If she could be stolen, honey, why, you don't want her anyhow."

Ezra just looked at her—bleak faced, grim, a walking ache of a man. She knew how he felt. Hadn't she been through it? She remembered from when her husband left—a wound, she'd been, a deep, hollow hole, surrounded by shreds of her former self.

She sweeps all the trash to the center of the floor, collects the bottles and the cigarette packs. Meanwhile, Ezra tapes squares of cardboard to the broken windowpanes. He works steadily, doggedly. She looks up once and sees how the sweat has made an eagle-shaped stain across his back. There are other cardboard squares on other panes, broken earlier. In a few more seasons, it occurs to her, they'll be working in the dark. It's as if they're sealing themselves in, windowpane by windowpane.

When Cody came back with Ruth, after the honeymoon, he was better-looking than ever, sleek and dark and well dressed, but Ruth was her same homely self: a little muskrat of a girl with wickety red hair and freckles, her skin that tissue-thin kind subject to lip sores and pink splotches, her twiggish body awkward in a matronly brown suit that must have been bought especially for this occasion. (Though Pearl was to find, in later years, that all Ruth's clothes struck her that way; nothing ever seemed as natural as those little-boy dungarees she used to wear with Ezra.) Pearl watched the two of them sharply, closely, anxious to come to some conclusion about their marriage, but they gave away no secrets. Ruth sat pressing her palms together; Cody kept his arm across the back of the couch, not touching her but claiming her, at least. He talked at length about the farm. They were heading out there directly, settling in that night. It was too late for sowing a garden but at least they could clean the place up, begin to make plans for next spring. Ruth was going to get started on that while Cody went back to New York. Ruth nodded at this, and cleared her throat and fumbled with the pocket of her suit jacket. Pearl thought she was reaching for one of her little cigars, but after a moment she stopped fumbling and placed her palms together again. And in fact, Pearl never saw her smoke another one of those cigars.

Then Ezra arrived—not whistling, oddly quiet, as he'd been since Ruth had left. He stopped inside the door and looked at them. "Ezra," Cody said easily, and Ruth stood up and held out her hand. She seemed frightened. This made Pearl like her, a little. (Ruth, at least, recognized the magnitude of what they'd done.) "How you doing, Ezra," Ruth said, quavering. And Ezra had said . . . oh, something or other, he'd managed something; and stood around a while shifting from foot to foot and answering their small talk. So it looked, on the surface, as if they might eventually smooth things over. Yes, after all, this choosing of mates was such a small, brief stage in a family's history.

But Ezra no longer played tunes on his recorder, and he continued to look limp and beaten, and he went to bed every night with no more than a "Good night, Mother." She grieved for him. She longed to say, "Ezra, believe me, she's nothing! You're worth a dozen Ruth Spiveys! A dozen of both of them, to be frank, even if Cody *is* my son. . . ." Though of course she loved Cody dearly. But from infancy, he had batted her away; and his sister had been so evasive, somehow; so whom did that leave but Ezra? Ezra was all she had. He was the only one who would let her in. Sometimes, in his childhood, she had worried that he would die young—one of life's ironic twists, to take what you valued most. She had watched him trudging down the street to school, his duck-yellow head bowed in thought, and she would have a sudden presentiment that this was the last she would see of him. Then when he returned, full of news about friends and ball games, how solid, how commonplace—even how irritating—he seemed! And sometimes, long ago when he was small, he might climb up into her lap and place his thin little arms around her neck, and she would drink in his smell of warm biscuits and think, "Really, this is what it's all about. This is what I'm alive for." Then, reluctantly, she allowed him to slip away again. (They claimed she was possessive, pushy. Little did they know.) As a child, he'd had a chirpy style of talking that was so cheerful, ringing through the house like a trill of water . . . when had that begun to change? As an older boy he grew shy and withdrawn, gazing out of shining gray eyes and saying next to nothing. She'd worried when he didn't date. "Wouldn't you like to bring someone home? Ask someone to Sunday dinner?" He shook his head, tongue-tied. He blushed and lowered his long lashes. Pearl wondered, seeing the blush, whether he thought much about girls and such as that. His father had left by then and Cody was no help, three years older, off tomcatting someplace or other. Then as a man, Ezra was . . . well, to be honest, he was not much different from when he was a boy. In a way, he was an *eternal* boy, never got boastful and brash like most men but stayed gentle, somber, contentedly running that restaurant of his and coming home peaceful and tired.

It was a shock when he introduced her to Ruth. What an urchin she was! But plainly, Ezra adored her. "Mother, I'd like you to meet my— meet Ruth." Pearl had stalled a little, at first. Maybe she had failed to act properly welcoming. Well, who could blame her? And now, seeing how things had turned out, who could say she'd been wrong? But she can't help wondering, anyhow . . . If she'd been a little more en- couraging, they might have married sooner. They might have married before Cody could work his mischief. Or if she had let herself *realize* . . . Yes, she wonders over and over again: if she'd mentioned Cody's plot to Ezra, stopped that situation that was not so much a courtship as a landslide, a kind of gathering and falling of events . . .

Ridiculous, of course, to imagine that anything she did could have mattered. What happens, happens. It's no one's fault. (Or it's only Cody's fault, for he has always been striving and competitive, a natural- born player of games, has had to win absolutely everything, even something he doesn't want like a runty little redhead far below his usual standards.)

She opens the farmhouse parlor to air it. It smells like skunk. She leaves the front door ajar, taking care not to step onto the porch, which could very well give way beneath her. She remembers how, toward the end of that first week after the honeymoon, she asked Ezra to bring out to Ruth a few odds and ends for the farm—some extra pans, some linens, a carpet sweeper she had no use for. Was there an ulterior motive in her suggestion? If not, why didn't she accompany him, visit the bride like any good mother-in-law? "Please, I don't want to," Ezra said, but she said, "Honey. Go." She hadn't had any conscious design— truly, none at all—but it was a fact that later that morning, dawdling over the dishes, she'd allowed herself a little daydream: Ezra coming up behind Ruth, setting his arms around her, Ruth protesting only briefly before collapsing against him . . . Oh, shouldn't it be possible to undo what was done? What all of them had done?

But Ezra when he returned was as subdued as ever, and only said that Ruth thanked Pearl for the pans and linens but was sending back the carpet sweeper as the farmhouse had no carpets.

Then Saturday, Cody came storming in with everything Ezra had taken to Ruth. "What's all this?" he asked Pearl.

"Why, Cody, pots and sheets, as you can surely see."

"How come Ezra brought them out?"

"I asked him to," she said.

"I won't have it! Won't have him hanging around the farm."

"Cody. It was at my request. Believe me," she told him.

"I do," he said.

She tried to get Ezra to go again the following week—taking the rug from the dining room and the carpet sweeper, once more—but he wouldn't. "I'm not comfortable there," he said. "There's no point. What's the point?" She supposed he was right. Yes, she thought, let Ruth wonder where he'd got to! People who leave us will be sorry in the end. She imagined Ruth alone in the farmhouse, roaming from room to room and peering sadly through the bare windows.

The next weekend, Pearl asked Ezra to drive her out. He couldn't very well refuse; he was her only means of transportation. They both, without discussing it, wore Sunday clothing—formal, guestlike clothing. They found the house looking sealed and abandoned. A lone hound nudged at a bone in the yard, but he surely didn't belong there.

Back home, Pearl placed a call to Cody in New York. "Aren't you coming to the farm any more?"

"Things are kind of busy."

"Won't Ruth be there during the week?"

"I want her here with me," he said. "After all, we just did get married."

"Well, when will we see you?"

"Pretty soon, not too long, I'm sure we'll be down in a while. . . ."

But they weren't; or if they were, they didn't tell Pearl, and she was too proud to ask again. The summer ended and the leaves turned all colors, but Ezra dragged himself along with no change. "Sweetheart," Pearl told him, as in his boyhood, "isn't there someone you'd like to have home? Some friend to dinner? Anyone," she said. Ezra said no.

From time to time, Pearl called Cody in New York again. He was courteous and noncommittal. Ruth, if she spoke, gave flustered replies and didn't seem to have her wits about her. Then in October, two full weeks went by when no one answered the phone at all. Pearl wondered if they'd gone to the farm, and she begged Ezra to investigate. But when he finally agreed to, he found nobody there. "Someone's shattered four windowpanes," he reported. "Threw rocks at them, or shot them out." This made Pearl feel frightened. The world was closing in on them; even here on her own familiar streets, she no longer felt safe. And who knew what might have become of Ruth and Cody? They could be lying dead in their apartment, victims of a burglary or some bizarre, New York–type accident, their bodies undiscovered for weeks. Oh, this was what happened when you broke off all ties with your family! It wasn't right; with your family, if with no one else, you have to keep on trying.

She called frantically, day after day, often letting the phone ring thirty or forty times. There was something calming about that faraway purling sound. She was, at least, connected—though only to an object in Cody's apartment.

Then he answered. It was late in October. She was so taken aback that she didn't know what to say. It seemed the monotonous ring of the phone had grown to be enough for her. "Um, Cody . . ." she said.

"Oh. Mother."

"Cody, where have you *been?*"

"I had a job to see to in Ohio. I took Ruth along."

"You didn't answer the phone for weeks, and we looked for you out at the farm and some of the windows were broken."

"Damn! I thought I was paying Jared to keep that kind of thing from happening."

"You can't imagine how I felt, Cody. When I heard about the windows I felt . . . You're letting that place go to rack and ruin and we never get to see you any more."

"I do have a job to do, Mother."

"I thought that once you married, you were moving down to Baltimore. You were doing over the farmhouse and planting a garden and all."

"Yes, definitely. That's a definite possibility," said Cody. "Get Ezra to tape those windows, will you? And tell him to speak to Jared. I can't have the place depreciating."

"All right, Cody," she said.

Then she asked about Thanksgiving. "Will you be coming down? You know how Ezra likes to have us at the restaurant."

"Oh, Ezra and his restaurant . . ."

"Please. We've hardly seen you," she said.

"Well, maybe."

So in November they returned—Cody looking elegant and casual, Ruth incongruous in a large, ornate blue dress. Her hair was so stubby, her head so small, that the dress appeared to be drowning her. She staggered in her high-heeled shoes. She still would not meet Ezra's gaze.

"What have you two been up to?" Pearl asked Ruth, as they rode in Cody's Cadillac to the restaurant.

"Oh, nothing so much."

"Are you decorating Cody's apartment?"

"Decorating? No."

"We've hardly seen it," Cody said. "I'm taking on longer-term jobs. In December I start reorganizing a textile plant in Georgia, a *big* thing, five or six months. I thought maybe Ruth could come with me; we could rent us a little house of some kind. There's not much point in commuting."

"December? But then you'd miss Christmas," said Pearl.

Cody looked surprised. He said, "Why would we miss it?"

"I mean, would you still make the trip to Baltimore?"

"Oh. Well, no, I guess not," he said. "But we're here for Thanksgiving, aren't we?"

She resolved to say no more. She had her dignity.

They sat at their regular family table, surrounded by a fair-sized crowd. (In those days—the start of the sixties—shaggy young people had just discovered Ezra's restaurant, with its stripped wood and pure, fresh food, and they thronged there every evening.) It was sad that Jenny couldn't come; she was spending the holiday with her in-laws. But Ruth, at least, rounded out their number. Pearl smiled across the table at her. Ruth said, "It feels right funny to be eating where I used to be cooking."

"Would you like to visit the kitchen?" Ezra asked. "The staff would enjoy seeing you."

"I don't mind if I do," she said. It was the first time since her marriage that she'd looked at him directly—or the first that Pearl knew about.

So Ezra scraped back his chair and rose, and guided Ruth into the kitchen. Pearl could tell that Cody wasn't pleased. He stopped in the act of unfolding his napkin and gazed after them, even taking a breath as if preparing to object. Then he must have thought better of it. He shook out the napkin angrily, saying nothing.

"So," said Pearl. "When do you move to the farm?"

"Farm? Oh, I don't know," he said. "Everything's so changed; the whole character of my work has changed." He looked again toward the kitchen.

"But you'd planned on raising a family there. It was all you ever talked about."

"Yes, well, and these long-term contracts," he said, as if he hadn't heard her.

Pearl said, "You had your heart just set on it."

But he continued watching the other two. He was not the least bit interested in what she might be saying. The kitchen was fully exposed, and could not have concealed the smallest secret. So why was Cody nervous? Ezra and Ruth stood talking with one of the cooks, their backs to the dining room. Ezra gestured as he spoke. He lifted both arms wide, one arm behind Ruth but not touching her, not brushing her shoulder, surely not encircling her or anything like that. Even so, Cody rose abruptly from his chair. "Cody!" Pearl said. He strode toward the kitchen, with his napkin crumpled in one fist. Pearl stood up and hurried after him, and arrived in time to hear him say, "Let's go, Ruth."

"Go?"

"I didn't come here to watch you and Ezra chumming it up in the kitchen."

Ruth looked scared. Her face seemed to grow more pointed.

"Come on," said Cody, and he took her elbow. "Goodbye," he told Pearl and Ezra.

"Oh!" said Pearl, running after them. "Oh, Cody, what can you be thinking of? How can you act so foolish?"

Cody yanked Ruth's coat from a brass hook in passing. He opened the front door and pulled Ruth into the street and shut the door behind them.

Ezra said, "I don't understand."

Pearl said, "Why does it always turn out this way? How come we end up quarreling? Don't we all love each other? Everything else aside," she said, "don't we all want the best for one another?"

"Certainly we do," Ezra said.

His answer was so level and firm that she felt comforted. She knew things were bound to work out someday. She let him lead her back to the table, and the two of them had a forlorn turkey dinner on the wide expanse of white linen.

Upstairs there are four bedrooms, sparsely furnished, musty. The beds are so sunken-looking, evidently even the courting couples have not been tempted by them. They're untouched, the drab, dirty quilts still smooth. But a dead bird lies beneath one window. Pearl calls down the stairwell. "Ezra? Ezra, come here this instant. Bring the broom and trash bag."

He mounts the stairs obediently. She looks down and sees, with a pang, that his lovely fair hair is thinning on the back of his head. He is thirty-seven years old, will be thirty-eight in December. He will probably never marry. He will never do anything but run that peculiar restaurant of his, with its hodgepodge of food, its unskilled waitresses, its foreign cooks with questionable papers. You could say, in a way, that Ezra has suffered a tragedy, although it's a very small tragedy in the eyes of the world. You could say that he and Ruth, together, have suffered a tragedy. Something has been done to them; something has been taken away from them. They have lost it. They *are* lost. It doesn't help at all that Cody in fact is a very nice man—that he's bright and funny and genuinely kind, to everyone but Ezra.

You could almost say that Cody, too, has suffered a tragedy.

In 1964, when she went out to Illinois to visit them, she felt in their house the thin, tight atmosphere of an unhappy marriage. Not a really terrible marriage—no sign of hatred, spitefulness, violence. Just a sense of something missing. A certain failure to connect, between the two of them. Everything seemed so tenuous. Or was it her imagination? Maybe she was wrong. Maybe it was the house itself—a ranch house in a development, rented for the four months or so that Cody would need to reorganize a plastics plant in Chicago. Plainly the place was expensive, with wall-to-wall carpeting and long, low, modern furniture; but there were no trees anywhere nearby, not even a bush or a shrub—just that raw brick cube rising starkly from the flatness. And outside it was so white-hot, so insufferably hot, that they were confined to the house with its artificial, refrigerated air. They were *imprisoned* by the house, dependent upon it like spacemen in a spaceship, and when they went out it was only to dash through a crushing weight of heat to Cody's air-conditioned Mercedes. Ruth, going about her chores every day, had the clenched expression of someone determined to survive no matter what. Cody came home in the evening gasping for oxygen—barely crawling over the doorsill, Pearl fantasized—but did not seem all that relieved to have arrived. When he greeted Ruth, they touched cheeks and moved apart again.

It was the first time Pearl had ever visited them, the first and only time, and this was after years of very little contact at all. They seldom came to Baltimore. They never returned to the farm. And Cody wrote almost no letters, though he would telephone on birthdays and holidays. He was more like an acquaintance, Pearl thought. A not very cordial acquaintance.

Once she and Ezra were driving down a road in West Virginia, on an outing to Harper's Ferry, when they chanced to come up behind a man in jogging shorts. He was running along the edge of the highway, a tall man, dark, with a certain confident, easy swing to his shoulders . . . Cody! Out here in the middle of nowhere, by sheer coincidence, Cody Tull! Ezra slammed on his brakes, and Pearl said, "Well, did you ever." But then the jogger, hearing their car, had turned his face and he wasn't Cody after all. He was someone entirely different, beefy jawed, nowhere near as handsome. Ezra sped up again. Pearl said, "How silly of me, I know full well that Cody's in, ah . . ."

"Indiana," said Ezra.

"Indiana; I don't know why I thought . . ."

They were both quiet for several minutes after that, and in those minutes Pearl imagined the scene if it really had been Cody—if he had turned, astonished, as they sailed past. Oddly enough, she didn't envision stopping. She thought of how his mouth would fall open as he recognized their faces behind the glass; and how they would gaze out at him, and smile and wave, and skim on by.

Whenever he phoned he was cheerful and hearty. "How've you been, Mother?"

"Why, Cody!"

"Everything all right? How's Ezra?"

Oh, on the phone he was so nice about Ezra, interested and affectionate like any other brother. And on the rare occasions when he and Ruth came through Baltimore—heading somewhere else, just briefly dropping in—he seemed so pleased to shake hands with Ezra and clap him on the back and ask what he's been up to. At first.

Only at first.

Then: "Ruth! What are you and Ezra talking about, over there?" Or: "Ezra? Do you mind not standing so close to my wife?" When Ezra and Ruth were hardly speaking, really. They were so cautious with each other, it hurt to watch.

"Cody. Please. What are you imagining?" Pearl would ask him, and then he would turn on her: "Naturally, *you* wouldn't see it. Naturally, he can do no wrong, can he, Mother. Your precious boy. Can he."

She had given up, finally, on ever being asked to visit. When Cody called and told her Ruth was pregnant, some two or three years into the marriage, Pearl said, "Oh, Cody, if she'd like it at all, I mean when the baby arrives . . . if she'd like me to come take care of things . . ." But evidently, she wasn't needed. And when he called to say that Luke was born—nine pounds, three ounces; everything fine—she said, "I can't wait to see him. I honestly can't wait." But Cody let that pass.

They sent her photos: Luke in an infant seat, blond and stern. Luke creeping bear-style across the carpet, on hands and feet instead of knees. (Cody had crept that way too.) Luke uncertainly walking, with a clothespin in each fat fist. He had to have the clothespins, Ruth wrote, because then he thought he was holding on to something. Otherwise, he fell. Now that photos were arriving, letters came too, generally written by Ruth. Her grammar was shocking and she couldn't spell. She said, *Me and Cody wrecken Luke's eyes are going to stay blue,* but what did Pearl care about grammar? She saved every letter and put Luke's pictures on her desk in little gilt frames she bought at Kresge's.

I think I ought to come see Luke before he's grown, she wrote. No one answered. She wrote again. *Would June be all right?* Then Cody wrote that they were moving to Illinois in June, but if she really wanted then maybe she could come in July.

So she went to Illinois in July, traveling with a trainload of fresh-faced boy soldiers on their way to Vietnam, and she spent a week in that treeless house barricaded against the elements. It was a shock, even to her, how instantly and how deeply she loved her grandson. He was not quite two years old by then, a beautiful baby with a head that seemed adult in its shape—sharply defined, the golden hair trimmed close and neat. His firm, straight lips seemed adult as well, and he had an unchildlike way of walking. There was a bit of slump in his

posture, a little droop to his shoulders, nothing physically wrong but
an air of resignation that was almost comical in someone so small.
Pearl sat on the floor with him for hours, playing with his trucks and
cars. "Vroom. Vroom. Roll it back to Granny, now." She was touched
by his stillness. He had a sizable vocabulary but he used it only when
necessary; he was not a spendthrift. He was careful. He lacked gaiety.
Was he happy? Was this a fit life for a child?

She saw that Cody had a sprinkling of gray in his sideburns, a more
leathery look to his cheeks; but that Ruth was still a scrappy little thing
in too-short hair and unbecoming dresses. She had not grown fuller
or softer with age. She was like certain supermarket vegetables that
turn from green to withered without ever ripening. In the evenings,
when Cody came home from work, Ruth clattered around the kitchen
cooking great quantities of country food that Cody would hardly touch;
and Cody had a gin and tonic and watched the news. The two of them
asked each other, "How was your day?" and "Everything fine?" but
they didn't seem to listen to the answers. Pearl could believe that in
the morning, waking in their king-sized bed, they asked politely, "Did
you sleep all right?" She felt oppressed and uncomfortable, but instead
of averting her gaze she was for some reason compelled to delve deeper
into their lives; she sent them out one night to a movie, promising to
watch Luke, and then ransacked all the desk drawers but found only
tax receipts, and bank statements, and a photo album belonging to the
people who really lived here. Anyway, she couldn't have said what it
was she was looking for.

Coming home, jouncing on the train amid another group of soldiers,
she felt weary and hopeless. She arrived in Baltimore seven hours late,
with a racking headache. Then as she entered the station, she saw Ezra
walking toward her in his plodding way and she felt such a stab of
. . . well, recognition. It was Luke's walk, solemn little Luke. Life was
so sad, she thought, that she almost couldn't bear it. But kissing Ezra,
she felt her sorrow overtaken by something very like annoyance. She
wondered why he put up with this, why he let things go on this way.
Could it be that he took some *satisfaction* in his grief? (As if he were
paying for something, she thought. But what would he be paying for?)
In the car, he asked, "How'd you like Luke?" and she said, "Don't
you ever think of just going there and trying to get her back?"

"I couldn't," he said, unsurprised, and he maneuvered the car laboriously from its parking slot.

"Well, I don't see why not," she told him.

"It's not right. It's wrong."

She wasn't given to philosophy, but during the drive home she stared
at the grimy Baltimore scenery and considered the question of right or
wrong: of theoretical virtue, existing in a vacuum; of whether there
was any point to it at all. When they reached home, she got out of

the car and entered the house without a word, and climbed the stairs
to her room.

Ezra scoops the dead bird onto a piece of cardboard and slides it
into the trash bag. Then he tapes the cardboard to the broken windowpane where the bird must have entered. Pearl, meanwhile, sweeps
up the shards of glass. She leaves them in a pyramid and goes downstairs
for the dustpan. Already, she sees, the house has a bit more life to
it—the sunny pattern of leaves shimmering on the parlor floor in front
of the open door, the smell of hot grass wafting through the rooms.
"It was never all that practical," Cody said on the phone just recently,
referring to the farm. "It was only a half-baked idea that I had when
I was young." But if he really meant that, why doesn't he go on and
sell? No, he couldn't possibly; she has spent so much time sweeping
this place, preparing it for him, opening and shutting bureau drawers
as if she'd find his secrets there. She can imagine Ruth in this kitchen,
Cody out surveying fence lines or whatever it is men do on farms.
She can picture Luke running through the yard in denim overalls. He
is old enough to go fishing now, to swim in the creek beyond the
pasture, maybe even to tend the animals. In August, he'll be eight. Is
it eight? Or nine. She's lost track. She hardly ever sees him, and must
conquer his shyness all over again whenever he and his parents pass
through Baltimore. Each visit, his interests have changed: from popguns
to marbles to stamp collecting. Last time he was here, some two or
three years back, she got out her husband's stamp album—its maroon,
fake-leather cover gone gray with mildew—only to find that Luke had
switched to model airplanes. He was assembling a balsa wood jet, he
told her, that would actually fly. And he was planning to be an astronaut.
"By the time I'm grown," he said, "astronauts will be ordinary. People
will be taking rockets like you would take a bus. They'll spend their
summers on Venus. They won't go to Ocean City; they'll go to beaches
on the moon." "Ah," she said, "isn't that wonderful!" But she was too
old for such things. She couldn't keep up, and the very thought of
traveling to the moon made her feel desolate.

And nowadays—well, who can guess? Luke must be involved in
something entirely different. It's so long since he was here, and she's
not sure he'll ever be back. During that last visit, Ezra got his old
pearwood recorder from the closet and showed Luke how to play a
tune. Pearl knows very little about recorders, but evidently something
happens—the wood dries up, or warps, or something—when they're
not played enough; and this one hadn't been played in a decade, at
least. Its voice had gone splintery and cracked. How startled she'd
been, hearing three ancient notes tumble forth after such a silence! Ezra
and Luke walked south on Calvert Street to buy some linseed oil. Not
two minutes after they left, Cody asked where they'd got to. "Why,
off to buy oil for Ezra's recorder," Pearl told him. "Didn't you see

them go?" Cody excused himself and went outside to pace in front of
the house. Ruth stayed in the living room, discussing schools. Pearl
hardly listened. She could look through the window and see Cody
pacing, turning, pacing, his suit coat whipping out behind him. She
could tell when Ezra and Luke returned, even before she saw them,
by the way that Cody stiffened. "Where have you been?" she heard
him ask. "What have you two been doing?"

Luke never did learn how to play the recorder. Cody said they had
to go. "Oh, but Cody!" Pearl said. "I thought you were spending the
night!"

"Wrong," he told her. "Wrong again. I can't stay here; this place is
not safe. Don't you see what Ezra's up to?"

"What, Cody? What is he up to?"

"Don't you see he's out to steal my son?" he asked. "The same way
he always stole everybody? Don't you *see?*"

In the end, they left. Ezra wanted to give Luke the recorder for keeps,
but Cody told Luke to leave it; he'd get him a newer one, fancier,
finer. One that wasn't all dried up, he said.

Pearl believes now that her family has failed. Neither of her sons is
happy, and her daughter can't seem to stay married. There is no one
to accept the blame for this but Pearl herself, who raised these children
singlehanded and did make mistakes, oh, a bushel of mistakes. Still,
she sometimes has the feeling that it's simply fate, and not a matter
for blame at all. She feels that everything has been assigned, has been
preordained; everyone must play his role. Certainly she never intended
to foster one of those good son/bad son arrangements, but what can
you do when one son is consistently good and the other consistently
bad? What can the sons do, even? "Don't you *see?*" Cody had cried,
and she had imagined, for an instant, that he was inviting her to look
at his whole existence—his years of hurt and bafflement.

Often, like a child peering over the fence at somebody else's party,
she gazes wistfully at other families and wonders what their secret is.
They seem so close. Is it that they're more religious? Or stricter, or
more lenient? Could it be the fact that they participate in sports? Read
books together? Have some common hobby? Recently, she overheard
a neighbor woman discussing her plans for Independence Day: her
family was having a picnic. Every member—child or grownup—was
cooking his or her specialty. Those who were too little to cook were
in charge of the paper plates.

Pearl felt such a wave of longing that her knees went weak.

Ezra has finished taping the glass. Pearl drifts through the other
bedrooms, checking the other windows. In the smallest bedroom, a
nursery, a little old lady in a hat approaches. It's Pearl, in the speckled
mirror above a bureau. She leans closer and traces the lines around
her eyes. Her age does not surprise her. She's grown used to it by
now. You're old for so much longer than you're young, she thinks.

Really it hardly seems fair. And then she thinks, for no earthly reason, of a girl she went to school with, Linda Lou something-or-other—such a pretty, flighty girl, someone she'd always envied. In the middle of their senior year, Linda Lou disappeared. There were rumors, later confirmed—an affair with the school's only male teacher, a married man; and a baby on the way. How horrified her classmates had been! It had thrilled them: that they actually knew such a person, had borrowed her history notes, helped her retie a loose sash, perhaps even brushed her hand accidentally—that hand that may have touched . . . well, who knew what. It occurs to Pearl, peering into the glass, that the baby born of that scandal must be sixty years old by now. He would have gray hair and liver spots, perhaps false teeth, bifocals, a tedious burden of a life. Yet Linda Lou, wearing white, still dances in Pearl's mind, the prettiest girl at the senior social.

"Don't you *see?*" Cody has asked, and Pearl had said, "Honey, I just can't understand you."

Then he shrugged, and his normal, amused expression returned to his face. "Ah, well," he said, "I can't either, I guess. After all, what do I care, now I'm grown? Why should it matter any more?"

She doesn't recall if she managed any reply to that.

She steps away from the mirror. Ezra comes in, bearing the trash bag. "All finished, Mother," he says.

"It looks a lot better, doesn't it?"

"It looks just fine," he tells her.

They descend the stairs, and close the door, and carry their supplies to the car. As they drive away Pearl glances back, like any good housewife checking what she's cleaned, and it seems to her that even that buckling front porch is straighter and more solid. She has a feeling of accomplishment. Others might have given up and let the trespassers take the place over, but never Pearl. Next season she will come again, and the season after, and the season after that, and Ezra will go on bringing her—the two of them bumping down the driveway, loyal and responsible, together forever.

7

DR. TULL IS NOT A TOY

"WHOEVER'S THE first to mention divorce has to take the children," Jenny said. "This has kept us together more times than I can count."

She was joking, but the priest didn't laugh. He may have been too

young to catch it. All he did was shift uncomfortably in his chair.
Meanwhile the children milled around him like something bubbling,
like something churning, and the baby dribbled on his shoes. He
withdrew his feet imperceptibly, as if trying not to hurt the baby's
feelings.

"Yet I believe," he said, appearing to choose his words, "that you
yourself have been divorced, have you not?"

"Twice," said Jenny. She giggled, but he only looked worried. "And
once for Joe here," she added.

Her husband smiled at her from the sofa.

"If I hadn't had the foresight to keep my maiden name," Jenny said,
"my medical diploma would read like one of those address books when
people have moved a lot. Names crossed out and added, crossed out
and added—a mess! Dr. Jenny Marie Tull Baines Wiley St. Ambrose."

The priest was one of those very blond men with glasslike hair, and
his color was so high that Jenny wondered about his blood pressure.
Or maybe he was just embarrassed. "Well," he said. "Mrs., um—or
Dr.—"

"Tull."

"Dr. Tull, I only thought that the . . . instability, the lack of stability,
might be causing Slevin's problems. The turnover in fathers, you might
say."

"In fathers? What are you talking about?" Jenny asked. "Slevin's not
my son. He's Joe's."

"Ah?"

"*Joe* is his father and always has been."

"Oh, excuse me," said the priest.

He grew even pinker—as well he ought, Jenny felt; for slow, plump
Slevin with his ashy hair was obviously Joe's. Jenny was small and
dark; Joe a massive, blond, bearded bear of a man with Slevin's slanted
blue eyes. (She had often felt drawn to overweight men. They made
her feel tidy.) "Slevin," she told the priest, "is Joe's by Greta, his
previous wife, and so are most of the others you see here. All except
for Becky; Becky's mine. The other six are his." She bent to take the
dog's bone from the baby. "Anyway . . . but Joe's wife, Greta: she
left."

"Left," said the priest.

"Left me flat," Joe said cheerfully. "Cleared clean out of Baltimore.
Parked the kids with a neighbor one day, while I was off at work.
Hired an Allied van and departed with all we owned, everything but
the children's clothes in neat little piles on the floor."

"Oh, my stars," said the priest.

"Even took their beds. Can you explain that? Took the crib and the
changing table. Only thing I can figure, she was so used to life with
children that she really couldn't imagine; really assumed she would

need a crib no matter where she went. First thing I had to do when I got home that night was go out and buy a fleet of beds from Sears. They must've thought I was opening a motel."

"Picture it," Jenny said. "Joe in an apron. Joe mixing Similac. Well, he was lost, of course. Utterly lost. The way we met: he called me at home in the dead of night when his baby got roseola. That's how out of touch he was; it's been twenty years at least since pediatricians made house calls. But I came, I don't know why. Well, he lived only two blocks away. And he was so desperate—answered the door in striped pajamas, jiggling the baby—"

"I fell in love with her the moment she walked in," said Joe. He stroked his beard; golden frizz flew up around his stubby fingers.

"He thought I was Lady Bountiful," Jenny said, "bearing a medical bag instead of a basket of food. It's hard to resist a man who needs you."

"Need had nothing to do with it," Joe told her.

"Well, who admires you, then. He asked if I had children of my own, and how I managed while I worked. And when I said I mostly played it by ear, with teen-aged sitters one minute and elderly ladies the next, my mother filling in when she could or my brother or a neighbor, or Becky sometimes just camping in my waiting room with her math assignment—"

"I could see she wasn't a skimpy woman," Joe told the priest. "Not rigid. Not constricted. Not that super-serious kind."

"No," said the priest, glancing around him. (It hadn't been a day when Jenny could get to the housework.)

Jenny said, "He said he liked the way I let his children crawl all over me. He said his wife had found them irritating, the last few years. Well, you see how it began. I had promised myself I'd never remarry, Becky and I would rather manage on our own, that's what I was best at; but I don't know, there Joe *was*, and his children. And his baby was so little and so recently abandoned that she turned her head and opened her mouth when I held her horizontal; you could tell she still remembered. Anyway," she said, and she smiled at the priest, who really was shockingly young—a wide-eyed boy, was all. "How did we get on this subject?"

"Uh, Slevin," said the priest. "We were discussing Slevin."

"Oh, yes, Slevin."

It was a rainy, blowy April afternoon, with the trees turning inside out and beating against the windowpanes, and the living room had reached just that shade of dusk where no one had realized, quite yet, that it was time to switch on the lights. The air seemed thick and grainy. The children were winding down like little clocks and fussing for their suppers; but the priest, lacking children of his own, failed to notice this. He leaned forward, setting his fingertips together. "I've been concerned," he said, "by Slevin's behavior at C.Y.O. meetings. He's not sociable at all, has no friends, seems moody, withdrawn. Of course it could be his age, but . . . he's fourteen, is he?"

"Thirteen," said Joe, after thinking it over.

"Thirteen years old, naturally a difficult . . . I wouldn't even mention it, except that when I suggested we have a talk he just wrenched away and ran out, and never returned. Now we notice that you, Mr. St. Ambrose, that you drop him off for mass every Sunday, but in fact he's stopped coming inside and simply sits out front on the steps and watches the traffic. He's, you might say, playing hooky, but—"

"Shoot," said Joe. "I get up specially on a Sunday morning to drive him there and he plays *hooky?*"

"But my point is—"

"I don't know why he wants to go anyhow. He's the only one of them that does."

"But it's his withdrawn behavior that worries me," the priest said, "more than his church attendance. Though it might not be a bad idea if, perhaps, you accompanied him to mass sometime."

"Me? Hell, I'm not even Catholic."

"Or I don't suppose *you*, Dr. Tull . . ."

Both men seemed to be waiting for her. Jenny was wondering about the baby's diaper, which bulged suspiciously, but she gathered her thoughts and said, "Oh, no, goodness, I really wouldn't have the faintest—" She laughed, covering her mouth—a gesture she had. "Besides," she said, "it was Greta who was the Catholic. Slevin's mother."

"I see. Well, the important thing—"

"*I* don't know why Slevin goes to church. And to Greta's church, her old one, clear across town."

"Does he communicate with his mother now?"

"Oh, no, she's never been back. Got a quickie divorce in Idaho and that's the last we heard."

"Are there any, ah, step-family problems?"

"Step-family?" Jenny said. "Well, no. Or yes. I don't know. There *would* be, probably; of course these things are never easy . . . only life is so rushed around here, there really isn't time."

"Slevin is very fond of Jenny," Joe told the priest.

"Why, thank you, honey," Jenny said.

"She won him right over; she's got him trailing after her anyplace she goes. She's so cool and jokey with kids, you know."

"Well, I try," Jenny said. "I do make an effort. But you never can be sure. That age is very secretive."

"Perhaps I'll suggest that he stop by and visit me," the priest said.

"If you like."

"Just to gab, I'll say, chew the fat . . ."

Jenny could see that it would never work out.

She walked him to the door, strolling with her hands deep in her skirt pockets. "I hope," she said, "you haven't got the wrong idea about us. I mean, Joe's an excellent father, honestly he is; he's always been good with Slevin."

"Yes, of course."

"Oh, when I compare him with some others I could name!" Jenny said. She had a habit, with disapproving people, of talking a little too much, and she knew it. As they crossed the hall, she said, "Sam Wiley, for instance—my second husband. Becky's father. You'd die if you ever saw Sam. He was a painter, one of those graceful compact *small* types I've never trusted since. Totally shiftless. Totally unreliable. He left me before Becky was born, moved in with a model named Adar Bagned."

She opened the front door. A fine, fresh mist blew in and she took a deep breath. "Oh, lovely," she said. "But isn't that a hilarious name? For the longest time I kept trying to turn it around, thinking it must make more sense if I read it off backward. Goodbye, then, Father. Thanks for dropping in."

She closed the door on him and went off to fix the children's supper.

This would be a very nice house, Jenny was fond of saying, if only the third-floor bathtub didn't drain through the dining room ceiling. It was a tall, trim Bolton Hill row house; she'd bought it back in '64, when prices weren't yet sky-high. In those days, it had seemed enormous; but seven years later, with six extra children, it didn't feel so big any more. It was inconvenient, warrenlike, poorly arranged. There were so many doors and radiators, it was hard to find space for the furniture.

She cooked at a sticky, stilt-legged stove, rinsed greens at a yellowed sink skirted with chintz, set plates on a table that was carved with another family's initials. "Here, children, everyone get his own silver, now—"

"You gave Jacob more peas than me."

"She did not."

"Did too."

"Did not."

"Did too."

"Take them! I don't even like them."

"Where's Slevin?" Jenny asked.

"Who needs Slevin anyhow, the old grouch."

The telephone rang and Joe came in with the baby. "That's your answering service, they want to know—"

"I'm not on; it's Dan's night on. What are they calling *me* for?"

"That's what I thought, but they said—"

He wandered off again, and returned a minute later to settle at the table with the baby in his lap. "Here's her meat," Jenny said, flying past. "Her spoon is on the . . ."

She left the kitchen, climbed the stairs to the second floor and called up to the third. "Slevin?" No answer. She climbed the rest of the way, quickly growing breathless. How out of shape she was! It was true, as her mother was forever telling her, that she had let herself go—a crime, her mother said, for anyone with Jenny's good looks. It was true that she'd become a bit haggard, slackened somewhat, her skin turning sallow and her eyebrows shaggy and her wide, amused mouth a dry brownish color now that she wore no lipstick. "Your hair!" her mother mourned. "Your lovely hair!"—which wasn't lovely at all: a thick, blunt, gray-threaded clump with boxy bangs. "You used to be such a beauty," Pearl would say, and Jenny would laugh. A fat lot of good it had done her! She liked to think that she was wearing her beauty out—using it up, she liked to think. She took some satisfaction in it, like a housewife industriously making her way through a jar of something she did not enjoy, would not buy again, but couldn't just discard, of course.

Panting, clutching a handful of denim skirt, she arrived on the third floor. It was the older children's floor, not her territory, and it had a musty, atticky smell. "Slevin?" she called. She knocked at his door. "Supper, Slevin!"

She opened the door a crack and peered in. Slevin lay on his unmade bed with his forearm over his eyes. A wide strip of blubbery belly showed, as it nearly always did, between jeans and T-shirt. He had his earphones on; that was why he hadn't heard. She crossed the room and lifted the earphones from his head. A miniature Janis Joplin song rang out tinnily: "Me and Bobby McGee." He blinked and gave her a puzzled look, like someone just waking. "Suppertime," she told him.

"I'm not hungry."

"Not hungry! What kind of talk is that?"

"Jenny, honest, I just don't want to get up."

But she was already pulling him to his feet—a burly boy nearly Jenny's height and considerably heavier but still babyish, creamy skinned. She propelled him to the door, pushing from behind with both palms flat on the small of his back. "You're the only one of them that I have to carry bodily to meals," she said. She sang him down the stairs:

> "Oh, they had to carry Harry to the ferry,
> And they had to carry Harry to the shore . . ."

"Seriously, Jenny," Slevin said.

They entered the kitchen. Joe made a trumpet of his hands above the baby's head and said, "Ta-ra! Ta-ra! He approaches!" Slevin groaned. The others didn't look up from their meal.

Sitting in her place next to Joe, gazing around at the tableful of children, Jenny felt pleased. They were doing well, she decided—even the older ones, who'd acted so wary and hostile when she had first met them.

Then she had an unsettling thought: it occurred to her that this would have to be her permanent situation. Having taken on these children, straightened their upturned lives and slowly, steadily won their trust, she could not in good conscience let them down. Here she was, forever. "It's lucky we get along," she said to Joe.

"It's extremely lucky," he said, and he patted her hand and asked for the mustard.

"Isn't it amazing how school always smells like school," Jenny told Slevin's teacher. "You can add all the modern conveniences you like—audiovisual things and computers—it still smells like book glue and that cheap gray paper they used to have for arithmetic and also . . . what's that other smell? There's another smell besides. I know it but I can't quite name it."

"Have a seat, Dr. Tull," the teacher said.

"Radiator dust," said Jenny.

"Pardon?"

"*That's* the other smell."

"I called you in for a purpose," said the teacher, opening the file that lay before her. She was a tiny thing, surely not out of her twenties, perky and freckled with horn-rimmed glasses dwarfing her pointed nose. Jenny wondered how she'd learned to be so intimidating so quickly. "I know you're a busy woman, Dr. Tull, but I'm genuinely anxious about Slevin's school performance and I thought you ought to be informed."

"Oh, really?" Jenny said. She decided she would feel better if she too wore glasses, though hers were only needed for reading. She dug through her purse and a pink plastic pacifier fell out. She pretended it hadn't happened.

"Slevin is very, very intelligent," the teacher said. She glared at Jenny accusingly. "He goes straight off the top of the charts."

"Yes, I figured that."

"But his English average . . ." the teacher said, flipping through papers. "It's F. Well, maybe D minus."

Jenny clicked her tongue.

"Math: C. History: D. And science . . . and gym . . . He's had so many absences, I finally asked if he'd been cutting school. 'Yes, ma'am,' he said—came right out with it. 'What did you cut?' I asked him. 'February,' he said."

Jenny laughed. The teacher looked at her.

Jenny straightened her glasses and said, "Do you think it might be puberty?"

"*All* these children are going through puberty," the teacher told her.

"Or . . . I don't know; boredom. You said yourself he's intelligent. Why, you ought to see him at home! Monkeying around with machinery, wiring stereos . . . He's got a tape recorder of his own, he worked for it and bought it himself, some superduper model, offhand I can't think of the name. I'm such a dunce about these things, when he talked about head cleaners I thought he meant shampoo; but Slevin knows all about it and—"

"Mr. Davies suggests," said the teacher, "—that's our assistant principal—he suggests that Slevin may be experiencing emotional problems due to the adjustments at home."

"What adjustments?"

"He says Slevin's mother abandoned him and Slevin was moved to your household almost immediately thereafter and had to get used to a brand-new mother and sister."

"Oh, that," said Jenny, waving her hand.

"Mr. Davies suggests that Slevin might need professional counseling."

"Nonsense," Jenny said. "What's a little adjustment? And anyhow, that happened a good six months ago. It's not as if . . . why, look at my daughter! She's had to get used to *seven* new people and she's never said a word of complaint. Oh, we're all coping! In fact my husband was saying, just the other day, we should think about having more children now. We ought to have at least one *joint* child, he says, but I'm not so sure myself. After all, I'm thirty-six years old. It probably wouldn't be wise."

"Mr. Davies suggests—"

"Though I suppose if it means so much to him, it's all the same to me."

"The same!" said the teacher. "What about the population explosion?"

"The what? You're getting me off the subject, here. . . . My point is," Jenny said, "I don't see the need to blame adjustment, broken homes, bad parents, that sort of thing. We make our own luck, right? You have to overcome your setbacks. You can't take them too much to heart. I'll explain all that to Slevin. I'll tell him this evening. I'm certain his grades will improve."

Then she bent to pick up the pacifier, and shook hands with the teacher and left.

On the wall in Jenny's office was a varnished wooden plaque: DR. TULL IS NOT A TOY. Joe had made it for her in his workshop. He was incensed by the scrapes and bruises that Jenny gathered daily in her raucous games with her patients. "Make them show some respect," he told her. "Maintain a little dignity." But the sign was all but lost among her patients' snapshots (on beaches, on seesaws, on photographers' blanketed tables, or behind lit birthday cakes) and the crayoned self-portraits they'd brought her. Anyhow, most of them were too young to read. She scooped up Billy Burnham and carried him, squawking and giggling, to the nurse for his tetanus shot. "Now, it's possible," she called back to Mrs. Burnham, "that tonight he'll experience a little soreness in his left—" Billy squirmed, and a button popped off Jenny's white coat.

The Albright baby was due for a DPT shot. The Carroll baby had to have her formula switched. Lucy Brandon's constant sniffle looked like an allergy; Jenny told Mrs. Brandon where she could take her for testing. Both the Morris twins' tonsils were swollen.

She asked the receptionist to order her a sandwich, but the receptionist said, "Aren't you eating out? Your brother's here; he's been waiting half an hour, at least."

"Oh, my Lord, I forgot all about him," Jenny said. She went into the waiting room. Ezra was seated on the vinyl couch, surrounded by pull toys and building blocks and oilcloth picture books. A family of Spanish-speaking children, probably patients of Dr. Ramirez, played at his feet, but you'd never mistake Ezra for a parent. His shaggy yellow hair was soft as a child's; he wore faded work clothes, and his face was wide and expectant.

"Ezra, honey," Jenny told him, "I clean forgot. My next appointment's in twenty minutes; do you suppose we could just grab a hamburger?"

"Oh, surely," Ezra said.

He waited while she took off her white coat and put on a raincoat. Then they rode the elevator down to the marble-paved lobby, and pushed through the revolving door onto a spattery, overcast street. There was a smell like wet coal. Huddled people hurried by and buses wheezed and cathedral bells rang far away.

"I feel dumb," Jenny said, "taking you of all people to a hamburger joint."

She was thinking of his restaurant, which always intimidated her a little. Recently, Ezra had remodeled the living quarters above it into a series of tiny, elegant private dining rooms like those in old movies— the velvet-hung compartments where the villain attempts to seduce the heroine. They'd be perfect for anniversary couples, Ezra said. (Like most unmarried men, he was comically, annoyingly sentimental about marriage.) But so far, only business groups and heavily jeweled Baltimore politicians had asked to use the rooms.

Now he said, "A hamburger's fine; I'm crazy about hamburgers." And when they walked through the plate glass doorway, into a slick, tiled area lined with glaring photos of onion rings and milkshakes, he looked around him happily. Secretaries clustered at some tables, construction workers at others. "It's getting like a collective farm," Ezra said. "All these chain places that everyone comes to for breakfast, lunch, sometimes supper . . . like a commune or a kibbutz or something.

Pretty soon we won't have private kitchens at all; you just drop by your local Gino's or McDonald's. I kind of like it."

Jenny wondered if there were any eating place he wouldn't like. At a soup kitchen, no doubt, he'd be pleased by the obvious hunger of the customers. At a urine-smelling tavern he'd discover some wonderful pickled eggs that he'd never seen anywhere else. Oh, if it had to do with food, he was endlessly appreciative.

While he ordered for them, she settled herself at a table. She took off her raincoat, smoothed her hair, and scraped at a Pablum spot on her blouse. It felt strange to be sitting alone. Always there was someone—children, patients, colleagues. The empty space on either side of her gave her an echoing, weightless feeling, as if she lacked ballast and might at any moment float upward.

Ezra returned with their hamburgers. "How's Joe?" he asked, sitting down.

"Oh, fine. How's Mother?"

"Doing well, sends her love . . . I brought you something," he said. He set aside his burger to rummage through his windbreaker pockets. Eventually, he came up with a worn white envelope. "Pictures," he said.

"Pictures?"

"Photos. Mother's got all these photos; I just discovered them. I thought maybe you'd be interested in having a few."

Jenny sighed. Poor Ezra: he was turning into the family custodian, tending their mother and guarding their past and faithfully phoning his sister for lunch. "Why don't you keep them," she said. "You know I'd just lose them."

"But a lot of these are of you," he said. He spilled the envelope onto the table. "I figured the children might like them. For instance, somewhere here . . ." He shuffled various versions of a younger, sterner Jenny. "Here," he said. "Don't you see Becky in this?"

It was Jenny in a plaid tam-o'-shanter, unsmiling. "Ugh," she said, stirring her coffee.

"You were a really nice little girl," said Ezra. He returned to his burger but kept the photo before him. On the back of it, Jenny saw, something had been written in pencil. She tried to make it out. Ezra noticed and said, "Fall, 1947. I got Mother to write the dates down. And I'm going to send Cody some, too."

Jenny could just imagine Cody's face when he got them. "Ezra," she said, "to tell the truth, I wouldn't waste the postage."

"Don't you think he'd like to compare these with how Luke looks, growing up?"

"Believe me," she said, "he'd burn them. You know Cody."

"Maybe he's changed," Ezra said.

"He hasn't," said Jenny, "and I doubt he ever will. Just mention something—one little harmless memory from our childhood—and his mouth turns down. *You* know how his mouth does. I said to him once, I said, 'Cody, you're no better than the Lawsons.' Remember the Lawsons? They moved into our neighborhood from Nashville, Tennessee, and the very first week all four children got mumps. Mrs. Lawson said, 'This city is unlucky, I believe.' The next week a pipe in their basement burst and she said, 'Well, that's Baltimore.' Then their daughter broke her wrist. . . . When they moved back to Tennessee, I went over to say goodbye. They were loading up their car trunk and they happened to slam the lid down smack on the fingers of their youngest boy. When they drove off he was screaming, and Mrs. Lawson called out, 'Isn't this a fitting way to leave? I always did say Baltimore was unlucky.' "

"Well, now, I'm trying to follow you, here," Ezra said.

"It's whether you add up the list or not," Jenny said. "I mean, if you catalogue grudges, anything looks bad. And Cody certainly catalogues; he's running his life with his catalogues. But after all, I told him, we made it, didn't we? We did grow up. Why, the three of us turned out fine, just fine!"

"It's true," said Ezra, his forehead smoothing. "You especially, Jenny. Look at you: a doctor."

"Oh, shoo, I'm nothing but a baby weigher," Jenny said. But she was pleased, and when they rose to go she took along the photographs to make him happy.

Joe said if they did have a baby, he'd like it to be a girl. He'd looked around and noticed they were a little short on girls. "How can you say that?" Jenny asked. She ticked the girls off on her fingers: "Phoebe, Becky, Jane . . ."

When her voice trailed away, he stood watching her. She was expecting him to speak, but he didn't. "Well?" she asked.

"That's only three."

She felt a little rush of confusion. "Have I left one out?"

"*No*, you haven't left one out. Has she left one out," he told the wall. He snorted. "Has she left one out, she asks. What a question! *No*, you haven't left one out. Three is all we have. Three girls."

"Well, there's no need to act so cross about it."

"I'm not cross, I'm frustrated," he said. "I'm trying to have a conversation here."

"Isn't that what we're doing?"

"Yes, yes . . ."

"Then where's the problem?"

He wouldn't say. He stood in the kitchen doorway with his arms folded tight across his chest. He gazed off to one side, scowling. Jenny was puzzled. Were they quarreling, or what? When the silence stretched on, she gradually, imperceptibly returned to slicing the cucumbers for supper. She brought the knife down as quietly as possible, and without a sound scooped the disks of cucumber into a bowl. (When she and Joe had first met, he'd said, "Do you put cucumber on your skin?" "*Cucumbers?*" she'd asked, astonished. "You look so cool," he told her, "I thought of this bottle of cucumber milk my aunt used to keep on her vanity table.")

Two of the children, Jacob and Peter, were playing with the Ouija board in front of the refrigerator. Jenny had to step over them when she went to get the tomatoes. "Excuse me," she told them. "You're in my way." But they ignored her; they were intent on the board. "What will I be when I grow up?" Jacob asked, and he set his fingertips delicately upon the pointer. "Upper middle class, middle middle class, or lower middle class: which?"

Jenny laughed, and Joe glared at her and wheeled and stamped out of the kitchen.

On the evening news, a helicopter crewman who'd been killed in Laos was buried with full military honors. An American flag, folded into a cushiony triangle, was handed to the parents—a gray-haired, square-chinned gentleman and his fragile wife. The wife wore a trim beige raincoat and little white gloves. It was she who accepted the flag. The husband had turned away and was weeping, would not even say a few words to the microphone somebody offered him. "Sir? Sir?" a reporter asked.

One white glove reached out and took the microphone. "What my husband means to say, I believe," the wife declared in a feathery, Southern voice, "is we thank all those who've gathered here, and we know we're just going to be fine. We're strong, and we're going to be fine."

"Hogwash," Slevin said.

"Why, Slevin," said Jenny. "I didn't know you were political."

"I'm not; it's just a bunch of hogwash," he told her. "She ought to say, 'Take your old flag! I object! I give up!' "

"My goodness," Jenny said mildly. She was sorting Ezra's photos; she held one out to distract him. "Look," she said. "Your Uncle Cody, at age fifteen."

"He's not my uncle."

"Of course he is."

"He's not my real uncle."

"You wouldn't say that if you knew him. You'd like him," Jenny said. "I wish he'd come for a visit. He's so . . . unbrotherly or something; I don't know. And look!" she said, alighting on another photo. "Isn't my mother pretty?"

"*I* think she looks like a lizard," Slevin said.

"Oh, but when she was a girl, I mean . . . isn't it sad how carefree she was."

"Half the time, she forgets my name," Slevin said.

"Well, she's old," Jenny told him.

"Not that old. What she's saying is, I'm not worth her bother. Old biddy. Sits at the head of the table with a piece of bread on her plate and sets both hands down flat and just stares around at us, stares around, face like one of those rotating fans, waiting for the butter but never asking, never saying a word. Till finally you or Dad says, 'Mother? Could we pass you the butter?' and she says, 'Why, *thank* you,' like she was wondering when you'd realize."

"She hasn't had an easy life," Jenny said.

"I wish just once we'd get all through the meal and nobody offer her the butter."

"She raised us on her own, you know," Jenny told him. "Don't you think it must have been hard? My father walked out and left her when I was nine years old."

"He did?" Slevin asked. He stared at her.

"He left her, absolutely. We never set eyes on him again."

"Bastard," Slevin said.

"Oh, well," said Jenny. She leafed through some more photos.

"Jesus! These people! They try to do you in."

"You're overreacting," Jenny told him. "I can't even remember the man, if you want to know the truth. Wouldn't know him if I saw him. And my mother managed fine. It all worked out. Look at this, Slevin: see Ezra's old-fashioned haircut?"

Slevin shrugged and switched the TV channel.

"And see what I was like at your age?" She handed him the picture with the tam-o'-shanter.

He glanced over. He frowned. He said, "Who did you say that was?"

"Me."

"No, it's not."

"Yes, it is. Me at thirteen. Mother wrote the date on the back."

"It's not!" he said. His voice was unusually high; he sounded like a much younger child. "It isn't! Look at it! Why, it's like a . . . concentration camp person, a victim, Anne Frank! It's terrible! It's so sad!"

Surprised, she turned the photo around and looked again. True, the picture wasn't particularly happy—it showed a dark little girl with a thin, watchful face—but it wasn't as bad as all that. "So what?" she asked, and she held it out to him once more. He drew back sharply.

"It's somebody else," he told her. "Not you; you're always laughing and having fun. It's not you."

"Oh, fine, it's not me, then," she said, and she returned to the rest of the photos.

* * *

"I want to talk to you about that oldest boy," her mother said on the phone. "What's his name? Kevin?"

"Slevin, Mother. Honestly."

"Well, he stole my vacuum cleaner."

"He did what?"

"Sunday afternoon, when you all came to visit, he slipped into my pantry and made off with my Hoover upright."

Jenny sat down on her bed. She said, "Let me get this straight."

"It's been missing all week," her mother said, "and I couldn't understand it. I knew we hadn't been burglarized, and even if we had, what would anyone want with my old Hoover?"

"But why accuse Slevin?"

"My neighbor told me, just this afternoon. Mrs. Arthur. Said, 'Was that your grandson I saw Sunday? Kind of hefty boy? Loading your Hoover upright into your daughter's car trunk?' "

"That's impossible," Jenny said.

"Now, how do you know that? How do you know what is or is not possible? He's hardly more than a stranger, Jenny. I mean, you got those children the way other people get weekend guests."

"You're exaggerating," Jenny told her.

"Well, all I ask is for you to go check Slevin's bedroom. Just check."

"What, this minute?"

"There's lint specks all over my carpet."

"Oh, all right," Jenny said.

She laid the receiver on her pillow and climbed from the second floor to the third. Slevin's door was open and he wasn't in his room, although his radio rocked with the Jefferson Airplane. She stepped stealthily over Slevin's knapsack, avoided a teetering pile of *Popular Science* magazines, opened his closet door, and found herself staring at her mother's vacuum cleaner. She would know it anywhere: an elderly machine with a gray cloth dust bag. Its cord was coiled neatly and it seemed unharmed. If he'd taken it apart to learn how it worked, she might have understood. Or if he'd smashed it, out of some rage toward her mother. But there it sat, entire. She stood puzzling over it for several seconds. Then she wheeled it out of the closet and lugged it down the stairs, to where her mother's voice was twanging impatiently from the receiver. "Jenny? Jenny?"

"Well, you're right," Jenny said. "I found it in his room."

There was a pause in which Pearl could have said, "I told you so," but kindly did not. Then she said, "I wonder if he might be calling for help in some way."

"By stealing a *vacuum* cleaner?"

"He's really a very sweet boy," Pearl said. "I can see that. Maybe he's asking for a psychologist or some such."

"More likely he's asking for a neater house," Jenny said. "The dust balls on his closet floor have started raising a family."

She pictured Slevin, in desperation, stealing an arsenal of cleaning supplies—this neighbor's broom, that neighbor's Ajax, gathered with the same feverish zeal he showed in collecting Indian head pennies. She was attacked by a sudden sputter of laughter.

"Oh, Jenny," her mother said sadly. "Do you have to see everything as a joke?"

"It's not *my* fault if funny things happen," Jenny said.

"It most certainly is," said her mother, but instead of explaining herself, she all at once grew brisk and requested the return of her vacuum cleaner by tomorrow morning.

Jenny and Joe and every child except the baby were watching television. It was long past bedtime for most of them, but this was a special occasion: the Late, Late Show was *A Taste of Honey*. Everyone in the house had heard of *A Taste of Honey*. It was Jenny's all-time favorite movie. She had seen it once, back in 1963, and never forgotten it. Nothing else had ever measured up to it, she was fond of saying, and after returning from some other movie she was sure to announce, "Well, it was all right, I guess, but it wasn't *A Taste of Honey*." By now, any one of the children could finish that sentence before she got it halfway out. They'd ask as soon as she walked in the door, "Was it *A Taste of Honey*, Jenny? Was it?" And Phoebe was once heard telling Peter, "I like the new teacher okay, I guess, but she isn't *A Taste of Honey*."

When they learned it was coming to television, they had all begged to stay up and watch. The older ones made cocoa and the younger ones set out potato chips. Becky and Slevin arranged a ring of chairs around the TV set in the living room.

"You know what's going to happen," Joe told Jenny. "After all this time, even *A Taste of Honey* won't be *A Taste of Honey*."

In a way, he was right. Not that she didn't still love it—yes, yes, she assured the children, it was just as she'd remembered—but after all, she was a different person watching it. The movie wrenched her with pity, now, when before it had made her feel hopeful. And wasn't it odd, wasn't it downright queer, that she'd never identified the story with her own? In 1963, she was a resident in pediatrics, struggling to care for a two-year-old born six weeks after her marriage dissolved. Yet she'd watched a movie about an unwed, unsupported pregnant girl with the most detached enjoyment, dreamily making her way through a box of pretzels. (And what had she been doing in a movie theater, anyway? How had she found the time, during such a frantic schedule?)

When it was over, she switched off the TV and shooed the children up the stairs. Quinn, the youngest, who had not been all that impressed with *A Taste of Honey*, was sound asleep and had to be carried by Joe.

Even the older ones were groggy and blinking. "Wake up," she told them. "Come on, now," and she tugged at Jacob, who had dropped in a bundle on the topmost step. One by one she guided them to their beds and kissed them good night. How noisy their rooms seemed, even in silence!—that riotous clamor of toys and flung-off clothes, their vibrant, clashing rock star posters and antiwar bumper stickers and Orioles banners. Three of the children wouldn't use sheets but slept in sleeping bags instead—garishly patterned, zippered cocoons sprawled on top of the blankets; and Phoebe didn't like beds at all but curled in a quilt on the floor, most often out in the hall in front of her parents' room. She lay across the doorway like a bodyguard, and you had to watch your step in the dark so as not to trip on her.

"I want that radio *down*," Jenny said, and she kissed the top of Becky's head. Then she peeked into Slevin's room, knocked on the frame of his open door, and entered. He wore his daytime clothes to bed, as always—even his wide tooled belt with the trucker's buckle— and he lay on top of the covers. She had been kissing him good night every night since she'd married Joe, but still he acted bashful. All she really did was brush her cheek against his, allowing him his dignity. "Sleep well," she told him.

He said, "I see you found the vacuum cleaner."

"Vacuum cleaner," she said, stalling for time.

"I'm sorry I took it," he said. "I guess your mom is pretty mad, huh? But it wasn't stealing; honest. I just needed to borrow it for a spell."

She sat on the edge of the bed. "Needed to borrow it for what?" she asked.

He said, "Well, for . . . I don't know. Just for . . . See, there it was in the pantry. It was exactly like my mother's. Just exactly. You know how you never think about a thing, or realize you remember it, and then all at once something will bring it all back? I forgot how it had that rubber strip around the edge so it wouldn't scuff the furniture, and that tall, puffy bag I used to be scared of when I was a kid. It even smelled the same. It had that same clothy smell, just like my mother's. You know? So I wanted to take it home. But once I got it here, well, it didn't work out. It's like I had lost the connection. It wasn't the same after all."

"That's all right, Slevin," she said. "Heavens, honey, that's all right." Then she worried her voice had shown too much, would make him bashful again, so she laughed a little and said, "Shall we get you a Hoover of your own for your birthday?"

He turned over on his side.

"Or we could have it made up in calico," she told him, giggling. "A tiny stuffed calico vacuum cleaner to take to bed with you."

But Slevin just closed his eyes, so after a while she wished him good
night and left.

She dreamed she was back with Sam Wiley, her second husband
and the one she'd loved the best. She'd made a fool of herself over
Sam. She dreamed he was twirling on that high wooden stool they
used to have in their kitchen in Paulham. He was preening the scrolls
of his handlebar mustache and singing "Let It Be." Which hadn't even
existed, at the time.

She opened her eyes and heard "Let It Be" on one of the children's
radios, sailing out across the dark hall. How often had she told them?
She got up and made her way to Peter's room—barefoot, stepping over
Phoebe. Radios late at night sounded so different, she thought—so far
away and crackling with static, almost gritty, as if the music had had
to travel above miles of railroad tracks and deserted superhighways,
past coal yards and auto dumps, oil derricks and factory smokestacks
and electrical transformers. She switched off the radio and pulled Peter's
sleeping bag up around his shoulders. She checked on the baby in her
crib. Then she returned to bed, shivering slightly, and huddled against
Joe's hulking back for warmth.

"Mack the Knife," Sam used to sing, and "Greenfields"—yes, that
had been around. She remembered how operatic he'd get, rolling his
eyes, pounding his chest, trying to make her laugh. (She'd been an
earnest young medical student, in those days.) Then she remembered
the tender, aching line that the examining table had pressed across the
mound of the baby, when Jenny was an intern bending over a patient.
Six months pregnant, seven months . . . By her eighth month the
marriage was finished, and Jenny was walking around in a daze. She
saw that she had always been doomed to fail, had been unlovable,
had lacked some singular quality that would keep a husband. She had
never known this consciously, before, but the pain she felt was eerily
familiar—like a suspicion, long held, at last confirmed.

She wore uniforms designed for male physicians with forty-inch
waists; there were no maternity lab coats. On rounds, professors would
give her doubtful glances and ask if she were sure she was up to this.
Sympathetic nurses brought her so many cups of coffee that she thought
she would float away. One of those nurses stayed with her through
most of her labor. Other women had their husbands, but Jenny had
Rosa Perez, who let her squeeze her fingers as hard as needed and
never said a word of complaint.

And what was the name of that neighbor who used to watch the
baby? Mary something—Mary Lee, Mary Lou—some fellow intern's
wife, as poor as Jenny and the mother of two children under two. She
baby-sat for a pittance, but even that was more than Jenny could afford.
And the schedule! Months of nights on duty, thirty-six hours on call

and twelve off, emergency room, obstetrics, trauma surgery . . . and her residency was not much better. Meanwhile, Becky changed from an infant to a little girl, an outsider really, a lively child with Sam Wiley's snapping black eyes, unrelated to Jenny. Though it was a shock, sometimes, to see her give that level, considering stare so typical of the Tulls. Was it possible, after all, that this small stranger might constitute a family? She learned to walk; she learned to talk. "No!" she would say, in her firm, spunky voice; and Jenny, trying to stay awake at three in the morning or three in the afternoon, whatever bit of time they had together, dropped her head in her hands. "No!" said Becky, and Jenny hauled off and slapped her hard across the mouth, then shook her till her head lolled, then flung her aside and ran out of the apartment to . . . where? (A movie, perhaps?) In those days, objects wobbled and grew extra edges. She was so exhausted that the sight of her patients' white pillows could mesmerize her. Sounds were thick, as if underwater. Words on a chart were meaningless—so many k's and g's, such a choppy language English was, short syllables, clumps of consonants, she'd never noticed; like Icelandic, maybe, or Eskimo. She slammed Becky's face into her Peter Rabbit dinner plate and gave her a bloody nose. She yanked a handful of her hair. All of her childhood returned to her: her mother's blows and slaps and curses, her mother's pointed fingernails digging into Jenny's arm, her mother shrieking, "Guttersnipe! Ugly little rodent!" and some scrap of memory—she couldn't quite place it—Cody catching hold of Pearl's wrist and fending her off while Jenny shrank against the wall.

Was this what it came to—that you never could escape? That certain things were doomed to continue, generation after generation? She failed to see a curb and sprained her ankle, hobbled to work in agony. She misdiagnosed a case of viral pneumonia. She let a green-stick fracture slip right past her. She brought Becky a drink of water in the middle of the night and then suddenly, without the slightest intention, screamed, "Take it! Take it!" and threw the cup into Becky's face. Becky shivered and caught her breath for hours afterward, even in her sleep, though Jenny held her tightly on her lap.

Then her mother called from Baltimore and said, "Jenny? Don't you write your family any more?"

"Well, I've been so busy," Jenny meant to say. Or: "Leave me alone, I remember all about you. It's all come back. Write? Why should I write? You've damaged me; you've injured me. Why would I want to write?"

Instead, she started . . . not crying, exactly, but something worse. She was torn by dry, ragged sobs; she ran out of air; there was a grating sound in her chest. Her mother said, calmly, "Jenny, hang up. You know that couch in your living room? Go lie down on it. I'll be there just as soon as Ezra can drive me."

Pearl stayed two weeks, using all of her vacation time. The first thing she did was call Jenny's hospital and arrange for sick leave. Then she set about putting the world in order again. She smoothed clean sheets on Jenny's bed, brought her tea and bracing broths, shampooed her hair, placed flowers on her bureau. Becky, who had hardly seen her grandmother till now, fell in love with her. Pearl called Becky "Rebecca" and treated her formally, respectfully, as if she were not quite sure how much she was allowed. Every morning she walked Becky to the playground and swung her on the swings. In the afternoon they went shopping together. She bought Becky an old-fashioned dress that made her look solemn and reasonable. She bought picture books—nursery rhymes and fairy tales and *The Little House*. Jenny had forgotten about *The Little House*. Why, she had loved that book! She'd requested it every evening, she remembered now. She'd sat on that homely old sofa and listened while her mother, with endless patience, read it three times, four times, five. . . . Now Becky said, "Read it again," and Pearl returned to page one, and Jenny listened just as closely as Becky did.

Sundays, when his restaurant closed, Ezra drove up from Baltimore. He was not, in spite of his innocent face, an open sort of person, and rather than speak outright of Jenny's new breakability he kept smiling serenely at some point just beyond her. She took comfort from this. There was already too much openness in the world, she felt—everyone raging and weeping and rejoicing. She imagined that Ezra was not subject to the ups and downs that jolted other people. She liked to have him read the papers to her (trouble in Honduras, trouble in Saigon, natural disasters in Haiti and Cuba and Italy) while she listened from a nest of deep blue blankets and a nightgown still warm from her mother's iron.

On the second weekend, Cody blew in from wherever he'd vanished to most recently. He traveled on a breeze of energy and money; Jenny was impressed. He used her telephone for two hours like the wheeler-dealer he always was and arranged to pay for a full-time sitter, a slim young woman named Delilah Greening who turned out to be better help than Jenny would ever have again. Then he slung his suit coat over one shoulder, gave her a little salute, and was gone.

She slept, sometimes, for twelve and fourteen hours straight. She woke dislocated, frightened by the sunlit, tickling silence of the apartment. She mixed up dreams and real life. "How did it happen—?" she might ask her mother, before she remembered that it hadn't happened (the Shriners' parade through her bedroom, the elderly gentleman hanging by his heels from her curtain rod like a piece of fruit). Sometimes at night, voices came vividly out of the dark. "Dr. Tull. Dr. Tull," they'd say, urgently, officially. Or, "Six hundred fifty milligrams of quinine sulfate . . ." Her own pulse thudded in her eardrums. She held her hand toward the light from the streetlamp and marveled at how white and bloodless she had become.

When her mother left and Delilah arrived, Jenny got up and returned to work. For a while, she carried herself as gently as a cup of liquid. She kept level and steady, careful not to spill over. But she was fine, she saw; she really was fine. Weekends, her mother and Ezra paid brief visits, or Jenny took Becky down to Baltimore on the train. They both dressed up for these trips and sat very still so as not to muss their clothes. Jenny felt purified, like someone who had been drained by a dangerous fever.

And the following summer, when she could have accepted more lucrative offers in Philadelphia or Newark, she chose Baltimore instead. She joined two older pediatricians, entered Becky in nursery school, and shortly thereafter purchased her Bolton Hill row house. She continued to feel fragile, though. She went on guarding a trembly, fluid center. Sometimes, loud noises made her heart race—her mother speaking her name without warning, or the telephone jangling late at night. Then she would take herself in hand. She would remind herself to draw back, to loosen hold. It seemed to her that the people she admired (one of her partners, who was a wry, funny man named Dan Charles; and her brother Ezra; and her neighbor Leah Hume) had this in common: they gazed at the world from a distance. There was something sheeted about them—some obliqueness that made them difficult to grasp. Dan, for instance, kept up such a steady, easy banter that you never could ask him about his wife, who was forever in and out of mental institutions. And Leah: she could laugh off the repeated failures of her crazy business ventures like so many pratfalls. How untouched she looked, and how untouchable, chuckling to herself and covering her mouth with a shapely, badly kept hand! Jenny studied her; you could almost say she took notes. She was learning how to make it through life on a slant. She was trying to lose her intensity.

"You've changed," her mother said (all intensity herself). "You've grown so different, Jenny. I can't quite put my finger on what's wrong, but *something* is." She wanted Jenny to remarry; she hoped for a dozen grandchildren, at least; she was always after Jenny to get out and mingle, socialize, make herself more attractive, meet some nice young man. What Jenny didn't tell her was, she simply couldn't be bothered with all that. She felt textureless, so that events just slid right off her with no friction whatsoever; and the thought of the heartfelt conversations required by a courtship filled her with impatience.

Then she met Joe with his flanks of children—his padding, his moat, his barricade of children, all in urgent need of her brisk and competent attention. No conversation *there*—she and Joe had hardly found a moment to speak to each other seriously. They were always trying to be heard above the sound of toy trucks and xylophones. She didn't even have time for thinking any more.

"Of course, the material object is nothing," said the priest. He winced at a squeal from the waiting room. "That's unimportant, the least of my concerns. Though it did have some historical value. It was donated, I believe, by the missionary brother of one of our parishioners."

Jenny leaned back against the receptionist's window and touched a hand to her forehead. "Well, I don't . . ." she said. "*What* did you say this was?"

"A rhinoceros foot," said the priest, "in the shape of an umbrella stand. Or an umbrella stand in the shape of a rhinoceros foot. It was an actual rhinoceros foot from . . . wherever rhinoceri come from."

A naked toddler shot out a door like a stray piece of popcorn, pursued by a nurse with a hypodermic needle. The priest stood back to give them room. "We know it was there in the morning," he said. "But at four o'clock, it was gone. And Slevin was in just previously; I'd asked him to come for a chat. Only I was on the phone when he arrived. By the time I'd hung up he was gone, and so was the rhinoceros foot."

Jenny said, "I wonder if his mother had a rhinoceros foot."

"Pardon?" said the priest.

She realized how this must have sounded, and she laughed. "No," she said, "I don't mean *she* had rhinoceros feet . . . oh, Lord . . ."

The priest said, "Dr. Tull, don't you see this is serious? We have a child in trouble here, don't you see that? Don't you think something ought to be done? Where do you *stand*, Dr. Tull?"

Jenny's smile faded and she looked into his face. "I don't know," she said, after a pause. She felt suddenly bereft, as if something were missing, as if she'd given something up. She hadn't *always* been like this! she wanted to tell him. But aloud she said, "I only meant, you see . . . I believe he steals what reminds him of his mother. Hoovers and umbrella stands. Doesn't that make sense?"

"Ah," said the priest.

"What's next, I wonder," Jenny said. She mused for a moment. "Picture it! Grand pianos. Kitchen sinks. Why, we'll have his mother's whole household," she said, "her photo albums and her grade-school yearbooks, her college roommate asleep on our bed and her high school boyfriends in our living room." She pictured a row of dressed-up boys from the fifties, their hair slicked down wetly, their shirts ironed crisply, perched on her couch like mannequins with heart-shaped boxes of chocolates on their knees. She laughed. The priest groaned. A little blue plastic helicopter buzzed across the waiting room and landed in Jenny's hair.

8
THIS REALLY HAPPENED

THE SUMMER before Luke Tull turned fourteen, his father had a serious accident at the factory he was inspecting. A girder swung around on its cable, hit Luke's father and the foreman standing next to him, and swept them both off the walkway and down to the lower level of the factory. The foreman was killed. Cody lived, by some miracle, but he was badly hurt. For two days he lay in a coma. There was a question of brain damage, till he woke and, in his normal, crusty way, asked who the hell was in charge around here.

Three weeks later, he came home by ambulance. His thick black hair had been shaved off one side of his head, where a gauze patch covered the worst of his wounds. His face—ordinarily lean and tanned—was swollen across one cheekbone and turning different shades of yellow from slowly fading bruises. His ribs were taped and an arm and a leg were in casts—the right arm and the left leg, so he couldn't use crutches. He was forced to lie in bed, cursing the game shows on TV. "Fools. Jackasses. Who do they think would be watching this crap?"

Luke's mother, who had always been so spirited, lost something important to the accident. First, in the terrible coma days, she drifted around in a wash of tears—a small, wan, pink-eyed woman. Her red hair seemed drained of color. Luke would say, "Mom?" and she wouldn't hear, would sometimes snatch up her car keys as if mistaking who had called and go tearing off to the hospital again, leaving Luke alone. Even after the coma ended, it didn't seem she came back completely. When Cody was brought home, she sat by his bed for hours saying nothing, lightly stroking one thick vein that ran down the inside of his wrist. She watched the game shows with a tremulous smile. "Jesus, look at them squawk," Cody said disgustedly, and Ruth bent down and laid her cheek against his hand as if he'd uttered something wonderful.

Luke, who had once been the center of her world, now hung around the fringes. It was July and he had nothing to do. They'd only been living here—in a suburb of Petersburg, Virginia—since the end of the school year, and he didn't know any boys his own age. The children on his block were all younger, thin voiced and excitable. It annoyed him to hear their shrieking games of roll-a-bat and the sputtery *ksh! kshew!* of their imaginary rifles. Toddlers were packed into flowered vinyl wading pools which they spent their mornings emptying, measuring cup by measuring cup, till every yard was a sea of mud. Luke could not remember ever being that young. Floating through the icy, white and gold elegance of the rented colonial-style house, he surfaced in various gilt-framed mirrors: someone awkward and unwanted, lurching on legs grown too long to manage, his face past cuteness but not yet solidified into anything better—an oval, fragile face, a sweep of streaky blond hair, a mouthful of braces that made his lips appear irregular and vulnerable. His jeans were getting too short but he had no idea how to go about buying new ones. He was accustomed to relying on his mother for such things. In the old days, his mother had done everything for him. She had got on his nerves, as a matter of fact.

Now he made his own breakfast—Cheerios or shredded wheat—and a sandwich for lunch. His mother cooked supper, but it was something slapped together, not her usual style at all; and mostly she would let Luke eat alone in the kitchen while she and Cody shared a tray in the bedroom. Or if she stayed with Luke, her *talk* was still of Cody. She never asked Luke about himself, no; it was "your daddy" this and "your daddy" that, never a thing but "your daddy." How well he was bearing up, how he'd always borne up, always been so dependable from the earliest time she had known him. "I was not but nineteen when I met him," she said, "and he was thirty years old. I was a homely chit of a girl and he was the handsomest thing you ever saw, so fine mannered and wearing this perfect gray suit. At the time, I was all set to marry Ezra, your daddy's brother. I bet you didn't know that, did you? Oh, I got around, in those days! Then your daddy stepped in. He was brazen as you please. Didn't care how it looked, didn't have an ounce of shame, just moved right in and claimed me for his own. Well, first I thought he was teasing. He could have had anyone, any girl he liked, somebody beautiful even. Then I saw he meant it. I didn't know which way to turn, for I did love your Uncle Ezra, though he was not so . . . I mean, Ezra was a much plainer person, more like me, you would say. But your daddy'd walk into the room and it seemed like, I don't know, the air just came alive, somehow. He put his hands on my shoulders one day and I told him please, I was engaged to marry Ezra, and he said he knew that. He stepped up close and I said really, Ezra was a good, good man, and he said yes, he was;· and we hugged each other like two people sharing some bereavement and I said, 'Why, you're near about my brother-in-law!' and he said, 'Very nearly, yes,' and he kissed me on the lips."

Luke lowered his lashes. He wished she wouldn't talk about such things.

"And if we've had our ups and downs," she said, "well, I just want you to know that it wasn't *his* fault, Luke. Look at me! I'm nothing but a little backwoods Garrett County farm girl, hardly educated. And

I'm not so easy to get along with, either. I'm not so easygoing. You mustn't blame him. Why, once—oh, you were in nursery school, I bet you don't remember this—I packed you up and left him. I told him he didn't love me and never had, only married me to spite his brother, Ezra, that he'd always been so jealous of. I accused him of terrible things, just terrible, and then while he was at work I carried you off to the railroad station and . . . this is funny now when I tell it, but it wasn't then; while we were waiting on the bench a Marine threw up in my pocketbook. Came time to board the train and I just couldn't make myself put my fingers in and get out the tickets, assuming they were still usable; and couldn't bear to reach in for the money to buy more tickets, either. So I called your daddy on the telephone, begged a dime from a nun and said, 'Cody, come and get me; this isn't really what I want to be doing. Oh, Cody,' I said, 'we've got so interwoven; even if you didn't love me at all, now we're so entwined. It's you I have to stay with.' And he left off work and drove down to collect me, all steady and sure in his fine gray suit, nothing like the rest of the world. Don't you remember that? You've forgotten all about it," she said. "It's just as well, I reckon. Luke, when you almost lose a person, everything comes so clear! You see how much he matters, how there's no one the least bit like him; he's irreplaceable. How he always puts us first; I mean, has never, in all his days, left you and me behind when he's off on business, but carts us to every new town he's called to because he won't do like his father, he says: travel about forgetting his own relations. It's not true that he brings us along because he doesn't trust me. He really cares for our welfare. When I think now," she said, "about your daddy kissing me that first time—'Very nearly, yes,' he said. 'Yes, very nearly your brother-in-law,' and kissed me so quiet but definite, insisting, like he wouldn't take no for an answer— why, I see now that's when my *life* began! But at the time I had no notion, didn't grasp the importance. I didn't know back then that one person can have such effect on another."

But if she was changed (if even Luke was changed—fading into someone transparent, he imagined), Cody was absolutely the same. After all, Cody hadn't suffered the strain of that coma; he'd been absent from it. He hadn't worried he would die, once he came to, because it wouldn't occur to him that he was the *type* to die. He'd sailed through the whole experience with his usual combination of nonchalance and belligerence, and now he lay thrashing on his bed wondering when he could get up again. "What I mainly am is mad," he told Luke. "This whole damn business has left me mad as hell. I felt that girder hit, you know that? I really felt it hit, and it hurt, and all the time I was flying through the air I wanted to hit it back, punch somebody; and now it seems I'm still waiting for the chance. When do I get to get even? And don't talk to me about lawsuits, compensation. The only thing I want to do is hit that girder back."

"Mom says would you like some soup," said Luke, wiping his palms nervously down his thighs.

"No, I wouldn't like soup. What's she always trying to feed me for? Listen, Luke. If your grandma calls again today, I want you to tell her I've gone back to work."

"To work?"

"I can't stand to hear her fret on the phone any more."

"But all along," Luke said, "you've been telling her you were too sick for company. Yesterday you were too sick and today you've gone back to *work*? What'll she think?"

"It's nothing to me what she thinks," said Cody. He never sounded very fond of Grandma Tull, who had called from Baltimore every day since the accident. Luke enjoyed her, the little he knew of her, but Cody said looks were deceiving. "She puts on a good front," he told Luke. "You don't know what she's like. You don't know what it was like growing up with her."

Luke felt he did know (hadn't he heard it all a million times?) but his father had got started now and wouldn't be stopped. "Let me give you an example," he said. "Listen, now. This really happened." That was the way he always introduced his childhood. "This really happened," he would say, as if it were unthinkable, beyond belief, but then what followed never seemed so terrible to Luke. "I swear it: your grandma had this friend named Emmaline that she hadn't seen in years. Only friend she ever mentioned. And Emmaline lived in . . . I forget. Anyhow, someplace far away. So one Christmas I saved up the money to buy a Greyhound bus ticket to wherever this Emmaline lived. I slaved and borrowed and *stole* the money, and presented my mother with the ticket on Christmas morning. I was seventeen at the time, old enough to take care of the others, and I said, 'You leave tomorrow, stay a week, and I'll watch over things till you get back.' And you know what she said? Listen; you won't believe this. 'But Cody, honey,' she said. 'Day after tomorrow is your brother's birthday.' "

He looked over at Luke. Luke waited for him to go on.

"See," Cody said, "December twenty-seventh was Ezra's birthday."

"So?" Luke asked.

"So she wouldn't leave her precious boy on his birthday! Not even to visit her oldest, dearest, only friend, that her other boy had given her a ticket for."

"I wouldn't like for Mom to leave me on my birthday, either," Luke said.

"No, no, you're missing the point. She wouldn't leave Ezra, her favorite. Me or my sister, she would surely leave."

"How do you know that?" Luke asked him. "Did you ever try giving her a ticket on *your* birthday? I bet she'd have said the same thing."

"My birthday is in February," Cody said. "Nowhere near any occasion for gift giving. Oh, I don't know why I bother talking to you. You're an only child, that's your trouble. You haven't the faintest idea what I'm trying to get across." And he turned his pillow over and settled back with a sigh.

Luke went out in the yard and threw his baseball against the garage. It thudded and bounced back, shimmering in the sunlight. In the old days, his mother had practiced throwing with him. She had taught him to bat and pitch overhand, too. She was good at sports. He saw glimpses in her, sometimes, of the scatty little tomboy she must once have been. But it had always seemed, when they played ball together, that this was only a preparation for the *real* game, with his father. It was like cramming for an exam. Then on weekends Cody came home and pitched the ball to him and said, "Not bad. Not bad at all," when Luke hit it out of the yard. At these moments Luke was conscious of adding a certain swagger to his walk, a certain swing to his shoulders. He imagined he was growing to be more like his father. Sauntering into the house after practice, he'd pass Cody's parked car and ask, "She still getting pretty good mileage?" He would stand in front of the open refrigerator and swig iced tea directly from the pitcher—something his mother detested. Oh, it was time to put his mother behind him now—all those years of following her through the house, enmeshed in her routine, dragging his toy broom after her big one or leaning both elbows on her dressing table to watch, entranced, as she dusted powder on her freckled nose. The dailiness of women's lives! He knew all he cared to know about it. He was exhausted by the trivia of measuring out the soap flakes, waiting for the plumber. High time to move to his father's side. But his father lay on his back in the bedroom, cursing steadily. "What the hell is the matter with this TV? Why bother buying a Sony if there's no one who will fix it?"

"I'll find us a repairman today," Ruth's new, soft voice floated out.

Ruth wore dresses all the time now because Cody said he was tired of her pantsuits. "Everlasting polyester pantsuits," he said, and it was true she didn't look as stylish as most other women, though Luke wasn't so sure that the pantsuits were to blame. Even after she changed to dresses, something seemed to be wrong. They were too big, or too hard-surfaced, or too shiny; they looked less like clothes than . . . housing, Luke thought. "Is this better?" she asked his father, and she stood hopefully in the doorway, flat on her penny loafers because in Garrett County, she said, they had never learned her to walk in high heels. By then, Cody had recovered from his mood. He said, "Sure, honey. Sure. It's fine." He wasn't *always* evil tempered. It was the strain of lying immobile. It was the constant discomfort. He did make an effort. But then, not two hours later: "Ruth, will you explain why

I have to live in a place that looks like a candy dish? Is it necessary to rent a house where everything is white and gold and curlicued? You think of that as class?"

It was the nature of Cody's job that he worked alone. As soon as he finished streamlining whatever factory had called him in, he moved on. His partner, a man named Sloan, lived in New York City and invented the devices that Cody determined a need for—sorting racks, folding aids, single hand tools combining the tasks of several. Consequently, there were no fellow workers to pay Cody visits, unless you counted that one edgy call by the owner of the factory where he'd had his accident. And they didn't know any of the neighbors. They were on their own, just the three of them. They might have been castaways. No wonder Cody acted so irritable. The only time Luke and his mother got out was once a week, when they went for groceries. Backing her white Mercedes from the garage, Ruth sat erect and alert, not looking behind her, already anxious about Cody. "Maybe I should've made you stay. If he needs to go to the bathroom—"

"He can good and *wait*," Luke said through his teeth.

"Why, Luke!"

"Let him pee in the bed."

"Luke Tull!"

Luke stared out the window.

"It's been hard on you," his mother said. "We've got to find you some friends."

"I don't need friends."

"Everybody needs friends. We don't have a one, in this town. I feel like I'm drying up. Sometimes I wonder," she said, "if this life is really . . ." But she didn't say any more.

When they returned, Cody was pleasant and cheerful, as if he'd made some resolutions in their absence. Or maybe he'd been refreshed by the solitude. "Talked to Sloan," he told Ruth. "He called from New York. I said to him, soon as I get this cast off I'm going to finish up at the factory and clear on out. I can't take much more of this place."

"Oh, good, Cody, honey."

"Bring me my briefcase, will you? I want to jot down some ideas. There's lots I could be doing in bed."

"I picked out some of those pears you like."

"No, no, just my briefcase, and that pen on the desk in my study. I'm going to see if my fingers are up to writing yet."

He told Luke, "Work is what I need. I've been *starved* for work. It's made me a little snappish."

Luke scratched his rib cage. He said, "That's all right."

"You make sure you get a job you enjoy, once you're grown. You've got to enjoy what you're doing. That's important."

"I know."

"Me, I deal with time," said Cody. He accepted a ball-point pen from Ruth. "Time is my favorite thing of all."

Luke loved it when his father talked about time.

"Time is my obsession: not to waste it, not to lose it. It's like . . . I don't know, an object, to me; something you can almost take hold of. If I could just collect enough of it in one clump, I always think. If I could pass it back and forth and sideways, you know? If only Einstein were right and time were a kind of river you could choose to step into at any place along the shore."

He clicked his pen point in and out, frowning into space. "If they had a time machine, I'd go on it," he said. "It wouldn't much matter to me where. Past or future: just out of my time. Just someplace else."

Luke felt a pang. "But then you wouldn't know *me*," he said.

"Hmm?"

"Sure he would," Ruth said briskly. She was opening the latches of Cody's briefcase. "He'd take you with him. Only mind," she told Cody, "if Luke goes too you've got to bring penicillin, and his hay fever pills, and his fluoride toothpaste, you hear?"

Cody laughed, but he didn't say one way or another about taking Luke along.

That was the evening that Cody first got his strange notion. It came about so suddenly: they were playing Monopoly on Cody's bed, the three of them, and Cody was winning as usual and offering Luke a loan to keep going. "Oh, well, no, I guess I've lost," said Luke.

There was the briefest pause—a skipped beat. Cody looked over at Ruth, who was counting her deed cards. "He sounds just like Ezra," he told her.

She frowned at Baltic Avenue.

"Didn't you hear what he said? He said it just like Ezra."

"Really?"

"*Ezra* would do that," Cody told Luke. "Your Uncle Ezra. It was no fun beating him at all. He'd never take a loan and he wouldn't mortgage the least little thing, not even a railroad or the waterworks. He'd just cave right in and give up."

"Well, it's only that . . . you can see that I've lost," Luke said. "It's only a matter of time."

"Sometimes it's more like you're Ezra's child, not mine."

"Cody Tull! What a thought," said Ruth.

But it was too late. The words hung in the air. Luke felt miserable; he had all he could do to finish the game. (He knew his father had never thought much of Ezra.) And Cody, though he dropped the subject, remained dissatisfied in some way. "Sit up straighter," he kept telling Luke. "Don't *hunch*. Sit straight. God. You look like a rabbit."

As soon as he could, Luke said good night and went off to bed.

The following morning, everything was fine again. Cody did some more work on his papers and had another talk with Sloan. Ruth cooked a chicken for a nice cold summer supper. Anytime Luke wandered by, Cody said something cheerful to him: "Why so long in the face?" he'd ask, or, "Feeling bored, son?" It sounded funny, calling Luke "son." Cody didn't usually do that.

They all had lunch in the bedroom—sandwiches and potato salad, like a picnic. The telephone, buried among the sheets, started ringing halfway through the meal, and Cody said not to answer it. It was bound to be his mother, he said. They kept perfectly silent, as if the caller could somehow hear them. After the ringing stopped, though, Ruth said, "That poor, poor woman."

"Poor!" Cody snorted.

"Aren't we awful?"

"You wouldn't call her poor if you knew her better."

Luke went back to his room and sorted through his old model airplanes. His parents' voices drifted after him. "Listen," Cody was telling Ruth. "This really happened. For my mother's birthday I saved up all my money, fourteen dollars. And Ezra didn't have a penny, see . . ."

Luke scrabbled through his wooden footlocker, the one piece of furniture that really belonged to him. It had accompanied all their moves since before he could remember. He was hunting the missing wing of a jet. He didn't find the wing but he did find a leather bag of marbles—the kind he used to like, with spritzy bubbles like ginger ale inside them. And a slingshot made from a strip of inner tube. And a tonette—a dusty black plastic whistle on which, for Mother's Day back in first grade, he'd played "White Coral Bells" along with his classmates. He tried it now: *White coral bells, upon a slender stalk . . .* It returned to him, note by note. He rose and went to his parents' room to play it through to the end. *Lilies of the valley deck my—*

His father said, "I can't stand it."

Luke lowered the tonette.

"Are you doing this on purpose?" Cody asked. "Are you determined to torment me?"

"Huh?"

"Cody, honey . . ." Ruth said.

"You're haunting me, isn't that it? I can't get away from him! I spend half my life with meek-and-mild Ezra and his blasted wooden whistle; I make my escape at last, and now look: here we go again. It's like a conspiracy! Like some kind of plot where someone decided, long before I was born, I would live out my days surrounded by people who were . . . nicer than I am, just naturally nicer without even having to try, people that other people preferred; and everywhere I go there's something, just that goddamn forgiving smile or some demented folk song floating out a window—"

"Cody, Luke will be thinking you have lost your senses," Ruth said.

"And you!" Cody told her. "Look at you! Ah, Lord," he said. "Some people fit together forever, don't they? And you haven't a hope in heaven of prying them apart. Married or not, you've always loved Ezra better than me."

"Cody, what are you *talking* about?"

"Admit it," Cody said. "Isn't Ezra the real, true father of Luke?"

There was a silence.

"You didn't say that. You couldn't have," Ruth told him.

"Admit it!"

"You know you don't seriously believe such a thing."

"Isn't it the truth? Tell me! I won't get angry, I promise."

Luke went back to his room and closed the door.

All that afternoon he lay on his bed, rereading an old horse book from his childhood because he didn't have anything else to do. The story struck him as foolish now, although once he'd loved it. When his mother called him for supper, he walked very firmly into the kitchen. He was going to refuse, absolutely, to eat in the bedroom with Cody any more. But his mother had already set two places at the kitchen table. She sat across from him while he ate, not eating much herself. Luke shoveled in various cold foods and refused to meet her eyes. The fact was that she was stupid. He didn't know when he'd seen such a weak and stupid woman.

After supper he went back to his room and listened to a radio show where people called up a tired-sounding host and offered their opinions. They discussed drunken drivers and battered wives. It grew dark, but Luke didn't turn on the light. His mother tapped hesitantly on his door, paused and left.

Then he must have fallen asleep. When he woke it was darker than ever, and his neck was stiff, and a woman on the radio was saying, "Now, I'm not denying I signed the papers but that was only his fast talk, only him talking me into it. 'Just put your John Doe right here,' he tells me . . ."

"I assume you mean John Hancock," the host said wearily.

"Whatever," said the woman.

Then beneath these voices, murmuring through the wall, came Cody's grumble and Ruth's pale answers. Luke covered his head with his pillow.

He tried to recall his Uncle Ezra. It was several years since they'd met. And even that was such a brief visit, his father taking them away in a huff before they'd got well settled. Finding Ezra was something like hunting through that footlocker; he had to burrow past a dozen other memories, and more came trailing up along with what he was after. He smelled the burned toast in his grandma's kitchen and re-membered Ezra's bedroom, which had once been Ezra's and Cody's together, where boyhood treasures (a football-shaped bookend, a peeling hockey stick) had sat in their places so long that to Ezra, they were invisible. Anything that caught Luke's attention, Ezra had seemed surprised to see. "Oh! Would you like to have that?" he would ask, and when Luke politely declined, not wanting to seem greedy, Ezra said, "Please. I can't think what it's still doing here." His room had been large—a sort of dormitory arrangement, occupying the whole third floor—but its stuffy smell of used sheets and twice-worn clothes had made it seem smaller. There was a lock inside the bathroom door downstairs, Luke recalled, that looked exactly like a little silver cashew; and the bathroom itself was tall and echoing, ancient, cold floored, with a porcelain knob in the tub reading WASTE.

He tried to picture his cousins—Aunt Jenny's children—but only came up with another room: his cousin Becky's ruffled bedroom, with its throng of shabby stuffed animals densely encircling her bed. How could she sleep? he had wondered. But she told him she had no trouble sleeping at all; and whenever she went away to spend the night, she said, she took the whole menagerie in a giant canvas suitcase and set it out first thing around the new bed, even before unpacking her pajamas; and most of her friends did the same. It was Luke's first inkling that girls were different. He was mystified and charmed, and he treated her protectively for the rest of that short visit—though she was a year older than he and half a head taller.

If Ezra were really his father, Luke thought, then Luke could live in Baltimore where houses were dark and deep and secretive. Relatives would surround him—a loving grandma, funny Aunt Jenny, those rafts of cousins. Ezra would let him help out in his restaurant. He would talk about food and how people need to be fed with care; Luke could hear his ambling way of speaking. Yes, now he had it: the memory homed in. Ezra wore a flannel shirt of soft blue plaid, washed into oblivion. His hair was yellow . . . why! It was Luke's kind of yellow, all streaky and layered. And his eyes were Luke's kind of gray, a full shade lighter than Cody's, and his skin had that same golden cast that caused it to blend into his hair almost without demarcation.

Luke let himself believe in some unimaginable moment between Ruth and Ezra, fourteen years ago. He skipped across it quickly to the time when Ezra would arrive to claim him. "You're old enough to be told now, son . . ."

Knitting this scene in the dark, doubling back to correct a false note or racing forward to a good part, Luke forgot himself and took the pillow off his head. Instantly, he heard Cody's voice behind the wall. "Everything I've ever wanted, Ezra got it. Anything in life I wanted.

Even things I thought I had won, Ezra won in the end. And he didn't
even seem to be trying; that's the hell of it."

"You won the damn *Monopoly* games, didn't you?" Luke shouted.

Cody said nothing.

The next morning, Cody seemed unusually quiet. Ruth took him into
the doctor's to get his walking cast—a moment they'd been waiting
for, but Cody didn't act interested now. Luke had to go along to serve
as a crutch. He flinched when Cody first laid his heavy arm cast across
his shoulders; he felt there was some danger hovering. But Cody was
a dead weight, grunting as he walked, evidently thinking about other
matters. He heaved himself into the car and stared bleakly ahead of
him. In the doctor's waiting room, while Luke and his mother read
magazines, Cody just sat empty faced. And after he got his walking
cast, he hobbled back to the car unassisted, ignoring Luke's offer to
help. He fell into bed as soon as they reached home and lay gazing
at the ceiling. "Cody, honey? Remember the doctor said to give that
leg some exercise," Ruth told him.

He didn't answer.

Luke went out to the yard and kicked at the grass a while as if he
were hunting for something. Next door, a cluster of toddlers in their
wading pool stared at him. He wanted to shout, "Turn away! Stop
looking at me; you have no business." But instead it was he who
turned, wandering out of the yard and down the street. More wading
pools; more round-eyed, judging stares. A Welsh corgi, squat and
dignified, bustled down the sidewalk, followed by a lady in a flowing
caftan. "Toulouse! Toulouse!" she called. The heat was throbbing; it
almost breathed. Luke's face became filmed with sweat and his T-shirt
stuck to his back. He kept wiping his upper lip. He passed rows of
colonial houses similar to his, each with some object featured like a
museum piece in the living-room window: a bulbous lamp, a china
horse, a vase of stiff-necked marigolds. (And what did his own window
have? He couldn't recall. He wanted to say a weeping fig tree, but that
was from an apartment they'd rented, three or four towns back.)
Sprinklers spun lazily. It was a satisfaction to stop, from time to time,
and watch a lawn soak up the spangled water drops.

Now here came some busy lady with her baby in a stroller, small
children all around her. He crossed the street to avoid them, took a
right turn, and arrived on Willow Bough Avenue with its whizzing
traffic, discount drugstores, real estate offices and billboards and service
stations. He waited at an intersection, pondering where to go ext. One
of the things about moving so often was, he never really knew where
he was. He believed his sense of direction had been blunted. He couldn't
understand how some people seemed to carry a kind of detailed, internal
map of the town they lived in.

A Trailways bus zipped past him reading BALTIMORE. Imagine hailing it. (Could you hail a Trailways bus?) Imagine boarding it—assuming he had the money, which he didn't—and riding off to Baltimore, arriving at Ezra's restaurant and strolling in. "Here I am." "*There* you are," Ezra would say. Oh, if only he'd brought his money! Another bus passed, but that was a local. Then a gigantic truck drew up, braking for an amber light. Luke, as if obeying orders, stuck out a thumb. The driver leaned across the seat and opened the door on the passenger side. "Hop on in," he told Luke.

NO RIDERS, a label on the window read. None of this was happening. Slowly, like someone being pushed from behind, Luke climbed into the cab. It was filled with loud music and a leathery, sweaty, masculine smell that made him feel instantly comfortable. He slammed the door and settled back. The driver—a knife-faced man, unshaven—squinted up at the traffic light and asked, "Whereabouts you headed, son?"

Luke said, "Baltimore, Maryland."

"Folks know you're going?"

"Sure," said Luke.

The driver shot him a glance.

"Why, my folks . . . *live* in Baltimore," Luke told him.

"Oh, then."

The truck started up again. They rumbled past the shopping mall where Luke's mother went for groceries. A green sign swung overhead, listing points north. "Well," said the driver, adjusting his mirror, "I tell you: I can carry you as far as Richmond. That's where I have to veer west."

"Okay," said Luke.

Even Richmond, after all, was farther than he'd ever meant to go.

On the radio, Billy Swan was singing "I Can Help." The driver hummed along in a creaky voice that never quite hit the right note. His thin gray hair, Luke saw, had recently been combed; it lay close to his skull in damp parallel lines. He held a cigarette between his fingers but he didn't light it. His fingernails were so thick and ridged, they might have been cut from yellow corduroy.

"In the summer of fifty-six," he said, "I was passing along this very road with my wife in a Safeway grocery truck when she commences to go into labor. Not but eight months gone and she proceeds directly into labor. Lord God! I recall to this day. She says, 'Clement, I think it's my time.' Well, I was young then. Inexperienced. I thought a baby came one-two-three. I thought we didn't have a moment to spare. And also, you know what they say: a seven-month baby will turn out good but an eight-month baby won't make it. I can't figure why *that* should be. So anyhow, I put on the brakes. I'm shaking all over. My brake foot is so shaky we're just wobbling down the highway. You see that sign over there? Leading off to the right? See that hospital sign? Well, that is where I taken her. Straight up that there road. I never come by here but what I recall it."

Luke looked politely at the hospital sign, and then swiveled his neck to go on looking after they had passed. It was the only response he could think of.

"Labor lasted thirty-two hours," the driver said. "Safeway thought I'd hijacked their rig."

"Well," said Luke, "but the baby got born okay."

"Sure," the driver told him. "Five-pound girl. Lisa Michelle." He thought a moment. Then he said, "She died later on, though."

Luke cleared his throat.

"Crib death is what they call it nowadays," said the driver. He swerved around a trailer. "Ever hear of it?"

"No, sir, I haven't."

"Sudden crib death. Six months old. Light of my life. Bright as a button, too—loved me to bits. I'd come home and she would just rev right up—wheel her arms and legs like a windmill soon as she set eyes on me. Then she went and died."

"Well, gosh," said Luke.

"Now I got others," the driver said. "Want to see them? Turn down that sun visor over your head."

Luke turned down the visor. A color photo, held in place by a pink plastic clothespin, showed three plain girls in dresses so new and starchy that it must have been Easter Sunday.

"The youngest is near about your age," the driver said. "What are you: thirteen, fourteen?" He honked at a station wagon that had cut too close in front. "They're nice girls," he said, "but I don't know. It's not the same, somehow. Seems like I lost the . . . attachment. Lost the knack of getting attached. I mean, I like them; shoot, I love them, but I just don't have the . . . seems to me I can't get up the energy no more."

A lady on the radio was advertising Chevrolets. The driver switched stations and Barbra Streisand came on, showing off as usual. "But you ought to see my wife!" the driver said. "Isn't it amazing? She loves those kids like the very first one. She just started in all over. I don't know what to make of her. I look at her and I can't believe it. 'Dotty,' I say, 'really it all comes down to nothing. It's not for anything,' I say. 'Dotty, how come you can go *on* like this?' See, me, I never bounced back so good. I pass that hospital road and you know? I halfway believe if I made the turnoff, things would be just like before. Dotty'd be holding my hand, and Lisa Michelle would be waiting to be born."

Luke rubbed his palms on his jeans. The driver said, "Well, now. Listen to me! Just gabbing along; I guess you think I talk too much." And for the rest of the trip he was quiet, only whistling through his teeth when the radio played a familiar song.

He said goodbye near Richmond, going out of his way to leave Luke at a ramp just past a rest center. "You wait right here and you'll get a ride in no time," he said. "Here they're traveling slow anyhow, and won't mind stopping." Then he raised his hand stiffly and drove off. From a distance, his truck looked as bright and chunky as a toy.

But it seemed he took some purpose with him, some atmosphere of speed and assurance. All at once . . . what was Luke *doing* here? What could he be thinking of? He saw himself, alone in the fierce white glare of the sun, cocking his thumb at an amateurish angle on a road in the middle of nowhere. He couldn't even visualize how far he had to go. (He'd never done well in geography.) Although it was hot—the peak of the afternoon, by now—he wished for a windbreaker: protection. He wished for his billfold, not so much for the small amount of money it held as for the i.d. card that had come with it when he bought it. If he were killed on this road, how would they know whom to notify? He wondered if—homeless, parentless—he would have to wear these braces on his teeth for the rest of his life. He pictured himself as an old man, still hiding a mouthful of metal whenever he smiled.

Then an out-of-date, fin-tailed car stopped next to him and the door swung open. "Need a lift?" the driver asked. In the back, a little tow-headed boy bounced up and down, calling, "Come on! Come on! Get in and have a ride. Come on in and ride with us!"

Luke got in. He found the driver smiling at him—a suntanned man in blue jeans, with deep lines around his eyes. "My name's Dan Smollett," he said. "That's Sammy in the back seat."

"I'm Luke."

"We're heading toward D.C. That do you any good?"

"It's fine," said Luke. "I guess," he added, still unsure of his geography. "I'm on my way to Baltimore."

"Baltimore!" said Sammy, still bouncing. "Daddy, can we go to Baltimore?"

"We have to go to Washington, Sammy."

"Don't we know someone in Baltimore too? Kitty? Susie? Betsy?"

"Now, Sammy, settle down, please."

"We're looking up Daddy's old girlfriends," Sammy told Luke.

"Oh," said Luke.

"We just came from Raleigh and saw Carla."

"No, no, Carla was in Durham," his father told him. "It was DeeDee you saw in Raleigh."

"Carla was nice," said Sammy. "She was the best of the bunch. You would've liked her, Luke."

"I would?"

"It's too bad she was married."

"Sammy, Luke doesn't want to hear about our private lives."

"Oh, that's all right," said Luke. He wasn't sure what he was hearing, anyhow.

They were back on the freeway by now, staying in the slow lane—perhaps because of the grinding noise that came whenever Dan accelerated. Luke had never been in a car as old as this one. Its interior was a dusty gray felt, the floors awash in paper cups and Frito bags. The glove compartment—doorless—spilled out maps that were splitting at the seams, along with loose change, Lifesavers, and miniature tractors and dump trucks. In the rear, Sammy bounced among blankets and grayish pillows. "Settle down," his father kept saying, but it didn't do any good. "He gets a little restless, along about afternoon," Dan told Luke.

"How long have you been traveling?" Luke asked.

"Oh, three weeks or so."

"Three weeks!"

"We left just after summer school. I'm a high school English teacher; I had to teach this grammar course first."

"Lookit here," Sammy said, and on his next bounce upward he thrust a wad of paper into Luke's face. Evidently, someone had been chewing on it. It was four sheets, mangled together, bearing typed columns of names and addresses. "Daddy's old girlfriends," Sammy said.

Luke stared.

"They are not," said his father. "Really, Sammy." He told Luke, "That's my graduating class in high school. Boys *and* girls. Last year they had a reunion; I didn't go but they sent us this address list."

"Now we're looking up the girls," Sammy said.

"Not all the girls, Sammy."

"The girls that you went out with."

"My wife is divorcing me," Dan told Luke. He seemed to think this explained everything. He faced forward again, and Luke said, "Oh." Another rest center floated by, a distant forest of Texaco and Amoco signs. A moving van honked obligingly when Sammy gave the signal out the window. Sammy squealed and bounced all the harder—a spiky mass of bones and striped T-shirt, flapping shorts, torn sneakers.

"What year are you in school?" Dan asked Luke.

"I'm going into ninth grade."

"Read any Hemingway? *Catcher in the Rye?* What are they giving you to read?"

"I don't know yet. I'm new," said Luke.

He could easily picture Dan as a teacher. He would wear his jeans in the classroom. He'd be one of those casual, comradely types that Luke had never quite trusted. Better to have him in suit and tie; at least then you knew where you stood.

"In Washington," Sammy said, "there's *two* girls, Patty and Lena."

"Don't say girls, say women," Dan told him.

"Patty Sears and Lena Sparrow."

"I'm better on the S's," Dan said to Luke. "They were in my homeroom."

"Lena we hear is separated," Sammy said.

Luke said, "But what do you do when you visit? What is there to do?"

"Oh, sit around," Sammy said. "Stay a few days if they ask us. Play with their dogs and their cats and their kids. Most of them do have kids. And husbands."

"Well, then," said Luke. "If they've got husbands . . ."

"But we don't know that till we get there. Do we," Sammy said.

"Sammy's a little mixed up," Dan said. "It's not as though we're hunting replacements. We're just traveling. This divorce has come as a shock and I'm just, oh, traveling back. I'm visiting old friends."

"But only *girl* friends," Sammy pointed out.

"They're girls I used to get along fine with. Not sweethearts, necessarily. But they liked me; they thought I was fine. Or at least, they seemed to. I assumed they did. *I* don't know. Maybe they were just acting polite. Maybe I was a mess all along."

Luke couldn't think what to say.

"So listen!" Dan told him. "You read *The Great Gatsby* yet?"

"I don't think so."

"How about *Lord of the Flies?* You get to *Lord of the Flies?*"

"I haven't read anything," said Luke. "I've been moved around a lot; anyplace I go they're doing *Silas Marner.*"

This seemed to throw Dan into some kind of depression. His shoulders sagged and he said no more.

Sammy finally stopped bouncing and sat back with a *Jack and Jill*. Pages turned, rattling in the hot wind that blew through the car. On the seat between Dan and Luke, Dan's address list fluttered. It didn't seem very long. Four or five sheets of paper, two columns to a sheet; it would be used up in no time. Luke said, "Um . . ."

Dan looked over at him.

"You must have gone to college," Luke said.

"Yes."

"Or even graduate school."

"Just college."

"Don't you have some addresses from there?"

"College isn't the same," said Dan. "I wouldn't be going far enough back. Why," he said, struck by a thought, "college is where I met my wife!"

"Oh, I see," Luke said.

Outside Washington, Dan stopped the car to let him off. On the horizon was a haze of buildings that Dan said was Alexandria. "Alexandria, Virginia?" Luke asked. He didn't understand what that had to do with Washington. But Dan, who seemed in a hurry, was already glancing in his side-view mirror. Sammy hung out the window calling, "Bye, Luke! When will I see you again? Will you come and visit when we find a place? Write me a letter, Luke!"

"Sure," said Luke, waving. The car rolled off.

By now it must be four o'clock, at least, but it didn't seem to Luke that he felt any cooler. His eyes ached from squinting in the sunlight. His hair had grown stringy and stiff. Something about this road, though—the foreign smells of tar and diesel fuel, or the roar of traffic— made him believe for the first time that he really was getting somewhere. He was confident he'd be picked up sooner or later. He thumbed a while, walked a few yards, stopped to thumb again. He had turned to begin another walk when a car slammed on its brakes, veering to the shoulder in front of him. "For God's sake," a woman called. "Get in this instant, you hear?"

He opened the door and got in. It was a Dodge, not nearly as old as Dan's car but almost as worn-looking, as if it had been used a great deal. The woman inside was plump and fortyish. Her eyes were swollen and tears had streaked her cheeks, but he trusted her anyhow; you'd think she was his mother, the way she scolded him. "Are you out of your mind? Do you want to get killed? Do you know the kind of perverts in this world? Make sure your door's shut. *Lock* it, dammit; we're not in downtown Sleepy Hollow. Fasten your seat belt. Hook up your shoulder harness."

He was happy to obey. He adjusted some complicated kind of buckle while the woman, sniffling, ground the gears and shot back into traffic. "What's your name?" she asked him.

"Luke."

"Well, Luke, are you a total idiot? Does your mother know you're hitching rides? Where are your parents in all of this?"

"Oh, ah, Baltimore," he said. "I don't guess you would be going there."

"God, no, what would I want with Baltimore?"

"Well, where *are* you going?"

"I don't know," she told him.

"You don't know?"

He looked at her. The tears were streaming down her cheeks again. "Um, maybe—" he said.

"Oh, relax. Never mind. I'll take you on to Baltimore."

"You will?"

"It's better than circling the Beltway forever."

"Golly, thanks," he said.

"They're letting infants out on their own these days."

"I'm not an infant."

"Don't you read the papers? Sex crimes! Muggings! Murders! Things that make no sense."

"So what? I've been traveling on my own a *long* time. Years," he said. "Ever since I was born, almost."

"For all you know," she told him, "I could be holding you for ransom."

This startled a laugh out of him. She glanced over and gave a sad smile. There was something reassuring about the comfortable mound of her stomach, the denim skirt riding up her stocky legs, the grayish-white tennis shoes. Periodically, she swabbed at the tip of her nose with her knuckles. He noticed that she wore a wedding ring, and had worn it for so long it looked embedded in her finger.

"Just two or three miles ahead, not a month ago," she said, "a boy in a sports car stopped to pick up a girl and she smashed in his skull with a flashlight, rolled him down an embankment, and drove away in his sports car."

"That proves it's you doing something dangerous, not me," he pointed out. (How easy it was to fall into the bantering, argumentative tone reserved for mothers!) "What did you pick me up for? I could be planning to kill you."

"Oh, indeed," she said, sniffling again. "You wouldn't happen to have a Kleenex on you, by any chance?"

"No, sorry."

"I'd never stop for just anyone," she told him. "Only if they're in danger—I mean young girls alone, or infants like you."

"I am not an—"

"Yesterday it was a girl in short shorts, can you believe it? I told her; I said, 'Honey, you're inviting trouble, dressed like that.' Day before, it was a twelve-year-old boy. He said he'd been robbed of his bus fare and had to get home as best he could. Day before that—"

"What, you drive here every day?"

"Most days."

He looked out the window at the vans and oil tankers, interstate buses, cars with their overloaded luggage racks. "I had sort of thought this was a long-*range* highway," he said.

"Oh, no. Heavens, no. No, I live right nearby," she told him.

"Then what are you driving around for?"

Her chin crumpled in. "None of your business," she said.

"Oh."

"What it is, you see, I generally do this from two or three in the afternoon till suppertime. Sometimes I go to Annapolis, sometimes off in Virginia someplace. Sometimes just round and round the Beltway. It all depends," she said. She tossed him a look, as if expecting him to ask what it all depended on, but he had been insulted and said nothing. She sighed. "Two or three o'clock is when my daughter wakes up. My daughter is fourteen years old. Just about your age, right? How old are you?"

He drummed his fingers and looked out the window.

"In the summer, she sleeps forever. My husband says, 'Jeepers, Mag.' He says, 'Why do you let her sleep so late?' Well, I'll tell you why. It's because she's impossible. Truly impossible. I mean, it isn't believable that she could be so awful. She comes downstairs in her bathrobe, yawning. Finds me in the kitchen. Says, 'Well, Ma, I see you're wearing your insecticide perfume again. DDT Number Five.' Then she floats away. Leaving me sniffing my wrists and wondering. I say, 'Liddie, are you going to clean your room today?' and she says, 'Listen to you, sniping and griping; you sound exactly like your mother.' I make a little joke; she says, 'Very funny, Ma. Ha ha. The big comedian.' I find she's stolen my best lace bra that I only wear on my anniversary and she flings it back all grimy at the seams: 'Take it, who wants it, it's too flat-chested anyhow.' To my face, she calls me a bitch, says I'm fat and homely, says she hates me, and I say, 'Listen here, young lady, it's time we got a few things straight,' but all she does is yawn and start chewing one of those plastic price-tag strings off the sleeve of her blouse. I tell my husband, 'Speak to her,' so he says, 'Liddie, *you* know how your mother gets. Why do you upset her?' I say, 'How I get? What do you mean, how I get?' and before you know, it's him and me fighting, which may have been her plan all along. Division. Disruption. Chaos. That's what she enjoys. She's got this boyfriend, treats him terribly. Finally he broke up with her, and she cried all night and asked a hundred times, 'Why did I act like I did? What can I do to change his mind?' I told her to be honest, just phone him and say she didn't know what had got into her; so next morning she phoned, and they made up, and everything was wonderful and she came and thanked me for my good advice. Her life was back in order, it looked like. So she sat at the table a while, calm as I've seen her. Then she started swinging her foot. Then she started picking her fingernails. Then she went and phoned her boyfriend again. Said, 'Roger, I didn't want to tell you this but I thought it's time you knew. The doctor says I'm dying of leukemia.' "

Luke laughed. She looked over at him innocently, but he noticed a wry, proud twist at the corners of her mouth. "Around two or three o'clock," she said, "I get in my car and start driving. At first, I'm talking out loud. You ought to see me. 'I'm never coming back,' I say. I'm cursing through my teeth; I'm honking at crippled old ladies. 'That little wretch, that pest, that spoiled brat,' I say. 'She'll be sorry!' I speed along—oh, you ought to see my traffic record! One more point on my license and I'll have to take that Saturday course on the evils of reckless driving; have to watch that movie where the lady ends up decapitated. Well, at least it'll get me out of the house. I sling the car around and don't let other cars ahead of me and I picture how my husband will come home and say, 'Liddie? Where is your mother? What did you *do* to her, Liddie?' and Liddie will feel just awful . . . but then I think of my husband. I have a really nice husband. It's not him I want to leave. And I wonder if I could sneak back home at night and tell him, 'Psst! Let's *both* leave. Let's elope,' I'll say. But I know he wouldn't do it. He's not as much involved. She annoys him but he's not around enough to make any serious mistakes with her. That's what kills me: making mistakes. Overreacting, letting her get to me . . . oh, I can think of so many! You could say that what I'm leaving behind is my own poor view of me, right? So then I start driving slower. I start remembering things. I think of Liddie when she was small: she always stood so straight. You could pick her out of a crowd by her straight little back. And for one whole year she would only eat with chopsticks. Click-click against her plate . . . you ought to have seen the mess! But I didn't mind. In those days, she liked me a lot. I was a really good mother, and she liked me."

"Maybe she *still* likes you," Luke said doubtfully.

"No," said the woman. "She doesn't."

They passed a sign for Baltimore. The countryside seemed endlessly the same—fields of high grass, then the backsides of housing developments with clotheslines and motorcycles and aboveground, circular swimming pools, then fields of high grass again, as if the scenery came around regularly on a giant conveyor belt.

"What it is," said the woman, "it's like I'm driving till I find her past self. You know? And *my* past self. Then mile by mile, I simmer down. I let up on the gas a bit more. So by suppertime, I'm ready to come home again."

Luke checked the clock on her dashboard. It was four thirty-five.

"Tonight I'll just fix a tuna salad," she said.

"Well, I appreciate your doing this."

"It's nothing," she said, and she gave a final swipe to her nose.

By five o'clock, they had reached the outskirts of Baltimore. It was something like entering a piece of machinery, Luke thought—all sooty and cluttered and churning. The woman seemed used to it; she drove without comment. "Now, tell me what to do after Russell Street," she said.

"Ma'am?"

"How do I find your house?"

"Oh," he said, "why don't you just drop me off downtown."

"Where downtown?"

"Anyplace will do."

She looked over at him.

He said, "I live so near, I mean . . ."

"Near to where?"

"Why, to anywhere."

"Now, listen, Luke," she said. "I'm getting a very odd feeling here. I want to know exactly where your parents are."

He wondered what she would do if he told her he had to look them up in the telephone book. He'd been away so long, he would say, at summer camp or someplace, the address had just slipped his . . . no. But the fact was, he had never known Ezra's street address. It was just a house they arrived at, Cody driving, Luke sitting in back.

"The thing of it is," he said, "they're both at work. They own this restaurant, the Homesick Restaurant. Maybe you could drop me off at the restaurant."

"Where is that?"

"Ah . . ."

"There is no such place, is there," she said. "I knew it! Homesick Restaurant, indeed."

"There is! Believe me," he said. "But it's new. They just did buy it, and I haven't been there yet."

"Look it up," she told him.

She stopped so suddenly, he was glad he'd fastened his seat belt. A telephone booth stood beside them. "Go on! Look it up," she told him. She must have thought she was calling his bluff.

Luke said, "All right, I will."

Then in the phone booth—the old, fully enclosed kind, a glass and aluminum boxful of heat—he ran a finger past *Homeland Racquet Club*, *Homeseekers Realty*, and found himself so surprised by *Homesick Restaurant* that it might have been a bluff after all. "It's on St. Paul Street," he said when he came back to the car. "You can drop me off anywhere; I'll find the number."

But no, she had to take him to the doorstep, though it meant a good deal of doubling back because St. Paul, it turned out, was one-way and she kept miscalculating the cross streets. When she parked in front of the restaurant, she said, "Well, I'll be! It exists."

"Thank you for the ride," Luke said.

She peered at him. "Are you going to be all right, Luke?" she asked.

"Of course I am."

"And you're certain your parents are here."

"Of course they are."

But she waited, anyhow. (It reminded him of the grade-school parties given by his classmates—his mother making sure he got in before she drove away.) He tried the restaurant's door and found it locked. He would have to go around to the rear. The woman leaned out her window and called, "What's the trouble, Luke?"

"I forgot, I have to use the kitchen entrance."

"What if that's locked, too?"

"It isn't."

"You listen, Luke," she called to him. "Everything is changing; things aren't safe like in the old days. Every alley in this city is full of muggers, are you hearing what I say? Every doorway and vacant building, Luke, every street in Baltimore."

He waved and disappeared. A moment later he heard her car take off again—but reluctantly, without its usual verve, as if she were still absorbed in her catalogue of dangers.

He knew the restaurant so well, he must have carried its image constantly within him: its clatter of pans and crash of china, smell of cut celery simmering in butter, broom-shaped bundles of herbs dangling from the rafters, gallon jars of wrinkly Greek olives, bushel baskets of parsley, steaming black kettles watched devotedly by a boy no older than Luke. Beyond the kitchen, hardly separate from it, stretched the dining room with its white-draped tables and dusty sunbeams. There were so many decorations in the dining room—gifts and mementos, accumulated over the years—that Luke was always reminded of someone's home, one of those teeming family houses where kindergarten drawings are taped above the mantel and then forgotten. He recognized the six-foot collage of Ezra's hearts-of-palm salad, presented by an artist who often ate here, and he saw the colored paper chain that he and his cousins had festooned around a light fixture for some long-ago Christmas dinner. (Ezra had never taken it down, though the dinner had broken off in a quarrel and the chain was now brittle and faded.) Luke knew that in one corner, out of his line of vision, sat a heavy antique bicycle that Ezra had bought in a Timonium flea market. MERCURIO'S CULINARY DELICACIES was lettered importantly across its wooden basket, which was filled with frosty glass pears and bananas contributed by a customer. Astride the bicycle stood a cardboard Marilyn Monroe with her dress blowing up—the prank of unknown persons, but no one had ever removed her and Marilyn rode on, her neck creased nearly to the breaking point, her smile growing paler season by season and her accordion-pleated skirt curling at the edges.

Hot, flushed workers darted around the kitchen, intent on their private tasks, weaving between the others like those Model T's in silent comedies—*zip!*, just missing, never once colliding, their paths crisscrossing but miraculously slipping past disaster. Luke stood in the doorway unnoticed. His trip had been such a process in itself; he had almost lost sight of his purpose. What was he doing here, anyhow? But then he saw Ezra. Ezra was piling biscuits in a crude rush basket. He wore not the blue plaid shirt that Luke remembered—which was flannel, after all, unsuitable for summer—but a chambray shirt with the sleeves rolled up. He thoughtfully set each biscuit in its place, his large, blunt hands deliberate. Luke made his way across the kitchen. He was

surprised by a flash of shyness. His heart was beating too fast. He
arrived in front of Ezra and said, "Hi."

Ezra looked up, still thoughtful. "Hi," he said.

He didn't know who this was.

Luke was stricken, at first. Then he began to feel pleased. Why, he
must have changed immeasurably! He'd shot up a foot; his voice was
getting croaky; he was practically a man. And there was some safety,
a kind of shield, in Ezra's flat gaze. Luke rearranged his plans. He
squared his shoulders. "I'd like a job," he said firmly.

Ezra grew still. "Luke?" he said.

"If that boy over there can tend the kettles—" Luke was saying. He
stopped. "Pardon?"

"It's Cody's Luke. Isn't it."

"How'd you guess?"

"I could tell when you did your shoulders that way, just like your
dad, just exactly like your dad. How funny! And something about the
tone of your voice, all set to do battle . . . well, Luke!" He shook
Luke's hand very hard. His fingers had a sandy feel from the biscuits.
"Where are your parents? Back at the house?"

"I'm here on my own."

"On your own?" Ezra said. He was smiling genially, uncertainly, like
someone hoping to understand a joke. "You mean, with nobody else?"

"I wanted to ask if I could stay with you."

Ezra stopped smiling. "It's Cody," he said.

"Excuse me?"

"Something's happened to him."

"Nothing's happened."

"I should have gone down; I knew I should. I shouldn't have let
him stop me. The accident was worse than they let on."

"No! He's fine."

Ezra surveyed him for a long, silent moment.

"He's already got his walking cast," Luke told him.

"Yes, but his other wounds, his head?"

"Everything's okay."

"You swear it?"

"Yes! Gosh."

"See, I don't have any other brothers," Ezra said.

"I swear. I cross my heart," said Luke.

"Then where is he?"

"He's in Virginia," said Luke. "I left him there. I ran away."

Ezra thought this over. A waitress sidled past him with a tray of
delicately clinking, trembling glasses.

"I didn't plan to," Luke told him. "But he said to me . . . see, he
said . . ."

Oh, there was no point in telling Ezra what Cody had said. It was nonsense, one of those remarks that pop up out of nowhere. And here was Luke, much too far from home, faltering under his uncle's kindly gaze. "I can't explain," he said.

But just as if he *had* explained, Ezra said, gently, "You mustn't take it to heart. He didn't mean it. He wouldn't hurt you for anything in the world."

"I know that," Luke said.

On the telephone with Ruth, Ezra was jocular and brotherly, elaborately casual, playing down what had happened. "Now, Ruth, I'm sitting here looking straight at him and he's perfectly all right . . . police? What for? Well, call them back, tell them he's safe and sound. A lot of fuss over nothing, tell them."

Luke listened, smiling anxiously as if his mother could see him. He laced the spirals of the telephone cord between his fingers. They were in Ezra's little office behind the kitchen. Ezra sat at a desk piled with cookbooks, bills, magazines, a pot of chives, a copper pan with a cracked enamel lining, and a framed news photo of two men in aprons holding an entire long fish on a platter.

Then evidently, Cody took over the phone. Ezra sounded more serious now. "We could maybe keep him a while," he said. "We'd like to have him visit. I hope you'll let him." In the directness and soberness of his tone, even in his short sentences, Luke read a kind of caution. He worried that Cody was shouting on the other end of the line; he dropped the cord and wandered away, pretending to be interested in the books in Ezra's bookcase. He felt embarrassed for his father. But there must not have been any shouting after all; for Ezra said serenely, "All right, Cody. Yes, I can understand that."

When he'd hung up, he told Luke, "They'll be here as soon as possible. He'd rather come get you now, he said."

Luke felt a little notch of dread beginning in his stomach. He wondered how angry his father was. He wondered how he could have thought of doing this—coming all this distance! So alone! It seemed like something he had floated through in a dream.

His grandmother's house still had its burned-toast smell, its dusky corners, its atmosphere of secrecy. If you moved in here, Luke thought, wouldn't you go on finding unexpected cubbyholes and closets for weeks or even months afterward? (Yes, imagine moving in. Imagine sharing the cozy living room, Grandma's peaceful kitchen.) His grandmother skittered around him, adding tiny dishes of food to what was already on the table. Ezra kept telling her, "Mother, take it easy. Don't fuss so." But Luke enjoyed the fuss. He liked the way she would stop in the midst of preparing something to come running over and cup his face. "Look at you! Just look!" She was shorter than he was, now. And she had aged a great deal, or else he'd been too young before to notice. There was something scratchy and flyaway about her little screwed-tight topknot, once blonde but now colorless, and her face sectioned deeply by pockets of lines and her wrinkled, spotted hands. He saw how much she loved him, purely from her hungry touch on his cheeks, and he wondered how his father could have misjudged her so.

"It's not right that your parents just come and take you back," she told him. "We'll make them stay. We'll just make them. I'll change the sheets in Jenny's old room. You can have the guest room. Oh, Luke! I wouldn't have known you. I wouldn't have dreamed it was you if I'd seen you on the street; it's been that long. Though I would have said . . . yes, I would have thought to myself as I passed, 'My, that child reminds me of my Cody years ago; doesn't he? Just fairer haired, is all.' I would have had this little pang and then forgotten, and then later maybe, making tea at home, I'd think, 'Wait now, something was disturbing me back there . . .'"

She tried to pour a bowl of leftover green beans into a saucepan but missed, and slopped most of the liquid onto the counter, and swabbed it with wads of paper towels while laughing at herself. "What an old lady! What a silly old lady, you're thinking. My eyesight isn't what it used to be. No, no, Ezra, I can manage, dear."

"Mother, why don't you let me take over?"

"I can certainly manage in my own kitchen, Ezra," she said. "Wouldn't you like to go back to the restaurant? No telling what those people of yours are up to."

"You just want to have Luke to yourself," Ezra teased her.

"Oh, I admit it! I admit it!"

She turned on the flame beneath the saucepan. "Everything is coming together," she told Luke. "I've been so worried, just sick with worry, picturing Cody in pain and longing to go to him, and of course he wouldn't let me; he's been like that ever since he was a baby, so . . . thorny, so bristly, just always has his back up. And now a little trouble or something—no, don't look so uneasy! I won't ask any questions, I promise; Ezra told me; it's none of our business, but . . . a little trouble of some kind brings you here to us, I don't know, maybe an argument? One of Cody's tempers?"

"*Mother,*" said Ezra.

"And so," she went on hastily, "we get to see him after all. He's really going to show himself. But, Luke. Be truthful. He isn't, he's not . . . scarred or anything, is he? His face, I mean. He hasn't got any disfiguring scars."

"Just bruises," said Luke. "Nothing that'll last. In fact," he added, "they're mostly gone by now."

It surprised him to find that he had held on to the picture of a broken Cody all this time, when really the bruises had faded, come to think of it, and the swellings had disappeared and the hair had almost completely grown over his head wound.

"He always was so handsome," Pearl said. "It was part of his identity."

Ezra moved around the table, setting out plates and silverware. The saucepan hissed on the stove. Luke sat down on a kitchen chair and tipped back against a radiator. Its sharply sculptured ribs and tall pipes made him think of old-fashioned, comforting places—a church he'd visited with a kindergarten friend, for instance, or his second-grade classroom, where once, when a snowstorm started during lunch hour, he had imagined a blizzard developing and keeping all the children snugly marooned for days, drinking cups of soup sent up from the cafeteria.

After supper, he and Pearl watched TV while Ezra went back to check the restaurant. Pearl kept the living room completely dark, lit only by the flickering blue TV screen. Both the front windows were open and they could hear the noises from the street—a game of prisoner's base, a Good Humor bell, a woman calling her children. Around nine o'clock, when the twilight had finally given way to night and the stuffy air had cooled some, Luke caught the distinctive, tightly woven hum of a Mercedes drawing up to the curb. He tensed. Pearl, who wouldn't have recognized the sound, went on placidly watching TV. "Who's that, dear?" she asked him, but it was some actor she referred to; she was peering at the television set. There were footsteps across the porch. "Eh?" she said. "Already?" She rose, fumbling first for the arms of her chair in two or three blind passes. She opened the front door and said, "Cody?"

Cody stood looming, larger than Luke had expected, his arm and leg casts glowing whitely in the dark. "Hello, Mother," he said.

"Why, Cody, let me look at you! And Ruth: hello, dear. Cody, are you all right? I can't make out your face. Are you really feeling better?"

"I'm fine," Cody told her. He kissed her cheek and then limped in.

"Hey, Dad," Luke said, rising awkwardly.

Cody said, "May I ask what you thought you were up to?"

"Well, I don't know . . ."

"Don't know! Is that all you have to say? You scared the hell out of us! Your mother's been beside herself."

"Oh, honey, we were so worried!" Ruth cried. She pulled him close and kissed him. Her dress—a magenta polyester that she wore on special occasions—crumpled its sharp ruffles against his chest. He smelled her familiar, grassy smell that he'd never really noticed before.

"We near about lost our minds," Ruth told Pearl. "I believe I must've aged a quarter-century. I felt if I looked out that same front window one more time I'd go mad, go stark, raving mad—same old curve in the road, same old sidewalk, empty. You just don't know."

"I do know. I do know," said Pearl.

She was feeling for the switch to a lamp that sat on a table. The silk shade rustled and tilted. Then Ezra arrived in the door. "Cody?" he said. "Is that you?" He strode in fast and first encountered Ruth— almost ran her down—and seized her hand and pumped it. "Good to see you, Ruth," he said. Meanwhile, Cody found the switch for his mother and turned the lamp on. It was coincidental; he was only being helpful, but Luke felt he'd turned on the lamp to *examine* them: Ruth and Ezra, face to face. Ezra blinked in the sudden light and then gave Cody a bear hug. Cody stood unresisting. "How's your arm? How's your leg?" Ezra asked. "What, no crutches?"

Cody went on studying Ruth and Ezra. "He says he can't use them," said Ruth. "He says with his opposite arm in a cast . . ." She reached out and smoothed Luke's T-shirt, which didn't need smoothing. She pushed his hair off his forehead. "And now that he's got this walking case . . ." she said absently. "Oh, Luke, sweetheart, didn't you think you'd be missed?"

Cody turned away and sank into an armchair. "Would you two like some iced tea?" Pearl asked.

"No, thanks," said Cody.

"Or coffee? A nice cup of coffee?"

"No! God. Nothing," said Cody.

Luke expected Pearl to look hurt, but she only gave Cody a curiously satisfied smile. "You always were a grump when you weren't feeling well," she told him.

In fact, how surprising this whole visit was!—low-keyed and uneventful, even boring. Luke started out sitting rigidly erect, but gradually he relaxed and let his attention drift to a variety show on TV. The grown-ups murmured around him without any emphasis, discussing money. Cody wanted Pearl to get a new furnace; he would pay for it, he said. Pearl said she had a little savings, but Cody kept insisting, as if there were something gratifying, something triumphant in buying a person a furnace. Oh, money, money, money. You'd think they could come up with some more interesting subject.

Luke pressed a lever in his armchair and found himself flung back, his feet raised suddenly on some sort of footrest. Now Pearl was asking where they would go after Petersburg, and Cody was saying he didn't know; Sloan and he were hoping to take on this cosmetics firm down in . . . His reasonable tone of voice made Luke feel hoodwinked, betrayed. Why, all this time he'd been hearing such terrible tales! He'd been told of such ill will and bitterness! But Cody and Pearl conversed pleasantly, like any civilized adults. They discussed whether the North or the South was a better place to live. They had a mild, dull, uninvested sort of argument about it, till it emerged that Pearl was assuming Baltimore was North and Cody was assuming it was South. She asked if this new factory might be as dangerous as the last one. "*Any* place is dangerous," said Cody, "if idiots are running it."

"Cody, I worry so," she told him. "If you knew how frantic I've been! Hearing my oldest, my firstborn son is in critical condition and I'm not allowed to come see him."

"Critical condition! I'm walking around, aren't I?"

"The walking *wounded*," she said, and she threw her hands up. "Isn't it ironic? I'd always thought disasters were . . . lower class. I would read these hard-luck stories in the paper: lady evicted when she's trying to raise the seven children of her daughter who was shot to death in a bar, and one of the children's retarded and another has to be taken for dialysis so many times per week by city bus, transferring twice . . . well, of course I feel sorry for such people but also, I don't know, impatient, as if they'd brought it on themselves some way. There's a limit, I want to tell them; only so much of life is luck. But now look: my eyesight's poorly and my oldest son's had a serious accident and *his* son's run away from home for reasons we're not told, and I haven't seen my daughter in weeks because she's all tied up with her little girl who's got that disease, what's it called, Anor Exia—"

"How's Becky doing, anyhow?" Cody asked, and Luke had an image of Cody's reaching into a wild snarl of strings and tugging on the one short piece that wasn't all tangled with the others.

"No one knows," Pearl said, rocking.

Ruth massaged her forehead, which had the strained, roughened look it always got after a difficult day. Ezra laughed at something on TV. Cody, who was watching the two of them, sighed sharply and turned back to his mother.

"We'd better be going," he told her.

She straightened. "What?" she said. "You're leaving?"

"We've got a long drive."

"But that's exactly why you're staying!" she told him. "Rest tonight. Start fresh in the morning."

"We can't," said Cody.

"Why can't you?"

"We have to . . . ah, feed the dog."

"I didn't know you had a dog."

"A Doberman."

"But Dobermans are vicious!"

"That's why we better hurry back and feed him," Cody said. "Don't want him eating up the neighbors."

He reached out a hand toward Luke, and Luke clambered off the reclining chair to help him to his feet. When Cody's fingers closed on his, Luke imagined some extra tightness—a secret handshake, a nudge at the joke they'd put over on Pearl. He kept his face deliberately expressionless.

"Listen, all," Ezra said. "It isn't long till Thanksgiving, you know." Everybody stared at him.

"Will you come back here for Thanksgiving? We could have a family dinner at the restaurant."

"Oh, Ezra, no telling where we'll be by then," said Cody.

"What," said Pearl. "You never heard of airplanes? Amtrak? Modern transportation?"

"We'll talk about it when the time gets closer," Cody said, patting her shoulder. "Ruth, you got everything? So long, Ezra, let me know how it's going."

There was a flurry of hugs and handshakes. Later, Luke wasn't sure he'd said thank you to Ezra—though what did he want to thank him for, exactly? Something or other . . . They made their way down the sidewalk and into Cody's car, which still had the stale, blank smell of air-conditioned air. Everyone called out parts of sentences, as if trying to give the impression that they had so much left to say to each other, there wasn't room to fit it all in. "Now, you be sure to—" "It sure was good to—" "Tell Jenny we wish—" "And drive defensively, hear?"

They pulled away from the curb, waving through the window. Pearl and Ezra fell behind. Luke, sitting in back, faced forward and found his father at the wheel. Ruth was in the passenger seat. "Mom?" Luke said. "Don't you think you ought to drive?"

"He insisted," Ruth said. "He drove all the way here, too." She turned and looked at Luke meaningfully, over the back of the seat. "He said he wanted it to be him that drove to get you."

"Oh," said Luke.

What was she waiting for? She went on looking at him for some time, but then gave up and turned away again. Trying his best, Luke sat forward to observe how Cody managed.

"Well, I guess it wouldn't be all that hard," he said, "except for shifting the gears."

"Shifting's easy," Cody told him.

"Oh."

"And luckily there's no clutch."

"No."

They passed rows and rows of houses, many with their porches full of people rocking in the dark. They turned down a block where there were stoops instead of porches, white stoops set close to the street. On one of these a whole family perched, with a beer cooler and an oscillating fan and a baby in a mesh crib on the sidewalk. A TV sat on a car hood at the curb so if you happened by on foot, you'd have to cross between TV and audience, muttering, "Excuse me, please," just as if you'd walked through someone's living room. Luke gazed back at that family as long as they were in sight. They were replaced by a strip of bars and cafés, and then by an unlit alley.

"Isn't it funny," Luke told his father, "no one's ever asked you to reorganize anything in Baltimore."

"Very funny," Cody said.

"We could live with Grandma then, couldn't we?"

Cody said nothing.

They left the city for the expressway, entering a world of high, cold lights and a blue-black sky. Ruth slid slowly against the window. Her small head bobbed with every dip in the road.

"Mom's asleep," Luke said.

"She's tired," said Cody.

Perhaps he meant it as a reproach. Was this where the scolding started? Luke kept very quiet for a while. But what Cody said next was, "It wears her out, that house. Your grandma's so difficult to deal with."

"Grandma's not difficult."

"Not for you, maybe. For other people she is. For your mother. Grandma believes your mother is 'scrappy.' She told me that, once. Called her 'scrappy and hoydenish.' " He laughed, recalling something, so that Luke started smiling expectantly. "One time," Cody said, "—I bet you don't remember this—your mother and I had this silly little spat and she packed you up and ran off to Ezra. Then as soon as she got to the station, she started thinking what life would be like with your grandma and she called and asked me to come drive her home."

Luke's smile faded. "Ran off to *where?*" he asked.

"To Ezra. But never mind, it was only one of those—"

"She didn't run to Ezra. She was planning to go to her folks," Luke said.

"What folks?" Cody asked him.

Luke didn't know.

"She's an orphan," Cody said. "What folks?"

"Well, maybe—"

"She was planning to go to Ezra," Cody said. "I can see it now! I can picture how they'd take up their marriage, right where ours left off. Oh, I believe I've always had the feeling it wasn't my marriage, anyhow. It was someone else's. It was theirs. Sometimes I seemed to enjoy it better when I imagined I was seeing it through someone else's eyes."

"Why are you *telling* me this?" Luke asked him.

"All I meant was—"

"What are you, crazy? How come you go on hanging on to these things, year after year after year?"

"Now, wait a minute, now . . ."

"Mom?" Luke shook her shoulder. "Mom! Wake up!"

Ruth's head sagged over to the other side.

"Let her rest," Cody said. "Goddammit, Luke—"

"Wake up, Mom!"

"Hmm," said Ruth, not waking.

"Mom? I want to ask you. Mom? Remember when you packed me up and left Dad?"

"Mm."

"Remember?"

"Yes," she murmured, curling tighter.

"Where were we going to go, Mom?"

She raised her head, with her hair all frowsy, and gave him a blurry, dazed stare. "What?" she said. "Garrett County, where my uncle lives. Who wants to know?"

"Nobody. Go back to sleep," Cody told her.

She went back to sleep. Cody rubbed his chin thoughtfully.

They sped through a corridor of light that was bounded on both sides by the deepest darkness. They met and passed solitary cars that disappeared in an instant. Luke's eyelids drooped.

"What I mean to say," Cody said. "What I drove all this way to say . . ."

But then he trailed off. And when he started speaking again, it was on a whole different subject: time. How time was underestimated. How time was so important and all. Luke felt relieved. He listened comfortably, lulled by his father's words. "Everything," his father said, "comes down to time in the end—to the passing of time, to changing. Ever thought of that? Anything that makes you happy or sad, isn't it all based on minutes going by? Isn't happiness expecting something time is going to bring you? Isn't sadness wishing time back again? Even *big* things—even mourning a death: aren't you really just wishing to have the time back when that person was alive? Or photos—ever notice old photographs? How wistful they make you feel? Long-ago people smiling, a child who would be an old lady now, a cat that died, a flowering plant that's long since withered away and the pot itself broken or misplaced . . . Isn't it just that time for once is stopped that makes you wistful? If only you could turn it back again, you think. If only you could change this or that, undo what you have done, if only you could roll the minutes the other way, for once."

He didn't seem to expect an answer, which was lucky. Luke was too sleepy to manage one. He felt heavy, weighted with other people's stories. He imagined he was slipping or falling. He believed he was gliding away, streaming down a great, wide, light-filled river of time along with all the people he had met today. He let his head nod over, and he closed his eyes and slept.

9
APPLE APPLE

ONE MORNING Ezra Tull got up and shaved, brushed his teeth, stepped into his trousers, and encountered a lump in the bend of his right thigh. His fingers glanced over it accidentally and faltered and returned. In the bedroom mirror, his broad, fair face had a frozen look. The word cancer came on its own, as if someone had whispered it into his ear, but what caused his shocked expression was the thought that flew in after it: All right. Let it happen. I'll go ahead and die.

He shook that away, of course. He was forty-six years old, a calm and sensible man, and later he would make an appointment with Dr. Vincent. Meanwhile he put on a shirt, and buttoned it, and unrolled a pair of socks. Twice, without planning to, he tested the lump again with his fingertips. It was nearly the size of an acorn, sensitive but not painful. It rolled beneath his skin as smoothly as an eyeball.

It wasn't that he really wanted to die. Naturally not. He was only giving in to a passing mood, he decided as he went downstairs; this summer hadn't been going well. His mother, whose vision had been failing since 1975, was now (in 1979) almost totally blind, but still did not fully admit it, which made it all the harder to care for her; and his brother was too far away and his sister too busy to offer him much help. His restaurant was floundering even more than usual; his finest cook had quit because her horoscope advised it; and a heat wave seemed to be stupefying the entire city of Baltimore. Things were so bad that the most inconsequential sights served to confirm his despair—the neighbor's dog panting on the sidewalk, or his mother's one puny hydrangea bush wilting and sagging by two o'clock every afternoon. Even the postman signified catastrophe; his wife had been murdered in a burglary last spring, and now he lugged his leather pouch through the neighborhood as if it were heavy beyond endurance, as if it would eventually drag him to a halt. His feet went slower and slower; his shoulders bent closer to the ground. Every day the mail arrived later.

Ezra stood with his coffee at the window and watched the postman moping past and wondered if there were any point to life.

Then his mother came downstairs, planting her feet just so. "Oh, look," she said, "what a sunny morning!" She could feel it, he supposed—warming her skin in squares when she stood next to him at the window. Or perhaps she could even see it, since evidently she still distinguished light from dark. But her dress was done up wrong. She had drawn her wispy gray-blond hair into its customary bun, and deftly applied a single spark of pink to the center of her dry, pursed lips, but one side of her collar stuck up at an angle and the flowered material pouched outward, showing her slip in the gap between two buttons.

"It's going to be another scorcher," Ezra told her.

"Oh, poor Ezra, I hate to see you go to work in this."

All she said carried references to sight. He couldn't tell if she planned it that way.

She let him bring her a cup of coffee but she turned down breakfast, and instead sat beside him in the living room while he read the paper. This was their only time together—morning and noon, after which he left for the restaurant and did not return till very late at night, long past her bedtime. He had trouble imagining what she did in his absence. Sometimes he telephoned from work and she always sounded so brisk— "Just fixing myself some iced tea," she would say, or "Sorting through my stockings." But in the background he would hear the ominous, syrupy strains of organ music from some television soap opera, and he suspected that she simply sat before the TV much of the day, with a cardigan draped graciously over her shoulders even in this heat and her chilled hands folded in her lap. Certainly she saw no friends; she had none. As near as he could recall, she had never had friends. She had lived through her children; the gossip they brought was all she knew of the outside world, and their activities provided her only sense of motion. Even back when she worked at the grocery store, she had not consorted with the customers or the other cashiers. And now that she had retired, none of her fellow workers came to visit her.

No, this was the high point of her day, no doubt: these slow midmorning hours, the rustling of Ezra's paper, his spotty news reports. "Another taxi driver mugged, it says here."

"Oh, my goodness."

"Another shoot-out down on the Block."

"Where will it all end?" his mother wondered.

"Terrorist bomb in Madrid."

Newspapers, letters, photos, magazines—those he could help her with. With those she let herself gaze straight ahead, blank eyed, while he acted as interpreter. But in all other situations, she was fiercely independent. What, exactly, was the nature of their understanding? She admitted only that her sight was not what it had once been—that it was impaired enough to make reading a nuisance. "She's blind," her doctor said, and she reported, "He thinks I'm blind," not arguing but managing to imply, somehow, that this was a matter of opinion—or of will, of what you're willing to allow and what you're not. Ezra had learned to offer clues in the casual, slantwise style that she would accept. If he were to say, for instance, "It's raining, Mother," when they were setting out for somewhere, she would bridle and tell him, "Well, *I* know that." He learned to say, "Weatherman claims this will keep up. Better bring your umbrella." Then her face would alter and smooth, adjusting to the information. "Frankly, I don't believe him," she would say, although it was one of those misty rains that falls without a sound, and he knew she hadn't detected it. She concealed her surprise so well that only her children, accustomed to her stubborn denial of anything that might weaken her, could have seen what lay behind that challenging gray stare.

Last month, Ezra's sister had reported that their mother had called to ask a strange question. "She wanted to know if it were true," she said, "that lying on her back a long time would give her pneumonia. 'What for?' I asked her. 'Why do you care?' 'I was only curious,' she said."

Ezra lowered his paper, and he cautiously placed two fingertips at the bend of his thigh.

After they'd finished their coffee, he washed out the cups and straightened the kitchen, which nowadays had an unclean look no matter what he did to it. There were problems he didn't know how to handle—the curtains graying beside the stove, and the lace doily growing stiff with dust beneath the condiment set on the table. Did you actually launder such things? Just throw them in the machine? He could have asked his mother, but didn't. It would only upset her. She would wonder, then, what else she'd missed.

She came out to him, testing her way so carefully that her small black pumps seemed like quivering, delicate, ultrasensitive organs. "Ezra," she said, "what are your plans for this morning?"

"No plans, Mother."

"You're certain, now."

"What is it you want to do?"

"I was thinking we could sort through my desk drawers, but if you're busy—"

"I'm not busy."

"You just say so if you are."

"I'll be glad to help."

"When you were little," she said, "it made you angry to see me sick or in need of aid."

"Well, that was when I was little."

"Isn't it funny? It was you that was the kindest, the closest, the sweetest child; the others were always up to something, off with their own affairs. But when I fell sick, you would turn so coldhearted! 'Does this mean we don't get to go to the movies?' you'd ask. It was your brother who'd take over then—the one I'd least expect it of. I would say, 'Ezra, could you just fetch me an afghan, please?' and you would turn stony and pretend not to hear. You seemed to think I'd done something *to* you—got a headache out of malice."

"I was very young then," Ezra said.

Although it was odd how clenched he felt, even now—not so much angry as defenseless; and he'd felt defenseless as a child, too, he believed. He had trusted his mother to be everything for him. When she cut a finger with a paring knife, he had felt defeated by her incompetence. How could he depend on such a person? Why had she let him down so?

He took her by the upper arm and led her back to the living room. (He was conscious, suddenly, of his height and his solid, comfortable weight.) He seated her on the couch and went over to the desk to remove the bottom drawer.

This was something he had done many times before. It wasn't, certainly, that the drawer needed cleaning, although to an outsider it might appear disorganized. Cascades of unmounted photos slid about as he walked; others poked from the moldy, crumbling albums stacked to one side. There was a shoe box full of his mother's girlhood diaries; an incomplete baby book for Cody; and a Schrafft's candy box containing old letters, all with the stamps snipped off the envelopes. There was a dim, lavender-colored corsage squashed as stiff and hard as a dried-up mouse carcass; a single kid glove hardened with age; and a musty-smelling report card for Pearl E. Cody, fourth year, 1903, with the grades entered in a script so elegant that someone might have laid A-shaped tendrils of fine brown hair next to every subject. Ezra was fond of these belongings. He willingly went over them again and again, describing them for his mother. "There's that picture of your Aunt Melinda on her wedding day."

"Ah?"

"You are standing next to her with a fan made out of feathers."

"We'll save it," said his mother. She was still pretending they were merely sorting.

But soon enough, she forgot about that and settled back, musing, while he recited what he'd found. "Here is a picture of someone's porch."

"Porch? Whose porch?"

"I can't tell."

"What does it look like?"

"Two pillars and a dark floor, clay pot full of geraniums . . ."

"Am I in it?"

"No."

"Oh, well," she said, waving a hand, "maybe that was Luna's porch." He had never heard of Luna.

To tell the truth, he didn't believe that relatives were what his mother was after. Ladies and gentlemen drifted by in a blur; he did his best to learn their names, but his mother dismissed them airily. It was herself she was hunting, he sensed. "Do you see me, at all? Is that the dinner where I wore the pale blue?" Her single-mindedness sometimes amused him, sometimes annoyed him. There was greed in the forward jutting of her chin as she waited to hear of her whereabouts. "Am *I* in that group? Was *I* on that picnic?"

He opened a maroon velvet album, each of its pulpy gray pages grown bright yellow as urine around the edges. None of the photos here was properly glued down. A sepia portrait of a bearded man was jammed into the binding alongside a Kodachrome of a pink baby in a flashy vinyl wading pool, with SEPT '63 stamped on the border. His mother poked her face out, expectant. He said, "Here's a man with a beard. I think it's your father."

"Possibly," she said, without interest.

He turned the page. "Here's a group of ladies underneath a tree."

"Ladies?"

"None of them look familiar."

"What are they wearing?"

"Long, baggy dresses," he told her. "Everything seems to be sagging at the waist."

"That would be nineteen-ten or so. Maybe Iola's engagement party."

"Who was Iola?"

"Look for me in a navy stripe," she told him.

"There's no stripes here."

"Pass on."

She had never been the type to gaze backward, had not filled his childhood with "When I was your age," as so many mothers did. And even now, she didn't use these photos as an excuse for reminiscing. She hardly discussed them at all, in fact—even those in which she appeared. Instead, she listened, alert, to any details he could give her about her past self. Was it that she wanted an outsider's view of her? Or did she hope to solve some mystery? "Am I smiling, or am I frowning? Would you say that I seemed happy?"

When Ezra tried to ask *her* any questions, she grew bored. "What was your mother like?" he would ask.

"Oh, that was a long time ago," she told him.

She hadn't had much of a life, it seemed to him. He wondered what, in all her history, she would enjoy returning to. Her courtship, even knowing how it would end? Childbirth? Young motherhood? She did speak often and wistfully of the years when her children were little. But most of the photos in this drawer dated from long before then, from back in the early part of the century, and it was those she searched most diligently. "The Baker family reunion, that would be. Nineteen-o-eight. Beulah's sweet sixteen party. Lucy and Harold's silver anniversary." The events she catalogued were other people's; she just hung around the fringes, watching. "Katherine Rose, the summer she looked so beautiful and met her future husband."

He peered at Katherine Rose. "She doesn't look so beautiful to *me*," he said.

"It faded soon enough."

Katherine Rose, whoever she was, wore a severe and complicated dress of a type not seen in sixty years or more. He was judging her rabbity face as if she were a contemporary, some girl he'd glimpsed in a bar, but she had probably been dead for decades. He felt he was being tugged back through layers of generations.

He flipped open tiny diaries, several no bigger than a lady's compact, and read his mother's cramped entries aloud. "*December eighth, nineteen-twelve. Paid call on Edwina Barrett. Spilled half-pint of top cream in the buggy coming home and had a nice job cleaning it off the cushions I can assure you . . .*" "*April fourth, nineteen-o-eight. Went into town with Alice and weighed on the new weighing machine in Mr. Salter's store. Alice is one hundred thirteen pounds. I am one hundred ten and a half.*" His mother listened, tensed and still, as if expecting something momentous, but all he found was *purchased ten yards heliotrope brilliantine*, and *made chocolate blanc-mange for the Girls' Culture Circle*, and *weighed again at Mr. Salter's store.* During the summer of 1908—her fourteenth summer, as near as he could figure—she had weighed herself about every two days, hitching up her pony Prince and riding clear downtown to do so. "*August seventh,*" he read. "*Had my measurements taken at the dressmaker's and she gave me a copy to keep. I have developed in every possible sense.*" He laughed, but his mother made an impatient little movement with one hand. "*September ninth,*" he read, and then all at once had the feeling that the ground had rushed away beneath his feet. Why, that perky young girl was this old woman! This blind old woman sitting next to him! She had once been a whole different person, had a whole different life separate from his, had spent her time *swinging clubs with the Junior Amazons* and *cutting up with the Neal boys something dreadful* and *taking first prize at the Autumn Recital Contest.* (*I hoped that poor Nadine would win,* she wrote in a chubby, innocent script, *but of course it was nice to get it myself.*) His mother sat silent, absently stroking the dead corsage. "Never mind," she told him.

"Shall I stop?"

"It wasn't what I wanted after all."

On his way to the restaurant, Ezra ducked into a bookstore and located a Merck Manual in the Family Health section. He checked the index for *lump*, but all he found was *lumpy jaw (actinomycosis).* Evidently you had to know the name of your disease first—in which case, why bother looking it up? He thought through what he remembered of his high school biology course, and decided to check under *lymph gland.*

The very phrase was reassuring; lymph glands swelled all the time. He had a couple in his neck that grew pecan sized anytime he developed a sniffle. But there were no lymph glands listed in the index, and it stopped him cold to see *lymphatic leukemia* and *lymphohematogenous tuberculosis*. He shut the book quickly and replaced it on the shelf.

Josiah had already opened the restaurant, and two helpers were busy chopping vegetables in the kitchen. A salesman in a plaid suit was trying to interest Josiah in some new product. "But," Josiah kept saying. "But I don't think—" Josiah was so gawky and confused-looking—an emaciated giant in white, with his black and gray hair sticking out in frenzied tufts as if he'd grabbed handfuls in desperation—that Ezra felt a rush of love for him. He said, "Josiah, what's the problem?" and Josiah turned to him gratefully. "Uh, see, this gentleman here—"

"Murphy's the name. J. R. Murphy," said the salesman. "I sell soy sauce, private brand. I sell it by the case."

"We could never manage a case," said Ezra. "We hardly ever use it."

"You will, though," the salesman told him. "Soy sauce is the coming thing; better get it while you can. This here is the antidote for radiation."

"For what?"

"Nucular accidents! Atom bums! Just take a look at the facts: those folks in Hiroshima didn't get near as many side effects as expected. Want to know why? It was all that Japanese food with soy sauce. Plain old soy sauce. Keep a case of this around and you'll have no more worries over Three Mile Island."

"But I don't even like soy sauce."

"Who says you've got to like it?"

"Well, maybe just a few bottles . . ." Ezra said.

He wondered if there were some cryptic, cultish mark on his door that told all the crazy people he'd have trouble saying no.

He went to check on the dining room. Two waitresses were shaking out tablecloths and spreading them with a crisp, ripping sound. Josiah was lugging in bales of laundered napkins. There was always a moment, this early in the day, when Ezra found his restaurant disheartening. He was chilled by the empty tables, the looming, uncurtained windows, the bitter smell of last night's cigarettes. What kind of occupation was this? People gulped down his food without a thought, too busy courting or arguing or negotiating to notice what they ate; then they went home and forgot it. Nothing amounted to anything. And Ezra was a middle-aged man with his hair growing transparent at the back of his head; but here he was, where he'd been at twenty, living with his mother in a Calvert Street row house and reading himself to sleep with cookbooks. He had never married, never fathered children, and lost the one girl he had loved out of sheer fatalism, lack of force, a willing assumption of defeat. (*Let it be* was the theme that ran through his life. He was ruled by a dreamy mood of acceptance that was partly the source of all his happiness and partly his undoing.)

Josiah came to stand before him. "See my boots?" he asked.

Ezra surfaced and looked down at Josiah's boots. They poked from beneath the white uniform—gigantic, rubber-coated canvas boots that could weather a flood, a snowstorm, an avalanche.

"L. L. Bean," Josiah said.

"Ah."

L. L. Bean was where Josiah got his mystery gifts. Once or twice a year they arrived: a one-man tent; a goose-down sleeping bag; hunting shoes in his unwieldy, hard-to-find size; an olive-drab poncho that could see him through a monsoon; a pocket survival kit containing compass, flint, signal mirror, and metallic blanket. All this for a man who'd been born and reared in the city and seemed inclined to stay there. There was never any card or note of explanation. Josiah had written the company, but L. L. Bean replied that the donor preferred to stay anonymous. Ezra had spent hours helping Josiah think of possibilities. "Remember that old lady whose walk you used to shovel? Maybe it's her."

"She'd be dead by now, Ezra."

"Remember Molly Kane, with her wheelchair? You used to wheel her to Algebra One."

"But she said, 'Let go my chair, you big ree-tard!' "

"Maybe now she regrets it."

"Oh, no. Not her. Not Molly Kane."

"Maybe just someone you changed a tire for and never gave it another thought. Someone you opened a door for. Maybe . . . I don't know . . ."

Ordinarily he enjoyed these speculations, but now looking down at Josiah's mammoth boots, he was struck by the fact that even Josiah—lanky, buck-toothed, stammering Josiah—had a human being all his own that he was linked to, whether or not he knew that person's name, and lived in a nest of gifts and secrets and special care that Ezra was excluded from.

"New Year's Day, nineteen-fourteen," Ezra read aloud. *"I hope this little diary will not get lost as last year's did. I hope I will not put anything foolish in it as I have been known to do before."*

His mother hid a smile, unsuccessfully. What foolishness could she have been up to so long ago? Ezra's eyes slipped down the page to a line that had been crossed out. "There's something here I can't read," he said.

"I never was known for my penmanship."

"No, I mean you scribbled over it with so many loops and things—"

"Apple apple," his mother said.

"Excuse me?"

"That's what we wrote over words that we wanted kept secret. *Appleappleapple* all joined together, so no one could guess what was written underneath."

"Well, it certainly worked," Ezra said.

"Move on," his mother told him.

"Oh. Um . . . *put a flaxseed poultice on my finger . . . started some gartlets of pale pink ribbon . . . popped some popcorn and buttered half, made cracker-jack of the rest . . ."*

His mother sighed. Ezra skimmed several pages in silence.

How plotless real life was! In novels, events led up to something. In his mother's diaries, they flitted past with no apparent direction. Frank brought her perfumed blotters and a box of "cocoa-nut" candy; Roy paid quite a call and couldn't seem to tear himself away; Burt Tansy took her to the comic opera and afterward presented her with a folio of the songs; but none of these people was ever mentioned again. Someone named Arthur wrote her a letter that was *the softest thing,* she said. *I didn't know he could be so silly. It was all in form though and I am not very mad.* A certain Clark Allensby promised to visit and did not; *I suppose it is all for the best,* she said, *but I can't understand his actions as to-morrow he is leaving.* And while she was stretching the curtains, she said, *the darkie announced a young man come to visit. I looked like a freak but went in anyhow and there sat Hugh McKinley. He was heading for the seed store so just HAPPENED to stop by, and staid some while . . .*

Ezra began to see that for his mother (or for the young girl she had been), there was a plot, after all. She had imagined a perfectly wonderful plot—a significance to every chance meeting, the possibility of whirlwind courtships, grand white weddings, flawless bliss forever after. *James Wrayson came to call most shockingly late,* she wrote. *Stole my picture off the piano and put it in his pocket. Acted too comical for words. I'm sure I don't know what will come of this.*

Well, nothing had come of it. Nothing came of anything. She married a salesman for the Tanner Corporation and he left her and never came back. "Ezra? Why aren't you reading to me?" his mother asked.

"I'm tired," he said.

He took her to an afternoon ball game. In her old age, she had become a great Orioles fan. She would listen on the radio if she couldn't attend in person, even staying up past her bedtime if the game went into extra innings. Baseball was the only sport that made sense, she said: clear as Parcheesi, clever as chess. She looked pleased with herself for thinking of this, but Ezra suspected that it had something in common too with those soap operas she enjoyed. Certainly she viewed each game as a drama, and fretted over the gossip that Ezra culled for her from the sports pages—players' injuries, rivalries, slumps, mournful tales of young rookies so nervous they flubbed their only chances. She liked to think of the Orioles as poverty-stricken and virtuous, unable to simply *buy* their talent as richer teams did. Players' looks mattered to her as deeply as if they were movie stars: Ken Singleton's high, shining cheekbones, as described by one of her granddaughters, sent her into a little trance of admiration. She liked to hear how Al Bumbry wiggled his bat so jauntily before a hit; how Stanhouse drove people crazy delaying on the mound. She wished Doug deCinces would shave off his mustache and Kiko Garcia would get himself a haircut. She thought Earl Weaver was not fatherly enough to be a proper manager and often, when he replaced some poor sad pitcher who'd barely had a chance, she would speak severely into the radio, calling him "Merle Beaver" for spite and spitting out her words. "Just because he grows his own tomatoes," she said, "doesn't necessarily mean a person has a heart."

Sometimes Ezra would quote her to his friends at the restaurant, and halfway through a sentence he would think, Why, I'm making her out to be a . . . character; and all he'd said would feel like a lie, although of course it had happened. The fact was that she was a very strong woman (even a frightening one, in his childhood), and she may have shrunk and aged but her true, interior self was still enormous, larger than life, powerful. Overwhelming.

They got to the stadium early so his mother could walk at her own pace, which was so slow and halting that by the time they were settled, the lineup was already being announced. Their seats were good ones, close to home plate. His mother sank down gratefully but then had to stand, almost at once, for the national anthem. For *two* national anthems; the other team was Toronto. Halfway through the second song, Ezra noticed that his mother's knees were trembling. "Do you want to sit down?" he asked her. She shook her head. It was a very hot day but her arm, when he took hold of it, was cool and almost unnaturally dry, as if filmed with powder.

How clear a green the grass was! He could see his mother's point: precise and level and brightly colored, the playing field did have the look of a board game. Players stood about idly swinging their arms. Toronto's batter hit a high fly ball and the center fielder plucked it from the sky with ease, almost absentmindedly. "Well!" said Ezra. "That was quick. First out in no time."

There was a knack to his commentary. He informed her without appearing to, as if he were making small talk. "Gosh. Look at that change-up." And "Call that a ball? Skimmed right past his knees. Call that a ball?" His mother listened, face uplifted and receptive, like someone at a concert.

What did she get out of this? She'd have followed more closely, he thought, if she had stayed at home beside her radio. (And she'd never *bring* a radio; she worried people might think it was a hearing aid.) He supposed she liked the atmosphere, the cheering and excitement and the smell of popcorn. She even let him buy her a Styrofoam cup of beer, which was allowed to grow warm after one sip; and when the bugle sounded she called, "Charge," very softly, with an embarrassed little half-smile curling her lips. Three men were getting drunk behind her—booing and whistling and shouting insults to passing girls—but Ezra's mother stayed untroubled, facing forward. "When you come in person," she told Ezra, "you direct your own focus, you know? The TV or the radio men, they might focus on the pitcher when you want to see what first base is doing; and you don't have any choice but to accept it."

A batter swung at a low ball and connected, and Ezra (eyes in every direction) saw how the field came instantaneously alive, with each man following his appointed course. The shortstop, as if strung on rubber bands, sprang upward without a second's preparation and caught the ball; the outfield closed in like a kaleidoscope; the second-base runner pivoted and the shortstop tagged him out. "Yo, Garcia!" a drunk yelled behind them, in that gravelly, raucous voice that some men adopt in ball parks; and he sloshed cold beer down the back of Ezra's neck. "Well . . ." Ezra said to his mother. But he couldn't think how to encompass all that had happened, so finally he said, "We're up, it looks like."

She didn't answer. He turned to her and found her caving in on herself, her head falling forward, the Styrofoam cup slipping from her fingers. "Mother? Mother!" Everyone around him rose and milled and fussed. "Give her air," they told him, and then somehow they had her stretched out on her back, lying where their feet had been. Her face was paper white, immobile, like a crumpled rock. One of the drunks stepped forward to smooth her skirt decorously over her knees, and another stroked her hair off her forehead. "She'll be all right," he told Ezra. "Don't worry. It's only the heat. Folks, make room! Let her breathe!"

Ezra's mother opened her eyes. The air was bright as knife blades, shimmering with a brassy, hard light, but she didn't even squint; and for the first time Ezra fully understood that she was blind. It seemed that before, he hadn't taken it in. He reeled back, squatting at the feet of strangers, and imagined having to stay here forever: the two of them, helpless, flattened beneath the glaring summer sky.

That night he dreamed he was walking among the tables in his restaurant. A long-time customer, Mr. Rosen, was dithering over the menu. "What do you recommend?" he asked Ezra. "I see you've got your stroganoff, but I don't know, that's a little heavy. I mean I'm not so very hungry, just peckish, got a little weight on my stomach right here beneath my rib cage, know what I mean? What do you think might be good for that? What had I ought to eat?"

This was how Mr. Rosen behaved in real life, as well, and Ezra expected it and always responded kindly and solicitously. But in the dream, he was overtaken by a most untypical panic. "I have nothing! Nothing!" he cried. "I don't know what you want! I don't have anything! Stop asking!" And he wrung his hands at the thought of his empty, gleaming refrigerator and idle stove.

He woke sweating, tangled in damp sheets. There was a certain white quality to the darkness that made him believe it was close to dawn. He climbed out of bed, hitching up his pajama bottoms, and went downstairs and poured a glass of milk. Then he wandered into the living room for a magazine, but the only ones he found were months old. Finally he settled on the rug beside his mother's desk and opened the bottom drawer.

A recipe for marmalade cake: *From the kitchen of . . .* with no name filled in. Someone's diploma, rolled and secured with a draggled blue ribbon. A clipping from a newspaper: *Bristlecone pines, in times of stress, hoard all their life in a single streak and allow the rest to die.* A photo of his sister in an evening dress with gardenias looped around her wrist. A diary from 1909, with a violet pressed between its pages. *Washed my yellow gown, made salt-rising bread, played Basket Ball,* he read. *Bought a hat shape at Warner's and trimmed it with green grosgrain. Preserved tomatoes. Went to Marching Drill. Learned progressive jackstraws.*

Her vitality hummed in the room around him. She was forever doing something to her "waists," which Ezra assumed to be blouses. Embroidering waists or mending waists or buying goods for a waist or sewing fresh braid on a waist, putting insertion on a waist, ripping insertion *off* a waist, tucking her red plaid waist until the tucker got out of fix, attaching new sleeves to a waist—even, for one entire week, attending a course called "Fashioning the Shirtwaist." She pressed a bodice, sewed a corset cover, darned her stockings, altered a girdle, stitched a comforter, monogrammed a handkerchief, cut outing flannel for skirts. (Yet in all the time he'd known her, Ezra had never seen her so much as hem a dish towel.) She went to hear a lecture entitled "Thunder Tones from the Guillotine." She pestered the vet about Prince's ailment—an injured stifle, whatever that was. She sold tickets to socials, amateur theatricals, and Mission Society picnics. She paid a call on her uncle but found his door double-locked and only a parlor window open.

In Ezra's slumbering, motionless household, the loudest sound came from fifteen-year-old Pearl, hitching up her underskirts to clamber through that long-ago window.

* * *

Daily, in various bookstores, he proceeded from the Merck Manual to other books, simpler to use, intended for laymen. Several were indexed by symptoms, including *lump*. He found that his lump could indeed be a lymph node—a temporary swelling in reaction to some minor infection. Or it could also be a hernia. Or it could be something worse. *Consult your doctor*, he read. But he didn't. Every morning, still in his pajamas, he tested the lump with his fingers and resolved to call Dr. Vincent, but later he would change his mind. Suppose it did turn out to be cancer: why would he want to endure those treatments—the radiation and the toxic drugs? Better just to die.

He noticed that he thought of dying as a kind of adventure, something new that he hadn't yet experienced. Like an unusual vacation trip.

His sister, Jenny, stopped by with her children. It was a Wednesday, her morning off. She took over the house with no trouble at all. "Where's your ironing? Give me your ironing," she said, and "What do you need in the way of shopping?" and "Quinn, get down from there." She had so much energy; she spent herself with such recklessness. In her worn-looking clothes, run-down shoes, with her dark hair lifting behind her, she flew around the living room. "I think you should buy an air-conditioner, Mother. Have you heard the latest pollution count? For someone in your state of health . . ."

Her mother, bleakly speechless, withstood this storm of words and then lifted one white hand. "Come closer so I can see your hair," she said.

Jenny came closer and submitted to her touch. Her mother stroked her hair with a dissatisfied expression on her face. "I don't know why you can't take better care of your looks," she said. "How long since you've been to a beauty parlor?"

"I'm a busy woman, Mother."

"How much time would you need for a haircut? And you're not wearing makeup, are you. Are you? In this light, it's hard to tell. Oh, Jenny. What must your husband think? He'll think you're not trying. You've let yourself go. I expect I could pass you on the street and not know you."

Her favorite expression, it seemed to Ezra: I wouldn't know you if I saw you on the street. She used it when referring to Jenny's poor grooming, to Cody's sparse visits, to Ezra's tendency to put on weight. Ezra caught a sudden glimpse of a wide, vacant sidewalk and his various family members strolling down it, their faces averted from one another.

Jenny's children ambled through the house, looking bored and disgusted. The baby chewed on a curtain pull. Jane, the nine-year-old, perched on Ezra's knee as casually as if he were a piece of furniture. She smelled of crayons and peanut butter—homely smells that warmed his heart. "What are you fixing in your restaurant tonight?" she asked.

"Cold things. Salads. Soups."

"Soups are hot," she said.

"Not necessarily."

"Oh."

She paused, perhaps to store this information in some tidy filing cabinet inside her head. Ezra was touched by her willingness to adjust—by her amiable adaptability. Was it possible, he sometimes wondered, that children *humored* grown-ups? If grown-ups insisted on toilet training, on *please* and *thank you*—well, all right, since it seemed to mean so much to them. It wasn't important enough to argue about. This is a transitive verb, some grown-up would say, and the children would go along with it; though to them it was immaterial, frankly. Transitive, intransitive, who cared? What difference did it make? It was all a foreign language anyhow.

"Maybe you could invite me to your restaurant for supper," Jane told Ezra.

"I'd be delighted to invite you for supper."

"Maybe I could bring a friend."

"Certainly."

"I'll bring Barbie."

"That would be wonderful," Ezra said.

"You bring a friend, too."

"All my friends work in the restaurant."

"Don't you ever date?"

"Of course I date."

"I don't mean just some one of those lady cooks you pal around with."

"Oh, I've dated in my time."

She filed that away also.

Jenny was criticizing their mother's doctor. She said he was too old, too old-fashioned—too general, she said. "You need a good internist. I happen to know a man on—"

"I've been going to Dr. Vincent as long as I've lived in Baltimore," her mother said.

"What's that got to do with it?"

"We don't all just change for change's sake."

Jenny rolled her eyes at Ezra.

Ezra said, "Maybe *you* could be her doctor."

"I'm her relative, Ezra."

"So much the better," Ezra said.

"Besides, my field is pediatrics."

"Jenny," said Ezra. "What would you say—"

He stopped. Jenny raised her eyebrows.

"What would you say is your patients' most common disease?"

"Mother-itis," she told him.

"Oh."

"Why do you ask?"

"It's not, um, cancer or anything."

"Why do you ask?" she said again.

He only shrugged.

After she'd collected the ironing, and made a shopping list, and rounded up the children, she said that she had to be off. She brushed her cheek against her mother's and patted Ezra's arm. "I'll walk you to the car," he said.

"Never mind."

He walked her anyway, relieving her of the laundry bag while she carried the baby astride her hip. They passed the mailman. He was bent so low to the ground that he didn't even notice them.

Out by the car, Ezra said, "I've got this lump."

"Oh?" said Jenny. "Where?"

He touched his groin. "In the morning it starts out small," he said, "but by evening it's so big, it's like a rock or something in my trouser pocket. I'm wondering if it's, you know. Cancer."

"It's not cancer. More likely a hernia, from the sound of it," she said. "Go see a doctor." She got in the car and buckled the baby into her carrier. Then she leaned out the open window. "Do I have all the children?" she asked.

"Yes."

She waved and drove off.

Back in the house, his mother was hovering at the window exactly as if she could see. "That girl has too big a family," she said. "I suppose her looks must be ruined by now."

"No, I haven't noticed it."

"And her hair. Honestly. Ezra, tell me the truth," she said. "How does Jenny seem to you?"

"Oh, the same as always."

"I mean, don't you think she's let herself go? What about what she was wearing, for instance?"

He tried to remember. It was something faded, but perfectly acceptable, he guessed. Was it blue? Gray? He tried to picture her hairdo, the style of her shoes, but only came up with the chiseled lines that had always, even in her girlhood, encircled her neck—rings of lines that gave her a lush look. For some reason, those lines made him sad now, and so did Jenny's olive hands with the ragged, oval fingernails, and the crinkles at the corners of her eyes, and the news that his life would, after all, go on and on and on.

"*February sixth, nineteen-ten,*" Ezra read aloud. "*I baked a few Scottish Fancies but they wouldn't do to take to a tea.*"

His mother, listening intently, thought that over a while. Then she made her gesture of dismissal and started rocking again in her rocker.

"*I hitched up Prince and rode downtown for brown silk gloves and an ice bag. Then got out my hat frames and washed my straw hat. For supper fixed a batch of—*"

"Move on," his mother said.

He riffled through the pages, glimpsing *buttonhole stitch* and *watermelon social* and *set of fine furs for $22.50.* "*Early this morning,*" he read to his mother, "*I went out behind the house to weed. Was kneeling in the dirt by the stable with my pinafore a mess and the perspiration rolling down my back, wiped my face on my sleeve, reached for the trowel, and all at once thought, Why I believe that at just this moment I am absolutely happy.*"

His mother stopped rocking and grew very still.

"*The Bedloe girl's piano scales were floating out her window,*" he read, "*and a bottle fly was buzzing in the grass, and I saw that I was kneeling on such a beautiful green little planet. I don't care what else might come about, I have had this moment. It belongs to me.*"

That was the end of the entry. He fell silent.

"Thank you, Ezra," his mother said. "There's no need to read any more."

Then she fumbled up from her chair, and let him lead her to the kitchen for lunch. He guided her gently, inch by inch. It seemed to him that he had to be very careful with her. They were traversing the curve of the earth, small and steadfast, surrounded by companions: Jenny flying past with her children, the drunks at the stadium sobering the instant their help was needed, the baseball players obediently springing upward in the sunlight, and Josiah connected to his unknown gift giver as deeply, and as mysteriously, as Ezra himself was connected to this woman beside him.

10
DINNER AT THE HOMESICK RESTAURANT

WHEN PEARL TULL died, Cody was off on a goose hunt and couldn't be reached for two days. He and Luke were staying in a cabin owned by his business partner. It didn't have a telephone, and the roads were little more than logging trails.

Late Sunday, when they returned, Ruth came out to the driveway. The night was chilly, and she wore no sweater but hugged herself as she walked toward the car, her white, freckled face oddly set and her faded red hair standing up in the wind. That was how Cody guessed something was wrong. Ruth hated cold weather, and ordinarily would have waited inside the house.

"It's bad news," she said. "I'm sorry."

"What happened?"

"Your mother's passed away."

"Grandma *died?*" asked Luke, as if correcting her.

Ruth kissed Luke's cheek but kept her eyes on Cody, maybe trying to gauge the damage. Cody himself, wearily closing the car door behind him, was uncertain of the damage. His mother had been a difficult woman, of course. But even so . . .

"She died in her sleep, early yesterday," Ruth said. She took Cody's hand in both of hers and gripped it, tightly, so that the pain he felt right then was purely physical. He stood for a while, allowing her; then he gently pulled away and went to open the car trunk.

They had not bagged any geese—the hunt had been a lame excuse, really, to spend some time with Luke, who was now a senior in high school and would not be around for much longer. All Cody had to unload was the rifles in their canvas cases and a duffel bag. Luke brought the ice chest. They walked toward the house in silence. Cody had still not responded.

"The funeral's tomorrow at eleven," said Ruth. "I told Ezra we'd be there in the morning."

"How is he taking it?" Cody asked.

"He sounded all right."

Inside the front door, Cody set down the duffel bag and propped the rifles against the wall. He decided that he felt not so much sad as heavy. Although he was lean bodied, still in good shape, he imagined that he had suddenly sunk in on himself and grown denser. His eyes were weighty and dry, and his step seemed too solid for the narrow, polished floorboards in the hall.

"Well, Luke," he said.

Luke seemed dazed, or perhaps just sleepy. He squinted palely under the bright light.

"Do you want to go to the funeral?" Cody asked him.

"Sure, I guess," said Luke.

"You wouldn't have to."

"I don't mind."

"Of course he's going," said Ruth. "He's her grandson."

"That doesn't obligate him," Cody told her.

"Of course it obligates him."

This was where they differed. They could have argued about it all night, except that Cody was so tired.

For their journey south, Cody drove Ruth's car because his own was still spattered with mud from the goose hunt. He supposed they would have to ride in some shiny, formal funeral procession. But when he happened to mention this to Ruth, halfway down the turnpike, she told him that Ezra had said their mother had requested cremation. ("Golly," Luke breathed.) There would only be the service, therefore— no cemetery trip and no burial. "Very sensible," Cody said. He thought of the tidy framework of his mother's bones, the crinkly bun on the back of her head. Did that fierce little figure exist any more? Was it already ashes? "Ah, God it's barbaric, however you look at it," he told Ruth.

"What, cremation?" she asked.

"Death."

They sped along—Cody in his finest gray suit, Ruth in stiff black beside him. Luke sat in the rear, gazing out the side window. They were traveling the Beltway now, approaching Baltimore. They passed trees ablaze with red and yellow leaves and shopping malls full of ordinary, Monday morning traffic. "When I was a boy, this was country," Cody said to Luke.

"You told me."

"Baltimore was nothing but a little harbor town."

There was no answer. Cody searched for Luke in the rear-view mirror. "Hey," he said. "You want to drive the rest of the way?"

"No, that's all right."

"Really. You want to?"

"Let him be," Ruth whispered.

"What?"

"He's upset."

"What about?"

"Your mother, Cody. You know he always felt close to her."

Cody couldn't figure how anyone could feel close to his mother— not counting Ezra, who was thought by some to be a saint. He checked Luke's face in the mirror again, but what could you tell from that impassive stare? "Hell," he said to Ruth, "all I asked was did he want to drive."

The city seemed even more ruined than usual, tumbling under a wan, blue sky. "Look at there," Cody said. "Linsey's Candy and Tobacco. They sold cigarettes to minors. Bobbie Jo's Barbecue. And there's my old school."

On Calvert Street, the row houses stood in two endless lines. "I don't see how you knew which one was home," Luke had told him once, and Cody had been amazed. Oh, if you lived here you knew.

They weren't alike at all, not really. One had dozens of roses struggling in its tiny front yard, another an illuminated madonna glowing night and day in the parlor window. Some had their trim painted in astonishing colors, assertively, like people with their chins thrust out. The fact that they were *attached* didn't mean a thing.

He parked in front of his mother's house. He slid from the car and stretched, waiting for Ruth and Luke.

By now, Pearl would have been out the door and halfway down the steps, reaching for the three of them with those eager, itchy fingers of hers.

"Is that your sister's car?" Ruth asked him.

"*I* don't know what kind of car she drives."

They climbed the steps. Ruth had her hand hooked in the back of Luke's belt. He was too tall for her to cup the nape of his neck, as she used to do.

When Cody first left home, he would knock when he returned for a visit. It was a deliberate, planned act; it was an insult to his mother. She had known that and objected. "Can't you walk straight in? Do you have to act like company?" "But company is what I am," he'd said. She had started outwitting him; she had lain in wait, rushing to meet him at the very first sound of his shoes on the sidewalk. (So it was, perhaps, not solely love that had sent her plunging down the steps.) Now, crossing the porch, Cody didn't know whether to knock or just open the door. Well, he supposed this house belonged to Ezra now. He knocked.

Ezra looked sad and exhausted, loosely filling a lightweight khaki suit that only he would have thought appropriate. As always, he seemed whiskerless, boy faced. There was a space between his collar and the knot of his tie. A handkerchief bunched messily out of his jacket pocket. "Cody. Come in," he said. He touched Cody's arm in that tentative way he had—something more than a handshake, less than a hug. "Ruth? Luke? We were starting to worry about you."

From the gloomy depths of the house, Jenny stepped forward to kiss everyone. She smelled of some complicated perfume but had her usual hastily assembled look—her tailored coat unbuttoned, her dark hair rough and tossed. Her husband ambled behind her, fat and bearded, good-natured. He clapped Cody on the shoulder. "Nice to see you. Too bad about your mother."

"Thank you, Joe."

"We're supposed to be starting for the church this very minute," Jenny said. "We have to leave early because we're picking up some of the children on the way."

"*I'm* all set," Cody said.

Ezra asked, "But don't you want coffee first?"

"No, no, let's get going."

"See," Ezra said, "I had planned on coffee and pastries before we started out. I'd assumed you'd be coming earlier."

"We've already had breakfast," Cody told him.

"But everything's on the table."

Cody felt his old, familiar irritation beginning. "Ezra—" he said.

"That was thoughtful of you," Ruth told Ezra, "but really, we're fine, and we wouldn't want to hold people up."

Ezra checked his watch. He glanced behind him, toward the dining room. "It's only ten-fifteen," he said. He walked over to a front window and lifted the curtain.

Now that it was apparent he had something on his mind, the others stood waiting. (He could be maddeningly slow, and all the slower if pushed.)

"It's like this," he said finally.

He coughed.

"I was kind of expecting Dad," he said.

There was a blank, flat pause.

"Who?" Cody asked.

"Our father."

"But how would he know?"

"Well, ah, I invited him."

"Ezra, for God's sake," Cody said.

"It wasn't *my* idea," Ezra said. "It was Mother's. She talked about it when she got so sick. She said, 'Look in my address book. Ask everybody in it to my funeral.' I wondered who she meant, at first. You know she never wrote anyone, and most of her relatives are dead. But as soon as I opened the address book I saw it: Beck Tull. I didn't even realize she knew where he had run off to."

"He wrote her; that's how she knew," Cody said.

"He did?"

"From time to time he sent these letters, boasting, bragging. *Doing fine . . . expecting a raise . . .* I peeked inside when Mother wasn't looking."

"I never even guessed," said Ezra.

"What difference would it have made?"

"Oh, I don't know . . ."

"He ditched us," Cody said, "when we were kids. What do you care about him now?"

"Well, I don't," said Ezra. And Cody, who had so often been exasperated by Ezra's soft heart, saw that in this case, it was true: he really didn't care. He looked directly at Cody with his peculiarly clear, light-filled eyes, and he said, "It was Mother who asked; not me. All I did was call him up and say, 'This is Ezra. Mother has died and we're holding her funeral Monday at eleven.' "

"That was *all?*" Cody said.

"Well, and then I told him he could stop by the house first, if he got here early."

"But you didn't ask, 'How are you?' or 'Where've you been?' or 'Why'd you go?'"

"I just said, 'This is Ezra. Mother has died and—'"

Cody laughed.

"At any rate," Jenny said, "it doesn't seem he's coming."

"No," said Cody, "but think about it. I mean, don't you get it? First he leaves and Mother pretends he hasn't. Out of pride, or spite, or something, she never says a word about it, makes believe to all of us that he's only on a business trip. A thirty-five-year business trip. Then Ezra calls him on the phone and does the very same thing. 'This is Ezra,' he says, as if he'd seen Dad just yesterday—"

Jenny said, "Can we get started now? My children will be freezing to death."

"Oh, surely," Ruth told her. "Cody, honey, her children are waiting on us."

"Mother would have done that, just exactly," Cody said. "If Dad had walked in she would have said, 'Ah, yes, there you are. Can you tell me if my slip is showing?'"

Joe gave a little bark of laughter. Ezra smiled, but his eyes filmed over with tears. "That's true," he said. "She would have. You know? She really would have."

"Fine, then, she would have," Jenny said. "Shall we go?"

She had been so young when their father left, anyhow. She claimed to have forgotten all about him.

At the funeral, the minister, who had never met their mother, delivered a eulogy so vague, so general, so universally applicable that Cody thought of that parlor game where people fill in words at random and then giggle hysterically at the story that results. Pearl Tull, the minister said, was a devoted wife and a loving mother and a pillar of the community. She had lived a long, full life and died in the bosom of her family, who grieved for her but took comfort in knowing that she'd gone to a far finer place.

It slipped the minister's mind, or perhaps he hadn't heard, that she hadn't been anyone's wife for over a third of a century; that she'd been a frantic, angry, sometimes terrifying mother; and that she'd never shown the faintest interest in her community but dwelt in it like a visitor from a superior neighborhood, always wearing her hat when out walking, keeping her doors tightly shut when at home. That her life had been very long indeed but never full; *stunted* was more like it. Or crabbed. Or . . . what was the word Cody wanted? Espaliered. Twisted and flattened to the wall—all the more so as she'd aged and wizened, lost her sight, and grown to lean too heavily on Ezra. That she was not at all religious, hadn't set foot in this church for decades; and though in certain wistful moods she might have mentioned the possibility of paradise, Cody didn't take much comfort in the notion of her residing there, fidgeting and finding fault and stirring up dissatisfactions.

Cody sat in the right front pew, the picture of a bereaved and dutiful son. But skeptical thoughts flowed through his head so loudly that he almost believed they might be heard by the congregation. He was back to his boyhood, it seemed, fearing that his mother could read his mind as unhesitatingly as she read the inner temperature of a roasting hen by giving its thigh a single, contemptuous pinch. He glanced sideways at Ruth, but she was listening to the minister.

The minister announced the closing hymn, which Pearl had requested in her funeral instructions: "We'll Understand It All By and By." Raising his long, boneless face to lead the singing, Reverend Thurman did appear bewildered—perhaps less by the Lord's mysterious ways than by the unresponsive nature of this group of mourners. Most were just staring into open hymnbooks, following each stanza silently. And there were so few of them: a couple of Ezra's co-workers, some surly teenaged grandchildren sulking in scattered pews, and five or six anonymous old people, who were probably there as church members but gave the impression of having wandered in off the streets for shelter, dragging their string-handled shopping bags.

When the service was finished, the minister descended from the pulpit and stopped to offer Cody, as firstborn, a handshake and condolences. "All my sympathy . . . know what a loss . . ."

"Thank you," said Cody, and he and Ruth and the minister proceeded down the aisle. Jenny and Joe followed, and last came Ezra, blowing his nose. By rights the grandchildren should have risen too, but if they had there would have been hardly any guests remaining.

Outside, the cold was a relief, and Cody was grateful for the lumbering noise of the traffic in the street. He stood between Jenny and Ruth and accepted the murmurs of strangers. "Beautiful service," they told him.

"Thank you," he said.

He heard a woman say to Ezra, over by the church doorway, "I'm so sorry for your trouble," and Ezra said, kindly, "Oh, that's all right"— although for Ezra alone, of the three of them, this death was clearly *not* all right. What would he fill his life with now? He had been his mother's eyes. Lately, he had been her hands and feet as well. Now that she was gone he would come home every night and . . . do what? What would he do? Just sit on the couch by himself, Cody pictured; or lie on his bed, fully dressed, staring into the swarming, brownish air above his bed.

Jenny said, "Did Ezra tell you we're meeting at his restaurant afterward?"

Cody groaned. He shook an old man's hand and said to Jenny, "I knew it. I just knew it." Hadn't he told Ruth, in fact? In the car coming down, he'd said, "Oh, God, I suppose there'll be one of those dinners. We'll have to have one of those eternal family dinners at Ezra's restaurant."

"He's probably too upset," Ruth said. "I doubt he'd give a dinner now."

This showed she didn't know Ezra as well as she'd always imagined. Certainly he would give a dinner. Any excuse would do—wedding or engagement or nephew's name on the honor roll. "Dinner at the Homesick Restaurant! Everyone in the family! Just a cozy family gathering"—and he'd rub his hands together in that annoying way he had. He no doubt had his staff at work even at this moment, preparing the . . . what were they called? The funeral baked meats. Cody sighed. But he suspected they would have to attend.

The old man must have spoken; he was waiting for Cody to answer. He tilted his flushed, tight-skinned face beneath an elaborate plume of silver hair that let the light shine through. "Thank you," Cody said. Evidently, this was the wrong response. The old man made some disappointed adjustment to his mouth. "Um . . ." said Cody.

"I said," the old man told him, "I said, 'Cody? Do you know me?' "

Cody knew him.

It shouldn't have taken him so long. There were clues he should have picked up at once: that fan-shaped pompadour, still thick and sharply crimped; the brilliant blue of his eyes; the gangsterish air of his pinstriped, ill-fitting navy blue suit.

"Yes," the old man said, with a triumphant nod. "It's your father speaking, Cody."

Cody said to Jenny, "I'm not sure if Ezra remembered to set a place for Dad."

"What?" Jenny said. She looked at Beck Tull. "Oh," she said.

"At the restaurant. Did he remember?"

"Oh, well, probably," she said.

"Nothing fancy," Cody told Beck.

Beck gaped at him.

"Just a light repast at the Homesick."

"What are you talking about?" Beck asked.

"Dinner afterward, of course, at the Homesick Restaurant."

Beck passed a hand across his forehead. He said, "Is this here Jenny?"

"Yes," Jenny told him.

"Jenny, last time I set eyes on you you were just about eight years old," said Beck. "Was it eight? Or nine. Your favorite song was 'Mairzy Doats.' You babbled that thing night and day."

"Oh, yes," Jenny said distantly. "And little lambs eat ivy."

Beck, who had drawn a breath to go on speaking, paused and shut his mouth.

"*You* remember Ruth," said Cody.

"Ruth?"

"My wife."

"Why should I remember her? I've been away! I haven't been here!"

Ruth stepped forward to offer her hand. "So Cody's married," said Beck. "Fancy that. Any children?"

"Well, Luke, of course," Cody said.

"I'm a grandfather!" He turned to Jenny. "How about you? Are you married?"

"Yes, but he's left to pick up the little ones," Jenny said. She waved goodbye to somebody.

"And Ezra?" Beck asked. "Where's Ezra?"

"Over there by the steps," Cody said.

"Ah."

Beck set off jauntily, running a hand through his crest of hair. Jenny and Cody gazed after him.

"If I just saw him on the street," Jenny said, "I would have passed him by."

"We *are* just seeing him on the street," Cody told her.

"Well. Yes."

They watched Beck arrive before Ezra with a bounce, like a child presenting some accomplishment. Ezra bent his head courteously to hear Beck's words, then gave him a mild smile and shook his hand.

"Imagine!" they heard Beck say. "Look at you! Both my sons are bigger than I am."

"Dinner is at my restaurant," Ezra told him calmly.

Beck's expression faltered once again, but recovered itself. "Wonderful!" he said. He moved toward the teen-agers, who had got wind of what was going on and stood in a clump nearby—silent, staring, hostile as usual. Beck seemed not to notice. "I'm your grandpa," he told them. "Your Grandpa Tull. Ever heard of me?" Probably they hadn't, unless they'd thought to inquire. He moved down the line, beaming. "I'm your long-lost grandpa. And you are—? What a handsome young fellow!"

He pumped the hand of the tallest teen-ager, who unfortunately was not a grandson at all but one of Ezra's salad boys.

Cody and Ruth and Jenny led the way to the restaurant on foot. The others lagged behind untidily. The first group turned onto St. Paul Street and passed various bustling little buildings—a dry cleaner's and a drugstore and a florist. All the other pedestrians were black; most held jangling radios to their ears, so that scraps of songs about love and jealousy and hardhearted women kept approaching and fading away. Then Ezra's wooden sign swung overhead, and the three of them climbed the steps and walked in.

In the chilly light from the windows, the restaurant seemed glaringly empty. One long table was covered with white linen, set with crystal and china. Thirteen places, Cody counted; for Jenny's Joe would be bringing more children, those too small to have sat through the service. A sweet-faced, plump waitress in a calico smock was drawing up a high chair for the baby. When she saw them come in, she stopped to give Jenny a hug. "I'm so sorry for your trouble," she said. "You and all your family, hear?"

"Thank you, Mrs. Potter," Jenny said. "Do you know my brother Cody? And this is Ruth, his wife."

Mrs. Potter clicked her tongue. "It's a terrible day for you," she said.

Cody turned toward the door in time to see Beck and Ezra enter, trailed by teen-agers. Ezra had obviously relaxed and grown talkative; he never could be cool to anyone for long. "So I tore out that wall there . . ." he was saying.

"Very nice. Very classy," said Beck.

"Stripped down these floors . . ."

"I hope you don't serve that kind of food a fellow can't identify."

"Oh, no."

"A *mish*mash of food, one thing not separate from another."

"No, never," Ezra said.

Cody watched with interest. (Ezra very often served such food.) Ezra led Beck through the room, waving an arm here and there. "See, these tables can be moved together if anyone should . . . and this is the kitchen . . . and these are two of my cooks, Sam and Myron. They've come in especially for our dinner. At night I have three more: Josiah, Chenille, and Mohammad."

"Quite an operation," said Beck.

The others, meanwhile, hung around their table. No one took a seat. Cody's son, Luke, and Jenny's son Peter—both unnaturally formal in white shirts and ties—wrestled together in an aimless, self-conscious way, tossing hidden glances at Beck. Probably these children saw him as a brand-new chance—a fresh start, someone to appreciate them at last. Yet when they finally sat down, no one chose a place near Beck. It was shyness, maybe. Even Ezra settled some distance away. Since Joe and the younger ones had still not arrived, this meant that Beck found himself flanked by several empty chairs. He didn't seem to notice. Kinglike, he sat alone, folding his hands before his plate and beaming around at the others. A tracery of red veins, distinct as mapped rivers and tributaries, showed in his cheeks. "So," he said. "My son owns a fancy restaurant."

Ezra looked pleased and embarrassed.

"And my daughter's a doctor," said Beck. "But Cody? What about you?"

Cody said, "Why, *you* know: I'm an efficiency consultant."

"A, how's that?"

Cody didn't answer. Ezra said, "He checks out factories. He tells them how to do things more efficiently."

"Ah! A time-study man."

"He's one of the very best," said Ezra. "He's always getting written up in articles."

"Is that so. Well, I sure am proud of you, son."

Cody had a sudden intimation that tomorrow, it would be more than he could manage to drag himself off to work. His success had finally filled its purpose. Was this all he had been striving for—this one brief moment of respect flitting across his father's face?

"I often wondered about you, Cody," Beck said, leaning toward him. "I often thought about you after I went away."

"Oh?" said Cody, politely. "Have you been away?"

His father sat back.

"*Anyhow,*" Ezra said. He cleared his throat. "Well. Dad. Are you still working for the Tanner Corporation?"

"No, no, I'm retired. Retired in sixty-five. They gave me a wonderful banquet and a sterling silver pen-and-pencil set. Forty-two years of service I put in."

Ruth murmured—an admiring, womanly sound. He turned to her and said, "To tell you the truth, I kind of miss it. Miss the contacts, miss the life . . . A salesman's life has a lot of action, know what I mean? Lot of activity. Oftentimes now it doesn't seem there's quite enough to keep me busy. But I do a bit of socializing, cardplaying. Got a few buddies at my hotel. Got a lady friend I see." He peeked around at the others from under his tufted eyebrows. "I bet you think I'm too old for such things," he said. "I know what you're thinking! But this is a really fine lady; she puts a lot of stock in me. And you understand I mean no disrespect to your mother, but now that she's gone and I'm free to remarry . . ."

Somehow, it had never occurred to Cody that his parents were still married. Jenny and Ezra, too, blinked and drew back slightly.

"Only trouble is this lady's daughter," Beck told them. "She's got this daughter, no-good daughter, thirty-five years old if she's a day but still residing at home. Eustacia Lee. No good whatsoever. Lost two fingers in a drill press years ago and never worked since, spent her compensation money on a snowmobile. I'm not too sure I want to live with her."

No one seemed able to think of any comment.

Then Joe arrived. He burst through the door, traveling in an envelope of fresh-smelling air, carrying the baby and towing a whole raft of children. Really there were only three, but it seemed like more; they were so chattery and jumbled. "Mrs. Nesbitt almost didn't let me out of school," and "You'll never guess what the baby ate," and "Phoebe had to stay in for being prejudiced in math." "Who's this?" a child asked, facing Beck.

"Your Grandpa Tull."

"Oh," she said, taking a seat. "Do us kids get wine?"

"Joe, I'd like you to meet my father," Jenny said.

"Really?" said Joe. "Gosh." But then he had to figure out the high-chair strap.

The last two children slipped into the empty chairs on either side of Beck. They twined their feet through the rungs, set pointy elbows on the table. Surrounded, Beck gazed first to his left and then to his right. "Will you look at this!" he said.

"Pardon?" Jenny asked.

"This group. This gathering. This . . . assemblage!"

"Oh," said Jenny, taking a bib from her purse. "Yes, it's quite a crowd."

"Eleven, twelve . . . thirteen . . . counting the baby, it's fourteen people!"

"There would have been fifteen, but Slevin's off at college," Jenny said.

Beck shook his head. Jenny tied the bib around the baby's neck.

"What we've got," said Beck, "is a . . . well, a crew. A whole crew."

Phoebe, who was religious, started loudly reciting a blessing. Mrs. Potter set a steaming bowl of soup before Beck. He sniffed it, looking doubtful.

"It's eggplant soup," Ezra told him.

"Ah, well, I don't believe . . ."

"Eggplant Soup Ursula. A recipe left behind by one of my very best cooks."

"On this day of death," Phoebe said, "the least some people could do is let a person pray in silence."

"She cooked by astrology," Ezra said. "I'd tell her, 'Let's have the endive salad tonight,' and she'd say, 'Nothing vinegary, the stars are wrong,' and up would come some dish I'd never thought of, something I would assume was a clear mistake, but it worked; it always worked. There might be something *to* this horoscope business, you know? But last summer the stars advised her to leave, and she left, and this place has never been the same."

"Tell us the secret ingredient," Jenny teased him.

"Who says there's a secret ingredient?"

"Isn't there always a secret ingredient? Some special, surprising trick that you'd only share with blood kin?"

"Well," said Ezra. "It's bananas."

"Aha."

"Without bananas, this soup is nothing."

"On this day of death," Phoebe said, "do we have to talk about food?"

"It is not a day of death," Jenny told her. "Use your napkin."

"The thing is," Beck said. He stopped. "What I mean to say," he said, "it looks like this is one of those great big, jolly, noisy, rambling . . . why, *families!*"

The grown-ups looked around the table. The children went on slurping soup. Beck, who so far hadn't even dipped his spoon in, sat forward earnestly. "A clan, I'm talking about," he said. "Like something on TV. Lots of cousins and uncles, jokes, reunions—"

"It's not really that way at all," Cody told him.

"How's that?"

"Don't let them mislead you. It's not the way it appears. Why, not more than two or three of these kids are even related to you. The rest are Joe's, by a previous wife. As for me, well, I haven't been with these people in years—couldn't tell you what that baby's name is. Is it a boy or girl, by the way? Was I even informed of its birth? So don't count *me* in your clan. And Becky down there, at the end of the table—"

"Becky?" said Beck. "Does she happen to be named for me, by any chance?"

Cody stopped, with his mouth open. He turned to Jenny.

"No," said Jenny, wiping the baby's chin. "Her name's Rebecca."

"You think we're a family," Cody said, turning back. "You think we're some jolly, situation-comedy family when we're in particles, torn apart, torn all over the place, and our mother was a witch."

"Oh, Cody," Ezra said.

"A raving, shrieking, unpredictable witch," Cody told Beck. "She slammed us against the wall and called us scum and vipers, said she wished us dead, shook us till our teeth rattled, screamed in our faces. We never knew from one day to the next, was she all right? Was she not? The tiniest thing could set her off. 'I'm going to throw you through that window,' she used to tell me. 'I'll look out that window and laugh at your brains splashed all over the pavement.' "

The main course was set before them, on tiptoe, by Mrs. Potter and another woman who smiled steadily, as if determined not to hear. But nobody picked up his fork. The baby crooned softly to a mushroom button. The other children watched Cody with horrified, bleached faces, while the grown-ups seemed to be thinking of something else. They kept their eyes lowered. Even Beck did.

"It wasn't like that," Ezra said finally.

"You're going to deny it?" Cody asked him.

"No, but she wasn't *always* angry. Really she was angry very seldom, only a few times, widely spaced, that happened to stick in your mind."

Cody felt drained. He looked at his dinner and found pink-centered lamb and bright vegetables—a perfect arrangement of colors and textures, one of Ezra's masterpieces, but he couldn't take a bite.

"Think of the other side," Ezra told him. "Think of how she used to play Monopoly with us. Listened to Fred Allen with us. Sang that little song with you—what was the name of that song you two sang? *Ivy, sweet sweet Ivy* . . . and you'd do a little soft-shoe. The two of you would link arms and soft-shoe into the kitchen."

"Is that right!" said Beck. "*I* didn't remember Pearl could soft-shoe."

Mrs. Potter poured wine into Cody's glass. He set his fingers around the stem but then couldn't lift it. He was conscious of Ruth, to his right, watching him with concern.

Then Ezra said, "So! What do you think of this wine, Dad?"

"Oh, afraid I'm not much for wine, son," said Beck.

"This is a really good one."

"Little shot of bourbon is more my style," said Beck.

"And best of all's the dessert wine. They make it with these grapes that have suffered from a special kind of mold, you see—"

"Well, wait now," Beck said. "Mold?"

"You're going to love it."

"And what is this here whitish stuff?"

"It's kasha."

"I don't believe I've heard of that."

"You'll love it," Ezra said.

Beck shook his head, but he looked gratified, as if he liked to think that Ezra had traveled so far beyond him.

Then Cody pushed his plate away. "I've got this partner, Sloan," he said. "A bachelor all his life. He never married."

Everyone took on an exaggerated attentiveness—even the children.

"Last year," Cody said, "Sloan ran into some old girlfriend, a woman he'd known years ago, and she had her little daughter with her. They were celebrating the daughter's birthday. Sloan asked which birthday it was, just making conversation, and when the woman told him, something rang a bell. He calculated the dates, and he said, 'Why! My God! She must be mine!' The woman looked over at him, sort of vaguely, and then she collected her thoughts and said, 'Oh. Yes, she is, as a matter of fact.' "

They waited. Cody smiled and gave them a little salute, implying that they could go back to their food.

"Well. What a strange lady," Beck said finally.

"Not at all," Cody told him.

"You'd think she'd at least have—"

"What she was saying was, the man had nothing to do with them. He wasn't ever there, you see, so he didn't count. He wasn't part of the family."

Beck drew back sharply. His eyes no longer seemed so blue; they had darkened to a color nearer navy.

Then Joe said, "The baby!"

The baby was struggling soundlessly, convulsively, mouth open and face going purple. "She's strangling," Jenny said. Several people leapt up and a wineglass overturned. Joe was trying to pull the baby from the high chair, but Jenny stopped him. "Never mind that! Let me at her!" It seemed the tray was strapped in place and they couldn't get the baby out from under it. An older child started crying. Something crashed to the floor. Jenny punched the baby in the midriff and a mushroom button shot onto the table. The baby wailed and turned pink. Hiccuping, she was dragged from the high chair and placed on her mother's lap, where she settled down cheerfully and started pursuing a pea around the rim of Jenny's plate.

"Will I live to see them grown?" Jenny asked the others.

"He's gone," said Ezra.

They knew instantly whom he meant. Everyone looked toward Beck's chair. It was empty. His napkin was tossed aside, one corner dipping into his plate and soaking up gravy.

"Wait here," Ezra said.

They not only waited; they suspended talk, suspended movement, while Ezra rushed across the dining room and out the front door. There was a pause, during which even the baby said nothing. Then Ezra came back, running his fingers distractedly through his hair. "He's nowhere in sight," he said. "But it's only been a minute. We can catch him! Come on, all of you."

Still, no one moved.

"Please!" said Ezra. "Please. For once, I want this family to finish a meal together. Why, every dinner we've ever had, something has gone wrong. Someone has left in a huff, or in tears, everything's fallen apart. . . . Come on! Everybody out, cover the area, track him down! We could gather back here when we find him and take up where we left off."

"Or," Cody pointed out, "we could finish the meal *without* him. That's always a possibility."

But it wasn't; even he could see that. One empty place at the table ruined everything. The chair itself, with its harp-shaped wooden back, had a desolate, reproachful look. Slowly, people rose. The children grouped around Ezra, who was issuing directives like a military strategist. "You and the little ones try Bushnell Street . . . rendezvous with Joe on Prima . . ." Then Ruth stood up too, to take the baby while Jenny put her coat on. They headed for the door. "Good hunting!" Cody called, and he tipped his chair back expansively and asked Mrs. Potter for another glass of wine.

Inwardly, though, he felt chastened. He thought of times in grade

school when he'd teased some classmate to tears, taken things a little
too far, and then looked around to find that all of his friends had
stopped laughing. Wasn't there the same hollow silence in this dining
room, among these sheeted tables? Mrs. Potter replaced the wine bottle
upon a silver-rimmed coaster. She stepped back and folded her hands
across her stomach.

"I believe I'll just go check on how they're doing," Cody told her.

Outside, the sky had deepened to a blue that was almost gaudy. A
weak sun lit the tops of the buildings, and it didn't seem so cold. Cody
stood with his hands at his hips, his feet spread wide—unperturbed,
to all appearances—and looked up and down the street. One section
of the search party was just disappearing around a corner: Joe and the
teen-agers. A stately black woman with her head wrapped in bandannas
had stopped to redistribute the contents of two grocery bags.

Cody took the alley to the right of the doorway, a narrow strip of
concrete lined with old packing crates and garbage cans battered shapeless. He passed the restaurant's kitchen window, where an exhaust fan
blew him a memory of Ezra's lamb. He skirted a spindly, starved cat
with a tail as matted as a worn-out bottle-brush. The back of his neck
took on that special alertness required on Baltimore streets, but he
walked at an easy, sauntering pace with his hands in his trouser pockets.

"Always have a purpose," his father used to tell him. "Act like
you're heading someplace purposeful, and none of the lowlife will mess
with you." He had also said, "Never trust a man who starts his sentences
with 'Frankly,'" and "Nine tenths of a good sidearm pitch is in the
flick of the wrist," and, "If you want to sell a person something, look
off elsewhere as you're speaking, not straight into his eyes."

"All we have is each other," Ezra would say, justifying one of his
everlasting dinners. "We've got to stick together; nobody else has the
same past that we have." But in that meager handful of advice offered
by Beck Tull—truly the sole advice Cody could remember from him—
there didn't seem much of a past to build on. From the sound of it,
you would imagine that the three of them shared only a purposeful
appearance, a mistrust of frankness, a deft wrist, and an evasive gaze.

Cody suddenly longed for his son—for Luke's fair head and hunched
shoulders. (He would rather die than desert a child of his. He had
promised himself when he was a boy: anything but that.) He thought
back to their goose hunt, where they hadn't had much to say to each
other; they had been shy and standoffish together. He wondered whether
Sloan would lend him the cabin again next weekend, so they could
give it another try.

He came out on Bushnell—sunnier than the alley and almost empty.
He shaded his eyes with his hand and looked around him and—why!
There was Luke, as if conjured up, sitting for some reason on the stoop
of a boarded-over building. Cody started toward him, walking fast.

Luke heard his footsteps and raised his head as Cody arrived. But it wasn't Luke. It was Beck. His silver hair appeared yellow in the sunlight, and he had taken off his suit coat to expose his white shirt and his sharp, cocked shoulders so oddly like Luke's. Cody came to a halt.

"I was just looking for the Trailways station," Beck told him. "I thought I could make it walking, but now I'm not so sure."

Cody took out his handkerchief to wipe his forehead.

"See, Claudette will be expecting me," said Beck. "That's the lady friend I mentioned. I figured I better go on and find a bus. Sorry to eat and run, but you know how it is with women. I told her I'd be home before supper. She's depending on me."

Cody replaced the handkerchief.

"I guess she'll want to get married, after this," said Beck. "She knows about Pearl's passing. She's sure to be making plans."

He held up his jacket, as if inspecting it for flaws. He folded it carefully, inside out, and laid it over his arm. The lining was something silky, faintly rainbow hued, like the sheen on aging meat.

"To tell the truth," Beck said, "I don't much want to marry her. It's not only that daughter; it's me. It's really me. You think I haven't had girlfriends before? Oh, sure, and could have married almost any one of them. Lots have begged me, 'Write your wife. Get a divorce. Let's tie the knot.' 'Well, maybe in a while,' I'd tell them, but I never did. I don't know, I just never did."

"You left us in her clutches," Cody said.

Beck looked up. He said, "Huh?"

"How could you do that?" Cody asked him. "How could you just dump us on our mother's mercy?" He bent closer, close enough to smell the camphorish scent of Beck's suit. "We were kids, we were only kids, we had no way of protecting ourselves. We looked to you for help. We listened for your step at the door so we'd be safe, but you just turned your back on us. You didn't lift a finger to defend us."

Beck stared past Cody at the traffic.

"She wore me out," he told Cody finally.

"Wore you out?"

"Used up my good points. Used up all my good points."

Cody straightened.

"Oh, at the start," Beck said, "she thought I was wonderful. You ought to have seen her face when I walked into a room. When I met her, she was an old maid already. She'd given up. No one had courted her for years; her girlfriends were asking her to baby-sit; their children called her Aunt Pearl. Then I came along. I made her so happy! There's my downfall, son. I mean with anyone, any one of these lady friends, I just can't resist a person I make happy. Why, she might be gap-toothed, or homely, or heavyset—all the better! I expect that if I'd got that divorce from your mother I'd have married six times over, just moving on to each new woman that cheered up some when she saw me, moving on again when she got close to me and didn't act so pleased any more. Oh, it's closeness that does you in. Never get too close to people, son—did I tell you that when you were young? When your mother and I were first married, everything was perfect. It seemed I could do no wrong. Then bit by bit I guess she saw my faults. I'd never hid them, but now it seemed they mattered after all. I made mistakes and she saw them. She saw that I was away from home too much and not enough support to her, didn't get ahead in my work, put on weight, drank too much, talked wrong, ate wrong, dressed wrong, drove a car wrong. No matter how hard I tried, seemed like everything I did got muddled. Spoiled. Turned into an accident. I'd bring home a simple toy, say, to cheer you all up when I came, and it would somehow start a fight—your mother saying it was too expensive or too dangerous or too difficult, and the three of you kids bickering over who got to play with it first. Do you recall the archery set? I thought it would be such fun, set up a target on a tree trunk and shoot our bows and arrows. But it didn't work out like I'd planned. First Pearl claims she's not athletic, then Jenny says it's too cold, then you and Ezra get in some kind of, I don't know, argument or quarrel, end up scuffling, shoot off an arrow, and wing your mother."

"I remember that," said Cody.

"Shot her through the shoulder. A disaster, a typical disaster. Then next week, while I'm away, something goes wrong with the wound. I come home from a sales trip and she tells me she nearly died. Something, I don't know, some infection or other. For me, it was the very last straw. I was sitting over a beer in the kitchen that Sunday evening and all at once, not even knowing I'd do it, I said, 'Pearl, I'm leaving.' "

Cody said, "You mean *that* was when you left?"

"I packed a bag and walked out," said Beck.

Cody sat down on the stoop.

"See," said Beck, "what it was, I guess: it was the grayness; grayness of things; half-right-and-half-wrongness of things. Everything tangled, mingled, not perfect any more. I couldn't take that. Your mother could, but not me. Yes sir, I have to hand it to your mother."

He sighed and stroked the lining of his jacket.

"I'll be honest," he said, "when I left I didn't think I'd ever care to see you folks again. But later, I started having these thoughts. 'What do you suppose Cody's doing now? What's Ezra up to, and Jenny?' 'My family wasn't so much,' I thought, 'but it's all there really is, in the end.' By then, it was maybe two, three years since I'd left. One night I was passing through Baltimore and I parked a block away, got out and walked to the house. Pretty near froze to death, standing across the street and waiting. I guess I was going to introduce myself or something, if anybody came out. It was you that came. First I didn't even know you, wondered if someone else had moved in. Then I realized it was just that you had grown so. You were almost a man. You came down the walk and you bent for the evening paper and as you straightened, you kind of flipped it in the air and caught it again, and I saw that you could live without me. You could do that carefree a thing, you see—flip a paper and catch it. You were going to turn out fine. And I was right, wasn't I? Look! Haven't you all turned out fine—leading good lives, the three of you? She did it; Pearl did it. I knew she would manage. I turned and walked back to my car.

"After that, I just stuck to my own routine. Had a few pals, a lady friend from time to time. Somebody'd start to think the world of me and I would tell myself, 'I wish Pearl could see this.' I'd even write her a note, now and then. I'd write and give her my latest address, anyplace I moved to, but what I was really writing to say was, 'There's this new important boss we've got who regards me very highly.' Or, 'There's a lady here who acts extremely thrilled when I drop by.' Crazy, isn't it? I do believe that all these years, anytime I had any success, I've kind of, like, held it up in my imagination for your mother to admire. Just take a look at *this*, Pearl, I'd be thinking. Oh, what will I do now she's gone?"

He shook his head.

Cody, searching for something to say, happened to look toward Prima Street and see his family rounding the corner, opening like a fan. The children came first, running, and the teen-agers loped behind, and the grown-ups—trying to keep pace—were very nearly running themselves, so that they all looked unexpectedly joyful. The drab colors of their funeral clothes turned their faces bright. The children's arms and legs flew out and the baby bounced on Joe's shoulders. Cody felt surprised and touched. He felt that they were pulling him toward them—that it wasn't they who were traveling, but Cody himself.

"They've found us," he told Beck. "Let's go finish our dinner."

"Oh, well, I'm not so sure," Beck said. But he allowed himself to be helped to his feet. "Oh, well, maybe this one last course," he said, "but I warn you, I plan to leave before that dessert wine's poured."

Cody held on to his elbow and led him toward the others. Overhead, seagulls drifted through a sky so clear and blue that it brought back all the outings of his boyhood—the drives, the picnics, the autumn hikes, the wildflower walks in the spring. He remembered the archery trip, and it seemed to him now that he even remembered that arrow sailing in its graceful, fluttering path. He remembered his mother's upright form along the grasses, her hair lit gold, her small hands smoothing her bouquet while the arrow journeyed on. And high above, he seemed to recall, there had been a little brown airplane, almost motionless, droning through the sunshine like a bumblebee.

MORGAN'S
PASSING

1967

THERE USED to be an Easter Fair at the Presbyterian church every year. Early Saturday morning the long, gentle hill out front would be taken over by tents, painted booths, mechanical rides on lease from the Happy Days Amusement Company, and large wooden carts slowly filling up their windows with buttered popcorn. A white rabbit, six feet tall, would bow in a dignified way as he passed out jellybeans from a basket. In the afternoon there would be an egg hunt behind the Sunday School building, and the winner was given a chocolate chicken. Music floated everywhere, strung-out wisps of one song weaving into another. The air always smelled like cotton candy.

But the Baltimore climate was unpredictable. Sometimes it was really too cold for a fair. One year, when Easter fell in March, so little was growing yet that the egg hunt was a joke. The eggs lay exposed and foolish on the bald brown lawn, and the children pounced on them with mittened hands. The grownups stood hunched in sweaters and scarves. They seemed to have strayed in from the wrong season. It would have been a better fair with no human beings at all—just the striped tents flapping their spring-colored scallops, the carousel playing "After the Ball," and the plaster horses prancing around riderless.

At the puppet show, in a green and white tent lit by a chilly greenish glow, Cinderella wore a strapless evening gown that made her audience shiver. She was a glove puppet with a large, round head and braids of yellow yarn. At the moment she was dancing with the Prince, who had a Dutch Boy haircut. They held each other so fondly, it was hard to remember they were really just two hands clasping each other. "You have a beautiful palace," she told him. "The floors are like mirrors! I wonder who scrubs them."

Her voice was wry and throaty, not at all puppet-like. You almost expected to see the vapor rising from her painted mouth.

The Prince said, "I have no idea, Miss . . . what was that name?"

Instead of answering, she looked down at her feet. The pause grew too long. The children shifted in their folding chairs. It became apparent that the ballroom was not a ballroom at all, but a gigantic cardboard carton with the front cut away and a gauze curtain at the rear. A child in the audience said, "I have to go to the bathroom."

"Ssh."

"Your name," said the Prince.

Why didn't she speak?

Really, the children saw, she was only a puppet. They sat back. Something had snapped. Even the parents looked confused.

Then Cinderella flopped onto her face in a very unnatural way, and a human hand emerged from her skirts and withdrew behind the scrim. The children stared. On the stage lay her dead and empty shell, with her arms flung back as if broken. "Is it over?" a child asked his mother.

"Hush. Sit still. You know that's not how it ends."

"Well, where's the rest, then? Can we go?"

"Wait. Here comes someone."

It was a grownup, but just barely. He felt his way through the bedsheet that hung at one side of the stage: a dark, thin boy in khakis and a rust-colored corduroy jacket, with a white shirt so old and well washed that all the life had gone out of it. There was something fierce about him—maybe the twist of his mouth, or the defiant way he kept his chin raised. "Ladies and gentlemen," he said, running a hand through his hair. "Boys and girls . . ."

"It's the Prince," said a child."

"Boys and girls, there's been . . . an illness. The play is over. You can get your money at the ticket booth."

He turned away, not even waiting to see how this would be taken, and fumbled at the sheet. But then he seemed struck by another thought, and he turned back to the audience. "Excuse me," he said. He ran a hand through his hair again. (No wonder it was so mussed and ropy.) "Is there a doctor in the house?" he asked.

They looked at each other—children, mostly, and most of them under five. Apparently there was no doctor. The boy gave a sudden, sharp sigh and lifted a corner of the sheet. Then someone at the rear of the tent stood up.

"I am a doctor," he said.

He was a lank, tall, bearded man in a shaggy brown suit that might have been cut from blankets, and on his head he wore a red ski cap—the pointy kind, with a pom-pom at the tip. Masses of black curls burst out from under it. His beard was so wild and black and bushy that it was hard to tell how old he was. Maybe forty? Forty-five? At any rate, older than you'd expect to see at a puppet show, and no child sat next to him to explain his being there. But he craned his head forward, smiling kindly, leading with his long, pinched nose and waiting to hear how he could help. The boy looked relieved; his face lost some of its tension.

"Come with me," he said. He lifted the sheet higher.

Stumbling over people's feet, sliding past the children who were already swarming toward the exit, the doctor made his way to the boy. He wiped his palms on his thighs and stooped under the sheet. "What seems to be the trouble here?" he asked.

"It's her," said the boy.

He meant the blond girl resting on a heap of muslin bags. She was small-boned and frail, but enormously pregnant, and she sat cradling her stomach—guarding it, looking up at the doctor out of level gray eyes. Her lips were so colorless, they were almost invisible.

"I see," said the doctor.

He dropped down beside her, hitching up his trousers at the knees, and leaned forward to set a hand on her abdomen. There was a pause. He frowned at the tent wall, weighing something in his mind. "Yes," he said finally. He sat back and studied the girl's face. "How far apart are the pains?" he asked.

"All the time," she said, in Cinderella's wry voice.

"Constantly? When did they begin?"

"About . . . an hour ago, Leon? When we were setting up for this performance."

The doctor raised his eyebrows—two black thickets.

"It would be exceedingly strange," he said, "if they were so close together this soon."

"Well, they are," the girl said matter-of-factly.

The doctor stood up, grunting a little, and dusted off his knees. "Oh, well," he said, "just to be on the safe side, I suppose you ought to check into the hospital. Where's your car parked?"

"We don't have one," the boy said.

"No car?"

The doctor looked around him, as if wondering how all their equipment had arrived—the bulky stage, the heap of little costumes, the liquor carton in the corner with a different puppet's head poking out of each cardboard compartment.

"Mr. Kenny brought us," said the boy, "in his panel truck. He's chairman of the Fund-Raising Committee."

"You'd better come with me, then," the doctor said. "I'll drive you over." He seemed fairly cheerful about it. He said, "What about the puppets? Shall we take them along?"

"No," said the boy. "What do I care about the puppets? Let's just get her to the hospital."

"Suit yourself," the doctor told him, but he cast another glance around, as if regretting a lost opportunity, before he bent to help the boy raise the girl to her feet. "What are they made of?" he asked.

"Huh?" said the boy. "Oh, just . . . things." He handed the girl her purse. "Emily makes them," he added.

"Emily?"

"This is Emily, my wife. I'm Leon Meredith."

"How do you do?" the doctor said.

"They're made of rubber balls," said Emily.

Standing, she turned out to be even slighter than she'd first appeared. She walked gracefully, leading the men out through the front of the tent, smiling at the few stray children who remained. Her draggled black skirt hung unevenly around her shins. Her thin white cardigan, dotted with specks of black lint, didn't begin to close over the bulge of her stomach.

"I take an ordinary, dimestore rubber ball," she said, "and cut a neck hole with my knife. Then I cover the ball with a nylon stocking, and I sew on eyes and a nose, paint a mouth, make hair of some kind . . ."

Her voice grew strained. The doctor glanced over at her, sharply.

"The cheapest kind of stockings are the best," she said. "They're pinker. From a distance, they look more like skin."

"Is this going to be a long walk?" Leon asked.

"No, no," said the doctor. "My car's in the main parking lot."

"Maybe we should call an ambulance."

"Really, that won't be necessary," the doctor said.

"But what if the baby comes before we get to the hospital?"

"Believe me," said the doctor, "if I thought there was the faintest chance of that, I wouldn't be doing this. I have no desire whatever to deliver a baby in a Pontiac."

"Lord, no," Leon said, and he cast a sideways look at the doctor's hands, which didn't seem quite clean. "But Emily claims it's arriving any minute."

"It is," Emily said calmly. She was walking along between them now, climbing the slope to the parking lot unassisted. She supported the weight of her baby as if it were already separate from her. Her battered leather pocketbook swung from her shoulder. In the sunlight her hair, which was bound on her head in two silvery braids, sprang up in little corkscrewed wisps like metal filings flying toward a magnet, and her skin looked chilled and thin and pale. But her eyes remained level. She didn't appear to be frightened. She met the doctor's gaze squarely. "I can feel it," she told him.

"Is this your first?"

"Yes."

"Ah, then," he said, "you see, it can't possibly come so soon. It'll be late tonight at the earliest—maybe even tomorrow. Why, you haven't been in labor more than an hour!"

"Maybe, and maybe not," said Emily.

Then she gave a sudden, surprising toss of her head; she threw the doctor a tilted look. "After all," she said, "I've had a backache since two o'clock this morning. Maybe I just didn't *know* it was labor."

Leon turned to the doctor, who seemed to hesitate a moment. "Doctor?" Leon said.

"All my patients say their babies are coming immediately," the doctor told him. "It never happens."

They had reached the flinty white gravel of the parking lot. Various people passed—some just arriving, holding down their coats against the wind; others leaving with balloons and crying children and cardboard flats of shivering tomato seedlings.

"Are you warm enough?" Leon asked Emily. "Do you want my jacket?"

"I'm fine," Emily said, although beneath her cardigan she wore only a skimpy black T-shirt, and her legs were bare and her shoes were ballet slippers, thin as paper.

"You must be freezing," Leon said.

"I'm all *right*, Leon."

"It's the adrenalin," the doctor said absently. He came to a stop and gazed off across the parking lot, stroking his beard. "I seem to have lost my car," he said.

Leon said, "Oh, God."

"No, there it is. Never mind."

His car was clearly a family man's—snub-nosed, outdated, with a frayed red hair ribbon flying from the antenna and WASH THIS! written in the dust on one fender. Inside, there were schoolbooks and dirty socks and gym bloomers and rucked-up movie magazines. The doctor knelt on the front seat and swatted at the clutter in the rear until most of it had landed on the floor. Then he said, "There you go. You two sit in back; you'll be more comfortable." He settled himself in front and started the engine, which had a whining, circular sound. Emily and Leon slid into the rear. Emily found a track shoe under her right knee, and she placed it on her lap, cupping the heel and toe in her fingers. "Now," said the doctor. "Which hospital?"

Emily and Leon looked at each other.

"City? University? Hopkins?"

"Whatever's closest," Leon said.

"But which have you reserved? Where's your doctor?"

"We haven't reserved anyplace," Emily said, "and we don't have a doctor."

"I see."

"*Anywhere*," said Leon. "Just get her there."

"Very well."

The doctor maneuvered his car out of the parking space. He shifted gears with a grinding sound. Leon said, "I guess we should have attended to this earlier."

"Yes, actually," said the doctor. He braked and looked in both directions. Then he nosed the car into the stream of traffic on Farley Street. They were traveling through a new, raw section barely within the city limits—ranch houses, treeless lawns, another church, a shopping mall. "But I suppose you lead a footloose sort of life," the doctor said.

"Footloose?"

"Carefree. Unattached," he said. He patted all his pockets with one hand until he'd found a pack of Camels. He shook a cigarette free and lit it, which involved so much fumbling and cursing and clutching at dropped objects that it was a wonder the other drivers managed to stay clear of him. When he'd finally flicked his match out, he exhaled a great cloud of smoke and started coughing. The Pontiac wandered from lane to lane. He thumped his chest and said, "I suppose you just follow the fairs, am I correct? Just follow the festivities, stop wherever you find yourselves."

"No, what happened was—"

"But I wish we could have brought along the puppets," the doctor said. He turned onto a wider street. He was forced to slow down now, inching past furniture shops and carpet warehouses, trailing a mammoth Mayflower van that blocked all view of what lay ahead. "Are we coming to a traffic light?" he asked. "Is it red or green? I can't see a thing. And what about their noses, the puppets' noses? How'd you make the stepmother's nose? Was it a carrot?"

"Excuse me?" Emily said. "Nose?" She didn't seem to be concentrating. "I'm sorry," she said. "There's some kind of water all over everything."

The doctor braked and looked in the rear-view mirror. His eyes met Leon's. "Can't you hurry?" Leon asked him.

"I *am* hurrying," the doctor said.

He took another puff of his cigarette, pinching it between his thumb and forefinger. The air in the car grew blue and layered. Up ahead, the Mayflower van was trying to make a left turn. It would take all day, at this rate. "Honk," Leon said. The doctor honked. Then he clamped his cigarette in his teeth and swung out into the right-hand lane, where a car coming up fast behind nearly slammed into them. Now horns were blowing everywhere. The doctor started humming. He pulled back into the left lane, set his left-turn signal blinking, and sped toward the next traffic light, which hung beside a swinging sign that read NO LEFT TURN. His cigarette had a long, trembly tube of ashes hanging from it. He tapped the ashes onto the floor, the steering wheel, his lap. *"After the ball is o-ver,"* he sang. He careened to the right again and cut across the apron of a Citgo station, took a sharp left, and emerged on the street he wanted. *"After the break of morn . . ."* Leon gripped the back of the front seat with one hand and held on to Emily with the other. Emily gazed out the side window.

"I always go to fairs, any fair in town," the doctor said. "School fairs, church fairs, Italian fairs, Ukrainian . . . I like the food. I also like the rides; I like to watch the people who run them. What would it be like, working for such an outfit? I used to take my daughters, but they're too old now, they say. 'How can that be?' I ask them. 'I'm not too old; how come you are?' My youngest is barely ten. How can she be too old?"

"The baby's here," Emily said.

"I beg your pardon?"

"The baby. I feel it."

The doctor looked in the mirror again. His eyes were more aged than the rest of him—a mournful brown, bloodshot and pouched, the skin beneath them the tarnished color of a bruise inside a banana. He opened his mouth, or appeared to. At any rate, his beard lengthened. Then it shortened again.

"Stop the car," Leon told him.

"Well . . . ah, yes, maybe so," the doctor said.

He parked beside a hydrant, in front of a tiny pizza parlor called Maria's Home-Style. Leon was chafing Emily's wrists. The doctor climbed out, scratching the curls beneath his ski cap and looking puzzled. "Excuse me," he said to Leon. Leon got out of the car. The doctor leaned in and asked, "You say you feel it?"

"I feel the head."

"Of course this is all a mistake," the doctor told Leon. "You know how long it takes the average primipara to deliver? Between ten and twelve hours. Oh, at least. And with a great deal more carrying on, believe me. There's not a chance in this world that baby could be here yet."

But as he spoke, he was sliding Emily into a horizontal position on the seat, methodically folding back her damp skirt in a series of tidy pleats. He said, "What in the name of—?" It appeared that her T-shirt was some sort of leotard; it had a crotch. He grimaced and ripped the center seam. Then he said, "She's right."

"Well, *do* something," Leon said. "What are you going to do?"

"Go buy some newspapers," the doctor told him. "Anything will be fine—*News American, Sun* . . . but fresh ones, you understand? Don't just accept what someone hands you in a diner, saying he's finished reading it . . ."

"Oh, my God. Oh, my God. I don't have change," Leon said.

The doctor started rummaging through his pockets. He pulled out his mangled pack of Camels, two lint-covered jellybeans, and a cylinder of Rolaids. "Emily," he said, "would you happen to have change for a dollar?"

Emily said something that sounded like yes, and turned her head from side to side. "Try her purse," the doctor said. They felt along the floor, among the gym clothes and soda straws. Leon brought up the purse by its strap. He plowed through it till he found a billfold, and then he raced off down the street, muttering, "Newspapers. Newspapers." It was a cheerful, jumbled street with littered sidewalks and a row of tiny shops—eating places, dry cleaners, florists. In front of one of the cafés were various newspapers in locked, windowed boxes.

The doctor stepped on his cigarette and ground it into the pavement.

Then he took off his suit jacket. He rolled up his sleeves and tucked
his shirt more firmly into his trousers. He bent inside the car and laid
a palm on Emily's abdomen. "Breathe high in your chest," he told her.
He gazed dreamily past her, humming under his breath, watching the
trucks and busses rumble by through the opposite window. The cold
air caused the dark hairs to bristle on his forearms.

A woman in high heels clopped down the sidewalk; she never even
noticed what was going on. Then two teenaged girls approached, sharing
fudge from a white paper sack. Their footsteps slowed, and the doctor
heard and turned around. "You two!" he said. "Go call an ambulance.
Tell them we've got a delivery on our hands."

They stared at him. Identical cubes of fudge were poised halfway to
their mouths.

"Well?" he said. "Go on."

When they had rushed into Maria's Home-Style, the doctor turned
back to Emily. "How're you doing?" he asked her.

She groaned.

Leon returned, out of breath, with a stack of newspapers. The doctor
opened them out and started spreading them under Emily and all
around her. "Now, these," he said conversationally, "will grant us some
measure of antisepsis." Leon didn't seem to be listening. The doctor
wrapped two newspapers around Emily's thighs. She began to blend
in with the car. He hung a sports section down the back of the seat
and anchored it to the window ledge with the track shoe she'd been
holding all this time.

"Next," he said, "I'll need two strips of cloth, two inches wide and
six inches long. Tear off your shirttail, Leon."

"I want to quit," Emily said.

"Quit?"

"I've changed my mind."

The cook came out of Maria's Home-Style. He was a large man in
an apron stained with tomato sauce. For a moment he watched Leon,
who was standing by the car in nothing but his jeans, shakily tugging
at his shirttail. (Leon's ribs showed and his shoulder blades were as
sharp as chicken wings. He was much too young for all this.) The cook
reached over and took the shirt and ripped it for him. "Thanks," said
Leon.

"But what's the use of it?" the cook asked.

"He wants two strips of cloth," said Leon, "two inches wide and six
inches long. *I* don't know why."

The cook tore again, following instructions. He gave the shirt to Leon
and passed the strips to the doctor, who hung them carefully on the
inner door handle. Then the cook propped a wide, meaty hand on the
car roof and bent in to nod at Emily. "Afternoon," he said.

"Hello," said Emily politely.

"How you doing?"

"Oh, just fine."

"Seems like he wants to come on and get born," the cook said, "and then he wants to go back in a ways."

"Will you get out of here?" Leon said.

The cook let this pass. "Those two girls you sent are calling the ambulance," he told the doctor. "They're using my free phone."

"Good," the doctor said. He cupped the baby's head in his hands— a dark, wet, shining bulge. "Now, Emily, bear down," he said. "Maria, press flat on her belly, just a steady, slow pressure, please."

"Soo now, soo now," the cook said, pressing. Leon crouched on the curb, gnawing a knuckle, his shirt back on but not buttoned. Behind them, a little crowd had gathered. The teenaged girls stood hushed, forgetting to dip into their fudge sack. A man was asking everyone if an ambulance had been called. An old woman was telling a younger one all about someone named Dexter, who had been a breech birth with multiple complications.

"Bear down," said the doctor.

There was a silence. Even the traffic noises seemed to have stopped.

Then the doctor stepped back, holding up a slippery, bleak lump. Something moved. There was a small, caught sound from someplace unexpected. So fast it seemed that everyone had been looking away when it happened, the lump turned into a wailing, writhing, frantic, indignant snarl of red arms and legs and spiraled telephone cord. "Oh," the crowd said, breathing again.

"It's a girl," said the doctor. He passed her to the cook. "Was a girl what you wanted?"

"Anything! Anything!" the cook said. "So long as she's healthy. Soo, baby."

"I was talking to Emily," the doctor said mildly. He had to raise his voice above the baby's, which was surprisingly loud. He bent over Emily, pressing her abdomen now with both palms. "Emily? Are you all right? Bear down again, please."

While he pressed, she couldn't get air to speak, but the instant he let up she said, "I'm fine, and I'd like my daughter."

The cook seemed reluctant to hand her over. He rocked the baby against his apron, thought a moment, and sighed. Then he gave her to the doctor. The doctor checked her breathing passages—the mashed-looking nose, the squalling cavern of a mouth. "With such a racket, how could she not be fine?" he asked, and he leaned in to lay her in Emily's arms. Emily nestled the baby's head against her shoulder, but the wailing went on, thin and passionate, with a hiccup at the end of each breath.

"What'd you do with those cloths?" the doctor asked Leon.

Leon was standing up now, so as to get a glimpse of the baby.

Something kept tugging his lips into a smile that he kept trying to bat down again. "Cloths?" he said.

"Those cloths you tore, dammit. We're nowhere near done here yet."

"You hung them on the door handle," someone in the crowd said.

"Oh, yes," said the doctor.

He took one cloth, leaned in, and tied it around the baby's cord. For all the blunt, clumsy look of his fingers, he did seem to know what he was doing. *"After the ball is over,"* he sang in his beard-blurred voice. While he was knotting the second cloth, a faraway cry started up. It sounded like an extension of the baby's cry—equally thin, watery-sounding in the wind. Then it separated and grew more piercing. "The ambulance!" Leon said. "I hear the ambulance, Emily."

"Send it back," Emily said.

"They're going to take you to the hospital, honey. You're going to be all right now."

"But it's over! Do I have to go?" she asked the doctor.

"Certainly," he said. He stepped back to admire his knots, which looked something like the little cloth bows on a kite tail. "Actually," he said, "they're coming in the nick of time. I have nothing to cut the cord with."

"You could use my Swiss Army officer's knife," she told him. "It's in my purse. It's the Woodsman style, with a scissors blade."

"Remarkable," said the doctor, and he rocked on his heels, beaming down at her. His teeth seemed very large and yellow behind the tangled beard.

The siren drew closer. A spinning red light wove through the traffic, and the ambulance screeched to a halt beside the doctor's car. Two men in white leaped out. "Where is she?" one asked.

"Here we are," the doctor called.

The men flung open the back doors of the ambulance and brought a stretcher crashing to the street—a wheeled bed, too long and narrow, like a coffin, with too much chrome. Emily struggled to a sitting position. The baby stopped in mid-cry, as if shocked. "Do I have to do this?" Emily asked the doctor. And while the attendants were helping her out of the car (chairing her onto the stretcher, newspapers and all), she kept her face turned toward the doctor and waited to be rescued. "Doctor? I can't stand hospitals! Do I have to go?"

"Of course," the doctor told her. He stooped for her purse and laid it on the stretcher.

"Is Leon coming too?"

"Certainly he's coming."

"Are *you?*"

"Me? Oh."

"Best if you would, Doc," the driver told him, unfolding a sheet over Emily.

"Well, if you like," the doctor said.

He closed his car door and followed the stretcher into the ambulance. There was another stretcher, empty, next to Emily's. He and Leon sat on it—both of them gingerly, just on the edge, with their knees jutting out. "Pretty fancy," the doctor said to Leon. He meant, presumably, the interior of the ambulance: the deeply carpeted floor, the gleaming tanks and gauges. When the men slammed the doors shut, there was a sudden, luxurious silence. The street noises faded, and through the tinted windows, the people on the sidewalk seemed as soundless and slow-moving as creatures on the ocean floor. They slid away. A café and a pawnshop glided past. Even the siren was muffled, like something on an old-fashioned radio.

"How're you feeling?" the doctor asked Emily.

"Fine," she said. She lay still, in a tangle of loosened braids. The baby stared severely at the ceiling.

"We really appreciate all you've done," Leon told the doctor.

"It was nothing," said the doctor, turning down the corners of his mouth. He seemed displeased.

"If Emily didn't have this thing about hospitals, we'd have made our arrangements sooner, I guess. But the baby wasn't due for another couple of weeks. We just kept putting it off."

"And I suppose you were on the move so much," the doctor said.

"No, no—"

"But the style of your lives: I don't imagine you can plan very far ahead."

"You have the wrong idea about us," Emily said.

Flattened on the stretcher, with the crisp sheet covering the newspapers and her sodden skirt, Emily seemed untouched, somehow—pristine and remote, with her gaze turned inward. "You think we're some kind of transients," she said, "but we're not. We're legally married, and we live in a regular apartment with furniture. This baby was fully planned for. We're even going to have a diaper service. I've already called to set it up, and they said to let them know when she came and they'd start delivery promptly."

"I see," said the doctor, nodding. He appeared to be enjoying this. The disorderly beard flew up and down, and the pom-pom on his ski cap bobbed.

"We've planned out every detail," Emily said. "We didn't buy a crib because cribs are extraneous. We're using a cardboard box for now, with padding on the insides."

"Oh, wonderful," said the doctor, looking delighted.

"When she gets too big for the box, we'll order this aluminum youth-bed rail we happened to see in a catalog. You can fit it onto any mattress. What's the point in all that equipment—cribs and strollers and Bathinettes? Besides, the youth-bed rail will even work in hotels and other people's apartments. It travels well."

"Travels, yes," the doctor echoed, and he clamped his hands between his knees, leaning with the ambulance as it sped around a curve.

"But we're not . . . I mean, it's only that we travel to give shows sometimes. There'll be someone wanting 'Snow White' or 'Cinderella' somewhere outside the city. But we're almost always home by night. We're never *shiftless*. You have the wrong idea."

"Did I say you were shiftless?" the doctor asked. He looked over at Leon. "Did I?"

Leon shrugged.

"We've thought of everything," Emily said.

"Yes, I see you have," the doctor said gently.

Leon cleared his throat. "By the way," he said, "we haven't discussed your fee."

"Fee?"

"For your services."

"Oh, emergency services aren't charged for," the doctor said. "Don't you know that?"

"No," said Leon.

He and the doctor seemed to be trying to stare each other down. Leon lifted his chin even higher. The light caught his cheekbones. He was one of those people who appear to be continually ready to take offense—jaw fixed, shoulders tight. "I'm not accepting this for free," he said.

"Who says it's free?" the doctor asked. "I expect you to name your baby for me." He laughed—a wheeze that ruffled his beard.

"What's your name?" Emily asked him.

"Morgan," said the doctor.

There was a silence.

"*Gower* Morgan," he said.

Emily said, "Maybe we could use the initials."

"I was only joking," the doctor told her. "Didn't you know I was joking?" He fumbled for his Camels and shook one out of the pack. "It was meant to be a joke," he said.

"About the fee," said Leon.

The doctor took his cigarette from his mouth and peered at the sign on the oxygen tank. "The fact is," he said, replacing the cigarette in its pack, "I had nothing better to do today. My wife and daughters have gone to a wedding; my wife's brother is getting married again." He clutched Leon's shoulder as they turned a corner. The ambulance was rolling up a driveway now. They passed a sign reading EMERGENCY ONLY.

"My daughters are growing up," the doctor said, "doing womanly things with their mother, leaving their father out in the cold. Each one when she was born seemed so new; I had such hopes; I was so sure we'd make no mistakes. Enjoy this one while you can," he told Leon. The baby started and clutched two bits of air.

"I had sort of thought she would be a boy," Leon said.

"Oh, Leon!" said Emily, drawing the baby closer.

"Boys, well," the doctor said. "We tried for a boy for years, ourselves. But you can always hope for next time."

"We can only afford the one," said Leon.

"One? One child," the doctor said. He fell into thought. "Yes, well, why not? There's a certain . . . compactness to it. Very streamlined. Very basic," he said.

"It's a matter of money," Leon said.

The ambulance bounced to a stop. The attendants flew out their front doors and around to the back, letting in the din of a gigantic, sooty machine just outside the emergency room, and the smell of hot laundry water and auto exhausts and wilted cafeteria food. They grabbed Emily's stretcher and rushed away with it, wheels shrieking. Leon and the doctor clambered to the pavement and trotted after it.

"Do you have dimes?" the doctor shouted.

"Time for what?"

"Dimes! Money!"

"No, I'm sorry," Leon said. "Could you use a dollar bill?"

"For you, I meant!" the doctor shouted. They passed through a set of swinging doors. He lowered his voice. "Not for me; for you. For the phone. You'll want to call about the baby."

"Who would I call?" Leon asked, spreading his arms.

The doctor stopped short. "Who would he call!" he repeated to himself. He wore the open, delighted expression he'd worn in the ambulance when he'd been told about the youth-bed rail.

Then a nurse lifted Emily's sheet, clucked at the blood-soaked newspapers, and ran alongside the stretcher as it rolled down a corridor. Another nurse took Leon's elbow and led him toward a typist in a glass compartment. Everything spun into action—polished, efficient, briskly clacketing. The doctor was left behind.

In fact, he was forgotten, for the moment. When Leon and Emily next thought of him, he was nowhere to be found. He'd just melted away. Had he left any word? Leon asked Emily's nurse. The nurse had no idea whom he was talking about. Another doctor had been called in, a resident in obstetrics. He said it was a fine delivery, healthy baby. All things considered, he said, Emily should be thankful. "Yes, and Dr. Morgan is the one we should thank," Leon told him. "Besides, we hadn't settled the fee." But the resident had never heard of Dr. Morgan. And he wasn't in the phone book, either. It seemed he didn't exist.

Later on (just a few weeks later, when their daughter's birth had faded and they felt she had always been with them), they almost wondered if they had imagined the man—just conjured him up in a time of need. His hat, Emily said, had made her think of a gnome. He really could have been someone from a fairytale, she said: the baby elf, the troll, the goblin who finds children under cabbage leaves and lays them in their mothers' arms and disappears.

1968

|

YOU COULD say he was a man who had gone to pieces, or maybe he'd always been in pieces; maybe he'd arrived unassembled. Various parts of him seemed poorly joined together. His lean, hairy limbs were connected by exaggerated knobs of bone; his black-bearded jaw was as clumsily hinged as a nutcracker. Parts of his life, too, lay separate from other parts. His wife knew almost none of his friends. His children had never seen where he worked; it wasn't in a safe part of town, their mother said. Last month's hobby—the restringing of a damaged pawnshop banjo, with an eye to becoming suddenly musical at the age of forty-two—bore no resemblance to this month's hobby, which was the writing of a science-fiction novel that would make him rich and famous. He was writing about the death of Earth. All these recent flying saucers, he proposed, belonged to beings who knew for a fact that our sun would burn out within a year and a half. They weren't just buzzing Earth for the hell of it; they were ascertaining what equipment would be needed to transfer us all to another planet in a stabler, far more orderly solar system. He had written chapter one, but was having trouble with the opening sentence of chapter two.

Or look at his house: a tall brick Colonial house in north Baltimore. Even this early on a January morning, when the sun was no more than a pinkish tinge in an opaque white sky, it was clear there was something fragmented about Morgan's house. Its marble stoop was worn soft at the edges like an old bar of soap, and heavy lace curtains glimmered in the downstairs windows; but on the second floor, where his daughters slept, the curtains were made from sections of the American flag, and on the third floor, where his mother slept, they were lace again, misting the tangle of ferns that hung behind them. And if you could see inside, through the slowly thinning gray of the hallway, you would find the particles of related people's unrelated worlds: his daughters' booksacks tumbling across the hall radiator, which also served as mail rack, sweater shelf, and message bureau; his wife's League of Women Voters leaflets rubber-banded into a tower on the living-room coffee table; and his mother's ancient, snuffling dog dreaming of rabbits and twitching her paws as she slept on the cold brick hearth. There was a cribbage board under the sofa. (No one knew this. It had been lost for weeks.) There was a jigsaw puzzle, half completed, that Morgan's sister, Brindle, filled her long, morose, spinsterish days with: a view of an Alpine village in the springtime. The church steeple was assembled and so were the straight-edged border and the whole range of mountains with their purple and lavender shadows, but she would never get to the sky, surely. She would never manage all that blank, unchanging blue that joined everything else together.

In the glass-fronted bookcase by the dining-room door, rows of books slumped sideways or lay flat: Morgan's discarded manuals reflecting various spells of enthusiasm (how to restore old paintings and refinish secondhand furniture; how to cure illness with herbs; how to raise bees in his attic). Beneath them sat his wife Bonny's college yearbooks, where Bonny appeared as a freckled, exuberant girl in several different team uniforms; and under those were his daughters' tattered picture books and grade-school textbooks and Nancy Drews, and his mother's tiny, plump autograph book, whose gilded title had been eaten away by worms or mildew or maybe just plain time, so that all that remained was a faintly shining trail of baldness as if a snail had crossed the crimson velvet in a tortuous script that coincidentally spelled out *Autographs*. (And on the first, yellowed page, in a hand so steely and elegant that you'd only see it now on a wedding invitation: *Louisa dearest, Uncle Charlie is not a poet so will only write his name hereunder, Charles Brindle, Christmas Day, 1911*—that awkward little shrug of inadequacy descending through the years so clearly, though the man had been dead a quarter-century or more and even Louisa might have had trouble recollecting him.) The bottom shelf held a varnished plaque of Girl Scout knots, a nearly perfect conch shell, and a brown cardboard photo album pasted with photographs so widely spaced in time that whole generations seemed to be dashing past, impatient to get it over with. Here was Morgan's father, Samuel, a boy in knickers; and next to him stood Samuel full-grown, marrying Louisa with her bobbed hair and shiny stockings. Here was little Morgan in a badly knitted pram set; and Morgan at eleven holding his infant sister, Brindle, as if he might have preferred to drop her (and look! was that the same pram set? only slightly more puckered and with some new stain or shadow down the front). And then suddenly Morgan at twenty-four, shorter-haired than he would ever be again, raw-necked, self-conscious, beside his plump, smiling wife with their first baby in his arms. (No telling where *their* wedding photo had got to, or that famous pram set either, for all Amy wore was a sagging diaper.) Now they stopped for breath for a moment. Here were fifteen solid pages of the infant Amy, every photo snapped by Morgan in the first proud flush of fatherhood. Amy sleeping, nursing, yawning, bathing, examining her fist. Amy learning to sit. Amy learning to crawl. Amy learning to walk. She was a sturdy child with her mother's sensible expression, and she appeared to be more real than anyone else in the album. Maybe it was the slowness with which she plodded, page by page, through the early stages of her life. She took on extra meaning, like the frame at which a movie is halted. (The experts lean forward; someone points to something with a long, official pointer . . .) Then the photos speeded up again. Here was the infant Jean, then the twins in their miniature spectacles, then Liz on her first day of nursery school. The film changed to Kodachrome, brighter than nature, and the setting was always the beach now— always Bethany Beach, Delaware, for where else could a man with seven daughters find the time for his camera? To look at the album, you would imagine that these people enjoyed an endless stream of vacations. Bonny was eternally sunburned, bulging gently above and below her one-piece Lastex swimsuit. The girls were eternally coconut-oiled and gleaming in their slender strips of bikinis, holding back handfuls of wind-tossed hair and laughing. Always laughing. Where were the tears and quarrels, and the elbowing for excessive amounts of love and space and attention? What about all those colds and tonsillectomies? Where was Molly's stammer? Or Susan's chronic night-mares? Not here. They sat laughing without a care in the world. At the edges of their bikinis, paler flesh showed, the faintest line of it, the only reminder of other seasons. And, oh yes, Morgan. One picture a year, taken aslant and out of focus by some amateurish daughter: Morgan in wrinkled trunks that flared around his thighs, whiskered all over, untouched by the sun, showing off his biceps and probably grinning, but how could you tell for sure? For on his head he wore an Allagash jungle hat from L. L. Bean, and mosquito netting in sweeps and folds veiled his face completely.

Now the light had reached the stairwell and sent a gleam along the banister, but the carpeted steps were still in darkness and the cat slinking up them was only a shadow, her stripes invisible, her pointed face a single spear of white. She crossed the hall floorboards without a sound. She strode to the north rear bedroom and paused in the doorway and then advanced, so purposeful that you could see how every joint in her body was strung. Next to Bonny's side of the bed, she rose up on her hind legs to test the electric blanket—pat-pat along the edge of the mattress with one experienced paw, and then around to Morgan's side and pat-pat again. Morgan's side was warmer. She braced herself, tensed, and sprang onto his chest, and Morgan grunted and opened his eyes. It was just that moment of dawn when the air seems visible: flocked, like felt, gathering itself together to take on color at any second. The sheets were a shattered, craggy landscape; the upper reaches of the room were lit by a grayish haze, like the smoke that rises from bombed buildings. Morgan covered his face. "Go away," he told the cat, but the cat only purred and sent a slitted stare elsewhere, pretending not to hear. Morgan sat up. He spilled the cat onto Bonny (a nest of tangled brown hair, a bare, speckled shoulder) and hauled himself out of bed.

In the winter he slept in thermal underwear. He thought of clothes— all clothes—as costumes, and it pleased him to stagger off to the bathroom hitching up his long johns and rummaging through his beard like some character from the Klondike. He returned with his face set in a brighter, more hopeful expression, having glimpsed himself in the bathroom mirror: there were decisions to be made. He snapped on the closet light and stood deciding who to be today. Next to Bonny's wrinkled skirts and blouses the tumult of his clothes hung, tightly packed together—sailor outfits, soldier outfits, riverboat-gambler outfits. They appeared to have been salvaged from some traveling operetta. Above them were his hats, stacked six deep on the shelf. He reached for one, a navy knit skullcap, and pulled it on and looked in the full-length mirror: harpooner on a whaling ship. He took it off and tried next a gigantic, broad-brimmed leather hat that engulfed his head and shaded his eyes. Ah, back to the Klondike. He tugged a pair of crumpled brown work pants over his long underwear, and added striped suspenders to hook his thumbs through. He studied his reflection awhile. Then he went to the bureau and plowed through the bottom drawer. "Bonny?" he said.

"Hmm."

"Where are my Ragg socks?"

"Your what?"

"Those scratchy, woolly socks, for hiking."

She didn't answer. He had to pad barefoot down the stairs, grumbling to himself. "Fool socks. Fool house. Nothing where it ought to be. Nothing where you want it."

He opened the back door to let the dog out. A cold wind blew in. The tiles on the kitchen floor felt icy beneath his feet. "Fool house," he said again. He stood at the counter with an unlit cigarette clamped between his teeth and spooned coffee into the percolator.

The cabinets in this kitchen reached clear to the high ivory ceiling. They were stuffed with tarnished silver tea services and dusty stemware that no one ever used. Jammed in front of them were ketchup bottles and cereal boxes and scummy plastic salt-and-pepper sets with rice grains in the salt from last summer when everything had stuck to itself. Fool house! Something had gone wrong with it, somehow. It was so large and formal and gracious—a wedding present from Bonny's father, who had been a wealthy man. Bonny had inherited a portion of his money. When the children stepped through the attic floor, it was Bonny who dialed the plasterers, and she was always having the broken windowpanes replaced, the shutters rehung when they sagged off their hinges, the masonry put back in chinks where the English ivy had clawed it away; but underneath, Morgan never lost the feeling that something here was slipping. If they could just clear it out and start over, he sometimes thought. Or sell it! Sell it and have done with it, buy a plainer, more straightforward place. But Bonny wouldn't hear of it—something to do with capital gains; he didn't know. It just never was the proper time, any time he brought it up.

The three smaller bedrooms, intended for a tasteful number of children, barely contained Morgan's daughters, and Brindle and Louisa shared an edgy, cramped existence on the third floor. The lawn was littered with rusty bicycles and raveling wicker furniture where Bonny's father had surely imagined civilized games of croquet. And nowadays apartment buildings were sprouting all around them, and the other houses were splitting into units and filling up with various unsortable collections of young people, and traffic was getting fierce. They seemed to be deep in the city. Well, all right. Morgan himself had been reared in the city, and had nothing against it whatsoever. Still, he kept wondering how this could have happened. As near as he could recall, he had planned on something different. He had married his wife for her money, to be frank, which was not to say he didn't love her; it was just that he'd been impressed, as well, by the definiteness that money had seemed to give her. It had hovered somewhere behind her left shoulder, cloaking her with an air of toughness and capability. She was so clear about who she was. Courting her, Morgan had specifically bought a yachting cap with an eagle on the front, and white duck trousers and a brass-buttoned blazer to wear while visiting at her family's summer cottage. He had sat outside on the terrace, securely defined at last, toying with the goblet of tropical punch that Bonny's father had insisted on mixing for him—although in fact Morgan didn't drink, *couldn't* drink, had never been able to. Drinking made him talk too much. It made him spill the beans, he felt. He was trying to stay in character.

Staying in character, he had asked her father for Bonny's hand. Her father gave his approval; Morgan had wondered why. He was only a penniless graduate student with no foreseeable future. And he knew that he was nothing much to look at. (In those days he wore no beard, and there was something monkeyish and clumsy about his face.) When he took Bonny out somewhere, to one of her girlfriends' parties, he felt he was traveling under false pretenses. He felt he had entered someone else's life. Only Bonny belonged there—an easygoing, pleasant girl, two or three years older than Morgan, with curly brown hair worn low on her neck in a sort of ball-shaped ponytail. Later, Morgan figured out that her father must have miscalculated. When you're rich enough, he must have thought, then it doesn't matter who you marry; you'll go on the same as ever. So he had nodded his blessing and given them this house, and expected that nothing would change. Luckily for him, he died soon after the wedding. He never saw the mysterious way the house started slipping downward, or sideways, or whatever it was that it was doing. He didn't have to watch as Bonny's dirndl skirts (once so breezy, so understated) began dipping at the hems, and her blouses somehow shortened and flopped bunchily out of her waistbands.

"Your father would have sold this house long ago," Morgan often told her. "Capital gains or no capital gains, he'd say you should get a new one."

But Bonny would say, "Why? What for?" She would ask, "What's wrong with this one? Everything's been kept up. I just had the roofers in. The painters came last May."

"Yes, but—"

"What is it that bothers you? Can you name one thing that's in disrepair? Name it and I'll fix it. Every inch is in perfect shape, and the Davey tree men just fertilized the trees."

Yes, but.

He went out front for the paper. Under his bare feet the spikes of frosty grass crunched and stabbed. Everything glittered. A single rubber flip-flop skated on the ice in the birdbath. He dashed back in, hissing, and slammed the door behind him. Upstairs an alarm clock burred, as if set off by the crash. They would be swarming everywhere soon. Morgan removed the news section and the comics section, laid them on a kitchen chair, and sat on them. Then he lit his cigarette and opened to the classified ads.

LOST. *White wedding dress size 10. No questions asked.*

He grinned around his cigarette.

Now here came Bonny, slumping in, still buttoning her housecoat, trying to keep her slippers on her feet. Her hair was uncombed and there was a crease down one side of her face. "Did it freeze?" she asked him. "Is there frost on the ground? I meant to cover the box-woods." She lifted a curtain to peer out the window. "Oh, Lord, it froze."

"Mm?"

She opened a cupboard door and clattered something. A blackened silver ashtray arrived inside the partition of Morgan's newspaper. He tapped his cigarette on it. "Listen to this," he told her. "FOUND. *Article of jewelry, in Druid Hill Park. Caller must identify.* I would call and say it was a diamond ring."

"How come?" Bonny asked. She took a carton of eggs from the refrigerator.

"Well, chances are no one wears real pearls to the zoo, or platinum bracelets, but plenty of people wear engagement rings, right? And besides, you can be so general about a ring. Yes, I would say a ring. Absolutely."

"Maybe so," said Bonny, cracking an egg on a skillet.

"LOST. *Upper denture. Great sentimental value,"* Morgan read out. Bonny snorted. He said, "I made it up about the sentimental value."

"I never would have guessed," Bonny told him.

He could hear bare feet pounding upstairs, water running, hairdryers humming. The smell of percolating coffee filled the kitchen, along with the crisp, sharp smoke from his Camel. Oh, he was hitting his stride, all right. He had managed it, broken into another day. He spread his paper wider. "I love the classifieds," he said. "They're so full of private lives."

"Are you going to get those shoes fixed this morning?"

"Hmm? Listen to this: M.G. *All is not forgiven and never will be."*

Bonny set a cup of coffee in front of him.

"What if that's me?" Morgan asked.

"What if what's you?"

"M.G. Morgan Gower."

"Did you do something unforgivable?"

"You can't help wondering," Morgan said, "seeing a thing like that. You can't help stopping to think."

"Oh, Morgan," Bonny said. "Why do you always take the papers so personally?"

"Because I'm reading the personals," he told her. He turned the page, "WANTED," he read. *"Geotechnical lab chief."*

(For the past nineteen years he had supposedly been looking for a better job. Not that he expected to find it.)

"Here's one. *Experienced go-go girls."*

"Ha."

He was employed by Bonny's family, managing one of their hardware stores. He had always been a tinkering, puttering, hardware sort of a man. Back in graduate school, his advisor had once complained because Morgan had spent a whole conference period squatting in the corner, talking over his shoulder while he worked on a leaky radiator pipe.

WANTED. *Barmaid, dog groomer, forklift operator.*

What he liked were those ads with character. (*Driver to chauffeur elderly gentleman, some knowledge of Homer desirable.*) Occasionally he would even answer one. He would even take a job for a couple of days, vanishing from the hardware store and leaving his clerk in charge. Then Bonny's Uncle Ollie would find out and come storming to Bonny, and Bonny would sigh and laugh and ask Morgan what he thought he was doing. He would say this for Bonny: she didn't get too wrought up about things. She just sloped along with him, more or less. He reached out for her, now, as she passed with a pitcher of orange juice.

He crooked an arm around her hips, or tried, to; she had her mind on something else. "Where's Brindle? Where's your mother?" she asked him. "I thought I heard your mother hours ago."

He laid the classified ads aside and tugged another section from beneath him: the news. But there was nothing worth reading. Plane crashes, train crashes, tenement fires . . . He flipped to the obituaries. *"Mrs. Grimm, Opera Enthusiast,"* he read aloud. *"Tilly Abbott, Thimble Collector.* Ah, Lord."

His daughters had begun to seep downstairs. They were quarreling in the hall and dropping books, and their transistor radios seemed to be playing several different songs at once. A deep, rocky drumbeat thudded beneath electric guitars.

"Peter Jacobs, at 44," Morgan read. "Forty-four! What kind of age is that to die?"

"Girls!" Bonny called. "Your eggs are getting cold."

"I hate it when they won't say what did a man in," Morgan told her. "Even 'a lengthy illness'—I mean, a lengthy illness would be better than nothing. But all they have here is *'passed on unexpectedly.'*" He hunched forward to let someone sidle behind him. "Forty-four years old! Of course it was unexpected. You think it was a heart attack? Or what?"

"Morgan, I wish you wouldn't put such stock in obituaries," Bonny said.

She had to raise her voice; the girls had taken over the kitchen by now. All of them were talking at once about history quizzes, boys and more boys, motorcycles, basketball games, who had borrowed whose record album and never given it back. A singer was rumored to be dead. (Someone said she would die herself if that were true.) Amy was doing something to the toaster. The twins were mixing their health-food drink in the blender. A French book flew out of nowhere and hit Liz in the small of the back. "I can't go on living here any more," Liz said. "I don't get a moment's peace. Everybody picks on me. I'm leaving." But all she did was pour herself a cup of coffee and sit down next to Morgan. "For heaven's sake," she said to Bonny, "what's that he got on his head?"

"Feel free to address me directly," Morgan told her. "I have the answer, as it happens. Don't be shy."

"Does he have to wear those hats of his? Even in the house he wears them. Does he have to look so peculiar?"

This was his thirteen-year-old. Once he might have been offended, but he was used to it by now. Along about age eleven or twelve, it seemed they totally changed. He had loved them when they were little. They had started out so small and plain, chubby and curly and even-tempered, toddling devotedly after Morgan, and then all at once they went on crash diets, grew thin and irritable, and shot up taller than their mother. They ironed their hair till it hung like veils. They traded their dresses for faded jeans and skimpy little T-shirts. And their taste in boyfriends was atrocious. Just atrocious. He couldn't believe some of the creatures they brought home with them. On top of all that, they stopped thinking Morgan was so wonderful. They claimed he was an embarrassment. Couldn't he shave his beard off? Cut his hair? Act his age? Dress like other fathers? Why did he smoke those unfiltered cigarettes and pluck those tobacco shreds from his tongue? Did he realize that he hummed incessantly underneath his breath, even at the dinner table, even now while they were asking him these questions?

He tried to stop humming. He briefly switched to a pipe, but the mouthpiece cracked in two when he bit it. And once he got a shorter haircut than usual and trimmed his beard so it was square and hugged the shape of his jaw. It looked artificial, they told him. It looked like a *wooden* beard, they said.

He felt he was riding something choppy and violent, fighting to keep his balance, smiling beatifically and trying not to blink.

"See that? He's barefoot," Liz said.

"Hush and pour that coffee back," Bonny told her. "You know you're not allowed to drink coffee yet."

The youngest, Kate, came in with a stack of schoolbooks. She was not quite eleven and still had Bonny's full-cheeked, cheery face. As she passed behind Morgan's chair, she plucked his hat off, kissed the back of his head, and replaced the hat.

"Sugar-pie," Morgan said.

Maybe they ought to have another baby.

With everyone settled around this table, you couldn't even bend your elbows. Morgan decided to retreat. He rose and ducked out of the room backward, like someone leaving the presence of royalty, so they wouldn't see the comics section he was hiding behind him. He padded into the living room. One of the radios was playing "Plastic Fantastic Lover" and he paused to do a little dance, barefoot on the rug. His mother watched him sternly from the couch. She was a small, hunched old lady with hair that was still jet black; it was held flat with tortoise-shell combs from which it crinkled and bucked like something powerful. She sat with her splotched, veined hands folded in her lap; she wore a drapy dress that seemed several sizes too large for her. "Why aren't you at breakfast?" Morgan asked.

"Oh, I'll just wait till all this has died down."

"But then Bonny'll be in the kitchen half the morning."

"When you get to be my age," Louisa said, "why, food is near about everything there is, and I don't intend to rush it. I want a nice, hot English muffin, split with a fork, not a knife, with butter melting amongst the crumbs, and a steaming cup of coffee laced with whipping cream. And I want it in peace. I want it in quiet."

"Bonny's going to have a fit," he said.

"Don't be silly. Bonny doesn't mind such things."

She was probably right. (Bonny was infinitely expansible, taking everything as it came. It was Morgan who felt oppressed by his mother's living here.) He sighed and settled next to her on the couch. He opened out his paper. "Isn't this a weekday?" she asked him.

"Yes," he mumbled.

She crooked a finger over the top of his paper and pulled it down so she could see his face. "Aren't you going to work?"

"By and by."

"By and *by*? It's seven-thirty, Morgan and you don't even have your shoes on. Do you know what I've done so far today? Made my bed, watered my ferns, polished the chrome in my bathroom; and meanwhile here you sit reading the comics, and your sister's sleeping like the dead upstairs. What is this with my children? Where do they get this? By and by you say!"

He gave up. He folded the paper and said, "All *right*, Mother."

"Have a nice day," she told him serenely.

When he left the room, she was sitting with her hands in her lap again, trustful as a child, waiting for her English muffin.

II

WEARING A pair of argyle socks that didn't go at all with his Klondike costume, and crusty leather boots to cover them up, and his olive-drab parka from Sunny's Surplus, Morgan loped along the sidewalk. His hardware store was deep in the city, too far to travel on foot, and unfortunately his car was spread all over the floor of his garage and he hadn't quite finished putting it back together. He would have to take the bus. He headed toward the transit stop, puffing on a cigarette that he held between thumb and forefinger, sending out a cloud of smoke from beneath the brim of his hat. He passed a row of houses, an apartment building, then a little stream of drugstores and newsstands and dentists' offices. Under one arm he carried a brown paper bag with his moccasins inside. They went with his Daniel Boone outfit. He'd worn them so often that the soft leather soles had broken through at the ball of the foot. When he reached the corner, he swerved in at Fresco's Shoe Repair to leave them off. He liked the smell of Fresco's: leather and machine oil. Maybe he should have been a cobbler.

But when he entered, jingling the cowbell above the door, he found no one there—just the counter with its clutter of awls and pencils and receipt forms, the pigeonholes behind it crammed with shoes, and a cup of coffee cooling beside the skeletal black sewing machine. "Fresco?" he called.

"Yo," Fresco said from the rear.

Morgan laid his package down and went behind the counter. He pulled out a copper-toed work boot. Where would one buy such things? They really would be useful, he felt; really very practical. The cowbell jingled again. A fat woman in a fur cape came in, no doubt from one of those new apartment buildings. All down the edge of her cape, small animals' heads hung, gnashing their teeth on their own spindly tails. She set a spike-heeled evening sandal firmly on the counter. "I'd like to know what you're going to do about this," she said.

"Do?" said Morgan.

"You can see the heel has broken again. It broke right off while I was walking into the club, and you were the people who'd repaired it. I looked like an utter fool, a clod."

"Well, what can I say?" Morgan asked her. "This shoe is Italian."

"So?"

"It has hollow heels."

"It does?"

They both looked at the heel. It wasn't hollow at all.

"Oh, we see a lot of this," Morgan told her. He stamped out his cigarette and picked up the sandal. "These shoes from Italy, they come with hollow heels so drugs can be smuggled in. So naturally they're weakened. The smugglers pry the heels off, take no care whatsoever; they don't have the slightest feeling for their work. They slam the heels back any old how, sell the shoes to some unsuspecting shop . . . but of course they'll never be the same. Oh, the stories I could tell you!"

He shook his head. She looked at him narrowly; faint, scratchy lines deepened around her eyes.

"Ah, well," he said, sighing. "Friday morning, then. Name?"

"Well . . . Peterson," she said.

He scrawled it on the back of a receipt, and set it with the sandal in a cubbyhole.

After she was gone, he wrote out instructions for his moccasins: GOWER. FIX! *Can't live without them.* He put the moccasins next to the sandal, with the instructions rolled inside. Then he trotted on out of the shop, busily lighting another cigarette beneath the shelter of his hat.

On the sidewalk his mother's dog was waiting for him. She had a cocked, hopeful face and two perked ears like tepees. Morgan stopped dead. "Go home," he told her. She wagged her tail. "Go home. What do you want of me? What have I done?"

Morgan set off toward the bus stop. The dog followed, whining, but Morgan pretended not to hear. He speeded up. The whining continued. He wheeled around and stamped one foot. A man in an overcoat halted and then circled Morgan at a distance. The dog, however, merely cowered, panting and looking expectant. "Why must you drag *after* me like this?" Morgan asked. He made a rush at her, but she stood her ground. Of course he should lead her home himself, but he couldn't face it. He couldn't backtrack all that way, having started out so speedy and chipper. Instead he turned and took off at a run, holding on to his hat, pounding down the sidewalk with the dog not far behind. The dog began to lose heart. Morgan felt her lose it, though he didn't dare turn to look. He felt her falter and then stop, gazing after him and spasmodically wagging her tail. Morgan clutched his aching chest and stumbled up onto a bus. Puffing and sweating, he rummaged through his pockets for change. The other passengers darted sidelong glances and then looked away again.

They passed more stores and office buildings. They whizzed through a corner of Morgan's old neighborhood, with most of the windows boarded up and trees growing out of caved-in roofs. (It had not done well without him.) Here were the Arbeiter Mattress Factory and Madam Sheba, All Questions Answered and Love Problems Cheerfully Solved. Rowhouses slid by, each more decayed than the one before. Morgan hunkered in his seat, clutching the metal bar in front of him, gazing at the Ace of Spades Sandwich Shop and Fat Boy's Shoeshine. Now he was farther downtown than he had ever lived. He relaxed his grip on the metal bar. He sank into the lives of the scattered people sitting on their stoops: the woman in her nightgown and vinyl jacket nursing a Rolling Rock beer and breathing frost; the two men nudging each other and laughing; the small boy in a grownup's sneakers hugging a soiled white cat. A soothing kind of emptiness began to spread through him. He felt stripped and free, like the vacant windows, frameless, glassless, on the upper floors of Syrenia's Hot Pig Bar-B-Q.

III

THE DOWNTOWN branch of Cullen Hardware was so old and dark and filthy, so thick with smells, so narrow and creaking, that Morgan often felt he was not so much entering it as *plunging* in, head first, leaving just his bootsoles visible on the rim. There was a raised platform at the rear, underneath the rafters, for his office: a scarred oak desk, files, a maroon plush settee, and a steep black Woodstock typewriter whose ribbons he had to wind by hand. This used to be Bonny's grandfather's office. This store was Grandfather Cullen's very first establishment. Now there were branches everywhere, of course. Nearly every shopping mall within a fifty-mile radius had a Cullen Hardware. But they were all slick and modern; this was the only real one. Sometimes Bonny's Uncle Ollie would come in and threaten to close it down. "Call this a store?" he would say. "Call this a paying proposition?" He would glare around him at the bulky wooden shelves, where the Black & Decker power tools looked foolish beside the old-fashioned bins of nails. He would scowl at the rusty window grilles, which had been twisted out of shape by several different burglars. Morgan would just smile, anxiously tugging his beard, for he knew that he tended to irk Uncle Ollie and he was better off saying nothing at all. Then Uncle Ollie would storm out again and Morgan would go back to his office, relieved, humming beneath his breath. Not that closing this branch down would have left him unemployed; for Bonny's sake, the Cullens would feel bound to find him something else. But here he had more scope. He had half a dozen projects under way in his office—lumber stacked against the stairs, a ball-peen hammer in his OUT basket. He knew of a good place to eat not far off. He had friends just a few blocks over. His one clerk, Butkins, did nearly all the work, even if he wasn't so interesting to talk to.

Once, a few years back, Morgan had had a girl clerk named Marie. She was a very young, round-faced redhead who always wore a loose gray smock to protect her clothes from the dust. Morgan started pretending she was his wife. It wasn't that he found her all that appealing; but he slowly built this scene in his mind where she and he were the owners of a small-town Ma-and-Pa hardware store. They'd been childhood sweethearts, maybe. Mentally, he aged her. He would have liked her to have white hair. He started wearing a wrinkled gray jacket and gray work trousers; he thought of himself as "Pa Hardware." The funny thing was, sometimes he could be looking right at her but daydreaming her from scratch, as if she weren't there. Then one afternoon he was standing on the ladder putting some shelves in order and she was handing him boxes of extension cords, and he happened to lean down and kiss her on the cheek. He said, "You look tired, Ma. Maybe you ought to take a little nap." The girl had gasped but said nothing. The next day she didn't show up for work, and she never came again. Her gray smock still hung in the stockroom. Occasionally, when he passed it, Morgan felt sad all over again for the days when he had been Pa Hardware.

But now he had this Butkins, this efficient, colorless young fellow already setting out a new display of Rubbermaid products in the window. "Morning," Morgan told him. He went on up to his office. He took off his parka, hung it on the coat tree, and sat down in the cracked leather swivel chair behind his desk. Supposedly, he would be dealing with the paperwork now—typing up orders, filing invoices. Instead he opened the center drawer and pulled out his bird-feeder plans. He was building the feeder for Bonny. Next Tuesday was their anniversary. They had been married for nineteen years; good God. He unrolled the plans and studied them, running a nicotine-stained finger across the angles of various levels and compartments. The feeder hung by a post

in which he would drill four suet holes—or peanut-butter holes, for
Bonny claimed that suet caused cholesterol problems. Morgan smiled
to himself. Bonny was a little crazy on the subject of birds, he thought.
He weighted the plans flat with a stapler and a pack of drill bits, and
went to find a good plank to begin on.

For most of the morning he sawed and sanded and hummed, occasionally pausing to push back his hat and wipe his face on his sleeve.
His office stairs made a fine sawhorse. At the front of the store a trickle
of shoppers chose their single purchases: a mousetrap, a furnace filter,
a can of roach spray. Morgan hummed the "W.P.A. Blues" and chiseled
a new point on his pencil.

Then Butkins went to an early lunch, leaving Morgan in charge.
Morgan had to rise and dust off his knees, regretfully, and wait on a
man in coveralls who wanted to buy a Hide-a-Key. "What for?" Morgan
asked. "Why spend good money on a little tin box? Do you see the
price on this thing?"

"Well, but last week I locked the keys inside my car, don't you
know, and I was thinking how maybe I could hide an extra key beneath
the—"

"Look," said Morgan. "All you do is take a piece of dental floss,
waxed. Surely you have dental floss. Thread your extra key on it,
double it for strength, tie it to your radiator grille and let the key hang
down inside. Simple! Costs you nothing."

"Well, but this here Hide-a-Key—"

"Are you not standing in the presence of a man whose wife perpetually mislays his car keys for him?" Morgan asked.

The man glanced around him.

"*Me*, I mean. She loses all I own," Morgan said, "and I've never
had a Hide-a-Key in my life."

"Well, still," the man said doggedly, "I think I'll just go on ahead
with this here."

"What is it?" Morgan asked. "You don't have dental floss? Never
mind! I tell you what I'll do: you come back this same time tomorrow,
I'll have a piece for you from home. Free, no charge. A gift. All right?
I'll bring you in a yard or two."

"For Christ's sake," said the man, "will you let me buy one cruddy
Hide-a-Key?"

Morgan flung his hands up. "Of course!" he said. "Be my guest!
Waste your money! Fill your life with junk!" He stabbed the cash-
register keys. "A dollar twenty-nine," he said.

"It's *my* dollar twenty-nine, I'll waste it however I like," said the
man, pressing the money into Morgan's palm. "Maniac."

"Junkie!"

The man rushed off, clutching his Hide-a-Key. Morgan muttered to
himself and slammed the cash register shut.

When Butkins came back, Morgan was free to go to lunch. He went to the No Jive Café; he liked their pickles. All the other customers were black, though, and they wouldn't talk to him. They seemed to spend their mealtimes passing tiny wads of money to the counterman, and then mumbling and looking off sideways under lowered lids. Meanwhile Morgan slouched over his plate and chewed happily on a pickle. It really was a wonderful pickle. The garlic was so strong it almost fizzed. But you only got one to a plate, alongside your sandwich. He'd asked time and time again for an extra, but they always said no; he'd have to order another hamburger that he didn't even want.

After he finished eating, he thought he'd take a walk. He had a regular pattern of places he liked to visit. He zipped his parka and set off. The day had not warmed up much; the passers-by had pinched, teary faces. Morgan was glad of his beard. He turned up his collar and held it close and proceeded almost at a run, squinting against the wind.

First to Potter, the used-instrument dealer, but Potter had someone with him—a gawky, plain young woman trying out a violin. "Father Morgan!" Potter cried. "Miss Miller, meet Father Morgan, the street priest of Baltimore. How's it going? How're your addicts? Come in and have some tea!"

But customers here were rare, and Morgan didn't want to interrupt. "No, no," he said, holding up a hand. "I must be on my way. Blessings!" and he backed out the door.

He cut through an alley and came out on Marianna Street. An exotic woman with a torrent of black hair stood beside a hot-dog cart. Her make-up was stupendous—a coppery glaze on her skin, a flaring red slash of a mouth, and mascara so heavily applied that each eyelash seemed strung with black beads. Now that it was winter, she was wrapped in old coats and sweaters, but Morgan knew from warmer seasons that underneath she wore a red lace dress and an armload of chipped, flaking, gold-tone bracelets. "_Zosem pas!_" he called out to her.

"Well, hey!" she said. She spoke extra brightly, exaggerating her lip movements. "How you today? Get a letter from home?"

Morgan smiled humbly and looked perplexed.

"Letter!" she shouted. She wrote on her palm with an imaginary pencil. "You get a letter?"

"Ah!" said Morgan, suddenly realizing. He shook his head. "_Pok,_" he said sadly. "_Kun salomen baso._" The corners of his mouth turned down; he scuffed a boot against the wheel of her cart.

"You poor man," she said. "Well, maybe tomorrow, huh?"

"_Brankuso,_" he told her. "_Zosem pas!_" and he waved and grinned and walked on.

At the corner of Marianna Street and Crosswell he hesitated. What he would really like was to turn down Crosswell—just ahead in that general direction. What harm could it do? He hadn't been in several weeks. He'd resisted temptation admirably. He shoved both hands in his pockets and set out.

CRAFTS UNLIMITED, the sign in the middle of the block said. It was an elderly building, four stories tall. The first-floor bay window was full of patchwork quilts, cornhusk dolls, samplers, woven goods, and puppets. The windows above it were narrower, dark and uncurtained. It was the third-floor windows that Morgan watched, from the shadow of a laundromat doorway—Emily and Leon Meredith's windows. He had learned their address with no trouble at all, just looked it up in the telephone book. He'd learned that along about now (just before the baby's nap, he supposed) one or the other of the Merediths would float up behind the window on the left and tug it open. A hand would trail out—Emily's pale hand or Leon's darker one—and there would be a still, considering moment while they pondered how to dress the baby for her outing. Morgan enjoyed that. (Bonny, with the last few children, had simply thrown whatever was closest into the stroller—a blanket, or some older child's jacket; anything would do). He imagined that the Merediths would also sprinkle a few drops of milk on their wrists before giving their daughter a bottle, and would test the water with the tip of an elbow before lowering her into her bath—whatever was instructed, he liked to believe. Whatever the proper method was. He waited, smiling upward, with both hands buried deep in his pockets.

Had he missed them? No, here they came, out the glass door beside the CRAFTS UNLIMITED sign. Leon carried the baby over his shoulder. (Naturally they would not have bought a carriage.) She must be nine or ten months old by now—a fat, apple-cheeked child in a thick snowsuit. Emily walked next to Leon, with her hand tucked through his arm and her face lifted and bright, talking to the baby and tripping along in her shabby trenchcoat and little black slippers. Morgan loved the way the Merediths dressed. It seemed they had decided, long ago, what clothes would be their trademark, and they never swerved from it. Leon always wore clean khaki trousers and a white shirt. Below the sleeves of his rust-colored corduroy jacket, a half-inch of immaculate white cuff emerged. And Emily wore one of three scoop-necked leotards—brown, plum, or (most often) black—with a matching wrap skirt of some limp material that flowed to mid-calf length. He had noticed such outfits in modern-dance productions on TV, and admired their fluidity. Now he saw that, worn on the street, they made fashion seem beside the point. In fact, the hemline was wrong for this year or even for this decade, he suspected, and who ever heard of such a young girl in such drab colors? But these costumes seemed to carry their own authority. She didn't look outdated at all. She looked stark, pared down. She had done away with the extras.

He enjoyed imagining their eat-in kitchen, with just two plates and two sets of silver and an earthenware bowl for the baby. He liked to think that their bathroom contained a bar of Ivory soap and three hotel towels. Well, and Leon's shaving things, of course. But nothing else. No bath oil, talcum tins, acne creams, hairdryers, children's orthodontic appliances, mingled bottles of perfume swearing at each other, dangling bras and nylons and lace-edged shower caps. He gazed longingly after the Merediths. Their two oval faces swung away, private and impenetrable. Their daughter's face was round as a coin, and stayed visible long after her parents had turned their backs on him, but she was no easier to read.

Of course, what he should have done was gallop across and catch up with them. "Remember me? Dr. Morgan. Remember? What a coincidence! I just chanced to be in the neighborhood, you see . . ." It wouldn't be difficult. He could take the baby's pulse, inquire about her DPT shots. Doctoring was so easy—a matter of mere common sense. It was almost *too* easy. He'd have more trouble sustaining the role of electrician, or one of those men who blow insulating material between the walls of houses.

Nevertheless, something stopped him. He felt awed by the Merediths—by their austerity, their certitude, their mapped and charted lives. He let them float away untouched, like people in a bubble.

IV

AFTERNOON DRIFTED over the store, and twilight sank into the corners. Butkins swallowed a yawn and mused at the window. Morgan invented an elaborate sort of paddlewheel device to tip squirrels off the bird feeder. He sanded each paddle carefully and fitted it into place. He felt comforted and steadied by this kind of work. It made him think of his father, a methodical man who might have been much happier as a carpenter than as an ineffectual high-school English teacher. "One thing our family has always believed in," his father used to say, "is the very best quality tools. You buy the best tools for the job: drop-forged steel, hardwood handles. And then you take good care of them. Everything in its place. Lots of naval jelly." It was the only philosophy he had ever stated outright, and Morgan clung to it now like something carved in stone. His father had killed himself during Morgan's last year of high school. Without a hint of despair or ill health (though he'd always seemed somewhat muted), he had taken a room at the Winken Blinken Motor Hotel one starry April evening and slit both wrists with a razor blade. Morgan had spent a large part of his life trying to figure out why. All he wanted was a reason—bad debts, cancer, blackmail, an illicit love affair; nothing would have dismayed him. Anything would have been preferable to this nebulous, ambiguous trailing off. Had his father, perhaps, been wretched in his marriage? Fallen under the power of racketeers? Committed murder? He rifled his father's correspondence, stole his desk key and his cardboard file box. He mercilessly cross-examined his mother, but she seemed no wiser than Morgan, or maybe she just didn't want to talk about it. She went around silent and exhausted; she'd taken a job at Hutzler's selling gloves. Gradually, Morgan stopped asking. The possibility had begun to settle on him, lately, as imperceptibly as dust, that perhaps there'd been no reason after all. Maybe a man's interest in life could just thin to a trickle and dry up; was that it? He hated to believe it. He pushed the thought away, any time it came to him. And even now he often pored over the file box he had stolen, but he never found more than he'd found at the start: alphabetized instruction sheets for assembling bicycles, cleaning lawnmowers, and installing vacuum-cleaner belts. Repairing, replacing, maintaining. One step follows another, and if you have completed step two, then step three will surely come to you.

He sanded the paddlewheel, nodding gently. He hummed without any tune.

Butkins came up the stairs to say, "I'm going now, if that's all you need. I'll see you tomorrow."

"Eh?" said Morgan. "Is it time?" He straightened and wiped his forehead with the back of his hand. "Well, yes, surely, Butkins," he said. "So long, then."

The store fell silent and grew fuzzy with darkness. Passers-by hurried home to supper without even glancing in. Morgan got to his feet, put on his parka, and made his way up the aisle. He switched off the lights and locked the three massive, burglar-proof locks. From outside, the place looked like an antique photograph: lifeless, blurred, the knobs and bulges in its window a mystery forever. Maybe Grandfather Cullen's ghost came here, nights, and roamed the aisles in a daze, ruminating over the rechargeable hedge clippers. Morgan turned his collar up and ran to catch the bus.

V

AT SUPPER the grownups sat bunched at one end of the table as if taking refuge from the children—Morgan in his hat, Bonny and Louisa, and Morgan's sister, Brindle, wearing a lavender bathrobe. Brindle had her mother's sallow, eagle face and hunched posture, but not her vitality. She sat idly buttering pieces of French bread, which she placed in a circle on the rim of her plate, while Louisa recounted, word for word, a cooking program she'd been watching on TV. "First he put the veal shanks endwise in a pot. Then he poured over them a sauce made of tomato paste, lemon zest, bits of celery . . . but everything was cut up ahead of time! *Naturally* it looks easy if you don't have to witness all the peeling and chopping."

Morgan reached across her for the salt.

"There's not enough real life on television," Louisa said.

"That's the whole point," Brindle told her.

"I'd like to see him try scraping the tomato paste out of that little tiny Hunt's can, too."

"Mother, you went through all this last week," Brindle said. "That's a re-run you were watching, and you made all the same objections too."

"I did not! I knew nothing about such programs last week."

"You told us every bit of it: the lemon zest, the celery . . ."

"Are you accusing me of a faulty memory?" Louisa asked.

"Ladies. Please," said Morgan. It was true there seemed to be some problem lately with his mother's memory. She had spells when she was doggedly repetitive; her mind, like an old record, appeared to stick in certain grooves. But it only made her nervous to have it brought to her attention. He scowled at Brindle, who shrugged and buttered another slice of bread.

Meanwhile his daughters ate in a separate flurry of gossip and quarrels and giggles—seven slim, blue-jeaned girls and then someone else, a little white-haired waif with rhinestone ear studs, some friend of Kate's. She sat between Kate and Amy and stared at Morgan narrowly, as if she disapproved of him. It made him nervous. He was never truly happy if he felt that even the most random passing stranger found him unlikable. He'd begun the meal in a fine mood, twirling his spaghetti theatrically on his fork and speaking in a broad Italian accent, but gradually he lost his enthusiasm. "What do you keep looking at?" he asked now. "Have we met before?"

"Sir?"

"This is Coquette," Kate told him.

"Ah. Coquette."

"Me and her are in the same class at school. We like the same boy."

Morgan frowned. "Same what?" he said.

"This boy named Jackson Eps."

"But you're only in fifth grade!"

"We liked him in fourth grade too."

"This is ridiculous," Morgan told Bonny. Bonny smiled at him; she never knew when to start worrying. "What are things coming to?" he asked his sister. "Where are we headed, here? It's all these Barbie dolls, Ken dolls, Tinkerbell make-up sets."

"*I* liked a boy in fifth grade," Brindle said.

"You did?"

"Robert Roberts."

"Oh, Lord, Brindle, not Robert Roberts again."

"Robert Roberts was in fifth grade?" Kate asked. She nudged Coquette. "Robert Roberts was Brindle's childhood sweetheart," she said.

"He was not only in fifth grade," said Brindle, "he was also in fourth, third, second . . . We used to have to share our reading-skills workbook; he was always losing his. In kindergarten we went shopping once at Bargain Billy's and he stuck a label on my cheek reading SLIGHTLY IMPERFECT. He also took me to my first school dance and my first car-date and my senior-class picnic."

Morgan sighed and tipped his chair back. Bonny helped herself to more salad.

"Then in college I broke it off," Brindle told Coquette. "I gave him back his high-school ring with the candle wax still in it to make it fit my finger—half a candle's worth, it looked like. I'd probably have drowned if I ever wore it swimming."

"Why'd you break it off?" Coquette asked her.

"I got married to someone else."

"But *why'd* you break it off? I mean, why marry someone else?"

Brindle pushed her plate away and set her elbows on the table. She said, "Well, I don't know if . . . When I talk about him, it sounds so simple, doesn't it? But see, even back in kindergarten he would sometimes act silly and sometimes bore me, and yet other times I was crazy about him, and when we grew up it got worse. Sometimes I liked him and sometimes I didn't like him, and sometimes I didn't even think of him. And sometimes he didn't like me, I knew it; we knew each other so well. It never occurred to me it would be that way with *anyone*. I mean, he was my only experience. You understand what I'm trying to say?"

Plainly, Coquette didn't understand a word. She was growing restless, glancing toward the plate of Oreos on the sideboard. But Brindle didn't see that. "What I did," she said, "was marry an older man. Man who lived next door to Mother's old house, downtown. It was a terrible mistake. He was the jealous type, possessive, always fearing I would leave him. He never gave me any money, only charge accounts and then this teeny bit of cash for the groceries every week. For seven years I charged our food at the gourmet sections of department stores— tiny cans of ham and pure-white asparagus spears and artichoke bottoms and hearts of palm, all so I could save back some of the grocery money. I would charge a dozen skeins of yarn and then return them one by one to the Knitter's Refund counter for cash. I subscribed to every cents-off, money-back offer that came along. At the end of seven years I said, 'All right, Horace, I've saved up five thousand dollars of my own. I'm leaving.' And I left."

"She had to save five thousand dollars," Morgan told the ceiling, "to catch a city bus from her house to my house. Three and a half miles—four at the most."

"I felt I'd been challenged," Brindle said.

"And it's not as if I hadn't offered to help her out, all along."

"I felt I wanted to show him, 'See there? You can't overcome me so easily; I've got more spirit than you think,' " Brindle said.

Morgan wondered if supplies of spirit were rationed. Did each person only get so much, which couldn't be replenished once it was used up? For in the four years since leaving her husband she'd stayed plopped on Morgan's third floor, seldom dressing in anything but her faded lavender bathrobe. To this day, she'd never mentioned finding a job or an apartment of her own. And when her husband died of a stroke, not six months after she'd left, she hardly seemed to care one way or the other. "Oh, well," was all she'd said, "I suppose this saves me a trip to Nero."

"Don't you mean Reno?" Morgan had asked.

"Whatever," she said.

The only time she showed any spirit, in fact, was when she was telling this story. Her eyes grew triangular, her skin had a stretched look. "I haven't had an easy time of it, you see," she said. "It all worked out so badly. And Robert Roberts, well, I hear he went and married a Gaithersburg girl. I just turn my back on him for a second and off he goes and gets married. Isn't that something? Not that I hold him to blame. I know I did it to myself. I've ruined my life, all on my own, and it's far too late to change it. I just set all the switches and did all the steering and headed straight toward ruin."

Ruin echoed off the high, sculptured ceiling. Bonny brought the cookies from the sideboard; the girls took two and three apiece as the plate went past. Morgan let his chair tip suddenly forward. He studied Brindle with a curious, alert expression on his face, but she didn't seem to notice.

VI

NOW HE and Bonny were returning from a movie. They slogged down the glassy black pavement toward the bus stop. It was a misty, damp night, warmer than it had been all day. Neon signs blurred into rainbows, and the taillights of cars, sliding off into the fog, seemed to contract and then vanish. Bonny had her arm linked through Morgan's. She wore a wrinkled raincoat she had owned since he first met her, and crepe-soled shoes that made a luff-luffing sound. "Maybe tomorrow," she said, "you could get the car put back together."

"Yes, maybe," said Morgan absently.

"We've been riding buses all week."

Morgan was thinking about the movie. It hadn't seemed very believable to him. Everyone had been so sure of what everyone else was going to do. The hero, who was some kind of double agent, had laid all these elaborate plans that depended on some other, unknowing person appearing in a certain place or making a certain decision, and the other person always obliged. Sentries looked away at crucial moments. High officials went to dinner just when they usually went to dinner. Didn't B ever happen instead of A, in these people's lives? Morgan plodded steadily, frowning at his feet. From out of nowhere the memory came to him of the hero's manicured, well-tended hands expertly assembling a rifle from random parts smuggled through in a leather briefcase.

They reached the bus stop; they halted and peered down the street. "Watch it take all night," Bonny said good-naturedly. She removed her pleated plastic rain-scarf and shook the droplets from it.

"Bonny," Morgan said, "why don't I own a corduroy jacket?"

"You do," she told him.

"I do?"

"You have that black one with the suede lapels."

"Oh, that," he said.

"What's wrong with it?"

"I'd prefer to have rust," he said.

She looked over at him. She seemed about to speak, but then she must have changed her mind.

A bus lumbered into view, its windows lit with golden lights—an entire civilization, Morgan imagined, cruising through space. It stopped with a wheeze and let them climb on. For such a late hour, it seemed unusually crowded. There were no double seats left. Bonny settled beside a woman in a nurse's uniform, and instead of finding someplace else Morgan stood rocking above her in the aisle. "I'd like a nice rust jacket with the elbows worn," he told her.

"Well," she said dryly, "you'd have to wear down your own elbows, I expect."

"I don't know; I might find something in a secondhand store."

"Morgan, can't you stay out of secondhand stores? Some of those people have *died*, the owners of those things you buy."

"That's no reason to let a perfectly good piece of clothing go to waste."

Bonny wiped the rain off her face with a balled-up Kleenex from her pocket.

"Also," Morgan said, "I'd like a pair of khaki trousers and a really old, soft, clean white shirt."

She replaced the Kleenex in her pocket. She jolted along with the bus in silence for a moment, looking straight ahead of her. Then she said, "Who is it this time?"

"Who is what?"

"Who is it that wears those clothes?"

"No one!" he said. "What do you mean?"

"You think I'm blind? You think I haven't been through this a hundred times before?"

"I don't know what you're talking about."

Bonny shrugged and turned her gaze out the window.

They were near their own neighborhood now. Lamps glowed over the entranceways of brick houses and apartment buildings. A man in a hat was walking his beagle. A boy cupped a match and lit a girl's cigarette. In the seat behind Bonny, two women in fur coats were having a conversation. "I guess you heard the news by now," one of them told the other. "Angie's husband died."

"Died?" asked the other.

"Just up and died."

"How'd it happen?"

"Well, he finished shaving and he put on a little aftershave and he came back into the bedroom and went to sit on the bed—"

"But what was it? His heart?"

"Well, I'm *telling* you, Libby . . ."

Morgan began to have an uncomfortable thought. He became convinced that his hand, which gripped the seat in plain view of these two women, was so repulsive to them that they were babbling utter nonsense just to keep from thinking about it. He imagined that he could see through their eyes; he saw exactly how his hand appeared to them—its knuckly fingers, wiry black hairs, sawdust ingrained around the nails. He saw his whole person, in fact. What a toad he was! A hat and a beard, on legs. His eyes felt huge and hot and heavy, set in a baroque arrangement of dark pouches. "He reached for his socks," the first woman said desperately, "and commenced to unroll them. One sock was rolled inside the other, don't you know . . ." She was looking away from Morgan; she was avoiding the sight of his hand. He let go of the seat and buried both fists in his armpits. For the rest of the trip he rode unsupported, lurching violently whenever the bus stopped.

And when they reached home, where the girls were doing their lessons on the dining-room table and Brindle was laying out her Tarot cards in the kitchen, Morgan went straight up the stairs to bed. "I thought you'd like some coffee," Bonny said. She called after him, "Morgan? Don't you want a cup of coffee?"

"No, I guess not tonight," he said. "Thank you, dear," and he continued up the stairs. He went to his room, undressed to his thermal underwear, and lit a cigarette from the pack on the bureau. For the first time all day, he was bare-headed. In the mirror his forehead looked lined and vulnerable. He noticed a strand of white in his beard. White hair! "Christ," he said. Then he bent forward and looked more closely. Maybe, he thought, he could pass himself off as one of those miracles from the Soviet Union—a hundred and ten, hundred and twenty, still scaling mountains with his herd of goats. He brightened. He could cross the country on a lecture tour. At every whistle stop he'd take off his shirt and show his black-pelted chest. Reporters would ask him his secret. "Yogurt und cigarettes, comrades," he cackled to the mirror. He took a couple of prancing steps, showing off. "Never anodder sing but yogurt und Rossian cigarettes."

Feeling more cheerful, he went to the closet for his cardboard file box, which he placed on the bed. He drew intently on his Camel as he padded around, getting arranged: turning on the electric blanket, propping up his pillow, finding an ashtray. He climbed into bed and set the ashtray in his lap. There was a little coughing fit to be seen through first. He scattered ashes down his undershirt. He pinched a speck of tobacco from his tongue. "Ah, comrades," he wheezed. He opened the file box, took out the first sheet of paper, and settled back to read it.

1. Familiarize yourself with all steps before beginning.
2. Have on hand the following: pliers, Phillips screwdriver . . .

He lowered the sheet of paper and gazed at the black windowpanes. Miles away from here, he imagined, the windows on Crosswell Street were blinking out, first the left one, then the right one. The baby would stir in her sleep. Leon's hand would drop from the light switch and he would cross the cold floor to their pallet. Then all daytime sounds would stop; there would only be the sifting breaths of sleepers, motionless and dreamless on their threadbare sheets.

Morgan turned his light off too, and settled down for the night.

1969

I

WHAT WAS it that he wanted of them? He was everywhere, it seemed—an oddly shaped, persistent shadow trailing far behind when they went for a walk, lurking in various doorways, flattening himself around the corner of a building. What they ought to do was simply wheel and confront him. "Why, Dr. Morgan!"—smiling, surprised—"how nice to run into you!" But the situation hadn't lent itself to that, somehow. The first time they'd seen him (or felt his presence, really), back when Gina was a baby, they hadn't realized who he was. Coming home from a shopping trip at twilight, they'd been chilled by a kind of liquid darkness flowing in and out of alleyways behind them. Emily had been frightened. Leon had been angry, but with Emily next to him and Gina in his arms he hadn't wanted to force anything. They had merely walked a little faster, and spoken to each other in a loud, casual tone without once mentioning what was happening. The second time, Emily had been alone. She'd left the baby with Leon and gone to buy felt for the puppets. Directly opposite their apartment building, in an arched granite doorway, a figure fell suddenly backward into the gloom of the laundromat. She hardly saw; she was calculating the yardage she would need. But that evening, as she was making a pointed hat for Rumpelstiltskin, the memory came swimming in again. She saw the figure fall once more out of sight—though he hadn't been wearing a pointed hat at all but something flat, a beret, perhaps. Still, where had she seen him before? She said, "Oh!" and laid her scissors down. "Guess who I think I saw today?" she said to Leon. "That doctor. That Dr. Morgan."

"Did you ask him why he never sent a bill?"

"No, he wasn't really . . . It wasn't a meeting, exactly. I mean, he didn't see me. Well, he saw me, but it seemed he . . . Probably," she said, "it wasn't Dr. Morgan at all. I'm sure he would have spoken."

A month or so later he followed her along Beacon Avenue. She stopped to look in the window of an infants'-wear shop and she felt someone else stop too. She turned and found a man some distance away, his back to her, gazing off down the street at nothing in particular. He might have stepped out of a jungle movie, she thought, with his safari shirt and shorts, his knee-high socks, ankle boots, and huge pith helmet. Extraneous buckles and D-rings glittered all over him—on his shoulders, his sleeves, his rear pockets. It was nobody dangerous. It was only one of those eccentric people you often see on city streets, acting out some elaborate inner vision of themselves. She walked on. At the next red light she glanced back again and here he came, hurrying toward her with a swaggering, soldierly gait to match the uniform, his eyes obscured by the helmet but his abundant beard in full view. Oh, you couldn't mistake that beard. Dr. Morgan! She took a step toward him. He looked up at her, clapped a hand on his helmet, and darted through a door reading LU-RAE'S FINE COIFFURES.

Emily felt absurd! She felt how open and glad she must look, preparing to call his name. But what had she done wrong? Why didn't he like her any more? He had seemed so taken with the two of them, back when Gina was born.

She didn't tell Leon. It would make him angry, maybe; you never knew. She decided that, anyhow, it had only been one of those unexplainable things—meaningless, not worth troubling Leon about.

So it got off on the wrong foot, you might say. There was a moment when they could have dealt with it straightforwardly, but the moment slipped past them. After several of these incidents (spaced across weeks or even months) in which one thing or another prevented them from going up to the man and greeting him naturally, it began to seem that the situation had taken a turn of its own. There was no way they could gracefully set it right now. It became apparent that he must be crazy—or, at least, obsessed in some unaccountable way. (Emily shivered to think of Gina's delivery at his hands.) Yet, as Leon pointed out, he did no harm. He never threatened them or even came within speaking distance of them; there was nothing to complain of. Really, Emily was taking this too fancifully, Leon said. The man was only something to be adjusted to, as a matter of course. He was part of the furniture of their lives, like the rowhouses looming down Crosswell Street, the dusty, spindly trees dying of exhaust fumes, and the puppets hanging in their muslin shrouds from the hooks in the back-bedroom closet.

II

NOW THAT it was winter, business had slacked off. There had been a little burst around Christmas (holiday bazaars, parties for rich people's children), but none of the open-air fairs and circuses that kept them so busy in the summer. Emily used the time to build a new stage—a wooden one, hinged and folded for portability. She repaired the puppets and sewed more costumes for them. A few she replaced completely, which led to the usual question of what to do with the old ones. They were like dead bodies; you couldn't just dump them in the trashcan. "Use them for spare parts," Leon always said. "Save the eyes. Save that good nose." Put Red Riding Hood's grandmother's pockmarked cork-ball nose on any other puppet? It wouldn't work. It wouldn't be right. Anyway, how could she tear that face apart? She laid the grandmother in a carton alongside a worn-out Beauty from "Beauty and the Beast"—the very first puppet she'd ever made. They were on their third Beauty at the moment, a much more sophisticated version with a seamed cloth face. It wasn't the plays that wore the puppets out; it was the children coming up afterwards, patting the puppets' wigs and stroking their cheeks. Beauty's skin was gray with fingerprints. Her yellow hair had a tattered, frantic look.

This whole room belonged to the puppets: the hollow back bedroom, with peeling silvery pipes shooting to the ceiling and a yellow rain stain ballooning down one wall. The window was painted shut, its panes so sooty that the sun set up an opaque white film in the afternoons. The wooden floor put splinters in Gina's knees and turned her overalls black. The china doorknob was hazy with cracks. The door hung crooked. Nights, when Emily worked late in the glow of one goose-necked lamp, the hall light that shone beneath the door was not a rod but a wedge, like a very long piece of pie.

She sat up late and repaired the witch, the all-purpose stepmother-witch that was used in so many different plays. No wonder she kept wearing out! One black button eye dangled precariously. Emily perched upon the stepladder that was the room's only furniture and tied a knot in a long tail of thread.

The puppets most in use were kept in an Almadén chablis box in the corner. They poked their heads out of the cardboard compartments: two young girls (one blonde, one brunette), a prince, a green felt frog, a dwarf. The others stayed in muslin bags in the closet, with name tags attached to the drawstrings: *Rip Van W. Fool. Horse. King.* She liked to change them around from time to time, assign them roles they were not accustomed to. Rip Van Winkle, minus his removable beard, made a fine Third Son in any of those stories where the foolish, kind-hearted Third Son ends up with the princess and half the kingdom. He fitted right in. Only Emily knew he didn't belong, and it gave a kind of edge to his performance, she felt. She ran him through his lines herself. (Leon played the older two sons.) She put an extra, salty twang in his voice. The real Third Son, meanwhile—more handsome, with less character—lay face-up backstage, grinning vacantly.

Emily had never actually planned to be a puppeteer, and even now both she and Leon thought of it as temporary work. She had entered college as a mathematics major, on full scholarship—the only girl her age in Taney, Virginia, who was not either getting married the day after graduation or taking a job at Taney Paper Products. Her father had been killed in an auto accident when Emily was a baby; then, early in Emily's freshman year at college, her mother died of a heart ailment. She was going to have to manage on her own, therefore. She hoped to teach junior high. She liked the cool and systematic process that would turn a tangle of disarranged numbers into a single number at the end—the redistributing and simplifying of equations that was the basis of junior-high-school mathematics. But she hadn't even finished the fall semester when she met Leon, who was a junior involved in acting. He couldn't *major* in acting (it wasn't offered), so he was majoring in English, and barely scraping by in all his subjects while he appeared in every play on campus. For the first time Emily understood why they called actors "stars." There really was something dazzling about him whenever he walked onstage. Seen close up, he was a stringy, long-faced, gloomy boy with eyes that drooped at the outer corners and a mouth already beginning to be parenthesized by two crescent-shaped lines. He had a bitter look that made people uneasy. But onstage, all this came across as a sort of power and intensity. He was so concentrated. His characters were so sharply focused that all the others seemed wooden by comparison. His voice (in real life a bit low and glum) seemed to penetrate farther than the other voices. He hung on to words lovingly and rolled them out after the briefest pause, as if teasing the audience. It appeared that his lines were invented, not memorized.

Emily thought he was wonderful. She had never met anyone like him. Her own family had been so ordinary and pale; her childhood had been so unexceptional. (His had been terrible.) They began spending all their time together—nursing a single Pepsi through an afternoon in the canteen, studying in the library with their feet intertwined beneath the table. Emily was too shy to appear in any plays with him, but she was good with her hands and she signed on as a set-builder. She hammered platforms and stairsteps and balconies. She painted leafy woods on canvas flats, and then for the next play she transformed the woods into flowered wallpaper and mahogany-colored wainscoting. Meanwhile, it seemed that even this slim connection with the theatre was making her life more dramatic. There were scenes with his parents, at which she was an embarrassed observer—long tirades from his father, a Richmond banker, while his mother wiped her eyes and smiled politely into space. Evidently, the university had informed them that Leon's grades were even lower than usual. If they didn't improve, he was going to flunk out. Almost every Sunday his parents would drive all the way from Richmond just to sit in Leon's overstuffed, faded dormitory parlor asking what kind of profession he could hope for with a high F average. Emily would rather have skipped these meetings, but Leon wanted her there. At first his parents were cordial to her. Then they grew less friendly. It couldn't have been anything she'd done. Maybe it was what she *hadn't* done. She was always reserved and quiet with them. She came from old Quaker stock and tended, she'd been told, to feel a little too comfortable in the face of long silences. Sometimes she thought things were going beautifully when in fact everybody else was casting about in desperation for something to talk about. So she tried harder to be sociable. She wore lipstick and stockings when she knew they were coming, and she thought up neutral subjects ahead of time. While Leon and his father were storming at each other, she'd be running through a mental card file searching for a topic to divert them. "Our class is reading Tolstoy now," she told Leon's mother one Sunday in April. "Do you like Tolstoy?"

"Oh, yes, we have it in leather," said Mrs. Meredith, dabbing her nose with a handkerchief.

"Maybe Leon ought to take Russian literature," Emily said. "We read plays too, you know."

"Let him pass something in his *own* damn language first," his father said.

"Oh, well, this is in English."

"How would that help?" Mr. Meredith asked. "I believe his native tongue is Outer Mongolian."

Meanwhile Leon was standing at the window with his back to them. Emily felt touched by his tousled hair and his despairing posture, but at the same time she couldn't help wondering how he'd got them into this. His parents weren't really the type to make scenes. Mr. Meredith was a solid, business-like man; Mrs. Meredith was so stately and self-controlled that it was remarkable she'd foreseen the need to bring a handkerchief. Yet every week something went wrong. Leon had this way of plunging into battle unexpectedly. He was quicker to go to battle than anyone she knew. It seemed he'd make a mental leap that Emily couldn't follow, landing smack in the middle of rage when just one second before he'd been perfectly level and reasonable. He flung his parents' words back at them. He pounded his fist into his palm. It was all too high-keyed, Emily thought. She turned to Mrs. Meredith again. "Right now we're on *Anna Karenina*," she said.

"All that stuff is Communist anyhow," said Mrs. Meredith.

"Is . . . what?"

"Sure, this tractor-farming, workers-unite bit, killing off the Tsar and Anastasia . . ."

"Well, I'm not . . . I believe that came a little later."

"What is it, you're one of these college leftists?"

"No, but I don't think Tolstoy lived that long."

"Of course he did," Mr. Meredith said. "Where do you think your friend Lenin would be if he didn't have Tolstoy?"

"Lenin?"

"Do you deny it? Look, my girl," Mr. Meredith said. He leaned earnestly toward her, lacing his fingers together. (He must sit this way at the bank, Emily thought, explaining to some farmer why he couldn't have a loan on his tobacco crop.) "The minute Lenin got his foot in the door, first person he called on was Tolstoy. Tolstoy this, Tolstoy that . . . Any time they wanted any propaganda written, 'Ask Tolstoy,' he'd say. 'Ask Leo.' Why, sure! They didn't tell you that in school?"

"But . . . I thought Tolstoy died in nineteen . . ."

"Forty," said Mr. Meredith.

"Forty?"

"I was in my senior year in college."

"Oh."

"And Stalin!" said Mr. Meredith. "Listen, *there* was a combination. Tolstoy and Stalin."

Leon turned suddenly from the window and left the room. They heard him going up the stairs to the sleeping quarters. Emily and Mrs. Meredith looked at each other.

"If you want my personal opinion," Mr. Meredith said, "Tolstoy was a bit of a thorn in Stalin's side. See, he couldn't *unseat* Tolstoy, the guy was sort of well known by then, but at the same time he was too old-line. You knew he was pretty well off, of course. Owned a large piece of land."

"That's true, he did," Emily said.

"You can see it must have been a little awkward."

"Well, yes . . ."

" 'The fact is,' Stalin says to his henchmen, 'he's an old guy. I mean, he's just a doddering old guy with a large piece of land.' "

Emily nodded, her mouth slightly open.

Leon came pounding down the stairs. He entered the parlor with a dictionary open in his hands. *"Tolstoy, Lev,"* he read out, *"1828–1910."*

There was a silence.

"Born in eighteen twenty-eight, died in nineteen—"

"All *right*," said Mr. Meredith. "But where is this getting us? Don't try to change the subject, Leon. We were talking about your grades. Your sloppy grades and this damn-fool acting business."

"I'm serious about my acting," Leon said.

"Serious! About *play*-acting?"

"You can't make me give it up; I'm twenty-one years old. I know my rights."

"Don't tell me what I can or cannot do," said Mr. Meredith. "If you refuse, I warn you, Leon: I'm withdrawing you from school. I'm not paying next year's tuition."

"Oh, Burt!" Mrs. Meredith said. "You wouldn't do that! He'd be drafted!"

"Army's the best thing that could happen to that boy," Mr. Meredith said.

"You can't!"

"Oh, can't I?"

He turned to Leon. "I'm driving home with you today," he said, "unless I have your signed and notarized statement that you will drop all extracurricular activities—plays, girlfriends . . ."

He flapped a pink, tight-skinned hand in Emily's direction.

"Not a chance," said Leon.

"Start packing, then."

"Burt!" Mrs. Meredith cried.

But Leon said, "Gladly. I'll be gone by nightfall. Not home, though— not now or ever again."

"See what you've done?" Mrs. Meredith asked her husband.

Leon walked out of the room. Through the parlor's front windows (small-paned, with rippling glass) Emily saw his angular figure repeatedly dislocating itself, jarring apart and drawing back together as he strode across the quadrangle. She was left with Leon's parents, who seemed slapped into silence. She had the feeling that she was one of them, that she would spend the rest of her days in heavily draped parlors—a little dry stick of a person. "Excuse me," she said, rising.

She crossed the room, stepped out the door, and closed it gently behind her. Then she started running after Leon.

She found him at the fountain in front of the library, idly throwing pebbles into the water. When she came up beside him, out of breath, and touched his arm, he wouldn't even glance at her. In the sunlight his face had a warm olive glow that she found beautiful. His eyes, which were long and heavy-lidded, seemed full of plots. She believed she would never again know anyone so decisive. Even his physical outline seemed to stand out more sharply than other people's. "Leon?" she said. "What will you do?"

"I'll go to New York," he said, as if he'd been planning this for months.

She had always dreamed of seeing New York. She tightened her hand on his arm. But he didn't invite her along.

To escape his parents, in case they came hunting him, they walked to a dark little Italian restaurant near the campus. Leon went on talking about New York: he might get something in summer stock, he said, or, with luck, a bit part Off-Broadway. Always he said "I," not "we." She began to despair. She wished she could find some flaw in his face, which seemed to give off a light of its own in the gloom of the restaurant. "Do me a favor," he told her. "Go to my room and pack my things, just a few necessities. I'm worried Mom and Dad will be waiting for me there."

"All right," she said.

"And bring my checkbook from the top dresser drawer. I'm going to need that money."

"Leon, I have eighty-seven dollars."

"Keep it."

"It's left over from the spending money Aunt Mercer gave me. I won't have any use for it."

"Will you please stop *fussing?*" Then he said, "Sorry."

"That's all right."

They walked back to campus, and while he waited beside the fountain, she went to his dorm. His parents weren't in the parlor. The two armchairs they had sat in were empty; the upholstery sighed as it rose by degrees, erasing the dents they had left.

She climbed the stairs to the sleeping quarters, where she'd rarely been before. Girls were allowed here, but they didn't often come; there was something uncouth about the place. A couple of boys were tossing a softball in the corridor. They paused grudgingly as she edged by, and the instant she had passed, she heard the slap of the ball again just behind her. She knocked at the door of 241. Leon's roommate said, "Yeah."

"It's Emily Cathcart. Can I come in and get some things for Leon?"

"Sure."

He was seated at his desk, tilted back, apparently doing nothing but shooting paper clips with a rubber band. (How would she ever love another boy after Leon left?) The paper clips kept hitting a bulletin board and then pinging into the metal wastebasket underneath it. "I'll need to find his suitcase," Emily said.

"Under that bed."

She dragged it out. It was covered with dust.

"Meredith leaving us?" he asked.

"He's going to New York. Don't tell his parents."

"New York, eh?" said the roommate, without much interest.

From the closet by Leon's bed Emily started taking the clothes she'd seen him wear most often—white shirts, khaki trousers, a corduroy jacket she knew he was fond of. Everything smelled of him, starchy and clean. She was pleased by the length of his trousers, in which she herself would be lost.

"You going with him?" the roommate said.

"I don't think he wants me to."

Another paper clip snapped against the bulletin board.

"I would if he asked me, but he hasn't," Emily said.

"Oh, well, you've got exams coming up. Got to get your A's and A-pluses."

"I'd go without a thought," she said.

"The man wants to travel light, I guess."

"Is this his bureau?"

He nodded and let his chair thud forward. "You don't think your picture'd be on *my* bureau," he said. "No offense, of course."

She glanced at the picture—her Christmas present to Leon. It stood behind an alarm clock, still in the deckle-edged cardboard folder supplied by the studio. The person it showed only faintly resembled her, she hoped. Emily hated being made to feel conscious of her physical appearance. She walked around most of the time peering out of the eye holes of her body without giving it much thought, and she found it an unpleasant shock to be pressed onto a piano bench with her head held at an unnatural angle, forced to reflect upon her too light skin and her pale lashes that had a way of disappearing in photographs. "Smile," the photographer had told her. "This is not a firing squad, you know." She had given a quick, nervous smile and felt how artificially her lips stretched across her teeth. When the man ducked behind his camera, she'd wiped the smile off instantly. Her face emerged sober and peering, netted by worry, the mouth slightly pursed like her spinster aunt's.

She didn't pack the photo. And when she got back to Leon at the fountain, she was lugging not only his suitcase but hers as well.

"I don't care what you say," she told him. She started calling this at some distance from him, she was so anxious to get it said. She was puffing and tottering between the two suitcases. "I'm coming with you. You can't leave me here!"

"Emily?"

"I think we ought to get married. Living in sin would be inconvenient," she said, "but if that's what you prefer, then I'd do that too. And if you tell me not to come, I'll come anyway. You don't own New York! So save your breath. I'll ride on the bus one seat behind you. I'll tell the taxi driver, 'Follow that cab!' I'll tell the hotel clerk, 'Give me the room next to his room, please.' "

Leon laughed. She saw she'd won him. She set down the suitcases and stood facing him, not smiling herself. In fact, what she'd won him with was a deliberate, calculated spunkiness that she really did not possess, and she was alarmed to find him so easily taken in. Or maybe he wasn't taken in at all, but knew that this was what the audience expected: that when some girl chases you down with her suitcase and behaves outrageously, you're to laugh and throw your hands up and surrender. Laughter was not his best expression. She had never seen him look so disjointed, so uneven. There was something asymmetrical about his face. "Emily," he said, "what am I going to do with you?"

"I don't know," she told him.

Already she was beginning to worry about that herself.

By evening they were on a Greyhound bus to New York City. By the next afternoon they were settled (it felt more like camping out) in a furnished room with a sink in one corner and a toilet down the hall. They were married Thursday, which was as soon as the law permitted. She'd seen more ceremony, Emily thought, when she got her driver's license. Marriage didn't cause as much of a jolt in her life as she'd expected.

Emily found a job as a waitress in a Polish restaurant. Leon—just for the moment—cleaned a theatre after shows. In the early evenings he hung out at various coffee-houses listening to actors and poets give readings. He took Emily along, whenever she didn't have to work. "Aren't they terrible?" he would ask her. "*I* can do better than that." Emily thought so too. Once they heard a monologue that was so inept that she and Leon got up and walked out, and the actor stopped halfway through a line to say, "Hey, you! Don't forget to leave some money in the cup." Emily would have done it—she'd do anything to avoid a scene—but Leon got angry. She felt him draw in his breath; he seemed to grow bigger. By now she knew how far his anger could take him. She lifted her hand to form the shape of his elbow, but she didn't actually touch him. You should never touch Leon when his temper was up. Then he let go of his breath again and allowed her to lead him away, with the actor still shouting after them.

It turned into a very hot summer, full of rainstorms and muggy black clouds. The heat in their room was like something alive. And they were continually on the brink of having no money whatsoever. Emily had never realized how much money mattered. She felt she had to breathe shallowly, conserve her energy, walk in a held-in, unobtrusive way as she sidled between people who were richer. She and Leon began to fight about how to spend what they did have. He was more extravagant—wasteful, she said. He said she was stingy.

In July, Emily had a scare and thought she might be pregnant. She felt trapped and horrified; she didn't dare tell Leon. So when she found she wasn't pregnant after all, she couldn't share her relief with him, either. She kept that experience in her mind. She kept examining it, trying to make sense of it. What kind of marriage was it if you couldn't tell your husband a thing like that? But he would have flown into a rage, and then sunk in on himself like over-risen bread. It was *her* idea, marrying, he'd say; and *she* was the one always harping on what they couldn't afford. She pictured the scene so clearly that she almost believed it had happened. She held it against him. Her eyes filled with tears sometimes as she recalled how badly he'd behaved. But he hadn't! He had never been given a chance! (he would say). She went on blaming him anyhow. She visited a family-planning clinic and she told them that her husband would kill her if she ever got pregnant. Of course she meant it figuratively, but she could tell from the way the social worker looked at her that in this neighborhood you couldn't always be sure of that. The social worker glanced at Emily's arms and asked her if she had any other problems. Emily wanted to talk about her separateness, about how she'd kept her pregnancy scare a secret from her own husband, but she knew that wasn't a serious enough problem. In this neighborhood, women were getting murdered. (She felt how frivolous she must seem to the social worker; she was wearing her leotard and wrap skirt from Modern Dance I.) Women were getting mugged in this neighborhood, or beaten up by their husbands. Emily's husband would never lay a finger on her. She was certain of that. She rested in a circle of immunity, she felt.

She herself was not an angry kind of person. The most she could manage was a little spark of delayed resentment, every now and then, when something had happened earlier that she really should have objected to if she'd only realized. Maybe if she'd had a temper herself, she would have known what string would pull Leon back down into calm. As it was, she just had to stand by. She had to remind herself: "He might hurt other people, but he's never laid a finger on me." This gave her a little flicker of pleasure. "He's crazy sometimes," she told the social worker, "but he's never harmed a hair of my head." Then she smoothed her skirt and looked down at her white, bloodless hands.

In August, Leon met up with four actors who were forming an improvisational group called Off the Cuff. One of them had a van;

they were planning to travel down the eastern seaboard. ("New York is too hard to break into," the girl named Paula said.) Leon joined them. From the start he was their very best member, Emily thought—otherwise they might not have let him in, with his deadwood wife who froze in public and would only take up space in the van. "I can build sets, at least," Emily told them, but it seemed they never used sets. They acted on a bare stage. They planned to get up in front of a nightclub audience and request ideas that they could extemporize upon. The very thought terrified Emily, but Leon said it was the finest training he could hope to have. He practiced with them at the apartment of Barry May, the boy who owned the van. There was no way they could truly rehearse, of course, but at least they could practice working together, sending signals, feeding each other lines that propelled them toward some sort of ending. They were planning on comedy; you could not, they said, hope for much else in a nightclub. They built their comedy upon situations that made Emily anxious—lost luggage, a dentist gone berserk—and while she watched she wore a small, quirked frown that never really left her, even when she laughed. In fact it was terrible to lose your luggage. (She'd once had it actually happen. She'd lain awake all one night before it was recovered.) And it was much too easy to imagine your dentist going berserk. She chewed on a knuckle, observing how Leon took over the stage with his wide, crisp gestures, his swinging stride that came from the hip. In one skit he was Paula's husband. In another he was her fiancé. He kissed her on the lips. It was only acting, but who knows: sometimes you act like a certain person long enough, you become that person. Wasn't it possible?

They started on tour in September. They left New York in the van with all their worldly goods piled on top, including Emily's and Leon's two fat suitcases and the fluted silver coffeepot that Aunt Mercer had sent for a wedding gift. They went first to Philadelphia, where Barry knew a boy whose uncle owned a bar. For three nights they played out their skits in front of an audience that did not stop talking once, and they had to cull their ideas from Emily, whom they'd fed a few suggestions and planted on a barstool just in case. Then they moved on to Haightsville, south of Philadelphia. They thought they had a connection there, but that fell through, and they ended up in a tavern called the Bridle Club that was decorated to look like a stable. Emily had the impression that most of the customers were married to other people waiting at home. It was a middle-aged crowd—squat men in business suits, women with sprayed and gilded hair and dresses that looked one size too small. These people, too, talked among themselves throughout the skits, but they did offer a few ideas. A man wanted a scene in which a teenager announced to her parents that she was quitting school to become an exotic dancer. A woman proposed that a couple have a quarrel about the wife's attempts to introduce a few gourmet foods to her husband. Both of these suggestions, when they were made, caused a little ripple of amusement through the room, and the group turned them into fairly funny skits; but Emily kept imagining that they might be true. The man did have the seedy, desolate look of a failed father; the woman was so frantically gay that she could very well have just escaped from a stodgy husband. What the audience was doing was handing over its pain, Emily felt. Even the laughter seemed painful, issuing from these men with their red, bunchy faces and the women bearing up bravely beneath their towering burdens of hair. For the third skit, a man sitting with three other men proposed the following: a wife develops the notion that her husband, a purely social drinker who can take it or leave it and quit whenever he wants to, supposing he ever did want to, is in fact an alcoholic. "Pretend like this woman gets more and more out of line," he said. "Pretend like she goes around watering the Jack Daniel's, calling up the doctor and the AA people. When he asks for a drink, she brings him ginger ale with a spoonful of McCormick's brandy extract stirred in. When he wants to go out for a friendly night with his buddies, she says—"

"Please!" said Barry, holding up a hand. "Leave something for us!"

Then everyone laughed, except Emily.

They were appearing at the Bridle Club for three nights, but the second night Emily didn't go. She walked around town instead, until almost ten o'clock, looking into the darkened windows of Kresge and Lynne's Dress Shoppe and Knitter's World. Periodically, carloads of teenagers shot by, hooting at her, but Emily ignored them. She felt so much older than they were, she was surprised she wasn't invisible to them.

In the drugstore, which was the only place still open, she bought a zippered cosmetic kit for traveling, completely fitted with plastic jars and bottles and a tiny tube of Pepsodent. She and Leon were almost penniless at this point. They were having to sleep apart—Emily and the two other women at the Y, the men in the van. The last thing they could afford was a $4.98 cosmetic kit. Emily rushed back to her room, feeling guilty and pleased. She started rearranging her belongings—carefully pouring hand lotion into one of the bottles, fitting her silver hairbrush into a vinyl loop. But she really didn't wear much make-up; the zippered bag took more room than her few cosmetics had taken on their own. It was a mistake. She couldn't even get her money back; she'd used the bottles. She began to feel sick. She went through her suitcase throwing things out—her white school blouses, her jeans, every bit of underwear. (If she wore only leotards, she wouldn't need underwear.) When she was done, all that remained in her suitcase were two extra wrap skirts, two extra leotards, a nightgown, and the cosmetic bag. The small cardboard wastebasket next to her bed was overflowing with filmy, crumpled, shoddy non-essentials.

Their third appearance at the Bridle Club was canceled in favor of the owner's cousin's girlfriend, a torch singer. "I didn't know there still were such things," Leon told Emily. He looked depressed. He said he wasn't sure this experience was as valuable as he'd once believed. But Barry May, who was more or less the leader of the group, refused to give up. He wanted to try Baltimore, which was full of bars, he said. Besides, one of the other members, Victor Apple, had a mother living in Baltimore, and they ought to be able to get a free place to stay.

Emily knew as soon as they arrived that Baltimore would not work out. Although they drove miles and miles of it (Victor managed to get them lost), the city continued to strike her as narrow and confining: all those gloomy rowhouses, some no wider than a single room; those alleys choked with discarded tires and bottles and bedsprings; those useless-looking, hopeless men slumped on their stoops. But she took to Victor's mother immediately. Mrs. Apple was a tall, cheerful, striding woman with clipped gray hair and a leathery face. She owned a shop called Crafts Unlimited, as well as the building that housed it, and various craftsmen filled her apartments, some paying only token rent until they could get on their feet. She gave the acting group a third-floor apartment, unfurnished and shabby but clean. It was split by a dark hall, with a living room and a bedroom on one side and a kitchen and a second bedroom on the other side. At the end of the hall was an antique bathroom, against whose window, long ago, the adjoining building had been constructed. You could stand at that window and see nothing but a sheet of old, spongy bricks. For some reason Emily found this comforting. It was the only view she had felt sure of lately.

It seemed to her now that adjusting to new places used up pieces of a person. Large chunks of her had been broken off and left behind in New York, in Philadelphia, in Haightsville—anyplace she had painstakingly set out her mother's silver-backed comb and brush on someone else's peeling bureau and contrived a pretense of familiarity with someone else's flaking walls and high, cracked ceiling. She followed Mrs. Apple everywhere; she couldn't help herself. She dusted the carvings and the handmade furniture down in the shop and she learned how to work the cash register. She waited on customers during busy periods—not for pay, but for the sunny smell of new wood and freshly woven fabrics, and the brisk, offhand friendliness of Mrs. Apple.

Emily and Leon slept in the front bedroom, in two sleeping bags. Victor spread his tangle of blankets in a corner of the living room. Barry and Paula and Janice slept in the back bedroom, three across. (Emily had given up trying to figure that out.) In the daytime Barry went looking for jobs while the others stayed home and played cards. They no longer practiced their skits or even mentioned them; but sometimes, watching them play poker, Emily had the feeling that to these people everything was a skit. When they lost, they groaned and tore their hair. When they won, they leaped up, flinging their cards to the ceiling, and trumpeted, "Tataa!" and took a bow. Their vowels were broader than most people's, and they italicized so much. You had to talk like that yourself sometimes, just to be heard above the din. Emily found herself changing. She heard herself coming down hard on her words, drawing them out. She caught sight of herself in a mirror once, unexpectedly—her small, dry face as wan as a ghost's, but one arm flung out grandly as if she were standing cloaked and hatted in the center of some stage. She stopped in mid-sentence and folded up again.

The bars in Baltimore were not the kind to want plays going on. They were *drinking bars,* Barry said, and this was a drinking city. At one place he would have had to step over a flatout body, either unconscious or dead, in the doorway; but he hadn't seen much point, he said, in applying there. A week passed, and then two weeks. They were living on a cheap brand of water-packed tuna, and Mrs. Apple had stopped inviting them so frequently to supper. Their greasepaint box somehow fell apart. Tubes of ghastly pink flesh-tone, like fat sticks of chalk, rolled into corners and stayed there, sending out their flowery old-lady smell. Janice and Paula stopped speaking to each other, and Janice moved her sleeping bag to the kitchen.

Then Barry found a job, but only for himself. A friend of a friend was putting on his own play. Emily wasn't there when he announced it. She'd been helping out at Crafts Unlimited. All she knew was that when she got back, there was Barry packing his knapsack. A swelling was rising on his lower lip, and Leon was gone. The others sat on the floor, watching Barry roll up his jeans with shaky hands. "That husband of yours is insane," he told Emily. Even his voice shook.

Emily said, "What happened?" and the others all started talking at once. It wasn't Barry's fault, they said; you have to watch out for number one in this world; what did Leon expect? Emily never did sort out the particulars, but she grasped the main idea. She was surprised at how little it bothered her. There was something satisfying about the damage done to Barry's lip. The skin had split where the swelling was highest; she was reminded of an overripe plum. "Oh, well," she said, "I suppose it's for the best."

"Mark my words," Barry told her, "you're living with a dangerous man. I don't know why you're not scared of him."

"Oh, he would never harm *me*," Emily said. She couldn't think why Barry was taking this so seriously. Didn't it often happen in these people's lives—drama, extravagant gestures? She removed some hairpins from her hair and pinned her braids higher on her head. The others watched her. She felt graceful and light-hearted.

Janice and Paula went back to New York; Janice planned to accept an old marriage proposal. "I just hope the offer's still open," she said. Emily had no idea what Paula was going to do, and she didn't care, either. She was tired of living in a group. She got on fine with them, right to the end, and she said goodbye to them politely enough, but underneath she felt chafed by every word they uttered.

That left Victor. Victor wasn't so bad. He was only seventeen, and he seemed even younger. He was a slight, stooped, timid boy with a frail tickle of a mustache that Emily longed to shave off. Once the others were gone, he moved his blankets to the rear bedroom. He showed up for meals looking shy and hopeful. It was a little like having a son, Emily thought.

By now they were completely out of money, so Emily started work as a paid assistant at Crafts Unlimited. Leon found a part-time job at Texaco, pumping gas. Victor just borrowed from Mrs. Apple. Mrs. Apple lent him the money, but gave out lectures with it. She wanted him to go back to school, or at least take the high-school-equivalency test. She threatened to send him to live with his father, whom Emily had always assumed to be dead. After these lectures Victor would slink around the apartment kicking baseboards. Emily commiserated with him, but she did think Mrs. Apple had a point. She couldn't understand how things had gone this far, even; everyone seemed to be living lives without shape, without backbone. "When you think of it," she told Victor, "it's amazing your mother ever let you go to New York in the first place. Really, she's a very . . . surprising woman."

"Sure, to you," said Victor. "Other people's mothers always look so nice. Up close, they're strict and grabby and they don't have a sense of humor."

Then Mrs. Apple came to Emily with an idea. (She probably felt that if she came to Victor, he'd turn it down automatically.) If they were so set on acting, she said, why not act at children's birthday parties? They could put an ad in the paper, get a telephone, borrow her Singer sewing machine to stitch a few costumes together. Mothers could call and order "Red Riding Hood" or "Rapunzel." (Emily would make a lovely Rapunzel, with her long blond hair.) They would gladly pay a good fee, she was certain, since birthday parties were such a trial.

Emily passed the idea on because it sounded like something she could manage. She would not, at least, freeze up onstage in front of a few small children. Victor was immediately willing, but Leon looked doubtful. "Just the three of us?" he asked.

"We could change costumes a lot. And there are always people around here, if we're really stuck for more characters."

"We could use my mother for a witch," Victor said.

"Well, I don't know," Leon said. "I wouldn't even call that acting, if you want to know the truth."

"Oh, Leon."

She dropped the subject for the next few days. She watched him weighing it in his mind. He came back from the Texaco station with his hands black, smearing black on the doorknobs and the switchplates. Even after he washed, black stayed in the creases of his skin and rimmed his fingernails. Sitting on the kitchen counter waiting for his tuna, he spread his hands on his knees and studied them, and then he turned them over and studied them again. Finally he said, "These children's plays, I suppose they'd do for a stopgap."

Emily said nothing.

He said, "It wouldn't hurt to give it a try, just so we don't get stuck in it."

Now, all this time Emily and Victor had been laying their plans, they'd been so sure he would change his mind. They'd already ordered a phone for the kitchen. It arrived the day after Leon gave in. They placed an ad in the papers and they made a large yellow poster to hang in Crafts Unlimited. *Rapunzel, Cinderella, Red Riding Hood,* the poster read. *Or . . . you name it.* ("Just so it doesn't take a cast of thousands," Leon said.)

Then they sat back and waited. Nothing happened.

On the sixth day a woman phoned to ask if they gave puppet shows. "I don't need a play; I need a puppet show," she said. "My daughter's just wild about puppets. She doesn't like plays at all."

"Well, I'm sorry—" Emily said.

"Last year I had Peter's Puppets come and she loved them, and all they charged was thirty-two dollars, but now I hear they've moved to—"

"Thirty-two dollars?" Emily asked.

"Four dollars a child, for seven guests and Melissa. I felt that was reasonable; don't you?"

"It's more than reasonable," Emily said. "For a puppet show we get five per child."

"Goodness," the woman said. "Well, I suppose we could uninvite the MacIntosh children."

In the two weeks before the party Emily borrowed Mrs. Apple's sewing machine and put together a Beauty, two sisters, a father, and a Beast, who was really just a fake fur mitten with eyes. She chose "Beauty and the Beast" because it was her favorite fairytale. Victor said he liked it too. Leon didn't seem to care. Plainly, as far as he was concerned, this was just another version of the Texaco job. He hardly noticed when Emily came prancing up to him with her hand transformed into Beauty.

She cut a stage from a cardboard box, and bought gauzy black cloth for the scrim. She and Victor clowned together, putting on doll-like voices to match the puppets' round faces. They had the two sisters sing duets and waltz on the kitchen windowsill. Leon just looked grim. He had figured out that most of their fee had already been spent on materials. "This is not going to make us rich," he said.

"But think of next time," Emily said, "when we'll already be equipped."

"Oh, Emily, let's not have a next time."

On the day of the party—a rainy winter afternoon—they loaded everything into Victor's mother's car and drove north to Mrs. Tibbett's stucco house in Homeland. Mrs. Tibbett led them through the living room to a large, cold clubroom, where Leon and Victor arranged the cardboard stage on a Ping-Pong table. Meanwhile Emily unpacked the puppets. Then she and Victor set the two sister puppets to whispering and snickering, trying to get Leon to join in. He was supposed to work the Beast, which he'd never even fitted on his hand; and he'd had to be told the plot during the drive over. He claimed the only fairytale he knew was "Cinderella." Now he ignored the puppets and paced restlessly up and down, sometimes pausing to lift a curtain and peer out into the garden. It was because of his parents, Emily thought. This house resembled his parents' house, which Emily had once visited during semester break. The living room had that same stiff, icy quality, with the pale rugs that no one seemed to have walked on and the empty vases, the ticking silence, the satin striped chairs, where obviously no children were ever allowed to sit. Mrs. Tibbett, even, was a little like Mrs. Meredith—so gracious and honeyed, her hair streaked, her mouth tight, with something unhappy beneath her voice if Leon would only hear it. Emily reached out to pat his arm, but then stopped herself and curled her fingers in.

The doorbell rang—a whole melody. "It's a goddamned cathedral," Leon muttered. The first guests arrived, and Melissa Tibbett, a thin-faced, homely child in blue velvet, went to greet them. These children were all five years old or just turning six, Mrs. Tibbett had said. They were young enough to come too early, with their party clothes already sliding toward ruin, but old enough, at least, not to cling tearfully to the birthday presents they'd brought. Emily supervised the opening of the presents. Mrs. Tibbett had vanished, and the two men seemed to think that dealing with the children was Emily's job. She learned the names that mattered—the troublemaker (Lisa) and the shy one who hid in corners (Jennifer). Then she settled them in front of the puppet show.

Victor was the father. Emily was each of the daughters in turn. Concealed behind the scrim, she didn't feel much stage fright. "What do you want me to bring you, daughter?" Victor squeaked.

"Bring me a casket of pearls, Father," Emily piped in a tiny voice.

Leon rolled his eyes toward the ceiling.

"What do you want me to bring *you*, Beauty?"

"Only a rose, Father. One perfect rose."

She could see the outlines of the children through the scrim. They were listening, but they were fidgety underneath, she thought. It made her nervous. She felt things were on the verge of falling into pieces. During the father's long scene alone in the palace, she saw Mrs. Tibbett's fluttery silhouette enter and stand watching. What a shame; she'd come during the dull part. "Oh. A table has been laid for me, with lovely foods," the father said. "And look: a fine gold bed with satin sheets. I wonder to whom this belongs." Mrs. Tibbett shifted her weight to the other foot.

Then the Beast arrived. Emily expected him to roar, but instead he spoke in a deep, chortling growl that took her by surprise. "Who's gobbled up all my food?" he asked plaintively. "Who's been sleeping in my bed?" (Oh, Lord, she hoped he hadn't confused this with "Goldilocks.") "My lovely bed, with the satin sheets to keep my hairdo smooth!" he groaned.

The children laughed.

An audience. She saw him realize. She saw the Beast raise his shaggy head and look toward the children. Their outlines were still now and their faces were craned forward. "Do *you* know who?" he asked them.

"Him!" they cried, pointing.

"What's that you say?"

"The father! Him!"

The Beast turned slowly. "Oho!" he said, and the father puppet shrank back, as if blown by the Beast's hot breath.

After the show the maid passed cake and punch around, but most of the children were too busy with the puppets to eat. Emily taught them how to work the Beast's mouth, and she had Beauty sing "Happy Birthday" to Melissa. Mrs. Tibbett said, "Oh, this was so much better than last year's 'Punch and Judy.'"

"We never do 'Punch and Judy,'" Leon said gravely. "It's too grotesque. We stick to fairytales."

"Just one thing puzzles me," said Mrs. Tibbett.

"What's that?"

"Well, the Beast. He never changed to a prince."

Leon glanced over at Emily.

"Prince?" Emily said.

"You had her living happily ever after with the Beast. But *that's* not how it is; he changes; she says she loves him and he changes to a prince."

"Oh," Emily said. It all came back to her now. She couldn't think how she'd forgotten. "Well . . ." she said.

"But I guess that would take too many puppets."

"No," Emily said, "it's just that we use a more authentic version."

"Oh, I see," Mrs. Tibbett said.

III

BY SPRING they were putting on puppet shows once or twice a week, first for friends of Mrs. Tibbett's and then for friends of those friends. (In Baltimore, apparently, word of mouth was what counted most.) They made enough money so they could start paying Mrs. Apple rent, and Leon quit his Texaco job. Emily went on working at Crafts Unlimited just because she enjoyed it, but she earned almost as much now from the extra puppets that she sold there. And gradually they began to be invited to school fairs and church fund-raisers. Emily had to sit up all one night, hastily sewing little Biblical costumes. A private school invited them to give a show on dental hygiene. "Dental hygiene?" Emily asked Leon. "What is there to say?" But Leon invented a character named Murky Mouth, a wicked little soul who stuffed on sweets, ran water over his toothbrush to deceive his mother, and played jump-rope with his dental floss. Eventually, of course, he came to a bad end, but the children loved him. Two more schools sent invitations the following week, and a fashionable pedodontist gave them fifty dollars to put on a Saturday-morning show for twenty backsliding patients and their mothers, who (Emily heard later) had to pay twenty-five dollars per couple to attend.

It was mostly Leon's doing, their success. He still grumbled any time they had a show, but the fact was that from the start he knew exactly what was needed: dignified, eccentric little characters (no more squeaky voices) and plenty of audience participation. His heroes were always dropping things and wondering where they were, so that the children went wild trying to tell them; always overlooking the obvious and having to have it explained. Emily, on the other hand, cared more for the puppets themselves. She liked the designing and the sewing and the scrabbling for stray parts. She loved the moment when a puppet seemed to come to life—usually just after she'd sewed the eyes on. Once made, a puppet had his own distinct personality, she found. It couldn't be altered or submerged, and it couldn't be duplicated. If he was irreparably damaged—or stolen, which sometimes happened—she could only make a new one to fill his role; she couldn't make the same one over again.

That was ridiculous, Leon said.

She imagined the world split in two: makers and doers. She was a maker and Leon was a doer. She sat home and put together puppets and Leon sprang onstage with them, all flair and action. It was only a matter of circumstance that she also had to be the voices for the heroines.

Victor was neither maker nor doer, or he was both, or somewhere in between, or . . . What was the matter with Victor? First he grew so quiet, and paused before answering anything she said, as if having to reel his mind in from more important matters. He moped around the apartment; he stared at Emily sadly while he stroked his wisp of a mustache. When Emily asked him what his trouble was, he told her he'd been born in the wrong year. "How can that be?" she asked him. She supposed he'd taken up some kind of astrology. "What difference does the year make?"

"It doesn't bother you?"

"Why should it bother me?"

He nodded, swallowing.

That night at supper he put down his plate of baked beans and stood up and said, "There's something I have to say."

They still had no furniture, and he'd been eating on the windowsill. He stood in front of the window, framed by an orange sunset so they had to squint at him from their places on the floor. He laced his fingers together and bent them back so the knuckles cracked. "I have never been a sneaky person," he said. "Leon, I'd like to announce that I'm in love with Emily."

Leon said, "Huh?"

"I won't beat around the bush: I think you're wrong for her. You're such a grouch. You're always so angry and she's so . . . un-angry. You think her puppets are nothing, a chore, something forced on you till you get to your real thing, acting. But if you're an actor, why don't you act? You think there's no theatre groups in this city? I know why: you had a fight with that guy Bronson, Branson, what's-his-name, when you went to try out. You've had a fight with everyone around. You can't try out for the Chekhov play because Barry May's in that and he'll tell all the others what you're like. But still you say you're an actor and you're so disadvantaged, so held back, wasting your talents here when there's other things you could be doing. *What* other things?"

Leon had stopped chewing. Emily felt her chest tightening up. Victor was smaller than Leon, and so young and meek he would never hit back. She imagined him cowering against the window, shielding his head with his arms, but she didn't know how to step in and stop this.

"I realize I'm not as old as Emily," Victor said, "but I could take much better care of her. I would treat her better; I'd appreciate her; I'd sit admiring her all day long, if you want to know. We'd live a real life, not like this, with her ducked over her sewing machine and you off brooding in some corner, paying her no attention, holding some grudge that no one can guess at . . . Well, I'll say it right out: I want to take Emily away with me."

Leon turned and looked at Emily. She saw that he wasn't angry at all. He was relaxed and amused, smiling a tolerant, kindly smile. "Well, Emily?" he said. "Do you want to go away with Victor?"

She felt suddenly flattened.

"Thank you, Victor," she said, pressing her palms together. "It's nice of you, but I'm fine as I am, thank you."

"Oh," said Victor.

"I appreciate the thought."

"Well," Victor said, "I didn't want to sneak around about it."

Then he sat back down on the windowsill and picked up his plate of beans.

The next morning he was gone—Victor and his tangle of blankets and his canvas backpack and his cardboard carton of LP records. He hadn't even said goodbye to Mrs. Apple. Well, it was a relief, in a way. How could they act natural after that? And she and Leon did need to be on their own. They were a married couple; it began to seem that they really were married. She was starting to think about a baby. Leon didn't want one, but in time he would come around. They could use Victor's room for a workshop now, and then for the baby later on. It was lucky Victor had left, in fact.

But she hated how his woodsy, brown boy-smell hung in the empty room for days after he had gone.

Several times in Emily's life, similar things had happened. Men had seemed to affix themselves to her—but not to her personally, she thought. What they liked was their idea of her. She remembered a boy in her logic class who used to write her notes asking if she would take down her hair for him. Her hair: a bunch of dead cells that had nothing to do with her. "Think of it as longer, thinner fingernails," she had written back coolly. She disliked being seen from outside that way— as someone with blond hair, someone with an old-fashioned face. Once, in New York, a man had started eating every day at the restaurant where she worked, and any time she so much as passed his table he would tell her about his ex-wife, who had also worn braids on top of her head. It was a continuing story: Emily would bring his rolls and he would say, "On our second date we went to the zoo." She'd refill his coffee cup and he would say, "I'm pretty certain she loved me to begin with." After a couple of weeks he went away, but Emily couldn't forget the ex-wife. She was Emily's other self; they would have understood each other, but she had slipped off and left Emily to take the blame. Now, with Victor, Emily wondered who he'd had in mind. Not Emily, she was sure—poking around in her linty old clothes, hunting up noses for her puppets. It must have been someone else who looked like Emily but had the capacity for a greater number of people in her life. Poor Victor! It was a pity, Emily thought. She was surprised at how much she missed him. She could not imagine loving anyone but

Leon, but when she'd put a puppet together and longed for someone to try him out on, she thought of Victor and their squeaky-voiced duets. She remembered Beauty's sisters clowning around at that first birthday party while Leon paced the floor.

It wasn't so easy to clown around with Leon.

IV

SHE DRESSED Gina in a T-shirt, pink corduroy overalls, and a snowsuit. She buckled her little red shoes on her feet. Gina was impatient to get going. "Can we swing on the swings?" she asked.

"Not today, honey."

"But I want to swing on the swings."

"Maybe tomorrow."

"*Why* can't we swing on the swings?"

She was almost two now. Terrible Two's: they had minds all their own. But that could be said of Gina at any age. Somehow, this one small child kept both of her parents continually occupied and teetering on the edge of exhaustion. They must be doing something wrong. It didn't look so hard for other people.

Emily put a coat on and tied a scarf over her hair. It was February, a damp, cold day. Even the apartment was cold. She poked her head into the kitchen to say goodbye to Leon. He was sitting at the chipped enamel table they'd bought from Goodwill, reading the *Village Voice*. "Leon?" she said. "I'm taking Gina for a walk."

"You want me to come along?"

"Oh, no, I'll be back soon."

He nodded and returned to his paper. Emily led Gina out the door. They went down the creaking stairway, past the side entrance of Crafts Unlimited, through the glass door at the front of the building. She checked the laundromat across the street. No one was there. She hoisted Gina into her arms and set off toward Beacon Avenue. Gina kept struggling to get down; she liked to go places under her own steam. (It took her all day.) By now she was so heavy that it was difficult to hold on to her. Emily went faster than she'd intended to, pulled forward by Gina's tilted weight. Her slippers made a rustling, patting sound.

They arrived at the E-Z Cafeteria five minutes early, but Leon's mother was already waiting, seated alertly at the foremost table with her hands crossed over her purse. When she saw Emily (when she saw Gina, really), she seemed to open like a flower. Her face lifted, her hands uncrossed themselves, and the feathers on her hat stirred. "Ah!" she cried. She rose and brushed her cheek against Emily's. "I wasn't sure you'd come," she told Emily. "I didn't know if you'd want to bring her out in this weather."

"Oh, she's out in any weather," Emily said.

Mrs. Meredith settled Gina in the high chair she'd already wheeled up. "Was she cold?" she crooned. "Did her little face get frozen?" She unwrapped her like a package, and patted Gina's thick, dark hair. "Oh, exactly like Leon's hair," she said. (She always did.) "Will you look at how she's grown? Just in this one month she's grown so that I never would have known her. Though of course I'd know her anywhere," she said, contradicting herself. Gina gazed at her reflectively. She was always quieter in her grandmother's presence.

The E-Z Cafeteria was not Mrs. Meredith's style, but it was one place they could manage Gina. They could wheel her down the food line instead of waiting for their order to arrive, and they could leave without delay any time she got restless. It had taken them a while to figure this out. They'd started off at the Elmwood—Mrs. Meredith's suggestion, a place near Towson, to which Emily had had to travel by bus. It was the only Baltimore restaurant Mrs. Meredith knew of. And, to be fair, she'd had no idea she was inviting a baby to lunch as well.

What had happened was, when Emily got married she had naturally informed her Great-Aunt Mercer, back in Taney. Aunt Mercer had not been very pleased, but she'd made the best of it. On her thick, silver-rimmed stationery, which smelled as if she'd kept it in her basement for the last ten years, she wrote to ask Emily who this young Meredith might be. *What's his daddy's name? Would I be likely to know any of his people? He isn't one of those Nashville Merediths, is he?* And once she had her answers, of course she felt duty-bound to write his parents a get-acquainted note. Next Leon received a letter from his mother, sent direct to his New York address: *Mr. Leon Meredith.* No mention of Emily. He threw it away unopened. "Oh, Leon!" Emily said. It was true she wasn't comfortable with his parents, but you couldn't just discard your only relatives. Leon said, "I told you that was a mistake, writing your aunt. I said it would be." And the letter stayed in the wastebasket.

They moved to Baltimore, but the letters followed, for all his mother had to do was ask Aunt Mercer for his new address. And Leon went on throwing the letters away. Maybe eventually he'd have opened one (this couldn't last forever, could it?), but then the Merediths did something unforgivable. They gave his forwarding address to his draft board.

It wasn't malicious, Emily was certain, but Leon thought it was. "That's my parents for you," he said. "They'd rather have me dead in the jungle than alive and happy without them." He went on cursing them even after he failed the physical. One leg was found to be an inch and a half shorter than the other, the result of a broken thighbone in his childhood. No one had ever noticed it before. He returned with a painful limp and said, "I'm free, but I won't forget what they tried to do to me." And he continued throwing their letters away.

If Emily's name had been on the envelopes too, she'd have opened them. She was pregnant by then and wishing for her mother. Aunt Mercer was no use—with her dim, steely handwriting: *The crocuses are late this year and the rodents have been at my galanthus bulbs*—and Mrs. Apple was sympathetic but had no recollection of childbirth. ("Perhaps I was put to sleep," she said. "Do they give anesthesia for such things? I may have been asleep the whole nine months, in fact.") Emily dreamed that Mrs. Meredith would suddenly arrive in person, miraculously plumper and more motherly, and she'd fold Emily into her lap and let her be a daughter again. But she never did.

Then, three months after Gina's birth, there it was: *Mrs. Leon Meredith.* Emily marveled at how long it had taken. She smuggled the letter into the bathroom and locked the door behind her to read it. *I know it must be you who's keeping our boy from us. I saw from the start you were a cold little person. But he is our only child. Think how we must feel.*

Emily was stunned. She couldn't believe that anyone would be so unfair. Her eyes blurred and the sheets of bricks shimmered in the window.

Why are you saying these things? she wrote back. *I have nothing to do with any of this and I don't understand it. It's between you and Leon.*

His mother said, *It seems you must have taken offense at something. Please, could we start over? Could we meet at the Elmwood this Wednesday at noon?*

Emily didn't want to meet her. She felt like ripping the letter to shreds. She looked at Gina, who lay crowing in her cardboard box, and she tried to imagine anything Gina could do—marrying, mismarrying, committing murder—that would sever her from Emily's life as Leon had severed himself from his parents'. There was nothing. She just wouldn't allow it. Gina was the whole point; even what Emily felt for Leon seemed pallid by comparison. She smoothed the letter on her lap and saw Mrs. Meredith's tense, powdery face, with the eyebrows plucked as thin as two arched wires and the lids beneath them always a little puffed, as if she were on the edge of tears.

There were certain rules, Emily had been taught. She would have to go just this once.

Mrs. Meredith came by taxi, all the way from Richmond. Evidently, she didn't drive, and had simply hired a cab for the day. The driver sat at the next table, spreading pâté on a cracker and reading *Male* magazine. Mrs. Meredith waited behind a foggy martini glass. Her back was very straight. Then Emily entered with Gina riding the way she liked to in those days—hanging over Emily's forearm, with her bottom propped against Emily's hip, frowning darkly at her own bare toes. "Oh!" Mrs. Meredith cried out, and one hand flew to her throat, knocking the martini glass into her lap.

Now that she thought back, Emily felt she really should have prepared

Mrs. Meredith. It was too theatrical—bursting in with an unannounced grandchild. It was more like something Leon would have done. She seemed to have caught some of Leon's qualities. He seemed to have caught some of hers. (He seldom spoke of moving on any more.) She was reminded of those parking-lot accidents where one car's fender grazes another's. It had always puzzled her that on each fender, some of the other car's paint appeared. You'd think the paint would only be on one car, not both. It was as if they had traded colors.

She tried to tell Leon about the lunch, once it had taken place. She led into it gradually. "Your mother's been writing *me* now, you know," she said.

But Leon said, "Emily, I don't want to hear about it and I don't want you to have anything to do with it. Is that clear?"

"All right, Leon," Emily said.

And, oddly enough, even Mrs. Meredith seemed content to let things be. It seemed she only wanted the connection; just who made the connection didn't matter so much. She liked to hear from Emily what Leon was up to. Did he help to care for Gina? "He walks her at night, and he baby-sits while I'm working in the shop," Emily told her, "but he can't yet bring himself to change a diaper."

"Exactly like Burt was," Mrs. Meredith said. "Oh, exactly!" But she never tried to press any closer than that. Maybe she found things easier as they were. She often retreated into stories about Leon's childhood, when he had been someone she could understand. "He was a beautiful baby," she said. "All the nurses told me so. Prettiest baby they'd ever seen! They couldn't believe their eyes!" Somehow, everything she said had a way of slipping out of her control. "Even the doctors stopped by to take a look. This one man, a heart surgeon, he came straight from an operation just to get a glimpse of him. 'Mrs. Meredith,' he said, 'I never saw a baby so beautiful in my life. Yes, sir, we're going to hear more of that young man. He's going to amount to something someday!' He called his wife on the telephone; I heard him in the hall. 'You ought to see this baby we've got here! Ought to see this baby!' " Next, Emily thought, there'd be a star beaming over the delivery room. She began to understand why Leon got so edgy around his mother. Mrs. Meredith's rouged face, gazing brightly at a boy no one else could see, seemed deliberately shuttered and obstinate.

In fact, she made Emily feel edgy as well, and Emily never enjoyed these lunches, or came any closer to liking Mrs. Meredith. Telling her a piece of news—or even speaking to Gina in Mrs. Meredith's presence— Emily heard her own voice take on a fulsome tone that wasn't hers at all. She felt that nothing she could say would ever live up to Mrs. Meredith's expectations. But what could she do? The very day after their lunch at the Elmwood, Mrs. Meredith started driving lessons. In a month she had her license and a brand-new Buick, and she drove the entire distance from Richmond to Baltimore, although, she said, she was scared to death of multi-lane highways and disliked going over thirty miles per hour. When she telephoned Emily from a corner booth, breathlessly announcing, "I did it! I'm here to take you to lunch," could Emily just say, "No, thank you," and hang up?

They settled into a schedule: the first Wednesday of every month. Emily never told Leon about it. She knew that, eventually, Gina would tell. Now that Gina could talk, it was only a matter of time. "When me and Grandma was eating . . ." she'd say, and Leon would say, "You and *who?*" and then all hell would break loose. Till then, Emily went dutifully to lunch, frowing slightly with concentration.

One time Mr. Meredith came too. He seemed baffled by the baby. He let his wife do all the talking, while he stared around at the dingy old men slurping soup in the E-Z Cafeteria. "So where's this son of mine?" he asked finally.

"He's . . . very busy at home," Emily said.

"Would you believe he was once the size of this little tyke?" he asked, jutting his chin at Gina. "I could carry him in the palm of my hand. Now we're not on speaking terms."

"Burt," said Mrs. Meredith.

"He was always quick to throw things away."

Later, when it was time to go, he asked Emily if she had all her equipment.

"Equipment?" Emily said.

"Equipment. You know."

Maybe he was asking if she were sane, marrying his son.

But then he said, "Crib, playpen, high chair, carriage . . ."

"Oh. We don't need all that," Emily said. "She sleeps in a cardboard box. It's perfectly comfortable."

"I'll send her a crib," Mr. Meredith said.

"No, Mr. Meredith, please don't do that."

"I'll send her one tomorrow. Imagine! A cardboard box!" he said, and he went away shaking his head and looking pleased, as if *his* expectations, at least, had every one been fulfilled.

The crib arrived: white, spooled, with an eyelet canopy. She'd never heard of such nonsense. Two delivery men came puffing up the stairs with it and leaned it, unassembled, against the wall in the hallway. She reached a finger inside a plastic bag and touched an eyelet ruffle. Then Leon walked in, tossing from hand to hand the cabbage she'd asked him to get at the market. "What's all this?" he asked.

"Your parents sent it," she said.

He took a step backward from the crib.

"Leon," she said. "While we're on the subject, I ought to tell you something."

He said, "I don't want to hear, I don't want to know, and I want this monstrosity gone by the time I get back."

Then he turned and left, still carrying the cabbage.

Emily thought it over. She mashed a banana for Gina's supper and fed it to her, absently taking a few bites herself. She looked out the kitchen doorway and into the hall, where the crib stood slanting elegantly. At that time Gina was six months old, and outgrowing her cardboard box. She slept more often with her parents, still munching drowsily on Emily's breast. It would be nice to have a safe container to keep her in, Emily thought. She scraped banana off Gina's chin and stuffed it back into her mouth. She looked at the crib again.

When Leon came back, the crib was still there, but he didn't mention it. Maybe he'd been doing some thinking himself. The following day Emily started assembling it. She would join two pieces and then leave it a while, as if it were only something to fiddle with—a crossword puzzle, a hoop of needlework. Then she'd come back and tighten a bolt; then she'd leaf through the paper. In a few days she had a completed crib. It seemed silly to leave it obstructing the hall, so she wheeled it into their bedroom. The effect was dazzling. All that white made the rest of the room seem drab. Their mattress on the floor had a lumpy, beaten look.

She went back to the hall for Gina and carried her into the bedroom and set her in the crib. Gina stared all around her at the eyelet ruffles, the decals, the bars. What a shock, she seemed to be saying. How did this imprisonment come about?

It came about inch by inch. These things just wear you down.

V

THIS CHILD had changed their lives past recognition, more than they had dreamed possible. You would think that someone so small could simply be fitted into a few spare crannies and the world could go on as usual, but it wasn't like that at all. From the start, she seemed to consume them. Even as a tiny infant she was aggressively sociable and noisy and enthusiastic, an insomniac who seldom took naps and struggled continually toward a vertical position. They would lay her down on her stomach for the night and instantly her head would bob up again, weaving and unsteady, her eyes so wide that her forehead seemed corrugated. She loved to be talked to, sung to, tossed in the air. As she grew older, she fell in love with Red Riding Hood's wolf and they had to give him up to her. If she slept at all, she slept with the wolf against her cheek and she dreamily twisted his red felt tongue. Periodically the tongue fell off and then she would go to pieces—crying and clinging to Emily till Emily sewed it back on. And she hated to be left. Hannah Miles, across the hall, was glad to baby-sit, but any time Emily and Leon went out, Gina wept as if her heart would break and Emily would have to stay. Or Leon would make her leave anyway, really insist, and she would go, but her thoughts remained with Gina, and all through the movie or whatever she would fidget, buttoning and unbuttoning her coat, not hearing a word. Then Leon would be angry with her and they'd have a fight and the outing would be wasted, but later when they returned, Gina would be wide awake and smiling, at eleven or twelve at night, reading books with Hannah and hardly noticing they were back.

They never asked, of course, whether she was worth it. They centered their lives on her. They could marvel forever at the small, chilly point of her nose, or her fat-ringed fingers or precisely cut mouth. When finally she fell asleep, the absence of all that fierce energy made the apartment feel desolate. Emily would drift through the rooms not knowing what to do next, though she'd wanted to do so much all day and never had a chance to begin. She wondered how they'd managed to produce such a child. She herself had always been so subdued and so anxious to please; Leon had Gina's fire but none of her joyous good nature. Where did she get that? She was a changeling. She had arrived with someone else's qualities. She was the gnome's baby, not theirs.

He stood in the laundromat doorway with his hat pulled low and he sank back into the darkness as they passed. Sometimes the hat was pointed, sometimes flat, sometimes broad-brimmed. Sometimes it seemed he had aged, was slackening, falling apart as certain people suddenly do; he was seen in gold-rimmed spectacles and his beard was cut to such a stubble that he might merely have neglected shaving himself. Then later he would reappear miraculously young again, the spectacles gone, the beard in full bloom. On occasion he was not gnomish at all but just a rather beakish, distinguished gentleman in suits so tidy you had the impression someone else had dressed him. On other occasions he could have stepped into a puppet show and not been out of place. He had a gait they would know anywhere, that seemed to belong to someone much younger—a reckless, bent-kneed, lunging gait, half running, landing on the balls of his feet. But once he was seen plodding out of a secondhand-clothing store with the resigned deliberation of a middle-aged man, and he had let his hair grow unsuitably long so it straggled in an unkempt and pathetic way over the back of his collar. At Christmas, Leon thought he saw him at a puppet show all the way over near Washington; but maybe it was just someone like him, he said. Then later he told Emily he'd been stupid—not for thinking it was he (the man was everywhere, after all), but for imagining there could be anyone else, anyplace, at any time, the faintest bit like Morgan.

1971

|

MORGAN'S OLDEST daughter was getting married. It seemed he had to find this out by degrees; nobody actually told him. All he knew was that over a period of months one young man began visiting more and more often, till soon a place was set for him automatically at suppertime and he was consulted along with the rest of the family when Bonny wanted to know what color to paint the dining room. His name was Jim. He had the flat, beige face of a department-store mannequin, and he seemed overly fond of crew-necked sweaters. And Morgan couldn't think of a thing to say to him. All he had to do was look at this fellow and a peculiar kind of lassitude would seep through him. Suddenly he would be struck by how very little there was in this world that was worth the effort of speech, the entanglements of grammar and pronunciation and sufficient volume of voice.

Then Amy started beginning every sentence with "we." *We* think this and *we* hope that. And finally: when we're earning a little more money; when we find a good apartment; when we have children of our own. This just crept in, so to speak. No announcements were made. One Sunday afternoon Bonny asked Morgan if he thought the back yard was too small for the reception. "Reception?" Morgan said.

"And it's not just the size; it's the weather," Bonny said. "What if it rains? You know how the weather can be in April."

"But this is already March," Morgan said.

"We'll all sit down this evening," said Bonny, "and come to some decision."

So Morgan went to his closet and chose an appropriate costume: a pinstriped suit he'd laid claim to after Bonny's father died. It stood out too far at the shoulders, maybe, but he thought it might have been what Mr. Cullen was wearing when Morgan asked him for permission to marry Bonny. And certainly he'd been wearing his onyx cufflinks. Morgan found the cufflinks in the back of a drawer, and he spent some time struggling to slip them through the slick, starched cuffs of his only French-cuffed shirt.

But when the four of them sat down for their discussion, no one consulted Morgan in any way whatsoever. All they talked about was food. Was it worthwhile calling in a caterer, or should they prepare the food themselves? Amy thought a caterer would be simplest. Jim, however, preferred that things be homemade. Morgan wondered how he could say that, having eaten so many suppers here. Bonny wasn't much of a cook. She leaned heavily on sherry—several glugs of it in any dish that she felt needed more zip. Everything they ate, almost, tasted like New York State cocktail sherry.

Morgan sat in the rocking chair and plucked out his beard, strand by strand. If he got up right now and left, he told himself, they might not even notice. He reflected on a long-standing grievance: there was one of Bonny's pregnancies that she'd forgotten to inform him about. It was the time she'd been expecting Liz, or maybe Molly. Bonny always said he was mistaken; of course she'd told him, she recalled it clearly. But Morgan knew better. He suspected, even, that she'd neglected to tell him on purpose: he tended to get annoyed by her slapdash attitude toward various birth-control methods. To his certain knowledge, the very first inkling he'd had of that pregnancy was when Bonny arrived in the kitchen one morning wearing the baggy blue chambray shirt she habitually used as a maternity smock. He was positive he would have remembered if she'd mentioned it to him.

"Amy will start down the stairs," Bonny said. Evidently, they were planning the actual ceremony now. "Her father will meet her at the bottom and walk her to the center of the living room."

"Daddy, promise me you won't wear one of your hats," Amy said.

Morgan rocked in his chair and plucked on, thinking of the tall black father-of-the-bride top hat he would purchase for the occasion. He knew just where he could find one: Tuxedo Tom's Discount Formal Wear. He began to feel slightly happier.

But later, when Jim and Amy had gone out, he sank into a spell of sadness. He thought of what a sunny child Amy had been when she was small. She'd had large, exaggerated curls swooping upward at each ear, so that she seemed to be wearing a Dutch cap. That Dutch-capped child, he thought, was whom he really mourned—not the present Amy, twenty-one years old, efficient secretary for a life-insurance company. He recalled how he had once worried over her safety. He'd been a much more anxious parent than Bonny. "You know," he told Bonny, "I used to be so certain that one of the children would die. Or all of them, even—I could picture that. I was so afraid they'd be hit by cars, or kidnapped, or stricken with polio. I'd warn them to look both ways, not to run with scissors, never to play with ropes or knives or sharp sticks. 'Relax,' you'd say. Remember? But now look: it's as if they died after all. Those funny little roly-poly toddlers, Amy in her OshKosh overalls—they're dead, aren't they? They did die. I was right all along. It's just that it happened more slowly than I'd foreseen."

"Now, dear, this is just an ordinary life development," Bonny told him.

He looked at her. She was seated at the kitchen table, working on the guest list for the wedding. On the wall above her was something like a hat rack—a row of short wooden arms. When you pressed a pearl pushbutton anywhere in this house, there was a clunk from the kitchen gong and one of the wooden arms would fly up, alerting a non-existent servant. Beneath each arm a yellowed label identified the room that had rung—or (in the case of bedrooms) the person. *Mr. Armand. Mrs. Armand. Miss Caroline. Master Keith.* Studying these labels, Morgan had the feeling that a younger, finer family lived alongside his, gliding through the hallways, calling for tea and hot-water bottles. Evenings, the mother sat by the fire in a white peignoir and read to her children, one on either side of her. A boy, a girl; how tidy. At dinner they discussed great books, and on Sunday they dressed up and went to church. *They* never quarreled. *They* never lost things or forgot things. They rang and waited serenely. They gazed beyond the Gowers with the placid, rapt expressions of theatregoers ignoring some petty disturbance in the row ahead.

"I'd like to invite Aunt Polly," Bonny said, "but that means Uncle Darwin, too, and he's so deaf and difficult."

She was peering through black-framed, no-nonsense glasses, which she'd just started wearing for reading. Morgan said, "So did *you* die, when you think of it."

"Me?"

"Where's that girl I used to take out walking? I used to hold on to your arm, high up, and you would look off elsewhere and get pink, but you wouldn't pull away."

Bonny added a name to her list. She said, "Walking? I don't remember that. I thought we always drove."

He slid his fingers down the inside of her upper arm, where the skin was silkiest. The back of his hand brushed the weight of one breast. She didn't seem to notice. She said, "Luckily, Jim doesn't have many relatives."

"She must be marrying him out of desperation."

Then she did look up. She said, "Couldn't you still love the girls anyhow? You don't stop loving people just because they change size."

"Of course I love them."

"Not the same way," she said. "It seems you get fixed on this one appearance of a person; I mean, this single idea you have." She clicked her ballpoint pen. "And anyway, why leap ahead so? They haven't *all* grown up. Molly and Kate are still in high school."

"No, no, they're gone, for all intents and purposes," Morgan said. "Out every evening, off somewhere, up to something . . . they're gone, all right." He brightened. "Aha!" he said. "Alone at last, my dollink!" But it called for too much effort. He drifted over to the stove, depressed, and lit a cigarette on a burner. "House feels so damn big, we needed a ride-'em vacuum cleaner."

"You always did want more closet space," Bonny told him.

"They've dumped their hamsters on us and gone away."

"Morgan. There were nine of us at dinner tonight, counting your mother and Brindle. When I was a little girl, any time there were nine at table we had to send downtown for Mattie Ida to come help serve."

"What we ought to do is move," Morgan said. "We could get a house in the country, maybe live off the land." He pictured himself in sabots and a rough blue peasant smock. The house would be a one-room cabin with a huge stone fireplace, a braided rug, and a daybed covered in some hand-woven fabric. Unbidden, Amy in her Dutch-cap curls bounced in the center of the daybed. He winced. "I'll take an early retirement," he said. "Forty-five feels older than I'd thought it would. I'll retire and we'll have some time to ourselves. Won't that be nice?"

"Now, don't go off on one of your crazy schemes," Bonny told him. "You'd die of boredom, retiring. You'd feel useless."

"Useless?" Morgan said. He frowned.

But Bonny was on the track of something new, thoughtfully tapping her pen against her teeth. She said, "Morgan, in this day and age, do you believe the bride's mother would still give the bride a little talk?"

"Hmm?"

"What I want to know is, am I expected to give Amy a talk about sex or am I not?"

"Bonny, do you have to call it *sex*?"

"What else would I call it?"

"Well . . ."

"I mean, sex is what it is, isn't it?"

"Yes, but, I don't know . . ."

"I mean, what would *you* say? Is it sex, or isn't it?"

"Bonny, will you just stop *hammering* at me?"

"Anyhow," she said, returning to her list, "in this day and age, I bet she'd laugh in my face."

Morgan rubbed his forehead with two fingers. Really, it occurred to him, if Bonny had been more serious, more responsible, none of this upheaval would be happening. Or at least it wouldn't be happening quite so soon. It seemed to him that she had let the children slip through her fingers in some sort of sloppy, casual, cheerful style that was uniquely hers. He recalled that once, while chaperoning Kate's sixth-grade class on a field trip to Washington, she'd lost all eight of her charges in the Smithsonian Institution. They'd been found among showcases full of savages, copying down the recipe for shrunken heads. At the school's annual mother-daughter picnic, where everyone else brought potato salad and lemonade, Bonny brought a sack of Big Macs and a thermos of chablis. Yes, and she had such a disastrous effect upon machinery; she had only to settle behind the steering wheel and instantly the car fell apart. Warning lights would blink, steam would issue from the radiator, the muffler would drop off, and hubcaps would roll in every direction and clang along the gutters and slither down storm drains. She'd make one simple right turn and the turn signal would never work again. No wonder he spent half his weekends on his back in the garage! And she'd passed all this on the girls too. The first driving lesson he gave Amy, the left front window had slid down inside the door and could not be retrieved. For that he'd had to go to the dealer.

And then there was his sister, who hadn't been out of that bathrobe of hers since Christmas. It hung on her like old orchid petals, wilted, striated, heavy-smelling. And his mother's memory was failing more than ever now, though she flew into a fury if anyone hinted as much. At supper, proving her sharpness, she'd recite whole portions of "Hia-watha" or the *Rubáiyát*. "Come, fill the Cup . . . !" she'd start up out of nowhere, slamming a fork against her glass, and Brindle would say, "Oh, Jesus, not again," and all the others would groan and fall into their separate, disorderly factions around the table.

Useless? Living this life of his was such hard work that even if he retired tomorrow, he had no hope of feeling useless.

II

AMY STOOD at the top of the stairs, wearing white and carrying roses. The hall window behind her lit her long, filmy skirt. At the bottom of the stairs Morgan waited with his hand on the newel post. He wore his new top hat and a pure-black suit from Second Chance. (There'd been a little fuss about the hat, but he'd held his ground.) He had trimmed his beard. Gold-rimmed spectacles (window glass) perched on his nose. He felt like Abraham Lincoln.

One of Morgan's failings was that formal, official proceedings— weddings, funerals—never truly affected him. They just didn't seem to penetrate. He'd lain awake half of last night mourning his daughter, but the fact was that now, with the ceremony about to begin, all that was on his mind was Amy's roses. He had distinctly heard the wedding-dress lady tell her to carry them low, at arm's length—*too* low, even, she said, because if Amy were nervous at all she'd tend to lift them higher. And now, before the music had even started, Amy had her bouquet at breast level. This didn't trouble Morgan (he couldn't see that it made the slightest difference), but he wondered why nervousness should cause people to raise their arms. Was it something to do with protecting the heart? Morgan experimented. He clasped his hands first low, then high. He didn't find the one any more comforting than the other. With his hands folded just beneath his beard, he tried a dipping rhythmic processional, humming to himself as he sashayed across the hall. *"Daddy,"* Amy hissed. Morgan dropped his hands and hurried back to the newel post.

Kate set the needle on the record. The wedding march began in mid-note. In the living room the guests grew suddenly still; all Morgan heard was the creaking of their rented chairs. He smiled steadily up at Amy, his spectacles catching the light and flashing two white circles across her face. With her hand trailing down the banister, weightless as a leaf, Amy set a pointed satin slipper in the center of each step. Her skirt caused a clinking sound among the brass rods that anchored the Persian carpet. Yesterday morning Bonny had taken a red Magic Marker and colored in the bare spots in the carpet. Then she'd used a brown Magic Marker for the rips in the leather armchair. (Sometimes Morgan felt he was living in one of those crayoned paper houses that the twins used to make.) Amy reached the hallway and took his arm. She was trembling slightly. He guided her into the living room and down the makeshift aisle.

On this same stringy rug he had walked her for hours when she was just newborn. He had nestled her head on his shoulder and paced the length of the rug and back, growling lullabies. The memory didn't stir him. It was just there, just another, lower layer in this room that was full of layers. He led her up to Bonny's minister, a man he disliked. (He disliked all ministers.) Amy dropped his arm and took a place next to what's-his-name, Jim. Morgan stepped back and stood with his feet planted apart, his hands joined behind him. He rocked a little to the lullaby in his head.

"Who gives this woman to be married?" the minister said. From the way the question rang in the silence, Morgan suspected it might have been asked once before without his noticing. He seemed to have missed part of the service. "Her mother and I do," he said. It would have been more accurate to say, "Her mother does." He turned and found his seat next to Bonny, who was looking beautiful and calm in a blue dress with a wide scoop neckline that kept slipping off one or the other of her shoulders. She laid a hand on top of his. Morgan noticed a gray thread of cobweb dangling from the ceiling.

Jim put a ring on Amy's finger. Amy put a ring on Jim's finger. They kissed. Morgan thought of a plan: he would go live with them in their new apartment. They didn't know a thing, not a thing. No doubt they'd have broken all their kitchen machines within a week and their household accounts would be a shambles, and then along would come Morgan to repair and advise. He would go as an old man, one of those really bereft old men with no teeth, no job, no wife, no family. In some small area he would act helpless, so that Amy would feel a need to care for him. He would arrive, perhaps, without buttons on his shirt, and would ask her to sew them on for him. He had no idea how to do it himself, he would tell her. Actually, Morgan was very good at sewing on buttons. Actually, he not only sewed on his own buttons but also Bonny's and the girls', and patched their jeans and altered their hemlines, since Bonny wasn't much of a seamstress. Actually, Amy was aware of this. She was also aware that he was not a toothless old man and that he did have a wife and family. The trouble with fathering children was, they got to know you so well. You couldn't make the faintest little realignment of the facts around them. They kept staring levelly into your eyes, eternally watchful and critical, forever prepared to pass judgment. They could point to so many places where you had gone permanently, irretrievably wrong.

III

THERE'D BEEN a compromise on the food. Bonny had ordered several trays from the deli, and then Morgan had picked up some cheese and some crackers which the girls had put together this morning. He'd been upset to discover that there was apparently no discount outlet for gourmet cheeses. "Do you know what these things *cost?*" he asked the groom's father, who had a hand poised over a cracker spread with something blue-veined. Then he wandered across the yard to check on the Camembert. It was surrounded by three young children—possibly Jim's nephews. "This one smells like a stable," the smallest was saying.
"It smells like a gerbil cage."
"It smells like the . . . elephant house at the zoo!"
The weather had turned out fine, after all. It was a warm, yellow-green day, and daffodils were blooming near the garage. A smiling brown maid, on loan from Uncle Ollie, bore a tray of drinks through the crowd, picking her way carefully around the muddy patches where the spring reseeding had not yet taken hold. The bride stood sipping champagne and listening to an elderly gentleman whom Morgan had never seen before. His other daughters—oddly plain in their dress-up clothes—passed around sandwiches and little things on toothpicks, and his mother was telling the groom's mother why she lived on the third floor. "I started out on the second floor," she said, "but moved on account of the goat."
"I see," said Mrs. Murphy, patting her pearls.
"This goat was housebroken, naturally, but the drawback was that I am the only person in this family who reads *Time* magazine. In fact, I have a subscription. And as coincidence would have it, the goat had only been trained on *Time* magazine. I mean, he would only . . . I mean, if the necessity arose, the only place he was willing to . . . was on a *Time* magazine spread on the floor. He recognized that red border, I suppose. And so you see if I were to lay my magazine aside even

for a second, why, along this animal would come and just . . . would up and . . . would . . ."

"He'd pee all over it," Morgan said. "Tough luck if she wasn't through reading it."

"*Oh*, yes," Mrs. Murphy said. She took a sip from her glass.

At Morgan's elbow, in a splintered wicker chair, an unknown man sat facing in the other direction. Maybe he was from the groom's side. He had a bald spot at the back of his head; fragile wisps of hair were drawn across it. He raised a drink to his lips. Morgan saw his weighty signet ring. "Billy?" Morgan said. He went around to the front of the chair. Good God, it was Billy, Bonny's brother.

"Nice wedding, Morgan," Billy said. "I've been to a lot, you know— mostly my own. I'm an expert on weddings." He laughed. His voice was matter-of-fact, but to Morgan it was the misplaced, eerie matter-of-factness sometimes encountered in dreams. How could this be Billy? What had happened here? Morgan had last seen Billy not a month ago. He said, "Billy, from the back of your head I didn't know you."

"Really?" Billy said, unperturbed. "Well, how about from the front?"

From the front he was the same as ever—boyish-looking, with a high, round forehead and dazzling blue eyes. But no, if you met him on the street somewhere, wouldn't he be just another half-bald businessman? Only someone who'd known him as long as Morgan had could find the bones in his slackening face. Morgan stood blinking at him. Billy seemed first middle-aged and anonymous; then he was Bonny's high-living baby brother; then he was middle-aged again— like one of those trick pictures that alter back and forth as you shift your position. "Well?" Billy said.

"Have some champagne, why don't you?" Morgan asked him.

"No, thanks, I'll stick to scotch."

"Have some cheese, then. It's very expensive."

"Good old Morgan," Billy said, toasting him. "Good old, cheap old Morgan, right?"

Morgan wandered away again. He looked for someone else to talk to, but none of the guests seemed his type. They were all so genteel and well modulated, sipping their champagne, the ladies placing their high heels carefully to avoid sinking through the sod. In fact, who here was a friend of Morgan's? He stopped and looked around him. Nobody was. They were Bonny's friends, or Amy's, or the groom's. A twin flew by—Susan, in chiffon. Her flushed, earnest face and steamy spectacles reminded him that his daughters, at least, bore some connection to him. "Sue!" he cried.

But she flung back, "I'm not Sue, I'm Carol."

Of course she was. He hadn't made that mistake in years. He walked on, shaking his head. Under the dogwood tree, three uncles in gray suits were holding what appeared to be a committee meeting. "No,

I've been letting my cellar go, these days," one of them was saying. "Been drinking what I have on hand. To put it bluntly, I'm seventy-four years old. This June I'll be seventy-five. A while back I was pricing a case of wine and they recommended that I age it eight years. 'Good enough,' I started to say. Then I thought, 'Well, no.' It was the strangest feeling. It was the oddest moment. I said, 'No, I suppose it's not for me. Thanks anyway.' "

At a gap in the hedge, Morgan slipped through. He found himself on the sidewalk, next to the brisk, noisy street, on a normal Saturday afternoon. His car was parked alongside the curb. He opened the door and climbed in. For a while he just sat there, rubbing his damp palms on the knees of his trousers. But the sun through the glass was baking him, and finally he rolled down a window, dug through his pockets for the keys, and started the engine.

These were his closest friends: Potter the musical-instrument man, the hot-dog lady, the Greek tavernkeeper on Broadway, and Kazari the rug merchant. None of them would do. For one reason or another, there wasn't a single person he could tell, "My oldest daughter's getting married. Could I sit here with you and smoke a cigarette?"

He floated farther and farther downtown, as if descending through darkening levels of water. All's Fair Pawnshop, Billiards, Waterbeds, Beer, First House of Jesus, SOUL BROTHER DO NOT BURN. Flowers were blooming in unlikely places—around a city trashcan and in the tiny, parched weed-patch beneath a rowhouse window. He turned a corner where a man sat on the curb flicking out the blade of his knife, slamming it shut with the heel of his hand, and flicking it out again. He traveled on. He passed Meller Street, then Merger Street. He turned down Crosswell. He parked and switched the engine off and sat looking at Crafts Unlimited.

It was months since he'd been here. The shopwindow was filled with Easter items now—hand-decorated eggs and stuffed rabbits, a patchwork quilt like an early spring garden. The Merediths' windows were empty, as always; you couldn't tell a thing from them. Maybe they'd moved. (They could move in a taxi, with one suitcase, after ten minutes' preparation.) He slid out of the car and walked toward the shop. He climbed the steps, pushed through the glass door, and gazed up the narrow staircase. But he didn't have what it took to continue. (What would he say? How would he explain himself?) Instead, he turned left, through a second glass door and into the crafts shop. It smelled of raw wood. A gray-haired, square-boned woman in a calico smock was arranging hand-carved animals on a table. "Hello," she said, and then she glanced up and gave him a startled look. It was the top hat, he supposed. He wished he'd worn something more appropriate. And why were there no other customers? He was all alone, conspicuous, in a roomful of quilted silence. Then he saw the puppets. "Ah, so!" he said.

"Ze poppets!" Surprisingly, he seemed to have developed an accent—from what country, he couldn't say. "Zese poppets are for buying?" he asked.

"Why, yes," the woman said.

They lay on a center table: Pinocchio, a princess, a dwarf, an old lady, all far more intricate than the first ones he'd seen. Their heads were no longer round, simple, rubber-ball heads but were constructed of some padded cloth, with tiny stitches making wrinkles and bulges. The old-lady puppet, in particular, had a face so furrowed that he couldn't help running his finger across it. "Wonderful!" he said, still in his accent.

"They're sewn by a girl named Emily Meredith," the woman told him. "A remarkable craftsman, really."

Morgan nodded. He felt a mixture of jealousy and happiness. "Yes, yes," he wanted to say, "don't I know her very well? Don't I know both of them? Who are you, to speak of them?" But also he wanted to hear how this woman saw them, what the rest of the world had to say about them. He waited, still holding the puppet. The woman turned back to her animals.

"Perhaps I see her workroom," he said.

"Pardon?"

"She leeve nearby, yes?"

"Why, yes, she lives just upstairs, but I'm not sure she—"

"Zis means a great deal to me," Morgan said.

Across from him, on the other side of the table, stood a blond wooden cabinet filled with weaving. Its doors were wavery glass, and they reflected a shortened and distorted view of Morgan—a squat, bearded man in a top hat. Toulouse-Lautrec. Of course! He adjusted the hat, smiling. Everything black turned transparent, in the glass. He wore a column of rainbow-colored weaving on his head and a spade of weaving on his chin. "You see, I also am artiste," he told the woman. Definitely, his accent was a French one.

She said, "Oh?"

"I am solitary man. I know no other artistes."

"But I don't think you understand," she said. "Emily and her husband, they just give puppet shows to children, mainly. They only sell puppets when they have a few extras. They're not exactly—"

"Steel," he said, "I like to meet zem. I like you to introduce me. You know so many people! I see zat. A friend to ze artistes. What your name is, please?"

"Well . . . Mrs. Apple," she said. She thought a moment. "Oh, all right. I don't suppose they would mind." She called to someone at the rear, "Hannah, will you watch for customers?" Then she turned to lead Morgan out the side door.

He followed her up the staircase. There was a smell of fried onions and disinfectant. Mrs. Apple's hips looked very broad from this angle. She became, by extension, someone fascinating: she must speak to the Merediths every day, know intimately their schedules and their habits, water their plants when they went on tour. He restrained the urge to set a friendly palm on her backside. She glanced at him over her shoulder, and he gave her a reassuring smile.

At the top of the stairs she turned to the right and knocked on a tall oak door. "Emily?" she called.

But when the door opened, it was Leon who stood there. He was holding a newspaper. When he saw Morgan, he drew the paper sharply to his chest. "Dr. Morgan!" he said.

Mrs. Apple said, "Doctor?"

She looked at Morgan and then at Leon. "Why," she said, "is this the doctor you told me about? The one who delivered Gina?"

Leon nodded.

"But I thought you were an artist!" Mrs. Apple said. "You said you were an artist!"

Morgan hung his head. He shuffled his feet. "I was embarrassed about my hat," he said. "I've just recently come from a wedding; I know I look ridiculous. I said I was an artist so you wouldn't laugh at me."

"Oh, you poor man," Mrs. Apple said. Then she did laugh. "You and your 'zis and zat.' Your 'zese and zose.' "

He risked a glance at Leon. Leon wasn't laughing. He was glaring at Morgan, and he kept the newspaper clamped to his chest as if guarding secrets.

"I do want to see your workroom," Morgan told him. "I may buy a large number of puppets."

"We don't have a large number," Leon said.

"Oh, come on, Leon," Mrs. Apple said. "Why not show him? What's the harm?" She nudged Morgan in the side. "You and your 'artistes.' Your 'poppets.' " She started laughing again. Her eyes grew rays of wrinkles at the corners.

Leon stood scowling at Mrs. Apple. Then, "Well," he said ungraciously, and he stepped back and turned to lead them down the hall.

Morgan peered swiftly into the room on his right—a flash of sunken sofa and a half-empty bookcase. On his left was the kitchen; he had an impression of cold, gleaming whiteness. The next door on the left led to the workroom. There was no real furniture at all—just a sewing machine beneath the window, and a stubby aluminum stepladder on which Emily sat snipping paper. Her black skirt drooped around her, nearly obscuring the ladder. The braids on top of her head picked up light from somewhere and glinted like flying sparks. "Emily," Leon said.

She looked up. Then she jumped off the stepladder and hid whatever she was doing behind her back. "What do *you* want?" she asked Morgan.

"Why, Emily. Goodness," Mrs. Apple said. "This is Dr. Morgan. Don't you recognize him? He's come to buy some puppets. A large *number* of puppets, Emily."

"Buy them downstairs," said Emily, white-faced.

You would think she had something against him.

Morgan tried not to feel hurt. He smiled at her. He said, "I like to see the process of things. Actually."

"There's no process going on here."

He stroked his beard.

Mrs. Apple said, "But . . . Emily? Show him the shadow puppets." She told Morgan, "She's trying something new, Doctor: shadow puppets, out of paper. See?" She crossed to the sewing machine and took something from one of its drawers. It was the silhouette of a knight in armor, attached to a slender rod. "You notice he's hinged at the joints," she said. "You work him behind a screen. He casts a shadow on the screen. Isn't that clever?"

"Yes, certainly," said Morgan. He looked around the room. He wondered what Emily sat on while she worked at the sewing machine. The stepladder, maybe? Even in his fondest fantasies he had not imagined such starkness. He was fascinated. "And will you be using shadow puppets in your shows now?" he asked Emily.

"Yes," she said shortly.

"No," Leon said.

There was a pause. Mrs. Apple gave a little laugh.

"With shadow puppets," Leon said, "it's all how they're hinged, nothing more. How Emily caused their joints to swing when she made them."

"So?" Emily said.

"You just scoot them along the ledge behind the screen, and their joints fall into place. There's nothing to *do*, even less to do than there is with the old kind of puppets."

"So?"

They stared at each other.

Morgan cleared his throat.

"Is that your child I'm hearing?" he asked.

Of course it was. She was singing something in a small, cracked voice, off in some other room. But nobody answered him. He poked his head out into the hall. Then he crossed the hall and went into the bedroom. There was a mattress in one corner and a bureau in another, and a narrow cot along one wall. A child sat on the cot, fitting Tinker Toys together. She sang, ". . . *how to get to Sesame Street* . . ." When she saw Morgan, she stopped.

Morgan said, "Hello there."

She looked at him doubtfully.

He heard the Merediths coming, and he said quickly, "Would you like my hat?" He tore his hat from his head and set it on hers, tilting it back so it wouldn't engulf her completely.

From the doorway, Emily said, "Gina! Take that off. You never try another person's hat on."

"It's my hat," Gina said. "He gave it to me."

"Take it off," Leon said.

"No."

She had a round face and a pointed chin; she had to keep her chin raised so the hat wouldn't slide down over her eyes. This made her look proud and challenging. In fact, she resembled Leon, Morgan thought. When Emily tried to lift the hat from her head, Gina fought her hands away. "It's *my* hat. It's mine."

Morgan said, "Surely. It's a gift."

Emily stopped struggling, but she continued to stand between Morgan and the child, shielding her. Her eyes were pale and cold. She had her arms folded tightly, and Leon stood firm beside her.

Mrs. Apple said, "Dr. Morgan?" She arrived breathless, and handed him another shadow puppet. This one was a king. He might have stepped out of a stained-glass window; red and blue transparent paper covered the pierced design in his robe. Lit behind a screen, he would cast jewel-like colored shadows. "Isn't he marvelous?" Mrs. Apple said. "It's art! You could hang it on the wall."

"That's true, I could," Morgan said. He stroked the colored paper with a thumb. Something about the precision of the design made him feel sad and deprived. His gaze slid off the king and away, landing finally on the bureau. Its top was nearly bare. There were no bottles or safety pins or ticket stubs; just a single framed photo of Leon and Emily holding hands in front of this building. Gina rode on Leon's shoulders. Her plump little calves bracketed his neck. All three of them were smiling squintily into the sunlight. Morgan stepped closer and bent over the photo, pinching his lower lip between his thumb and index finger. The king hung forgotten in his left hand. Bemused, he peered into a drawer that was partway open. Then he opened it further and studied its contents: three white shirts and a box of Kleenex. "Dr. Morgan!" Emily said sharply.

"Yes, yes."

He followed the others out of the room, laying a hand on Gina's head as he passed. Her hair was so soft, it seemed to cling to his fingers for several seconds afterward.

Back in the workroom, he said, "What do you do with Gina while you're giving your puppet shows?"

Emily turned away, refusing to answer, but Leon said, "We take her along."

"And? Does she help with the productions?"

"Oh, no. She's just barely turned four."

"She knows the ropes, though," Morgan suggested. "She was raised backstage, after all. She knows to stay quiet while a play is going on."

"Gina?" Leon said. He laughed. "Gina's never been quiet a full minute in her life. We have to keep hushing her all through the show, and if it's a birthday party, it's worse. She cries when someone else gets to blow out the candles. She hates it when Emily pays attention to other children."

"Oh, you ought to see one of their shows," said Mrs. Apple. She slid the king out of Morgan's hand. Without noticing, he'd rucked up one corner of the colored paper. "They're getting so well known! They've been all the way to Washington. And a man who runs an entertainment company wanted to just take them over, make them part of his troupe, like professionals. What did you ever tell that man, Leon? Did you ever answer his letter?"

"I threw it away," Leon said.

"Threw it away!"

"It was some kind of Bible group. Gospel singers and things."

"But—threw it away! You could at least have answered it."

"And off in some poky town," Leon said. "Tinville, Tindale . . ."

"I doubt you *ever* answer letters," Morgan said. He felt suddenly pleased and excited.

Leon said, "Oh, well . . ."

"Really, what's the point? Why complicate your lives? You go downstairs to clear out the mailbox every now and then, and you glance at what's there and toss it all in the wastebasket and come back empty-handed."

"Well, sometimes," Leon said.

"When?" Emily asked him. Then she turned to Morgan and said, "We're not who you believe we are."

"Eh?"

"We're not who you imagine."

"Come look at Rip Van Winkle," Mrs. Apple said.

"We live like anyone else. We manage fine. We like to be left alone," said Emily. "Let me show you to the door."

"Oh, but Emily!" Mrs. Apple said. "He hasn't seen all the puppets!"

"He's seen enough."

"He wanted to buy a large number!"

"No, no, that's all right . . . I really must be going," Morgan said. "Thank you anyhow."

Emily spun through the door, a swirl of black skirt, and he followed her. They went down the hallway single-file—Emily, Morgan, Leon. Mrs. Apple stayed behind, no doubt looking around at the puppets in bewilderment. "Maybe some other time?" she called after him.

"Yes, maybe so . . ."

He skidded on a Tinker Toy and said, "Oh, excuse me," and lurched against the wall. He clapped a hand to his head. "I'd better go home and change," he said.

"Change?" Leon asked.

"Yes, I . . . need another hat."

His voice was echoing now; they'd reached the stairs. But instead of starting down, he looked at the door across the landing. "Who lives there?" he asked.

"Joe and Hannah Miles," said Leon, but Emily said, "No one."

"Miles? Are they craftsmen also?"

"We'll see you to the street," Emily told him. She pushed forward, edging him toward the stairs, and when he took his first step down, she followed so closely that he felt hounded. "I don't understand you," she said. (He should have known. She would not veil anything; she was as uncurtained as her windows.) "What do you want of us? What are you after? Why did you trail us all those months and lurk in doorways and peer around corners?"

"Oh? You noticed?" Morgan said. He staggered with embarrassment and grabbed the banister.

"You could have come straight up and said hello, like ordinary people."

"Yes, but I was so . . . I'd built up this idea of you. I almost preferred watching, don't you see. My own household is impossible. Very confusing, very tedious," he said. He stopped, halfway down the last flight of stairs. "Oh, *you* think it's all so romantic, I suppose," he said. "Big-city doctor! Saving lives. But mostly it's a treadmill. I work too far downtown; I attract a low class of patient. Twice I've had my office robbed by addicts looking for drugs, and one of those times I was present. They tied my secretary to her chair with a raincoat belt and they made me go through all my desk drawers. It was unnerving. There I was, tumbling out sample packs of decongestants, sinus tablets, pediatric nosedrops . . . I'm not a brave man. I gave them all I had. I tell you this to show you what sort of existence I lead, Emily, Leon . . ."

He was out of breath. He felt a white space inside his head, as if he were standing at an unaccustomed altitude. "Just hear what happened last summer," he said. "I had this patient who'd been stabbed. Stabbed in front of a Fells Point bar, something to do with a woman. They brought him in and woke me in the dead of night. That's the kind of practice I have—such fine patients. And no answering service, no condominium in Ocean City where I can vanish over the weekend . . . Anyhow. He had a long, shallow cut all down the left side, from the ribcage to the hipbone, fortunately clear of the heart. I laid him on the table in my office and stitched him up right then and there. Took me an hour and a quarter—a tiresome job, as you might imagine. Then just as I'm knotting the last stitch, wham! The door bursts open. In comes the man who stabbed him. Pulls out a knife and rips him down the *right* side, ribcage to hipbone. Back to the needle and thread. Another hour and a quarter."

Leon gave a sudden snort of laughter, but Emily just nudged Morgan forward. Morgan resumed his descent, leaning heavily on the banister like someone old and rheumatic. He said, "They come to me with headaches, colds, black eyes . . . self-healing things. A man who does sedentary work—a taxi driver, say—will spend the weekend moving furniture and then call me out of bed on a Sunday night. 'Doc, I got the most terrible backache. Do you think it could be a disk? A fusion? Will I need an operation?' For this I went to medical school!"

"Here," said Emily. They had reached the front door. She pushed it open for him and held out her hand. "Goodbye," she told him. Leon grinned anxiously behind her, as if trying to ease the insult. Morgan took her hand and was startled by its lightness and its dryness.

"You don't want to be friends at all, do you?" he said.

"No," Emily told him.

"Ah," he said. "And why would that be?"

"I don't like how you try to get into our lives. I hate it! I don't like being pried into."

"Emily," Leon said.

"No, no," Morgan told him. "It's quite all right. I understand." He looked away, toward his dusty, sagging car. He had no feelings whatsoever. It seemed he'd been emptied. "Maybe you could meet my wife," he said with an effort. "Would you like to meet Bonny? Have I told you about her? Or you might like my children. I have very nice children, very normal, very ordinary; they seem *determined* to be ordinary . . . Two are in high school. One's grown, really, a secretary; and four others are in college, here and there. Most of the year, they're gone. We hardly hear from them. But that's the way it is, right? Every parent says that. You can see that I'm a family man. Does that help? No, I guess it doesn't." It seemed he was still holding Emily's hand. He dropped it. "The oldest girl's getting married," he said. "I'm not a doctor. I work in a hardware store."

Emily said, "What?"

"I manage Cullen Hardware."

"But . . . you delivered our baby!" she said.

"Ah, well," he told her, "I haven't witnessed three of my daughters' births for nothing." He patted all his pockets, hunting cigarettes, but when he found a pack, he just stood holding it and looking into their stunned faces. "That stabbing business, well, I read it in the paper," he said. "I presented myself untruthfully. I do that often, in fact. I often find myself giving a false impression. It's not something I intend, you understand. It almost seems that other people conspire with me, push me into it. That day you called for a doctor in the house: no one else came forward. There was this long, long silence. And it seemed like such a simple thing—offer some reassurance, drive you to the hospital. I had no inkling I'd actually have to deliver a baby. Events just . . . rolled me forward, so to speak."

He wished they would say something. All they did was stare at him. Meanwhile a girl in an old-fashioned dress climbed the front steps and said, "Hello, Emily, Leon." But they didn't even glance at her, or move aside when she slipped past them and through the open door.

"Please. It's not entirely my fault," he said. "Why are people so willing to believe me? Just tell me that. And this is what's depressing: they'll believe me all the quicker if I tell them something disillusioning. I might say, for instance, that being a movie star is not what it's cracked up to be. I'll say the lights are so hot that my make-up runs, and there's forever this pinkish-gray stain around the inside of my collar that my wife despairs of. Clorox has no effect on it; not even Wisk does, though she's partially solved the problem by prevention. What she does, you see, is rub my collar with a bar of white bath soap before I put a shirt on. Yes, that seems to work out fairly well, I'll say."

"This is crazy," Leon told him.

"Yes," said Morgan.

"You must be crazy!"

But Emily said, "Well, I don't know. I see what he means, in a way." Both men turned to stare at her. Leon said, "You do?"

"He just . . . has to get out of his life, sometimes," she said.

Then Morgan gave a long, shaky sigh and sank down on the stoop. "My oldest daughter's getting married," he said. "Could I sit here with you and smoke a cigarette?"

1973

I

THE NEWSPAPER said, *Crafts Revival in Baltimore? Festival Begins June 2.* There was a picture of Henry Prescott, ankle-deep in wood chips, carving one of his decoys. There was a picture of Leon Meredith holding up a puppet, with his wife beside him and his daughter at his feet. He was a grim, handsome, angular man, and his mouth was sharply creviced at the corners. He was not a young boy any more. It took a photo to make Emily see that. She placed the paper on the kitchen table, pushing away several breakfast dishes, and leaned over it on both elbows to study it more closely. The porous texture of the newsprint gave Leon a dramatic look—all hollows and steel planes. Next to him, Emily seemed almost featureless. Even Gina failed to show how special she was.

"The whole idea," Leon was quoted as saying, "is improvisation. We take it moment by moment. We adapt as we go along. I'm talking about the plays, you understand—not the puppets. The puppets are my wife's doing. She makes them according to a fixed pattern. *They're* not improvised."

This was true, in a way, and yet it wasn't. Emily did have a homemade brown-paper pattern for the puppets' outlines, but the outlines were the least of it. What was important was the faces, the dips and hills of their expressions, which tended to develop unexpected twists of their own no matter how closely she guided the fabric through the sewing machine. Yes, definitely, the puppets were improvised too. She wished she'd spoken up when that reporter was interviewing them—said something to defend herself.

"The heads are padded," Leon said, "and stiffened with some kind of sizing. My wife mixes the sizing. She has her own recipe, her own way of doing things. I'm allowed to help with the props sometimes, but my wife insists on making the puppets totally by herself."

Emily folded the paper and laid it aside. She went down the hall to the back room. It was Gina's room now. The sewing machine and the muslin bags had been moved to the room Leon and Emily shared; Gina's belongings had multiplied too far to be contained in one small corner. Her unmade bed was laden with stuffed animals, books, and clothes. In the rocking chair by the window sat a Snoopy dog bigger than Gina. Grandma and Grandpa Meredith had brought it for her sixth birthday. Emily felt it was ridiculous to give a child something that size—not to mention the cost. What could they have been thinking of? "Oh, well," Leon had told her, "that's just how they are, I guess. *You* know how they are."

Gina was under the bed. She emerged, frowsy-haired, with a sneaker in her hand. "Aren't you ready yet?" Emily asked her. "It's time to go."

"I was looking for my shoe."

Emily took the sneaker from her and loosened a knot in the lace. "Now, Gina, listen," she said. "We've got a play to give out in the county today, and we're leaving before you get back. When kindergarten's over, you walk home with the Berger girls and wait in the shop till we come. Mrs. Apple says she'll keep an eye on you."

"Why can't I stay home and go with you?"

"Summer will be here soon enough," Emily told her. "You'll be home all the time, come summer."

She slipped the sneaker on Gina's foot and tied it. Gina's socks were

already creased and soiled and falling down her ankles. Her blouse
had egg on the front. Emily had known children like Gina when she
was a child herself. They had a kind of extravagant squalor; there was
something lush about the tumbled appearance of their clothing. She
had always assumed their mothers were to blame, but now she knew
better. Not half an hour ago Gina had been neat as a pin; Emily had
made certain of it. She plucked a dust ball from Gina's hair, which
was rich and thick-stranded like Leon's. "Come along," she told her.
"You'll be late."

She slung her purse on her shoulder and they left the apartment,
clicking the latch very gently because Leon was still asleep. They walked
down the stairs, where everyone's breakfast smells hung in the air—
bacon, burned butter, the Conways' kippered herrings. They passed
the door of the shop, which was still dark, and stepped out into the
street. It was a warm, sunny morning. The city looked freshly washed,
with gold-lit buildings rising through a haze in the distance, women
in spring dresses sweeping their stoops, green ivy flooding through the
windows of an abandoned rowhouse. Gina hung on to Emily's hand
and skipped and sang:

> *Miss Lucy had a baby,*
> *She called it Tiny Tim,*
> *She put it in the bathtub*
> *To see if it could swim . . .*

Emily said good morning to Mrs. Ellery, who was shaking out her
dust mop, and to the ancient blind man whose daughter, or granddaughter it must have been, set him on his stoop every fair day with
a grayish quilt wrapped around his legs. "Nice weather," Emily called,
and the old man nodded, turning his sealed-looking eyelids toward the
sun like a plant in the window. She stopped on the second corner to
wait for the Berger girls. Helena Berger shooed them out the door—
two little freckled redheads in plaid dresses. They ran ahead with Gina,
and at the next intersection Emily had to call, "Stop! Wait!" She hurried
up, out of breath, while they lurched and teetered on the edge of the
curb. She held out her hands, and the younger Berger girl took one
and Gina took the other. The Berger child was all bones; Emily felt a
rush of love for Gina's warm, chubby fingers, which were slightly sticky
in the creases. She waded across the street, embroiled in children, and
turned them loose on the other side. They scattered ahead again,
skipping disjointedly.

> *Miss Lucy called the doctor,*
> *Miss Lucy called the nurse,*
> *Miss Lucy called the lady*
> *With the alligator purse . . .*

Emily sensed a presence nearby, the shape of someone familiar, and she turned and found Morgan Gower loping along beside her. He tipped his battered green Army helmet and smiled. "Morgan," she said. "How come you're out so early?"

"I couldn't sleep past five o'clock this morning," he said. "There's too much excitement at the house."

At Morgan's house there was always too much excitement. She'd never been there, but she pictured a bulging, seething box of a place—the roof straining off, the side seams splitting. "What is it this time?" she asked him.

"It's Brindle. My sister. Her sweetheart came back."

Emily hadn't known his sister had a sweetheart. She shaded her eyes and called, "Children! Wait for me!" Then she said, "Did Kate get out of her leg cast yet?"

"Who?" he asked. "Oh, yes. Yes, that's all . . . but see, at seven or so last night, just at the end of supper, the doorbell rang and Bonny said, 'Brindle, go see who that is, will you?' since Brindle was nearest the door, so Brindle went and then . . ."

They'd reached the intersection. Emily held out her hands and the children swarmed around her, knocking Morgan backward a pace. When she'd crossed to the other side and turned to look for him, he was picking up his helmet from the gutter. He polished it with his sleeve, sadly, and set it on his head. It matched his splotchy camouflage jacket and his crumpled olive-drab jungle pants. He was always dressing for catastrophes that were unlikely to occur, she thought. "These are guaranteed, certified, snake-proof boots," he said now. He stopped to hold up one green foot. "I bought them at Sunny's Surplus."

"They're very nice," she said. "Children! Slow down, please."

"How come you have those other two girls?" Morgan asked. "I don't remember seeing them before."

"I'm trading off with their mother. She's walking Gina home today so that I can do a show."

"Well, it all seems so disorganized," Morgan said. "I come to you people for peace and quiet and I find this disorganization. Look at Gina: she hasn't even said hello to me."

"Oh, she will; you know she loves to see you. It's only that she's with friends."

"I prefer it when you both come and Gina walks between you, just the one of her. Where's Leon? Why isn't he here?"

"He's sleeping. He was out late last night, trying for a part in a play."

"It's too disorganized," Morgan said glumly. He stopped and peered down the front of his jacket. Then he reached inside and brought up a pack of cigarettes. "So Brindle goes to the door," he said, "and nothing more happens. There's nothing but silence. Well, we thought she might have faded off somewhere. Forgot where she was headed. Lost her way or something. You know Brindle. Or at least, you know *about* her: always in that bathrobe, moping. 'How was your day?' you ask, and she says, 'Day?' She acts surprised to hear there's been one. 'Go see where she's got to,' Bonny tells me. 'She's *your* sister; see what she's up to.' So I push away from the table and go to find her and there she is in the entrance hall being kissed by a total stranger. It's one of those long, deep, wrap-around kisses, like in the movies. I was uncertain what to do about it. It seemed rude to interrupt, but if I turned and left they'd no doubt hear the floorboards creak, so I just stood there flossing my teeth and the two of them went on kissing. Heavy-set man with slicked-down hair. Brindle in her bathrobe. Finally I ask, 'Was there something you wanted?' Then they pulled apart and Brindle said, 'It's Robert Roberts, my childhood sweetheart. Don't you know him?' "

"Children!" Emily called. They'd reached another intersection. She ran ahead to take their hands. Morgan followed, muttering something. "Known him all his life, of course" was what it sounded like. "Knew him when he was a *bit* of a thing, coming to play roll-a-bat with Brindle in the alley. Called her 'Idiot. Dumbhead. Moron,' in that fond, insulting way that childhood sweethearts have . . ."

The school loomed up, a gloomy building surrounded by cracked concrete, teeming with shabby children. Emily bent to kiss Gina good-bye. "Have a good day, honey," she said, and Morgan said, "How about old Morgan? No kiss for Uncle Morgan?"

He bent over, and Gina threw her arms around his neck and kissed his cheek. "Come by after school and help me again with my yo-yo," she said.

"All right, sugar-pie."

"You promise?"

"Absolutely. Have I ever let you down?"

When she ran off, he stood watching after her, smiling and tapping cigarette ashes across the toes of his boots. "Ah, yes. Ah, yes," he said. "What a darling, eh? I wish she'd stay this size forever."

"I hate that school," Emily said.

"Why! What could be wrong with it?"

"It's so crowded; classes are so big, and I doubt I'll ever feel safe letting her walk here alone. I'd like to send her someplace private. Leon's parents have offered to pay, but I don't know. I'd have to think how to bring it up with Leon."

"No, no, leave her here. Don't forsake your principles," Morgan said. He took her elbow and turned her toward home. "I never thought you'd send your daughter to a private school."

"Why not? What principles?" Emily asked. "You sent yours to private school."

"That was Bonny's doing," Morgan told her. "She has this money. We never see it, never buy anything inspiring with it, but it's there, all right, for things that don't show—new slate roof tiles and the children's education. Her money is so well behaved! I would have preferred a public school, myself. Why, surely. You don't want to cart her off to some faraway place, all these complicated carpools—"

"Dad Meredith happened to mention it while Leon was out of the room," Emily said. "On purpose, I guess. He must be hoping I'll wear Leon down, so when the subject comes up again Leon will be used to it. But I haven't said a word, because Leon's so proud about money. And you know what a temper he has."

"Temper?" Morgan said.

"He might just explode."

"Oh, I can't picture that."

"He's always had this angry streak."

"I can't picture that at all," Morgan said.

He stopped and looked around him. "I would offer to take you for a drive," he said, "just to celebrate the return of Robert Roberts, don't you know. I'm much too keyed up to work today. But, unfortunately, my car's been stolen."

"Oh, that's terrible," Emily said. "When did it happen?"

"Just now," he told her.

"Now? This morning?"

"This instant," he said. He pointed to an empty place at the curb, beside a mailbox. "I parked it here, where I thought you might be passing. Now it's disappeared."

Emily's mouth dropped open.

"There, there, I'm not upset," he said. "As you would say: what's a car, after all?" He spread his arms, smiling. "It's only an encumbrance. Only another burden. Right? I'm better off without it."

Emily didn't know how he could talk that way. A car was very important. She and Leon had been saving for one for years. "You ought to call the police immediately," she told him. "Come back with me and use our telephone. Time really matters."

"There'd be no point," he said. "I've never had much faith in policemen." He took her elbow again to lead her on. The grip of his tense, warm fingers reminded her of Gina. "Last summer," he said, "while we were driving to the beach, a state trooper flagged us down and asked us for a lift. He said his patrol car had been stolen. Can you imagine? He got in the rear with Molly and Kate and my mother . . . those big, shiny boots, gun in a holster . . . he leaned over the front seat and saw Bonny, saw her eating an apple core. 'You want to watch it with those seeds,' he told her. He said, 'My cousin Donna used to love appleseeds. Best part of the apple, she claimed. One year me and my brother saved up all our seeds in a Baby Ben alarm-clock

box and gave them to her for Christmas. She was thrilled. She ate
them every one, and by evening she was dead. Here's where I get off,'
he said; so I stopped the car and out he climbed and that was the last
we saw of him. It seemed he'd only popped in to bring us this message,
you know? And then departed. I said to Bonny, I told her, 'Think of
it, the lives of ordinary citizens in the hands of a man like that. Walking
around with a gun,' I said. 'No doubt loaded, no doubt cocked, or
whatever it is you do with a gun.' "

"Yes, but . . ." Emily said.

She was about to tell him that surely the next policeman wouldn't
be so peculiar. But then she wondered. Some people, it appeared, attract
the peculiar all their lives. "Well, anyway," she said, "it wouldn't hurt
just to give the police a phone call."

"Maybe not, maybe not," Morgan said. He was reading a chipped
and peeling sign: EUNOLA'S RESTAURANT. "Is this place any good?" he
asked.

"I've never tried it."

"Lived right here in the neighborhood and never tried Eunola's?"

"It's a matter of money."

"Let's go in and have some coffee," Morgan said.

"I thought you had to open your store."

"Oh, Butkins will do that. He's happier without me, to tell the truth.
I get in the way." He pulled open the door and shepherded Emily in
ahead of him. There were four small tables and a counter where a row
of men in hard hats sat drinking their coffee under a veil of cigarette
smoke. "Sit," Morgan said, guiding her to a table. He settled opposite
her. "Do you know what this means, this Robert Roberts business? Do
you see the implications? Why, it's wonderful! First the years go by
and Brindle stays in her bathrobe, moping, scuffing about in her slippers,
wondering when the next meal is. 'Fix it yourself, if you're hungry,'
I've told her, but she says, 'Well,' she says, 'I don't know where
anything's kept, the food and utensils and such.' Understand, this is a
house she's been living in since nineteen . . . was it sixty-four? Or
maybe sixty-five, she moved in. Kate was already in school, I remember.
Sue had started her piccolo lessons . . . Then here comes Robert
Roberts! Here he comes, out of the blue. He says his wife is dead now.
And anyhow, he says, his heart was always with Brindle. I can't imagine
why. She's very plain to look at and she's not at all good-natured. But
his heart was always with her, he says. And he was the very person
she's been telling us about at the dinner table, every night of our lives.
Why, our children knew Robert Roberts's name before they knew their
own! They knew all his favorite board games and his batting average.
And here he comes, with an armload of roses, the most colossal heap
of roses; the whole entrance hall took on that rainy, dressed-up smell

that roses have . . . and asking her to marry him! Isn't life . . . symmetrical? I'd really underestimated it."

A waitress stood over them, tapping her pencil. Emily cleared her throat and said, "I'll have coffee, please."

"Me too," said Morgan. "Yes, it was quite a night. The two of them sat up till dawn, discussing their plans. I kept them company. They want to get married in June, they say."

"You certainly have a lot of weddings in your family," Emily told him.

"Oh, not really," he said. He reached across the table for her purse, opened it, and peered inside. "There was Amy's, of course, and then Jean's, but I don't count Carol's; she got divorced before she'd finished writing her thank-you notes." He turned the purse upside down and shook it. Emily's wallet fell out, followed by a key ring. He shook the purse again, but it was empty. "Look at that!" he said. "You're so orderly."

Emily retrieved her belongings and put them back in her purse. Morgan watched, with his head cocked. "I too am orderly," he told her.

"You are?"

"Well, at least I have an interest in order. I mean, order has always intrigued me. When I was a child, I thought order might come when my voice changed. Then I thought, no, maybe when I'm educated. At one point I thought I would be orderly if I could just once sleep with a woman."

He took a napkin from the dispenser and unfolded it and smoothed it across his knees.

Emily said, "Well?"

"Well, what?"

"Did sleeping with a woman make you orderly?"

"How can you ask?" he said. He sighed.

Their coffee arrived, and he seized the sugarbowl and started spooning out sugar. Four teaspoons, five . . . he stirred after each spoonful, and dripped coffee on the tabletop and into the bowl. Caramel-colored beads grew up across the surface of the sugar. Emily looked at them and then at Morgan. Morgan bared his teeth at her encouragingly. She looked away again.

Why put up with him? He was really so strange that sometimes, out in public, she felt an urge to walk several paces ahead so that no one would guess they were acquainted. Or when the three of them were together, she'd make a point of taking Leon's arm. But it was funny how he grew on a person. He added something; she couldn't say just what. He made things look more interesting than they really were. Sometimes he accompanied the Merediths when they went to put on a puppet show, and from the squirrel-like attention he gave to all they

did she would understand, suddenly, how very exotic this occupation
was—itinerant puppeteers! Well, not itinerant, exactly, but still . . .
and she'd look at Leon and realize what a flair he had, with his deep,
dark eyes and swift movements. She herself would feel not quite so
colorless; she would notice that Gina, who sometimes struck her as a
little blowzy, was just like one of those cherubic children on a nineteenth-century chocolate box.

"Leon's picture was in the paper," she told Morgan now.

"Eh?"

She leaned forward. She saw that this must be why she'd agreed to
stop for coffee. "There was an article," she said, "in the morning paper,
all about our puppets."

"Oh, I missed it," he said. "I left the house too early."

"They had a picture of the three of us, but really it was Leon's
article," she said.

Morgan lit a cigarette and tipped his chair back, studying her.

"He talked about the puppets, how they're . . . oh, not improvised.
How they're cut from a pattern." She folded her hands and examined
her knuckles. "He meant something by that. It's hard to explain. If I
tell you what it meant, you'll think I'm imagining things."

"You probably are," Morgan said.

"And last night, this play he went to try for . . . what he used to
do in the old days was, he'd memorize a part for tryouts. He wouldn't
just go and read it, like other people. He had this very quick memory.
It always made an impression. So yesterday afternoon he started to
learn the part he wanted, and it turned out he couldn't do it. He'd
memorize one line and go on to the next, but when he put the two
together he found he'd forgotten the first one and he'd have to begin
all over again. It kept happening. It was eerie. *I* knew the lines, finally,
just from hearing them; but he still didn't. And he blamed me for it.
He didn't say so outright, but he did. I know."

"You're imagining things," Morgan said.

"It's true that he's changed since he met me," Emily said.

Morgan rocked on his chair legs, smoking and frowning. He said,
"Did I ever tell you I was married once before?"

"What? No, I don't think so. And now he's so friendly with his
parents. Well, of course he can say that's all my doing; I used to be
the only one who spoke to them. But now it seems . . . well, truthfully,
they visit a little too much. He gets on with them a little too well."

"I married during my senior year in college," Morgan said. "Her
name was Letitia. We eloped and never told a soul. But as soon as we
got married, we lost interest in each other. It was the funniest thing.
We took up with different crowds; Letitia became involved in an antique-
music group and went off to New York over Christmas vacation . . .
we drifted apart, as they say. We went our separate ways."

Emily couldn't see why he was telling her this. She made an effort and sat straighter in her chair. "Is that right?" she said. "So you got a divorce?"

"Well, no."

"What happened, then?"

"Nothing happened," Morgan said. "We just went our ways. No one knew about the elopement, after all."

Emily thought back over what he'd told her. She said, "But then you'd be a bigamist."

"Technically speaking, I suppose I am," Morgan said cheerfully.

"But that's illegal!"

"Well, yes, I guess it is, in a way."

She stared at him.

"But it's really very natural," he told her. "It's quite fitting, when you stop to consider. Aren't we all sitting on stacks of past events? And not every level is neatly finished off, right? Sometimes a lower level bleeds into an upper level. Isn't that so?"

"Honestly," Emily said. "What has this got to do with anything?" She reached for her purse and stood up. Morgan stood too and came lunging around to pull her chair back, but she was too quick for him. She didn't even wait for him to pay the cashier. She walked on out the door and left him at the register, and he had to run to catch up with her.

"Emily?" he said.

"I have to be getting home now."

"But I seem to have strayed from my point. All your talk of bigamy, legalities, you made me forget what I wanted to say."

"Half the time, Morgan," Emily said, "I believe you're telling out-and-out lies. I believe you just told me one. You did, didn't you? Did you? Or not?"

"See, Emily," Morgan said, "of course he's changed. Everybody does; everyone goes bobbing along, in and out of inlets, snagging on pilings, skating down rapids . . . Well, I mustn't get carried away. But, Emily, you're still close. You haven't parted directions. You're still very much alike."

"Alike!" said Emily. She stopped in front of a newsstand. "How can you say that? We're totally different. We come from totally different backgrounds. Even our religions are different."

"Really?" said Morgan. "What religion is Leon?"

"Oh, Presbyterian, Methodist . . ." She started walking again. "We're nothing at all alike."

"To me you are," Morgan said. "And you get along so well."

"Ha," said Emily bitterly.

"You have the happiest marriage I know of, Emily. I love your marriage!"

"Well, I can't think why," Emily said.

But she let herself fall into step with him.

They passed a woman painting her front door a bright green. "Apple green, my favorite color!" Morgan called, and the woman laughed and bowed like someone on a stage. They passed an open window where Fats Domino sang "I'm Walkin'," and Morgan spread his arms and started dancing. The fact that he had a cigarette clamped in his teeth made it look difficult and precarious; he reminded Emily of those Russians who dance with a glass of vodka on their heads. She stood to one side, awkwardly swinging her purse and smiling. Then Morgan stopped and took his cigarette from his mouth. "Why, look at that," he said. He was staring at something just behind her. She turned, but it was nothing—a car parked next to a mailbox.

"My car!" he said.

"Your what?"

"It's my car!"

"Are you sure?"

But that was a silly question; even Emily was sure. (And why would he claim such a ruined object, otherwise?) Morgan rushed around it, breathing rapid puffs of smoke. "See?" he said. "There's Lizzie's tennis racket, my turban, my sailor suit that I was bringing home from . . . See that Nehi bottle? It's been rolling up and down the back window ledge for the past six months. Or," he said, pausing, "is it possible that someone else might have a car just like this?"

"Really, Morgan," Emily said. "Of course it's yours. Go call the police."

"What for? Why not just steal it back?"

"Well, you want the thief arrested, don't you?"

"Yes," he said, "but meanwhile it's parked in a No Parking zone and I might be given a ticket."

"When it wasn't you that parked it there?"

"You can never tell, in this world," he said. "I promised Bonny I wouldn't run up more traffic fines." He was trying all the doors, but they were locked. He walked around to the front of the car and settled on his haunches before the grille. "I don't suppose you have your Swiss Army knife with you," he said.

"My what? No."

He plucked at a string that was looped through the grille. Then he set his face close and started gnawing at the string. The woman who'd been painting lowered her brush and turned to watch. "I don't understand what you're after," Emily said.

"The key," Morgan said. Something clinked to the ground. He groped beneath the car for it.

"Over to your right," Emily told him. "Closer to the wheel."

Morgan stretched out on his stomach, with his legs trailing behind

him. (The soles of his snake-proof boots were as deeply ridged as snow
tires.) He reached farther under the car. "Got it," he said. A little three-
wheeled mail truck the size of a golf cart bounced up and stopped.
"Help!" Morgan shouted, and he raised his head. She heard his helmet
clang against the underside of the bumper. "I'm hit!" he said.

"Morgan?"

"I'm run over! It's my leg!"

A mailman descended from the truck, whistling, and started toward
the mailbox. Emily grabbed his sleeve and said, "Move."

"Huh?"

"Move the truck! You've run a man over."

"Sheesh," said the mailman. "Don't he see the No Parking sign?"

"Move that truck this instant, I tell you!"

"All right, all right," the mailman said. He turned back to his truck,
glancing down at Morgan on the way. Morgan showed him a face that
seemed all teeth.

"Hurry," said Emily, wringing a handful of skirt.

Meanwhile the woman with the paintbrush arrived, dripping apple
green. "Oh, that poor, poor man," she said. Emily knelt next to Morgan.
She had a sick weight on the floor of her stomach. But at least there
was no blood. Morgan's leg, pinned at the shin beneath the toy tire,
looked flattened but still in one piece. He was breathing raggedly. Emily
laid a hand on his back. "Are you in pain?" she asked him.

"Not as much as you might expect."

"He's going to move the truck."

"Of all the damn-fool, ridiculous—"

"Never mind, it could happen to anyone," Emily said, patting his
back.

"I was talking about the mailman."

"Oh."

The mailman released his brake. The truck gave a grinding sound
and inched backward. "Oof!" said Morgan. He rolled free. He sat up
and inspected his leg. A dusty, wedge-shaped mark ran down the green
fabric.

"Is it broken?" Emily asked him.

"I don't know."

"Rip his pants," the woman with the paintbrush suggested.

"Not the pants!" said Morgan. "They're World War Two."

Emily started folding up the cuff, working gingerly, tensed for what
she might have to see. By now, two old ladies with shopping bags
had joined them, and the mailman was telling them, "I could report
him for illegal parking, if I was that bad of a guy."

"There's nothing here," Emily said. She was inspecting Morgan's
pale, hairy shin. "Can you wiggle your toes?"

"Yes."

"Can you stand?"

He attempted it, with an arm around Emily for support. He was heavier than he looked, hard-muscled, warm, and he gave off the harsh gray smell of someone who'd been smoking for a very long time. "Yes," he said, "I can stand."

"Maybe he just ran over your trousers."

He drew back from her. "That's not true at all," he said.

"But there's no blood, the bone's not broken . . ."

"I felt it. I felt the pressure, a pinch, so to speak, at one side of my calf. You think I don't know when I'm hit? Not all hurts show up from outside. You can't just stand outside and pass judgment on whether I've been injured or not. You think I don't know when a U.S. Government mail truck pins me flat to the pavement?"

"Jesus," said the mailman.

The two old ladies went on their way, and the woman returned to her painting. The mailman unlocked the mailbox. Morgan held up a hand; something glittered. "But at least I've got the key," he told Emily.

"Oh, yes. The key."

He opened the door on the passenger side. "Quick. Jump in," he said.

"Me?"

"Jump in the car. What if the thief comes? All this racket, this hullabaloo . . ."

He waited till she'd climbed in, and then he closed the door and came around to the driver's side. "I've had too much excitement lately," he told her. "I don't know why things can't go a little more smoothly." He settled himself with a grunt and leaned forward to fit the key in the ignition. "Now look," he said. "Another difficulty."

The key wouldn't go. A second key was already there, and a dangling leather case. "What are these?" he asked Emily.

"They must have been locked in the car," she said.

"I'm always amazed," Morgan said, "by how incompetent your average criminal is."

"But maybe the car wasn't stolen at all," Emily told him.

"How could that be?"

"Maybe you just *thought* you parked in that other block."

"No, no," he said impatiently. "That would be ridiculous." He started the motor, veered out around the mail truck, and headed up the street. It sounded as if he were in the wrong gear. "Come back with me and meet Bonny," he said.

"Oh, Leon will be wondering where I am. And anyway, don't you have to go to work?"

"I can't work today; I only had an hour of sleep last night. It was Brindle, this business with Brindle. Have you ever heard of such a thing? Robert Roberts, after all these years!"

Emily hoped he wouldn't start on Robert Roberts again. She felt exhausted. It seemed to her that those few blocks from Gina's school had taken hours, days; she'd expended years' worth of energy on them. The sight of Morgan beside her (humming "I'm Walkin'" and tapping the steering wheel, fresh as a daisy, without a care in the world) made her head ache.

But then her apartment building approached. Crafts Unlimited was just opening, and its fluorescent lights were fluttering on and off as if unable to gather strength. The windows above it were dark. You could imagine that the building was nothing but an empty shell. Morgan sailed past, still humming. Emily didn't try to stop him.

II

EMILY AND LEON had given a good deal of thought to Morgan's wife— to what she must be like, considering the amount of time he spent away from her. He was always dropping in on the Merediths for a visit, mentioning other places he'd just come from and still others where he was heading afterward. Was he ever home at all, in fact? Even weekends? For on Saturdays he engaged in his own unique style of shopping. He would travel to the depths of Baltimore and return with unlikely items: dented canned goods, or knobby packages wrapped in brown paper and tied all around with string in a dozen clumsy knots. (You would think they hadn't heard of bagging yet, where Morgan shopped.) Sundays he went to fairs and festivals. At events where Emily and Leon took their puppets, they might even run into him purely by chance. They'd look through the scrim at the seated audience—no more than a long, low hillock—and find him standing at the rear, this sudden jutting peak topped by some outlandish hat, always alone, always brooding over something and puffing on a cigarette. (But when they came out afterward to take their bows, he'd be beaming mightily and clapping like a proud parent.) Winters, when the fairs died down, he'd go to church bazaars and grade-school fund-raisers. No occasion was too small for him. He was never too busy to stop and contemplate the appliquéd felt Christmas-tree skirts or the Styrofoam snowmen with sequin eyes. So who was this Bonny, whom he was so eager to leave? Maybe she nagged him, Leon said. Maybe she was one of those tight, crimped ladies holding court alone in her careful living room, among the polished figurines that Morgan mustn't touch and the crystal ashtrays he mustn't flick his ashes into. But Emily didn't think so. Putting together all that Morgan said (his rush of accidents and disasters, his admiration of the Merediths' stripped apartment), she imagined Bonny as a slattern, in a zip-front housedress and a headful of pincurls. She wasn't surprised when Morgan parked his car in front of a well-kept brick Colonial house—after all, she'd known there was money, and slate tiles for the roof—but she blinked when she stepped out and found a brown-haired woman in a neat skirt and blouse weeding petunias along the front walk. Well, maybe it was the sister. But Morgan said, "Bonny?"

Bonny straightened and wiped her forehead with the back of her wrist. There were a few faint smile lines around her eyes. Her lipstick was a chipped, cracked, glossless red. She looked cheerful but non-committal; she seemed to be waiting for Morgan to explain himself.

"Bonny, this is Emily Meredith," Morgan said.

Bonny went on waiting.

"Emily and her husband run a puppet show," Morgan said.

"Oh, really?"

It hadn't occurred to Emily that Bonny wouldn't have heard of her. (She had heard of Bonny, after all.) She felt a little hurt. She held out her hand and said, "How do you do, Mrs. Gower."

Bonny shook her hand. She said, "Well, are . . . you here to see Morgan? Or what?"

"She's here to see *you*," Morgan told her.

"Me?"

Morgan said, "What happened was, my car was stolen, but then I stole it back, by and by, but still there was so much excitement, what with Robert Roberts and all . . ."

"You mean, you asked her to come inside the house?"

"Oh!" Emily said. "Well, of course I don't want to interrupt your work."

"It's all right," Bonny said. "Why don't you roll down your pants leg, Morgan?" She turned to lead them up the walk.

"But, Mrs. Gower—"

"Stay, stay," Morgan urged, from a bent position. He flattened his cuff around his ankle. "She's just surprised. You've come this far; stay!"

Emily followed Bonny up the steps. She felt she had no choice, although she would rather have been anywhere else. They passed a clay pot in which herbs were growing—chives and maybe marjoram or thyme. Emily looked at them wistfully. Under other conditions, she thought, Bonny might very well have been someone she was fond of, but they'd got started wrong. It was Morgan's fault. He was so thought-less and abrupt. She felt irritated by his dishpan-shaped helmet, bound-ing along beside her. "Notice Bonny's roses," he said. It could have been a hint—a clue to Bonny's soft spot—but Bonny said, without turning. "How can she? They're not blooming yet."

The three of them entered the hall. On the radiator were a stack of library books with scummy plastic covers, a watering can, and a box of Triscuits. Emily had to watch her step through a little turmoil of shoes and sneakers, and by then they'd reached the living room. "Look!"

Morgan said, pouncing on a vase. "This is what Amy made at camp, the summer she was ten."

"It's very pretty," Emily said. It was lopsided, and a crack ran down from the rim.

"I wish you could meet her, but she lives in Roland Park now. You can meet Mother and Brindle, though."

"Brindle's out shopping for a wedding ring," Bonny said.

"A ring! Yes, I've told Emily all about that. And see, here's Molly's picture on the mantel. Isn't she beautiful? It's from her school play; they say she has a talent for acting. I can't imagine where she got it. There's never been an actor in our family. What do you think of her? Bonny, don't we still have Jeannie's wedding album?"

There was something feverish about him, Emily thought. He darted around the room, rummaging through various overloaded shelves. Emily and Bonny stood in the doorway watching him. Once they happened to glance at each other, but when Emily saw Bonny's expression— oddly hooded—she looked away again. "Please," she told Morgan, "I ought to be going. I'll just catch a bus and go, please."

"But you haven't met my mother!" he said, stopping short. "And I wanted Bonny to get to know you; I wanted you two to . . . Bonny, Emily was in the paper today."

"Was she?" Bonny said.

"Where's the paper? Did you throw it out?"

"I think it's in the kitchen."

"Come to the kitchen. Let's all go! Let's all have some coffee," he said. He raced away. Bonny straightened from the door frame to follow him, and Emily trailed behind. She wished she could just vanish. She thought of ducking out soundlessly, slipping away before they noticed. She dodged a mobile of homemade paper sailing ships and stepped into the kitchen.

The counters in the kitchen were stacked with dirty dishes, and several animals' feeding bowls cluttered the floor. One wall was shingled with yellow cartoons and news clippings and hockey schedules, recipes, calendars, photographs, telephone numbers on torn corners of paper, dental appointment cards, invitations—even someone's high-school diploma. Emily felt surrounded, flooded. Over by the back door Morgan was plowing through a stack of newspapers. "Where is it? Where is it? Did it come?" he asked. "Aha!" He held up a paper. He laid it flat on the floor, licked his thumb, and started turning pages. "News . . . editorials . . . crafts revival in Baltimore!"

Peering over his shoulder, Emily saw Leon's sober face. He seemed to be staring at her out of another world. "Bonny, here's Leon. Emily's husband," Morgan said. "And here's her daughter, Gina. See?"

"Very nice," said Bonny, setting out coffee cups.

"You know," Morgan said thoughtfully, "I once looked a little like Leon."

Bonny glanced at the photo. "Like that man there? Never," she said. "You're two totally different types."

"Well, yes," he said, "but there's something about the eyes, maybe; I don't know. Or something around the mouth. Or maybe it's the forehead. I don't know."

He stood up, abandoning the paper, and pulled out a chair from the table. "Sit down, sit down," he told Emily. He took a seat opposite, as if demonstrating, and fixed her with an urgent, focused look till she sat too. She felt trapped. The dishes on the counters towered so far above her that she imagined they might teeter and topple, swamping her. A typewriter stood in a puddle of orange juice on the table, with a sheet of paper in the carriage . . . *resolution was passed by a show of hands*, she read, and *Matilda Grayson requested that* . . . Bonny placed a carton of cream in front of her and a crumpled sack of Pantry Pride sugar.

"Were you working on something special?" asked Emily, motioning toward the typewriter.

"Yes," Bonny said. She handed Emily a cup of coffee and sat down next to her.

"Um . . . what do you do for a living, Mrs. Gower?"

"I'm Morgan's wife for a living."

"Oh, I see."

"Yes," Bonny said, "but do you see that it's a full-time job? It keeps me busy every minute, I tell you. Oh, from outside he seems so comic and light-hearted, such a character, so quaint, but imagine dealing with him. I mean, the details of it, the coping, stuck at home while he's off somewhere, wondering who he thinks he is now. Do you suppose we couldn't all act like that? Go swooping around in a velvet cape with a red satin lining and a feathered hat? That part's the easy part. Imagine being his wife, finding a cleaner who does ostrich plumes. Keeping his dinner warm. Imagine waiting dinner while he's out with one of his cronies that I have never met—Salvation Army bums or astrologists or whatever other awestruck, smitten people he digs up."

Emily set her cup down.

"You think I don't appreciate him. You wonder why he married me," Bonny said.

"No, no," said Emily. She looked across at Morgan, who seemed unperturbed. He was tipping contentedly in his chair, like a child who is confident he's the center of attention, and puffing on a cigarette. Twisted ropes of smoke hung around his head.

"Emily," Bonny said.

Emily turned to her.

"Emily, Morgan is the manager of a hardware store."

Emily waited, but that was the end of it. Bonny seemed to be expecting her to speak. "Yes," Emily said, after a minute.

"Cullen Hardware," Bonny said.

"She knows that, Bonny," Morgan said.

"She does?"

Bonny stared at him. Then she asked Emily, "You don't think he's a . . . rabbi or a Greek shipping magnate?"

"No," Emily said.

She decided not to mention how they'd met.

Bonny pressed her fingers to her lips. There were freckles, Emily saw, dusting the back of her hand. After all, she was a pleasant woman; she gave a little laugh. "You must think I've lost my mind," she said. "Crazy Bonny, right? Morgan's crazy wife, Bonny."

"Oh, no."

"It's just that I worried you might have been . . . misled. Morgan's such a, well, prankster, in a way."

"Yes, I know about that."

"You do?" Bonny said.

She glanced over at Morgan. Morgan smiled seraphically and blew out a whoosh of smoke.

"But I think he's trying to give it up," said Emily.

"Oh, I hope so!" Bonny said. "Why! It takes so much ingenuity to manage some of that foolishness . . . think what he could accomplish if he used that brain for sensible things! If he straightened out. If he decided to go straight."

"Not much," said Morgan cheerfully.

"What, dear?"

"There's not much I could accomplish. What do you imagine I'd be doing instead?"

"Oh, why . . . just *attending* to things. I mean, attending to where you belong." She turned to Emily. "There's nothing wrong with a hardware store. Is there? My family's always done well in hardware; it's nothing to be sneezed at. But Uncle Ollie says Morgan's heart's not in it. What's the good of a store, he says, where you have to positively wrest the merchandise from the manager? Assuming you can find the manager. I tell Uncle Ollie, 'Oh, leave him alone. Cullen Hardware is not the be-all and end-all,' I tell him, but it's true that Morgan could get more narrowed in. He doesn't know how to say no. He never refuses to be swept along."

"Mostly it's muscles," Morgan said.

This must have been something he'd told her before; Bonny rolled her eyes at Emily. Morgan turned to Emily and repeated it. "It's a matter of muscles," he said.

"I don't understand."

"A matter of following where they lead me. Have you ever gone

out to the kitchen, say, and then forgotten what for? You stand in the
kitchen and try to remember. Then your wrist makes a little twisting
motion. Oh, yes! you say. That twist is what you'd do to turn a faucet
on. You must have come for water! I just trust my muscles, you see,
to tell me what I'm here for. To drop me into my true activity one
day. I let them lead me."

"He lets them lead him into saying he's a glassblower," Bonny said,
"and a tugboat captain for the Curtis Bay Towing Company, and a
Mohawk Indian high-rise worker. And that's just what I happen to
hear; heaven knows what more there is." Her lips twitched, as if she
were hiding some amusement. "You're walking down the street with
him and this total stranger asks him when the International Brotherhood
of Magicians is meeting next. You're listening to a politician's speech
and suddenly you notice Morgan on the platform, sitting beside a
senator's wife with a carnation in his buttonhole. You're waiting for
your crabs at Lexington Market and who's behind the counter but
Morgan in a rubber apron, telling the other customers where he caught
such fine oysters. It seems he has this boat that was handed down
from an uncle on his mother's side, a little bateau with no engine—"

"Engines disturb the beds," said Morgan. "And I don't like mechanical
tonging rigs, either. What was good enough for my uncle on my mother's
side is good enough for me, I say."

Bonny smiled at him and shook her head. "You step out for two
minutes to buy milk, leaving him safe home in his pajamas, and coming
back you pass him on the corner in a satin cap and purple satin shirt,
telling four little boys the secret that made him the only undefeated
jockey in the history of Pimlico. A jockey, six feet tall! Why do they
all believe him? He never used a crop, you see, but only whispered
in the horse's ear. He whispered something that *sounded* like a crop.
What was the word?"

"Scintillate," Morgan said.

"Oh, yes," said Bonny. She laughed.

Morgan trotted in his chair, holding imaginary reins. "Scintillate,
scintillate," he whispered, and Bonny laughed harder and wiped her
eyes.

"He's impossible," she told Emily. "He's just . . . impossible to
predict, you see."

"I can imagine he must be," Emily said politely.

She was beginning to like Bonny (her pink, merry face, and the
helpless way she sank back in her chair), but she thought less of
Morgan. It had never occurred to her that he knew exactly how people
saw him, and that he enjoyed their astonishment and perhaps even
courted it. She frowned at him. Morgan pulled his nose reflectively.

"She's right," he said. "I make things difficult. But I plan to change.
Hear that, Bonny?"

"Oh, do you, now?" Bonny said. She stood up to raise the kitchen window. "I don't know what to make of my garden," she said, looking out at the yard. "I was certain I'd planted vegetables someplace, but it seems to be coming up all flowers."

"I mean it," Morgan said. He told Emily, "She doesn't believe me. Bonny, don't you see what's here in front of you? Here's Emily Meredith; I brought her home. I brought her to our house. I told her and Leon, both, exactly who I was. I told about you and the girls. They know about Amy's new baby and the time Kate smashed the car."

"Is that right?" Bonny asked Emily.

Emily nodded.

"Well, I can't think what for," Bonny said. "I can't think why he bored you with all that."

"I'm combining my worlds!" Morgan said, and he raised his coffee cup to Bonny.

But Bonny said, "There's a catch to it somewhere. There's something missing. I don't understand what he wants."

Emily didn't understand either. She shook her head; Bonny shook hers. In fact, it seemed that Bonny and Emily were the old friends and Morgan was the newcomer. He sat slightly apart, perched under his helmet like an elf under a mushroom, turning his face from one to the other while the women watched, narrow-eyed, to see what he was up to.

1975

|

EVEN WHEN Morgan fell asleep, he didn't truly lose consciousness. Part of him slept while the rest of him stayed alert and jittery, counting things—thumbtacks, mattress buttons, flowers on a daughter's dress, holes in a pegboard display of electrical fittings. A plumber came in and ordered some pipes: six elbows and a dozen nipples. "Certainly," said Morgan, but he couldn't help laughing. Then he was competing in a singing contest. He was singing a song from the fifties called "Moments to Remember." He knew the words, but was unable to pronounce them properly. *The ballroom prize we almost won* came out *the barroom brawl we almost won.* His partner was not a good dancer anyway, and in fact they were nowhere close to winning. Why! His partner was Laura Lee Keller, the very first girl he had ever loved— someone he had lost track of long, long before the days of "Moments to Remember." After the prom, he and Laura Lee had driven to the beach with half the senior class and lain kissing on a blanket by the ocean. Still, even now, even after all these years, the sound of the ocean reminded him of possibilities unfolding: everything new and untried yet, just around the corner. He opened his eyes and heard the ocean just a few blocks distant, the very same ocean he'd lain beside with Laura Lee, but he himself was middle-aged and irritable and so was Laura Lee, he supposed, wherever she was; and his mouth had a scorched taste from smoking too much the night before.

It was six o'clock in the morning in Bethany Beach, Delaware, in the buckling tarpaper cottage they rented from Uncle Ollie every July. Tongue-and groove walls, painted a dingy blue too long ago, rose high above the swaybacked bed. A tattered yellow shade rustled in the window. (Where else but near the ocean would you see this kind of window—the cheap aluminum frame stippled by salt air, the bellying screen as soft and sleazy as some synthetic fabric? Where else would the screen doors and porches have those diagonal wooden insets at the corners, so that no right angles appeared to exist within earshot of the Atlantic?) The room was full of castoffs: a looming wardrobe faced with a flecked, metallic mirror; a bow-fronted bureau topped with a mended dresser scarf (every one of the drawers stuck, and several of the cut-glass knobs were missing); a pink shag rug as thin and wrinkled as a bathmat; and a piecrust table beside the bed with a cracked brown plastic clock radio on the doily at its center. Morgan sat up and switched on the radio. He had just missed the Six O'Clock Sermonette; Guy and Ralna were singing "What a Friend We Have in Jess." Next to him, Bonny stirred and said, "Morgan? What on earth . . . ?"

He lowered the volume a little. He inched out of bed, took a sombrero from the wardrobe, and put it on without looking in the mirror. Barefoot, in his underpants, he slogged down the hall to the kitchen. Already the air was so warm and heavy that he felt used up.

The cottage had four bedrooms, but only three were occupied. His mother slept in the second and Kate, their last remaining child, in the third. It used to be that the place was overflowing. The girls would share beds and couches; Brindle roomed with Louisa; various daughters' boyfriends lined up in sleeping bags out on the porch. Morgan had complained of the confusion at the time, but now he missed it. He wondered what point there was in coming any more. Kate was hardly present—she was eighteen years old now, busy with her own affairs, forever off visiting friends in the ugly new condominium south of town. As for Louisa, the trip seemed to shake her memory loose; she was even more dislocated than usual. Only Bonny appeared to enjoy herself. She padded along the shoreline with a bucket, hunting shells. The bridge of her nose developed a permanent pink, peeling patch. Sometimes she sat at the edge of the breakers and dabbled like a child, with her legs in a V—a rash of red on top, pale underneath. Then Morgan would pace the sand just behind her with his thumbs hooked in the waistband of his trunks, braving the sun and the sticky spray, for he was never comfortable when a member of his family was in the water. He considered swimming (like sailing, like skiing) to be unnatural, a rich person's contrivance to fill up empty hours. Although he could swim himself (a taut, silent breast stroke, with his mouth tightly closed, not wetting so much as the tip of his beard), he would never swim just for pleasure. And he would surely never swim in the ocean. His distrust of the ocean was logical and intelligent, he felt. He kept sensibly away from the edge, wearing stout shoes and woolen socks at all times. He only listened to the breakers, and plummeted into a deep, slow trance where once again he lay with Laura Lee Keller on a blanket beneath the stars.

It was too hot for coffee, but he'd get a headache if he tried to do without it. He made instant, using water straight from the tap. Beneath the taste of Maxwell House and sugar he caught the thick, dark taste of beach water, but he drank it anyway, from a jelly-glass painted with clowns. Then he rinsed the glass. Then he took Bonny's purse from the kitchen table and put it in the freezing compartment of the refrigerator. (Another folly of rich people was their belief that in resort towns, crime does not exist. Morgan knew better. He sensed danger all around, and would have felt more secure in the heart of Baltimore.)

He went back to the bedroom and found Bonny sitting against her pillow. "What are you up so early for?" she asked him. "And why was the radio on?"

"I wanted to hear the news," he said.

It wasn't true; he never felt the news had anything to do with him. What he'd wanted was to drown out the sound of the ocean. This was Tuesday. They'd been here three days. There were eleven days remaining. He sighed and sat on the edge of the bed to pull his socks on. "I'll bring breakfast from the bakery," he told Bonny. "Anything you want while I'm in town?"

"The bakery's not open yet."

"I'll go and wait. I'll buy a paper. It's too quiet here."

"Well, bring some of those bow-tie things with cherries, then . . ." She yawned and ruffled her hair. A pillow mark ran down her left cheek. "Lucky you," she said. "You fell asleep right away, last night."

"I had a terrible sleep."

"You fell asleep instantly."

"But the whole night long I dreamed," Morgan said, "and woke, and checked the clock. I can't remember now what I dreamed. A man in a tailcoat stepped out of the wardrobe. I think this house is haunted, Bonny."

"You say that every year," Bonny told him.

"Well, it's haunted every year." He pulled a striped T-shirt over his head. When he emerged, he said, "All these wakeful nights, peculiar thoughts . . . the most I hope for, from a vacation, is a chance to rest up once it's over."

"Today's the day my brother comes," Bonny said, climbing out of bed.

Morgan zipped his hiking shorts, which were new and full of pockets and flaps that he hadn't yet explored. Attached to one pocket was a metal clasp. It was probably meant for a compass. "I don't suppose you brought along a compass," he told Bonny.

"Compass?"

He glanced at her. She was standing before the wardrobe in a short, plain nightgown that he happened to be fond of. He was even fond of the grapy veins in her calves, and her rumpled knees. He considered slipping up to kiss the pulse in her throat, but then he felt laden by the heat and the waves and the tongue-and-groove walls. "Ah, God. I have to do something about this *life* of mine," he said.

"What about it?" she asked, sliding a blouse off a hanger.

"It's come to nothing. It's come to nothing."

She looked over at him, and parted her lips as if about to ask a question. But then he said, "Bow-tie pastries, right? With cherries."

He was gone before she could ask whatever it was she had planned.

II

WITH ONE hand under his mother's elbow, he steered her along the boardwalk. It was nearly noon, and she wore a great black cartwheel of a hat to guard against sunburn. Her striped terry beach robe was long-sleeved and ankle-length, and it concealed not a bathing suit but an ordinary street dress, for she could no more swim than fly, she always said. Her face was pale and pursed, even in this heat, and her fingertips were cold when she touched his arm. She touched his arm to tell him to stop for a second. She wanted to look at a house that was under construction. "What an unusual shape," she said.

"It's called an A-frame," Morgan said.

"Why, it's practically all garret."

Morgan summoned his thoughts together. At moments like this, when Louisa seemed fully in touch with her surroundings, he always made an effort to have a real conversation with her. "The cost," he said, "is considerably lower than for other houses, I believe."

"Yes, I should think so," she said. She patted his arm again, and they walked on. She said, "Let's see now. How long have we been here?"

"Three days, Mother."

"Eleven more to go," she said.

"Yes."

She said, "Heavens."

"Maybe our family wasn't cut out for vacations," Morgan said.

"Maybe not."

"It must be the work ethic," he said.

"Well, I don't know what *that* is. It's more like we vacation all year round on our own."

"How can you say that?" Morgan asked. "What about my hardware store?"

She didn't answer.

"We're city people," Morgan said. "We have our city patterns, things to keep us busy . . . It's dangerous, lolling around like this. It's never good just to loll around and think. Why, you and Father never vacationed in your lives. Did you?"

"I don't recall," she said.

She would not remember anything about his father, ever. Sometimes Morgan wondered if her failing memory for recent events might stem from her failing memory of her husband; selective forgetfulness was an impossibility, maybe. Having chosen to forget in one area, she had to forget in all others as well. He felt a sudden urge to jolt her. He wanted to ask: am I aging in the same direction my father did? have I journeyed too far from him? am I too near? what do I have to go on, here? I'm traveling blind; I'm older now than my own father ever lived to be. Instead, he asked, "Didn't you and he go to Ocean City once?"

"I really wouldn't know," she said primly.

"Jesus! You're so *stubborn!*" he shouted, slapping his thigh. His mother remained unmoved, but two girls walking ahead in bikinis looked over their shoulders at him. "Do you ever think how I must feel?" he asked his mother. "Sometimes I feel I've just been *plunked* here. I have no one from the old days; I'm just a foreigner on my own. You can't count Brindle; she's so much younger, and anyway so wrapped up in that husband of hers . . ."

"But there's always me," his mother said, picking her way around a toddler with a bucket.

"Yes," he said, "but often you sort of . . . vacate, Mother; you're not really there at all."

He had hurt her feelings. He was glad of it only for an instant; then he felt deeply remorseful. His mother raised her head high and looked off toward someone's A-frame cottage, where beach towels flapped on the balcony railing. "Why!" she said. "Wasn't that speedy."

"What was, Mother dear?"

"They've finished construction on the A-frame," she said. "It seems like no time at all." And she jutted her chin at him with a triumphant, bitter glare.

"So it does, dear heart," he said.

III

MORGAN WENT out to get a pizza for their supper and returned to find that Bonny's brother had arrived. He'd brought his new wife, Priscilla, a pretty girl with short, straight blond hair caught back in a silver barrette. They had been married only a few weeks. They wore similar crisp, new-looking white slacks and pastel shirts, like honeymooners. Morgan hadn't even met Priscilla up till now—or people seemed to assume he hadn't, for Billy introduced her and she shook Morgan's hand formally. Bonny said, "Priscilla went to Roland Park Country School with the Semple-Pearce girls, Morgan."

"Oh, yes," Morgan said, but the truth of the matter was, he could have sworn that Billy had been married to Priscilla once before. He seemed to remember her. He thought she might even have visited this cottage. But she acted as if everything were new to her. "What a sweet place," she said. "What a lot of . . . character," and she walked around the living room fingering the seashell ashtrays like a stranger, and peering at the photograph of Uncle Ollie's 1934 lacrosse team, and reading all the titles on the *Reader's Digest* book condensations. Morgan was cagy; he went along with it. Then as soon as possible he cornered Bonny, who had taken the pizza out to the kitchen.

"Bonny," he whispered, "isn't that girl an ex-wife of his?"

"No, dear, she's his present wife."

"But didn't Billy marry her another time, earlier?"

"What are you talking about?"

"I know he did," he said. "He married her and brought her here; it was the same time of year."

Bonny straightened up from the oven. She looked hot; the hair around her temples was damp. She said, "Morgan, I am not in the mood for any of your jabs at my brother."

"Jabs? What jabs?"

"Just because he may have a fondness for one particular type of girl—" Bonny said.

"I'm not talking *types*, Bonny. I mean this. He brought her here several years ago and she had that little dog Kelty, Kilty, . . . why deny it? There's nothing wrong with marrying her twice. Lots of people go back, retrace, try to get it right the second time around. Why cover it up?"

She only sighed and returned to the living room. Morgan followed her. He found Billy and Priscilla on the wicker couch, talking with

Morgan's mother. Billy looked old and foolish in his vivid clothes, with
his bald pink skull, his pale hair straggling behind his ears. He had
hold of one of Priscilla's hands and was stroking it, like something
trapped, in his lap. Priscilla was pretending the hand did not belong
to her. She leaned forward earnestly, listening to Louisa discuss the
drive to Bethany. "I took along a thermos of Lipton tea," Louisa said,
"and two nice, juicy nectarines, and a box of arrowroot biscuits that
Bonny sometimes buys for my digestion." Priscilla nodded, her face
alight with interest and enthusiasm. She was very young. She couldn't
possibly have been married several years ago; several years ago she
would still have been a schoolgirl in a royal-blue Roland Park Country
School jumper. Morgan felt confused. He sat down in a rocking chair.

Louisa said, "Traffic was held up on the Bridge, so we stopped and
I got out and sat in the grass by the side of the road. There was a
little boy there, just a tot, and I shared one of my nectarines with him
and he gave me a nice speckle pear."

"*Seckel* pear," Morgan murmured. He could not bear to have her
laughed at.

"A speckle pear, this one was. I finished half of it and put the other
half in a Baggie. Then we got back in the car and drove across the
Bridge, but in Delaware we stopped again where the Kiwanis Club was
barbecuing chickens and I had half a chicken, a Tab, and a sack of
potato chips. They were out of bread-and-butter pickles. At Farmer
John's Vegetable Stand . . ."

Priscilla's purse was one of those button-on things with a wooden
handle. Bermuda bags, he believed they were called. You could button
on an infinity of different covers to match different outfits. He would
bet that her suitcase was full of covers—seersucker pink, yachting blue
. . . he lost his train of thought. He wondered what had possessed
him to leave his camera at home, hanging by its leather strap in the
downstairs closet. For the first time in twenty years he would not have
pictures of their vacation. On the other hand, what was the use of
such pictures? They were only the same, year after year. Same waves,
same sunburns, same determined smiles . . .

"After we reached Bethany, I started feeling a little peckish, so I
walked to the market with Kate and picked out a watermelon. It was
a wonderful melon, really fat and thumpy-sounding, and once we got
it back to the cottage all we had to do was touch a knife point to it
and it crackled all the way open. But it had no taste. Can you believe
it? Had no taste whatsoever. Such a lovely color and not a scrap of
taste. I just don't understand that," Morgan's mother said.

Morgan suddenly remembered another of last night's dreams. He'd
been standing on a lawn beside a beautiful, graceful woman he'd never
seen before. She led him toward a child's swing hanging from a tree
limb. They settled on it—the woman sitting, Morgan standing, enclosing

her with his feet. They started swinging over a cliff. Tiny yellow flowers dotted a field far below them. Morgan knew that when they were swinging high enough, they would leap. He would die. He wasn't upset about it. Then the woman tipped her head back against him, and he felt the length of her between his legs—the curve of her ribcage, the satiny coolness of her clothing. He was like a boy again, trembling. He saw that as long as he felt this way, he wanted to go on living, and all at once he was afraid of the leap. He woke abruptly, with his heart beating so hard that his whole body seemed to vibrate.

IV

IN THE PAST few years Morgan had become a letter-writer. He couldn't have said exactly why. It just seemed, sometimes, that he grew restless and ill-contained; he couldn't sit still; there was something he wanted to tell someone, but he couldn't think what it was and he had no particular person in mind. Then he would sit down and write letters— although even that was not quite it; it was only second best. At work, he used his Woodstock typewriter, which produced an uneven, sooty print that danced all over the page. He plodded away with two index fingers, stopping after every word or so to pry up the A key, which wouldn't spring back on its own. At home, he wrote with a leaky fountain pen whose cartridge he refilled with a plastic hypodermic needle. (He'd salvaged the needle from an emergency-room wastebasket during one of the children's accidents. Buying cartridges already filled was an extravagance, he felt.) He wrote all his daughters, even those still living in Baltimore. He wrote the traveling salesmen who came to the store, and his friends Kazari and the Greek tavern-keeper. Because he did not often have anything to say, he gave advice, as a rule. *It has come to my attention that your company's plant-sprayer bottles work exceedingly well for dousing fireplace logs at bedtime. Simply fill the bottle with water, adjust the nozzle to setting 4 . . .*

Or:

Dear Amy,
    I notice that you appear to be experiencing some difficulty with household clutter.
    Understand that I'm not blaming you for this, your mother has the same problem. But as I've been telling her for years, there is a solution.
    Simply take a cardboard box, carry it through the rooms, load into it everyone's toys and dirty clothes and such, and hide it all in a closet. If people ask for some missing object, you'll be able to tell them where it is. If they *don't* ask (now, here is the important

part), if a week goes by and they don't notice the object is gone, then you can be sure it's non-essential, and you throw it away. You would be surprised at how many things are non-essential. Throw everything away, all of it! Simplify! Don't hesitate!

All my love, sweetheart,

Daddy

That night, after the others had gone to bed, Morgan sat at the kitchen table and wrote a postcard to Potter, the musical-instrument man . . . *weather has been fair and warm, a high in the 80's all three days . . . must thank the good Lord for in Rehoboth I hear they had 1¾ inches of rainfall in 47 minutes . . . Yours in Christ, Gower Morgan, S.J.* He wrote Todd, his three-year-old grandson, a fine, masculine letter: *The new pickup is doing well and the baggage space comes in handy, believe me. Was able to take our entire set of Encyclopedia Britannica to the beach. Now have 15,010 miles on the odometer with the fuel cost per mile being 2.1¢ and total operating costs per mile being 4.76¢. If you assume a 30% depreciation each year . . .*

He addressed the letter to Todd and laid it on top of Potter's postcard. He sat there blankly for a moment. Then he reached for another sheet of paper. *Dear Emily, Leon, and Gina,* he wrote. *Have been having pleasant weather and temperatures in the 80's . . .*

But it never helped to write the same things over. He crossed the sentence out and wrote, *Why not come Friday for the weekend? Simply take the Bay Bridge and continue to Wye Mills, switching there to Highway 404 and then to Highway 18 . . .*

V

LATE THURSDAY morning Brindle showed up. No one had expected her. Morgan was on the front porch, slouching in a painted rocker and leafing through a volume of the encyclopedia. He happened to glance toward the street and there, just coming to a halt, was the little red sports car that Robert Roberts had given Brindle on their wedding day. Brindle yanked the emergency brake and got out, streaming tears. Her head was swathed in the white chiffon scarf she always slept in to calm her hair down, and she wore some kind of oversized, ankle-length white coat. In fact, she reminded Morgan of an early automobile driver. "Oh, I like that very much," he told her as she climbed the porch steps. "The veil, the duster . . ."

"It's not a duster, it's a bathrobe," Brindle said. She blew her nose in a soggy-looking Kleenex. Crying had turned her soft and full, almost pretty. Her eyelids were shiny and her sallow skin had a faint pink glow. She sank into the chair next to Morgan's and folded her Kleenex to a dry spot. "I got it last week at Stewart's," she said. "Sixteen forty-nine, marked down from thirty-two ninety-eight."

"Half-price; not bad at all," said Morgan. "Here, dear, have a cigarette."

"I don't smoke," she told him.

"Have one, sweetheart. It'll do you good."

He extended the pack and shook it invitingly, but she only blotted her eyes. "I can't stand it any more," she said. "I must have been out of my mind, marrying that . . . tree, that boulder; all he does is sit there mourning. I can't stand it."

"Have a Rolaid. Have a coughdrop. Have some Wrigley's spearmint gum," Morgan said. He tore through his pockets.

"He keeps my graduation photo on the television set. Half the time that he pretends he's watching TV, he's really watching my photo. I see him clicking his eyes back in focus when I walk into the room. When he thinks I'm busy with something else, he'll go over to the photo and pick it up and study it. Then he'll shake his head and set it down again."

Her face fell apart and she started sobbing. Morgan gazed off toward the street. He wasn't exactly humming, but he went, "Mm-mm, mm-mm," from time to time, and drummed his fingers on his open book. A little boy rode by on a bicycle, tinkling a bell. Two ladies in skirted swimsuits carried a basketful of laundry between them.

"Of course, every situation has its difficult moments," Morgan said. He cleared his throat.

Then Bonny came out on the porch. "Brindle!" she said. "What are you doing here?"

"Bonny, I just can't stand it any more," Brindle said.

She reached out her arms, and Bonny came over to hug her and tell her, "There now, Brindle, never mind." (She always knew better than Morgan what to say.) "Never you mind, now, Brindle."

"It's getting so I'm jealous of my own self," Brindle said, muffled. "I'm jealous of my photograph, and the silver-plated ID bracelet I gave him when I was thirteen. He never takes that bracelet off. He sleeps with it; he bathes with it. 'Let it *go*,' I feel like saying. 'Can't you ever forget her?' He sits in that TV room staring at my photo . . . there's times I've even seen tears in his eyes. I say, 'Robert, talk to me, please,' and he says, 'Yes, yes, in a minute.' "

Bonny smoothed a lashing of Brindle's hair back under the white scarf. Morgan said, "Oh, but surely this will pass."

"It will never pass," said Brindle, sitting up and glaring at him. "If it hasn't passed in two years, how can you think it ever will? I tell you, there's nothing worse than two people with the same daydream getting together, finally. This morning I woke up and found he hadn't come to bed. I went down to the TV room and there he was, sound asleep with my photo in the crook of his arm. So I picked up my keys from the counter and left. I didn't even bother dressing. Oh, I was like someone half-crazy, demented. I drove all the way to your house and parked and got out before I remembered you were in Bethany. Do you know that idiot paper-boy is still delivering your papers? They were everywhere, clear across the lawn. Sunday's was so old and yellow, you'd think it was urine-stained—and maybe it was. Listen, Morgan, if you're burglarized while you're gone, you have every right to sue that paper-boy. You remember what I said. It's an open invitation to any passing criminal."

"But things started off so well," Morgan said. "I had so much hope when Robert Roberts first came calling. Ringing the doorbell, bringing you roses—"

"What roses? He never brought roses."

"Of course he did."

"No, he didn't."

"I *remember* he did."

"Morgan, please," said Bonny. "Can't you let this be?"

"Oh, very well. But sweeping you into his arms . . . remember?"

"It was all an act," said Brindle.

"An act?"

"If he'd been halfway truthful," she said, "he'd have swept my *graduation* photo into his arms. And kissed it on the lips. And given it a sports car."

Her chin crumpled in again, and she pressed the damp knot of Kleenex to her mouth. Bonny gazed over Brindle's head at Morgan, as if expecting him to take some action. But what action would that be? He had never felt very close to Brindle; he had never understood her, although of course he loved her. They were so far apart in age that they were hardly brother and sister. At the time of her birth he already had his school life, and his street life, and his friends. And their father's death had not drawn them together but had merely shown how separate they were. They had mourned in such different ways, Brindle clinging fiercely to her mother while Morgan trudged, withdrawn and stubborn, through the outside world. You could almost say that they had mourned entirely different people.

He sat forward slowly, and scratched the crown of his sombrero. "You know," he said, "I was certain he brought roses."

"He never brought roses," Brindle said.

"I could swear he did: red ones. Armloads."

"You made those roses up," said Brindle. She tucked the Kleenex into her bathrobe pocket.

"What a pity," Morgan said sadly. "That was the part I liked best of all."

VI

FOR LUNCH he made spaghetti, which was Brindle's favorite dish. He put on his short-order-cook's clothes—a dirty white apron and a sailor cap—and took over the kitchen, while Bonny and Brindle sat at the table drinking coffee. "Spaghetti à la Morgan!" he said, brandishing a sheaf of noodles. The women merely stared at him, blank-faced, with their minds on something else. "I had hints from the very beginning," said Brindle, "but I wouldn't let myself see them. You know how it is. Almost the first thing he said to me, that first day he showed up, was . . . he pulled back from me and took both my hands and stared at me and, 'I can't understand it,' he said. 'I don't know why I've kept thinking of you. It's not as if you're a beauty, or ever were,' he said. 'Also I'm getting older,' I told him, 'and my dentist says my teeth are growing more crooked every year.' Oh, I never held anything back from him. I never tried to be what I wasn't."

Bonny clicked her tongue. "He doesn't properly appreciate you," she said. "He's one of those people who's got to see from a distance before he knows how to feel about it—from the past or out of other people's eyes or in a frame kind of thing like a book or a photo. You did right to leave him, Brindle."

Morgan felt a little itch of anxiety starting in his temples. "But she didn't *leave* him; she's just taking a little holiday from him," he told Bonny.

Bonny and Brindle gazed into space. Probably they hadn't even heard what he said.

Last spring Bonny's old college roommate had divorced her husband of twenty-seven years. And of course there were those wives of Billy's (every one of whom had left him, some without so much as a note) and Morgan's own daughter Carol, who just one week after her wedding had returned, in very good spirits, to settle back into the apartment she'd been sharing with her twin sister. Also, Morgan knew for a fact that two of Bonny's closest friends were considering separations, and one had actually spoken with a lawyer. He worried that it was contagious. He feared that Bonny might catch the illness; or it was more like catching a piece of news, catching *on;* she would come to her senses and leave him. She would take with her . . . what? Something specific hung just at the edge of his mind. She would take with her the combination to a lock, it felt like—a secret he needed to know that Bonny knew all along without trying. When Bonny came back from lunch with a friend, Morgan was always quick to point out the friend's faults and ulterior motives. "She's discontented by nature; any fool can see that. How that poor lunk of a husband ever fell for her . . . Don't believe a word she tells you," he would say. Oh, it was women friends you had to watch out for, not men at all but women.

He rattled a spatula on a frying pan, trying to claim Bonny's attention. He did a little short-order-cook's dance. "Cackles on a raft for Number Four!" he called. "BLT, hold the mayo!"

Bonny and Brindle gave him identical flat, bemused stares, unblinking, like cats.

"Bonny, I don't see any garlic cloves," he said, switching tactics.

"Use dehydrated."

"Dehydrated! Dried-out garlic chips? Unthinkable."

"No one will know the difference."

"I wish you'd learn to make grocery lists," he said. "You want to get organized, Bonny. Keep a list on the door of the fridge and write down whatever item you finish off."

Bonny ran her fingers through her hair. She made it look like some kind of weaving—searching out a strand, lacing it into other strands behind her ear.

"Here's what we'll do," he told her. "Next week, when we get back to Baltimore, I'm going to take a pad of paper to the supermarket. I'm going to map out all the aisles. Aisle one: olives, pickles, mustard. Aisle two: coffee, tea . . . nothing will be omitted. Then you can get it Xeroxed two hundred and sixty times."

Her fingers paused. "How many?"

"Five times fifty-two. Five years' worth."

She looked into his face.

"After five years I'll make you a new one," Morgan said. "Things may have changed in the store by then."

"Yes, they very well may have," Bonny said.

She threw Brindle a quick, tucked glance, and they smiled at each other. It was a smile so sunny and bland, and so obviously collusive, that all of Morgan's uneasiness returned. It occurred to him that often they must discuss him behind his back. "Oh, you know Morgan," they must say, rolling their eyes. "You know how he is."

"Well, anyway," he said, "all I intended was . . . See, if we check items off on this list, shopping would be so simple. Everything would go the way it ought to. Don't you agree?"

"Yes, yes."

"Should I be the one to get it Xeroxed?"

"No, dear, I'll do it," Bonny said. Then she sighed and laughed, in that way she had, and drank the last of her coffee. "For now," she told Brindle, "let's you and me go into town and buy the garlic."

"Never mind; I'll use dehydrated," Morgan said hastily.

But she said, "Oh, the walk will do us good. We'll take your mother, too." She rose and looked under a stack of magazines. Then she looked in the oven, and finally in the refrigerator. She took out her purse and kissed Morgan. "Anything else you want?" she asked him.

"You could get cream."

"We have cream."

"Yes, but with more people coming tomorrow, and they might be as early as breakfast time—"

"Who might?"

"The Merediths."

"Merediths?"

"At least, I *think* they might," he said. "I just dropped them this note, you see, because Brindle wasn't here and I hadn't known Billy was staying through the weekend. I'd thought there'd be enough room. And there will be. Why, of course there will be! Where'd we put those sleeping bags?"

"Morgan, I wish you would check with me before you do these things," Bonny said.

"But you like them! You always say you like them."

"Like who?" Brindle asked. "Who're we talking about, here?"

Bonny said, "Oh, the . . . you remember them, Brindle: the Merediths. You've seen them at the house, several times. Leon and Emily Meredith. Well, certainly I like them. I'm very fond of both of them, you know that, but still—"

"*I* found them a little dry, personally," Brindle said. "Her, at least. No, I don't think she'd be a barrel of fun at the beach."

"Oh, Emily's not dry at all, just—"

"And anyhow," Morgan told Brindle, "I don't remember asking what you thought. For that matter, I don't remember asking you to Bethany, so you're in a fine position to criticize my guest list."

"Now, Morgan," Bonny said.

"Oh, well," said Brindle, "they won't come. Don't worry, Bonny. Emily won't like sand. She won't like mess. She won't want to go into that messy, sticky ocean. I know the type; they can't come to the banquet," she said.

Then she set out with Bonny, so cheered by her own perceptiveness that her face looked peaky and alight with pleasure, and Robert Roberts might never have existed.

VII

BUT THEY DID come. They arrived the next day in midmorning, driving the little black VW that Leon had picked up secondhand. Morgan was not quite adjusted yet to the thought of their owning a car. (Though if it had to happen, he supposed that this tiny, bell-shaped machine was the most appropriate. And black; that was a nice touch. Yes, and, after all, what was wrong with itinerants possessing some form of transportation? Maybe they should buy a trailer, as well.) Morgan stood in the yard, rocking from heel to toe, watching as they parked. Emily got out first, and pulled the front seat forward for Gina. Emily had the wrong kind of shoes on—Docksiders. Morgan could hardly believe his eyes. With her black leotard and her flowing black skirt, there was something almost shocking about those cloddy, stiff brown loafers with the white rubber soles. And Gina, when she emerged, wore the squinty, grudging expression of someone yanked from sleep. Leon's face had a clenched look and there was a shaving cut in the cleft of his chin, plastered with a tiny square of toilet paper. No, they were definitely not at their best. It seemed Morgan had only to leave town and they fell apart, rushed ahead without him, tossed aside all their old charm, and invested in unsuitable clothing. (Leon's new polo shirt was electric blue, almost painful to the sight.) Still, Morgan stepped forward, putting on a smile of welcome. "Why! How nice to see you," he said, and he kissed Emily's cheek. Then he hugged Gina and shook hands with Leon. "Have a good trip? Much traffic? Bad on the Bridge?" he asked. Leon muttered something about senior-citizen drivers and jerked the trunk lid open.

"It was an easy trip, but I don't know what the scenery was like because Leon drove so fast it blurred together," Emily said.

"Emily thinks I'm speeding if she can't read all the small print on every billboard," Leon said, "every road sign and circus poster. If she can't count all the fruit in all the fruit stands."

"Well, I didn't notice that patrolman disagreeing with me."

"The fellow's speedometer was way off base," Leon said, "and I'm going to tell them so when it comes to court." He took out a small suitcase and slammed the trunk lid shut. "These people just have a quota to fill. They'll pick up anyone, if they haven't passed out enough tickets that day."

"Ah, well," Morgan said soothingly. "You got here safely; that's what's important." He took the suitcase from Leon. It weighed more than he'd expected. "Come on in the house," he said. "Bonny! The Merediths are here!"

He led them up the front steps and into the living room. The house's smell—mildew and kerosene—struck him for the first time as unfriendly. He noticed that the cushions in the rattan chairs were flat as pancakes, soggy-looking, and the rattan itself was coming loose in spirals from the arms. Maybe this hadn't been such a good idea. Emily and Leon stared around uncertainly. Gina slouched near the door and peeled a thumbnail. This was her summer to thin out, it seemed. Her halter top sagged pathetically around her flat little chest. Morgan felt he was suddenly viewing everyone, himself included, in terms of geometry: an ill-assorted collection of knobs and bulges parked in meaningless locations. Then Emily said, "I brought a camera."

"Eh?" said Morgan. "Oh, a camera!"

"Just a Kodak."

"But that's wonderful!" he said. "I left mine at home this year. Oh, it's wonderful that you thought of it!" And just then Bonny emerged from the kitchen, smiling, wiping her palms on her skirt. He saw that things would be fine after all. (Life was full of these damp little moments of gloom that came and went; they meant nothing.) He beamed and watched as Bonny hugged everyone. Behind her came his mother, also smiling. "Mother," he said, "you remember the Merediths."

"Of course," she said. She held out a hand, first to Leon and then to Emily. "You brought me that fruitcake last Christmas," she told Emily.

"Oh, yes."

"It had the most marvelous glaze on the top."

"Why, thank you," Emily said.

"And did your husband ever recover from his stroke?"

"Excuse me?"

Morgan saw in a flash what must have happened. His mother had Emily confused with Natalie Czernov, a next-door neighbor from Morgan's childhood. Mrs. Czernov had also made fruitcake at Christmas. He was so fascinated by this slippage in time (as if the fruitcake were a kind of key that opened several doors at once, from several levels of history) that he forgot to come to Emily's rescue. Emily said, "This is my husband right here, Mrs. Gower."

"Oh, good, he's better, then," Louisa said.

Emily looked at Morgan.

"Maybe I should show you where you're staying," he said.

He picked up their suitcase again and led them down the hall to Kate's room. The bed had been freshly made and there was a sleeping bag on the floor for Gina. "The bathroom is next door," he said. "There are towels above the sink. If you need anything else . . ."

"I'm sure we'll be fine," Emily said. She opened the suitcase. Morgan glimpsed several new-looking squares of folded clothing. Leon, meanwhile, crossed the room abruptly and looked out the window. (All he would see was a row of dented trashcans.) Then he moved on to the picture that hung over the bed: a dim blue sea, flat as glass, on which rode a boat made of real shells. "We shouldn't have come," he said, peering at a clamshell sail.

"Oh, Leon, we need a rest," Emily told him.

"We have to give a puppet show on Monday morning. That means either we fight the Sunday traffic on the Bridge, or we go back at crack of dawn on Monday, driving like hell to meet the schedule, and Lord help us if we have a flat or any little tie-up on the way."

"It's nice to get out of the city," Emily told Morgan. She removed a camera from the suitcase and closed the lid again. "Leon thought we couldn't take the time, but I said, 'Leon, I'm tired. I want to go. I'm tired of puppets.'"

"She's tired of puppets," Leon said. "Whose idea were they, I'd like to know? Whose were they in the first place? I'm only doing what you said to, Emily. You're the one who started this."

"Well, there's no good reason we can't leave them for a weekend, Leon."

"She thinks we can just leave whenever we like," Leon told Morgan.

Morgan passed a hand across his forehead. He said, "Please. I'm sure this will all work out. Don't you want to come see the ocean now?"

Neither Leon nor Emily answered him. They stood facing each other across the bed, their backs very straight, as if braced for something serious. They didn't even seem to notice when Morgan left the room.

VIII

NO, IT HADN'T been such a good idea to ask them here. The weekend passed so slowly, it didn't so much pass as *chafe* along. It ground to a stop and started up again. It rasped on Morgan's nerves. Actually, this was not entirely the Merediths' fault. It was more the fault of Brindle, who faded into tears a dozen times a day; or Bonny, who overdid her sunbathing and developed a fever and chills; or Kate, who was arrested in Ocean City on charges of possessing half an ounce of marijuana. But Morgan blamed the Merediths anyhow. He couldn't help but feel that Leon's sulkiness had cast some kind of evil spell, and he was irritated by the way Emily hung around Bonny all the time. (Who had befriended Emily first, after all? Who had first discovered her?) She had changed; just wearing different shoes on her feet had somehow altered her. He began to avoid her. He devoted himself to Gina—a sad, sprouty child at an awkward age, just the age to tear at his heart. He made her a kite from a Hefty bag, and she thanked him earnestly, but when he looked into her face he saw that she was really watching her parents, who were arguing in low voices at the other end of the porch.

He began reflecting on Joshua Bennett, a new neighbor back in Baltimore. This Bennett was an antique dealer. (Now, *there* was an occupation.) He looked like Henry the Eighth and he lived a gentlemanly life—eating small, expensive suppers, then reading leather-bound history books while twirling a snifter of brandy. Early last spring, when Bennett first moved in, Morgan had paid a call on him and found him in a maroon velvet smoking jacket with quilted satin lapels. (Where would one go to buy a smoking jacket?) Bennett had somehow received the impression that Morgan had descended from an ancient Baltimore shipping family and owned an atticful of antique bronzes, and he had been most cordial—offering Morgan some of his brandy and an ivory-tipped cigar. Morgan wondered if Bennett would have accepted an invitation to the beach. He began plotting his return to Baltimore: the friendship he would strike up, the conversations they would have. He could hardly wait to get back.

Meanwhile the weekend dragged on.

Kate had disgraced the family, Bonny said. Now she was on the police files, marked for life. Bonny seemed to take this very seriously. (Her sunburn gave her a hectic, intense look.) Because the cottage had no telephone, the Ocean City police had had to call the Bethany police and have them notify the Gowers. Naturally, therefore, the news would be everywhere now. Saturday, at breakfast, Bonny laid a blazing hand on Louisa's arm and asked Kate, "How do you think your grandma feels? Her late husband's name, which up till now has been unbesmirched." Morgan had never heard her use the word "unbesmirched" before, and he wasn't even sure that it existed. He took some time thinking it over. Louisa, meanwhile, went on calmly spooning grapefruit. "What do you say, Mother?" Bonny asked her.

Louisa peered out of her sunken eyes and said, "Well, I don't know what all the fuss is about. We used to give little babies marijuana any old time. It soothed their teething."

"No, no, Mother, that was belladonna," Bonny said.

Kate merely looked bored. Brindle blew her nose. The Merediths sat in a row and watched, like members of a jury.

And on the beach—where the ocean curled and flattened beneath a deep blue bowl of sky, and gulls floated overhead as slow as sails—this group was a motley scramble of blankets, thermoses, sandy towels, an umbrella that bared half its spokes every time the wind flapped past, a squawking radio, and scattered leaves of newspaper. Kate, who had been grounded for the rest of her vacation, flipped angrily through *Seventeen.* Bonny sweated and shivered in layers of protective garments. The white zinc oxide on her nose and lower lip, along with her huge black sunglasses, gave her the look of some insect creature from a science-fiction movie. Gina dug a hole in the sand and climbed into it. Billy and Priscilla made a spectacle of themselves, lying too close together on their blanket.

And Emily, in an unbecoming pale blue swimsuit that exposed her thin, limp legs, took pictures that were going to turn out poorly, but she would not yield her camera to Morgan. She worried that he would snap *her,* she said. Morgan swore he wouldn't. (She was already pasted in his mind as he would like her to be forever—wearing her liquid black skirt and ballet slippers. He would surely not choose to record this other self she had become.) "All I want to do," he told her, "is photograph some groups. Some action, don't you see." He couldn't bear her finicky delays, the stylized poses she insisted on. Morgan himself was a photographer of great speed and dash; he caught people in clumps, in mid-motion, mid-laugh. Emily picked her way across the sand to one person at a time, stopping every step or so to shake her white feet fastidiously, and then she would take an eternity getting things just right, squinting through the camera, squinting at the sky— as if there were anything that could be done, any adjustments at all to aid a Kodak Instamatic. "Be still, now," she would tell her subject, but then she'd wait so long that whoever it was grew strained and artificial-looking, and more than once Morgan cried, "Just *take* it, dammit!" Then Emily lowered her camera and turned, eyes widening, lips parting, and had to begin all over again.

Sunday afternoon the Merediths had a quarrel about when they were going home. Emily wanted to wait till Monday, but Leon wanted to leave that evening. "Lord, yes," Morgan longed to say. "Go!"—not only to the Merediths but to everyone. They could abandon him on the beach. Fall would come and he'd be buried under drifting threads of sand and a few brown leaves blown seaward. He pictured how calm he would grow, at last. The breakers would act for him, tumbling about while he lay still. He would finally have a chance to sort himself out. It was *people* who disarranged his life—Louisa in her striped beach robe like a hawk-nosed Bedouin, Brindle in an old stretched swimsuit of Bonny's that fell in vacant folds around her hunched body. He sat beneath the umbrella in his sombrero and trunks and his shoes with woolen socks. His bare chest felt itchy and sticky. He chewed a match and listened to the Merediths quarrel.

Leon said that if they left Monday, they might very well miss their show. Emily said it was only a puppet show. Leon asked how she could say *only*. Wasn't it what she'd set her heart on, dragged him into, held his nose to—damn puppets with their silly grins—all these years? She said she had never held his nose to anything and, anyway, it was Leon's business what he did with his life. She had certainly not forced him into this, she said. Then Leon jumped to his feet and went striding southward, toward town. Morgan watched after him, idly observing that Leon had developed a roll of padded flesh above the waistband of his trunks. He was a solid, weighty man now, and came down hard on his heels. Flocks of slender girls parted to let him pass. He pushed on through them, not giving them a glance.

Possibly, Billy and Priscilla were quarreling too, for they sat apart from each other and Billy drew deep circles in the sand between his feet. The women melted closer together; the men remained on the outskirts, each alone, stiff-necked. The women's soft voices wove in with the rush of the ocean. "Look at the birds," Emily told Gina. "Look how they circle. Look how they're hunting for fish."

"Or maybe they're just cooling off their underwings," Louisa said.

Bonny, gazing at the horizon from behind her dark glasses, spoke in a tranquil, faraway voice. "It was here on this beach," she said, "that I first knew I was a grownup. I had thought of myself as a girl for so long—years after I was married. I was twenty-nine, pregnant with the twins. I'd brought Amy and Jeannie to the beach to play. I saw the lifeguard look over at me and then at some spot beyond me, and I realized he hadn't really seen me at all. His mind told him, 'Lady. Children. Sand toys,' and he passed on. Oh, it's not as if I were ever the kind that boys would whistle at. It's not as if I were used to hordes of men admiring me, even back when I was in my teens. But at least, you see, I had once been up for consideration, and now I wasn't. I was reclassified. I felt so sad. I felt I'd had something taken away from me that I was so certain of, I hadn't even noticed I had it. I didn't know it would happen to me too, just to anyone else."

Morgan noticed someone walking toward them: a man in a business suit that was made of some dull gray hammered-metal fabric. Everyone he passed stared after him for a moment. He ruffled their faces like a wind, and then they turned away again. It was Robert Roberts. Morgan said, "Brindle." Brindle seemed to comprehend everything, just from the sound of her name. She hunched tighter on her blanket and hugged her knees and frowned, not looking. It was up to Morgan. He rose and spat his match out. "Why, Robert Roberts!" he said, and offered his hand, too soon. Robert had some distance to travel yet. He came lurching up the slope a little untidily, in order not to keep Morgan waiting. His palm was damp. His face glistened. He was a man without visible edges or angles, and his thin brown hair was parted close to the center and plastered down. It appeared that he was sinking into the sand. There was sand across the creases of his shoes, and more sand filling his trouser cuffs. He gripped Morgan's hand like a drowning man and stared fixedly into his eyes—but that was his salesman's training, no doubt. "It's Bob," he said, panting.

"Beg pardon?"

"I'm Bob. You always call me Robert Roberts, like a joke."

"I do?"

"I came for Brindle."

Morgan turned to Brindle. She hugged her knees harder and rocked, staring out to sea.

"It's the same thing all over, isn't it?" Robert said to Morgan. "It's the same old story. Once again she leaves me."

"Ah, well . . . have a seat, Robert, Bob. Don't be such a stranger."

Robert ignored him. "Brindle," he said, "I woke up Thursday morning and you were gone. I thought maybe you were just miffed about something, but it's been four days now and you never came back. Brindle, are we going round and round like this all our lives? We're together, you leave me, we're together, you leave me?"

"You do still have my photograph," Brindle told the ocean.

"What's that supposed to mean?"

Brindle got to her feet. She brushed sand off the seat of her bathing suit; she adjusted a strap. Then she went up to Robert Roberts and set her face so close to his that he drew back. "Look," she said, tapping her yellow cheekbone. "This is *me*. I am Brindle Gower Teague Roberts. All that string of names."

"Yes, Brindle, of course," Robert said.

"You say that so easily! But since you and I were children, I've been married and widowed. I married old Horace Teague next door and moved into his rowhouse; I bought little cans of ham in the gourmet sections of department stores—"

"You've told me all that, Brindle."

"I am not the girl in the photograph."

She was not. The skin below her eyes was the same damaged color as Morgan's. The dimple in one cheek had become a dry crack— something Morgan had never noticed. She was thirty-eight years old. Morgan stroked his beard.

"Brindle, what is it you're saying?" Robert Roberts asked. "Are you saying you don't love me any more?"

In the little group of women (all gazing politely in other directions) there was the softest rustle, like a laugh or a sigh. Robert looked over at them. Then he turned to Morgan. "What is she saying?" he asked.

"I don't know," said Morgan.

Louisa said, "If they marry, I hope I won't be sent to live with them."

"They *are* married, Mother dear," Morgan told her.

"You have no idea how hard it is," Louisa said, "not knowing where you'll be shipped to next."

"Mother, have we ever shipped you anywhere? Ever in all your life?"

"Haven't you?" she asked. She considered, retreating into the hood of her beach robe. "Well, somehow it feels like you have, at least," she said. "No, I prefer to stay on with you. Bonny, you won't let him send me off to Brindle's, will you? Morgan's difficult to live with but . . . eventful, I suppose you'd say."

"Oh, yes," said Bonny dryly.

"Promise?"

"Mother," said Morgan. "They're married. They're already married, and no one's shipped you anywhere. Tell her, Brindle. Tell her, Robert, Bob . . ."

But Robert faced the sea, not listening. His hair blew up stiffly, in spikes, which made him look desperate. While the others watched, he bent to dust the sand from his trousers. He pulled his shirtcuffs a proper length below the sleeves of his coat. Then he started walking toward the water.

He circled a child with a shovel and he stepped over a moat and a crenellated wall. But his powers of observation seemed to weaken as he drew nearer the sea, and he stumbled into a shallow basin that three little boys were digging. He climbed out again, ignoring their cries. Now his trouser legs were dark and sugary-looking. He accidentally crushed a paper cup beneath his heel. He reached the surf and kept going. A young man, lifting a screaming girl in the air and preparing to dunk her, suddenly set her down and stood gaping. Robert was knee-deep in seething white water. He was waist-deep. When the breakers curled back for a new assault, he was seen to be clothed in heavy, dragging vestments that looked almost Biblical.

Up until now, no one had moved. They might have been little specks of bathers on a postcard. But then Brindle screamed, "Stop him!" and all the women clambered to their feet. The lifeguard stood on his high wooden chair, with a whistle raised halfway to his mouth. Billy barreled past. Morgan hadn't even heard him get up. Morgan threw his sombrero into Bonny's lap and followed, but the lifeguard was faster than both of them. By the time Billy and Morgan hit the water, the lifeguard was in to waist level, heaving his orange torpedo at Robert. Robert brushed it away and plunged on.

A breaker crashed around Morgan's knees, colder than he had expected. He hated the feeling of wet woolen socks. However, he kept going. What he had in mind was not so much rescuing Robert as defeating him. No, Robert would never get away with this; he couldn't escape so easily; it must not be allowed. Morgan swarmed in the water, his limbs wandering off in several directions. A surprised-looking woman lifted both flaps of her bathing cap and stared. The lifeguard took a stranglehold on Robert from behind, and Robert (who so far had not even got his hair wet) flailed and fell backward. He was engulfed by a wave and came up coughing, still in the lifeguard's grasp. The lifeguard hauled him in. Morgan followed with his arms out level, his head lunging forward intently. The lifeguard dragged Robert up on the sand and dumped him there, like a bundle of wet laundry. He prodded Robert with one long, bronzed foot. "Oh, me," Morgan said wearily, and he sat down beside Robert and looked at his ruined shoes. Billy sank next to him, out of breath. Robert went on coughing and shrugging off the people who crowded around. "Stand back, stand back," the lifeguard said. He asked Morgan, "What was he, drunk?"

"I wouldn't have the faintest idea," Morgan said.

"Well, I got to make a report on this."

"Really, that won't be necessary," Morgan said, rising. "I'm from the Bureau."

"The what?"

"Parks and Safety," Morgan said. "What's your name, son? Of course I plan to mention this to the board."

"Well, Hendrix," the lifeguard said. "Danny Hendrix, with an x."

"Good work, Hendrix," Morgan said. He briskly shook the lifeguard's hand. The lifeguard stood around a minute, scratching his head, and then he went down to the water to watch his orange torpedo float out to sea.

They propped Robert up and draped him across their shoulders— one arm circling Morgan's neck, one arm circling Billy's. Robert seemed uninjured, but he was heavy and lethargic and his shoes dragged behind him. "*Come* on, fellow," Billy said cheerfully. He looked pleased; perhaps he was reminded of his fraternity days, which he'd once told Morgan were the happiest of his life. Morgan himself stayed silent. He wished he had a cigarette.

They hauled Robert past the blanket, where the women were packing their belongings. Brindle was smoothing out towels and folding them. She would not look at Robert. Morgan felt proud of her. Let Robert see whom he was dealing with here! Let him see how they could handle it—all of them together. For this was no mere marital quarrel, no romantic tiff. No, plainly what had happened was a comment upon their whole family—on the disarray of their family life. Robert had been standing right beside this blanket, had he not, listening to Louisa forget where she was in time, Morgan arguing with her, all the others grouping into battle squads . . . and then he'd made his break, escaped. The scoundrel. He'd insulted every one of them, each and every one. Morgan felt a flash of anger. Pretending to be concerned about Hendrix, he stopped without warning and ducked away from Robert's arm and turned toward the ocean. Robert tilted and nearly fell. Morgan shaded his eyes. Hendrix was sending signals to the lifeguard on the next beach. Morgan could not read signal flags, but he could easily imagine the conversation that was taking place. WHAT WAS PROBLEM, the neighbor would ask, and Hendrix would answer, MIXUP CHAOS MUDDLE . . .

Kate was watching too. (No doubt she found Hendrix handsome.) Morgan said, "Can you tell what he's saying?"

She shrugged. "It's just the clear sign," she said.

"The what?"

"You know—all clear, everything in order."

"Little does he know," Morgan said.

IX

BONNY TOLD Morgan they were running out of beds. Were the Merediths leaving tonight or tomorrow morning? she asked him. This conversation took place in the kitchen, late in the afternoon, while Bonny was emptying ice-cube trays into a pitcher. Above the crackle and clink of ice, she whispered that it would certainly solve a great deal if the Merediths left before bedtime. Then she could put Brindle and Robert in their room. But Morgan didn't think Brindle would want to share a room with Robert anyhow. "Let it be, Bonny," he said. "Send Robert out on the porch with a sleeping bag."

"But, Morgan, they're married."

"The man's a lunatic. She's better off without him."

"You're the one who was against her leaving him," Bonny said. "Now, just because he walks into the surf a ways—"

"With all his clothes on. With his suit on. Making us look like some kind of institutional outing, a laughingstock . . ."

"Nobody laughed," Bonny said.

"It's a mark of how badly this vacation is going," Morgan said, "that, lately, I've been wondering how the hardware store is doing."

"He was just showing her he cared," said Bonny.

"I've half a mind to call Butkins in the morning and see if he's restocked those leaf bags yet. With fall coming on—"

"What are you talking about? It's July."

Morgan pulled at his nose.

"Go ask Emily what they've decided," Bonny said.

"You want me to tell them to leave?"

"No, no, just ask. If they're staying on, we'll work out something else."

"Maybe *we* could leave," he said hopefully. "The others could stay and we could go."

Bonny gave him a look.

He wandered into the living room, where his mother and Priscilla were playing Scrabble. Kate was painting her fingernails at a little rattan table. The smell of nail polish filled the room—a piercing, city smell that Morgan liked. He would have preferred to settle here, but he said, "Anyone seen Emily?"

"She's out front," Priscilla told him.

He went to the porch, letting the rickety screen door slam shut behind him. Emily was taking pictures again. She photographed Gina, who was lining up a row of oyster shells on the railing. She photographed Robert, who sat stiff and humiliated in a rocker, wearing borrowed clothes—Billy's wedding-white slacks and candy-striped shirt. Then she photographed Morgan. Morgan had to stand still for a long, long moment while Emily squinted through the camera at him. He did his best not to show his irritation. At least, he was glad to see, Emily had got out of that swimsuit. She wore her black outfit and no shoes at all. She was her old, graceful, fairy-dancer self. As soon as Morgan heard the shutter click, he said, "Now I'll snap one of you, since you're looking so fine and pretty." He came down the front steps and took the camera from her hands. She put up no resistance, for once. She seemed tired. Even when he drew away and aimed the camera at her, she didn't smooth her hair or lighten her expression.

He snapped the picture and handed the camera back to her. "Ah

. . . Bonny was just wondering," he said. "Should we count on having you three for the night?"

"I don't know," she said. She rolled the film forward with a little zipping sound. "I'll have to talk to Leon," she said finally.

"Oh? Where *is* Leon?"

"He never came back from his walk. I was planning to go into town and look for him."

"I'll come with you," Morgan said. "Gina? You want to take a walk?"

"I'm busy," Gina said, laying out another row of shells.

"Robert?"

"I'm waiting for Brindle."

Morgan and Emily started down the street. It was narrow and patchily surfaced; they could walk in the center of it without much fear of traffic. They passed a woman hanging out beach towels and a little girl blowing soap bubbles on her steps. The houses were so close together that it almost seemed the two of them were proceeding through a series of rooms—hearing Neil Diamond on the radio and then an oboe concerto, catching a whiff of coffee and frying crabcakes, watching a man and a boy sort out their fishing tackle on a green porch glider. Emily said, "He'll have a mighty long wait."

"Who will?" Morgan asked.

"Robert Roberts. Brindle's gone back to Baltimore."

"She has?"

"Billy drove her to the bus in Ocean City."

"But her car's parked right out front!"

"She doesn't want it any more, she said."

"Oh," said Morgan. He thought that over. "So it's my house she's gone to, is it?"

"I didn't ask," Emily said.

"It serves him right," said Morgan. "Yes, I was on his side till now, the way he rang our doorbell, bringing roses . . . but, oh, this ocean business. No. People imagine they can hold you with such things. They cause themselves some damage and assume that we'll accept responsibility. But they underestimate us. They fail to realize. No, Brindle will never forgive him for that."

Emily said nothing. He glanced down at her and found her drawn and pale, walking alongside him with her camera held tight in one bluish hand. How had she managed to avoid a sunburn? She'd been out on the beach as long as the others. He wiped his sweaty forehead on his sleeve. "Well," he said, "I suppose you must find us very tiring. Right?"

"I've had a wonderful time," she told him.

"Eh?"

"I've had a wonderful time."

"Yes, well, that's sweet of you, but . . . never mind, I know this wasn't what you're used to. There's no economy to our life. Don't think I haven't noticed that."

"It was wonderful. It was a real vacation," Emily said. "As soon as we got your letter, I was so excited—I went out and bought us all new clothes. It's been years since I've been to the beach. Not since high school."

"Ah, yes, high school," Morgan said, sighing.

"He never thinks we can spare the time. He'd rather stay at home. We either give our shows or stay home. Sometimes I think he's doing it for spite—he's saying, 'You wanted to marry and settle, didn't you? Well, here we are, and we're never going anywhere again.' It's funny: I hoped I'd grow more like him—more, oh, active—but it seems instead he's more like me. We just sit home. I sit in that room with that sewing machine; I feel like someone in a story, some drudge. I feel like the miller's daughter, left to spin gold out of straw. Visiting here was just what we needed—so much going on, so many things happening—"

"Oh, dear, oh, dear," Morgan said. He felt very uncomfortable, and had forgotten to bring his cigarettes. They passed a man smoking on his front steps and Morgan drew a chestful of sharp gray air from him. "Doesn't the sun set differently here," he said, "so long and level; the light's so flat, somehow—" He walked faster. Emily kept up. They turned east and passed the first of a string of shops.

"He puts me in such a position," she said. "He always makes it seem that everything was my idea, that I'm the one who organized our lives this way, but I'm not. I mean, if he just *sat*, what was I to do? Tell me that!"

Morgan said, "I honestly don't believe I can last another day in the place."

"In Bethany?" Emily asked. She looked around her. "But it's beautiful," she said.

"It smells of dead fish."

"Why, Morgan."

They passed a gift-shop window hung with yellow nets and filled with spiky, varnished conch shells from Florida and pewter sand dollars, seahorses locked in Lucite paperweights, racks of pierced earrings shaped like starfish and dolphins. They climbed a set of weathered wooden stairs, and on the way up the ramp to the boardwalk Morgan glanced into the dark plate glass of the Holiday House restaurant. "Oh! My God," he said.

Emily turned to him.

"Look!" he said, feeling his cheeks, peering into the glass. "I'm so old! I'm so ruined! I seem to have . . . fallen apart."

She laughed.

"Well, I don't see anything funny," he told her.

"Morgan, don't worry. You're fine. It's always like that, if you haven't braced your face first."

"Yes, but now my face is braced," he said. "And look! Still!"

She stopped laughing and put on a sympathetic expression. But, of course, he couldn't expect her to understand. Her skin seemed filmed with gold; the metal filings of her hair glinted in the sunlight. She started walking again and after a moment he followed, still testing different parts of his face with his fingertips.

"I thought he'd be right around here somewhere," Emily said, gazing up and down the boardwalk.

"Maybe he stopped at a café."

"Oh, he'd never do that on his own."

This interested him. "Why not?" he asked. "What would he have against it?"

She didn't answer. She set her hands on the boardwalk railing and looked out at the ocean. It was five o'clock at least, maybe later, and only one or two swimmers remained. A single white Styrofoam raft skated away on the surf. Couples strolled along the edge, dressed in clean, dry clothing that gave them the lovingly tended look of small children awakened from naps. There were flattened squares of sand where families had been camped on blankets, and abandoned drip-castles and bucket-shaped towers. But no Leon. "Maybe he's back at the cottage," Morgan said. "Emily?"

She was crying. Tears rolled singly down her cheeks while she faced straight ahead, wide-eyed. "Why, Emily," Morgan said. He wished Bonny were here. He put an arm around Emily, clumsily, and said what he supposed Bonny might say. "There, now. Never mind," he told her, and when she turned toward him, he folded her in to him and said, "Never you mind, Emily." Her hair smelled like fresh linen that had hung to dry in the sun all day. The camera, which she clutched to her chest, made a boxy shape between them, but elsewhere she was soft and boneless, surprisingly slight; there was nothing to her. He was startled by a sudden ache that made him tighten his arms and pull her hard against him. His head grew light. She made some sound, a kind of gasp, and tore away. "Emily, wait!" he said. It was difficult to get his breath. He said, "Emily, let me explain," but she had already backed off, and Morgan was left reeling and hot-faced with shame, and before he could straighten out this new catastrophe, he looked down and saw Leon passing below them, absorbed in the evening paper.

X

THEY LOST their good weather on Monday and didn't see the sun again till Thursday, and by then it was too late; everyone remaining in the cottage was annoyed with everyone else. Billy and Priscilla left early, in a huff—Priscilla driving Brindle's car. Louisa quarreled with Kate about some blueberry muffins, and Bonny told Morgan that he'd have to take Louisa in the pickup, going home. She certainly couldn't travel with the two of them together. But Morgan didn't want to take her. He looked forward to making the trip alone, with an extra-early start and no stops along the way. Then as soon as he reached home, he figured, he would pay a call on Joshua Bennett, the antique dealer. And maybe afterward he'd wander on downtown, just to see what he'd missed. No, there wasn't any room for Louisa in his plans. So Saturday morning, while the others were still packing, he threw his encyclopedia into the truck-bed. "Goodbye, everybody," he said, and he left. Traveling down their little street, before he turned onto the highway, he could look in the rear-view mirror and see Kate chasing after him, and Bonny descending the porch steps calling something, and Louisa shading her eyes in the door. In this family, you could never have a simple leavetaking. There were always threads and tangles trailing.

He drove slightly over the speed limit, once even swerving to the shoulder of the road to bypass a line of cars. He had only a few minutes' wait at the Kent Narrows and none at all on the Bridge. Skimming across the Bridge, he felt he was soaring. He reached the city limits at eleven, and was home by eleven-twenty—long before Bonny and the others.

The yard was overgrown, littered with rolled newspapers. The house was cool and musty-smelling behind its drawn shades, and there was a mountain of mail in the hall beneath the mail slot. In the dining room Brindle sat playing solitaire. Coffee stains yellowed the front of her bathrobe. She trilled her fingers absently when he walked in, and then she laid a jack of diamonds on a queen of spades. "Pardon my not bringing in the papers," she said, "but I didn't want to go outside because Robert Roberts was parked in front of the house for most of the week."

"Persisting, is he?" Morgan said. He sat down next to her to sort the mail.

"I couldn't even go for milk, or to buy a loaf of bread, so I managed on what was here. Sardines and corned-beef hash, mainly. I feel like someone on a submarine; I have this craving for lettuce. But it wasn't so bad. I didn't really mind. It made me think of back when we were kids, when we were poor. Morgan," she said, pausing with a ten of clubs in mid-air, "weren't we happier, in some ways, when we were up against it?"

"As far as I'm concerned, we're still up against it," Morgan said.

There was a dainty blue envelope from Priscilla that must contain a thank-you note. It made him tired to think of it. He passed on to a thicker one that looked more promising, and ripped it open. Inside was a sheaf of photographs, wrapped in a letter. He checked the signature:

Emily. Now what? *Dear Morgan and Bonny,* she wrote, in a neat, italic hand that struck him as stunted. *Thank you again for a lovely vacation. I hope we did not put you to too much trouble. Toward the end we were so rushed, getting off in time to beat the dark, that I didn't feel we properly said goodbye. But it was so nice of you to have us and we all had such a . . .*

Morgan grimaced and turned to the photos. He flipped through them idly. Then he sat straighter and went through them again. He laid one on the dining room table and another one beside it, and another. Bonny, Robert, Brindle, Kate . . .

Each person sat alone, suspended in an amber light that surely did not exist in Bethany Beach, Delaware. Bonny folded her arms across her stomach and smiled a radiant smile. Robert Roberts shone like a honeymooner in his borrowed shirt, and Brindle's skin had the mellow glow of a priceless painting. Kate with her stubborn pout was as sultry and mysterious as a piece of exotic fruit. Morgan's sombrero, pushed back, was a halo, and the white streaks in his beard gave him the depth and texture of something carved. Well, it was only the film. It was cut-rate film, or out of date, or underexposed.

But each person gazed out so steadily, with such trust, such concentration. Emily herself, marble-pale in folds of black, met his scrutiny with eyes so clear that he imagined he could see through them and behind them; he could see what she must see, how his world must look to her. A buoyant little bubble of hope began to rise in him. Over and over, he sorted through the pictures, rearranging them, aligning them, dropping them, smiling widely and sighing and laughing, ignoring his sister's astonished stare: a man in love.

1976

I

WHEN SPRING came, Emily started walking. She walked all spring and summer, down alleyways, across tattered rags of parks, through stores that smelled of pickles and garlic. She went in the front doors and out the back, emerging on some unknown street full of delivery trucks, stacked wooden crates, construction workers with pneumatic drills tearing up the pavement. Her ballet slippers, nearly soundless, tripped along in time to the music in her head. She liked songs about leaving, about women who packed up and left, and men who woke to find their beds unexpectedly empty. *If you miss the train I'm on, you will know that I am gone . . .* She slipped between two children sharing popcorn from a bag. *One of these mornings, it won't be long, you'll call my name and I'll be gone . . .* She brushed against an old lady with a shopping bag full of bottles, did not apologize, kept going. *I know you, rider, going to miss me when I'm . . .* Gone, gone gone: her slippers thumped it out. She had a spiky step to begin with, but every day, all over again, she softened; she would slow down bit by bit, and wilt, and grow calm. She would think of how Leon's jacket hung across that broad, subtle curve between his shoulder blades. How complete his words sounded—more certain than other people's, spoken in an even voice that carried some special weight. How he always kept his mouth closed, not tightly clamped but relaxed and gentle, giving her, for some reason, an impression of secrets working within him.

She sighed and turned home, after all.

Often, on these walks, she was followed by Morgan Gower—a wide leather hat and a tumult of beard, loping along behind her. If she paused till he caught up, he'd make a nuisance of himself. He had entered some new stage, developed a new fixation. It was harmless, really, but annoying. He might declare himself to her anywhere—fling out his arms in the middle of the Broadway Fish Market, beam down at her, full of joy. "Last night I dreamed you went to bed with me." She would click her tongue and walk away. She would march on out and down the block, cut through an alley past a grinding garbage truck, and he would follow, but he kept his distance. His hat rounded corners like a flying saucer, level and spinning, the rest of him sauntering beneath. Glancing back, she had to laugh. Then she turned away again, but he'd already noticed; she heard him laugh too. Didn't he realize she had problems on her mind? She was overhung by thoughts of Leon, like someone traveling under a cloud. First marching, then drifting, she paced out the knots and snarls of life with Leon. Love was not a comedy. But here came Morgan, laughing. She gave in and stopped once more and waited. He arrived beside her and pointed at the neon sign that swung above their heads. "Look! *La-Trella's Rooms. Weekly! Daily!* Let's just nip upstairs."

"Really, Morgan."

And even in front of Leon—what did Morgan imagine he was doing? In front of glowering, dark Leon, he said, "Emily, fetch your toothbrush. We're eloping." When there was music, anywhere—a car radio passing on the street—he would seize her by the waist and dance. He danced continually, nowadays. It seemed his feet could not keep quiet. She had never known him to act so silly.

Fortunately, Leon didn't take him seriously.

"You'd be getting more than you bargained for," he said to Morgan.

Still, she said, "Morgan, I wish you wouldn't joke like that in front of Leon. What must he think?"

"What should he think? I'm stealing you away," Morgan said, and he circled the kitchen, where Emily happened to be washing dishes, and threw open all the cupboards. "Which things are you bringing with you? These plates? This bowl? This two-quart vinyl orange-juice pitcher?"

She rested her soapy hands on the sink and watched him. "Morgan," she said. "Don't you ever get self-conscious?"

"Well," he said.

He closed a cupboard door. He stroked his beard.

"That's a very interesting question," he said. "I'm glad you asked me that. The fact is . . . ah, yes, I do."

She blinked. "You do?"

"The fact is," he said, "with you: well, yes, I do."

He stood before her, smiling. There was something clumsy about him that made her see, suddenly, what he must have been like as a boy—one of those bumbling boys who can't think what to talk about with girls; or who talk too much, perhaps, out of nervousness—compulsively relating the entire plots of movies or explaining how the internal-combustion engine works. It was a shock; she had never pictured him that way. And anyhow, she was probably wrong, for an instant later he was back to the Morgan she had always known: a gray-streaked, twinkling clown of a man, swinging into a soft-shoe dance across her kitchen floor.

At least he could make her laugh.

II

SHE WALKED through summer and into fall. She did other things too, of course—gave puppet shows, sewed costumes, cooked, helped Gina with her homework. But at night, when she closed her eyes, she saw a maze of streets and traffic, the way compulsive chess-players see chessboards in their dreams. She was revisited by the smallest details of her walks—by the clank of a foot on a manhole cover, the spark of mica in concrete, and the Bicentennial fire hydrants sticking out their stunted arms like so many defective babies. She opened her eyes, sat up, rearranged her pillow. "What's the trouble?" Leon would ask.

There were any number of answers she could give, all true. She said, sometimes, that she thought their marriage had something badly wrong with it, something out of step, she couldn't say just what. Maybe so, said Leon, but what did she want him to do about it? He did not believe, he said, that there was anything in the world that would make her really happy. Unless, perhaps, she could bring the whole solar system into line exactly her way, not a planet disobeying. What was it that she expected of him? he would ask. She was silent.

Or sometimes she said that she worried about Gina. It didn't seem right for a nine-year-old to act so serious, she said. It broke her heart to see her so unswervingly alert to their moods, watching from a distance, smoothing over quarrels. But Leon said Gina was growing up, that was all. Naturally, he said. Let her be, he said.

Also, Emily said, their puppet shows never went well any more. Running through every play was some kind of dislocation—characters stepping on each other's speeches, unsynchronized, ragged, or missing cues and gawking stupidly. Fairytales fell into fragments, every line a splinter. When Cinderella danced with the Prince, their cloth bodies clung together, but the hands inside them shrank away. Emily believed that the audience could guess this. She was certain of it. Leon said that was ridiculous. They were making more money than they ever had before; they had to turn down invitations. Things were going wonderfully, Leon said.

In her sleep, she dreamed she walked a revolving pavement like a merry-go-round, and she was still tired when she woke.

Often, when she had some work that could be done by hand, she'd spend her mornings down in Crafts Unlimited. She'd perch on a stool behind the counter and listen to Mrs. Apple while she sewed. Mrs. Apple knew hundreds of craftsmen, all their irregular, colorful lives, and she could talk on and on about them in her cheery way, stringing together people Emily had never heard of. Emily relaxed, expanded, watched well-dressed grandmothers buying her puppets. Once Mrs. Apple's son Victor came to visit. He was living in D.C. now and had driven over unannounced. He'd gained a good deal of weight and shaved off his mustache. His wife, a pretty woman with flossy blond hair, carried their small son in her arms. "Well, well, well," Victor said to Emily, and he hooked his thumbs into the tiny pockets of his vest. "I see you're still making puppets."

She felt she had to defend herself. "Yes," she said, "but they're much different now. They're a whole different process."

Getting off her stool, though, going to a table to show him a king with a gnarled face, she was conscious of how dreary she must seem to him—still in the same building, the same occupation, wearing the same kind of clothes. Her braids, she felt suddenly, might as well have solidified on her head. She wished she had not let Morgan Gower persuade her to go back to ballet slippers. She wished she had Gina here—all the change that anyone could ask for. Victor bounced slightly on the balls of his feet, examining the king. Melissa, Emily thought suddenly. Melissa Tibbett—that was the name of the birthday child at their very first show, when Victor had been the doll-voiced father wondering what to bring back from his travels. Melissa must be in her teens by now—sixteen years old, at least; long past puppets. Emily set the king back on the table and smoothed his velvet robe.

"How about Leon?" Victor asked. "Is he doing any acting?"

"Oh, well, not so very much. No, not so much at the moment," she said.

He nodded. She hated the understanding way he looked into her eyes.

That afternoon she pulled a cardboard box from the closet and unpacked her marionettes. She'd been experimenting with marionettes for several years. She liked the challenge: they were harder to work. She had figured out her own arrangement of strings, suspended from a single cross of Popsicle sticks. There were two strings for the hands, two more for the knees, and one each for the head and the lower back. (At fairs she'd seen double and triple crosses, like biplanes, and half a dozen additional strings, but none of it seemed essential.) She took a Red Riding Hood, her most successful effort, and went into the living room. Leon was on the couch, reading the afternoon paper. Gina was writing a book report. "Look," Emily said.

Leon glanced up. Then he said, "Oh, Emily, not those marionettes again."

"But look: see how easy?"

She pranced Red Riding Hood across the floor, up the couch, into Gina's lap. Gina giggled. Then Red Riding Hood skipped away, swinging a small yellow basket that snapped cleverly over her arm. "What do you think?" Emily asked Leon.

"Very nice, but not for us," Leon said. "Emily, our old puppets can do that, and more besides. They can set the basket down and pick it up again. They don't have all those strings in the way."

"Oh, it's just like with my shadow puppets. You won't try anything new," she said. "I'm tired of the old ones."

"So?" he asked her. "You can't just switch the universe around, any time you're tired of it."

She packed the marionettes in their box. She went for a walk, though she ought to be starting supper. At the corner of Crosswell and Hartley she paused for a traffic light and Morgan Gower came up beside her. He was wearing a tall black suit, a high-collared shirt, and a bowler hat so ancient it looked rusty. He bowed and tipped his hat. She laughed. A grin spread behind his beard, but he seemed to guess her mood and he didn't speak. In fact, when the light turned green he dropped back again, though she was conscious of his presence—keeping a measured distance behind, humming a little tune and watching over her.

III

IN OCTOBER, Emily's second cousin Claire called to say that her great-aunt had died in her sleep. She'd donated her remains to the cause of medical science, Claire said (just like Aunt Mercer; she would put it in just those words), but still there'd be a service at the Meetinghouse. Emily thought she ought to attend it. She hadn't seen Aunt Mercer in twelve years—not since before her marriage. They had only exchanged Christmas cards, with polite, fond notes beneath the signatures. Going now, of course, was pointless; but even so, Emily canceled a puppet show and left Gina with Leon and took the Volkswagen south.

She was nervous about making the four-hour trip alone, but as soon as she'd merged on the interstate she felt wonderful. It seemed that the air here was thinner and lighter. She was even pleased by all the traffic she encountered—so many people skimming along! No doubt they were out here day and night, endlessly circling the planet, and now at last she had joined them. She smiled at every driver she passed. She was fascinated by the private, cluttered worlds she glimpsed— maps and stuffed animals on window ledges; a passenger sleeping, open-mouthed; a pair of children combing out their dog.

She turned off the interstate and traveled smaller and smaller roads, winding through rich farm country and then poor country, passing unpainted shacks bristling with TV antennas, their yards full of trucks on blocks and the hulls of cars, then speeding through coppery wood- lands laced with underbrush and discarded furniture. She reached Taney in the early afternoon. The town was still so small that several of the men hunkering before the Shell station were familiar to her—not even any older, it seemed; just painted there, dreamily holding their hand- rolled cigarettes. (Their names swam back to her: Shufords and Grind- staffs and Haithcocks. She'd had them stored in her memory all these years without knowing it.) Autumn leaves scuttled down Main Street. She turned up Erin Street and parked in front of the squat little house that she and her mother had shared with Aunt Mercer.

The yard was shadowed by great old trees. No real grass grew there— just patchy bits of plaintain in the caked orange dirt, weeds trailing out of a concrete urn, and a leaf-littered boxwood hedge giving off its dusky, pungent smell. Where were Aunt Mercer's flowerbeds? She would generally have something blooming, even this late in the year. Emily climbed the front-porch steps and paused, uncertain whether to knock or to walk on in. Then the door swung open and Claire said, "Emily, honey!"

She hadn't changed. She was plump and kind-faced, with little gray curls in a pom-pom over her forehead and another pom-pom at the back of her neck. She wore a stiff, wide, navy-blue dress that barely bent to accommodate her, and heavy black shoes with open toes. "Honey, don't just stand there. Where's your little family?"

"I left them home," Emily said.

"Left them! Came all this way by yourself? Oh, and we were counting on seeing your sweet daughter . . ."

Emily couldn't imagine Gina in this house. It wouldn't work; the two wouldn't meet in her mind. She followed Claire through the hall, with its smell of old newspapers, and into the parlor. The furniture was dark and ungainly. It so completely filled the room that Emily almost failed to notice the two people sitting on the puffy brown sofa— Claire's husband, Claude, and Aunt Junie, Claire's mother, the mountainous old woman who also lived here. Neither one was a blood relation, but Emily bent to kiss their cheeks. She'd last seen them when she came home after her mother's death, and they'd been sitting on this very sofa. They might have remained here ever since—abandoned, sagging, like large cloth dolls. When Claude reached up to pat her shoulder, the rest of him stayed sunk in the cushions; his arm seemed disproportionately long and distant from his body. Aunt Junie said, "Oh, Emily, look at you, so grown up . . ."

Emily sat on the sofa between them. Claire settled in a rocker. "Did you eat?" she asked Emily. "You want to wash up? Have a Coke? Some buttermilk?"

"I'm fine," Emily said. She felt *sinfully* fine, larger and stronger and less needy than all three of them put together. She folded her hands across her purse. There was a silence. "It's good to be back," she said.

"Wouldn't Aunt Mercer be pleased?" asked Claire.

There was a little bustle of motion; they'd found their subject. "Oh, wouldn't she just love to see you sitting here," Aunt Junie said.

"I wish she could have known," said Claire. "I wish you could have come before she passed."

"But it was painless," Claude said.

"Oh, yes. It's the way she'd have wanted to go."

"If she had to go, well, that's the way."

Claire, said, "All those troubles with her joints, Emily; you never saw. Arthritis swolled her up so, she got extra knobs and knuckles. Times she had a job just fixing her meals, but you know how she was: she wouldn't give in. Times she couldn't button her buttons or dial on the telephone, and Mama with that elbow of hers . . . I would say, 'Aunt Mercer, let me come over and stay a while,' but she said, 'No,' said, 'I can do it.' She just had to do it her way. She always liked to feed that cat of hers herself, said it wouldn't eat from anyone else, which was only what she liked to believe; and she was bound and determined to write her own letters. At Christmas—remember, Emily? How she always wrote you, longhand? And sent a little something for the baby. And Easter, why, that was her day to have us all over, and do every bit herself. Polished the silver, set the table . . . but she had to see to it some time ahead, in case the arthritis, you know . . . I stopped by on Good Friday and there was the cloth on the table and the very best china laid out. I said, 'Aunt Mercer, what's all this in aid of?' 'I just want to be sure it's ready,' she said, 'for your mama can't manage a thing with that elbow and I do like to get organized.'

See, she would never even mention her arthritis. Doctor had to tell us what was what; said, 'She is in more pain than she lets on.' She hated to put us out, never cared to lean on others. In some ways, it was best that she was taken when she was."

"Oh, it was all for the best," Aunt Junie said.

Claude said, "It was a mercy."

"I should have come before," Emily said. "I never knew. She never mentioned it in her letters."

"Yes, well, that was how she was."

"But she'd be proud that you came now," Aunt Junie said.

"And you'll want to go through her things, surely—so many of her nice things that I know she would want you to keep," Claire said.

"I don't have room in the car," said Emily. But suddenly she felt she would like this whole house—the wallpaper patterned with wasp-waisted baskets of flowers, the carpet always rubbed the wrong way, the china high-heeled slipper filled with chalky china roses. She imagined moving in. She pictured resuming her life where she'd left off, drinking her morning cocoa from the celery-green glass mug she'd found in a cereal box when she was eight. And when Claire said, "But her jade bar pin, Emily, *that* wouldn't need any space," she instantly pictured the bar pin, streaked with a kind of wood grain and twined at one end with blackened gold leaves. She was amazed at how much was still lodged in her mind. Like the Shufords, the Grindstaffs, and the Haithcocks, Aunt Mercer's house lived on in Emily, every warped shingle and small-paned window, whether she took it out to examine it or not. She would let the bar pin go to Aunt Junie, who wore such things, but in a sense she would continue owning it forever, and she might catch an accidental glimpse of it, barely noticed, some moment while waking or falling asleep fifty years from now.

"I don't have room even for that," she said.

Then she spread her hands and looked down at them—the parched white backs of them, the gold wedding ring as thin as wire.

At four o'clock they got to their feet and prepared to walk over to the Meetinghouse. Everyone seemed to have a great many coats and scarves, although it was a warm day. They helped each other, like handicapped people. Claire smoothed Claude's collar for him and straightened his lapels. "Don't you have a wrap, dear?" Aunt Junie asked Emily. "Your . . . what is that . . . skirt and top; it's so thin. Won't you borrow a sweater? You don't want to take a chill." But Emily shook her head.

Walking up Erin Street, they did meet a few young people, wearing boot-cut jeans and those velvet blazers that were popular in Baltimore too. This town was not so isolated as Emily had imagined. But the Meetinghouse—the only Friends Meeting in Taney County—was as small and poor as ever, a gray frame cubicle huddled in the back yard of the Savior Baptist Church; and everyone approaching it was old. They mumbled and clung to each other's arms, climbing the front steps. Emily hoped to see the friends she'd gone to First Day School with—never more than three or four of them in the best of times—but they must have moved away. There was no one under fifty. She took her seat on a straight-backed bench, between Aunt Junie and Claude. She looked around the little room and counted fourteen people. The fifteenth entered and closed the door behind him. A hush fell like the hush on a boat when the engine is cut off and the sails are raised.

In this quiet Emily had grown up—not a total silence but a ticking, breathing quiet, with the occasional sound of cloth rubbing cloth, little stirrings, throats cleared, people rustling coughdrop packets or fumbling through their purses. She expected nothing from it. (She had never been religious.) She wondered, for the hundredth time, what that dusty red glass was on the ledge above the east window. It was nearly overflowing with something that looked like wax. Maybe it was a candle. She always came to that conclusion. (But first she thought of something brewing—a culture, yogurt, dough, something concocting itself out of nothing.) She tried to name all the states in the Union. There were four beginning with A, two with C . . . but the M's were hard; there were so many: Montana, Missouri, Mississippi . . .

An old man with cottony hair rose and stood leaning on his cane. "Mercer Dulaney," he said, "once walked two and one-half miles in rheumatism weather to feed my dogs while I was off visiting my sister in Fairfax County. I reckon now I'll take that cat of hers and tend it, if it don't get on too bad with my dogs."

He sat down, groped for a handkerchief, and wiped his lips. "Ah, ah," he said. It made her think of Morgan Gower; he sometimes said that. She was surprised to remember her other life—its speed, its modernness, the great rush of noisy people she knew. She thought of Morgan hurtling down the street behind her, her daughter (daughter!) hailing a city bus; Leon tossing coins on the bureau before he undressed. She remembered the first time she ever saw Leon. He had walked in the door of the library reading room, wearing that corduroy jacket of his. He had stood there looking around him, hunting someone, and had not found whoever it was and turned to go; but in turning, he caught sight of Emily and paused and looked at her again, and then frowned and went on out. She had not actually been introduced to him for another week. But now it seemed to her that at his entrance—swinging through the library door, carrying a single book in his hand (his fingers fine-textured and brown, his shirtcuffs so perfectly white)—her life had suddenly been set in motion. Everything had started up, as if complicated wheels and gears had finally connected, and had raced along in a blur from then on. It was only now, in this slowed-down room, that she had a chance to examine what had happened.

Why! Her mother had died! Her mother, and she'd never truly mourned her. She thought of the last time they'd spoken, on the long-distance phone in the dormitory lobby. ("It's raining here," her mother had said. "But I don't want to waste our three minutes on the weather. Did you get that skirt I mailed you? But I don't want to waste this time on clothes, my goodness . . .") She thought about her dormitory room with its two narrow iron bedsteads and the stuffed white unicorn on her pillow. She had once collected unicorns; she'd loved them. What had happened to her unicorn collection? Her roommate must have got it, or Goodwill had come, or it had simply been discarded. And think what else was gone: her favorite books she'd brought with her to college, her diary, her locket with her only picture of her father in it— a young man, laughing. She ached for all of them. She felt they had just this minute been ripped away from her. She thought of Aunt Mercer with her long-chinned, sharp, witty face, her pale, etched mouth always fighting back a smile. It was such a loss; she was so lost without Aunt Mercer.

"When she and I were girls," Aunt Junie said, dragging herself to her feet, plunking her purse in Emily's lap, "we used to walk to school together. We were the only two girls from the Meeting and we kept to ourselves. Little did I guess I would be marrying her brother, in those days! I thought he was just a pest. We had these plans for leaving here, getting clean away. We were going to join the gypsies. In those days there were gypsies everywhere. Mercer sent off for a book on how to read the cards, but we couldn't make head nor tail of it. Oh, but I still have the cards someplace, and the string puppets from when we planned to put on shows in a painted wagon, and the elocution book from when we wanted to take up acting . . . and of course we had thoughts of becoming reporters. Lady news reporters. But it never came to anything. What if we'd known then how it would turn out? What if someone had told us what we'd *really* do—grow old in Taney, Virginia, and die?"

She sat down then, and retrieved her purse from Emily, and closed her eyes and went back to waiting.

IV

THAT EVENING they had supper at Claire's—casseroles brought over by other members of the Meeting, fruit pies with people's last names adhesive-taped to the tins. No one ate much. Claude chewed a toothpick and watched a small TV on the kitchen counter. He was an educated man, a dentist, but there was something raw-boned and countrified about him, Emily thought, when he gave his startled barks of laughter at a re-run of "The Brady Bunch." Claire toyed with a piece of pie.

Aunt Junie studied her plate and chewed the inside of her lip. Later, when the dishes were done, they moved to the larger TV in the living room. At nine o'clock Aunt Junie said she was tired, and Emily helped her next door to Aunt Mercer's, where both of them planned to sleep.

"I suppose we'll have to sell this place," Aunt Junie said, moving laboriously along the sidewalk. "There isn't much point in keeping up two houses now."

"But where will you live, Aunt Junie?"

"Oh, I'd move in with Claire and Claude," she said.

Emily thought of something dark, like an eye, contracting and getting darker. There once had been three houses, long ago when Emily's father was still alive.

Aunt Junie shuffled ahead of Emily through the front door. A lamp glowed in the hall, casting a circle of yellow light. "You ought to pick out what you want here," Aunt Junie said. "Why, some of it's antiques. Pick out what you'd like to take home."

She leaned on Emily's arm, and they made their way to the living room. Emily turned a light on. Furniture sprang into view, each piece with its sharp shadow—a drop-leaf table with its rear leaf raised against the wall; a wing chair; a desk with slender, curved legs that used to remind Emily of a skinny lady in high-heeled shoes. She could have taken all of this, heaven knows. Offered, in general terms, a desk or a sofa, she would have said, "Oh, thank you. Our apartment does seem bare." A little itch of greed might have started up, in fact. But when she stood in this room and saw the actual objects, she didn't want them. They were too solid, too thickly coated by past events, maybe; she couldn't explain it. She said, "Aunt Junie, sell it. You could surely find some use for the money."

"Take something small, at least," Aunt Junie said. "Emily, honey, you're our only young person. You and your little daughter: you're all we've got to pass things on to."

Emily pictured Gina reading in the wing chair, twining a curl at her temple the way she always did when she was absorbed. (Was she in bed yet? Had she brushed her teeth? Did Leon know she still liked a nightlight, even if she wouldn't say so?) She missed Gina's watchful eyes and her delicate, colorless, chipped-looking mouth—Aunt Mercer's mouth. Emily had never realized. She stopped dead, struck by the thought.

Meanwhile, Aunt Junie traveled around the room, holding her crippled arm with her good hand. "This china slipper, maybe. Or these little brass monkeys: hear no evil, see no evil . . ."

"Aunt Junie, really, we don't lead that kind of life," Emily told her.

"What kind of life? What kind of life must it take just to put a few brass monkeys on your coffee table?"

"We don't *have* a coffee table," Emily said, smiling.

"Take Mercer's, then."

"No. Please."

"Or jewelry, a watch, a brooch. Pin her bar pin on your collar."

"I don't have a collar, either," Emily said. "I only wear these leotards, and they're made of something knit; they can't be pinned."

Aunt Junie turned and looked at her. She said, "Oh, Emily, your mother sent you off so nice. She read up in *Mademoiselle* and made you all those clothes for college. She was worried you'd be dressed wrong. No one *else* in your class went away to school, none of those Baptists, those Haithcocks and Biddixes. She wanted you to go off nice and show them all, come back educated, settle down, marry someone good to you like my Claire did; see my Claire? And she fixed you that sweet paisley dress with the little white collar and cuffs. Now, *that* you could pin a brooch on. She said you could wear it to Meeting. You said, 'Mama, I do not intend to go to Meeting there and all I want is blue jeans. I'm getting out,' you said, 'I'm going to *join*, get to be part of some big group, not going to be different ever again.' What a funny little thing you were! But of course she paid you no mind, and rightly so, as you can see; quite rightly so. Now, I don't know what you call this: leotard? Is that it? Well, I'm sure it's all very stylish in Baltimore, but Emily, honey, it can't hold a candle to that paisley dress your mother made."

"That paisley dress is gone," Emily said. "It's twelve years old. It's cleaning windows now."

Aunt Junie turned her face away. She looked stony and blind with hurt. She groped through the furniture—chair, desk, another chair—and reached the sofa and lowered herself into it.

"But of course I wore it," Emily said, lying.

She pictured it still hanging in her dormitory closet, a ghost passed on to each new freshman class. ("This dress belonged to Miss Emily Cathcart, who vanished one Sunday in April and was never seen again. College authorities are still dragging Sophomore Pond. Her spirit is said to haunt the fountain in front of the library.")

She sat down beside Aunt Junie. She touched her arm and said, "I'm sorry."

"Oh, what for?" Aunt Junie asked brightly.

"If you like, I'll take the bar pin. Or something little, anything, or— I know what: the marionettes."

"The—?"

"String puppets is what you called them. Didn't you say you'd kept them?"

"Yes," said Aunt Junie, without interest. "Someplace or other, I guess."

"I'll take one home with me."

"Yes, I recollect now you said you give some kind of children's parties," Aunt Junie said. She adjusted her paralyzed arm beneath the shelf of her bosom. "It's been a tiring day," she said.

"You want me to help you to bed?"

"No, no, you run along. I can manage."

Emily kissed her on the cheek. Aunt Junie didn't seem to notice.

In the room that Emily and her mother had once shared—such an intertwined, unprivate life that even now she didn't feel truly alone here—she untied her skirt and stepped out of her shoes. Her own younger face, formless, smiled from a silver frame on the bureau. She switched off the light, folded back the spread, and climbed into bed. The sheets were so cold they felt damp. She hugged herself and clenched her chattering teeth and watched the same old squares of moonlight on the floor. Aunt Junie, meanwhile, seemed to be moving around in some other part of the house. Drawers slid open, latches clicked. Emily thought she heard the rafters creak in the attic. Oh, this leaden, lumbering world of old people! She slid away into a patchwork kind of sleep. Her mother seemed to be rearranging the bedroom. "Let's see, now, if the chair were here, the table here, if we were to put the bed beneath the window . . ." Emily sat up once to pull the spread back over her shoulders for warmth. An owl was hooting in the trees. This time when she slept, it was like plummeting into someplace bottomless.

She woke and found the room filled with a pearly gray, pre-dawn light. She got up, staggering slightly, and reached for her skirt and tied it around her. She put on her shoes and went out to the hall, which was darker. From Aunt Junie's room a snoring noise came. Oh, Lord, they would probably all sleep for hours yet. She felt her way to the living room to find her purse, where she'd stashed a comb and toothbrush. It was on the coffee table. Something knobby poked from it. She turned the lamp on, blinked, and lifted out an ancient female marionette in a calico dress.

The head and hands were plaster, crudely colored. She had a large, faded mouth and two dim circles of rouge. Her black thread hair was in braids. Her tangled strings were tied to a single-cross control bar, just like the one that Emily had invented. Or maybe (it began to seem) she had not invented it after all, but had remembered it from her childhood. Though she couldn't recall ever having been shown this little creature. Maybe it was something that was passed in the dark through the generations—the very thought of giving puppet shows, even. And here she imagined she'd come so far, lived such a different existence! She saw her Red Riding Hood scene in a whole new light now, as something crippled. She held the marionette by its snarl of strings. The blue eyes stared at her flatly. The plaster hands—one finger chipped—were suspended in a gracious, stiff position.

Out in the kitchen a clock ticked with a muffled sound, as if buried. There was barely enough room to walk between chairs and occasional tables. Everything was so stuffed and smothering. She set the marionette on the sofa and picked up her purse and left the room. Fresh air, she thought, might clear her head. She opened the door and stepped out on the porch, where instantly the cold pierced all she wore. But still the stuffy feeling didn't leave her. She descended the steps. She went out to the street and stood shivering and looking at the car—Leon's car, compact and gleaming. After a moment she opened the door and slid inside and took a deep breath of its leathery smell. Then she found her keys in her purse. Then she switched the engine on, but not the headlights, and slipped away.

In Baltimore it was a crowded, clamorous morning in the middle of the week, with the sun flashing off a sea of metal and everyone honking and darting in and out of lanes. Emily turned down Crosswell Street and parked somewhere, anywhere, she didn't know. She flew from the car and ran inside the building and up the stairs, and then couldn't find the proper key and was jingling her way through a ring of them when Leon opened the door. He stood there looking down at her, holding a book in one hand, and threw her arms around him and pressed her face to his chest. "Emily, love," he said. "Emily, is something wrong?" She only shook her head, and hung on tight.

V

ALMOST DAILY she had letters from Morgan, whether or not he came in person. *Dear Emily, Am enclosing this Sears ad, you really need a pipe wrench and Sears are better than any Cullen Hardware sells . . .* For he had taken over the care of their apartment, moving in on the disrepair that lurked in all its corners; he clanked blithely among the mysteries beneath the kitchen sink. *Dear Emily, Came across a hint last night that just might solve that trouble with your toaster. Simply cut a piece of heavy paper, say a matchbook cover, 1" × 1" . . .*

He was the Merediths' own personal consumer advocate, composing disgusted notes to Radio Shack on his tinny, old-fashioned typewriter, storming into auto-repair shops—solving whatever little discontent Emily mentioned in passing. She began to rely on him. Sometimes she said, "Oh, I really shouldn't ask you to do this—" but he would say, "Why not? Who would you rather ask instead? Ah, don't hurt my feelings, Emily."

Once she had a problem with her tape recorder, the portable recorder she'd bought to use in their shows. Morgan didn't happen to be around, and while Emily fiddled with the buttons she caught herself wondering, irritably, where *was* he? How could he leave her alone like this, to cope without him when he'd led her to depend on him? She grabbed up the recorder and ran the several blocks to Cullen Hardware. She

arrived breathless; she slapped the recorder on the counter between
Morgan and a customer. "Listen," she said, jabbing a button. In blew
the trumpet for "The Brementown Musicians"—but blurred and bleary,
with some kind of vibration in the speaker. The customer stepped back,
looking startled. Morgan sat on his high wooden stool and nodded
thoughtfully. "It's driving me crazy!" Emily told him, switching it off.
"And if you think it sounds bad now, you ought to hear it when the
volume's up, in the middle of a show. You can't tell if it's a trumpet
or a foghorn."

Morgan went to a revolving rack for a paintbrush, and he came back
and took the recorder onto his lap and slowly, tenderly, brushed the
plastic grooves that encased the speaker. Grains of something white
flew out. "Sugar, perhaps. Or sand," he said. "Hmm." He pressed the
button and listened again. The trumpet sound was clear and pure. He
gave the machine back to Emily and returned to adding up the customer's purchases.

Like a household elf, he left behind him miraculously mended electrical cords, smooth-gliding windows, dripless faucets, and toilet tanks
hung with clever arrangements of coat-hanger wire to keep the water
from running. "It must be wonderful," Emily told Bonny, "to have him
with you all the time, fixing things," but Bonny just looked blank and
said, "Who, Morgan?"

Well, Bonny had her mind on other matters. She was helping one
of her daughters through a difficult pregnancy. The baby was due in
February but kept threatening to arrive now, in early November; the
daughter had come home to lie flat on her back for the next three
months. It was all Bonny could talk about. "When she sits up just a
little, to straighten a pillow," she said, "I have this picture of the baby
falling, just tumbling out of her like a penny out of a piggy-bank, you
know? I say, 'Lizzie, honey, lie down this instant, please.' It's turning
around my view of things. I used to think of pregnancy as getting
something ready, growing something to finish it; now all I think of is
holding something back that is going to come regardless. And Morgan!
Well, you know Morgan. Always off somewhere, he really has no
comprehension . . . At night he comes home and reads her stories
from the operas. He's taken up an interest in the opera, has he told
you? Such a crazy man . . . 'Don Giovanni encounters a statue and
invites it home to supper,' he reads. 'Sounds like something *you* would
do,' I tell him. He reads on. I believe he thinks that Liz is still a child,
in need of bedtime stories; or maybe he just likes an excuse to read
them himself—but for day-to-day things! For bringing trays to her and
emptying bedpans!"

Emily nodded gravely. She sympathized with Bonny; he must be
exasperating to live with. But, after all, it wasn't Emily who had to
live with him.

She recalled how odd he'd seemed when they first knew him—his hats and costumes, his pedantic, elderly style of speech. Now he seemed . . . not ordinary, exactly, but understandable. She was beginning to want to believe his assumption that events don't necessarily have a reason behind them. Last month she and Leon were sitting with him in Eunola's Restaurant when Morgan glanced out the window and said, "How funny, there's Lamont. I thought he was dead." He didn't act very surprised. "That happens more and more often," he said cheerfully. "I often think I see, for instance, my mother's father, Grandfather Brindle, walking down the street, and he's been dead for forty years. I tell myself he might not really have died at all—just got tired of his old existence and left to start a new one without us. Who's to say it couldn't happen? Someplace there may be a whole little settlement—even a town, perhaps—full of people who supposedly died but really didn't. Have you thought of that?"

Then Leon gave a tired hiss, the way he did when Emily said something silly. Well, why shouldn't there be such a town? What was so impossible about it? Emily sat straighter, and looked guiltily into her lap. "The world is a peculiar place," Morgan said. "Tottery old ladies, people you wouldn't trust to navigate a grocery cart, are heading two-ton cars in your direction at speeds of seventy miles per hour. Our lives depend on total strangers. So much lacks logic, or a proper sequence."

"Jesus," said Leon.

But Emily felt encouraged; everything looked brighter. (This was shortly after she'd come back from Taney. Morgan's kind of spaciousness sounded wonderful to her.) She smiled at him. He smiled back. He was wearing a furry Russian hat, now that the weather had turned. It sat on his head like a bear cub. He leaned across the table to Leon and told him, "Often I fall into despair. You may find that funny. I seem to be one of those people whose gloominess is comical. But to me it's very serious. I think, in ten thousand years, what will all this amount to? Our planet will have vanished by then. What's the point? I think, and I board the wrong bus. But when I'm happy, it's for no clearer reason. I imagine that I'm being very witty, I have everyone on my side, but probably that's not the case at all."

Leon let out his breath and watched the waitress refilling their cups.

"Oh, I'm annoying you," Morgan said.

"No, you're not," Emily told him.

"Somehow, it appears I am. Leon? Am I annoying you?"

"Not at all," Leon said grimly.

"I tend to think," Morgan said, "that nothing real has ever happened to me, but when I look back I see that I'm wrong. My father died, I married, my wife and I raised seven human beings. My daughters had the usual number of accidents and tragedies; they grew up and married and gave birth, and some divorced. My sister has undergone *two* divorces, or terminations of marriage, at least, and my mother is aging and her memory isn't what it ought to be . . . but somehow it's as if this were all a story, just something that happened to somebody else. It's as if I'm watching from outside, mildly curious, thinking, So this is what kind of life it is, eh? You would suppose it wasn't really mine. You would suppose I'd planned on having other chances—second and third tries, the best two out of three. I can't seem to take it all seriously."

"Well, I for one have work to do," Leon said, rising.

But Emily told Morgan, "I know what you mean."

I *wish* I knew, was what she should have said.

His manners were atrocious (she often thought); he smoked too much and suffered from a chronic cough that would surely be the death of him, ate too many sweets (and exposed a garble of black fillings whenever he opened his mouth), scattered ashes down his front, chewed his cuticles, picked his teeth, meddled with his beard, fidgeted, paced, scratched his stomach, hummed distractingly whenever it was someone else's turn to speak; he was not a temperate person. He wore rich men's hand-me-downs, stained and crumpled and poorly kept, and over them an olive-drab, bunchy nylon parka, its hood trimmed with something matted that might be monkey fur. He smelled permanently of stale tobacco. When he wore glasses, they were so fingerprinted and greasy you couldn't read his eyes. He was excitable and unpredictable, sometimes nearly manic, and while it was kind of him to manage their affairs, the fact was that he could often become . . . well, presumptuous was the word—pushy, managerial, bending the Merediths to his conception of them, which was not remotely rooted in reality, taking too much for granted, assuming what he should not have assumed. He talked too much and too erratically, or grew stuffy and bored them with lengthy accounts of human-interest items from the paper, grandchildren's clever remarks, and *Consumer Reports* ratings; while at moments when he should have been sociable—when the Merediths had other guests, at their Halloween party, for instance—he would as likely as not clam up completely and stand around in some corner with his hands jammed deep in his pockets and a glum expression on his face. And *his* parties! Well, the less said, the better. Combining garbage men with philosophy professors, seating small children next to priests with hearing aids . . .

But once, passing a bookstore, Emily happened to notice a blown-up photo of the first successful powered flight, and the sight of Wilbur Wright poised on the sand at Kitty Hawk—capped and suited, strangely stylish, suspended forever in that tense, elated, ready position—reminded her for some reason of Morgan, and she suddenly felt that she had never given him full credit. And another time, when she switched on a cassette tape to see if it were the music for "Hansel and Gretel," she found that Morgan must have been playing with it, for his gruff, bearded voice leaped forth, disguised in a German accent. "Nu? Vhere is de button?" he said, and then she heard a Japanese "Ah so!" and two clicks, where he must have pressed the button off and on again. "Tum, te-tum," he said, singing tunelessly, rustling cellophane. There was the sound of a match being struck. He blew a long pull of air. "Naughty boy, Pinocchio!" he said in a chirping voice. "I see you've been untruthful again. Your nose has grown seven inches!" Then he gave his smoker's laugh, breathy and wheezing, "Heh, heh," descending into a cough. But Emily didn't laugh with him. She listened intently, with her forehead creased. She bent very close to the machine, unsmiling, trying to figure him out.

VI

SHE AND LEON were invited to the Percy School's Thanksgiving Festival, where they'd never been before. She wasn't sure what show they should put on. "Rapunzel"? "Thumbelina"? Late one afternoon, just a few days before the Festival, she took Rapunzel from her muslin bag and propped her on the kitchen table. Rapunzel had not been used for a while and had an unkempt, neglected look. Her long, long braids had grown frazzled. "I suppose I should make her another wig," Emily told Gina. Gina was doing her homework; all she said was, "Mmm."

But then Leon came in and said, "Rapunzel? What's she doing here?"

"I thought we'd take her to the Festival."

"Last night you said we'd do 'Sleeping Beauty.'"

"I did?"

"I suggested 'Sleeping Beauty' and you said that would be fine."

"How could I have?" Emily asked. "We can't give 'Sleeping Beauty.' There are thirteen fairies. Not even counting the king, the queen, the princess . . ."

"I said, 'Emily, why not let's do something different for a change?' and you said, 'All right, Leon—'"

"But never 'Sleeping Beauty,'" Emily said.

"I said, 'How about "Sleeping Beauty"?' and you said, 'All right, Leon.'"

He was making it up. Except that Leon never made things up. There was no way Emily could have held that conversation, not even half asleep. Why, if you counted the old woman at the spinning wheel, Prince Charming . . . It was out of the question. They couldn't begin to handle a cast of that size. She considered the possibility that he had discussed the subject with someone else, mistakenly. They always seemed to miss connections these days. They started every morning so courteous, so hopeful, but deteriorated rapidly and ended up, at night, sleeping with their backs to each other on the outermost edges of the bed.

She noticed that two vertical grooves had started to appear in Leon's cheeks. They were not so much lines as hollows, such as you would see in a man who habitually kept his jaw set too far forward.

Then he said, "How about taking Gina? *She* could work some of the fairies."

"But it's on Wednesday afternoon," Emily said. "Gina would still be in school."

"Oh, I don't mind missing school," Gina said.

Emily suspected she was only trying to keep peace. Gina loved school. "Well, *I* mind," Emily told her.

"Oh, Mama."

"And thirteen fairies! Even if we owned that many, how would just one more pair of hands help run them all?"

"We could bring them on a few at a time, maybe," Leon said.

Emily started pacing around the table. Gina and Leon watched her. Gina chewed a pencil and swung her feet, but Leon stayed motionless. Then Emily wheeled on him and said, "Are you doing this on purpose?"

"I beg your pardon?"

"I mean, is this supposed to prove something, Leon? Are you just trying to show me I'm . . . oh, set in my ways? You want me to say I refuse to give a play with eighteen puppets in it, and my daughter playing hooky, and that will mean I'm rigid, narrow-minded?"

"All I know is, I said, 'How about "Sleeping Beauty," Emily—' "

"You never did."

Leon closed his mouth, shrugged, and walked out of the room. Emily looked over at Gina, who was watching, but Gina abruptly stopped chewing her pencil and buried herself in her homework.

Then Emily took her coat from the hook in the hall and left the apartment, jabbing her arms into her sleeves as she stalked down the stairs. It was late enough so the smell of different suppers had begun to fill the stairwell: cabbage, green peppers, oil—stifling smells. Crafts Unlimited was already dark and dead-looking. She slammed out into the street. Twilight had drained the color from the buildings. An old woman paused on the corner to set down all her bundles and rearrange them. Emily swerved around her, keeping her fists knotted in her coat pockets. She crossed against a red light and walked very fast.

He was impossible. There was no hope for either of them. She had locked herself in permanently with someone she couldn't bear.

She passed a boy and girl who were standing in the center of the sidewalk, holding hands, the girl pivoting on her heels and giving the boy a shy smile. It was heartbreaking. She would have stopped to set them straight, but of course they wouldn't believe her; they imagined they were going to do everything differently. She met a child, some friend of Gina's. "Hello, Mrs. Meredith." "Hello, um, Polly," she said—motherly, matronly, indistinguishable from any other woman.

Sometimes she thought the trouble was, she and Leon were too well acquainted. The most innocent remark could call up such a string of associations, so many past slights and insults never quite settled or forgotten, merely smoothed over. They could no longer have a single uncomplicated feeling about each other.

Then she heard footsteps behind her. They kept coming. She slowed, and the corners of her mouth started turning up without her say-so, but when she looked back it was no one she knew—a man on his way to someplace in a hurry. He kept his face buried in his collar. She let him pass her. Then she looked back again. But no matter how long she stood watching, the sidewalk was empty.

She took a right on Meller Street and walked with more purpose. She crossed another street and turned left. Now there was a stream of people bundled up, intent, rushing home to supper. It occurred to her that Cullen Hardware might be closed by now. She slowed, frowning. But no, its windows were still lit with that faded light that always seemed filmed by dust. She pushed through the door. Butkins was bent over a sheet of paper at the counter. "Has Morgan gone home?" she asked him.

Butkins straightened and passed a hand across his high forehead. "Oh, Mrs. Meredith," he said. (He was so determinedly formal, though she'd known him for years.) "No, he's up in his office," he said.

She headed down an aisle of snow shovels and sidewalk salt, and climbed the steps at the rear. Every board whined beneath her feet. On the landing, Morgan's office seemed unusually still—no sawing, hammering, drilling, no flurry of wood chips. Morgan was lying on the maroon plush sofa. He was hatless, for once, and wore a satin-lapeled smoking jacket that very nearly matched the sofa. His hair looked flat and thin. His face was a pale glimmer in the dusk. "Morgan? Are you sick?" Emily asked.

"I have a cold," he said.

"Oh, just a cold," she said, relieved. She took off her coat and laid it on the desk.

"Just a cold! How can you say that?" he asked her. His energy seemed to be returning. He sat up, indignant. "Do you have any idea how I feel? My head is like a beachball. This morning I had a temperature of ninety-nine point nine, and last night it was a hundred and one. I lay awake all night, and had fever dreams."

"You can't do both," Emily said. "Lie awake, and dream as well."

"Why not?" he asked her.

He always had to throw his whole self into things—even into illness. His office looked like a hospital room. A Merck Manual lay open on the filing cabinet, and his desk was a jumble of medicines and cloudy

drinking glasses. On the floor beside the couch were a bottle of cough
syrup, a sticky teaspoon, and a cardboard box spilling papers. She bent
to pick up one of the papers. It was a photograph of the oldest,
homeliest washing machine she'd ever laid eyes on, the kind with a
wringer attached. *Model 504A,* she read, *can easily be connected to any
existing . . .* She replaced the paper and sat down in the swivel chair
at the desk. Morgan sneezed.

"Maybe you ought to be home in bed," she told him.

"I can't rest at home. It's a madhouse there. Liz is still flat on her
back trying to hang on to that baby. She gets the wicker breakfast tray;
I end up with the tin meat platter. And people have already started
arriving for Thanksgiving."

Butkins called something. Morgan said, "Eh?"

"I'll be going now, Mr. Gower."

"He ought to know I can't hear a thing with this cold," Morgan told
Emily.

"He says he's going," Emily said. "Do you want me to help lock
up?"

"Oh, thank you. It's true that I'm not myself."

But he went on sitting there, blotting his nose with a handkerchief.
Emily heard the front door shutting behind Butkins.

"When Butkins leaves the store," Morgan said, "I sometimes wonder
if he dematerializes. Ever thought of that?"

She smiled. He watched her soberly, not smiling himself. "What's
wrong?" he asked.

"What? Nothing," Emily said.

"The tip of your nose is white."

"It's nothing."

"Don't lie to me," he said. "I've known you nine years. When the
tip of your nose is white, something's wrong. It's Leon, I suppose."

"He thinks I'm narrow-minded," Emily said.

Morgan sneezed again.

"He thinks I'm rigid, but *he's* the one. He never tries out for plays
now, and that gospel-troupe man is still after us but Leon won't even
talk to him. I'm getting claustrophobic. I can't drive after dark any
more because the space is too small—you know, the lighted space the
car travels in. I think I must be going crazy from irritation, just from
little petty nameless irritations. Then he says that I'm the one who's
narrow."

Morgan shook a cigarette from an unfamiliar green pack. "See? We'd
better elope," he said.

"Do you think you ought to be smoking?"

"Oh, these are all right. They're menthol."

He lit up and started coughing. He stumbled to his feet, as if reaching
for more air, and wandered around the office, coughing and thumping

his chest. Between gasps, he said, "Emily, you know I'm always here
for you."

"You want some Robitussin, Morgan?"

He shook his head, gave a final cough, and settled on his desk top.
Medicine bottles clinked all around him. Emily wheeled her chair back
slightly to allow him more room. His socks, she saw, were translucent
black silk, and he wore pointy black patent-leather slippers that reminded her of Fred Astaire. He was sitting on her coat, rumpling it,
but she decided not to point that out.

"I know you must find me laughable," he told her.

"Oh, well, I wouldn't say *laughable*, really—"

"But I'm serious," he said. "Let's stop fooling, Emily. I love you."

He slid off his desk, disentangling himself with difficulty from her
coat, which had somehow twisted itself around one of his legs. Emily
stood up. (What did he have in mind?) He was, after all, a grown man,
real, lean-bodied. The hunger with which he drew on his cigarette
caused her to step behind her chair. But he went on past her. He was
only pacing. He walked to the railing, looked over the darkened store
below him, and walked back.

"Of course," he said, "I don't intend any harm to your marriage. I
admire your marriage very much. I mean, in a sense, I love Leon as
well, and Gina; the unit as a whole, in fact . . . Who *is* it I love? But
you, Emily . . ."

He flicked his ashes onto the floor. "I am fifty-one years old," he
said. "You're what, twenty-nine or thirty. I could easily be your father.
What a joke, eh? I must look ridiculous."

Instead he looked sad and kind, and also exhausted. Emily took a
step in his direction. He circled her, musing. "I think of you as an
illness," he said. "Something recurrent, like malaria. I push the thought
of you down, you see. Whole weeks go by . . . I imagine that I'm
somehow deeper when I manage to overcome it. I feel stronger and
wiser. I take some pleasure, then, in doing what I'm supposed to do.
I carry the garbage out; I arrive at work on time . . ."

She touched his arm. He dodged her and went on pacing, head
lowered, puffing clouds of smoke.

"I persuade myself," he said, "that there is some virtue in the trivial,
the commonplace. Ha! What a notion. I think of those things on TV,
those man-in-the-street things where the ordinary triumphs. They stop
some ordinary person and ask if he can sing a song, recite a poem
. . . they stop a motorcycle gang. I've seen this! Black-leather motorcycle
gang and ask, 'Can you sing all the words to "Some Enchanted Evening"?' And up these fellows start, dead serious, trying hard—I mean,
fellows you would never expect had *heard* of 'Some Enchanted Evening.'
They stand there with their arms around each other, switchblades poking

out of their pockets, brass knuckles in their blue jeans, earnestly, sweetly singing . . ."

He'd forgotten all about her. He was off on this track of his own, tearing back and forth across his office. Emily sat down on the couch and looked around her. There was a bulletin board on the wall above the filing cabinet, and it was covered with clippings and miscellaneous objects. An Adlai Stevenson button, a frowsy red feather, a snapshot of a bride, a blue silk rose . . . She imagined Morgan rushing in with them, the spoils of some mysterious, private war, and tacking them up, and chortling, and rushing out again. She was struck, all at once, by his separateness. He was absolutely unrelated to her. She would never really understand the smallest part of him.

"They stop this fat old lady," he was saying. "A mess! A disaster. Gray and puffy like some failed pastry, and layers of clothes that seem to have melted together. 'Can you sing "June Is Bustin' Out All Over"?' they ask, and she says, 'Certainly,' and starts right up, so obliging, with this shiny grin, and ends with her arms spread and this little stamp-stamp finish—"

He bit down on his cigarette and stopped his pacing long enough to demonstrate—both hands outflung, one foot poised to stamp. "*Just . . . because . . . it's* JUNE!" he sang, and he stamped his foot.

"I love you too," she told him.

"JUNE!" he sang.

He paused. He took the cigarette from his mouth.

"Eh?" he said.

She smiled up at him.

He tugged his beard. He shot her a sidelong glance from under his eyebrows, and then he dropped his cigarette and slowly, meditatively ground it out with his heel. When he sat on the edge of the couch, he still seemed to be thinking something over. When he bent to kiss her, he gave off a kind of shaggy warmth, like some furred animal, and he smelled of ashes and Mentholatum.

1977

I

MORGAN'S DAUGHTER Liz finally, finally had her baby, on the coldest night in the coldest February anyone could remember. It was Morgan who had to get up and drive her to the hospital. Then of course her husband, Chester, arrived from Tennessee, and when Liz was released from the hospital, she and Chester and the baby stayed on in her old room a few days till Liz was strong enough to travel. Meanwhile the house filled further, like something flooding upward from the basement. Amy and Jean kept stopping by with their children, and the twins drifted in from Charlottesville, and Molly and her family from New York, and by the time Kate arrived with her boyfriend, there was nowhere to put the boyfriend but the storeroom on the third floor, underneath the eaves. This was on a weekend. They'd be gone by Monday, Morgan reminded himself. He loved them all, he was crazy about them, but life was becoming a little difficult. The daughters who hadn't got along in the past didn't get along any better now. The new baby appeared to be the colicky type. And there was never any time to see Emily.

"If we feed the children in the kitchen," Bonny said, counting on her fingers, "that makes sixteen grownups in the dining room, or fifteen if Lizzie wants a tray in bed, but then the mothers would have to keep running out to check on them, so maybe we should feed the children early. But then the children would be tearing around like wild things while we were trying to eat, and I just remembered, Liz said her old college roommate was coming at seven-thirty, so we can't eat too late, or maybe she meant she was coming for supper; do you think so? and in that case we'd be *seven*teen at table, assuming Liz does not want a tray in bed, and naturally she wouldn't if her roommate's eating downstairs, but we only have service for sixteen; so we'll have to divide it up, say you and me and Brindle and your mother in the first shift and then the girls and their husbands and . . . oh, dear, David is Jewish, I think. Is it all right I'm serving ham?"

"Who's David?" Morgan asked.

"Katie's boyfriend, Morgan. Pay attention. This is really very simple."

Then after supper one of the grandsons either broke a toe or didn't break a toe, no one could be sure, though everyone agreed that broken toes required no splints anyhow, so there wasn't much point in troubling a doctor outside office hours. Actually, Morgan would not have minded driving the boy to the hospital, which by now he could have found in his sleep. He needed air. The living room was a sea of bodies— people reading, knitting, wrestling, quarreling, playing board games, poking the fire, lolling around, yawning, discussing politics. The shades had not been drawn, and the darkness pressing in made the house seem even murkier. Louisa's black Labrador, Harry, had chewed a Jiffy bag into little gray flecks all over the carpet.

Morgan went upstairs to his bedroom, but two toddler girls were standing at the bureau trying on Bonny's lipstick. "Out! Out!" he shouted. They lifted their smeared faces to him like tiny, elderly drunks, but they didn't obey. He left, slamming the door behind him. In the hall he was hit by the lingering smell of ham, which made him feel fat. He heard the baby fussing in an edgy voice that clawed at the small of his back. "It's too much," he told this what's-his-name, this David, a thin, studious young man who was just descending the third-floor stairs with a paperback book in his hand. David was too polite to say anything, but there was something about the way he fell in with Morgan, going down the next flight of stairs, that made Morgan feel he sympathized.

Bonny was walking the baby in the entrance hall, which seemed to be the only space left. "Could you take Pammy for a while?" she asked.

"Pammy. Ah. The baby."

He didn't want her, but Bonny looked stretched and gray with fatigue. He accepted the baby in a small, warm, wilted clump. No doubt she would spit all over the shoulder of his pinstriped, head-of-the-family suit that he always wore for these occasions. "Bonny, I think we may have carried things too far, this visit," he said.

"Now, Morgan, you always tell me that. Then the next day after they leave you wander through the house like a dog that's lost its puppies."

"Yes, but every visit there are more, you see," he said, "and they seem to hang around for a longer spell of time."

Molly came through from the kitchen, carrying a bucket. "Christopher's thrown up," she said.

"How does the world strike you so far?" Morgan asked the baby.

The doorbell rang. Bonny said, "Who can that be?"

"It must be Liz's roommate."

"Morgan, honestly. Liz's roommate is sitting in the living room."

"She is?"

"She just had supper with us, Morgan."

Morgan opened the door, one-handed. Emily stood waiting. She landed in his vision like a pale, starry flash of light. He felt everything around him lift and brighten. "Oh," he told her. She smiled at him. She was holding a package tied with pink yarn. (In some illogical way, it seemed the gift was for him. It seemed *she* was the gift.)

Then Bonny said, "Emily!" and stepped forward to kiss her. Emily looked at Morgan over Bonny's shoulder. Grave as a child, she drew away and turned to him and patted the baby's bare foot.

"She's beautiful," she said.

She was gazing into his eyes.

The baby had been cranking up to cry again, but gave a sudden hiccup and fell silent—taken aback, maybe, by the icy wind from the door, or by the touch of Emily's cold hand. "Come on inside," Bonny told Emily. "You must be frozen! Did you drive? Have you ever seen such weather?"

She led Emily into the living room. Morgan followed. He felt that

Emily was the single point of stillness. Everyone milled around her while she stood upright at the center. There was something wonderfully prim about the way she offered her package to Liz, as if she weren't sure it would be accepted. But Liz was already exclaiming as she took it. (Motherhood had enlarged her, fuzzed her edges; she was a flurry of bathrobe and milky smells.) And of course she loved the lamb puppet inside. Everyone had to pass it around and try to work it. The lamb's quilted face was nuzzled to the baby's cheek. The baby started and batted the air with both fists. "Offer Emily a drink, will you?" Bonny told Morgan.

Morgan stooped to lay the baby in Louisa's lap. Louisa took her uncertainly, one gnarled hand still clutching a glass of port. "What *is* this?" she asked.

"It's a baby, Mother."

"Is it mine?"

He reconsidered, took the baby back, and gave her to Brindle. Brindle was reading a mail-order catalog and passed her on to a twin. Throughout all this the baby looked better entertained than she had the whole day.

"She's the image of Liz," Emily said. "Isn't she? She's just like her. But with Chester's eyes."

"Emily, honey, where's Leon?" Bonny asked. "And where's Gina? Didn't she want to see the baby?"

"She has a science report due Monday. She's been working on it all weekend."

Morgan imagined the hush in their apartment: the bare, clean living room, Gina concentrating on a single book.

"But Leon, at least," Bonny said. "You could have brought Leon."

"He wanted to watch this program on TV. If I waited till it was finished, the baby would have gone to bed, I figured."

Two years ago the Merediths had bought a small television set. Morgan tended to forget that. Every time Emily referred to it, he mentally blinked; he felt himself having to make some disruptive inner adjustment. He went to the sideboard and poured her a glass of sherry—the only drink she'd ever been known to ask for. When he handed it to her, she was just slipping out of her coat. "Let me hang that up," he told her.

"Oh, I'll keep it. I can only stay a minute."

She sat on the couch, talking to Bonny and Liz, and Morgan harumphed his way around the living room. He stepped over a Monopoly game, threw another log on the fire. He wound the clock on the mantel. He squatted, grunting, and picked up the discarded paper from Emily's gift and folded it carefully for future use. She must have decorated the paper herself, or bought it from Crafts Unlimited. It was patterned with a block print of little bells. He loved her old-time, small-town manners—

her prompt gifts and cards and thank-you notes, her Christmas fruitcake, her unfailing observance of every official occasion. She was the most proper person he had ever met. (A while back, she had angled a night away from home—their one whole night together. They were so tired of snatched moments. She'd told Leon she was going to Virginia. She'd met Morgan at the Patrician Hotel and insisted on signing her true name in the register—her name and address and telephone number, all written with the pen held perpendicular to the page in a stiff, quaint manner that delighted him. He'd asked later, why not a false name? It wouldn't be right, she had said.)

"I parked the car at the corner," she was telling Bonny, "and just as I got out I saw this little family. A man, a woman, two children. One of the children had fallen, he was crying, and I slowed down to check on him; you know how it is when you hear a child cry. Well, it was only a scrape or something, a scabby knee. But evidently the father was blind. He didn't seem to know what had happened. He just kept saying, 'What is it, Dorothy? Dorothy, what is it? Dorothy, what's gone wrong?' and Dorothy wouldn't answer. She picked up the child that was crying and then she got the older one, really much too big a child to carry, hoisted on her other hip, and she was so swaddled around with winter coats and scarves and also she had a big purse and some huge kind of tote bag, I don't know, groceries or things; it was hard to tell by the streetlight. She was *staggering*, just tottering along. And he was still asking, 'What is it?' and feeling all around him, frantic. She said, 'Look, you wait here, I've got to go bring the car. Nicholas can't walk.' He said, '*Why* can't he walk? For God's sake, what's happened?' and she got all exasperated and said, 'Just wait, I tell you; keep calm. Stay right here and I'll be back. Jason, you weigh a ton. Hang on to Mommy, Nicholas . . .' I wanted to tell the man, 'It's a scrape. It's nothing.' I wanted to tell the woman, 'Why bring the car? Why are you doing this? Or if you do have to bring the car, why not leave the children with him, and the bags and things? He can manage those. Why wade off like that, *why?* Why make things, oh, so ingrown, so twisted?' "

"Oh, when you see how other people have such handicaps," Bonny said, "you have to thank your stars our own lives are so easy. Don't you?"

She'd missed the point. So had everyone else, Morgan supposed. They went on rattling their dice, clicking their needles. A log fell in the fire, sending out a shower of sparks. The dog stirred and half-heartedly thumped his tail. Brindle turned the pages of her catalog, with its garish, blurred illustrations. *Amazing Soap Cradle!* Morgan read. *Remarkable Perma-Tweezers! Astounding Hair Trap Saves Costly Repair Bills!* He lifted his eyes and met Emily's. She looked beautifully remote to him, so distinct from everyone else that she seemed smaller even than the children.

Then when she had to go, it was Bonny who told Morgan to walk her to the car. Operating on her own misguided version of events, Bonny said, "Now, make sure she locks her doors, Morgan. You heard what peculiar people are running around loose." Emily let Morgan help her into her coat, and she waved good night to the others and kissed Bonny on the cheek. "Come back on a weekday," Bonny said. "Have lunch with me one day while Gina's at school. It's been so long since we've had lunch! What's become of you?" Emily didn't answer that.

She and Morgan went down the front steps, out to the street. It was such a cold night that there was something flinty about the air, and Morgan's heels rang as if on metal. He was bundled into his parka, with the hood up; but Emily's coat didn't look warm and, although she wore black tights, her papery little shoes were probably no protection at all. He took her hand. She had tiny, precise knuckles and a cluster of chilly fingers. "Tomorrow's Sunday," he said. "I guess you can't get away."

"No, I guess not."

"Maybe Monday."

"Maybe."

"Come out at suppertime, to buy milk or something. I'll stay on late at the store."

"But I've done that so often."

"He hasn't said anything, has he?"

"No."

They dropped hands, separated by that "he"—a word that pointed out their furtiveness. In private, they no longer mentioned Leon. Morgan could not picture him without an inner twinge of sorrow and remorse. It seemed he liked Leon even better than before, and appreciated more fully the sober dignity of his high-cheekboned face, which was—come to think of it—admirably stoical, like an American Indian's. (Leon had a way of looking at Morgan, lately, with his long black eyes expressionless, lusterless, impassive.) But with Bonny, strangely enough, Morgan felt no guilt at all. He had sealed her off in another compartment. Coming home to her, he would be as pleased as ever by her easy chuckle and her heavy breasts and the absentminded hugs she gave him as she slid past him in the choked and crowded corridors of their house.

He and Emily reached her car. She started into the street, to the driver's side, but he stopped her and drew her in to him. She smelled clear and fresh, like snow, and there was sherry on her breath. He kissed the curve of her jaw, just below one earlobe. "Morgan," she whispered, "someone will see." (She had an exaggerated fear of rumor; she imagined that people were more observant than they really were.)

He felt he was trying to fill up on her. He kissed her mouth—a dry, sharp, wrinkled mouth, oddly touching—and unbuttoned her coat to slip his hands inside and circle her. Her body was so thin and pliant that it always seemed he was missing something, leaving part of it behind. "Stay longer," he said in her ear.

"I can't," she said, but she held on for a moment, and then she pulled away and ran to climb into her car. The headlights lit up. The engine coughed and started. Morgan stood watching after her, pinching his lower lip between his fingers and thinking of what he should have said: Come even if it's Sunday. Promise you'll come Monday. Why don't you wear gloves? Mornings, now, when I wake up, I have this springy, hopeful feeling, and I see that everything is worth it, after all.

II

As SOON as the weather thawed, Emily started jogging. It was a strange thing for her to do, Morgan thought—not really her type of activity. She bought a pair of clumsy yellow running shoes and a pedometer that she strapped to her waist with an old leather belt of Leon's. Several times, when Morgan was on his way to see her, he caught sight of her approaching at the other end of the block, wearing her unrunner-like skirt from which her legs flew out like sticks. Her yellow feet seemed the biggest part of her. She always looked as if she just *happened* to be running—as if she had a bus to catch or had suddenly remembered a pot left boiling on the stove. Maybe it was her tripping gait, which lacked seriousness. Maybe it was the flip and swing of her skirt. As she drew near, she would call out, not breaking stride, "Be with you in a minute! Once more around the block!" But when she stopped, finally, her pedometer would surprise him: four miles. Four and a half miles. Five. Always pressing her limits.

Once Morgan asked what she was running for.

"I just am," she told him.

"I mean, your heart? Your figure? Your circulation? Are you training for a marathon?"

"I'm just running," she said.

"But why push yourself?"

"I'm not pushing myself."

She was, though. After a run, there was something intense about her. She'd be glossy with sweat, strung up, a bundle of wiry muscles, vibrating. Her hair, loosened, flew out in an electric spray, each strand as crinkled as her amber-colored, crinkly hairpins. She was so different from other women that Morgan didn't know quite how to go about her. He was baffled and moved and fascinated, and he loved to slide his fingers down the two new, tight cords behind each of her knees.

He couldn't imagine what it felt like to be Emily.

In the hardware store one afternoon he closed his eyes and said, "Tell me what you see. Be my seeing eye." She said, "A desk. A filing cabinet. A couch." Then she seemed to give up. He opened his eyes and found her looking helpless, wondering what he wanted of her. But that was all he wanted: her pure, plain view of things. Not that he would ever really possess it.

Morgan himself wasn't so fond of exercise. He hated exercise, to tell the truth. (Oh, to tell the truth, he was a much, much older man, and not in such very good condition.) And Leon had no interest in it either. Leon was one of those people who seem permanently athletic without effort. He was in fine shape, heavy and solid, sleekly muscled. He watched Emily's jogging distantly, with a tolerant expression on his face. "She's going about it all wrong," he told Morgan. "She's driving herself too hard."

"Ah! Didn't I say the same thing?"

"She has to be in charge so. Has to win."

They were sitting on the front stoop of the apartment building on a sunny day in March. The weather felt tentative. After this bitter, shocking winter, people seemed to view spring as a trick. They went on wearing woolen clothes, and removed them piece by piece each day as they grew warmer. Bonny still had her boxwoods shrouded in burlap. She mourned for her camellia buds, which had been fooled into emerging and would surely drop off with the next freeze. But spring continued. The camellia buds opened out triumphantly, a vivid pink with full, bloused petals. Morgan and Leon sat in their shirtsleeves, almost warm enough, too lazy to go in for their jackets, and around the corner came Emily: a little black butterfly of a person with yellow feet, far away. There was something about her running that seemed eternal. She was like the braided peasant girl in a weatherhouse, traveling forever on her appointed path, rain or shine, endearingly steadfast. Morgan felt himself grow weightless with happiness, and he expanded in the sunlight and beamed at everything with equal love: at Leon and the spindly, striving trees and Emily jogging up and away and the seagull wheeling overhead, floating through the chimneys in a languid search for the harbor.

III

LEON'S FATHER had a heart attack, and Leon drove to Richmond to see him. Morgan visited Emily that evening. In the kitchen Gina was mixing a cake for her school's bake sale. She kept coming into the living room and asking where the vanilla was, or the sifter, or prancing around Morgan and checking all his pockets for the coughdrops she was fond of. Morgan was patient with her. He held his arms out passively while she searched him. Then when she returned to the kitchen, he and Emily made casual, artificial conversation. He might have lounged on the couch beside her in the old days, not giving it a thought, but now he was careful to sit some distance from her on a straight-backed chair. He cleared his throat and said, "Bonny told me to ask if you wanted to borrow her car."

"Oh, that's very nice of her. No, thank you."

"What if he's gone a long time? You might need it."

"No."

"What if he's gone through the weekend and it interferes with a puppet show?"

"I'll cancel it."

"Or I could come in his place. Why not? I'll come as Leon."

"I'll just cancel."

They looked at each other. Emily seemed paler than usual. She kept smoothing her skirt, but when she saw him watching she stopped abruptly and folded her hands in her lap. The strain was affecting her, he supposed. She was not accustomed to deceit. Neither was he, really— not to this kind. He wished they could just tell everyone and have done with it. Leon would say, "I understand," and Morgan could move in and the four of them would be happy as larks, complete at last; they would laugh at how secretive they had been at first, how possessive, how selfish.

There was a blue tinge around Emily's eyes that gave her a raccoon look.

He stood up and said, "I have to go. Will you see me out?"

"Yes, certainly," Emily said, and she stood too, smoothing her skirt again with a nervous gesture that wasn't like her.

They went down the hall, passing the kitchen, where Emily poked her head in and said, "Gina, I'll be right back."

"Oh. Okay," Gina said. She was covered with flour and she looked harassed and distracted.

Morgan took Emily by the hand and led her out the door. But halfway down the stairs they heard footsteps coming up and he let go of her. It was Mrs. Apple in a bushy Peruvian poncho, briskly jingling her keys. "Oh! Emily. Dr. Morgan," she said. "I was just stopping in to ask about Leon's father. Is he going to be all right? Have you had any news?"

"Not so far," Emily said. "Leon said he'd phone me tonight."

"Well, I know how anxious you must be."

Morgan leaned against the banister, exasperated, waiting for this to end.

"Oh, but with modern medicine," Mrs. Apple said, "these things are nothing. A heart attack's so simple. Everything's replaceable; they'll give him a Teflon tube or a battery or something and he'll go on for years yet. Tell Leon he'll go on forever. Right, Dr. Morgan?"

"Right," said Morgan, staring at the ceiling.

If he inched his hand up the banister, he could just touch the back of Emily's skirt—a slink of cool, slippery cloth with a hint of warmth beneath it. His fingertips rested there, barely in contact. Mrs. Apple didn't notice. "If he's not home by tomorrow night," she was telling Emily, "you and Gina come for supper. Nothing fancy; you know I'm a vegetarian now . . ."

When she finally let them go, Morgan strode rudely down the stairs and out the door without saying goodbye. Emily had to run to catch up with him. "I can't abide that woman," he said.

"I thought you liked her."

"She repeats herself."

They walked fast, crossing the street and heading up the block toward Morgan's pickup. It was a cool, windy night with a white sky overhead. A few people were out on the sidewalk—teenagers hanging around a lamppost, some women on their stoops. When Morgan reached the pickup, he took hold of the door handle and said, "Let's go someplace."

"I can't."

"Just a short way. Just to be alone."

"Gina will start wondering."

He sagged against the door.

"I don't know what to do," she said.

"Do?"

He looked at her. She stood with her arms folded, gazing at some fixed point across the street. "I'm thinking of leaving," she said. "Getting out."

It must be Leon again. Morgan thought she'd stopped being bothered by all that, by whatever it was . . . he had never quite understood, although he'd tried. It seemed he kept missing some clue. Were they talking about the same marriage? Emily, what is your *problem*, exactly? he sometimes wanted to ask, but he didn't. He leaned against the pickup door and listened carefully, tilting his Panama hat forward over his eyes.

"I'm even packed," she said, "or half-packed. I've been packed for years. This morning I woke up and thought, 'Why don't I just leave, then? Wouldn't it be simpler?' These clothes are so foldable and non-crushable. They take up a single drawer and they'd fit with no trouble at all in the suitcase in the closet. I still have this cosmetic kit that I bought when I was first married. I'm set! It seems I always knew that I might have to be. I've worked it so I could grab my bag up any time and go."

Morgan was interested. "Yes, yes," he said, nodding to himself. "I see what you mean."

Emily rattled on, like somebody clacking away in a fever. "When I jog, you know what I imagine? I imagine I'm in training for some emergency—a forced flight, a national disaster. It's comforting to know that I'm capable of running several miles. Nights, sometimes, I wake with a jolt, scared to death, heart just racing. Then I tell myself, 'Now, Emily, you can manage. You are very good at surviving. You can run five miles at a stretch, if you have to, and your suitcase can be ready in thirty seconds flat—' "

"What you need is a backpack," Morgan said. "An Army surplus backpack to leave your hands free."

Emily said, "I am seventeen days overdue."

"Seventeen days!" Morgan said.

He thought at first she was referring to some new jogging record. Then even after he understood, he seemed to have trouble absorbing it. (It was years since he and Bonny had had to concern themselves with such things.) "Think of that!" he said, stalling for time, nodding more rapidly.

"Of course, it could be a false alarm."

"Oh, yes, a false alarm."

"Will you please stop echoing?"

It hit him all at once. He straightened and yanked the truck's handle, and the door swung out, flooding Emily's face with light. She looked sleepy and creased; her eyes had adjusted to the dark. But she met his gaze firmly. "Emily," he said, "what are you telling me?"

"What do you think I'm telling you?"

He noticed that her face was pinched, as if from fear. He saw this suddenly from her viewpoint—seventeen days of waiting, not telling a soul. He shut the door again and laid an arm around her, heavily. "You should have mentioned this earlier," he said.

"I'm scared of what Leon will say."

"Yes, well . . ." He coughed. "Ah . . . will he realize? That is, will he realize that, ah, this is not his doing?"

"Of course he will," Emily said. "He does know how to count."

Morgan thought this over—all that it revealed. He patted her shoulder and said, "Well, don't worry, Emily."

"Maybe it's nerves," Emily said.

"Oh, yes. Nerves." He saw that he was echoing again and he quickly covered it up. "These things are vicious circles. What's the word I want? Self-perpetuating. The greater the delay, the more nervous you become, of course, and so the delay is even greater and you become even more—"

"I do believe in abortion," Emily said, "but I don't believe in it for me."

"Oh?" he said.

He frowned.

"Well, for who, then?" he asked.

"I mean, I don't think I could go through with the actual process, Morgan."

"Oh, yes. Well—"

"I just couldn't do it. I couldn't."

"Oh. Well, naturally. Of course not," he said. "No, naturally not."

He noticed that he was still patting her—an automatic gesture that was beginning to make his palm feel numb. "We shouldn't stay out here, Emily," he said. "You'd better go in now."

"I thought I was so careful," she told him. "I don't understand it."

Bonny used to say that—long, long ago in a younger, sunnier world. He had been through it all before. He was a grandfather several times over. He steered Emily back to her building at a halting, elderly pace. "Yes, well, yes, well," he said, filling the silence. On her front steps he thought to say, "But we could always ask a doctor. Get some tests."

"You know I can't stand doctors. I hate to just . . . hand myself over," Emily said.

"Now, now, don't upset yourself. Why, tomorrow you may find this was all a mistake—nerves or a miscalculation. You'll see."

He kissed her good night, and held the door while she slipped inside, and smiled at her through the glass. He was calm as a rock. And why shouldn't he be?

None of this was happening.

IV

NOW EVERY day that passed meant another blank on the calendar, another whispered conversation on the phone or in Cullen Hardware. Leon was back from Richmond; they couldn't talk in the apartment. But Emily's sheeted eyes, when Morgan stopped in for a visit, told him all he cared to know.

A week went by, and then two weeks, "What's the matter with Emily?" Bonny asked. "Have you seen her? She never comes around any more."

Morgan thought of answering her. Just simply answering her. "Well," Bonny might say, "these things happen, I suppose." Or maybe, airily, "Oh, yes, I guessed as much." (She was his oldest friend. She had known him over thirty years.) But he said nothing—or something offhand, inconsequential; nothing that mattered.

Once he met Emily by accident in the Quick-Save Grocery. She was choosing a can of soup. Instantly, without even a greeting, they fell upon her signs and symptoms. ("I'm not the slightest bit morning-sick. And I would be, don't you think? I was terribly sick with Gina.") In the middle of the aisle Morgan set his fingertips precisely within the neckline of her leotard and gave a clinical frown into space, but her breasts were as small and tight as ever. He dismayed himself by longing, suddenly, to take her away to his faded office couch again. But he didn't suggest it. No, if this turned out to be a false alarm, he promised, they would become the brightest, gayest, most aboveboard of companions—he and Emily and Leon, racketing along in a merry threesome, and he and Emily would not so much as hold hands except to . . . what, to help each other out of boats, through the windows of burning buildings.

He turned these thoughts over continually, plowing them under, digging them up again, but the odd part was that he still felt sublimely, serenely distant. He seemed to have grown removed from everything. Even his own house, his family, he suddenly saw from outside. Often he paused in a doorway, say the door to his room, and looked in as if he were judging someone else's life. It was not a bad place: the window open, curtains fluttering. He observed how lovely Bonny was when she fell into helpless laughter, which she was always doing. He noticed that when the house was full of women, there was a sound like water flowing in and out of the upstairs rooms. His mother and his sister spoke their chosen lines, which were as polished as the chorus of a poem. "This is the time when the artichokes begin, those spiky little leaves with a lemon-butter sauce . . ." "If Robert Roberts had not taken all my energy, all the care I ever had to give . . ." One of the twins—Susan, who had never married—was home recovering from a bout of hepatitis, and she lay peacefully in her old spool bed, knitting Morgan a beautiful long stocking cap from every color of scrap wool in the house. As for his other daughters—why, it began to seem he'd finally found a place in their eyes, basking among their clamorous children. What had been embarrassing in a father, it appeared, was lovably eccentric in a grandfather. Yes, and on second thought, even his work was not so terrible—his hardware store smelling of wood and machine oils, and Butkins perched on a stool behind the counter. Butkins! He was a skeletal, hay-colored man, with a nose so pointed that it seemed a clear drop hung perpetually at its tip. He had once been young—twenty-three when Uncle Ollie hired him. In Morgan's mind he'd stuck at that age forever after, but now Morgan took a closer look and found him nearing forty, bowed by his wife's ill health and the death of his only child. He seemed collapsed at the center, cavernous. His eyes were the palest, milkiest blue that Morgan had ever seen, celestially mild and accepting. Morgan felt he had wasted so much time, had nearly let this man slip through his fingers unnoticed. He took to hunkering on his office steps and bemusedly smoking cigarettes while he studied Butkins at work, till Butkins grew flustered and spilled coins all over the counter as he was making change.

Emily phoned him at the hardware store. "I'm calling from home," she said. "Leon's gone out."

"How are you?" Morgan asked her.

"Oh, well."

"Are you all right?"

"Yes, but my back is starting to ache."

"Backache. Well, good! Yes, that's a good sign, I'm certain of it."

"Or else not," Emily said. "And anyhow, I may be just imagining things."

"No, no, how can you imagine a backache?"

"It's possible. There's nothing so strange about that."

"Well, what are you feeling, exactly?"

"I don't know, it may be all in my mind."

"Just tell me what you're feeling, please, Emily."

"Morgan, don't snap at me."

"Sweetheart, I wasn't snapping. Just tell me."

"You always get this . . . older tone of voice."

He lit a cigarette. "Emily," he said.

"Well, I have a dragginess in my back, you see, a really tired dragged-outness. Do you think that's hopeful? I tried to jog this morning and I couldn't do more than a block. Right now I have to go to Gina's gymnastics meet, and I was thinking, 'I'll never make it, I know I'll never make it. All I want to do is crawl into bed and sleep.' Oh, but that's a terrible sign, sleepiness. I just remembered. It's the worst sign I could have."

"Nonsense," Morgan told her. "You're feeling the strain, that's all. Why, naturally. You ought to get some rest, Emily."

"Well, maybe after Gina's meet."

"What time is that? I'll go in your place."

"Oh . . . in half an hour. But she's expecting me."

"I'll tell her you weren't feeling well and she'll have to take me instead."

"But I'm always letting her down, these days—"

"Emily, go to bed," he said. He hung up.

He told Butkins he would be out for a while. Butkins nodded and went on alphabetizing packets of flower seeds. When all this was over, Morgan decided, he was really going to devote himself to the hardware store. He'd start bringing a sandwich and staying here through lunch hour, even. He set his beret at a steeper angle and went to find his pickup.

Gina's school was in the northern part of town—St. Andrew's, a girls' school that Leon's parents had selected for her. They were paying her tuition and had the right to choose, Morgan supposed. Still, he didn't think much of St. Andrew's. He'd have preferred her to stay on at public school. He thought Leon's parents were a bad influence: last

Christmas they'd bought Emily an electric mixer. If Emily didn't watch out, that apartment would be as overstuffed as anyone's. These things could creep up on you, Morgan told her.

He turned down the shady driveway of St. Andrew's and parked beside a school bus. The gym must be the building straight ahead. He recognized the hollow sound that voices take on in a gymnasium. He crossed the playground, tucking in his workshirt and combing his beard with his fingers, hoping he made a good showing. (Gina was ten yers old now—the age when you had to start watching your step. Any little thing could mortify her.)

Evidently, he was late. The meet had already begun. In acres of echoing hardwood that smelled of varnish, little girls were teetering on a high chrome frame. Morgan crossed to the bleachers and settled himself on the lowest level, alongside a scattering of mothers. All the mothers wore blazers and blond, pageboy haircuts. He tried to picture Emily sitting here with them. He hunched forward in his seat and looked around for Gina. It took a moment (there were swarms of little girls in blue leotards and swarms in lavender, and he didn't even know which color was St. Andrew's), but he spotted her, finally. She was the one in blue with the cloud of curls. Her face was still round and opulent—he would know those heavy-lidded eyes anywhere, and that pale, delicate mouth—but her body had become a stick, the narrow hips pathetically high above legs so long and thin that he could see the workings of her kneecaps when she walked. She came over to him, her bare toes gripping the floor. Ordinarily she would hug him, but in front of friends she never did. "Where's Mama?" she asked him.

"She doesn't feel well."

"She never comes to anything any more," Gina said, but without much concern; her attention had already wandered elsewhere. She turned to study the girls on the other team. Then, "Morgan!" she screeched, spinning on him. "You can't smoke in here!"

She must have eyes in the back of her head. Morgan muttered, "Sorry," and replaced his cigarette in the pack.

"I could die of embarrassment," she said.

"Sorry, sweetheart."

"Are you giving me a ride home afterward?"

"I will if you like."

"That red-haired girl is Kitty Potts. I hate and despise her," Gina said. She ran off.

Morgan watched a series of girls perform slow and trembling labors on a balance beam. Periodically, one would fall off and have to climb back on. Gina, when it was her turn, fell off twice. By the time she'd finished, Morgan's muscles ached; he'd been holding his breath. He remembered that his daughter Kate had also liked gymnastics, a few years back. She'd won several ribbons. In fact, he didn't believe he'd ever seen her fall or make an error, not once in any meet that he'd attended. He might have just forgotten, of course. But he was sure that her scores had been better. Gina's was a 4.3, read off by a bored-looking woman at a microphone. Coming here today was an unnatural act, Morgan decided. He really had nothing to do with any of this— the unfamiliar gym, the blazered mothers, someone else's daughter in a leotard. He wished he could get up and go back to the hardware store.

They'd finished with the balance beam and moved in the horse for vaulting. Morgan thought vaulting was a monotonous event to watch. He tucked his boot in off the floor so the girls could run past him, one by one, for two leaps each. Their arms and legs looked stretched with concentration, and their faces were comically intense. Gina raced by with her eyes tightly focused. She sprang up and cleared the horse, but then she did something wrong. Instead of landing upright, she fell in a twisted heap on the mat.

The mothers went rigid; one laid her needlepoint aside. Morgan leaped to his feet. He was certain Gina'd broken her neck. But no, she was all right, or nearly all right—in tears, but not seriously injured. She rose holding on to one wrist. A young woman in shorts, with a whistle dangling from her neck, bent over her to ask her questions. Gina answered inaudibly, blotting her tears on her sleeve.

The woman led her up the floor again for her second try, though Gina was shaking her head and sobbing. The woman was saying something in a coaxing, reasoning voice. She smoothed Gina's hair, speaking urgently. It was barbaric. Morgan hated sports. He sat down and put an unlit cigarette in his mouth with a trembling hand.

Gina shrugged the woman away, drew herself up, and narrowed her eyes at the horse. There was still a little catch in her breath. It was the loudest sound in the gym. Everyone leaned forward. Gina set her jaw and started running. By the time she passed Morgan she was a steely, pounding blur. She cleared the horse magnificently and landed in perfect form, with her arms raised high.

Morgan jumped up and flung away his cigarette. He galloped in her footsteps all the way to the horse, and veered around it to hug her. Tears were streaming down his cheeks. "Sweetheart, you were wonderful," he said. She said, "Oh, Morgan," and giggled. (She was unscathed; she had forgotten everything.) She slipped away from him to join her teammates. Morgan returned to his seat, beaming and wiping his eyes. "Wasn't she wonderful," he told the mothers. He blew his nose in his handkerchief. He felt suddenly joyous and expansive. What could he not accomplish? He was a wide, deep, powerful man, and it was time he took some action.

V

"How was the meet?" Emily asked Gina.

"It was all right."

"I'm sorry I couldn't be there. Morgan, do you want to come in?"

"Yes, thank you," Morgan said. Emily's appearance shocked him. Four days ago—the last time he'd seen her—she'd been a little drawn, yes, but now her skin had the yellow, cracked look of aged chinaware. "Emily, dear," he said. Emily slid her eyes sideways, reminding him of Gina, but he ignored her. He didn't even glance around for Leon, who might very well have returned by now. "I've come to take you to a doctor," he said.

"Is Mama really sick?" Gina asked.

"She needs a check-up. You stay here, Gina. We won't be long."

He started hunting through the closet for a sweater or a jacket, something light, but all he found was Emily's winter coat. He took it off the hanger and helped her into it. She stood docilely while he buttoned the buttons.

"It's not that cold," Gina told him.

"We have to take good care of her."

He led Emily out the door, closing it behind him. Halfway down the stairs, he heard the door swing open again. Gina hung over the banister. "Can I have that last banana?" she asked her mother.

Morgan said, "Yes. For God's sake. Anything you like." Emily was silent. Like someone truly ill, she made her way faltering down the stairs.

In the truck she said, "Do we have an appointment?"

"We'll make one when we get there."

"Morgan, it takes weeks."

"Not today it won't," he said, pulling out of the parking space.

He drove to St. Paul Street, to Bonny's old obstetrician. He couldn't remember the number, but recalled very clearly the upholsterer's establishment next to it, and when he found a display window full of dusty velvet furniture, he stopped immediately, blocking an alley, and assisted Emily from the truck.

"How do you know this person?" Emily asked, looking around her at the gaunt, grimy buildings.

"He delivered all my daughters."

"Morgan!"

"What?"

"We can't go in there."

"Why not?" he asked.

"He knows you! I mean, we have to find someone else. We have to assume an alias or something."

Morgan took her elbow and guided her up the front steps, through the brass-trimmed door, and into a carpeted lobby. "Never mind all that," he told her, punching a button for the elevator. "This is no time to play around, Emily."

The elevator door slip open. A very old black man in a purple and gold uniform weas sitting on a stool in the corner. Morgan hadn't realized that elevator men still existed. "Three," he said. He stepped in beside Emily. The silence in which they rode was dense and charged. Emily kept twisting her top button.

In the waiting room Morgan told the receptionist, "Morgan Gower. Emergency."

The receptionist looked at Emily.

"We have to see Dr. Fogarty right away," Morgan said.

"Doctor is booked solid. Would you care to make an appointment?"

"It's an emergency, I tell you."

"What seems to be the trouble?"

"I'll discuss the trouble when I see Fogarty."

"Dr. Fogarty is very busy, sir. Perhaps if you leave a number where he can call when he's through with his patients—"

Morgan stepped past her, around her desk, and through the oak door behind her. Often, biding his time in various waiting rooms, he had imagined doing this, but he had always assumed it would be necessary to wrestle the receptionist to the floor first. In fact the receptionist was a tiny, mousy girl with limp hair, and she didn't even stand up when he came through. He barreled down a short white corridor, into a room full of instruments, out again, and into another room. There an older, grayer Dr. Fogarty was seated behind a kidney-shaped desk, placing his fingertips neatly together, holding a discussion with a very young couple. The couple looked bashful and pleased. The girl was leaning forward, about to ask some earnest question. Rushed though he was, Morgan had time for a little spasm of pity. How shallow they seemed! Probably they thought this was the most significant moment in history. "Pardon me," Morgan told them, "I hate to interrupt this way."

"Mr. Gower," the doctor said, unsurprised.

"Ah! You remember me."

"How could one forget?"

"This is an emergency," Morgan said.

Dr. Fogarty let his chair rock forward at last, and parted his fingertips. "Is something wrong with Bonny?" he asked.

"No, no, it's Emily, someone else. This is Emily." He should have brought her in with him. What could he have been thinking of? He grabbed a hank of his hair. "It's terribly important. She's going to pieces, believes she's pregnant . . . Fogarty, if she's right, we need to know it now, this instant, not at two-fifteen next Tuesday or Wednesday or Friday."

"Mr. Gower, honestly," the doctor said. He sighed. "Why you have to take every stage of your life so much more to heart than ordinary people—"

Immediately, Morgan felt reassured. So this was merely a stage, then! He turned to the couple and said, "I beg your pardon. Have I told you that? I'm sorry to seem so rude." The couple stared at him with blank, unformed faces.

"Show her into the room next door," the doctor said. "I'll be with you in a minute."

"Oh, thank you, Fogarty," Morgan said.

He felt a rush of affection for the man—his benign expression and his puffy gray mustache. It must be wonderful to view events so matter-of-factly. Maybe Morgan ought to shave his beard off and wear only a mustache. He stumbled out of the office, tentatively fingering his whiskers. He went back to the waiting room, where Emily was sitting alert, ready to fly, on a loveseat next to a pear-shaped woman in a smock. The receptionist didn't even glance at him. (Maybe this happened every day.) He beckoned to Emily, and she rose and came toward him. He led her to the room beside the doctor's office, the one that was full of equipment, and he helped her take her coat off. There was no place to hang it. He folded it into a wrinkled, oval bundle and set it on an enameled cabinet. "Didn't I tell you?" he asked Emily. "Everything will be all right. I'll take care of you, sweetheart."

Emily stood looking at him.

"Sit down," he told her. He steered her toward the examining table. She sat gingerly on the foot of it, smoothing her skirt around her.

Then Morgan started circling the room. All the instruments struck him as gruesome—tongs and pincers. What a world of *innards* women lived in! He shook his head. In one corner he found a hospital scale. The last person to stand on it had weighed a hundred and eighty-two pounds. "Mercy," he said disapprovingly. He slid the weights to the left. They felt solid and authoritative. "Ahem, young lady," he told Emily, "if you'll just hop on our scales, please . . ."

"I should have called a clinic. Family Planning or something," Emily said, as if to herself. "I meant to, every day, but I don't know, lately it seems I've got locked in place, frozen."

"Would you like a johnny coat?" Morgan asked, rooting through the cabinet. "Look here, they're pink. Just slip into our Schiaparelli johnny coat, Miss . . ."

Emily didn't respond. She was holding herself tense, with her hands clasped tightly in her lap.

Morgan went over and touched her arm. "Emily. Don't worry," he said. "This will all work out. Emily? Am I getting on your nerves? Do you want me to leave? Yes, I'll go outside and wait for you, that's a good idea . . . Emily, don't feel bad."

She still didn't answer.

He left and went to sit in the waiting room. He chose a chair in the corner, as far as possible from the pear-shaped woman. Even so, she seemed to be pressing in on him. She gave off a swelling, insistent warmth, although she pretended not to and seemed immersed in a *Baby Talk* magazine. Morgan let his head drop and covered his eyes with his fingers. Everything was a bluff. He knew the truth by now, however long it might take Fogarty to prove it scientifically. This was it. This was it.

He was done for.

The woman flipped the pages of her magazine, and car horns honked in the distance, and the telephone rang with a muted, purring sound. Morgan raised his head and stared at the oak door. He began to see the situation from another angle. An assignment had been given him. Someone's life, a small set of lives, had been placed in the palm of his hand. Maybe he would never have any more purpose than this: to accept the assignment gracefully, lovingly, and do the best he could with it.

VI

ON WEDNESDAY morning, after Emily heard from the doctor, Morgan came home from work to tell Bonny. Bonny had launched one of her spring-cleaning attacks that always made the house seem untidier than before. Morgan could smell the dust flying the minute he walked in. She was in the dining room, wearing a kerchief over her hair, washing down her ancestors' portraits with Spic and Span. Various scowling gentlemen in nineteenth-century frockcoats leaned against the chairs. Bonny was not intimidated. She scrubbed their faces with the same brisk energy she had once shown in scrubbing her children. Morgan stood in the doorway watching.

She wrung out a sponge, wiped her forehead with the back of her wrist, and then looked over at him. "Morgan? What is it?" she asked.

He said, "Emily's pregnant."

In the second it took her to absorb it, he saw he had worded it wrong. She could easily misunderstand. She might say, "Why, isn't that nice! They must be thrilled. But no, she understood, all right. Her mouth dropped open. She took on a white, opaque look. She reared back and threw the sponge at him. It skimmed his cheekbone, wet and warm and rough like something alive. Partly, he was impressed. (What a woman! Direct as some kind of electrical charge—undiffused.) But he had never been able to tolerate being hit in the face. He felt bitterly, gloriously angry, and free. He turned and walked out of the house.

At the hardware store he pushed past Butkins and went to use the phone. "Emily? Can you talk?" he asked.

"Yes. Leon's loading the car."

"Well, I told her," he said.

"What'd she say?"

"Nothing, in fact."

"Was she very angry?"

"No. Yes. I don't know," he said. "Emily, have you talked to Leon?"

"No. I'm going to."

"When?"

"Soon," she said. "Right now we've got a show at the library. I have to wait till after it's done."

"Well, I don't know why," Morgan said.

"Maybe I could tell him tonight."

"Tonight? Sweetheart, you'd better get this over with," he said.

"It's just . . . you know, just a matter of finding the proper moment."

After he had hung up, Morgan had a sudden fear that she would *never* tell Leon. He pictured having to sleep on the couch in his office forever—a man unkempt, uncared for. Like someone who had fallen between two stepping stones in a river, he'd let go of Bonny without yet being certain of Emily. He could not imagine life as a bachelor.

He sat a while drumming his fingers on his desk. He had an urge to write letters. But whom would he write to? He wondered how he could get hold of his cardboard file box. Surely Bonny wouldn't do anything rash with it, would she?—burn it? set it out for the trashmen? She knew how much it meant to him.

Finally he rose and went downstairs. Butkins was outdoors, helping a customer. In the spring they put some of their merchandise on the sidewalk—flats of seedlings, giant bags of mulch and fertilizer. Morgan peered through the window and saw Butkins tenderly fitting a marigold plant into a brown paper bag. He turned away and went into the stockroom. There were cartons of garden tools here, waiting to be unpacked. He opened one and pulled out the trowels, dozens of them, which he heaped on the floor. He opened others and pulled out hedge trimmers, then cultivators, then shiny-toothed wheels for edging lawns. The stockroom became a tangle of chrome blades and painted wooden handles.

Butkins came in and said, "Um . . ."

Morgan surveyed all he had unpacked. Then he pried up another flap and reached for a pair of grass shears in a cardboard sheath.

Butkins said, "Mr. Gower, there's some things of yours on the sidewalk."

"Things?"

"It looks like . . . belongings. Clothing. Also a dog."

"How'd they get there?"

"Mrs. Gower, ah, dumped them there."

Morgan straightened up and followed Butkins through the store and out onto the sidewalk, which was a sea of hats and clothes. An elderly woman with a cane was trying on a pith helmet. Harry, who had never been much of a watchdog, was smiling at her with his tongue hanging out. He was sitting on Morgan's red-and-white-striped, 'twas-the-night-before-Christmas nightshirt. "I'm sorry, Mr. Gower, I didn't know what to do," Butkins said. "It happened so fast. She *threw* them, like. Knocked over half the seedlings."

"Yes, but why the dog?" Morgan asked.

"Pardon me?"

"The dog, the dog. It's not my dog; it's my mother's. I never even liked him. He dribbles. Why did she send me the dog?"

"Well, and there's some articles of clothing here too, you see."

"It isn't fair. I don't want a dog."

"There's hats and nightwear."

"Come back here!" Morgan told the old lady. She was making off with his pith helmet. She wore it tipped too far forward—had no idea of the proper angle. "Come back with my helmet!" he cried. She walked faster and faster, as if on little wheels. Considering her age and her cane, Morgan had to marvel.

"Shall I go after her?" Butkins asked.

"No, help me bring in the rest of the things. People will be all over them," Morgan said. Butkins stooped for an armload of clothing, but stopped when Morgan told him, "She won't even know to dampen it, I'll bet."

"Pardon?"

"You dampen the helmet in hot weather. It cools your head by the process of evaporation."

"Shall I go after her, then?"

"No, no."

"Are these boots yours too?"

"Everything," said Morgan. He scooped up an armload of hats and followed Butkins inside. "Actually, I don't think she brought nearly my whole wardrobe, though. Where's my gnome hat? Where's my sombrero?"

"Are you and Mrs. Gower experiencing some difficulty?" Butkins said.

"Not at all. Why do you ask?" said Morgan. He went outside for another armload, chasing away two small boys who were interested in a sheepskin vest. "Come in, Harry," he told the dog. "Butkins, we'll need those cartons from the stockroom."

They made a total of six trips. Bonny had not, in fact, forgotten anything. Morgan found his file box under a cloak. He found his gnome hat and sombrero, and also a Napoleonic tricorne he'd forgotten all

about. He blew the dust off and tried it on. He checked his reflection
in the nickel surface of the cash register. Under the cocked brim his
bearded face peered out hollowly. He was sickened. What a farce! How
ridiculous! He had always, even in infancy, been a fool for hats. As a
child, he'd worn firemen's helmets and Indian headdresses to bed at
night. This was no better. He tore the tricorne off and flung it on the
floor.

"Oh!" said Butkins. "It's an antique."

"I hate it."

"You don't want to get it dusty," Butkins said, picking it up.

"It's already dusty. You can have it."

Butkins did not seem to want it, however. He gave the hat a doubtful,
troubled look, and placed it cautiously on the counter beside a flashlight
display.

VII

AT LUNCHTIME, when Morgan was alone in the store, he dialed the
Merediths' number again. Nobody answered. They must not have
returned from their puppet show. He let the phone ring on and on.
Harry lay at his feet, his nose between his paws, rolling his eyes at
Morgan.

When Butkins came back, Morgan decided not to go to lunch himself.
He wasn't hungry. And he didn't climb the stairs to his office, but
stayed close to Butkins, drawing some kind of comfort from him, mutely
watching the dull, homely transactions that took place: the purchasing
of paint, nails, a screen-door hook, the return of a defective light switch.
He noticed that when Butkins had no customers, he fell into a kind
of trance; he gazed into space, sighing, and absently fingered an earlobe.
Perhaps he was thinking of his wife. She had some slow, creeping
illness; Morgan couldn't think of the name. Something to do with her
muscles. She was no longer able to walk. And the child who died had
been struck by a hit-and-run driver. Morgan remembered the funeral.
He wondered how Butkins endured it, where he found the strength to
open his eyes every morning and dress himself and force down a little
food and set out for the hardware store. He must feel nothing but
contempt for Morgan. But when Butkins came out of his trance and
found Morgan's eyes on him, he only gave his gentle smile. "Why
don't you leave?" Morgan asked. "Take the afternoon off."

"But it's not my day; it's Wednesday."

"Leave anyhow."

"Oh, I might as well stay."

It was lucky he did, as it happened. Around three o'clock Jim showed
up—Amy's husband. From the focused way he strode in the door,

wearing his slim gray lawyer suit, carrying his calfskin briefcase, Morgan guessed that he'd been sent by Bonny. Plainly, he knew everything. His face was pulled downward by long, severe lines. "Where can we talk?" he asked Morgan.

"Why, my office, I suppose."

"Let's go there."

Jim led the way himself. Morgan followed. He didn't so much walk as drift, dimly touching T-squares and hammers as he passed down the aisle. He wondered, idly, how Jim would handle this. What had ever prepared him for such a discussion? He trailed Jim up the stairs. Jim took a seat in Morgan's swivel chair. Morgan had to sit on the couch, like an applicant for something. (They must teach you this strategy in law school.) Morgan prinked the creases of his trousers and smiled at Jim, showing all his teeth. Jim didn't smile back.

"Well, I heard the news," he told Morgan.

"Yes, I figured you had."

"It's not clear to anyone what you plan to do next, Morgan."

"Do?"

"What steps you plan to take."

"Ah."

Jim waited. Morgan went on smiling at him.

"Morgan?"

"Well, for the moment I may have to sleep on this couch," Morgan said. "It's not the best of beds, as you see—damn buttons, tufting, whatever you want to call it—"

"I'm not inquiring about your *mattress*, Morgan. I'm asking what arrangements you contemplate."

"Arrangements?"

"Have you told this other woman you're assuming responsibility?"

"She's not 'this other woman,' Jim. She's Emily. You've met Emily. And of course I'm assuming responsibility."

"Morgan, I don't like to be tactless—"

"Then don't be," Morgan said.

Jim sat back in the swivel chair, studying him. He had his briefcase set across his knees like a desk. Although he had long ago traded his crew-neck sweaters for suits, he had never lost his mannequin look. Even now that he was graying, Morgan saw, he was doing it in a mannequin's style—handsome silvery wings above his ears. Jim tapped his briefcase thoughtfully. "You realize," he told Morgan, "that you're not the first man this has happened to."

"Oh? I'm not?"

"Well, I fail to see what's so humorous, Morgan."

"No, no . . . What I mean to say is, I *am* the first man it's happened to in quite this way. Or rather, it's the first time it's happened to *me*, and to her. There's no point trying to fit us on a graph."

Jim sighed. "Let's start all over," he said.

"Certainly."

"You know, Morgan, that Bonny was pretty upset this morning when she heard the news. But it's not the end of the world, I told her. It's not what you'd break up a marriage for. Is it? Get a hold of yourself, I told her. Oh, sure, she'll take a while forgiving you. It's a shock to everybody—Amy, Jean . . . they might be hard on you at the moment . . ."

Morgan nodded, trying to look reasonable. Of course, he should have realized the girls would be involved. They were loyal to Bonny, naturally, and it must look terrible, what he'd done. Oh, he didn't blame them at all. But still he felt a little hurt, picturing Bonny surrounded by clucking daughters. How they rushed to scenes of tragedy and melodrama! He was reminded of Susan, their most difficult child, who had spent a tiresome, extended adolescence bickering with Bonny. She would drive home from college for weekends and he'd barely have unloaded the laundry from her car when she'd be storming out again. "I'll never come back here, never. I was an idiot to try." "But what happened?" he would ask, astonished. She would yank her laundry bag from his hands and flounce into her car and grind the engine. "And how did it happen so *fast*?" he would call after her departing taillights. Spontaneous combustion! Flint rocks, miraculously magnetized! They rushed to battle with such enthusiasm.

It was just as well he was done with all that. In his mind Emily shone as clear and still as a pool.

"I plan to ask Bonny for a divorce," he told Jim.

"Morgan. Christ, Morgan. Look, man . . ."

"I don't suppose you give discounts to family members, do you?"

"I don't handle divorces."

"Oh."

"And anyhow . . . Christ, Morgan, what's got into you? You're throwing everything away!"

"I've already told Emily," Morgan said, "that I'll take care of her and Gina and the baby. She could never just stay with her husband; she's said that. And she has nobody else to rely on. See, I realize I'm behaving badly, Jim, but this is one of those times when, whatever you do, it's bad from one angle and good from another. I mean, I can't be virtuous on every front in this situation. Can I?"

"Listen," Jim said. He hunched forward over his briefcase, as if about to pass on a secret. "Life is not always X-rated, Morgan."

"I beg your pardon?"

"I mean, generally it's more like . . . oh, a low R, I'd say: part bed, part grocery-shopping. You don't want to ruin everything for the sake of, ah . . ."

Morgan fished for his cigarettes. What did Jim imagine? Life with

Bonny, after all, was not exactly rated G. He decided not to say that out loud. He offered Jim a cigarette. Jim, who didn't smoke, took one and waited for Morgan to strike a match. "See, what I'm getting at—" he said.

"I know what you're getting at," said Morgan, "but you miss the point. I've already made my mind up, Jim. I'm not going to change it. I have this feeling of . . . swerving, like seizing my boat and wrenching it around, steering it off course and onto a whole new, unlikely one. It's not bad! It's not a bad feeling! You aren't going to make me give it up!"

And as he spoke, he felt drunk with his own decisiveness. He could hardly wait for Jim to leave, so that he could go find Emily and settle this forever.

VIII

HE HAD trouble coaxing the dog into the pickup. Harry didn't like traveling. He had to be dragged across the sidewalk with his nails scritching. But Morgan couldn't leave him behind, because Butkins had begun to sneeze. He heaved Harry into the truck, tucked his tail in, and closed the door. Then he went back to the store to tell Butkins, "I'm not sure how long I'll be. If I'm still away by closing time, lock up, will you? And don't let anyone bother my clothes."

It was the time of afternoon when children were coming home from school—neat little grade-schoolers with satchels, junior-high boys in baggy Army jackets and girls with plastic combs sticking out of their jeans pockets. Teenagers milled at intersections, making driving difficult.

On Crosswell Street the mothers were waiting on their stoops. They shaded their eyes and discussed the weather, the Orioles, what they planned to serve for supper. A fat woman in a dress like a petticoat had opened a can of beer and was passing it around. Burnished lavender pigeons clustered at a sack of spilled popcorn.

Morgan pushed through the door of the Crafts Unlimited building and pulled Harry after him. Harry hung back, whining, but Morgan hauled him up the stairs with a length of rope he'd borrowed from the store. He knocked on the Merediths' door. Emily opened it. "Good, you're back," he said. He walked in.

"Morgan? What are you doing here?"

"I've come to get this settled." He paused in the hall and glanced around for Leon. "Where is he?"

"He's picking up Gina. It's our turn for the carpool."

"Have you told him yet?"

"No."

He turned to look at her. She was twisting her hands. "I can't," she said. "I'm scared. You don't know what a temper he has."

"Emily . . . Sit, Harry. *Sit*, dammit. Emily, what are you saying?" he asked. It cost him some effort, but he said, "Would you rather not do this at all? Rather go on the way you were, work it out somehow— the two of you? You should say so now, Emily, if that's true. Just tell me what you want of me."

"I want to be with you," she said. "I wish we could just run away."

"Ah," he said. He was immediately taken with the idea. "Yes! Run away. No luggage, no fixed destination . . . Will Gina come willingly, do you think?"

"I don't know," she said. She swallowed. "It's telling him face to face I mind. Maybe I could go to a pay phone and call him up, tell him from a distance."

"Well, that's a thought."

"Or you could tell him."

"Me?"

"You could . . . get behind a table or something where he couldn't hit you and then break the news to him."

"I preferred the running-away plan," Morgan said.

"But taking Gina: I couldn't do that to Leon. And I'd never leave her behind."

"All right," Morgan said. "I'll tell him myself."

He assumed it was all arranged then, and went into the kitchen to sit down and wait for Leon. But Emily floated after him, still twisting her hands, and said, "Oh, no, what am I thinking of? I don't know why I'm such a coward. Of course I have to be the one to do it. Go away and come back later, Morgan."

"That's impossible," he said. "I'm lugging this dog around."

"I feel sick," she said.

"Dear heart. This is really very simple," he told her. "We're all adults. We're reasonable beings. What do you imagine will happen? Could I have some water for Harry, please?"

She took a bowl from the cupboard and filled it at the sink. She set the water in front of Harry, who started slurping it up. Then she shifted her purse from a chair and sat next to Morgan. "If we ran away, I would have to find some other kind of work," she said. "Something I couldn't be traced by. It's so easy to track down a puppet show, at any fair or church bazaar."

"Well, then. You can't run away," he said. "What would you do without your puppets?"

"I could manage fine without my puppets," she said.

"No, no . . ."

"I never planned to stick with them forever."

"Oh, of course you'll stick with them, Emily, dear."

She slumped in her chair, massaging her temples with her fingertips.

Harry raised his head and shook water all over the kitchen floor. "Mind your manners," Morgan told him. He reached across the table for Emily's purse. It had an interesting weight to it. Most days, all it contained was keys and her billfold, but whenever she had a puppet show she loaded it with carefully selected equipment. You could live in the wilderness for a month off that purse, Morgan thought. He rummaged through it and came up with a ball of string, a roll of Scotch tape, her Swiss Army knife, a pair of needle-nosed pliers . . . "What's this for? And this?" he kept asking.

"I think I'm going to throw up," she said.

"What's this little Baggie full of Cheerios?"

"They're the doughnuts for Red Riding Hood's basket."

"Oh, yes. Oh, excellent."

He began to feel very happy. He piled everything back in the purse and started humming, patting his knees, looking around for something new. "How's your burner doing?" he asked.

"It's fine."

"See? I told you all it needed was unclogging."

He hummed a few more bars. Then he said, "Don't you want to know why I have this dog with me?"

She didn't seem to. He continued anyway. "Bonny brought him. Threw everything out on the sidewalk: hats, clothes, vacuum-cleaner instructions . . . and Harry. But Harry belongs to Mother. Mother's always owned a dog. This must be her tenth or twentieth. Who did she have when you first met us—Elmer? Lucille? She pays them no mind at all, never looks at them, it's me who walks them . . . but she's always had one, so she always will. That's the way they work things, back home. The extras! The stacks of unnecessary extras! The stacks of unnecessary extras! This Harry, you see, is Bonny's revenge. Oh, she knew what she was doing, all right. Cluttering up my leaving, even. I'm surprised she didn't bring the cat as well."

"I always did want a dog," Emily said unexpectedly.

"Eh?"

"But I couldn't because my mother was allergic."

"Yes, that's Butkins' trouble, too. Allergic."

"Butkins?"

They heard the front door open. Emily sat up straighter. "Mama," said Gina, bouncing in, "guess what I got on my science test. Hello, Morgan, what's Harry doing here?"

"I brought him in for a drink. Well, Miss Gina," Morgan said. "What'd you get on your science test?"

"A-plus," she said. She twined an arm around him and looked down at Harry, who was scratching fleas. Leon walked in.

"Hello, Morgan," he said.

"Leon."

"Taking the afternoon off?"

"Yes, well, there's something I want to discuss with you."

"What's that?" asked Leon.

Morgan glanced over at Gina. She had dropped her arm but continued to stand there, so close that he could smell her salty, summery smell of fresh sweat and chewing gum. He scratched his head. "Leon," he said, "would you like to . . . come walk the dog with me?"

"Do what?"

"Walk the dog."

Leon looked at the dog, who grinned.

"Don't if you don't want to," Morgan said. "Do you want to?"

"All right, Morgan," Leon said calmly.

Morgan stood up, tucking in his shirt, adjusting his Panama hat. They went out of the apartment together. Just as Leon was closing the door, Gina called, "Wait!"

"What's the matter?"

"You forgot the dog."

"Oh," Morgan said. He shuffled back to the door and took Harry's rope from her.

They went down the stairs and outside. The rush-hour traffic was just beginning. Trucks rumbled past, and cars with single, determined drivers, and taxis carrying ladies submerged in packages. It took a while to cross the street. Then they started north. Leon led, with both hands loose at his sides in an easy, unquestioning way that gave Morgan a sudden pang.

"Well," Morgan said.

He waited for Harry to sniff out the proper spot in the grass. Leon straightened a sign that had pivoted on its post.

"I find myself in a little difficulty," Morgan said.

"Say it, Morgan."

"It's Emily."

They walked on. Morgan thought of the old women in the neighborhood where he had grown up—how they never announced a death straightforwardly but prepared the bereaved first, planting tiny seeds of news and allowing them to sprout on their own, no faster than the bereaved could handle. Emily's name, he hoped, might be such a seed all by itself. Certainly Leon seemed to be turning it over in his mind. They stopped and waited for a light to change, although no cars were coming.

"Emily and I . . ." Morgan said.

They crossed the street. They avoided a shattered whiskey flask.

"She's expecting a child," Morgan said.

Leon didn't slow down. Morgan cast a sideways glance at him and found his face unmoved. "You knew all along," Morgan said.

"No," said Leon. "Not about the child."

"But the rest of it, you knew."

"Yes."

"Well . . . how?"

"Osmosis, maybe," Leon said. "Something or other."

"You have to believe me," Morgan said. "I never intended any harm. I really can't explain . . . I mean, day by day, you see, it didn't seem so terrible. But I know how it must appear from outside."

"What are your plans?" Leon asked politely.

They paused, facing each other, with Harry on his haunches between them. If Leon was going to get violent, now was the time. But he didn't, of course. Morgan had never understood why Emily thought he would. She must have been mistaken, suffered one of those funny blind spots married people often have. Or maybe she was talking about an earlier Leon; that possibility occurred to him. Morgan gazed off, seeing the last of someone he'd been hearing about for years. He sighed and pulled his nose.

"Well," he said, "if you're willing, I suppose I'll move her and Gina to some other town. I don't know."

"Do you want the apartment?"

"*Your* apartment?"

"Do you want the puppets, the equipment, the job? Want me to be the one to go?"

"Oh, well, no, I couldn't ask—"

"Really, what do I need with all that? Take it," Leon said.

"Oh,"

"Take it."

"Well, if you're sure," said Morgan.

Then Leon said, "Aah, God, Morgan." He spoke wearily, disgustedly, but not with any sharpness.

Even so, Morgan flinched.

When they resumed walking, it was in the other direction, homeward. They passed Eunola's Restaurant, where the three of them had so often stopped for coffee. Then they came to the laundromat where Morgan had stood, countless times, watching Leon and Emily setting out with their baby. Perhaps, he thought, this was not so much a love story as a friendship story, and he felt saddened by Leon's patient, trudging figure beside him. (Where was that thin, olive-skinned boy parting the curtains to call for a doctor? Would Emily ever again, in the future, wear that tilted look she had first tossed Morgan?)

They crossed the street and entered the building. When Morgan saw the long stairway, he believed, for a moment, that he might not make it. He was exhausted, and his chest ached. But a strange thing happened. As he climbed, it seemed his spirits climbed too. He speeded up, leaving Leon behind, taking steps two at a time. He wanted to get on with this. He wanted to begin his new life.

1978

I

CINDERELLA WAS dancing with the Prince, nestled in his brown felt arms, gliding across the walnut desk in somebody's father's study. Over her head, blue satin swoops hung from the folding wooden stage. There was a scrim at the rear that didn't entirely conceal the puppeteers, but the audience was too entranced to notice. It was a very young audience— mostly four-year-olds. The birthday child wore a gilt paper crown that resembled the Prince's.

"Mercy," Cinderella said, "it must be getting late. I'm sure it's nearly midnight."

"Midnight? So what?" the Prince asked in his gruff, rasping voice. "We'll dance till dawn. We'll dance all the next day!"

"Um, well, but you see, Your Majesty . . ."

They were stalling for time. Where was the clock? "The clock!" Emily whispered. Gina was off in a trance again, holding the cassette recorder just beyond Emily's reach and gazing dreamily at the audience. Joshua, who was supposed to be in Gina's care, was creeping under the desk. He gurgled to himself and dribbled on a nest of extension cords.

"Ding, ding!" Emily called in desperation. "Ding, ding, ding . . ."

Somewhere in there she lost count, but she trusted that the audience wouldn't catch it. She could hardly wait to whisk Cinderella off the stage so she could rescue the baby. The instant the curtain was lowered, she snatched him up. He wore only a grayish diaper. His solid little trunk, barrel-shaped, was faintly sticky, and he trailed a silvery, cool thread of spit down the back of Emily's hand.

"Gina, honey," Emily said, "I thought you were going to watch him for me. 'Oh, I can manage both,' you told me, 'mind Josh and do the props too . . .'"

Morgan, meanwhile, was digging through a pile of objects on the floor. "Fireplace, fireplace," he muttered. "What's happened to the fireplace?"

"Gina had it last."

But Gina was busy with thoughts of her own. Eleven years old, tall and secretive, languorous from half a summer of lolling about in the heat, she sat on a leather chair with her knees cocked and hummed the waltz that Cinderella had been dancing to. "Here we are," Morgan said. He straightened, puffing, and held up the cardboard fireplace. Joshua reached for it, but Morgan was too quick for him. He set the fireplace in one corner of the stage. "Now, where's the stepmother?" he asked Emily. "Where are the sisters?"

"Gina? Take Josh for me, will you?"

Gina unfolded herself with a sigh and accepted the baby. He grabbed at her shiny hair clasp. He grabbed at Morgan's sailor cap, in passing, but was borne away to the leather chair. "Tra la la," Gina sang, rocking him too hard.

Out front, the audience grew hushed and expectant. Emily slipped off Cinderella's ballgown, exposing her burlap rags. She held her up, ready to go, and smiled at Morgan. He nodded and raised the curtain.

II

"YOU KNOW that Kate's home," Bonny said.

"Oh, really?" said Emily. "I hadn't heard." She switched the receiver to her other ear. She was trying to stir a stew and talk on the phone simultaneously. "Has something happened?" she asked.

Instead of answering, Bonny let out a long, thin breath. All of a sudden, this late in her life, Bonny had taken up smoking. She didn't smoke very competently and always seemed to be inhaling or exhaling at exactly the wrong moment, leaving her listeners suspended. She had also developed other new habits. She continually joined strange philosophical societies and women's groups, began unpromising jobs and then resigned almost at once, and telephoned Emily at any hour she pleased. Although she never mentioned Morgan without biting his name off, she seemed not to blame Emily at all. This was a relief, of course, but it was also a little insulting. (It implied that Emily was powerless, without a will of her own.) When Bonny paused for one of her cigarette breaths, Emily pictured the humming wires that linked them. Bonny was knotted into her line, knotted into her whole existence. Even if Emily were to hang up, Bonny's phone would still connect hers because Bonny was the one who'd placed the call.

"She has this back," Bonny said. "This sprained or twisted back, or something. The way it came about was, she and her husband were involved in a head-on collision. David walked away from it without a scratch, but Kate did something to her back."

"What happened to the other driver?" Emily asked.

"What other driver?"

"The driver of the other car."

"David was the driver of the other car."

"You mean she collided with her husband?"

"Yes, and got this injured back, this sprained or twisted back; I'm telling you," Bonny said.

"Oh, now I see."

"Well, I wanted her to come home because I can nurse her better than David could. Heaven knows I've had the practice. And besides that, I've been attending these lectures on a whole different kind of nutrition, a diet that heals any sort of ailment. It works on physical problems, mental problems, depressions, infections, tumors . . . You may not remember this, but last winter, when Molly was mugged in Buffalo while she was taking her son to the emergency room . . ."

Salting the stew, tasting it, listening with half an ear, Emily considered the Gowers' accidents: their wrecks, falls, and fires, all those events through which they slid so blithely. To Emily, who had no accidents whatsoever, their lives sounded catastrophic; but to Bonny, sheer custom must have leveled everything out. Emily tried to imagine reaching such a stage. She couldn't begin to.

Even now that Morgan's household had moved to hers, she thought— his mother and sister and dog, his hats and suits—she herself didn't seem to have been transformed in any way at all.

III

EMILY TOOK Gina shopping. Gina was going to Camp Hopalong in Virginia for the month of August, at Leon's parents' expense. It was time she learned to live away from home, they said. Emily was uneasy about it. She didn't like doing without Gina for so long, and also she was afraid that in Virginia, near Leon and his parents, Gina would somehow be stolen from her—turned against her. They would point out that Emily was immoral or deceitful or irresponsible, oh, any number of things, she just knew it; and Emily would not be there to explain herself. But she didn't tell Gina that. Instead, she said, "You're so young, you might get lonesome. Remember how Morgan had to bring you back from Randallstown? You couldn't make it through a simple slumber party."

"Oh, Mama. That was at Kitty Potts's house and she had that group of girls that didn't like me."

"Still," Emily said.

"*Everybody* goes to camp. I'm not a baby any more."

Emily hoisted Joshua on her hip and walked Gina down Crosswell Street to Merger Street, to Poor John's Basement. Holding Camp Hopalong's checklist in her free hand, she informed the salesgirl that they needed six pairs of white shorts. Six pairs! It was lucky Leon's parents were paying for the clothes as well. Gina took a stack of shorts into a curtained booth, while Emily waited outside. (Recently, Gina'd turned modest.) The salesgirl, awkward on her platform sandals as some frail, hoofed animal, hung in the background, clutching one elbow. Joshua started fussing and leaning out of Emily's arms, but she couldn't put him down because the floor was filthy—blackened boards permanently stamped with scraps of foil and gray disks of chewing gum. Joshua grew heavier and heavier. Emily called, "Gina? Honey, hurry, please. It's nearly lunchtime."

There was no answer. She knocked on the wall near the booth and then drew the curtain aside. Gina was standing before a full-length mirror, wearing a stained T-shirt and a pair of blinding white shorts with cardboard tags dangling from a belt loop. Tears rolled down her face. She seemed to be watching them in the mirror. "Honey!" Emily said. "What's wrong?"

"I look like a freak," Gina said.

"Oh, Gina."

"I'm fat."

"Fat! You're skin and bones."

"Look: great bobbles of fat. Obese! And my knees don't match."

"That's ridiculous," Emily said. She looked to the salesgirl for help. "Isn't that ridiculous?"

The salesgirl blew a perfect pink bubble.

"I wish I were dead," Gina said.

"Honey, would you rather not go to camp?"

Gina sniffed and said, "No, I'll go."

"You don't have to, you know."

"I want to."

"They can't force you."

"I *want* to," Gina said. "I want to get out of here! And never come back. I'm sick of everything always so messy, babies and diapers and those two old ladies taking up my bedroom. You just let them move right in on me. You acted glad to have them. Nobody *else* at St. Andrew's sleeps on a fold-out bed. And that dog that snores, and Morgan's stupid tools and things anyplace I want to sit. I'm fed up with him! Does he have to wear those hats all the time? Does he have to make such a show of himself?"

"Why, Gina!" Emily said.

But later, when they'd walked home, it was to Morgan that Gina acted friendliest. At lunch she kept giggling with him, and then flashing some kind of challenge at Emily with her flat, black, unreadable eyes.

IV

"I'M MUCH more free than I used to be," Bonny said. "I mean, he used to color my world so. You know how that is?"

There was something wrong with the telephone. Other lines seemed to be spilling into it. Emily heard faint laughter and a burble of distant voices. "No," she said, worming a screwdriver out of Joshua's grasp. "No, not exactly."

"Oh, he was so tiring! Everything had to be larger than life, extravagant, grandiloquent. Take my brother, Billy. You've met Billy. He hasn't been lucky in marriage. He's had three wives. But three is not an impossible number. I mean, the way Morgan always spoke of him, you'd think Billy'd been married *dozens* of times. 'Now, who is his wife at the moment?' he'd ask. 'Do I know her name?' And somehow we all fell in with it. Even Billy, it seemed, came to believe that he'd had this great, long train of wives. He made jokes about it, acted like a drop-in guest at his own weddings. There! See? I'm talking as if he had a wedding every week."

Something was boiling over on the stove. At the kitchen table Brindle slouched in her long, white, dingy bathrobe, laying out her Tarot cards, and when she heard the hiss of steam she looked up, but she did nothing about it. Emily stepped over the dog, stretched to the end of her cord, and took the pan off the stove and set it in the sink. "Bonny, I'm cooking supper now," she said.

"He only feels he's real when he's in other people's eyes," Bonny told her. "Things have to be *viewed*. All alone in the bathroom, he's no one. That's why his family doesn't count. They tend not to see him; you know how families are. So he has to go out and find himself in someone else's line of vision. Oh, how wearing he was! I blame it on his mother. She expected so much of him—especially after his father died. 'You can be anything,' she told him. He must have misunderstood. He thought she said, 'You can be *every*thing.' "

"He's wonderful with Gina," Emily said.

"I feel sorry for you," Bonny said.

V

TRUNKS AND dress forms, a rusty birdcage, barrels containing a gigantic cup-and-saucer collection muffled in straw, stacks of *National Geographics*, Brindle's catalogs, Louisa's autograph book, a samovar, a carton of records, a lady's bicycle, a wicker elephant. And this was only what lined the hall, which had once been as empty as a tunnel. In the living room: two sets of encyclopedias (one general, one medical), a spread-out jigsaw puzzle, Louisa's platform rocker with several yards of knitting coiled in the seat, and half a dozen runny watercolors of peaches, pears, and grapes—products of an art course Brindle had taken twenty years ago, back when she was married to her first husband. The husband himself (pink-faced, with a windowpane of white painted on his bald skull like the shine on an apple) hung in a curly gold frame above a bookcase full of manuals.

In Gina's room there was almost no floor—just a field of bureaus and unmade beds. In Morgan's and Emily's room were more bureaus (two and a half for Morgan alone), the bed, the sewing machine, Gina's old, yellowed crib with the tattered eyelet canopy they'd brought up from the basement for Joshua, and puppets dangling from the picture rails, since there wasn't space in the closet. The closet held Morgan's clothing. There, also, no floor was evident—no air, even. Step inside and you'd be impacted in a solid, felty darkness, faintly smelling of mothballs.

Emily loved it all.

She began to understand why Morgan's daughters kept coming home when they had to convalesce from something. You could draw vitality from mere objects, evidently—from the seething souvenirs of dozens of lives raced through at full throttle. Morgan's mother and sister (both, in their ways, annoying, demanding, querulous women) troubled her not a bit, because they weren't hers. They were too foreign to be hers. Foreign: that was the word. All she touched, dusted, and edged around was part of a foreign country, mysterious and exotic. She drew in deep breaths, as if trying to taste the difference in the air. She was fascinated by her son, who did not seem really, truly her own, though she loved him immeasurably. At meals, she tended to keep silent and to watch everybody with a small, pleased smile. At night in bed, she never lost her surprise at finding herself alongside this bearded man, this completely other person. She felt drawn to him by something far outside herself—by strings that pulled her, by ropes. Waking in the dark, she rolled toward him with a kind of stunned sensation. She was conscious of their two surfaces meeting noticeably: oil and water.

But Morgan said they had to move to some place bigger—a place with more bathrooms, at least. He was sorry, he said, to be putting her through this. He knew she had never bargained on having his female relatives dumped at her door like stray cats. (Actually, they had climbed the stairs themselves, wearing gloves, but it was true that Bonny'd just dropped them off in front of the building.) He would like, he said, a house in the country—a large, bare farmhouse. However, there was the matter of money. Even keeping this apartment was difficult, nowadays. Mrs. Apple had raised the rent. She was not as friendly as she'd once been, Emily thought. And Morgan had lost his job. Emily felt that this was spitefulness on Bonny's part. Why should Morgan's private arrangements affect his work at Cullen Hardware? But Morgan said that was Uncle Ollie's doing, not Bonny's. In fact, he said, Uncle Ollie had seemed to leap at the opportunity—had rushed to the store as soon as he heard the news and flung Morgan's wardrobe onto the sidewalk, the selfsame wardrobe Bonny had flung there earlier. (People were so eager to get rid of his *clothes*, Morgan mourned.) It so happened that Morgan was out, at the time. He returned to find Uncle Ollie planted in front of the store, rising from a billow of hats. "Is it true what they tell me?" "Yes." "Then you're fired." If he had said, "No," Morgan claimed, Uncle Ollie would no doubt have been disappointed. He must have been waiting all along for such a chance.

Now Morgan had no steady employment, although a couple of times a week he clerked at the plumbing-supply store down the street. Emily tried to make more and more puppets, faster and faster, working late at night while Josh was asleep. Whenever Morgan saw her bent over her sewing machine, he apologized. He said, "You look like someone in an ad for unions." What he didn't understand was that Emily felt happier now than she'd ever felt before. She rattled inside this new life like . . . well, like Morgan in one of his hats, she supposed. But he went on apologizing. He couldn't believe she didn't mind.

When the time arrived for Leon to drive to Baltimore and pick up Gina, Emily cleaned the apartment so he wouldn't imagine she had let things go. But she didn't try to straighten the clutter, or get Brindle out of her bathrobe. And she didn't hide Morgan's collection of outdated Esso maps or his latest woodworking project—a formless bundle of two-by-fours leaning in a corner of the bathroom.

It was a Saturday he was coming. Saturday morning she got up early, not that she had any choice: Joshua woke her. She took him out to the kitchen and fed him, balancing his warm, damp weight in her lap. He waved his fists and pedaled with his feet as soon as he saw his cereal. His four lower teeth, as crisp as grains of rice, clicked against the spoon. He was a beautiful baby—dark and creamy-skinned, like Gina, but easier than she had been. Leon had never met him.

Gina came in, wearing her new white shorts and a Camp Hopalong T-shirt. "How come you're up so early?" Emily asked her.

"Brindle's snoring."

"Don't you want to save your new clothes till later in the day? You'll get them dirty before Daddy sees them."

"He said he was starting out at crack of dawn."

"Oh."

Emily looked at the kitchen clock. She wiped Joshua's mouth with a corner of his bib, scooped him up, and carried him off to his bath.

When she brought him back to the bedroom, dripping wet, Morgan was standing in front of a bureau threading a belt through his jeans. He was humming a polka. Then he stopped. Emily looked up from toweling the baby and found Morgan watching her in the mirror, his eyes darkened and sobered by a black felt cowboy hat. "What's wrong?" she asked him.

"Should I go?"

"Go where?"

"When he comes, I mean. Do you want me to leave you two alone?"

"No. Please. I need you to stay," she said.

Morgan saw Bonny all the time. Any dull moment Bonny had, it seemed, she would come unload something new on them—some belonging of Brindle's or Louisa's, some piece of furniture she'd suddenly decided was really more Morgan's than hers. But Emily hadn't seen Leon since the day he moved out. Even at Christmas she'd just put Gina on a Greyhound bus.

Morgan came over to stand opposite her. Lately, he had started wearing rimless, octagonal spectacles—real ones, not mere window glass. They gave him an expression of kindness and patience. He said, "I'll do whatever you want, Emily."

"I have to have you here. I can't go through it without you."

"All right."

His calm unnerved her.

"Not that this means anything to me," she said. "His coming: I don't care."

"No."

"It couldn't matter less."

"I understand."

He went back to the bureau and slipped his cigarettes into his pocket. On the bed Joshua flapped his arms and suddenly crowed.

Louisa and Brindle were having breakfast in the kitchen while Emily did the dishes. Louisa chewed her toast in a mincing way. Brindle sat with her chin in her fist and stirred her coffee aimlessly. "Last night I dreamed of Horace," she told Emily. Horace was her first husband. "He said, 'Brindle, what'd you do with my socks?' I felt terrible. It seems I'd thrown them out. I said, 'Oh, why, Horace, they're right where they belong. Just use your eyes,' I said. Then, while he was looking again, I went running to the garbage cans and dug through everything, hunting."

"I dreamed of chili," Louisa said. "My, Morgan used to love chili. He was one of those boys that, you know, likes to hang over pots in the kitchen. Always took an interest in what I cooked. Many's the time he asked me exactly what I'd put in something. 'Why do you brown the onions first?' Or, 'Which is better in spaghetti—tomato sauce or tomato paste?' 'Neither one,' I'd tell him, 'you cook down your own tomatoes, from scratch.' Well, that's another story. Chili is what he loved best. But nowadays, I don't know, I make this extra-special effort to talk about food with him the way he used to enjoy so much and it seems he doesn't take the same interest. Hardly bothers to answer. Hardly even listens, it sometimes seems to me. But of course I may be wrong."

The doorbell rang. Emily turned from the sink and looked at Brindle.

"Who could that be?" Brindle asked her.

"I don't know."

"Maybe it's Leon."

"But this is so early," Emily said.

"Well, for heaven's sake, go see. You always act so *wooden*," Brindle said.

Emily wiped her hands and went to the door. Leon stood there in a new gray suit. He looked more polished than she'd remembered— his hair cut very close to his head, his skin dark and sleek—and he'd grown an oversized, droopy mustache. Emily had seen so many of those mustaches, exactly the same shape, on young men with briefcases, lawyers, executives. She could almost believe it was a borrowed mustache, pasted on. "Leon?" she said.

"Hello, Emily."

She took a step back. (She hadn't had time to get into her shoes yet.)

"Is Gina ready?" he asked her.

"Yes, I think so."

Then Morgan appeared, swinging Joshua in the air, saying, "Ups-a-daisy . . ." He stopped and said, "Why, Leon."

"Hello, Morgan."

"Won't you come in?"

"I can't stay," Leon said, but he stepped inside. Emily shut the door behind him. After a moment's hesitation, Leon followed Morgan down the hall to the living room.

Emily wished Morgan would take his spectacles off. Wearing them, he looked humble and domesticated. He held the baby slung over his shoulder and padded around the room, arranging seats. "Here, I'll just move these, find someplace for this knitting . . . Well, ah, shall I call Gina?"

"If you will, please."

Morgan gave Emily a look she couldn't read and left, still carrying Josh.

"So!" Leon said.

"How are you, Leon?" Emily asked him.

"I'm fine."

"You look well."

"You do too."

There was a pause.

"You know I'm taking courses at the college," Leon said.

"Oh, really?"

"Yes, when I get my degree, I'm enrolling in this training program at Dad's bank. It's interesting work, when you see it up close. You'd think it would be dull, but it's really very interesting."

"That's nice," Emily said.

"So I'd like to keep Gina year-round."

"You *what?*"

"Now, Emily, don't be hasty. Think this over. I've got a good apartment, stable life, schools nearby. I promise she could visit you any time she liked; I swear it. Emily, you have your son now. You have another child."

"Gina stays with me," Emily said. Her teeth were chattering.

"What kind of set-up is this for her?"

"It's a fine set-up."

Louisa appeared in the door, navigating the floorboards as if they lay under a foot of water. She made her way to Leon and said, "You're sitting in my chair."

"Oh, sorry," Leon said.

He stood up. Emily said, "Um, do you remember Leon, Mother Gower?"

"Yes, perfectly," she said.

Leon moved to the sofa next to Emily. He smelled of aftershave— not his own smell at all. Louisa arranged herself in her rocker and spread her skirt all around her.

Then Brindle entered with a large, cracked mug of coffee. She sat on the end of the sofa nearest Leon. "So what have *you* been up to?" she asked him.

"I'm planning to enroll in this training program at the bank."

"Oh, yes. Training program. Well, things have been in a fine pickle here, I can tell you."

"Brindle—" Emily said.

But Louisa suddenly interrupted. "And where's your pretty wife?" she asked Leon.

"Excuse me?"

"Where's that girl that used to bring me fruitcake?"

Leon looked at Emily.

"I'll go check on Gina," Emily said.

Even the flow of her skirt, as she walked out, seemed strained.

She found Gina and Morgan standing together among the unmade beds, fiddling with Gina's camp flashlight. "Naturally it doesn't work," Morgan was saying. He tipped the batteries into the palm of his hand. "You've filled it wrong."

"How could I have filled it wrong? I used what they said to use, D size."

"Yes, but the poles are not reversed, Gina."

"What poles?"

"You know that batteries are polarized," he said.

Gina said, "No . . . but I have to leave now, Morgan." She was jittery and restless, twisting a piece of hair, glancing toward the hall. Joshua had worked his way to a bureau and was tugging a satin strap from a drawer. Morgan noticed none of this. He was busy with the flashlight.

"Observe," he said, holding up a battery. "A plus sign on the positive end. A minus sign on the negative end."

Emily felt wrenched by his elderly, instructive tone of voice. She came over to him and kissed his cheek. "Never mind that," she told him. "We're making Leon wait. Gina, run say hello to Daddy. We'll fix your flashlight."

Gina left—released, like something snapped from a rubber band. Morgan shook his head and dropped the batteries in place. "Eleven years old and doesn't know batteries are polarized," he said. "How will she manage in the modern world?"

"Morgan," she said, just above a whisper. "Leon wants to keep her."

"Keep her? Hand me that cap, please."

"You don't think he can make us give her up or anything, do you? In some court of law?"

"Nonsense," Morgan said, screwing the flashlight shut.

"Morgan, I don't understand how he and I switched sides here," Emily said. "He used to claim I tied him down. Now all at once he's going to work in a bank, and I lead an unstable life, he says."

"How can you have a more stable life than ours?" Morgan asked her. He dropped the flashlight into Gina's trunk, closed the lid, and snapped the locks down.

But in the living room it seemed that everyone was conspiring to seem as unstable as possible. Gina was sitting on Leon's knee, which she had not done in years. She looked awkward and precarious. Louisa was knitting her eternal scarf. The dog was asking to go out: he paced up and down in front of Leon, his toenails clicking on the floor. And Brindle had somehow worked around to her favorite subject: Horace. "I never thought we had much in common because he was a gardening man, always messing in his garden. He owned the rowhouse next to ours when I was just a girl. We only had a little puddle of a yard, but he had a corner lot, with roses and azaleas out back and some of those tiny fruit trees that you flatten to a wall—tortured, I always said. I never liked that kind of tree. And a real little fountain with a statue of a goddess. Well, not real; just plaster or something, but still. He came out every morning and watered his flowers, pruned his shrubs if the merest sprig was out of place. I laughed at him for that. Then he brought me fresh-picked roses with the dew and the aphids still on them and I would say, 'Oh, thanks,' hardly caring, but if he didn't come I started noticing. What doesn't leave an empty space, if you're used to it and it goes? I think he was lonesome. He said I put him in mind of his plaster goddess, but that just made me laugh more. One of her bosoms was hanging out and she didn't have a nipple. And he was an *old* fellow, really, or seemed old then, these knotted white legs in gardening shorts . . . but when he came calling he wore trousers, and a white shirt with one of those collars that spread wide, like wings. Oh, I sincerely miss him still," she said, "and I suppose I always will. Now it's me that's bringing roses, when I go to visit his grave."

"Everything's packed," Emily told Leon.

"Good."

He set Gina aside and stood up.

"What's funniest," said Brindle, rising also, "is I'm older now than Horace was when he started courting me. Can you believe it?"

Leon gave Emily a long, stern look. It was plain what he was saying: Call this a fit life for a child? As if she understood, Louisa lifted her chin and fixed him with a glare.

"Usually," she told him, "I would be in a much more elegant place, I want you to know."

Then Brindle wheeled on her and said, "Oh, Mother, hush. Wouldn't every one of us? Be quiet."

Still Emily wouldn't answer what Leon was asking her.

Leon and Morgan together carried the trunk through the hall. Harry led the way, in a joyful rush, and Gina followed with her sleeping bag. Emily had Joshua astride her hip. Already, so soon after his bath, he had a used look. Emily pressed her cheek to him and drew in his smell of milk and urine and baby powder. She trailed the others down the stairs.

"I brought my father's Buick because I knew we'd need the luggage space," Leon was telling Morgan. "But maybe still I'll have to get a rope from somewhere. I'm not so sure the lid will close."

"You want to keep a rope in your car at all times," Morgan said. "Or better yet, one of those nylon-coated cords with hooks at either end. Simply go to any discount camping store, you see . . ."

Leon set down his end of the trunk and rummaged through his pockets for the keys. The sun gave his hair a hard blue shine, like bits of coal. Emily studied him from the doorway. The odd thing was that although she no longer loved him, she had the feeling this was only another step in their marriage: his opening his father's Buick, Morgan helping him load the trunk in, Gina tossing her sleeping bag alongside. They were linked, in some ways, forever. He turned back to her and held out a hand. It was probably the first time in her life that she had shaken hands with him.

"Emily," he said, "think about my suggestion."

"I can't," she said. She lifted the baby's weight. Barefoot, with one hip slung out, she felt countrified and disadvantaged.

"Just think about it. Promise."

Instead of answering, she went over to the car and bent to kiss Gina through the window. "Honey, be careful," she said. "Have a good time. Call me if you're homesick; please call."

"I will."

"Come back," she said.

"I *will*, Mama."

Emily stepped away from the car, and stood in the crook of Morgan's arm, smiling hard and holding Josh very close.

VI

"I'VE DECIDED to become a writer," Bonny said. "I've always had a bent in that direction. I'm writing a short story composed entirely of thirty years' worth of check stubs and budget-book entries."

"What kind of story would that make?" Emily wondered. She sat down in the nearest kitchen chair, holding the receiver to her ear.

"You'd be surprised at how a plot emerges. I mean, checks to the diaper service, then to the nursery schools, then to the grade schools . . . but it's sad to see things were so cheap once. It seems pathetic that I spent ten dollars and sixteen cents on groceries for the second week of August nineteen fifty-one. Did Morgan see my personal?"

"What personal?" Emily asked.

(Of course he'd seen it.)

"My personal in the classified section. Don't tell me he doesn't read the papers any more."

"Oh, did you put a personal in?"

"It said, MORGAN G.: *All is known.* Didn't he see it?"

"Morgan can't be bothered reading every notice in the paper."

"I thought that would really get him," Bonny said. "How he would hate for all to be known!"

She was right. He'd hated it. He'd said, "What does this mean? Of course I realize it must be Bonny's doing, but . . . do you think it might be someone else? No, of course it's Bonny. What does she mean, all is known? *What's* known? What is she talking about?"

"He likes to think he's going through life as a stranger," Bonny said. Emily said, "I believe I hear the baby crying."

"Sometimes," Bonny said, "I wonder if there's even any point in blaming him. It's the way he *is*, right? It's in his genes, or . . . None of his family has ever seemed quite normal to me. I didn't know his father, of course, but what kind of man must he have been? Killing himself for no good reason. And his grandfather . . . and his great-great-uncle! Has he told you the story of his great-great-uncle? Uncle Owen, the black sheep. What would it take to be the black sheep of that family? You wonder. No one ever says, if they know. This was when the family was still in Wales. Uncle Owen was such an embarrassment, they sent him off to America. Sort of a . . . remittance man, is that what they call them?"

"I'd better hang up," Emily said.

"When they sailed into New York Harbor, Uncle Owen was so excited he started dancing all over the deck," Bonny said. "The sight of the Statue of Liberty drove him wild. He started jumping up and down too close to the railing. Then he fell overboard and drowned." She started laughing. "Do you believe it? This is a documented fact! It really happened!"

"Bonny, I have to go now."

"Drowned!" said Bonny. "What a man!" And she went on laughing and laughing, no doubt shaking her head and wiping her eyes, for as long as Emily stood listening.

VII

ONE NIGHT in August the doorbell rang with a stutter—two quick burrs before it fell silent. Morgan had gone out shopping. Emily thought he might be the one at the door, maybe too burdened to manage his key. But when she answered, she found a young, pale, fat boy, sweating heavily, teetering on dainty feet and holding a bouquet of red carnations. He said, "Mrs. Meredith?"

"Yes."

"Will the dog bite?"

She didn't want to say he wouldn't, though it should have been obvious. Harry sat beside her, no more interested than was polite, slapping his tail against the floor with a rubbery sound.

"Well, fella. Down, fella," the boy said, advancing. Emily stepped back. "You don't know me," he told her. "My name is Durwood Linthicum from Tindell, Maryland."

The shine on his forehead gave him a desperate, determined look. She thought he couldn't be more than eighteen. She wondered if the flowers were for her. But then he said, "I brought these to give your husband."

"My husband?"

"Mr. Meredith," he said, pressing farther inward. She took another step back and bumped into a china barrel. "My father was Reverend R. Jonas Linthicum," he said. "He's passed now. Passed in June."

"Oh, I'm sorry to hear that," she said. "Mr. Linthicum, my husband isn't here just now—"

"I see the name don't strike a chord," he said.

"Um . . ."

"Never mind, your husband will know it."

"Well, but, um . . ."

"My father and Mr. Meredith used to correspond. Or at least, my father corresponded. My father ran the Holy Word Entertainment Troupe."

"Oh, yes," Emily said.

"You've heard of it."

"I remember your father wanted us to come . . . give Bible shows, wasn't it?"

"Now you got it."

"Well, you see, Mr. Linthicum—"

"Durwood."

"See, Durwood . . ."

Behind him, the door opened wider and Morgan stepped in, carrying a twenty-five-pound keg of powdered skim milk with a water stain at one edge. "Mr. Meredith!" said Durwood. "These are for you."

"Eh?" said Morgan. He set down the keg and took the carnations. He was wearing his tropical outfit—white Panama hat and white suit. Next to all that white, the carnations were startling, too bright to be real, like a liquor ad in an expensive magazine. Morgan buried his beard in them and took a long, thoughtful sniff.

"I been wanting to meet you since I was thirteen, fourteen years of age," Durwood said. "Any time we came near Baltimore, I begged and pestered my father to let me see one of your shows. Durwood Linthicum," he said, producing the name with a flair. He held out a large, soft hand. Emerald and ruby (or colored glass) rings were embedded in his fingers. "I know *you* know me, all those letters you received."

"Ah. Linthicum," said Morgan. He shook the hand, looking past Durwood to Emily.

"Holy Word Entertainment Troupe," Emily said.

"*Oh*, yes."

"Not to speak ill of the dead," said Durwood, "but my father didn't always have such very good business sense. Like, he saw one of your shows and thought right much of it, saw those articles about you in the papers, but all he thought was, 'That fellow could put on some fine, fine Bible stories. Daniel in the lions' den and Ruth and Naomi.' Right? Why, *I* knew that you would say no! You do other things besides, you do 'Red Riding Hood' and 'Beauty and the Beast.' *I'm* aware of that!"

Morgan stroked his beard.

"Could we maybe take a seat?" Durwood asked. "I got something to lay out before you."

"Why, surely," said Morgan.

He went down the hall to the living room, and Durwood followed. Emily came last, unwillingly. Some moment had slipped past her, here. She'd intended to clear all this up, but now it seemed too late.

In the living room Louisa was rocking and knitting. She glanced at Durwood and cast her yarn busily over her needle. "Mother," Morgan said, "this is Durwood Linthicum."

"It's a pleasure," said Durwood. He sat down on the couch and leaned toward her, lacing his fingers in front of him. "Ma'am, I guess you know what kind of son you got here."

Louisa looked over at Morgan, her shaggy black eyebrows like two sharp roofs.

"I been telling my father for years," Durwood said. " 'Daddy, you take that fellow however you can obtain him. We want to branch out, anyhow; nobody cares for this Bible stuff these days. With all our connections—schools, clubs, churches—we got a sure thing!' I said. 'We got everything we need!' There's this other group I like too—the Glass Accordion. I'm just crazy for their music. But he said no, we're only booking gospel music here. Wouldn't give them the time of day. Wouldn't even come hear them. Well, that's another story. I plan to pay them a visit right after I leave you folks. But it's you I feel this special interest in. Mr. Meredith, sir, you are near about my idol! I been following all the news of you. I think you're wonderful!"

"Why, thank you," said Morgan, smelling his carnations.

"Only, it's funny: you don't much look like your photos."

"I grew a beard, you see."

"Yes, a beard will do it, I guess." Durwood looked over at Emily. He said, "But I hope it don't mean you've . . . gone hippie, or some such."

"No, no," Morgan said.

"Well, good! Well, good! Because, now, maybe me and my father didn't always see eye to eye on every little thing, but, you know, I still want a Christian outfit, still want a fine, upstanding group we wouldn't be ashamed to take to a school auditorium . . ." He trailed off, suddenly frowning. He said, "I surely hope those Glass Accordion folks are not on drugs. Do you think?"

"Oh, no, no, I shouldn't imagine they are," Morgan said soothingly.

"You're going to like it in Tindell, Mr. Meredith."

"Tindell?"

"Well, you wouldn't want to keep on living in Baltimore, would you? We got connections all over the state of Maryland, and clear through southern Pennsylvania."

Louisa said, "I've been to Tindell."

"Well, there now!" said Durwood.

"Hated the place."

"Hated *Tindell?*"

"Didn't seem truly populated."

"Well, I don't know how you can say that."

"Empty as a graveyard. Stores all closed."

"You must have gone on a Sunday."

"It *was* a Sunday," she said. "Sunday, March sixth, nineteen twenty-one. Morgan had not been born yet."

"Who's Morgan?"

"Him," she said, jabbing her chin at Morgan.

"It's a family nickname," Morgan said. "A sign of affection. Emily, could you show Mother off to bed now?"

"Bed?" said his mother. "It's not even nine o'clock yet."

"Well, you've had a hard day. Emily?"

Emily rose and went over to his mother. She set a hand under her wiry arm and helped her gently to her feet. "What's got into him?" Louisa said. "Don't forget my knitting, Emily."

"I have it."

She led the old woman down the hall and into her room. Brindle was already there, writing in her diary. She looked up and said, "Bedtime already?"

"Morgan has a guest."

Louisa said, "I wish we were back at Bonny's house. A person had breathing room at Bonny's house. Here I'm shunted around like an extra piece of furniture."

"I'm sorry, Mother Gower," Emily said. She went to the closet for Louisa's nightgown, which hung on a hook. Brindle's and Louisa's silky dresses packed the rod. At the far end were Gina's things: two school jumpers, two white blouses, and a blue quilted bathrobe. It made Emily sad to see them. She removed the nightgown from its hook and closed the door. "Can you help her with her buttons?" she asked Brindle. "I'd better get back to the living room."

But when she left, she didn't go to the living room after all. She stood in the hall a moment, listening to Durwood's breathy voice— Mr. Meredith this, Mr. Meredith that. "Used to be I didn't even *like* a puppet show, never liked that Punch-and-Judy stuff, but your puppets, Mr. Meredith, they're another matter altogether."

She crossed the hall and went into her own room. First she closed the door partway, so that only a thin crack of light showed, and then she changed into her nightgown and slipped between the sheets. Across from her, Joshua stirred in his crib and gave a snuffling sigh. The window was open and she heard all the sounds of summer—a police siren, someone whistling "Clementine," music from a passing radio. Durwood said, "Think how it'd free you! Think on it, Mr. Meredith. We do the booking; we do the billing, let you attend to more essential things. Why, we even got Master Charge. Got BankAmericard. Got NAC, I tell you."

There was something about a sound heard from a lying-down position: it was smaller, but clearer. She even heard Morgan's match strike when he lit a cigarette. She smelled his sharp smoke. She was reminded of houses she had visited as a child—the rough, ragged smoke of hand-rolled cigarettes and the smells of fried fatback and kerosene in the Shufords' and Biddixes' kitchens, where she had been ill at ease, an outsider. Shrinking inwardly, as her family would have expected her to, she had waited barely within the door for some schoolmate to snatch up a spelling book and a couple of cold biscuits for lunch. But she had longed, all those years, to step farther into those kitchens and to have them open up to her. She smiled now, in the dark, and fell asleep listening to Morgan's rumbling answers.

Then the apartment was suddenly still and Morgan was in the

bedroom. He stood in the light from the hall, gazing into the mirror above one bureau. His Panama hat was still on his head. He took off his glasses and rubbed the bridge of his nose. He emptied his pockets of change, a crackling pack of Camels, and something that rolled a short distance and fell to the floor. He stooped for it, grunting. She said, "Morgan?"

"Yes, sweetie."

"Has he gone?"

"Yes."

"All this 'Mr. Meredith' business," she said. "Why didn't you tell him?"

"Oh, well, if it makes him happy . . ."

He came to sit on the edge of the bed. He bent over to kiss her (still in his hat, which seemed about to topple onto her), but just then, slow, unsteady footsteps started across the hall. He straightened up. There was a tiny knock.

In the lighted doorway Louisa stood silhouetted. Her long white nightgown outlined two stick legs. "Morgan?" she said.

"Yes, Mother."

"I fear I may have trouble sleeping."

"Jesus, Mother, you've barely got to bed yet."

"Morgan, what was the name of the man we used to see so much of?"

"What man, Mother?"

"He was always around. He lived in our house. Morgan, what was his name?"

"Mother! Christ! Go to bed! Get out of here!"

"Oh, excuse me," she said.

She wandered away again. They heard her in the living room—first in one part, then in another, as if she were walking without purpose. The springs in the sofa creaked, directly behind their heads.

"You shouldn't be so rude to her," Emily told Morgan.

"No," he said. He sighed.

"Shouting like that! What's wrong with you?"

"I can't help it. She never sleeps. She's down to three hours a night."

"But that's the way old people *are*, Morgan."

"We don't have any chance to be alone," he said. "Mother, Brindle, the baby . . . it's like a transplant. I transplanted all the mess from home. It's like some crazy practical joke. Isn't it? Why, I even have a teenaged daughter again! Or near teenaged; nowadays they're adolescents earlier, it seems to me . . ."

"I don't mind it," Emily said. "I kind of enjoy it."

"That's easy for you to say," he told her. "It's not your problem, really. You stay unencumbered no matter what, like those people who can eat and eat and not gain weight. You're still in your same wrap skirt. Same leotard."

Little did he know how many replacement leotards she had had to buy over the years. Evidently, he imagined they lasted forever. She smoothed his hair off his forehead. "You'll feel better when we move," she told him. "Naturally it's difficult, six people in two bedrooms."

"Ah! And what will we use for money, for this move?"

"I'll find some other places to sell my puppets. I don't think Mrs. Apple pays me enough. And I'll start making more of them. And Brindle—why can't Brindle work?"

"What doing? Pumping gas?"

"There must be something."

"Emily, hasn't it occurred to you that Brindle's not all that well balanced?"

"Oh, I wouldn't say—"

"We're living in a house of lunatics."

She was silent. It was as if he'd twisted some screw on a telescope.

"Anyway," he said, more gently, "she has to help out with Mother. She may be a total loss other ways, but at least she saves you some of that—Mother's little mental lapses and her meals and pills."

He nudged her over on the bed and lay down next to her, fully dressed, with his head propped against the wall. "What we want to do," he said, "is desert."

"Do what?"

"Just ditch them all," he said, "and go. We want a place that's smaller, not bigger."

"Oh, Morgan, talk sense," she said.

"Sweetheart, you know that Gina would be better off with Leon."

She sat up sharply. "That's not true!" she said.

"What kind of life is this for her? Strange ladies in her bedroom . . . You mark my words. After that luxury camp, after she's visited Leon a couple of days and gone out sailing with Grandpa Meredith and shopping for clothes with Grandma, she's going to call and ask to stay. You want to bet? She's at that age now; she disapproves of irregularity. She'll like Leon's apartment swimming pool and tennis courts and whatever else. He may even have a sauna bath! Ever thought of that?"

"I can't do without Gina, Morgan."

"And the others," he said. "Mother and Brindle. You think Bonny wouldn't take them back? If we walked out of here and left them, Brindle would be on the phone to Bonny before we hit the pavement. 'Bonny, dear, they've left us!' " Morgan said in a high, gleeful voice. " 'Goody, now we can get back to color TV and civilization!' And Bonny would say, 'Oh, God, I suppose it's up to me now,' and here she'd come, rolling her eyes and clucking, but secretly, you know that she'd be pleased. She likes a lot of tumult. A lot of feathers flying in her nest. I'd ask her for a divorce again and this time she'd agree to it. No, I can't do that, I don't want her knowing where we are. I don't want her driving after us with hats and dogs and relatives. I'll bring one suit, one hat, and you and Josh. We'll just clear out—pull up our tent and go."

"Yes? Where to?" Emily asked. She was lying flat again, with her eyes closed. There was no point taking him seriously.

"Tindell, Maryland," he told her. "Join up with that fellow Durwood."

"It was Leon he was asking for."

"*I* am Leon, for all he knows."

"Oh, Morgan, really."

He was silent. He seemed to be thinking. Finally he said, "Isn't it funny? I've never changed my name. The most I've done is reverse it. My name has been the one last thing I've hung on to."

She opened her eyes. She said, "I mean this, Morgan. I do not intend to leave Gina."

"Oh, all right, all right."

"I absolutely mean that."

"I was only talking," he said.

Then he rose and went to the closet, and she heard his Panama hat settle among the other hats with a dim, soft, whiskery sound.

VIII

"IT'S ALL very easy for you," Bonny said, "because Morgan's in a position of certainty by now. You know what I mean? He's . . . solidified. You inherited him when he was old and certain. You have never got lost in a car together and yelled at each other over a map; he will always seem in charge, to you."

Emily stood in pitch dark, lifting first one foot and then the other from the cool, slick kitchen floor. She said, "Bonny, why do you keep calling?"

"Hmm?"

"This is just not natural. Why are we always on the phone this way?"

Bonny let out a whoosh of smoke. She said, "Well, I'm worried about his eyes."

"His eyes?"

"I'm reading this book. This book by some Japanese expert. Everything's in the eyes, it says. If you can see a rim of white below someone's iris, you can be sure that person's in trouble. Physically, emotionally . . . and you know Morgan's eyes. That's not just a *rim* of white, it's an ocean! His lower lids sag like hammocks. I don't think he's eating right. He needs more vegetables."

"I feed him plenty of vegetables."

"You know he has a sweet tooth. And he drinks so much coffee, chock-full of sugar. Deadly! Refined white sugar, processed sugar. It's a wonder he's lasted as long as he has. Oh, Emily! He should be eating alfalfa sprouts and fresh strawberries, organically grown."

"There's nothing wrong with Morgan's diet."

"He should cut down on red meats and saturated fats!"

"I have to hang up now, Bonny."

"If he were properly fed," said Bonny, "don't you think he'd act different? I mean, basically he's a good man, Emily. Basically he's warm-hearted and open. Openness is his problem, in fact. Oh, Emily, if I had him back, don't you think I would feed him better now?"

IX

EMILY FELT her way down the dark hall, stubbing her toe against the wicker elephant. She arrived in the bedroom and found Morgan wide awake, propped against the wall, silently smoking a cigarette. He didn't say anything. She got into bed beside him, smoothed her pillow, and lay down. The telephone rang in the kitchen.

"Don't answer," Morgan said.

"What if it's someone else?"

"It's not."

"What if it's Gina? An emergency?"

"It won't be. Let it ring."

"You can't say that for sure."

"I'm almost sure."

At this hour, in this mood, "almost" seemed good enough. She took the chance. She didn't get up. There was something restful about simply giving in, finally—abdicating, allowing someone else to lead her. The phone rang on and on, first insistent, then resigned, faint and forlorn, rhyming with itself, like the chorus of a song.

1979

I

HE WAS standing in Larrabee's Drugstore, waiting for his change. He'd bought a pack of Camels, a box of coughdrops, and a *Tindell Weekly Gazette*. The saleslady rang up his purchases, but then fell into conversation with another customer. It surely was cold, she agreed. It was much too cold to be March. Her cat wouldn't leave the stove and her dog was having to wear his little red plaid coat. She kept Morgan's change in her cupped hand, jingling it absently. Morgan stood waiting— an anonymous, bearded, bespectacled man of no interest to her. Finally he gave up and opened out his paper. He liked the *Gazette* very much, although it didn't carry Ann Landers. He scanned the personals. *I will not be responsible, I will not be responsible . . .*

In the Lost and Found he learned that someone had lost a rubber plant. The things that some people mislaid! The carelessness of their lives! A complete set of Revereware cooking pots had been found in the middle of North Deale Road. A charm bracelet in the high-school parking lot.

Now for the obituaries. Mary Lucas, Long-Time Tindell Resident. Also Pearl Joe Pascal, and Morgan Gower, and . . .

MORGAN GOWER,
HARDWARE STORE MANAGER

Morgan Gower, 53, who maintained a home at
the Tindell Acres Trailer Park, died yesterday after
a lengthy illness.
Mr. Gower had served as manager of the downtown branch of Cullen Hardware, in Baltimore.
He is survived by . . .

He raised his head and looked around him. The drugstore was of old, dark wood, its shelves sparsely stocked. In some spots there was only one of an item—one box of Sweet 'n Low packets, its corners dented; one tube of Prell shampoo with a sticky green cap. It was definitely a real place. It smelled of damp cardboard. The saleslady was ancient, her skin so wrinkled that it seemed quilted, and her glasses hung on a chain around her neck.

. . . is survived by his wife, the former Bonny
Jean Cullen; seven daughters, Amy G. Murphy,
of Baltimore; Jean G. Hanley, also of Baltimore;
Susan Gower, of Charlottesville, Virginia . . .

"Sir," the saleslady said, holding out his change.
He closed the newspaper and pocketed the money.
Outside, a cold, damp wind hit him. It was Sunday morning. The streets were empty and the sidewalks seemed wider and whiter than usual. All the other stores were closed—the little dimestore, the grocery store, the barbershop. He walked past them slowly. His pickup was parked in front of the Hollywood Stars Beautician. The red plywood box constructed over its truckbed (MEREDITH PUPPET CO. arching across

each side) creaked in the wind. Morgan climbed into the cab. He opened his pack of cigarettes and lit one. Coughing his habitual, hacking cough, he spread out the paper again.

> . . . Carol G. Haines, also of Charlottesville; Eliz-
> abeth G. Wing, of Nashville, Tennessee . . .

He set it down and started the engine.

Fool paper; fool backwoods editors. Even they, you'd think, would have the common sense, the decency, to check a thing like that before they printed it. Where were their standards? You call that journalism?

He drove up Main Street, puffing rapidly on his cigarette. At Main and Howell the traffic light was red. He braked, and glanced sideways at the paper.

> . . . Molly G. Abbott, of Buffalo, New York; Kath-
> leen G. Brustein, of Chicago . . .

Someone behind him honked, and he started off again. He veered from Howell into an alley, a moonscape of bleached, stubbled clay with a few empty beer bottles tossed in the weeds, and from there to the state highway. Up ahead lay the trailer park. A flaking metal sign spelled out TINDELL ACRES MONTHLY RATES J. PROUTT PROPRIETOR. He turned left on the gravel road and passed the office—a streamlined aluminum trailer whose cinderblock steps and flowerboxes attempted to give it a rooted look. *Also his mother, Louisa Brindle Gower,* a persistent voice continued in his mind; *a sister, Brindle G. T. Roberts, and eleven grandchildren.* Behind the office, a dozen smaller trailers sat at haphazard angles to one another. They might have been tossed there by a fractious child, along with the items of scrap all around them—discarded butane tanks, a rust-stained mattress, a collapsed sofa with a sapling growing up between two of its cushions. Morgan drove past an old woman in a man's tweed overcoat. He parked in front of a small green trailer and got out. The woman turned to look after him, brushing wisps of gray hair from her eyes. It was obvious she planned to start a conversation. Morgan would not admit she was there. He rushed toward the trailer, keeping his head ducked. His mouth felt too large. He had, he observed detachedly, all the physical symptoms of . . . shame; yes, that was it. How peculiar. He felt insufficiently shielded by his cap, which was trim, narrowly visored, of no particular character. He turned up the collar of his jacket before he fumbled at the door.

"Cold enough for you?" the woman called in a thin, carrying voice.

He bowed lower over the lock.

"Yoo-hoo! Mr. Meredith!"

Services will be private.

Emily was cooking breakfast. He smelled bacon, a special Sunday treat. Josh was toddling through the living room in a pair of sodden corduroy overalls with one strap trailing. Morgan scooped him into his arms and Josh chuckled.

"Did you get the paper?" Emily asked.

He set Joshua down again. "No," he said.

He had left it in the truck. He would dispose of it later on.

There was no reason to feel so embarrassed. Bonny was the one who ought to feel embarrassed. (For it was Bonny who had done it, he assumed. Of course it was. Wasn't it?) What a silly reaction to have! He considered himself with a remote, bemused curiosity. Even his posture seemed furtive—the way he walked the length of the trailer with as little noise as possible, stooped, head ducked, as if trying not to disturb the air. He went from the living room (one couch beneath a small, louvered window) through the narrow aisle between a table and the counter that was their kitchen. Sliding past Emily, he kissed the back of her neck. She had a ripple of bones down her nape that reminded him of the scalloped spines of some seashells.

He continued into the bedroom, with its single built-in bureau and bed. A Port-a-Crib took all the remaining space. To reach the little curtained closet in one corner, he had to clamber across the bed. He took his cap off and set it on the shelf next to Emily's suitcase. He took his jacket off and hung it on a hanger. He had bought the jacket last November at a place called Frugal Fred's. Having left his extra clothes behind when he fled Baltimore, he had found himself with nothing warm enough to get him through the winter, and he'd paid five dollars for this heavy blue jacket that must once have been part of an Air Force uniform, although it was bland and dull now, undercoated. All the insignia seemed to have been removed, leaving empty stitches on the sleeves and across one pocket. He supposed that was some sort of regulation. They wouldn't want anyone impersonating an officer, naturally. Yes, it was only sensible. But sometimes he liked to imagine that the insignia had been *ripped* away. He pictured a scene in a field—the ranks of men standing at attention, the bugle call, the drums, Morgan stepping smartly forward, his commanding officer stripping him of his stripes in a single dramatic gesture. Whenever he thought of this, he walked straighter in his jacket and took on an impassive expression: the look of a man who had willfully, recklessly directed his life on a collision course toward ruin. However, he knew it was a jacket that no one would glance at twice. And his cap was what they called a Greek sailor cap, but not really Greek-looking, not seaworthy-looking; everybody wore them nowadays, even teenaged girls at the local high school, tilting the visors over their jumbles of curls.

He washed his hands in the tiny bathroom and returned to the kitchen. Emily was dishing out breakfast. He sat down at the table and watched her lay two strips of bacon on his plate. "Come eat, Josh," she called.

Josh was running a tin trolley car along the edge of the couch. He brought the trolley to the table with him, swaggering along in his rocking-horse gait, studiously silent. (He was the quietest, most accepting child Morgan had ever known.) In his layers of shirts and sweaters he seemed to be having trouble bending his chunky arms. Emily picked him up and set him in his chair. "What's that?" he asked, pointing to his cup.

"It's orange juice, Josh."

Josh took a bite from a strip of bacon, fed another bite to the front window of his trolley car.

"Did you mail my letter?" Emily asked Morgan, sitting down across from him.

"What letter?"

"My letter to Gina, Morgan."

"Oh, yes," Morgan said. "I took it to that box in front of the Post Office."

"It'll reach Richmond by Tuesday, then," Emily said.

"Well, or Wednesday."

"If she writes me back the same day, I might get a letter on Friday."

"Mm."

"She hardly ever writes the same day, though."

"No."

"I wish she were a better letter-writer."

He said nothing. She looked up at him.

"Is something wrong?" she asked.

"Wrong?"

"You seem different."

"I'm fine," he said.

She went back to buttering her toast. Her hands were white with cold, the nails bluish. The curve of her lashes cast faint shadows on her cheeks. It struck him how unchanged she was. Year after year, while everyone around her grew older, Emily kept her young, pale, unlined face, and her light-colored eyes gave her a look of perpetual innocence. She wore the same clothes. Her hair was the same style, piled in braids on top of her head with a few stray tendrils corkscrewing at her neck to give her a hint of some secret looseness—always possible, never realized—that could stir him still.

Well, he would go to the editors. Of course he would. He'd go storming in with the paper. "See here, what's the meaning of this? Don't you people ever check your facts? *Morgan Gower, Hardware Store Manager!* Where's your sense of responsibility? *I* am Morgan Gower. Here I stand before you."

But they would say, "Aren't you that fellow Meredith? One that works for young Durwood?"

In fact, he had no case.

ll

EMILY ZIPPED Josh into his jacket for a walk, but Morgan decided not to go with them. "Don't you feel well?" she asked him.

"I'm fine, I tell you."

"Did you pick up those coughdrops?"

"Yes, yes, somewhere here . . ."

He slapped his pockets and beamed at her, intending reassurance. She went on frowning. "Don't forget we have that show tonight," she told him.

"No, I haven't forgotten."

After they left, he watched them through the living-room window— Emily a fragile little thread of a person, Josh in his fat red jacket trudging along beside her. They were heading north, across a field, toward the scrubby pine woods that ran along the highway. The field was so lumpy and rutted that sometimes Joshua stumbled, but Emily had hold of his hand. Morgan could imagine her tight, steady grip— the steely cords in her wrist, like piano wire.

He turned away from the window a fraction of a second before the phone rang, as if he'd been expecting it. Maybe he just wouldn't answer. It was sure to be someone pushing in, someone who'd found him out: "So! I hear you died." But, of course, no one had any way of knowing. He made himself go into the bedroom, where the phone sat on the bureau. It rang six times before he reached it. He lifted the receiver, took a breath, and said, "Hello."

"Is that you, Sam?" a man asked.

"Yes."

"It is?"

"Yes."

"You don't sound like yourself."

"I've got a cold," Morgan said.

Morgan grinned into the mirror.

"Well, I guess you heard what happened to Lady."

Then a strange thing happened. It felt as if the floor just skated a few feet away from him. Not that he lost his balance; he stood as firm as ever, and his head was perfectly clear. But there was some optical illusion. His surroundings appeared to glide past him. He might have been riding one of those conveyor belts that carry passengers into airport terminals. Come to think of it, he had felt this way once before in an airport near Los Angeles. He'd gone to fetch Susan—it must have been four or five years ago; she'd had some kind of crack-up over a broken love affair—and after flying all one day he'd landed but gone on flying, it felt like. Or everything had flown around him, as if he'd been traveling so long, such a distance, that a sudden stop was impossible. He blinked, and reached out for the bureau.

"Sam?" the man asked.

"I'm not Sam. Please. You have the wrong number."

He hung up. He looked around the trailer, and found it stable again.

Then he took his cap and jacket from the closet and put them on, and he wrote a note to Emily: *Gone on an errand. Back soon.* He let himself out the door and crossed the yard to his truck and climbed in.

It was a forty-five-minute drive to Baltimore, and all through it he talked steadily underneath his breath. "Silly damn Bonny," he muttered, "damn meddler; stupid, interfering meddler, thinks she's so—" He glanced in the rearview mirror and swung out to pass a van. "Sitting there rubbing her hands together, laughing at me; thinks she got *to* me somehow. Ha, that's how much she knows, yes . . ."

He wondered how she'd found out what town he lived in. He had never told her. He considered the possibility that she had put the item in every paper in the state of Maryland—every paper in the country, even. Lord, all across the continent, for anyone to see. He pictured her telephoning hundreds and thousands of editors, rushing into their offices, trailing balls of Kleenex and rough drafts on the backs of cash-register tapes—a woman with her accelerator stuck. She had always lived a headlong kind of life. Any mental image he had of her (he thought, honking at a wandering sports car) showed her breathless, with her hair in her eyes and her blouse untucked. Look how she'd thrown his clothes out, and his mother and his sister and the dog! Cursing to himself, slamming on his brakes, he forgot that she had thrown them out at different times. He imagined that she'd dumped them all at once. He seemed to remember Brindle and Louisa, deposited in front of the hardware store, waiting on little camp stools till he could collect them. Or, why camp stools, even? Lying on their backs, like overturned beetles, in an ocean of discarded costumes. He recalled that Bonny often seemed to be held together by safety pins. Safety pins connected a slip strap to her slip, a buttonhole to the thready place where a button should have been, and her watch to its black ribbon band. And the watch was almost never wound. And the gaps in her hems were repaired with Scotch tape that rustled when she walked; no, when she ran; no, when she galloped by. She had never been known to just walk.

This used to be all farmland, but now each town was linked to the others by a frayed strand of filling stations and shopping malls. Morgan sped along. The superstructure on his truckbed moaned. The padlock on its rear door clanked whenever he slowed down.

"Thinks she's so clever, thinks I care. Thinks it matters what fool thing she does to me."

He entered the outskirts of Baltimore. They'd put up more apartment buildings. You couldn't turn your back, it seemed. At a traffic light a boy braked beside him in a long, finned Dodge that must have been twenty years old. All the windows were closed, but the music on his radio was so loud that it sailed out anyhow—the "Steadily Depressing, Low-Down, Mind-Messing, Working at the Carwash Blues." In spite of himself, Morgan beat time on the steering wheel.

At least there was a little sun here—a pale, weak, late-winter sun lighting white steeples and empty sidewalks. He drove north on Charles, passing a stream of small shops and then the University, deserted-looking, its buildings clean and precisely placed like something built of toy blocks. He turned into a corridor of large houses, cafés, apartment buildings, and parked on Bonny's street but some distance from her house, so she wouldn't easily see the truck from her windows. Then he got out and lit a cigarette and started waiting.

It was cold, even in the sunlight. He raised his collar around his ears. He saw the newspaper on Bonny's front walk. Ten-something in the morning and she hadn't brought it in yet; typical. A cardinal was sitting in the dogwood tree, a drop of red in a net of black branches. Morgan wondered if it could be one of those who'd hatched in that net in the mock-orange bush a few years back. He felt some proprietary interest. All one summer he'd chased the cat away; the parent birds would alert him, fluttering and giving their anxious chirps that sounded like the clink of loose change in a pocket. But didn't cardinals migrate? His cigarette tasted like burning trash. He ground it out.

Then here came Billy's wife, Priscilla, tapping up the walk in her spiffy white coat, carrying her basket-shaped purse that was sure to have a whale carved on its lid. She disappeared into the house. (She had to step right over the paper.) She was extraneous, no one he ever gave much thought to; he dismissed her instantly. He leaned forward and watched the door open again. Out popped a boy. His grandson? Todd? If so, he'd grown. He was carrying a yellow skateboard, and when he reached the street he just skated away—here one second, gone the next, for Morgan didn't watch after him. He was centered on that door still.

A long time went by. He leaned against the hood of the truck and listened to the engine ticking as it cooled.

The door first darkened, drawing inward, and then vanished altogether. Bonny stepped out on the stoop. Beneath her matted brown cardigan she wore something peasantish, unbecoming—a gauzy, full blouse, and a gathered skirt that made her look fat. Morgan assumed she was heading for the paper, but she ignored it as the others had and continued down the walk. Morgan slid around behind the truck.

She didn't even look in his direction. She turned west, bustling along. He saw something flash in her hand—her red billfold, no doubt over-stuffed as always with credit cards, outdated photos, and wrinkled little wads of money.

For a while he followed, keeping well back. He knew where she was going, of course. On a Sunday morning, with Priscilla there, and Todd, and who knew how many other people, she'd be off to the bakery for cinnamon rolls. But he followed anyway, and fixed his eyes on her. She'd let her hair grow, he noticed—a mistake. The puffy little clump at the back of her neck had turned into a sort of oval, with tattered ends.

What was going on in that head?

This was why he'd come: to find out. He'd driven here without wondering what for, and was confronted with it now so abruptly that he stopped short. All he wanted to ask was, why had she *done* it?

Was some meaning implied?

Did she imagine . . . ?

No, surely not.

Did she imagine he really had passed away?

"Passed away" was all he was up to just now. "Died" would stick in his throat. No, he couldn't ask that.

He continued to stand there while Bonny went on racing toward the bakery.

Then he turned and went back to the house. He circled around it. (The front door opened to the center hall, where anyone might see him enter.) He walked to the side, toward the screen porch, reached through a rip in the screen and raised the rusty hook and let himself in. The moldy smell of the wicker furniture—like mice, like cheap magazines—reminded him of summer. He tried the knob of the glass-paned door that led to the living room. It was unlocked. (He'd warned them a thousand times.) Soundlessly, he slipped in.

The room was empty. Last night's Parcheesi game lay scrambled in front of the cold gray fireplace. A cup was making a ring on the coffee table. He crossed to the hall. From the kitchen Priscilla called, "Bonny? Back so soon?"

He darted toward the stairs, keeping to carpets, where his footsteps would be softest. He mounted the stairs so swiftly that he scared himself—the blurred speed of his climb was too hushed, too spooky. In the upstairs hall his heel clicked once on the floorboards by accident. He ducked into the bedroom and clapped a palm to his pounding chest.

No one came.

Her bed was unmade and her nightgown was a spill of soiled ivory nylon across the rug. All the bureau drawers were open. So was the closet. He tiptoed to the closet. How unlike itself it seemed: so much space. You couldn't say it was bare, exactly (those clothes of hers she never would give up, skirts with the hemlines altered a dozen different times, Ship 'n Shore blouses from the fifties with their dinky Peter Pan collars), but certainly it was emptier than it used to be. The shelf where he'd kept his hats now held a typewriter case, a hairdryer, and a shoebox. He opened the shoebox and found a pair of shoes, the chunky kind so out of date they were coming back into fashion.

He opened the drawer in her nightstand and found a tube of hand cream and a book of Emily Dickinson's poems.

He opened the drawer in *his* nightstand (once upon a time) and found a coupon for instant coffee, a light-up ballpoint pen, and a tiny leather notebook with *Night Thoughts* written in gilt across the cover. Aha! But the only night thoughts she'd had were:

> Woolite
> Roland Park Florist
> Todd's birthday?

Something clamped his wrist—a claw. He dropped the book. "Sir," said Louisa.

"Mother?"

"I've forgotten the number for the police."

"Mother," he said, "I've only come to . . . pick up a few belongings."

"Is it 222–3333? Or 333–2222."

She still had hold of his wrist. He couldn't believe how strong she was. When he tried to squirm away, she tightened her fingers. He could have struggled harder, but he was afraid of hurting her. There was something brittle and crackling about the feel of her. He said, "Mother dear, please let go."

"Don't call *me* Mother, you scruffy-looking, hairy person."

"Oh," he said. "You really don't know me."

"Would I be likely to?" she asked him.

She wore her Sunday black, although she never attended church—a draped and fluted black dress with a cameo at the throat. On her feet were blue terrycloth scuffs from which her curved, opaque toenails emerged—more claws. She encaged his wrist in a ring of bone.

"I said to the lady downstairs," she said, " 'There's burglars on the second floor.' She said, 'It's only those squirrels again.' I told her, 'This time it's burglars.' "

"Look. Ask Brindle if you don't believe me," said Morgan.

"Brindle?" She considered. "Brindle," she said.

"Your daughter. My sister."

"She told me it was squirrels," Louisa said. "At night she asks, 'What's that skittering? What's that scuttling? Is it burglars?' I say, 'It's squirrels.' Now I say, 'Hear that burglar on the second floor?' She says,

'It's only squirrels, Mother. Didn't you always tell me that? They're hiding their acorns in the rafters in the attic.' "

"Oh? You have rodents?" Morgan asked.

"No, squirrels. Or *something* up there, snickering around . . ."

"You want to be careful," Morgan told her. "It could very well be bats. The last thing you need is a rabid bat. What you ought to do, you see, simply take a piece of screening—"

His mother said, "Morgan?"

"Yes."

"Is that you?"

"Yes," he said.

"Oh, hello, dear," she said serenely. She let go of his wrist, and kissed him.

"It's good to see you, Mother," he said.

Then Bonny said, from the doorway, "Get out."

"Why, Bonny!" said Morgan.

"Out."

She was carrying her sack from the bakery, and gave off the mingled smells of cinnamon and fresh air. Her eyes had darkened alarmingly. Yes, she meant business, all right. He knew the signs. He edged away from his mother. (But there was only one door, and Bonny blocked it.)

"I was just leaving, Bonny," he said. "I only came to ask you something."

"I won't answer," she said. "Now go."

"Bonny—"

"Go, Morgan."

"Bonny, why'd you put that piece in the paper?"

"What piece?"

"That . . . item. What you call . . . obituary."

"Oh," she said. There was a sudden little twist to her mouth that he remembered well—a wry look, something between amusement and regret. "Oh, *that*," she said.

"What made you do it?"

She thought it over.

His mother said, "I'm certain it's not bats, because I hear their little feet."

"To tell the truth," Bonny said, "I'd forgotten all about it. Oh, dear. I really should have canceled it; I meant to all along; it was only one of those impulses that just hit sometimes—"

"I can't figure out how you knew where I lived," Morgan said.

"I called Leon in Richmond and asked," she said. "I guessed you'd tell Leon at least, because of Gina."

"But what was the point, Bonny? An *obituary*, for God's sake."

"Or do bats have feet too?" said his mother.

"It was meant to be an announcement," Bonny said.

"What kind of announcement?"

She colored slightly. She touched the dent at the base of her throat. "Well, I'm seeing someone else now," she said. "Another man."

"Ah," he said.

"A history professor."

"That explains printing my obituary?"

"Yes."

Well, yes.

He took pity on her then—her pink cheeks, and the clumsy, prideful, downward look she wore. "All right," he said. "That's all I had to ask. I'll be going now."

She drew back to let him pass. Already she'd collected herself—lifted and straightened. He stepped into the hall. Then he said, "But, ah, God, Bonny, you don't know how it felt! Really, such an . . . embarrassment, an item like that in a public place, all on account of some whim you get, some halfcocked notion!"

The twist in her mouth returned, and deepened. No doubt she found this hilarious.

"It's probably not even legal," he said.

He started coughing. He searched his pockets for his handkerchief.

"Do you want a Kleenex?" she asked. "What's the matter with you, Morgan? You don't look well."

"I could probably have you arrested," he told her. He found his handkerchief and pressed it to his mouth.

"Let's not talk about what we could arrest each other for," Bonny said.

So he went down the stairs at last, not even saying goodbye to his mother or giving her a final glance. Bonny followed. He heard the rustle of her bakery sack close behind his ear—an irritating sound. An irritating woman. And this banister was sticky to the touch, downright dirty. And you could break your neck on the rug in the entrance hall.

At the door, when his thoughts were flowing toward the pickup truck (get gas, check tires) and the journey home, Bonny suddenly seemed to have all the time in the world. She brushed a piece of hair off her forehead and said, "His name is Arthur Amherst."

"Eh?"

"This man I'm seeing. Arthur Amherst."

"Good, Bonny, good."

"He's very steady and solid."

"I'm glad to hear it," he said, jingling his keys in his pocket.

"You think that means he's dull, I suppose."

"I know it doesn't mean that," he said.

He pulled out his keys then, and turned to leave, but was struck by something and turned back. "Listen," he said. "Those really may be bats, you know."

"What?"

"Those creatures Mother's hearing in the attic."

"Oh, well, they're not harming anybody."

"How can you be sure of that? You ought to do something about it. Don't put it off; they could chew through the wiring."

"*Bats?*" she asked.

"Or whatever," he said.

He hesitated, and then touched his cap in a salute and left.

Now there was church traffic, old men in felt hats driving carloads of tinkly old ladies, sidewalks ringing with the clop of high heels. He traveled downtown in a suspended state of mind, shaking off the annoyances of the morning. He traveled farther and farther, not out of the city but deeper into it. It wouldn't hurt to take a look at Cullen Hardware. There was always the possibility that Butkins would be there, even on a Sunday, maybe sorting stock or just standing idly, dimly, at the window as he sometimes did.

But the hardware store was gone. There was only a blank space between the rug store and Grimaldi Brothers Realty—not even a hole, just a vacant lot. Weeds grew on it, even. The wastepaper crumpled in its hillocks had already begun to yellow and dissolve. A billboard on the rear of the lot read: AT THIS LOCATION, NIFF DEVELOPMENT CORP. WILL BE CONSTRUCTING A . . .

He considered a minute, settled his glasses higher on his nose, and drove on. But what about Butkins? Where was Butkins? He turned left. He cut over to Crosswell Street. Crafts Unlimited was still there, closed for Sunday but thriving, obviously. The ranks of pottery jars in its window gave it an archeological look. The third-floor windows above it were as dark and plain as ever. He half believed that if he were to climb the stairs, he'd find Emily and Leon Meredith still leading their pure, vagabond lives, like two children in a fairytale.

III

"I'M CERTAIN I can fit into it," the second stepsister said. "It's only that I've been shopping all day and my feet are a little swollen."

"Madam. Please," the Prince said in his exhausted voice.

"Well, maybe I could cut off my toes."

"What about you, young lady?" asked the Prince. He was looking at Cinderella, who peeked out from the rear of the stage. Dressed in burlap, shy and fragile, she inched forward and approached the Prince. He knelt at her feet with the little glass slipper, or it may have been a shimmer of cellophane. All at once her burlap dress was mysteriously cloaked in a billow of icy blue satin. "Sweetheart!" the Prince cried, and the children drew their breaths in. They were young enough still. Their expressions were dazzled and blissful, and even after the house lights came on they continued sitting in their chairs and gazing at the stage, open-mouthed.

It was the Emancipation Baptist Church's Building Fund Weekend. There'd been two puppet shows on Saturday, and this evening's was the last one. Then Morgan and Emily could pack up their props and leave the church's Sunday School hall, which had the biting, minty smell of kindergarten paste. They could say goodbye, at least temporarily, to the Glass Accordion and the Six Singing Simonsons and Boffo the Magician. Emily set the puppets one by one in their liquor carton. Joshua staggered down the aisle with one of Boffo's great brass rings. Morgan folded the wooden stage, lifted it onto his shoulder with a grunt, and carried it out the side entrance.

It was a pale, misty night. The sidewalk gleamed under the streetlights. Morgan loaded the stage into the back of the pickup and slammed the door shut. Then he stood looking around him, breathing in the soft, damp air. A family passed—cranky children, kept awake past their bedtime, wheedling at their mother's edges. A boy and girl were kissing near a bus stop. On the corner was a mailbox, which reminded Morgan of his letter to Bonny. He'd carried it with him all evening; he might as well get it sent off. He took it from the pocket of his Air Force jacket and started across the street. (. . . *simply strew a handful of mothballs*, the letter whispered, *a. along the attic floor beams; b. in the closets beneath the eaves* . . .)

His boots made a gritty sound that he liked. Cars hissed past him, their headlights haloed. He flattened the envelope, whose corners had started curling. *But if it's bats . . .* he should have said. He'd forgotten to mention bats. *You don't want to close all the openings till you're certain the bats are . . .* and he also should have said, *Remember that Mother's vitamins are tax-deductible*, and *Don't rush into anything with this professor fellow*, and *Just loving him is not all it takes, you know.* He should have added, *I used to think it was enough that I was loving; yes, I used to think, at least I am a sweet and loving man, but now I see that it matters also who you love, and what your reasons are. Oh, Bonny, you can go so wrong . . .*

He stood at the mailbox, shaking his head, stunned. It took an auto horn to bring him to his senses, and he had the feeling that this wasn't the first time it had honked. A woman leaned out of a Chevrolet, her hair a bobbled mass of curlers. "Well? Will they or won't they?" she asked him.

"I beg your pardon?"

"Will my letters get there by Tuesday, I said, or will they drag their feet and loiter like the last ones did? You folks are always saying next-day-delivery-this, next-day-delivery-that; then it's me that gets stuck with the finance charges when you drag into BankAmericard with my credit payment two, three, four days late . . ."

She was waving a pack of letters out the window. Morgan tipped his visored cap and took them from her. "Absolutely," he said. "It was Robinson who was doing all that and now they've let him go. From here on out, you can trust the U.S. Mail, ma'am."

"I bet," she said.

She rolled up her window and screeched off.

Morgan dropped Bonny's letter in the slot. Then he went through what he'd been handed by the woman. Patti Jo's Dress Shop, LeBolt Appliances . . . he dropped them in too. Clarion Power and Light. He dropped that in. The rest were personal, addressed in a lacy, slanted script to a woman in Essex, a woman in Anneslie, and a married couple in Madison, Wisconsin. He would mail them too, but first he might just take a little glance inside. He started walking back toward the church, coughing dryly, tapping the envelopes against the palm of his hand. They were crisp and thick, weighted with secrets. They whispered *spent Monday letting that dress out some* and *labor pains so bad she like to died* and *least you could have done is have the decency to tell me.* Up ahead, Emily stood at the curb beside a cardboard carton. Josh rode astride her hip. For some reason Morgan felt suddenly light-hearted. He started walking faster. He started smiling. By the time he reached Emily, he was humming. Everything he looked at seemed luminous and beautiful, and rich with possibilities.

THE
TIN CAN TREE

1

AFTER THE funeral James came straight home, to look after his brother. He left Mr. and Mrs. Pike standing on that windy hillside while their little boy wandered in circles nearby, and the only one who saw James go was Joan. She looked over at him, but she didn't say anything. When he was a few steps away he heard her say, "We have to go home now, Aunt Lou. We have to go down." But Mrs. Pike was silent, and all James heard for an answer was the roaring of the wind.

Going down the hill he took big steps—he was a tall man, and the steepness of the hill made him walk faster than he wanted to. It was too hot to walk fast. The sun was white and glaring and soaked deep in through the mat of his black hair, and his face felt slick when he wiped it with the back of his hand. Partway down the hill he stopped and took off his suit jacket. While he was rolling up his shirt sleeves he looked back at the grave to see if the others were coming, but their backs were still turned toward him. From here it seemed as if that wind hardly touched them; they stood like stones, wearing black, with their heads down and their figures making straight black marks against the sky. The only thing moving was little Simon Pike, as he picked his way down through the dry brambles toward James. Simon looked strange, dressed up. He had always worn Levi's and crumpled leather boots, but today someone had made him put his suit on. That would be Joan. Mrs. Pike had looked at nothing but the ground for two days now, and couldn't notice what Simon wore. Joan would have polished those white dress-shoes that Simon was getting all grass-stained, and taken out the last inch of cuff on his sleeves so that they could cover his wrists. There was a thin faint line above each of his cuffs where the old hem had been; James could see it clearly when Simon came up even with him. He stood staring at the cuffs for a long time, and then he shifted his eyes to Simon's face and saw Simon frowning up at him, his eyebrows squinched into one straight line across his forehead and his mouth held tight against the wind.

"I'm coming too," he told James. His voice had a low, froggy sound; he was barely ten, but in a year or two his voice would begin to change.

James nodded and finished rolling up his shirt sleeves. There was a band of dampness beneath his collar. He loosened his tie and unbuttoned the top button of his shirt, and then he began walking again with Simon beside him. Now he went more slowly, bracing himself against the steepness of the hill. Each time he took one step Simon took two, but when he looked over at Simon to see if he was growing tired, Simon ignored him and walked faster. He wasn't sweating at all. He looked cold. James wiped his face on his shirt sleeve and followed him down between the rocks.

"Getting near lunchtime," he said finally.

Simon didn't answer.

"Want to eat with Ansel and me?"

"Well."

"Don't worry about your mother. I'll tell her where you are."

Simon said something to his shoes, but James couldn't hear.

"What's that?" he asked.

"I wouldn't bother."

"We'll tell your cousin Joan then," said James. "Soon as she gets back."

The wind was so hot it burned his face; it made lulling sounds around his ears so that he couldn't hear his own footsteps. He pushed his hair off his forehead but it fell into his eyes again, hanging in a tangled web just at the top of his range of vision. Beside him, Simon was letting his hair do what it wanted. He had greased it down with something (it needed cutting, but Joan had been too busy with her aunt to see about that) and now it ruffled up in thick strings and stood out wildly in every direction. When James turned to look at him he nearly smiled. With his face sideways to the wind the roaring sound was quieter, so he kept looking in Simon's direction until Simon grew uneasy.

"What you staring at?" he asked.

"Nothing," said James. "Some wind we got." He looked straight ahead again, and the roaring sound came back to hammer at his ears.

The ground they were treading was wild and weedy, with rocks sticking up here and there so white they might have been painted. There was no path to follow. Below them was the whole town of Larksville—the main street hidden by trees, but the outlying houses and the tobacco fields laid bare to the sun. At the foot of the hill was the white gravel road where Simon and James both lived. They lived in a three-family house that looked like only a long tin roof from here. No houses stood near it. James's brother Ansel said whoever built their house must have been counting on Larksville's becoming a city someday, but Larksville was getting smaller every year. When anyone went away to college it was taken for granted they'd never be back again, not for any longer than it took to eat a Christmas dinner in the house they'd started out in. Yet the long crowded house sat there, half a mile from town as a bird flies and a mile by car, and its three chimneys were jumbled tightly together with the smoke intermingling in wintertime.

The sight of that green part of town was cool and inviting; it made

James think of cold beers in the tavern opposite the post office. He looked down at Simon, but Simon was hunched into the jacket of his suit and he still seemed cold.

"Do you like sardines?" James asked him.

"Not much."

"Or cold cuts?"

"No."

They stepped through a tangle of briars, with the thorns making little ripping sounds against their clothes. "I could eat a pizza," Simon said.

"You better talk to Ansel, then. He makes pizzas."

Simon tripped and caught himself. He looked down at the small rock that had tripped him and then began kicking it ahead of him down the hill, swerving out of his course to recover it every time the rock rolled sideways. Gray streaks began to show on his shoes, but James didn't try to stop him.

When they reached the gravel road they turned right and began heading in the direction of the house. Simon's rock rolled into a ditch; he left it lying there. It looked as if they might get all the way home this way—not talking much, and not saying anything when they *did* talk, just as if this were an ordinary walk on an ordinary day. That suited James. He had been thinking too much, these last two days—turning things over and over, figuring out how if just some single incident had happened, or hadn't happened, things might have been different. Now he ached all over, and thinking made him sick. He was just beginning to feel easier, ambling along in silence beside Simon, when Simon turned and began walking backwards ahead of James, fixing his frowning brown eyes on a point far down the road. He opened his mouth and closed it, and then he opened it again and said, "James."

"What."

"How far down in the ground before it starts getting cold?"

"Pretty soon," said James.

"*How* soon."

"Pretty soon."

"I'm just thinking," Simon said.

To keep him from thinking any more, James said, "But then it gets hot again, down towards the center of the earth. That's beyond digging distance."

"Six feet under is stone, stone cold," said Simon.

"Well, yes."

"Good old Janie Rose, boy."

"Now, wait," James said. "Now, Janie Rose don't feel if it's cold or it's not, Simon. Get that all straight in your mind."

"I know that."

"Get it straight *now*, before you go bothering your mother about it."

"I know all about that," said Simon. He spun around and began walking forward again, still ahead of James. Strands of his hair rose up and floated behind him, like the tail plumes of some strange bird. "You don't get what I mean," he called back.

"Maybe not."

"Now, you know Janie Rose."

"Yes," said James, and without his wanting it the picture of Janie Rose came to him, sharp and clear—Janie Rose looking exactly the way he thought her name sounded, six years old and blond and fat, with round pink cheeks and round thick glasses. He hadn't been planning to think about it. He said, *"Yes, I know,"* and then waited for whatever would follow, keeping part of his mind far away.

"She just hated cold," said Simon. "Playing 'Rather' in the evenings after supper—which would you rather be, blind or deaf; which would you rather die of, heat or cold—she chose heat any day. She had a twenty-pound comforter on her bed, middle of summer."

"I already said to you—" James began.

"Well, I *know*," said Simon, and he started walking faster then and whistling. He whistled off-key, and the tune was carried away by the wind.

When they reached their house, which stood slightly swaybacked by the road with its one painted side facing forward, James stopped to look in his mailbox. There was only a fertilizer ad, which he stuck in his hip pocket to throw away later. "See what your mail is, why don't you," he told Simon.

Simon was walking in small neat circles around the three mailboxes. He stuck out a hand toward the box with "R. J. Pike" painted on it and flipped the door open, and then made another circle and came to a stop in front of the box to peer inside. "Fertilizer ad," he said. He pulled it out and dropped it on the roadside. "Letter for Mama." He pulled that out too, and dropped it on top of the first. "She'll never read it."

James picked the letter up and followed Simon along the dirt path to the house. Halfway through the yard the path split into three smaller ones, each leading to a separate door on the long front porch. Simon took the one on the far left, heading toward James's door, and James took the far right to deliver the Pikes' letter. The Pikes' part of the porch had a washing machine and an outgrown potty-chair and a collection of plants littering it; he had to watch his step. When he bent to slide the letter under the door he heard a scratching sound and a little yelp, and he stood up and called to Simon, "Your dog wants out, all right?"

"All right."

He opened the door and a very old, fat Chihuahua slid through, dancing nervously on stiff legs as if her feet hurt her. "Okay, Nellie," he said, and bent to pat her once and then stepped over her and continued down the porch. On his way he passed the Potter sisters' window and waved to Miss Faye, smiling and shaking his head to show her he couldn't come in. She was sitting behind closed glass, full face to the window and as close to it as she could get, and when James shook his head the corners of her mouth turned down and she slumped back in her chair. Neither she nor Miss Lucy could climb that hill to the funeral, and they were counting on James to tell them about it.

Simon was standing at James's door, his hands in his pockets. "Why didn't you go on in?" James asked him, and Simon just shook his head.

"I reckoned I'd wait," he said.

"Ansel'd let you in."

"Well, anyway," said Simon, and stood back to let James open the door for him.

The inside of the house was cool and dim. It had unvarnished wooden floorboards, with no rugs, and when Simon walked in he clicked his heels sharply against the wood the way he did when he was wearing his boots. Walking that way, swinging his thin legs in heavy, too-big strides, made him look younger, like a small child entering a dark room. And he didn't look to his left, although he knew James' brother would be on the couch where he always was.

"Ansel?" James said.

"Here I am."

James closed the screen door behind him and looked toward the couch. Ansel was sitting there, with his back very straight and his feet on the floor. Usually he spent the day on his back (he had anemia, the kind that never got much better or much worse so long as he was careful), but today he had made a special effort to be up. He was wearing his Sunday black suit, and he had slicked his pale hair so tightly down with water that it was the same shape as the narrow bones of his head. Probably he had thought that was the least he could do for Janie Rose. When James came in Ansel didn't look in his direction; he was watching Simon. He waited until Simon finally turned around and faced him, and then he stood up and stooped toward him in what looked like a bow. "I hope this day wasn't too hard on you," he said formally, and then sat down and waited while Simon stood frowning at him.

"We got back before the others," James said. "I promised Simon lunch."

"Oh. Well, I doubt that he— Here, you want to sit down?"

He patted the couch where he sat, which meant that he was extending special privileges. Ordinarily he didn't like people sitting there. After a minute Simon shrugged and clicked his heels over to the couch, and Ansel moved aside to give him room.

"I haven't really talked to you since the, uh— It's been quite a few days. But I wanted to say—"

"I been busy," said Simon.

"Well, sure you have," Ansel said. "I know that." He was sitting forward now, placing the tips of his fingers together, gazing absently at the floor with those clear blue eyes of his. It made James nervous (Ansel had been known to get too serious at times like this) but before he could change the atmosphere any, Ansel had begun speaking again. "Uh, I wanted to tell you," he said, "I been meaning to say to you— sheesh! James, will you close the door?"

James gave the inner door a push and it clicked shut.

"Too much wind," Ansel said. "Well. I been meaning to, um, give you my condolences, Simon. And tell you how sorry I am not to go to the funeral. James said I shouldn't, but you don't know how I—"

"You didn't miss much," said Simon.

"What? Well, I just wish I could've come and paid my respects, so to speak. That's what I told James. But James said—"

Simon sat tight, his hands pressed between his knees and his eyes straight ahead. When James started into the kitchen Simon half stood, with that squinchy little frown on his face again, so James stopped and leaned back against the wall. He wasn't sure why; always before this it was Ansel that Simon followed, leaving James to Janie Rose. But now Simon sank back in his seat again, looking easier, and began kicking one foot lazily in the direction of the coffee table. Ansel rambled on, his speech growing more certain.

"I had never been so shocked by *any* news," he said. "I was saying that to James. I said, 'Why, she and Simon were over here not but a while ago,' I said. 'Why, think how Simon must *feel*.' "

"I feel all right," Simon said.

"I mean—"

"I feel all right."

Ansel rubbed the bridge of his nose and looked over at James, and James straightened up from his position against the wall. "Mainly he feels hungry," he told Ansel. "I promised him lunch."

"Why, sure," said Ansel. "If he wants it. But I doubt he does. You hungry, Simon?"

"I'm starved," Simon said.

"You going to eat?"

"I *reckon* I am."

"I see," said Ansel.

Simon stood up and came over to James. When he got to James's side he just stood there and waited, with his eyes straight ahead and his back to Ansel. "We going to get that pizza?" he asked.

"Anything you want."

"Pizza?" Ansel said, and Simon turned then and looked up at James.

"That's what I promised him," James said.

"Why, Simon—"

"Hush," said James. "Now, Simon, we got three kinds of pizza mix out there. Sausage, and cheese, and something else. I forget. You go choose and then we'll cook it up. All right?"

"All right," Simon said. He turned and looked back at Ansel, and then he went on into the kitchen. When he was gone, James came over and sat down beside Ansel.

"Listen," he said.

Away from outsiders now, Ansel slumped back in his seat and let his shoulders sag. There were tired dark marks underneath his eyes; he hadn't slept well. "You're on my couch," he said automatically. "Do I have to tell you, James? Sitting like that makes the springs go wrong."

"Simon's folks are still on the hill," said James. "We've got to keep him here; I promised Joan he wouldn't sit in that house alone."

"Ah, sitting alone," Ansel said. He sighed. "That's no good."

"No. Will you help keep him busy?"

"The couch, James."

James stood up, and Ansel swung his feet around and slid down until he was lying prone. "I don't see how he can eat," he said.

"He's hungry."

"I *wonder* about this world."

"People handle things their own ways," James said. "Don't go talking to him about dying, Ansel."

"Well."

"Will you?"

"Well."

There was a crash of cans out in the kitchen. A cupboard door slammed, and Simon called, "Hey, James. I've decided."

"Which one?"

"The sausage. There was only just the two of them." He came into the living room, carrying the box of pizza mix, and Ansel raised his head to look over at him and then grunted and lay back and stared at the ceiling. For a minute Simon hesitated. Then he walked over to him and said, "*You're* the pizza-maker."

"Who said?" Ansel asked.

"Well, back there on the hill James said—"

"All right." Ansel sat up slowly, running his fingers through his hair. "It's always something," he said.

"Well, maybe—"

"No, no. I don't mind."

And then Ansel smiled, using his widest smile that dipped in the middle and turned up at the corners like a child's drawing of a happy man. When he did that his long thin face turned suddenly wide at the cheekbones, and his chin became shiny. "We'll make my speciality," he said. "It's called an icebox pizza. On refrigerator-defrosting days that's the way we clean the icebox; we load it all on a pizza crust and serve it up for lunch. You want to see how I make it?"

He was standing now, smoothing down his Sunday jacket and straightening his slumped shoulders. When he reached for the pizza mix Simon walked forward and gave it to him, not hanging back now but looking more at ease. Ansel said, "This is something every man should know. Even if he's married. He can cook it when his wife is sick and serve her lunch in bed. Do you want an apron?"

"No," said Simon.

"Don't blame you. Don't blame you at all. Well—" and he was heading for the kitchen now, reading the directions as he walked. His walk was slow, but not enough to cause James any worry. James could judge the way Ansel felt just by glancing at him, most of the time. He had to; Ansel would never tell himself. When he felt his best he was likely to call for meals on a tray, and when he was really sick he might decide to wallpaper the bedroom. He was a backward kind of person. James had a habit of looking at him as someone a whole generation removed from him, although in reality he was twenty-six, only two years younger than James himself. He was thinking that way now, watching with narrow, almost paternal eyes as Ansel made his way into the kitchen.

"Naturally there are no really *rules*," Ansel was saying, "since you never know what might be in the icebox." And Simon's voice came floating back: "Fruit, even? Lettuce?" "*Well*, now . . ." Ansel said.

James smiled and went over to the easy chair to sit down, stretching his legs out in front of him. It felt good to be home again. The house was a dingy place, with yellow peeling walls and sunken furniture. And it was so rickety that whenever James had some photography job that required a long time-exposure he had to run around warning everyone. "Just *sit* a minute," he would say, and he would pull up chairs for everybody in the house and then go dashing off to take his picture before people started shaking the floors again. But at least it was a comfortable house, not far from town, and Ansel had that big front window in the living room where he could watch the road. He would sit on the couch with his elbows on the sill, and everything he saw passing—just an old truck, or a boy riding a mule—meant something to him. He had been watching that long, and he knew people that well.

Thinking of Ansel and his window made James look toward it, to see what was going on, but all he saw from where he sat was the greenish-yellow haze of summer air, framed by mesh curtains. He rose and went over to look out, with his hands upon the sill, and peered down the gravel road toward the hill he had just come from. No one was in sight. Maybe it would be hours before they returned; Joan might still be standing there, trying to make her aunt and uncle stop staring at that grass. But even so, James went on watching for several minutes. He could still feel the wind, gentler down here but strong enough to push the curtains in.

For a long time now, wind would make him think of today. He had climbed that hill behind all the others, and seen how the wind whipped the women's black skirts and ruffled little crooked parts down the backs of their hairdos. And when the first cluster of relatives had taken their leave at the end, stopping first to touch Mrs. Pike's folded arms or murmur something to Mr. Pike, the words they said were blown away and neither of the parents answered. Though they might not have answered anyway, even without the wind. The day that Janie Rose died, when James had spent thirty-six hours in the hospital waiting room and finally heard the news with only that tenth of his mind that was still awake, he had gone to Mrs. Pike and said, "Mrs. Pike, if there's anything I or Ansel can do for you, no matter what it is, we will want to do it." And Mrs. Pike had looked past him at the information desk and said, "Just falling off a *tractor* don't make a person die," and then had turned and left. So James had let them be, and went home and told Ansel to keep to himself a while and not go bothering the Pikes. "Not even to give our sympathy?" asked Ansel, and James said no, not even that. He hadn't liked the thought of Ansel's going to the funeral, either. Ansel said he had half a mind to go anyway—he could always rest on the way, he said—but James could picture that: Ansel toiling up the hill, clasping his chest from the effort and gasping out lines of funeral poetry, calling out for the whole procession to stop the minute he needed a rest. So James had gone alone, and quietly, and had promised to report to Ansel the minute it was over. The only one there that he had spoken to was Joan; the only two sounds he carried away with him were Joan's low voice and the roaring of the wind. He thought he would never like the sound of wind again.

Out in the kitchen now, Janie Rose's brother was talking on and on in his froggy little voice. "I never saw *peanut* butter on a pizza," he was saying. "You sure you know what you're doing, Ansel?"

"Just wait'll you taste it," Ansel said.

James left the window and went out to the kitchen. "How's it going?" he asked.

"It's coming along," Ansel said. He was swathed in a big checked dishtowel, wrapped right over his suit jacket and safety-pinned at the back, and on the counter stood the almost finished pizza that Simon was decorating. The kitchen was rippling with heat. James took his shirt off and laid it on the counter, so that he was in just his undershirt, and he opened the back door.

"Aren't you hot?" he asked Simon.

But Simon said, "No," and went on laying wiener slices down. On the floor at his feet were little sprinklings of flour and Parmesan, and the front of his suit was practically another pizza in itself, but the important thing was keeping him busy. It was too bad the pizza-making couldn't go on for another hour or so, just for that reason; they would have to find something else for him to do.

Ansel said, "Now the olives, Simon."

"I don't think I like olives."

"Sure you do. Olives are good for the brain. Will you look at your shirt?"

Simon looked down at his shirt and then shrugged.

"It'll wash," he said.

"Your mama'll have a fit."

"Ah, she won't care."

"I bet she will."

"She won't care."

"*Any* mother would care about *that*," said Ansel. "Makes quite a picture."

"Pictures," James said suddenly. He straightened up. "Hey, Simon. You seen my last photographs?"

"No," said Simon. "You get another customer?"

"Not in the last few days, no. But I took a bunch on my own a while ago. When you're done I'll show you."

"Okay," said Simon.

"Olives," Ansel reminded him.

James went over to the back window and looked out. There was the Pikes' Nellie, burrowing her way through a tangle of wild daisies and bachelor's buttons. He had been planning to pick Joan a bunch of those daisies, before all this happened. They were her favorite flowers. Now he couldn't; the house would be stuffed with hothouse funeral flowers. And anyway, he couldn't just walk in there with a bunch of daisies in his hand and risk disturbing the Pikes. The daisies would have grown old there, waving in the sunshine on their long green stems, before he could go back to doing things like that again.

The pizza was in the oven. Ansel slammed the door on it and wiped his hands and said, "*There*, now."

"How much longer?" Simon asked.

"Oh, I don't know. Fifteen-twenty minutes. We'll go out where it's cool and wait on it. You coming, James?"

James followed them out to the living room. It seemed very dark and cool here now. Ansel settled down on his couch with a long contented groan, and Simon went over to Ansel's window and stood watching the road.

"Anybody seen those people?" he asked James.

"What people?"

"My mama and them. Anybody seen them?"

"No, not yet."

"Well, anyway," said Simon, "I reckon I'll just run on over and have a look, see if maybe they haven't—"

"I think we'd have seen them if they'd come," said James. "Or heard them, one."

"*Still* and all, I guess I'll just—"

"You two," Ansel said. "Do you have to stand over me like that?" He was lying full length now, with his head propped against one of the sofa arms. "Kind of overwhelming," he said, and James moved Simon gently away by one shoulder.

"I almost forgot," he said. "You want to see my pictures?"

"Oh, well I—"

"They're good ones."

"Well."

James went down the little hallway to his darkroom. There was a damp and musky smell there, and only the dimmest light. He headed for the filing cabinet in the corner, where he kept his pictures, and opened the bottom drawer. The latest ones were at the front, laid away carefully (taking pictures for fun wasn't something he could afford very often), and when he pulled them out he handled them gently, examining the first two alone for a minute before he returned to the living room.

"Here you go," he said to Simon. "Your hands clean?"

"Yes."

His hands were covered with tomato sauce, but he held the pictures by the rims so James didn't say anything. The first picture didn't impress Simon. He studied it only a minute and then sniffed. "One of those," he said. James grinned and handed him the next one. Neither Simon nor Janie Rose had ever liked anything but straight, posed portraits— preferably of someone they could recognize, which always made them giggle. But when James wasn't taking wedding pictures, or photographs for the Larksville newspaper, he turned away from portraits altogether. He had the idea of photographing everyone he knew in the way his mind pictured them when they weren't around. And the way people stuck in his memory was odd—they were doing something without looking at him, usually, wheeling a wheelbarrow up a hill or hunting under the dining-room table for a spool of thread. Old girlfriends of his used to object to being photographed in their most faded blue jeans, the way he remembered them from some picnic. But almost always he won out in the end; the pictures of people in his mind and in his filing cabinet were nearly identical. Joan he imagined in a dust storm, the way he had first seen her (she had come down the road with two suitcases and a drawstring handbag, spitting dust out of her mouth and turning her face sideways to the wind as she walked). For a long time now he had waited for another dust storm, and last week one had come. That was in those first two pictures, the ones that Simon had barely glanced at. Even when James said, "That's your cousin Joan, if you don't know," thinking to make Simon look twice, Simon only raised his eyebrows. It was the third picture he liked. In that one Ansel was lying on his couch, looking up at the sky through the window and absently playing with the cord of the shade. "Ansel!" Simon said, and Ansel turned his head and looked at him.

"What now?" he asked.

"I just seen your picture here."

"*Oh*, yes," Ansel said.

"Of you on your couch and all."

"Oh, yes. Here, let me look." He raised himself up on one elbow, reaching out toward the picture, and Simon brought it over to him. "That's me, all right," said Ansel. He studied it for a while, smiling. "It's not bad," he said.

"I think it's a right good picture."

"Yep. Not bad at all." He handed the picture back and lay down again, staring up at the ceiling and still smiling. "They're wonderful things, pictures," he said.

"Well, some of them."

"Very *remaining* things, you know?"

"I don't like them other kind, though," Simon said. "Dust clouds and all. I can't see what *they're* for."

"They're for me," said James. "Here, I got another one of Ansel."

"James," Ansel said, "do your legs ever get to feeling kind of numb? Kind of achey-numb?"

"Prop them up."

"Propping *up* won't do it."

"It's what you get for not having your shots," James said.

"Oh, well. Right behind the knee, it is." He propped his legs against the back of the couch and slid farther down, so that his feet were the highest part of him. "This couch is too short," he said. "Here, Simon. Hand me the next one."

The next picture had Ansel sitting up, looking self-conscious. When Ansel saw it he smiled his dippy little smile again and brought the picture closer to examine it. "This is one I posed myself," he said. "Had James take it like I wanted. James, I believe it's my *shoes* aggravating that feeling."

James set the rest of the pictures beside Simon and reached over to untie Ansel's shoes. "If you'd get the right *size*," he said.

"No, it's to do with my illness. I can tell."

"It's on Wednesdays you get your shots," said James. "This is Saturday. That's five times you missed."

"Lot you care. Listen—" He twisted around, so that he was facing

Simon. "What was I talking about? The picture. That's right. I was about to say, in my estimation this picture is the best of the lot. The one of me sitting up." He tilted the picture toward the light. "Heroic, like," he said. "Profile to the window and all."

"The other one's better," said Simon.

"What other one?"

"The first one. You lying down."

"That's because you're used to me lying down," Ansel said. He sighed and tossed the picture onto the coffee table. "Everyone's used to it. When I stand up they hardly recognize me. Faces change, standing up. Become more bottom-heavy. Pass me the next one."

"I think the pizza must be done," said James. "Hey, Ansel?"

"Well, take it out. This one of Mr. Abbott—I'd be insulted if I was him. Troweling up the garden plot with his back to the camera and his rear end sticking out."

James got up and went to the kitchen. The pizza-smell filled the whole room, and when he opened the oven he thought it looked done. From a hook on the wall he took a pot-holder and then hauled the pizza out and set it on the counter, burning one finger on the way. "Ansel!" he called. He came to the living room doorway. Ansel was just bending over a picture, rocking slightly back and forth and frowning at it, and Simon was sorting through the rest of them. "Ansel," James repeated.

"This one here," said Ansel, "ought not to've been included."

"Which one?" Simon asked.

"I'm ashamed of James. You ought not to see it."

"Well, I just *saw* it," said Simon. "What's the matter with it?"

"Nothing's the matter. I'll just set it aside."

He pulled himself up and lay the picture face down on the back of the couch, looking over his shoulder to make sure Simon hadn't seen. "Shamed of James," he said.

"Well, for heaven's sake," James said from the doorway. "What's all that about, Ansel?"

"It ought never to've been included, that picture."

James crossed the living room and picked up the picture. It was a perfectly ordinary one—he'd done it as a favor for Miss Faye, who wanted her screened back porch photographed now that her nephew had spent half the summer building it. She had led James way behind the house, deep into the wild grass that grew there among scattered piles of rusted stoves and old car parts, and she directed him to photograph the whole long house so that her people in Georgia could get an idea how the porch was proportioned. "I think this is too *far*, ma'am," James told her, but she insisted and this was what had come of it—a wild, weedy-looking picture, with the house rising above a wave of grass like a huge seagoing barge. Miss Faye's porch was only a little bump sticking out along with a lot of other bumps—Janie Rose Pike's tacked-on back bedroom, the woodshed under James and Ansel's bathroom window, and the rusted old fuel barrel on its stilt legs beside the middle chimney. He hadn't shown the picture to Miss Faye yet, for fear of disappointing her. But it wasn't all *that* bad; he couldn't see what was upsetting Ansel.

"I don't get it," he said.

"Well, never you mind. Just give it back."

"What you trying to pull, Ansel?"

"Will you give it back?"

James handed it across, but before Ansel's fingers had quite touched it Simon reached out and took it away. He swung away from the couch, avoiding Ansel's long arm, and wandered out into the middle of the room with his eyes fixed frowningly on the picture. Ansel groaned.

"You see what you done," he told James.

"Ansel, I don't know why—"

"Then *listen*," Ansel said. He leaned forward, talking in a whisper now. "James, someone *departed* is in that picture—"

"Where?" Simon asked.

"Oh, Lord."

"Well, I don't see."

"Me neither," said James. "What're you up to, Ansel?"

Ansel stood up, supporting himself with both hands on the arm of the couch. When he walked over to Simon he walked like a man wading, sliding his stocking feet across the floor. He poked his finger at one corner of the picture, said "There," and then waded back again. "I'm going to lie down," he said to no one in particular.

"Ah, yes," said James. "I see."

"I don't," Simon said.

"Right here she is."

He pointed. His forefinger was just touching the Model A Ford that stood behind the house, resting on cinder-blocks that were hidden by the tall waving grass. All that could really be seen of the Ford was its glassless windows and its sunken roof—it had been submerged in that sea of grass a long time—and in the front window on the driver's side, no bigger than a little white button, was Janie Rose's moon-round face. She was too far away to have any expression, or even to have her spectacles show, but they could see the high tilt of her head as she eyed James and the two white dots of her hands on the steering wheel. She was pretending to be some haughty lady driving past. Yet when James drew back from the picture he lost her again immediately; she could have been one of the little patches of Queen Anne's lace that dotted the field. "I don't see how you found her," he told Ansel.

"No trouble."

Simon stared at the picture a while and then tilted it, moving Janie

Rose out of his focus. "She just blurs right in again," he said. "She comes and goes. Like those pictures in little kids' magazines, where you try and find the pig in the tree."

"The *what?*" Ansel said. He raised his head and looked at Simon, open-mouthed.

"But it's here, sure enough," said James. "Isn't that something? I never saw her. Not even when I was enlarging it, and I looked it over right closely then."

"It's funny," Simon said.

"You hungry, Simon?"

"I guess." But he went on staring at the picture. He seemed not so much to be looking at Janie Rose as turning the whole thing over in his mind now, holding the picture absently in front of him. With his free hand he was pulling at a cowlick over his forehead.

"When our mother died," Ansel said suddenly, "I was beside myself." Simon looked over at him.

"I couldn't think about her. I couldn't think her name. Yet people are different these days. I see that."

"Oh, well," Simon said. He returned to his picture. "James, is there such a thing as X-ray cameras? Could you take a picture of our house, like, and have the people show up from inside?"

"I don't know," said James. "I doubt it."

A fly buzzed in, humming its way in zigzags through the room, and Ansel followed it with his eyes. When the fly had disappeared into the kitchen he lay back again, gazing upwards. "I'm doing all my dying in one room now," he told the ceiling.

"Oh, stop that," James said.

"It's true. I'm getting contained in smaller and smaller spaces. First it was the whole of North Carolina; then this town; then this room. Soon no place. We *all* got to go."

"Look," James said. "I know of one stone-cold pizza in the kitchen. What do I do with it? Throw it out?"

"Well," said Ansel. He sat up and peered over at Simon. "Why do you keep looking at that picture?"

Simon put the picture down. He looked from Ansel to James, and then he stood up and stuck his hands in his pockets. "When I come to think of it," he said, "I don't want no pizza."

"Well you don't have to eat it," said James.

"I think I'll just pass it up."

"All right."

"It's hard to say what's happening to people," Ansel said. "They don't seem to realize, no more. Don't think of *themselves* being dead someday; don't mourn no more. It's hard to say what they *do* do, when you stop and consider."

"Don't die of anemia no more, either," said James.

"What do you know about it?"

Simon was tilting gently back and forth, from his toes to his heels and his heels to his toes, with his shoulders hunched high and his eyes on a spot outside Ansel's window. He didn't seem to be listening.

"Nobody's perfect," Ansel said. "Janie wasn't exactly a pink-pinafore type, I admit it. Rattling through her prayers in purple pajamas: Deliver us from measles. But she's under the earth like you'll be someday, have you thought of that? *You* in that clay, and your survivors calling you a pig in a tree?"

"Ansel, there's not a thing in this world you do right," James said.

But Ansel waved him aside and sat forward, on the edge of his couch. "What will you do about *me?*" he asked. "How *about* that, now? When I am—"

Simon was crying. He was still rocking back and forth, still keeping his hands jammed tightly in his pockets, but there were wet paths running through the flour on his cheeks and his eyes were frowning and angry. "Well—" he said, and his voice came out croaky. He took a breath and cleared his throat. "Well, I reckon I'll be getting on home," he said.

"Oh, now," said Ansel.

But James said, "All right. It's all right."

He crossed over to open the door and Simon went out, stumbling a little. James followed him. He stood on the porch and watched Simon all the way down to his end of the house, hoping Simon might look back once, but he never did. He walked stiffly and blindly, with his sharp little shoulder-bones sticking out through the back of his jacket. When he reached his own door he hesitated, with his hand on the knob and his back still toward James. Then he said, "Well," again, and pulled the door open and went on in. The screen door slammed shut and rattled once and was still. James could hear Simon's footsteps clomping on across the hollow floor of the parlor.

The aluminum porch chair was still beneath the window, where Ansel had been sitting in it to watch the funeral go by. After a minute James went over and sat down on it. He let his arms rest along the arms of the chair and the metal burned him, making two lines of sunbaked heat down the inside of his forearms. Behind him was the soft sound of the mesh curtains moving, and the sleeves of Ansel's rough black suit sliding across the splintery windowsill. "Hot out," Ansel said.

James squinted toward the road.

"I wish it was the season for tangerines."

There were no people passing now, only the yellow fields across the way rippling in the wind and one gray hound plodding slowly through the yard. In the house behind James were the soft, humming sounds of other people, murmuring indistinct words to one another and moving gently around. James closed his eyes.

"Hey, James."
He didn't answer.
"James."
"What."
"James, I told you he wouldn't eat."
The wind began again, and James rose from his chair to go inside. He didn't want to sit here any more. Here it was too still; here there was only that wind, rushing over and around the house in its solitary position among the weeds.

2

JOAN PIKE was twenty-six years old, and had lived in bedrooms all her life. She lived the way a guest would—keeping her property strictly within the walls of her room, hanging her towel and washcloth on a bar behind her door. No one asked her to. Her aunt had even said to her, once, that she wished Joan would act more at home here. "You could at *least* hang your coat in the downstairs closet," she said. "Could you do that much?" And Joan had nodded, and from then on hung her coat with the others. But her towel stayed in her own room, because nobody had mentioned that to her. And she read and sewed sitting on her bed, unless she was expressly invited downstairs.

If they had asked her, point-blank, the way they must have wanted to—if they had asked, "Why do you have to be invited?" she wouldn't have known the answer. It was what she was used to; that was all. When she was born, her parents were already middle-aged. They weren't sure what they were supposed to do with her; they treated her politely, like a visitor who had dropped in unexpectedly. If she sat with them after supper they tried to make some sort of conversation, or gazed at her uneasily over the tops of their magazines until she retreated to her room. So now, a hundred miles from home and on her own, it felt only natural to be living in another bedroom, although she hadn't planned it that way. She had come here planning just to stay with the Pikes a week or two, until she found a place of her own, and then the children made her change her mind. When Janie Rose's hamster ran away, and Janie Rose stayed an hour in the bathroom shouting that it wasn't important, brushing her teeth over and over with scalding hot water that she didn't even notice and crying into the sink, Joan was the only one who could make her come away. After that the Pikes asked if she would like to live with them, and she said yes without appearing to think twice. This bedroom wasn't like the first one, after all. Here there was always something going on, and a full family around the supper table. When she went walking with Simon and Janie Rose, she pretended to herself that they were hers. She played senseless games with them, toasting marshmallows over candles and poking spiders in their webs to try and make them spin their names. For four years she had lived that way. Nine months of each year she worked as a secretary for the school principal, giving some of her salary to the Pikes and sending some home to her parents, and in the summers she worked part-time in the tobacco fields. In the evenings she sat with James, every evening talking of the same things and never moving forwards or backwards with him, and she spent a little time with the Pikes. But she still lived in her bedroom; she still waited for an invitation, and when any of the Pikes wanted to see her they had to go knock on her door.

Today no one knocked. Her aunt and uncle had gone straight to their room after the funeral and were there now—the sound of Mr. Pike's murmuring voice could just be heard—and Simon was alone in his room and seemed to be planning to stay there. That left Joan with a piece of time she knew would be her own, with no one interrupting, and at first she thought it was what she needed. She could sit down and get things sorted in her mind, and maybe catch some sleep later on. There was still that heavy feeling behind her eyes from the long aching wait in the hospital. But when she tried sorting her thoughts she found it was more than she could do just now, and then when she tried sleeping her eyes wouldn't shut. She lay on top of her bedspread, with her shoes off but her dress still on in case her aunt should call her, and her eyes kept wandering around the bland, motel-like cleanness of her room. It seemed every muscle she owned was tensed up and waiting to be called on. If she were alone in the house she would have gone down and scrubbed the kitchen floor, maybe, or at least had a long hot bath. But who knew whether her aunt would approve of that on a day like today?

When she finally thought of what she could do, she sat up quickly and frowned at herself for not thinking of it sooner. It was the one thing her aunt had asked of her all day: she had been sitting at the breakfast table, digging wells in her oatmeal and staring out into the back yard, and suddenly she had caught sight of Janie Rose's draggled blue crinoline flapping on the clothesline. "Take everything away, Joan," she said.

"What?"

"Take Janie's things away. Put them somewhere."

"All right," said Joan, but she was hunting raisins for Simon's oatmeal and hadn't really been thinking about it. Now she wasn't sure how much time she would have; Simon might come in at any moment. She wanted to do the job alone, keeping it from the rest of the family, because different things could bother different people. With her it had been Janie Rose's pocket collection—modeling clay and an Italian stamp and a handful of peas hidden away during supper, sitting on the edge of the tub where they had been dumped before a bath five nights ago. She didn't think any more could bother her now.

She opened her door and looked out into the hallway. No one was there. Behind the Pikes' door the mumbling voice still rambled on, faltering in places and then starting up again, louder than before. When Joan came out into the hall in her stocking feet, a floorboard creaked beneath her and the murmuring stopped altogether, but then her uncle picked up the thread and continued. Joan reached the steps and descended them on tiptoe, and when she got to the bottom she closed the door behind her and let out her breath.

Janie Rose's room opened off the kitchen hall. It had had to be built on for her especially, because the Pikes had never planned for more than one child and the room that was now Joan's had been taken up by a paying lodger at the time. Janie didn't like her room. She liked Simon's, with the porthole window in the closet and the cowboy wallpaper. When Simon wasn't around she did all her playing there, so that her own room looked almost unlived in. On her hastily made-up bed sat an eyeless teddy bear, tossed against the pillow the way Janie Rose must have seen it in her mother's copies of *House and Garden*. And her toys were neatly lined on the bookshelves, but wisps of clothes stuck out of dresser drawers and her closet was one heap of things she had kicked her way out of at night and thrown on the floor.

It was the closet Joan began with. She pulled back the flaps of a cardboard box from the hall and then began to fold the dresses up and lay them away. There weren't many. Janie Rose hated dresses, although her mother had dreams of outfitting her in organdy and dotted swiss. The dresses Janie chose for herself were red plaid, with the sashes starting to come off at the seams because she had a tendency to tie them too tightly. Then there were stacks of overalls, most of them home-sewn and inherited from Simon, and at the very bottom were the few things her mother had bought when Janie Rose wasn't along—pink and white things, with "Little Miss Chubby" labels sewn into the necklines. While she was folding those Joan had a sudden clear picture of Janie Rose on Sunday mornings, struggling into them. She dressed backwards. She refused to pull dresses over her head, for fear of becoming invisible. Instead she pulled them up over her feet, tugging and grunting and complaining all the way, and sometimes ripping the seams of dresses that weren't meant to be put on that way. She had a trick that she did with her petticoat, so that it wouldn't slide up with her dress—she bent over and tucked it between her knees, and while she was doing all this struggling with the dress she would be standing there knock-kneed and pigeon-toed, locking the petticoat in place and usually crying. She cried a lot, but quietly.

When Joan had finished with the closet, the cardboard box was only two-thirds full. The closet was bare, and the floor had just a few hangers and bubble gum wrappers scattered over it. It looked worse that way. She reached over and slammed the closet door shut, and then she dragged the box over to the dresser and began on that.

Upstairs, a door slammed. She straightened up and listened, hoping it was only the wind, but there were Simon's footsteps down the stairs. For a minute she was afraid he was coming to find her, but then she heard the soft puffing sound that the leather chair made when someone sat in it, and she relaxed. He must not want to be with people right now. She pushed her hair off her face and opened the next dresser drawer.

Janie Rose had more sachet bags than Joan thought existed. They cluttered every drawer, one smell mixed with another—lemon verbena and lavender and rose petals. And tossed in here and there were her mother's old perfume bottles with the tops off, adding their own heavy scent, so that Joan became confused and couldn't tell one smell from another any more. She wondered why Janie Rose, wearing all this fragrant underwear, had still smelled only of Ivory soap and Crayolas. Especially when she wore so *much* underwear. On Janie Rose's bad days, when she thought things were going against her or she was frightened, she would pile on layer upon layer of undershirts and panties. Her jeans could hardly be squeezed on top of it all, and if she wore overalls the straps would be strained to the breaking point over drawersful of undershirts. Sometimes her mother made her take them off again and sometimes she didn't ("She's just hopeless," she would say, and give up), but usually, if the day turned better, Janie peeled off a few layers of her own accord. On the evenings of her bad days, when Simon came in for supper, he had a habit of reaching across the table and pinching her overall strap to see how many other straps lay beneath it. It was his way of asking how she was doing. If Janie was feeling all right by then she would just giggle at him, and he would laugh. But other days she jumped when he touched her and hunched up her shoulders, and then Simon would say nothing and fix all his attention on supper.

Out in the parlor now Joan heard the squeaking of leather as Simon rose, and the sound of his shoes across the scatter rug. She stopped in the act of closing the box and waited, silently; his footsteps came closer, and then he appeared in the doorway. "Hey, Joan," he said. There was something white on his face.

"Hey."

He looked at the cardboard boxes without changing expression, and then he went over to the bed and sat down, picking up the teddy bear in one hand. "Hey, Ernest," he said. He laid Ernest face down across his lap, circling the bear's neck with one hand, and leaned forward to watch Joan.

"I'm packing things away," she told him.

"Well, I see you are."

She folded the flaps of the box down, one corner over another so as to lock them, and then stood up and pushed the box toward the closet. "Some of your things're on the shelves there," she told Simon while she was opening the closet door. The box grated across the hangers on the floor. "You better take out what's yours, before I pack it away."

"None of it is," said Simon, without looking at the shelves.

"Some is. That xylophone."

"I don't play that any more. Don't you know I've stopped playing with that kind of thing?"

"All right," Joan said.

"I gave it for keeps."

"All right."

"Unliving things last much longer than living."

"That's true," Joan said. She chose an armload of things from the shelves—dolls, still shining and unused, a pack of candy Chesterfields, and an unbreakable yellow plastic record ordered off a cereal box. She dumped them helter-skelter into a second box and returned for another armload. "James give you a good lunch?" she asked.

"No."

"What was wrong with it?"

"Nothing," said Simon. "There just wasn't any. Because I didn't eat it."

"Oh."

"If I *had* of eaten it, it would have been a pizza."

"I see."

She dumped another armload in the box. It was half full now, and junky-looking, with the arms of dolls and the wheels of cars tangled together.

"I better make you a sandwich," she said finally.

"Naw."

"You want an apple?"

"Naw."

He crossed over to where she was standing and laid the bear gently on top of the other things. "James has got this photograph," he said, and went back to sit on the bed. "That Ansel, boy."

"What about him?"

"I just hate him. I hate him."

When it looked as if he weren't going to say any more, Joan began removing the last few things from the shelf. Every now and then she looked Simon's way, but he sat very quiet with his back against the wall and his face expressionless. Finally she said, "Well, Ansel has his days. You know that." But Simon remained silent.

The room was bare now; all that remained were the things on the clothesline. She pushed the second box into the closet and then said, "I'm going out back a minute. After that I'll fix you a sandwich." Simon stood up to follow her. "I'm only going for a minute," she said, but Simon came with her anyway, and they went down the hall and through the kitchen and out the back screen door.

It was hot and windy outside, with the acres of grass behind the house rumpling and tangling together. The few things on the line— Simon's bathing suit and Janie Rose's crinoline and Sunday blouse— were being whipped about by the wind so that they made little cracking sounds. While Joan unpinned Janie's things, Simon wandered nearby snapping the heads off the weeds.

"Simon," she called to him, "what kind of sandwich you want?"

"I ain't hungry."

"I'll just make you a little one. And go call your mama and daddy; they have to eat too."

"I wish *you* would."

"Come on, Simon."

He shrugged and started toward the house, still walking aimlessly and kicking at things. "All right," he said. "But I'll tell them it's your fault I came."

"They won't mind you coming."

"You think not?"

He banged the screen door behind him. After he was gone Joan stood in the yard awhile, clutching Janie's things against her stomach, feeling the dampness soak into her stocking feet. She wished she could just walk off. If it weren't for Simon, she would; she would go find some place to sit alone and think things out. But her feet were growing cold, and there were sandwiches to make; she shook her hair off her forehead and started back toward the house. The closer to the house she came the quieter the wind sounded, and when she stepped back into the kitchen there was a sudden silence in her ears that felt odd.

She put the things from the clothesline into the closet, and then she returned to the kitchen and leaned against the refrigerator while she planned a meal. The room was so cluttered it made thinking difficult. Small objects lay here and there, gathering dust because no one had ever found a place for them. The kitchen windows were curtainless, and littered with lost buttons and ripening tomatoes. And the wall behind the stove was covered with twenty or thirty drawings, scotch-taped so closely together they might have been wallpaper. Most of them were Simon's—soldiers and knights and masked men with guns. His mother thought he might be an artist someday. Scattered among them were Janie Rose's drawings, all of the same lollipop-shaped tree with hundreds of tiny round apples on it. She said it was the tree out back, but that was only a tiny scrubby tree with no leaves; it had never borne fruit and wouldn't have borne apples even if it had, since it was some other kind of tree. Once her mother said, "Janie, honey, why don't you draw something *else?*" and Janie had run out crying and wouldn't come down from the attic. But the next day she had said she would draw something different. She came into the kitchen where they were all sitting, carrying a box of broken crayons and a huge sheet of that yellow pulpy paper she always used. "What else *is* there to draw?" she asked, and her mother said, "Well, a house, for instance. Other children draw houses." Then they all hung over her, and she drew a straight up-and-down line and a window, and then a green circle above it with lots of red apples on it. Everybody sat back and looked at her; she had drawn an apple tree with a window in it. "*Oh,* my," she said apologetically, and then she smiled and began filling in the circle with green crayon. After that she never tried houses again. She labored away at apple trees, and signed them, "Miss J.R. Pike" in the corner, in large purple letters. Simon never signed his, but that was because his mother said she would recognize his style anywhere in the world.

When Simon came downstairs again he had changed into his boots; he was trying to make the floor shake when he walked. "Daddy's coming and Mama ain't," he said. "She ain't hungry."

"Did you ask if she wants coffee?"

"She didn't give me a chance. She said go on and let her rest."

"Well, run up again and ask her."

"*No,* sir," Simon said. He sat down firmly in one of the chairs.

"Just run up, Simon—"

"I won't do it," he said.

Joan thought a minute, and then she said, "Well, all right." She reached out to smooth his hair down and for a minute he let her, but just barely, and then shrugged her hand away.

"Daddy wants just a Co-Cola," he told her.

"He's got to have more than that."

"No. He said— Hey, Joan."

"What."

"I got an idea."

"All right."

"Why not you and me go *out* and eat. You like that?"

"We can't," Joan said.

"We could go to that place with the chicken."

"We have to stay home, Simon."

"I would pay for it."

"No," Joan said, and she touched one upright piece of his hair again. "Are you the one that doesn't like using other people's forks? That makes twice in two days you've had that idea."

"Well, anyway," said Simon. But he must have been expecting her to say no; he sat back quietly and began drumming his fingers on the table. Above them was the sound of Mr. Pike's footsteps, crossing the hall and beginning to descend the stairs, and Joan remembered why she was in the kitchen and went back to the refrigerator. She opened the door and stared inside, at shelves packed tightly with other people's casseroles. At the kitchen doorway her uncle said, "I only want a Coke, Joan," and came to stand beside her, bending down to peer at the lower shelves.

"You have to eat something solid," Joan told him.

"I can't." He straightened up and rubbed his forehead. He was a lean man, all bones and tough brown skin. Ordinarily he did construction work, but for the month of July he had been laid off and was spending his time the way Joan did, helping Mr. Terry get his tobacco in. Years of working outdoors had made his face look stained with walnut juice, and his eyes were squinted from force of habit even when he wasn't in the sun. They were narrow brown slits in his face, the same shade as Simon's, and they were directed now at Joan while he waited for her to speak.

"There's a chicken salad here from Mrs. Betts," said Joan.

"No, thank you."

"The kind you like, with pimento."

"No."

"Now, eat a *little* something," she said. "I could be perking coffee for you to take Aunt Lou, if you'd sit down a minute."

"Oh, well," he said.

He sat down awkwardly, across from Simon, giving his Sunday pants a jerk at each knee to save the crease. "How you been getting along?" he asked Simon.

"Okay."

"Not giving Joan any trouble."

"No, sir."

"He's been just fine," said Joan. She set the salad out and laid three plates on the table. Her uncle studied his own plate seriously, hunching his shoulders over it and working his hands together.

"I'm glad to hear it," he said finally. When Joan looked over at him he said, "About Simon, I mean. James and Ansel feed you okay, boy?"

"No, sir."

"Well. Joan, Dr. Kitt left a prescription for your aunt but I don't see how I can go into town and leave her. I wonder, would you mind too much if—"

"I'll see to it after we eat," Joan said.

"All right."

He accepted his chicken salad wordlessly, keeping his eyes on Joan's hands as she dished his share out. When she had passed on to the next plate, he said, "Thank you," and the words came out hoarse so that he had to clear his throat. "Thank you," he said again. Even then his voice was muffled-sounding. In the last three days he had been talking steadily, always mumbling something into Mrs. Pike's ear to keep her going. It was probably the most he had talked in a lifetime. Ordinarily he sat quiet and listened, with something like awe, while his wife rattled on; he seemed perpetually surprised and a little proud that she should have so much to say.

When Joan had sat down herself, after filling the others' plates and passing out forks, she said, "Eat, now." She looked at the other two, but neither of them picked up his fork. "*Come* on," she said, and then Simon sighed and tucked his paper napkin into his collar with a rustling sound.

"This feels like Sunday-night supper," he said.

"It does."

"Not like afternoon. Why're we eating in the afternoon? What the *day* feels like, is Wednesday."

"Wednesday?"

"Feels like Wednesday."

"Why does it feel like—?"

"She blames it on herself," said Mr. Pike.

"What?"

"It breaks my heart. She keeps saying how she was hemming Miss Brook's basic black at the time—I never *have* liked that Miss Brook— and Janie Rose comes up and says, 'Mama,' she says, 'I'm going off to—' and Lou just never did hear where. Miss Brook was going on about her bunions. 'Lou,' I told her, I said, 'Lou, *I* don't think that would have—' but Lou says that's how it come to happen. She *never* let Janie Rose play with those Marsh girls. Never would have let her go, if she had known. But she was—"

"Never let her ride no tractors, either," said Simon. "Shakes a girl's insides all up."

"Hush," Joan told him. "Both of you. There's not even a dent made in that chicken salad."

Her uncle picked his fork up and then leaned across the table toward her. "She *blames* herself," he said.

"I know."

"She keeps—"

"*Eat*, Uncle Roy."

He began eating. His fork made steady little clinking sounds on the plate, and he chewed rapidly with the crunchy sound of celery filling the silence. When he was done, Joan put another spoonful of salad on his plate and he kept on without pause, never looking up, making his way doggedly through the heap of food. Simon stopped eating and stared at him, until Joan gave his wrist a tap with her finger. Then he started eating again, but he kept his eyes on his father. When Mr. Pike reached for the bowl and dished himself another helping, still crunching on his last mouthful, chewing without breathing, like a thirsty man drinking water, Simon looked over at Joan with his eyes round above a forkful of food and she frowned at him and cleared her throat.

"Um, Mrs. Hammond phoned today," she said. "She's a very *cheering* person, Uncle Roy; maybe Aunt Lou could talk to her later on. I told her to call back in a day or—"

"Remember Janie Rose?" Simon asked.

His father stopped chewing. "Remember *what?*" he said.

"Remember how she did on the telephone? Never answering 'Hello,' but saying, 'I am listening to WKKJ, the all-day swinging station,' in case WKKJ was ever to call and give her the jackpot for answering that way. Only you know, WKKJ never *did* call—"

"Simon, I *mean* it," Joan said.

"Lou is breaking my heart," said Mr. Pike.

"Wouldn't you feel funny, if you was to call someone that answered like that? 'I am listening to—' "

"It wasn't her *fault,*" Mr. Pike said. "Janie never *asked* for no special attention, like. She just kind of—"

"God in heaven," Joan said.

The doorbell rang. It made a sharp, burring noise, and Joan stood up so quickly to answer it that her chair fell over backwards behind her. She let it stay. She escaped from the kitchen and crossed the parlor floor, smoothing her skirt down in front of her, making herself walk slowly. Behind the screen, standing close together with their faces side by side and peering in, were the Potter sisters from next door. They stepped backwards simultaneously so that Joan could swing the door open, and then Miss Faye entered first with Miss Lucy close behind her.

"We only stopped by for a minute," said Miss Faye. "We wanted to bring your supper."

"Well, come on in," Joan said. "Really, do. Come out to the kitchen, why don't you."

"Oh, I don't think—"

"No, I mean it." She took Miss Faye by one plump wrist, almost pulling her. "You don't know how glad I am to see you," she said.

"Well, if you really think—"

They walked on tiptoe, bearing their covered dishes before them like sacred offerings. When they reached the kitchen door, Mr. Pike stood up to greet them and his chair fell backwards too, so that the room with its overturned furniture looked stricken. "Why, Miss, um, Miss

Lucy," he said. "And Miss Faye. I declare. Come in and have a—"
and he bent down and pulled the chairs up by their backs, both at
the same time. "Sit down, why don't you," he said.

Joan drew up the chair from beside the stove, and Miss Lucy sat
down in it with a sigh while Miss Faye went to sit beside Simon. "We
only mean to stay a minute," said Miss Lucy. She plopped the bowl
she was carrying down on the table in front of her and then sat back,
sliding her purse strap to a more comfortable position on her wrist.
The Potter sisters always carried handbags and wore hats and gloves,
even if they were going next door. They were small, round women,
in their early sixties probably, and for as long as Joan had known them
they had had only one aim in life: they wanted to have swarms of
neighborhood children clamoring at their door for cookies, gathering
in their yard at the first smell of cinnamon buns. And although no one
came ("Children nowadays prefer to buy Nutty Buddies," Miss Faye
said), they still went on baking, eating the cookies themselves, growing
fat together and comparing notes on their identical heart conditions. It
was those heart conditions that Miss Faye was discussing right now.
She was saying, "Now, you and Lou know, Roy, how much we wish
we could have climbed that hill today. If there was *any* way, the merest
logging trail, we would've got there. But as it was, it would just have
meant more tragedy. You know that."

And Mr. Pike was saying, "Well, I know, I know," and nodding
gently without seeming to be listening. There was chicken salad on his
chin, which meant that both the Potters kept staring tactfully down at
their gloves instead of looking at him. Joan passed him a paper napkin,
but he ignored it; he sat forward on his chair and said, "It surely was
nice of you to come. Nice to bring us supper."

"It's the *least* we could do," said Miss Lucy. She looked around her,
toward the kitchen door, and then lowered her voice. "Tell me," she
whispered. "How is she now? How's Lou?"

"It just breaks my heart," said Mr. Pike.

"Oh, my."

"Not a thing I can do, seems like. She just sits. If she would stop
all this *blaming* herself—"

"They all do that," said Miss Faye.

"She said Janie was the one she never paid no mind to."

"Will you listen to that."

"Never gave her a fair share."

"If it's not one reason it's another," Miss Lucy said. "I've seen that
happen plenty of times."

"Maybe if you talked to her," said Mr. Pike. He pushed his plate
away and straightened up. "You think you could just run up there a
minute?"

"Well, not *run*, no, but—"

"I didn't mean that," he said. "No, you can take the stairs as slow as you want to. But if you two would talk to her a minute, so long as you don't mind—"

"Why, we don't mind a bit," said Miss Faye. "We'd be proud." She reached up to set her flowered hat straighter, as if she might like to put an extra hat on top of the first one for such a special visit. And Miss Lucy pulled gloves to perfect smoothness, and then folded her hands tightly over her purse.

"I just don't like to trouble you," Mr. Pike said.

"You stop that, Roy Pike."

They rose simultaneously, with their backs very straight. But even making the trip across the kitchen they walked slowly, preparing themselves for the stairs. "Be careful," Joan told them. "Just see they don't get out of breath, Uncle Roy."

"I will."

But Simon was frowning as he watched them leave. "Hey, Joan," he said.

"Hmmm?"

"When they go up to bed at night, it takes them half an hour. They take two steps and then rest and talk; they bring their knitting along."

"Well, that's kind of silly," said Joan.

"Could they crumple up and die on our stairs?"

"No, they could not," she said. "It would take more than that."

"How do you know?"

"I heard Dr. Kitt tell them so. They just shouldn't get too out of breath, is all, or run in any marathons. He said—"

"I got an idea," Simon said.

"What?"

"Listen." He stood up from his place at the table and came around to face her, with his hands hitched through his belt loops. "How about us going to a movie," he said. "That Tarzan movie."

"We're not supposed to."

"Well, I got to get out," he said.

She looked down at him, considering. His face had a thin, stretched look; patches of flour still clung to it like some sort of sad clown makeup and his hair stuck up in wiry tangles. "Well, I do have to get Aunt Lou's prescription," she said. "Would you comb your hair first?"

"Sure."

"All right, we'll go."

"Right now?"

"If you want to."

He nodded, but with his face still wearing that strained look, and turned to go upstairs and then turned back again. "I'll wash downstairs," he said.

"There's no soap here."

"I don't care."

He turned on the water in the kitchen sink and splashed his face, and then he reached spluttering for the dishtowel. "My allowance money's all the way upstairs," he said. "I'll pay you back tomorrow, if you'll lend me the money."

"All right."

She went into the living room, with Simon following, and handed him a comb from her pocketbook. While he was combing his hair she went upstairs for her shoes. Mrs. Pike's door was open now. She was lying on her bed, with her head propped up on two pillows and the sisters beside her talking steadily, and when Joan walked past, her aunt followed her with her soft blue eyes but only vaguely, as if she weren't seeing her, so Joan didn't stop in to say anything. She put on her shoes and picked up a scarf and went downstairs, where Simon was waiting with his hand on the newel post and his face strained upward.

"What're they doing?" he asked her.

"I don't know."

"Are they crying?"

"I don't think so."

"Well. I *would*'ve gone upstairs," he said. "You know."

"I know."

"Did you think I wouldn't?"

"No." She sighed suddenly, looking back toward the stairs. "*I* don't know how to comfort people," she said.

"Well."

They went out the front door, across the porch, and down the wooden steps. It was beginning to get cool outside. Joan could hear tree frogs piping far away, and the wind had died down enough so that the sound of cars on the east highway reached her ears. She clasped her hands behind her back and followed Simon, cutting across the road and through the field toward town.

"Remember I've got heels on," she called.

"I remember."

"Remember that makes it hard walking."

He slowed down and waited for her, walking backwards. Behind him and all around him the field stretched wide and golden, with bits of tall yellow flowers stirring and glimmering like spangles in the sunlight. And when Joan came up even with him, so that he turned and walked forward again by her side, she could look down and see how his hair, bleached lighter on top, took on a varnished look out here and the little line of fuzz down the back of his neck had turned shiny and golden like the field he was walking in. "Right about here . . ." he said, but the wind started up just then and blew his words away.

"What?" she asked.

"Right about here is where I lost that ball. Will you keep a lookout for it?"

"I will."

"Do you reckon I'll ever find it?"

"No."

"I don't either," Simon said.

But they walked slowly anyway, keeping their eyes on the ground, kicking at clumps of wild wheat to see what might turn up.

3

"*HOLD* STILL," James said.

He bent over and peered through the camera. No one was holding still. Line upon line of Hammonds, from every corner of the state, littered the Larksville Hammonds' front lawn, sitting, kneeling, and standing, letting arms and legs and bits of dresses trail outside the frame of his camera. Whole babies were being omitted; they had crawled to other patches of grass. Yet the grown-ups stood there with their dusty blue, look-alike eyes smiling happily, certain that they and their children were being saved intact for future generations. James straightened up and shook his head.

"Nope," he said. "You've moved every which-away again. Close in tighter, now."

He waited patiently, with his hands on his hips. For five years he had been going through this. Every year there was a picture of the Hammond family reunion to be put in the Larksville paper, and another two or three for the Hammonds themselves to choose for their albums. By now he was resigned to it; he had even started enjoying himself. He smiled, watching all those hordes of Hammonds close in obligingly with sideways steps while their eyes stayed fixed on the camera. Moving like that made them look like chains of paper dolls, bright and shimmering in the heat. Eyelet dresses and seersucker suits blurred together; their whiteness was blinding. James shaded his eyes with one hand, and then he said, "Okay," and bent down over his camera again. But someone else was moving. It was Great-Aunt Hattie in the front row; she had started coughing. She was sitting in a cane-bottom chair, with children and animals tangled at her feet and the grown-ups forming a protective wall behind her. When she began her coughing fit, they closed in still tighter in a semicircle and the oldest nephew leaned down with his head next to hers. The coughs grew farther apart. After a minute the nephew raised his head and said, "She's sorry, she says." The others murmured behind him, saying it didn't matter. Swallowed down the wrong throat," said the nephew.

Someone called out, "Give her brown bread." And someone else said, "No, rock candy will do it." But the aunt spread her old hands out in front of her, palms down and fingers stretched apart, signifying she was better now and wanted to hear no more about it. "Back in your places," James said, and the twenty or thirty Hammonds closest to him drifted back to their original positions and made their faces stern again. Mothers looked anxiously down the rows, gripping their neighbors' arms and peering around them to make sure their children were at their best, and fathers hooked their thumbs into their belts and glared into the lens. "Hold it," James said. When he snapped the picture there was a little stirring through the group, and everyone relaxed. "That's the second," he called to the hostess. "You want another?"

"One more, James."

While he was fiddling with the camera people began talking again, still standing in their set places, and some lit cigarettes. He peered through the view-finder at them. If this were any other picture he would snap it now, catching them at their ease, but family pictures were different. He liked the way they stood so straight in jumbled, self-conscious rows, and molded themselves to make a block of tensed-up faces. "I'm ready," he warned them, and they did it again—closed their mouths and narrowed their eyes and set their shoulders. He snapped the picture that way. Then he said, "That's all," and watched the children as they shook themselves and scattered off to play.

The hostess walked up to him, trailing white lace, sinking into the ground at every step in her high-heeled pumps. "There's one more I want, James," she said, and then stopped and let her eyes wander after her youngest child. "Joey, you *know* not to ride that dog," she called.

"Yes, ma'am."

"I want you to photograph Great-Aunt Hattie alone," she told James. "She's getting old. Can you do that?"

"If she's willing," said James.

"She's not."

"Then maybe we should—"

"Now, don't you worry," said Mrs. Hammond. "I'll talk her around. They're serving up the ice cream over there. You go and get you some, and when you're through I'll have Aunt Hattie ready. Hear?"

"Well, okay," James said. But Mrs. Hammond hadn't stayed to hear his answer.

He folded his equipment up and put it on the porch, out of the way of the children. Then he went across the yard to the driveway, where the others were standing in line for ice cream. They looked different now, quick-moving and flexible, with the paper-doll stiffness gone. In a way James was sorry. Some of the best pictures he had were these poker-straight rows of families, Hammonds and Ballews and Burnetts; he kept copies of them filed away in his darkroom, and sometimes on long lonesome days he pulled them out and looked at them a while, with a sort of faraway sadness coming up in him if he looked too long. He might have seen any one of those families only that morning in the hardware store, but when he looked at their faces in pictures they seemed lost and long ago. ("I just wish once you'd take a *giggly* picture," Ansel said. "You make me so sorrowful.") Thinking about that made James smile, and the girl in front of him turned around and looked up at him.

"I'm thinking," he told her.

"That's what it looked like," she said. Her name was Maisie Hammond, and she lived across town from here and sometimes came visiting Ansel. She thought Ansel was wonderful. James was just considering this when she said, "How's that brother of yours?" and he smiled at her.

"Just fine," he said. "He's home reading magazines."

"Well, say hello to him." She moved up a space in line, still facing in James's direction and walking backwards. Standing out in the sunlight like this she was pretty, with her towhead shining and her white skin nearly transparent, but Ansel had always said she was homely and only out to catch a good husband (it was rumored James and Ansel came from an old family). Whenever she came visiting, Ansel turned his face to the wall and played sicker than he was. That was how he planned to scare her off, but Maisie only stayed longer then and fussed around his couch. She liked taking care of people. She would fetch pillows and ice-water, and Ansel would wave them away. When she was gone, James would say, "Ansel, what you want to treat her like that for?" But by that time Ansel had fooled even himself, and only tossed his head on the pillow and worried about how faint he felt. To make it up to Maisie now (although she wasn't aware there *was* anything to be made up), James stepped closer to her in the line and said, "Maisie, it's been a good two weeks since you've been by."

"Two *days*," said Maisie. "Day before yesterday I was there."

"I never heard about it."

"You were off somewhere. Taking care of some arrangements for the Pikes."

The man ahead of her left with his Dixie cup of ice cream, and Maisie turned forward again and took two cups from the stack on the table. "Here," she said. She passed him a fudge ripple, with a little paper spoon lying across the top of it. "The children got to the strawberry before us."

"That's all right," said James. "I don't like strawberry."

He followed her back across the lawn, preferring to stick with her rather than interrupt the little individual reunions that were going on among the others. When she settled on the porch steps, fluffing her skirt out around her, he said, "You mind if I sit with you?" She shook her head, intent on opening her ice cream. "I'm going to take a picture of your great-aunt," he said.

"Oh, her."

"Do you like sitting out in the sun like this?"

"Yes," she said. But she looked hot; she was too thin and bird-boned, and being the slightest bit uncomfortable made her seem about to topple over. James was used to Joan, who was unbreakable and built of solid flesh.

When he had pried the lid off his own ice cream, and dipped into it with his paper spoon, he said, "It's sort of melty-looking." Maisie didn't answer. She was staring off across the yard. "Better eat yours before it turns to milk," he told her.

But Maisie said, "Ansel was laying down, when I went to see him."

"He does that," said James.

"I mean laying still. Not doing anything."

"Well, it was nice of you to come," he said.

She shrugged impatiently, as if he hadn't understood her. "You were out doing something," she told him. She seemed to be starting all over again now, telling the story a second time. "You weren't around."

"I was helping Mr. Pike with some arrangements," said James.

"That's what Ansel said."

"I'm sorry I wasn't around."

"Well. When I came in I said, 'Hey, Ansel,' and Ansel didn't even hear me. He was just laying there. I said, 'Hey!' and he jumped a foot, near about. He was a million miles away."

James was making soup out of his ice cream. He had it down to a sort of pulpy mess now, the way he liked it, and then he looked up and saw Maisie wrinkling her nose at it. He stopped stirring and took his first bite. "Ansel's a great one for daydreaming," he said with his mouth full.

"He wasn't daydreaming."

"Oh."

"He was crying, near about."

"*Ansel?*"

"Well, almost," said Maisie. She sat forward, with the ice cream still untasted in her hand. "I said, 'Ansel, *what's* the matter?' But he never did say. His eyes were all blurry."

"You got to remember Janie Rose," James said. "It was only three days ago."

"Well, I thought of that. But then I thought, no, Janie wasn't all that much to him. She was right bothersome, as a matter of fact. We had her over for supper just a month ago, her and her family; we gave them chicken. Mama forgot about Janie being vegetarian. Janie said, 'This chicken's *dead*,' and her daddy said, 'Well, I *hope* so,' and everybody laughed, but Mama's feelings were a little hurt. Though she went to the funeral and all, just like anyone else. I said, 'Ansel, is that what's bothering you? Janie Rose Pike being taken?' But the way he was acting, I don't think that was the real reason."

"His feet hurt him sometimes," said James.

"This is *serious*, James."

"I'm being serious."

"Anyway," Maisie sighed, and she took the first mouthful of her ice cream. It bothered him, the way she ate it; she chewed, slowly and carefully, even though the ice cream was nothing but liquid now. When she had swallowed, she said, "All he would talk about was dying. He said he could see how it would all turn out; they would mourn him like they mourn Janie Rose, not sad he died but sorry they hadn't liked him more. He'd rather they be sad he died, he said."

"Oh, now," said James. "He's been on that for days. It'll pass."

"Will you listen? I can't hardly sleep nights, for thinking about it. I keep wondering if he's all right."

"Of course he's all right," James said.

But Maisie was still hunching over, frowning into space. Her ice cream was forgotten. A child ran by, chased by another child, grabbing Maisie's knee for support as he pivoted past her, and Maisie only brushed his hand away absentmindedly. "Those times he goes away," she said finally, "those times he starts to get better and then goes off drinking for a night and can't be found till morning. He'll die of it."

"He won't die," said James. "He could lead a life like any other man, if he wasn't so scared of needles."

"He *might* die," Maisie said. "What if one of those nights of his, he don't come back?"

But James was getting tired of this. "Look," he said firmly. He swallowed the last of his ice cream and said, "Ansel only goes so far, you notice. Only enough to worry people. You ever thought of that?"

"What? Well, if that isn't the *coldest* thing. How do you know how far he'll go?"

"I just do," James said. "I been through this."

"Can you say for *sure* how far he'll go?"

"I been through it *hundreds* of times."

"I believe you don't even give it a thought," said Maisie. "That's what Ansel said. He said, 'What does *James* care—' "

"Well, we've got to be clearheaded about this," James said.

"You're clearheaded, all right." She jabbed her spoon into her ice cream and left it there, standing straight up in the middle of the cup.

" 'What does James care,' he said, and then just lay there with his eyes all blurry—"

"I do everything I can think of," said James.

"Oh, foot."

"I try everything I know."

"Then tell me this, if you do so much all-fired good. Can you say that never, never once in all your life, have you thought about Ansel's going off and letting you be someday?"

"Well, for—"

"Never thought how nice it would be to live on your own for a change, just one little old TV dinner to pop into the—"

"I try *everything* I *know!*" James shouted, and then noticed how loud his voice was and lowered it. "I mean—"

But Maisie just folded in the rim of her Dixie cup with all her concentration, as if her mind was made up. Then she rose and said, "Well, I'll be seeing you." Her skirt was rumpled in back, but she didn't bother smoothing it down. When she walked away James stood up, from force of habit, and waited until she was halfway across the yard before he sat down again. Inside he felt slow and heavy; he was chewing on his lower lip, the way he did when he didn't know what to say. All the way across the yard he watched her, and turned his empty ice cream cup around and around in his hands.

In front of him some children were playing statues. An out-of-town boy was flinging the others by one arm and then crying, "Hold!" so that they had to freeze there, and when he came to Janice Hammond, who was the littlest, he swung her around so hard that she spun halfway across the lawn and landed against Mrs. Hammond, who was heading over toward James. "Hold!" the boy said. Mrs. Hammond looked down at Janice, who was clutching her around the middle. She said, "*Oh*, Janice," tiredly, and was about to pull away, but the other children stopped her. "No, Janice has got to stay that way," said the out-of-town boy, and Mrs. Hammond seemed too tired to argue. She stood still, rising above Janice's circled arms like the figure of someone passively drowning, and called out, "James, we're ready with Aunt Hattie."

"Where is she?" he asked.

"Over there. Standing up. We wanted her to sit but she says no, she'll do it standing. Die with her boots on. She doesn't like cameras." She came to life suddenly and disentangled herself from Janice, ignoring the other children's protests. "She's fading," she said. James looked over at Janice, surprised, and Mrs. Hammond caught his look and shook her head. "Aunt Hattie, I mean," she said. "Just fading away."

"I'm sorry to hear that," said James. He gathered up his equipment and came after her. "She looked all right to me."

"Well, she fades out and then in again."

They circled a little group of women, all standing in identical positions with folded arms while they watched the children playing statues. "I don't like doing this if she don't want me to," James called. "Some people just have an allergy to cameras."

But Mrs. Hammond smiled brightly at him over her shoulder and kept walking. Out here on the grass the sun was still hot, and the back of Mrs. Hammond's powdered neck glistened faintly. She had the same brittle little bones as her niece Maisie, only covered now with a solid layer of flesh. James looked away from her and shifted his equipment to the other shoulder. "Right here would be a good place," he said. He hadn't really looked around; he just wanted to stop and not do anything any more. The heaviness inside was weighing him down. He set the camera on its tripod and then leaned on it, with his chin propped on his hand, and Mrs. Hammond said, "You all right?"

"I'm fine," James said.

"You look kind of tired."

He straightened up and tucked his shirt in. There was Great-Aunt Hattie, only a few yards away now, being led gingerly by Mrs. Hammond. Aunt Hattie looked neither to the right nor to the left; she seemed to be pretending Mrs. Hammond wasn't there. The closer they got to the camera, the farther away her eyes grew.

"Right here would be a good place," said Mrs. Hammond. "Don't you think so, James? In front of the roses?"

"Fine," James said. He had started adjusting his camera and wasn't really looking now. But when he raised his eyes again he saw that the old woman had been placed directly in front of a circular flower bed; she seemed to be rising from the middle of it, like an intricately sculptured garden decoration. James smiled. "I've changed my mind," he said. "I don't think she should have those flowers behind her."

"They're so pretty, though," Mrs. Hammond said sadly.

"Well. But I think she should have just grass behind her. You mind moving over, Miss Hattie?"

"I have just one thing to say," Miss Hattie said suddenly.

"Ma'am?"

"Don't push me. You can tell me where to go, but don't push me around."

"Oh, I won't," said James.

"The *last* time I had my picture taken—"

"I think he wants you to move over," Mrs. Hammond said. "Could you step this way, dear?"

The aunt stepped stiffly, jerking her chin up. "I was saying, Connie," she said, "the *last* man that took my picture was in need of an anatomy lesson. I told him so. He came right up to me and pushed my face sideways but my shoulders full-front, and my knees sideways but my feet full-front, so I swear, I felt like something on an Egyptian wall.

You should have seen the photograph. Well, I don't have to tell you how it looked. I said—"

"If I were you I'd let my beads show," said Mrs. Hammond. "They're such nice ones."

"Well, just for that I won't," snapped Aunt Hattie. She raised her hands, heavy with old rings, and fumbled at the neck of her crepe dress until she had closed it high around her throat, hiding the beads from sight. "Now *no* one can see them," she said, and Connie Hammond sighed and turned to James with her hands spread hopelessly.

"I try and I try," she told him, and he looked up from fiddling with his camera and smiled.

"Why don't you go on and see to the others," he said, "and I'll call you when I'm through. I bet you haven't even had your ice cream yet."

"No. No, I've been so busy. Well, I might for just a minute, maybe—" She trailed off across the yard, looking relieved, and the last part of her to fade away was her voice, which still flowed on and on.

"She's putting on weight, don't you think?" Aunt Hattie asked.

James had the camera ready now, but he was waiting because he wanted the picture to be just right. He bent down and cleared away a dandelion from one of the tripod legs, and then over his shoulder he called, "You comfortable like that? Don't want to sit down?"

"No. I'll stand."

Connie Hammond wouldn't like that, but James was glad. To him Aunt Hattie looked just right this way—standing against a background of bare grass, holding her shoulders high to hide the beads and jutting her chin out at him. She had terrified high school students for forty years that way, back when she taught Latin I. People still told tales about her. She had declined her nouns in a deafening roar and slammed her yardstick against her desk on the ending of every verb. While students could lead other teachers off their subjects just by asking how they'd met their husbands, Miss Hattie had only strayed from Latin once a year, at Christmastime, when she read aloud from a condensed version of *Ben Hur*. James could picture that. He wished he had her in a classroom right now, to photograph her the way she stood in his mind. But all he had was this wide lawn, and he would have to make do with that. He stood there, pressing a dandelion between his fingers and squinting across at her. "That's right," he told her. "That's what I want."

She shifted her feet a little. "How many prints you plan to make of this?" she asked.

"Ma'am?"

"How many copies?"

"Oh. As many as you want."

"Well, I want *none*," she said. "I'd like to request that you make the one picture asked of you and have that be that."

"Oh, now."

"Connie can have one, if she wants it so much. But that's because I don't like her. Nothing she could *do* would make me like her; I just constitutionally don't. Danny can't have one."

"Danny who?" he asked. "Raise your chin a little, please."

"Danny Hammond. Is there anyone in this world whose last name isn't Hammond?" She raised her chin but went on talking; James leaned his elbow on his camera and waited. "Danny I put up with," she said. "How long will they hide him away from me?"

"Danny *Hammond?* Why, I saw him only last—"

"*You* saw him. You saw him. But do you think *I* do? They rush him away the moment I come around; he looks back over his shoulder all bewildered. He's only seven."

"Could you turn more toward me?" asked James.

"They think he insulted me last Valentine's Day."

"Oh, I don't think Danny would—"

"Made me a present. None of these easy-breaking things from the gift shop. Made me a ceramic saltshaker in school, and it was the exact shape of my head, with even the wrinkles painted in."

"That's nice," said James.

"Do you know where the salt comes out?"

"Well, no."

"My nose. Ho, out my nose. Two little holes punched for nostrils, and out came the salt. Can you picture Connie's face?"

James laughed. "I sure can," he said.

"Well, of course she hadn't *seen* the thing, prior to my unwrapping it. She thought it was a bobby-pin holder or something. She said, 'Danny *Hammond!*' and made a grab for it, but I was too quick for her. I meant to *keep* it; it's not often I get such a personal present. But Connie rushed him off like I would eat him and there I sat, all alone with my saltshaker. No one to thank."

"Maybe you could—"

"I still use it, though."

"Ma'am?"

"The saltshaker. I use it daily."

"Well, I would too," said James.

"Then you see why he shouldn't have my picture."

That stumped him; he had to consider a minute. (If Miss Hattie Hammond was fading out, should he not just let it pass and agree with her?) But Miss Hattie seemed the same to him as ever, as sharp as a rock against the green of the lawn. "I don't see what you mean," he said.

"Ah well."

"I don't understand what pictures have got to do with it."

"Not much," she said. "But they're photographing me because I'm old, you know. They think I'm dying. (I'm not.) They think they'll have something to remember me by. But pictures are merely one way, Mr. Green. Should a person that I *like* have a picture of me?"

"I wouldn't let it worry me," said James. "I find no one ever looks at pictures anyway, once they get hold of them."

"*I* don't want Danny remembering just a picture. Remembering something flat and of one tone. What is ever all one way?"

"Well," James said. He frowned down at his fingers, sticky now with dandelion milk. "Well, *plenty* of—"

"Photographs," said Miss Hattie, "are the only thing. Don't interrupt. Everything else is a mingling of things. Photographers don't agree, of course. Why else would they take pictures? Press everything flat on little squares of paper—well, that's all right. But not for people that you'd like to stay *interested* in you. Not for Danny Hammond."

"Now, wait a minute," said James, but Miss Hattie held up her hand.

"I already know," she said. "*I* know photographers."

James grinned and bent over his camera again. "As far as things that're all one way," he called, "I can name—"

"No. Not a thing, not a person, Mr. Green. Take your picture."

He gave up. Through the frame of his viewfinder he saw her standing just the way he wanted her, old-fashioned-looking and symmetrical, with her hands across her stomach and her mouth tight. Her face was like a turtle's face, long and droopy. It had the same hooded eyes and the same tenacious expression, as if she had lived for centuries and was certain of living much longer. Yet just in that instant, just as his hand tightened on the camera and his eyes relaxed at seeing the picture the way he had planned it, something else swam into his mind. He thought of Miss Hattie coughing, in the center of that family reunion— not defiant then but very soft and mumbling, telling them all she was sorry. He frowned and raised his head.

"Well?" said Miss Hattie.

"Nothing," James said.

He bent down again, and sighted up the haughty old turtle-face before him and snapped the picture. For a minute he stayed in that position; then he straightened up. "I'm done," he said.

"I should hope so."

"I'll get one copy made, for Mrs. Hammond."

"I'm going in then. I'm tired."

"All right," he said. "Goodbye, Miss Hattie."

"Goodbye."

She nodded once, sharply, and turned to go, and James watched after her as long as she was in sight. Then he stared down at his camera. Just to his right Connie Hammond materialized—he caught a fold of lace out of the corner of his eye—but he didn't look at her.

"Well, now!" Mrs. Hammond said brightly. She was out of breath and looked anxious. She came around in front of him and went to stand where Miss Hattie had stood, with her eyes intent on the ground, as if by tracking down the print of Miss Hattie's Wedgies she could suddenly come to some understanding of her. "I'm sure it'll come out good," she called over her shoulder.

"Well."

"What's that?"

"Yes, I'm sure it will," James said. He folded up his tripod and gathered the rest of his equipment together. "I'm leaving now," he told her.

"Oh, are you?"

"I'll have the pictures ready in a day or two."

"That'll be fine," said Mrs. Hammond. But she was still staring at the ground and looking anxious; she didn't turn around to say goodbye.

James's pickup truck was parked on the road at the edge of the lawn. He circled around the children, being careful to stay clear of the ones playing statues. Their game was growing rougher now. Little Janice Hammond was frozen in the exact stance of a baseball pitcher, her right arm drawn back nearly out of joint, and even her face was frozen—she was grimacing wildly, showing an entire set of braces on her teeth. But she unfroze just as James passed her; she shook out her arms and smiled at him and he smiled back.

"I want to come out *pretty* in them pictures," she said. "You see what you can do about it."

"I'll see."

He placed the camera on the leather seat of the pickup and then went around to the driver's side and climbed in. It was like an oven inside. First he started up the motor and then he rolled down his window, and while he was doing that he caught sight of Maisie Hammond. She was standing high up on the lawn, waving hard to him and smiling. He waved back. This time when the heavy feeling hit his stomach he didn't shrug it off; he sat turning it over in his mind, letting the motor idle. As long as he sat there, Maisie went on waving. And when he had shifted into first and rolled on down to the bottom of the hill, he looked in the rear-view mirror and saw her still waving after him. He thought suddenly that she must be having two feelings at once—half one way and half another. Half angry at him, and half sorry because she had told him so. And now she had to keep on waving.

He looked down beside him at the camera, where Miss Hattie was so securely boxed now in her single stance. But the fields he drove through shimmered uncertainly in the sunlight; the road was misted with dust, and he was driving home now not knowing if he wanted to go there or not, not knowing for sure what he thought about anyone. All he could do was put the heavy feeling out of his mind, and let only the road and the fields alongside it occupy his thoughts.

4

THAT SUNDAY, Joan began thinking about Simon's hair. She started out by saying, "Simon, tomorrow morning first thing I want to find you in that barber's chair," but Simon said, "Aw, Joan, I don't want to go downtown." Since that movie yesterday he had changed his mind about town; he hadn't even asked to eat in a restaurant today, and Joan could see his point. Going downtown meant people murmuring over him and patting his head, asking Joan in whispers, "How is he taking it? Is his mother coming out of it?" while Simon stood right next to them, his chin tilted defiantly and his eyes on their faces. Little boys who were usually his friends circled him widely, looking back over their shoulders in curious, half-scared glances. They had never seen someone that close to funerals before, not someone their own age. When Simon and Joan were coming out of the movie theater a member of Mrs. Pike's church had stopped smack in front of them and said to her friend, "Oh, that poor little boy!" Her voice had rung out clearly and hung in the air above them, making other people stop and stare while Simon pulled on Joan's hand to rush her home. She could understand it if he had never went downtown again.

So instead of insisting, she said, "Well, all right. But we've got to cut your hair at home then. Today."

"It's not so long," he said.

"Curls down over your ears."

"Well, we've got nothing to cut it with."

"Scissors," Joan reminded him. "Your mother's sewing scissors. *Anything.*"

"Okay. Tomorrow, then," said Simon. "Bright and early."

"Tomorrow's a tobacco day; I won't be here. You know that."

"*Other* boys have hair *lots* longer."

"Orphans do," said Joan. "Will you fetch the scissors?"

He slid off the couch, grumbling a little, and went for his mother's sewing basket. It sat in one corner of the living room, gathering dust, odds and ends of other people's clothing poking out of it every which-way. (Mrs. Pike was a seamstress; she made clothes for most of the women in Larksville.) The materials on the top Simon threw to the floor, making a huge untidy pile beside the basket, and he rummaged along the bottom until he brought up a large pair of scissors. "These them?" he asked, and walked away from the basket with that heap of material still lying beside it. Joan let the mess stay there. She followed Simon into the kitchen, a few steps behind him, with her eyes on the back of his head. Where it had been pressed against the couch his hair was as matted as a bird's nest. It would take a sickle to cut all that off.

In the kitchen she found an apron and tied it around his neck, to keep the hair from tickling, and then she had him sit on the high wooden stool beside the kitchen table. He revolved on it slowly, making the seat of it squeak, while Joan looked him over and debated where to start. "I don't know where you *got* all that hair," she told him. "When was the last time you went to the barber's?"

"I don't know."

"It couldn't have been all that long ago."

"You sure you know how to cut hair?" Simon asked.

"Of course I do."

"Whose have you cut?"

"Well, my own," Joan said.

He stopped revolving and looked at her hairdo. "It's a little choppy at the ends," he told her.

"It's supposed to be."

"Will mine come out like that?"

"I surely hope not."

"If it does, what will we—"

"Now, Simon," Joan said, "I don't want to hear any more about it. Let's just get it over with."

He sighed then and gave in, but with his shoulders squinched up and his neck drawn into itself as if he thought she might slip and cut his head off. His hair grew in layers, lapping downwards like hay on a haystack. When Joan cut too much from one of the sun-yellowed upper layers it sprang straight up, choppy and jagged-edged, and she quickly pressed it down again and shot a look at Simon to see if he had noticed. He hadn't. He sat slumped on the stool, idly swinging one boot and gazing out the window. The only sound now was the steady snipping of scissors.

Out in the back yard Joan could see her uncle—just his head and his crumpled blue shirt. He was tilting back on an old kitchen chair in the sunshine, with one hand resting absently on Nellie's neck. That was the way he had been sitting all day. When Joan called him for his meals he came in docilely and ate everything set before him, and then he went out back again. Twice he had gone upstairs to see his wife, but that had taken only a minute; he must have given up trying to talk to her. Even Joan had given up. When she went to her aunt's bedroom, to where she was lying on her back with the covers pulled up around her, and asked her to come down for a bite to eat, her aunt only said, "No," and closed her eyes. Saying that one word seemed to take all the strength she could muster; Joan didn't dare argue with her. In the back of her mind she kept trying to think up little plots, planning ways to get her aunt interested in something, but she wasn't the kind of person who could do that. The most she could do was try and take care of the house for a while, and feed Mr. Pike and Simon. Even that was hard; she had never learned how to keep house.

The top part of Simon's hair was cut now. She squinted at it, not sure if this was how it was supposed to be or not. It seemed a little homemade-looking. But then she shrugged and began on the shaggy part along the back of his neck. She could always even it up later on.

Outside, Ansel called, "Is anybody home?" His voice was thin and wavered in the wind. Simon gave a sudden start and turned his head, so that Joan nearly gouged him in the neck. "Hold *still*, Simon," she said, and Ansel called again, "Is anybody home?"

"It's him," Simon said.

"Who do you mean? It's Ansel."

"I know. It's him."

"Just stop wiggling," said Joan. She raised her voice and called out, "We're out here, Ansel."

"Out where?"

"Out *here*."

"Well, is someone going to come and let me in?"

"It's not locked," Joan said, and returned to her cutting. She didn't like Ansel and had never pretended to; he could open his own doors. When he came ambling out to the kitchen, walking in that shuffling way of his and stooping to get through the doorway, she didn't even turn around to look at him. "How are you," she said, making it a statement.

"Oh, not so bad, I guess."

"Turn a little to the left, Simon."

"Hey, Simon," Ansel said.

Simon frowned at his boots.

"*Hey*, boy."

"He's having his hair cut," said Joan.

"Ah, I see. That makes it impossible for him to speak."

"Will you have a seat?"

"I might," he said. He pulled out one of the chairs from the table and sat down, facing Joan and Simon. He was looking better than usual today. The yellowish pallor of his face had faded and he sat nearly erect, with his arms folded across his chest. When he saw Simon frowning at him he smiled his dippy smile and said, "What's the matter with the barber, boy?"

"What?"

"Barber sick?"

But Simon only shrugged and didn't answer. Joan said, "I'm cutting his hair myself this time."

"I see that."

"I'm using the sewing scissors."

"I see."

That seemed to leave nothing more to be said. Joan hesitated a minute, with the scissors in mid air, and then she said, "Turn around, Simon."

"Are we done?" Simon asked.

"Almost. I want to think what to do about the front part of it."

"Where's Mr. and Mrs. Pike?" said Ansel.

"Uncle Roy's out back."

"Where's *Mrs.* Pike?"

Joan was frowning at Simon's hair, trying to figure out how to begin on that front shock. Any way she managed it, it was almost sure to end up looking like bangs. She snipped gingerly at one piece and held what she had cut off up to the light to examine it. Then she said, "Ansel, what're you here for?"

"Who, me?"

"Didn't James tell you not to bother her? Where *is* James?"

"He's taking pictures of the Hammonds."

"Didn't he tell you not to come around here?"

"Well, yes, he did," Ansel said. "He *suggested* that I not. But I was sitting reading on the couch and it occurred to me: I thought I might just wander over and see how you all are doing."

"We're doing fine," said Joan. She snipped off another piece of hair.

"Joan, you're ruining that boy."

"It'll turn out all right."

"Well. I was sitting reading a *Guideposts*," Ansel said, "and after that two outdoor-type magazines, and then I read them again. I would've read them a third time, if I hadn't come on over here. I read even the smallest inch-long ads for worm farms; I read the list of editors at the front and the entire information about the subscriptions. Then I thought I might come and see you."

"Simon, maybe you better get a mirror," Joan said. "I'm not sure what you're going to think of this."

"Aw, I don't care," said Simon. "Is it done?"

"You go look in a mirror and *see* if it is."

Simon stood up and little rags of hair fell around him, spilling off the apron around his neck. When he walked out of the room he trailed fuzz in a long path behind him.

"He won't thank you for this," Ansel said.

"I don't think it's so bad."

"Twice before, I started to come," Ansel said. "I got up and headed for the door and then I thought, 'No.' I cut my fingernails. I cleaned out my wallet. Then I thought I might as well come over. I thought—"

When he talked he had a way of leaning slightly forward and placing his fingertips together, as if words came hard to him and he had to consider. Yet in reality the words came flooding from him; it always made her feel swept away and drowned, with so many useless words spilling around her. Sometimes she could even get interested in what he said, but she never lost that drowned feeling. While he talked she stood silently by the stool, keeping her face blank and idly snipping at thin air with her scissors, but inside she was thinking, I wish you would *go*. The pale thinness of his face irritated her. She thought about all the long evenings of three long years, with James sitting next to her on the porch and never taking one step forward, never asking for more than tonight's kiss and tomorrow's date and never mentioning marriage or a family or any of those other things she was sitting there waiting to hear. And the reason for it all was Ansel, who hung limp and heavy in his brother's living room and expected to die any day, although actually he was stronger than any of them. He had that flood of words, after all, and that sad dippy smile, and that way of placing his fingers together as if asking people to be patient while he fumbled for what to say. "I thought I would come offer sympathy and then leave again," he was saying, and Joan snapped, "Well, you've offered it. Are you leaving?"

"Huh?" Ansel said. He looked up, bewildered. "Joan, I ain't even seen your Aunt *Lou* yet—"

Simon came in, with his hair plastered down by water. "It looks kind of like I expected it to," he said.

"You don't like it?"

"Well, yes. It'll grow out."

"I could trim it around the edges a little more," Joan said.

"No, that's all right. Thank you anyway."

"Or maybe tomorrow you could—"

"Hush!" Ansel said. He sat up straight, listening, and when the other two turned toward him he pointed at the ceiling. "Footsteps," he said.

It was the slow, clapping sound of Mrs. Pike's mules, crossing the upstairs hallway. "She's only going over to the bedroom," Joan said, but then the sound continued to the stairs, and Ansel said, "She's coming down." He stood up, preparing to meet her. Joan reached out and touched his arm. "Let her be," she said. "Why don't you go home?"

"I wanted to say hello."

"Do it some other time."

"No, I want—"

The footsteps descended slowly, like a child's—both feet meeting on the same step, then another hesitant step downwards. Joan left the kitchen, with a wave of her hand toward Ansel to show that he should stay there. He did, which surprised her a little. She crossed through the parlor alone and came to stand at the bottom of the stairs, looking up. Her aunt had just barely reached the halfway point. She was holding on to the railing and gazing steadily at Joan, her face blank without its makeup, her dark yellow hair straggly and uncurled, and her plump body wrapped in a chenille bathrobe. The grayness of her made her blend into the dark stairwell. She said, "Joan," and her voice came out blurred and gray also, without expression.

"What?" Joan said.

But her aunt didn't answer. She continued down the stairs laboriously, and when she reached the bottom she would have gone straight into the kitchen except that Joan took hold of her by one arm.

"Don't you want to sit in the parlor a while?" she asked. "I'll bring coffee."

"No."

"*Ansel's* out there in the kitchen."

"No."

Mrs. Pike went on walking, not pulling away from Joan but just walking off, so that Joan had to drop her arm or follow her. She dropped it. Her aunt said, "No," again, as if some new question had been raised, but Joan was trailing behind her now in silence, frowning at Mrs. Pike's back. Her back was soft and shapeless, and folded in upon itself at the waist where her sash was tightened. When she walked the hem of her robe fluttered out and Joan could see the dinginess where it had dragged across the floor.

Ansel was standing, ready to greet her. He said, "Mrs. Pike, I been waiting to see you," and Mrs. Pike said, "Ansel," and crossed to one of the kitchen chairs. Over by the window Simon stood with his back to her, his hands jammed awkwardly in his pockets and his chopped-at, straggly head wearing a stiff and listening look.

"I only came to tell you how I feel," Ansel said gently. "Then I'll leave."

"Where is Roy?" asked Mrs. Pike.

"Out back. You want I should get him?"

"No."

Mrs. Pike was sitting craned forward a little, with her hands on her stomach as if it hurt her. After a minute Ansel sat down opposite her, but Joan remained standing and Simon stayed by the window. Mrs. Pike didn't look at any of them. "I thought I would come downstairs a little," she said.

"That's the way," said Ansel. "You shouldn't sit alone."

"I wasn't sitting."

"What I actually came to say," Ansel said, "was how bad I feel about all this. That's all I wanted to tell you. I told James, I said, 'It's

like the tragedy has struck at our own lives. I know just how she feels,'
I said. I said—"

"No," said Mrs. Pike.

"Ma'am?"

But Mrs. Pike only looked away then, toward the screen door. Behind
her, Simon picked up the cord of the paper window shade and began
tying knots in it, small tight knots running up and down the length
of the cord.

"What was you saying no for?" Ansel asked.

Mrs. Pike didn't answer.

"Was you saying I *don't* know how you feel? Mrs. Pike, I know how
you feel better than you do yourself. I been through this before."

"Ansel," Joan said, "you've offered your sympathy now. I think you'd
better leave."

"But I've got so much I want to *say* to her—"

"I came down to eat," said Mrs. Pike, "but I don't think I will."

Joan turned away from Ansel and looked down at Mrs. Pike. She
said, "Why, Aunt Lou, there's all kinds of things to eat in the icebox.
Everyone's been bringing things."

"No," her aunt said.

"I know that when my mother died," said Ansel, "everyone kept
trying to snap me out of it. They said that mourning has never brought
the dead back. But it's only right to mourn; it's only natural. People
have their faults but when they're dead you mourn them, and you
expect to be mourned yourself someday."

"Janie Rose didn't have no faults," said Mrs. Pike.

"No, ma'am, of course she didn't. When my—"

"We don't know how it might have turned out. She was a little
chubby but not, you know, really fat. She might have slimmed down
some later on. I never *said* to her she was fat. I don't know what she
thought I said but really I didn't. Never a word."

"When my mother died," said Ansel, "I thought of all the bad things
I ever said about her. I got in a real swivet about it. She was a fine
woman, but scared of everything. Wouldn't stand up against my father
for us. When some sort of crisis was going on she had a way of sort
of humming underneath her breath, slow and steady with no tune, and
sewing away at someone's overalls without looking up. My father
was—"

Joan came over and stood between Ansel and Mrs. Pike, bending
down low so as to make her aunt look into her face. "I want you to
eat something, now," she said. "There's a stew. Would you like that?"

"No."

"There's a whole icebox of things."

"No."

"My father was not what you'd call a man of *heart*," said Ansel, placing his fingertips together. "Very strict. We always kept two goats around the place, to eat off the underbrush—"

"Isn't it funny," Mrs. Pike said, "that no one sent roses. Roses are a very normal flower, yet nobody sent them. Everything but, in fact."

"It's a little hot for good roses," Joan said.

"In the spring, when the goats had kids," said Ansel, "we would fatten them up for eating. Only by the time they were fat they'd be good pets, and we would beg for my father not to kill them. We would cry and make promises. But my mother sat humming (though she loved those goats the best of all and had names for every one of them) and my father always killed them. Only there was one thing that made up for that—"

"Ansel," Joan said, "will you go home?"

"Wait a minute. When my mother brought a roasted kid in, or any part of it, holding it high on a wooden platter with potatoes around it, she always dropped it just in the doorway between the kitchen and the dining room. It never failed. The meat on the floor, and the potatoes rolling about like marbles and leaving little buttery paths behind them. 'Pick it up,' my father always said, but she would begin talking about germs and never let us eat it. I haven't *yet* tasted a piece of roasted goat. I think about that often now; it makes up for that humming, almost. I'm sorry I ever—"

Someone knocked on the front door. Joan said, "Ansel, will you go see who that is?"

"Why, Joan, it's *your* house."

"I don't care; just go."

"I'm not *well* enough to go bobbing up and down for people," said Ansel. But he rose anyway, moving slowly like an old man and holding his chest. "Who is it?" he called.

"Is that you, Ansel?"

It was James, with his voice sounding loud and steady even though he was still outside the house. Hearing him made Joan straighten up and feel suddenly more cheerful, and Simon turned around and let the window-shade cord slip out of his hand. "Ansel, what are you doing here?" James called.

"What're *you* doing here?"

"I'm looking for you. I been looking all over."

James had let himself in now, seeing that Ansel wasn't advancing to the door very quickly. He crossed the parlor in long strides, and appeared in the kitchen entrance with his hands on his hips.

"I'm taking you home for supper," he told Ansel. "I'm sorry about this, Mrs. Pike."

Mrs. Pike only gazed at him unblinkingly, without appearing to hear him. Joan said, "I wish you would, James."

"Come on, Ansel."

"Supper in the after*noon?*" asked Ansel.

"It's getting on towards sunset."

"Well, I don't feel so good, James. I'm not hungry."

"What's the matter with you?" James asked.

"My head is swimming."

"You been resting enough?"

"Well, yes. But after lunch this blackness started floating in, and then a little later this, um—"

Joan leaned back against the table, watching. She had never seen James actually *listen* to all this before; it seemed strange, and she couldn't figure out why he was doing it. The more James listened, the more Ansel's symptoms expanded and grew in detail; even his face looked paler. But James kept on nodding, saying "Hmm," every now and then. Finally he said, "I'll put you in bed. You can have your supper on a tray, if you want."

"Oh, I think I'll just stay here and—"

"It's time to go, Ansel."

Ansel sighed and let himself be led toward the doorway by one elbow. To Mrs. Pike he called, "I hope you're feeling better, ma'am. I'll be back tomorrow, maybe, or the next day—"

"Come on," James said.

They stopped trying to be graceful about it. James gave Ansel's arm a good tug and Joan followed close behind, almost on Ansel's heels, to hurry him out. After her came Simon, with his face looking small and curious under his ragged haircut. Mrs. Pike didn't go with them. She sat quietly in her chair, with her hands still pressed to her stomach, and it wasn't until the others were all the way into the parlor that she spoke.

"*Nobody* knows," she said distinctly.

Ansel wheeled around, fighting off Joan's and James's hands, and shouted, "*What's* that?"

Mrs. Pike didn't answer.

"Let's go," James said.

"I just want to tell you," Ansel shouted toward the kitchen, "I know better than you can *imagine*, Mrs. Pike. You're just sorry now you weren't nicer to her, but I know how it feels to *really* miss someone. I remember—"

Both James and Joan stopped then, looking first at Ansel and then back toward the kitchen. But all they heard was the creaking of a chair, as if Mrs. Pike had changed positions. And that seemed to show Ansel what they had been trying to tell him all along: that Mrs. Pike wasn't listening right now, and that nothing he could say would do her any good or any harm. So he shrugged and let himself be led the rest of the way out. When Joan stepped back a pace, indicating that he should go first and that she was staying in the house, he nodded good-bye to her gravely.

"One thing I'd like to make clear, Joan," he said. He was facing her squarely, acting very formal and dignified. "I *do* know," he told her.

"All right," Joan said absentmindedly.

"I *remember* how it feels. My memory's excellent."

"I believe you."

"Clutters my mind at night, it's so excellent."

James pulled him gently.

"When I want to sleep, it does. Clutters my mind."

"All right, Ansel," James said.

He led him on out to the porch. When he passed Joan she could smell the smoky, outdoors smell of James's and he bent closer to her and said, "If you need anything, I want you to tell me."

"I will."

"And when you can get away, come over and see us."

"I will."

She stood in the doorway with her hand on Simon's shoulder and watched after them—Ansel tall and thin and leaning against James, who was solider and could bear his weight. She heard Ansel say, "Right through my temples it is, James. A sort of spindle of dizzy-feeling, right through my temples."

James said, "We'll lie you down. You feel tired?"

"Naw. I was thinking—"

"You sure now," James said.

"Huh?"

"I want you to tell me."

"Tell you what?" Ansel asked.

But James didn't answer that. And Joan, listening with a frown because it was so strange to her, felt suddenly lost and uncertain. She retreated into the parlor again, letting the screen door swing slowly shut behind her. But there was no one to listen to what was bothering her. Only Mrs. Pike, staring at the wall in the kitchen, and Simon beside her with his funny new haircut.

5

"Now, I can have my ideas," said Missouri, "and you can have yours. Mind what you're doing there, Miss Joan. First off, I don't believe in sitting. I have never believed in sitting. Minute a person sits his mind gives way. Will you *watch* what you're *doing?*"

Joan sighed and handed her the next bunch of tobacco leaves. It was Monday afternoon, late in the day but hot, and even here under the shade of the pecan trees she could feel the sweat trickling down between her shoulder blades. Beside her stood three other women—two handing to Mrs. Hall, who was the fastest tobacco-tier in the county, and the other helping Joan do the handing to Missouri. Missouri was huge and black, and every move she made was a wide slow arc, but she could tie nearly as fast as Mrs. Hall. She stood at the end of her rod with her broad bare feet spraddle-toed in the dust, and first she yanked a handful of leaves from her daughter Lily and then from Joan, wrapping each handful to the rod with one sure circling of the twine so that the leaves hung points-down and swinging. If Joan or Lily was too slow with the next hanging she would click her tongue and stand there disgusted, holding the twine taut in her fingers, and when the leaves were ready she would take them with an extra hard yank and bind them so hard that the twine cut into the stems. Now it was Joan who was slow (they were down to the last of this tableload, and she was having trouble finding a full handing of leaves) and Missouri made her clicking sound and shifted her weight to the other foot.

"What it is," she called down the table to Mrs. Hall, "I bind *across* the stick. You bind on the same side, and I declare I don't see how. With Miss Joan on the left, I take her leaves and bind them on the right, and backwards from that with Lily. You follow my meaning?"

"Yes, and I think it's just as *inefficient*," Mrs. Hall said. She stopped her tying to brush a piece of wispy blond hair off her face. "That's three inches wasted motion every bunch you tie, Missouri."

"Ha. Fast as *I* move, who cares about three inches."

"It adds up. You see if it don't."

"Ha."

She yanked Joan's bunch from her and lashed it to the rod. That finished up the stick; it looked now like one long chain of hanging green leaves, with the rod itself hidden from sight by the thick stems that stuck up on either side. "You!" she said without looking, and Jimmy Terry raised himself from the side of the barn and set down his Coke bottle. By the time he had ambled over to Missouri she had lifted the stick from its notched stand and stood making faces because of the weight of it, holding it very carefully so as not to crush the leaves. "Watch it, now," she said, and thrust it at him, and he started back to the drying-barn while she bent to take another rod and lay it in the notches. "I was saying something," she said. She tied the white twine around the end farthest from her and then snapped it off at a length of five feet or so, while Mrs. Hall stopped tying to watch her. (Mrs. Hall spent every day of every tobacco season trying to figure out how Missouri snapped off her twine ahead of time without measuring it.) "I was talking about sitting," Missouri said, grandly ignoring Mrs. Hall. "This table is *bare*, Lord; when they going to bring us more? Now, when you sit, your blood sort of sits along with you. It don't go rushing around your brain no more. Consequently, it takes that much more time to get rid of some sad idea in your mind. The process is slowed considerable. Whereas if you hurry your blood *up* some . . . There is a sizable amount of people could benefit from what I know. I could just go on and on about it. But do you get what I mean up to now?"

"Well, so far," Joan said.

"Good. Now, what started me on that—well, I do say. Took you long enough."

She was looking off toward the dirt driveway, where the men were just coming with the mule. Behind the mule was a huge wooden sled piled high with tobacco leaves, and it must have been heavy because the mule was objecting. He had stopped trying and began to amuse himself by blowing through his nose at the flies circling his head, and when Mr. Terry slapped his back he only switched his tail and gave an extra hard wheeze through his nose. Mr. Terry pulled out a bandanna and wiped his face.

"You stop that and bring him here," Missouri commanded. "We're out of leaves and getting paid for standing here with our arms folded."

"Well, I wouldn't want *that*," Mr. Terry said, but he went on wiping his face with his back to the mule. He was an easygoing man; it was a wonder to the whole countryside how he ever got his tobacco in. Behind the sled was James Green, filling in for the day because Mr. Pike was at home with his wife, and he wasn't doing anything about the mule either. His face was dark from the sun and glistening, and his hair hung in a wet mop over his forehead. When he saw Joan he grinned and waved, but he didn't look as if he gave a hang whether that mule *ever* moved, so Missouri heaved a huge sigh and laid down her twine.

"I never," she said, and circled the long picnic table where the women were standing and headed for the mule. "Jefferson, you no-good, you," she told the mule, "you going to keep us waiting all day?"

"*That's* not Jefferson," Mr. Terry said. "That's my brother Kerr's mule, Man O'War. He's only a distant cousin to Jefferson."

"I don't care who he is." She reached up and grabbed the mule by one long ear, as if he were a little boy, and pulled in the direction of the table. The mule followed, sighing sadly. "In the end, it's the women that work," Missouri told him. "Stand still now, you hear?"

"I wish it *was* Jefferson," said Mr. Terry. "He was some good mule, old Jefferson."

"He sick?" Missouri asked.

"Nah. Dead."

"That's why this one is doddering around so, then. They know, them mules."

"Mr. Graves shot him down," Mr. Terry said. He and James were both at work now, lifting armloads of leaves from the sled and carrying them over to the table. "He says he has the right, because Jefferson kicked his boy."

"Nah, that ain't so. Only if Jefferson *killed* the boy, outright. Takes more than that to kill Sonny Graves. Sonny ain't dead, is he?"

"Oh, no."

"Well, you go on and sue then. Go on and do it."

"Well," Mr. Terry said. He took the mule and turned him around, and when he slapped him this time the mule headed back toward the fields with the empty sled skittering behind him. "We'll let Saul take care of him," Mr. Terry told James. To the women at the table he called, "That was the last load, there. Me and the men are going to cut out and have a beer up at the house."

"Don't you give Lem more than one," Missouri said.

"You know how he gets."

"Well."

He headed toward the house, wiping his face again with the bandanna, and James turned and said, "You yell when you're ready to go, Joan."

"All right," Joan said.

When the men had left there was a different feeling in the air, blanker and stiller. The smell of sweat and mule and hot sun had drifted away, and for a minute the women just stood looking after them with their faces expressionless. Then Missouri said, "Well," and she and Mrs. Hall took their places at their rods again and the others turned to the new heap of leaves on the table.

"That James stays out in the sun much more, he's going to change races," Missouri said to Joan.

"I guess he might," Joan said.

"He's a good man. Though a bit too quiet—don't let things show through."

"No."

Missouri waited, still without going back to her work. Finally she said, "Just where is he from?"

The others looked up. Joan said, "Oh . . . from around here he says."

"Well, so are we all," said Missouri. "But what *town?*"

"He doesn't talk much about it."

"*That's* kind of peculiar," Mrs. Hall called. "You ever asked him?"

"He's not *wanted* or nothing, is he?" said Missouri.

"No."

"You never know. I'd been married two and a half years before I found out Lem had been married before. Mad? I tell you—"

"If I were you I'd ask him," Mrs. Hall said.

"Well, I did," said Joan. She was beginning to feel uncomfortable. "He *told* me where he was from but it was just an ordinary town, like Larksville—"

"Then why don't he say so?"

"Well, you know Ansel," Joan said.

"There's an odd one."

"He doesn't like for James to talk about it. He's afraid James'll send him back."

"Good thing if he did," said Mrs. Hall. "You ever been invited to meet their family?"

"Well, no."

"They had some kind of falling-out," Missouri's daughter Lily said. Everyone looked at her, and she said, "Well, that's what Maisie Hammond said."

"Maisie Hammond don't know beans," Missouri said. "Haven't you learned not to listen to gossip?"

"If I was you, Joan," said Mrs. Hall, "I'd just march right up and ask him. I'd say, 'James, will you take me to meet your family?' Just like that, I'd ask."

"No," Joan said.

They went on watching her, waiting for her to say more, but she didn't. She concentrated on grouping the leaves together by the stems, a small cluster at a time, so that they lay flat against each other, and then she held them out to Missouri and waited patiently until Missouri gave up and started tying again. Each time Missouri took the leaves from her there was a funny numb feeling in Joan's fingertips, from the leaves sliding across layers and layers of thick tobacco gum on her skin. Tobacco gum covered her hands and forearms, and it had worked in between the straps of her sandals so that there was black gum on the soles of her feet. Tonight when she walked barefoot through the house she would leave little black tracks behind her. She rubbed the tip of her nose against a clean spot on the back of her hand, and Missouri clicked her tongue at her to tell her to hurry. "I want to get *home*," she told Joan, and Joan swooped down on another bunch of leaves and handed them to her. In her sleep she would see tables full of tobacco leaves, stack upon stack of yellow-green leaves with their fine sticky coating of fuzz and their rough surfaces that reminded her of old grained leather on book covers. Whenever she told her aunt about that, about dreaming every night of mules and leaves and drying barns, her aunt thought she was complaining and said, "Nobody *asked* you to do it. I even told you, I said it right out, I didn't want you doing it. Secretaries don't work tobacco, honey." But then Joan only laughed and said she liked seeing leaves in her sleep. "There's lots worse I could dream of," she said, and Mrs. Pike had to agree.

Missouri had started talking again, now that she saw Joan wasn't going to answer any more questions. "Let's get back to sitting," she said. "What led me to speak of it was, your working and all so soon after that, uh, tragedy occurred. Now, honey, don't you mind Mrs. Pike. I know her, she feels like even James shouldn't of come. Feels like it shows disrespect. But look at it head-on and—"

"Well, not disrespect," Mrs. Hall called across. "Not that, exactly. But I see Lou's point. *I* wouldn't have come today, Joan. I don't mind telling you."

"What would I do at home?" Joan asked. "Sit?"

"Exactly what led me to my discussion," said Missouri. "What *sitting* does, is—"

"You could have stayed around and helped out," Mrs. Hall said. "Made tea and things. A person needs company at a time like this. And James there, why, he is very close to being Janie's cousin-in-law, or once removed, or whatever you call it—"

Once again they all looked at Joan, but she went on grouping leaves and they sighed and turned back to the table.

"*Any*way," said Mrs. Hall, "with his own brother on the verge of—"

"Well, this is sort of pointless," Joan said. "You just think one way, and me another. I don't think she wants any more than her own husband there, and that's what she's got. And Simon too, if she wants him."

"Ain't *that* a funny thing," Lily said suddenly. "Up to last week, it was Janie *Rose* she never paid no attention to—"

"You hush," Missouri said. "This is Miss Joan's *relatives* we're talking about."

"Well, I know that. Now, won't it Simon she used to brag on all the time? Won't it Simon that was spoiled so rotten he—"

"Hush."

"My feet are killing me," said Mrs. Hall.

Her second hander, the pale one named Josephine, looked down at Mrs. Hall's feet and gave one of them a gentle kick with the toe of her sneaker. "With me it's sneakers or barefoot," she said. "What you wearing leather shoes for?"

"Because I'm older than you. I have to look decent." She snapped off her twine and turned to the barn. "Boy!" she called.

"Will you look?" said Missouri. "She's a stick and a half ahead of me, and you two are poking along. Hurry it up, Lily."

Lily handed her the next bunch and then stretched, raising her thin black arms an enormous length above her head. To show her disapproval Missouri jerked her string with a twanging sound, and one of Lily's leaves fell out of its bunch on the stick and landed in the dust. "Oh,

Lord," Missouri said. She handed her string to Joan and bent to pick
up the leaf, holding the small of her back with one hand. A pink slip
strap slid down over her shoulder. "Four hours ago it was four o'clock,"
she said when she had retrieved the leaf. "Now it's four thirty. When'll
it ever be five?"

"Won't help you if it is," called Mrs. Hall, "so long as you've still
got leaves on your table."

"Well, I can't help it if they loaded the most leaves on me." She
pulled her strap up again and took the end of the twine away from
Joan. "I was saying something," she said. "I have that fidgety feeling,
like I wasn't finished."

"Sitting," Joan reminded her.

"Sitting? Oh, sitting. My lord, how long I been *on* that? Well, anyway."
She snapped her fingers at Lily, who was gazing open-mouthed at a
pecan tree, and Lily jumped and handed her another bunch of leaves.
"Originally," Missouri said, "I was getting around to a remedy for Mrs.
Pike. Well, now I've gotten to it. Mrs. Pike is going to have to start
working again."

"Working?" Lily said. "*I* didn't know Mrs. Pike worked."

"Will you *hush?*" Missouri switched the twine to her left hand and
reached across to slap Lily's arm. "I don't know where you spend all
your time, Lily," she said. She took up the twine in her right hand
again and snatched Joan's leaves from her. "Well, it so happens she
does work. She's a seamstress. Teen-iney stitches and a Singer for her
machine work. Miss Joan can tell you. Most of it's altering things, but
she makes things from scratch also. Reason you might not know," she
told Lily, "is she does it at home. Works in. A lot of right important
people go there. Mrs. Lawrence, the judge's wife, does—saw her drive
up to the door once. Do you see what I'm getting at, Miss Joan?"

"Well, yes," said Joan. "You're saying this would snap her out of it.
But being a seamstress is like working in a beauty shop—you have to
carry on a conversation. And Aunt Lou just isn't capable right now."

"Of *course* not," said Mrs. Hall. "Why, she just don't have the heart
to do that. Will you *look* at you people?"

"I got the answer," Mrs. Hall's first hander called. "I don't see why
you are all worrying." She kept on handing as she spoke, thrusting
precisely neat bunches at Mrs. Hall with lightning speed. "It's like
when you've been sick," she said. "They have to walk you around by
the elbow a while. Well, Mrs. Pike needs to be walked around too,
only in the talking sense. Joan here only works every other day; she
can spare the time. She can greet the customers and tell them the news
and all, so's they won't even notice how quiet Mrs. Pike is. Then by
and by Mrs. Pike'll start to get interested in what Joan is talking about.
She'll begin uncurling and saying a few words herself. That's why she
was such a favorite before, Mrs. Pike was; she could talk up a storm."

Missouri was watching her with her mouth open. "Charleen," she said, when Charleen had finished speaking, "you are just as silly as you look, Charleen. You must think Miss Joan is some kind of a walking newspaper. Do you? She don't say two words in a day, Joan don't. Customers would drop off like apples in the fall, and Mrs. Pike would have one more reason not to get a grip on things."

"Silly yourself," Charleen muttered, and bent closer over her pile of leaves.

"Mrs. Pike's no worse than my sister Mary was," said Mrs. Hall. "When Mary's oldest died she sat on the porch seven days and seven nights and it rained on her. I thought she'd *mold*, before we got her in again. Mrs. Pike is at least talking some."

"Not much," Josephine said. She was scraping tobacco gum off her hands with a nail file while Mrs. Hall tied a knot at the end of her stick. "I went up to her at the burying and, 'Mrs. Pike,' I said. 'I surely am sorry.' And you know what she said? She said, 'This is where Simon's bedroom was going to be.' I tell you, it scared me."

"Well, they were going to build a house there," Mrs. Hall said. She slammed another stick in the stand. "I say they should have put Janie Rose by the church, but that's a individual matter."

Missouri took off her straw hat and began fanning her face with it. "You can rest," she told Joan and Lily. "We're even now. Boy?"

"Yes'm."

"Well, come on and get it."

Joan and Lily leaned back against the table, half sitting on it, and Missouri tilted her head back so that she could fan her neck. "Sun's about gone," she said, "but still working. What was it I was thinking, now? Lily?"

"Well, I'm sure *I* don't know," Lily said.

"Hush. Wait, now—oh." She stopped fanning herself, clamped her hat on her head again, and bent for another rod. "Stop that standing around," she commanded. "Charleen, I take it back."

"What?"

"What I said. I take it back. You only half silly."

"Oh, why, *thank* you."

"Only half as silly as you look. Stand up straight, Lily, you're a mess. What's that all over your hands?"

"It's tobacco gum, what you think?"

"Oh." She snapped off her length of twine, with Mrs. Hall watching closely, and reached for Joan's leaves. "I'm a little vague, but I'm thinking," she said. Then she frowned into space for a while. Finally she said, "Growing old surely do damage a person."

"Well, is *that* what you've been getting ready to say?" Mrs. Hall asked irritably.

"*Oh* no," Missouri said. "It was something entirely different. I was working up to something."

"You were talking about Aunt Lou," Joan reminded her.

"Well, I know I was. If you all would just let me—"

"Personally," said Mrs. Hall, "I think this is a lot of fuss for nothing. You think it's something wrong if Mrs. Pike sticks to herself a few days. Well, something *is* wrong. Somebody died. And that's all I'm going to say."

"It's just as well," said Missouri. "You keep distracting my mind."

"Why, Missouri—"

"You *said*," Missouri reminded her, "you said that was all you was going to—"

Mrs. Hall sighed and turned her back, muttering something but not attempting to argue any more, and Missouri nodded to herself several times. "There now," she said. "Now, what was I—?" But when Lucy clicked her tongue in exasperation, exactly like her mother, Missouri waved her free hand at her to tell her not to speak. "Now I remember," she said. "Growing old surely do— Well. Anyway. Now, of course we're not saying anything's wrong with Mrs. Pike. Sure she's sad. Going to go right on being that way, always a little sad to the end of her days. But that don't stop us from trying to make her feel better; that's just natural. We all got reasons. Maybe we want to stop remembering the dead ourselves. Or a host of other reasons."

She bent down and slapped a fly on her leg. "Oh, you," she said to the fly, and then reached out for Joan's leaves. Joan was holding the leaves too high and far away, and Missouri had to snap her fingers at her. "*Come* on," she said. Joan came to life and handed the leaves over.

"*Any*how," said Missouri. "Now I've lost my place again. Where was I?"

"Mrs. Pike," Joan said.

"Mrs. Pike? Oh, her. Well, no, I was passing on to someone else. What's-his-name. What's his name?"

"*Mr.* Pike?" Lily suggested.

"Just hush. Though he's in this too, of course. No, just hush—Simon. That boy of theirs. You know him, Joan?"

"He's my cousin," said Joan.

"Oh, yes. Yes. Simon. Going to go to pieces if things go on this way. Do you see now what I'm getting at?"

"Well, no."

"It's as plain as the nose on— Boy? Come on, now, quit that poking. I'm saying it's Simon should be in her beauty shop with her."

"In her—?"

"I mean in her sewing shop. Look what you done now, got me all confused. Well, that's who you want."

"You mean he should entertain the customers," Joan said.

"That was my point."

"Well—"

"He's the only one can help now. Not hot tea, not people circling round. Not even her own husband. Just her little boy."

"I don't see how," said Joan.

Missouri made an exasperated face. "*You* don't know," she told her. "You don't know how it would work out. Bravest thing about people, Miss Joan, is how they go on loving mortal beings after finding out there's such a thing as dying. Do I have to tell you that?"

She snapped her twine tight and held it there while she watched Joan scrape up the last of the leaves. "I despise finishing the day on half a stick," she said.

"Well, I'll be," said Charleen. She leaned back against the table, shaking her head and watching Mrs. Hall tie the end of her stick. "I never. Was *that* what you did all this talking to say?"

"It was," said Missouri.

At the other end of the table, Mrs. Hall suddenly looked up. "That's true," she said slowly, but when they turned toward her she only shook her head. "That's true," she said again, and lifted her tobacco rod gently from its notches and handed it to the waiting boy.

6

JAMES WAS halfway through his second beer before he saw Joan coming toward him. He was sitting on Mr. Terry's porch, leaning back against the side of the house in a folding chair and lazily listening to the other men talking, and the beer can was making a cold wet ring on his knee. There were four other men there, all sitting just like he was in a line against the house. Maybe if Joan hadn't come he would have sat with them till supper, just to rest up from the long day's work and let the breeze dry his damp shirt. But then Mr. Terry said, "If you'll look out yonder—" and James raised his eyes toward the fields and saw Joan padding down the dirt driveway in bare feet with a sandal swinging from each hand. "Out yonder to the east is what I mean to cultivate year after next," Mr. Terry went on. He had been saying that for as long as James had known him. "I aim to extend the alfalfa a bit. No sense in letting good land grow wild, I say." James only nodded, not really listening. He squinted his eyes so as to see better—Joan was still far away—and watched how she picked her way so quickly and gently along the dusty wheel-tracks. Her head was bent, so that her hair fell forward and nearly hid her face. Way behind her were the other women, going in the opposite direction toward town, and once they turned back and waved at Joan but she didn't see them. The women bobbed on, farther and farther, until all that showed of them was their bright dresses between the tobacco rows and two huge black umbrellas shading Lily and Missouri from the sun.

"I also been thinking about the eight acres out back," said Mr. Terry. "They're Paul Hammond's, but he's not using them."

"No," James said.

"You listening?"

Joan had reached the edge of the Terrys' front yard. She crossed onto the grass, sliding her feet a little as if she liked the coolness of it, and Mr. Terry stopped talking and the others sat forward and took their hats off.

"Hey, Joan," said Mr. Terry.

"Hey." She stopped at the bottom of the steps and smiled up at them. "Lem," she said, "Missouri sent you a message. She said to come right on home."

Lem tipped back again in his chair, shaking his head. "Must be a mistake somewheres," he said. His eyes were faraway and dreamy, and the others laughed softly.

"Well, anyway," said Joan. "I came to see if you're ready to go yet, James. Or do you want to stay on a while."

"No, I'm ready."

He finished his beer in one gulp and stood up. Down at the end of the porch, Howell Blake looked up from cleaning his fingernails with a pocket knife and said, "You coming tomorrow?"

"Depends on Roy Pike, I guess. Looks like he'll be sitting with his wife a while."

"Well, just so's *one* of you makes it," said Mr. Terry. "You tell Roy I know how it is. *You* tell him, Joan."

"I will."

James went down the steps toward Joan, and she switched one sandal to the other hand so that he could take her free hand in his. Both of them were coated with tobacco gum. The gum had lost its stickiness by now but it still clung to their skin in heavy layers, so that it was like holding hands with rubber gloves on. He kept hold of her anyway, and turned partway back to nod at the others. "See you tomorrow, I guess," he said. "I or Roy, one."

"Okay. So long."

"So long."

They crossed the yard together and then they were on the dirt driveway again, heading toward the gravel road. When James looked down, he could see the dust rising in little puffs around Joan's toes every time she took a step. Her toes were gum-covered too, and the dust had stuck to them like a layer of sugar frosting.

"I have to have a bath," Joan said, as if she had been following his eyes.

"No. I like you this way."

"I'm serious. You have to have one too, and then we can sit outside and cool off."

"Okay," James said. He pulled her along faster, because he liked the idea of just the two of them sitting out on the porch a while. But Joan slowed him down again.

"I have to put on my sandals to walk fast," she said. "Do you want me to?"

"No, that's all right."

But she bent down anyway, and James stood waiting while she slid her feet into the sandals. She was wearing bermudas and a faded blue shirt with the tails out, and when a breeze started up it ballooned out the back of her shirt and made her look humpbacked. He put one hand on the hump. It vanished, pressed flat by the weight of his hand, and he could feel the ripple of her backbone through the thin cloth of her shirt. It seemed to him he knew Joan's clothes by heart. He could tell the seasons by them, and if she bought something new, he felt uneasy and resentful toward it until it had become worn-looking. When spring came he never really felt it until those old cotton shirts had come out again, though for days he might have known about the bits of green on the trees and the flowering Judas buds by the side of the road. He smiled down at Joan now and she straightened up and looked at him, not knowing anything about what was going on in his mind.

"What're you thinking?" she asked him.

"Nothing."

They turned onto the gravel road, holding hands again. A station wagon drove past, clanking and rattling as if it would fall apart before their eyes, and Joan waved at whoever was driving but James didn't look up. He was concentrating on the gravel beneath his feet, and on steering Joan into the sandiest part of the road. Finally he said, "I've got an idea."

"What?"

"How about coming over and cooking supper tonight? We could sit out and eat it on the porch."

"You know I can't cook."

"Well, hot dogs is all right."

He dropped her hand and put his arm around her, so that he could feel her shoulder moving against his rib cage as they walked. They were going very slowly now; he had stopped caring if they never got

anywhere at all. He would like to go on down this road indefinitely,
with everything around him shining and wearing a clean, finished, end-
of-the-day look. The sun picked things up slantwise, and the fields
were very still in between the gusts of breeze. When they rounded the
bend and their house appeared, long and shabby with its tin roof batting
the sunshine into their eyes, it seemed surprising and out of place.
Both of them slowed down still more to stare at it. Then Joan said,
"Well, I'll race you home."

"Now?"

"Come on."

She started running, moving in bursts of uneven speed and letting
her hands stay open instead of doubling them into fists the way most
people did. Beside her, James ran at a slow easy pace because he didn't
want to leave her behind. When he ran like this he was scarcely
breathing hard, but Joan was out of breath and laughing. They reached
the edge of the yard, and she stopped to tuck her shirttails in. "You
weren't even trying," she told him. "That was no race."

But he reached out for a tall blue spiky flower and presented it to
her gravely, as if she had won, and she accepted it.

"When you coming over?" he asked.

"In an hour or so. I have to take a bath and see that the others
eat."

"Can you leave your aunt?"

"I'll see how she is," Joan said. She bent over suddenly and clapped
her hands together, with the stem of the flower between them. "Hey,
Nellie," she said. "That you?"

The bushes beside the lawn rustled and the dog poked just her head
out, her nose pointed upwards. "Where you been?" Joan asked her.
She made little coaxing motions with her hands. For a minute James
watched, and then when it looked as if Nellie would be a long time
making up her mind to come he turned toward the house.

"I'm going on in," he called.

"All right. Come on, Nellie."

James crossed the yard and climbed the steps at his end of the porch.
In the seat of Ansel's chair was a rumpled magazine, which he picked
up to take inside with him. "I'm home, Ansel," he said in the doorway.
But Ansel didn't answer, and his couch was bare. "Hey, Ansel?"

On the coffee table was Ansel's entire collection of seashells, all laid
out neatly with the hollow sides up. This must have been one of his
bored days, spent wandering aimlessly through the house with an
occasional pause to glance over some possession of his before he grew
tired of it and began wandering again. But he hadn't been flipping
through James's photographs, the way he usually did on those days.
And he wasn't in the kitchen, or up in his room. "Ansel?" James called

once more, and his voice rang out into a waiting, ticking silence that worried him.

He went outdoors again. Joan was still in the yard, sitting on her heels and patting Nellie. When she saw James she said, "You're supposed to be in the tub by now," but James only shook his head.

"I can't find Ansel," he said.

Joan stood up then and came over to the porch. "He's probably just gone visiting," she told him. "Did you look for a note?"

"*Ansel* don't leave notes."

"Well, he'll be back."

"I don't know. I want you to check your aunt's for me; I don't like bothering her."

"All right." She turned and made a kissing sound at Nellie, who danced after her toward the porch. "It's time for your supper," Joan told her, and then led her through the Pikes' door by snapping her fingers high above Nellie's head. After they had disappeared into the house James stayed out on the porch, waiting to see if Joan had found his brother. If she had, she would need help coaxing him out. He had a sudden clear picture of Joan backing out the door again, snapping her fingers at Ansel to lead him forward the way she had led Nellie. He smiled, and then relaxed and swung one foot up onto the porch railing.

But when Joan came she came alone. "He's at the Potters'," she said, before James could ask. "Uncle Roy said he came calling, but Simon wouldn't let him in. He went on to the Potters'."

"Well, maybe I'll just check," said James.

"Oh, he's all right, James. What's got into you lately?"

"I just want to make sure," he told her. "I wish you'd come with me. If I go alone I'll *never* get out, once they start to talking."

"Well, all right."

She came over to stand beside him, and he knocked on the Potters' door. There was no screen on it, because they didn't need one; they kept the inner door shut. Summer and winter their part of the porch had a closed, unbreathing look, and they had long ago paid James two dozen cinnamon buns for taking the baggy old screen door off its hinges and carting it out back. When James knocked there was first a faint movement of the paper shade—they had to make sure who it was—and then there was the sound of two bolts sliding back. The door cracked open; Miss Faye poked her round face out.

"Why, James," she said.

"Hello, Miss Faye."

"And Joan too. Both of you together. Joan, honey, don't you look fresh and outdoorsy today. I was saying to Miss Lucy just a—well, step on inside, step in."

"Actually," James said, "I just wanted to see if you had Ansel here."

"Ansel?" She had the door wide open now, and was throwing back
one arm to show that they were welcome. James kept trying to peer
past her, hoping to see Ansel, but the way the Potters' house was
arranged made it impossible. They had set up a labyrinth of tall black
folding screens with needlework flowers on them, so that the house
was divided into a dozen or more tiny rooms. No matter how James
craned his neck around Miss Faye, all he saw was the screen behind
her and more screens behind that. "Oh, Ansel," Miss Faye was saying.
"James, I worry about that boy. I was saying just a while ago; I said—
are you coming in? Don't stand outside; come on in."

"We've only got a minute," Joan said gently. "Is Ansel here?"

"Well, let's see." She stepped further back, leaving them the whole
doorway to enter through and after a minute the two of them came
in. Who could tell what might be hidden in this maze of screens? The
air was dark and stale, from being separated into so many cubicles in
a tightly closed house. And there was a thick feeling to the walls that
must have come from the heavy tapestries, because every place else
in this house was shell-thin. When they were inside, Miss Faye shut
the whole world behind them out; she said, *"Now,"* and slammed the
door and slid the two locks into place. James frowned (it made him
uneasy, being locked in this way) but Joan only looked amused.

"You were going to tell us if Ansel's here," she reminded Miss Faye.

"Yes. Yes, I was saying—Lucy? Lucy, are you coming to say hello?"

They heard Miss Lucy's footsteps, sounding very faint and taking a
long time to weave in and out among the screens. First she came close
and then went farther away again, and suddenly she popped out right
behind Miss Faye. She wore a huge white apron with jokes about
outdoor barbecues printed all over it.

"Lucy, look who's here," said Miss Faye.

"Well, isn't this nice?" Miss Lucy came towards them with both
hands outstretched, making James wonder, just as he always did, what
he was supposed to do when she reached him—hug her?—but Joan
saved the day by stepping up and taking both Miss Lucy's hands in
her own. "You're looking just as *healthy,*" Miss Lucy told her, and
then gave a little giggle and shook her tight cap of curls. "We've had
so much company today that I'm getting all—"

"Well, that's really what we came to talk about," said James.

"Aren't you going to sit down?"

"We wanted to ask—"

"You *have* to sit down." She began backing around the first screen,
still holding Joan's hands. James glanced over at a puffy plush chair,
with its layers and layers of antimacassars, and then shook his head.

"I'm sorry," he said, "but it looks like Ansel isn't here, and that's
what we came about."

"*Oh* yes. Yes, he was here."

"When?" James asked.

"At three o'clock today, on the nose. No, more like three fifteen. I forget, Faye . . ."

"It was three twenty exactly," said Miss Faye. "It was my turn to wear the brooch-watch today. I had looked down at it, while checking to see if my blouse was clean, just before I answered the door. And it was Ansel at the door. Will you sit down, please?"

"That was nearly two hours ago," James said.

"No, you're wrong, James."

"Well, it's way past five."

"Oh, it was nearly two hours ago that he *came*, all right. But it was more recently that he left, because he stayed to have a jam braid."

"Well—"

"Also a glass of milk. I said, 'Ansel, we've got to get some meat on your bones.' So did Miss Lucy. She said so too. Ansel said, 'Oh, Miss Faye, I just don't know.' He was feeling sad."

"What about?" asked James.

"He didn't say. Well, you know how he is. Some days the world is just too much for him. That's how he put it. 'Miss Faye,' he said, 'some days the world is just too much for me.' He told Lucy that too. 'Miss Lucy,' he said, 'some days the—' "

"Did he say where he was going?"

"Why, home, I reckon."

"I have to leave," James said.

"Oh, now. You only just—"

"I'm sorry, Miss Faye. Come on, Joan."

He reached the door before Miss Faye could, and he slid the bolts back himself, with Miss Faye's hands fluttering anxiously above his. Then he shot out on the porch, not even trying to be polite about it. Joan followed, but with her head turned toward the Potters, her voice drifting back to them as she tried to smooth everything over. "I'm sorry we have to leave this way," she said, "but I know you see how it is—" and the Potters made thin, sad little sounds to show that they did.

"Just please come back," Miss Faye told them, and James nodded tiredly and let the door swing shut. The two bolts slid back into place.

When they were outside again James just stood there, trying to think where to begin. Joan didn't seem worried at all. She said, "I got tobacco gum all over Miss Lucy's hands."

"That's too bad," James said absently.

"She was staring at her hands all funny-like; that's how I noticed. Little bits of black were sticking to them."

James turned around and looked at her. "Will you *listen?*" he told her. "I can't find Ansel."

"I'm sorry, James." She grew serious, and came over to stand beside him. "He'll come back," she said.

"I don't know."

"He always has before."

"Well, I just don't *know*," James said. He knelt to tie his shoe and then stayed that way, looking down the porch to see who might be coming along the road. No one was in sight. "We don't know *what* might have happened," he said.

Joan squatted down beside him and said, "Well, he's come back every other time, James."

"You already said that."

"I just meant—"

"I *know* he comes back. I been through this a hundred times. If I didn't even go looking for him, he'd come back. But I can't be a hundred per cent sure of that."

Down the road came a red hen, strutting importantly, sticking her neck far out as if she were heading someplace definite. As she walked she talked to herself, in little conversational clucks. James and Joan watched after her until she had disappeared.

"Somehow I can't get what Maisie said off my mind," James said finally. "How would I feel if just once he went too far? There'd be no one to blame but me, if that happened."

"Maisie who?" Joan asked.

"Maisie Hammond."

"Well, if you *did* go after him, you know how it'd be. You ever seen Ansel standing on a street corner waiting for you? He goes somewhere you'd never think to look, James. You go up and down town all night searching for him, waking every drinking man to ask him if he knows, and where does it get you? You always end up right here, waiting for him to decide to come back."

"I like to think I looked," James said.

"I know that." She stood up again, and the cotton smell of her shirt floated past him. "I can see it better than you can," she told him. "I don't like him. I can see easier than you how he will always come back."

"You can't see."

"Look," Joan said. "What's got into you? Things were getting better for a while. You weren't fussing over him, and he had almost stopped wandering off. Why have you started acting this way?"

He stared down at her feet, long and dirty in sandals that had molded themselves to the curl of her toes. Her feet made him so angry that he almost didn't answer her. But then she looked down at him, with her face worried and unsure, and he said, "I don't know."

"Well, there's got to be some reason."

"Will you stop asking me that? *You* don't have a brother."

"Maybe not," Joan said, "but there is nothing I like or understand about you going to look for Ansel all the time. If he wanted he could have done a full day's work today, and been off at a dance right now."

"No, he couldn't."

"Yes, he could. He could be dancing and you and I could be going someplace. We could be doing something. We could be someone besides an old familiar couple that'll be courting when they're seventy and the town's fondest joke. Are you listening?"

"No," James said.

He got up off his knees and went down the porch steps. Bits of tobacco gum and dust from the floorboards clung to the knees of his pants, but he didn't brush them off. The sunset glowed red and dull across the roof of the pickup. "Don't bother fixing supper," he called.

"I wouldn't *think* of fixing supper."

He stopped and looked back at her. She was standing at the edge of the porch now, with her arms folded and her feet planted solidly apart. "I wish you'd wear some real *shoes* once," he said.

"What?"

"I'm sick of those sandals."

"Well, I'm sick of everything," Joan said.

Her voice was flat now, and only sad-sounding. It made him look back at her one more time, but by then she had turned away and was walking down the porch. "Joan?" he said. She went on walking, not answering. From behind, her folded arms gave her a thin, round-shouldered look, and she stepped in that gentle way she had, with her bare pointed heels rising and falling delicately across the long gray porch.

7

AT NIGHT, when everyone was in bed, the house seemed to belong to one family instead of three. The separate sleeping-sounds mingled and penetrated through all the thin walls, and by now James could identify each sound exactly and where it came from. He knew Miss Faye's snore, as curlicued and lacy as she herself was, and the loud, honking sound that Mr. Pike made. He knew Miss Lucy's rat-a-tat on the walls, first on Mr. Pike's wall when the snoring grew too noisy and then on his own wall if he talked in his sleep. He thought it must be a thimble she tapped with. Because there was a big room's width between his end of the house and the Pikes' end, he wasn't sure of the softer sounds there—Simon's snoring, for instance, or Mrs. Pike's. And he had always wondered if Joan snored. But he had heard Janie Rose's nightmares often enough. They came through loud and clear, drifting up from the open window of her tacked-on bedroom downstairs. *"That's* not something you should be doing," she would say reasonably. And then, "Daddy, would you come *quick?"* and the floundering thuds across the floor as Mr. Pike began groping his way toward her voice in the dark. But if Simon talked in his sleep, he must have talked quietly. All James heard of him was in the morning, when they tried to wake him and he bellowed out, "Oh, *fine,* I'll be right there! I already got my socks on. Ain't this some day?"—yet all the while sound asleep, and just trying to fool people. Sometimes Mr. Pike shouted too. He would have too many beers on a Saturday night and throw all the pillows out the window. "Ninety-nine point two per cent of all the people in the southern *states* die of smothering," he would roar to the night, and then Miss Lucy would rap on the wall. Miss Lucy never slept at all; James was convinced of that. She spent her time policing the area. On nights when Ansel was restless, when he tossed around on his old wooden bed across the room from James (he wouldn't sleep in the other bedroom, for fear of waking alone and finding his feet numb), and when he kept calling, "James, how long has this night been going *on?"* Miss Lucy would tap very gently and ask if Ansel wanted her hot water bottle. "No, ma'am," James always said, and Miss Lucy would go back to her quiet, patient pacing. Sometimes James had a great urge to go see what she was wearing. He pictured her in a twenty-pound quilted robe with lead weights at the bottom, like the ones sewn into curtains, because it dragged so loudly across the floor at every step she took. But once he had had a horrible nightmare, right after eating two pizzas. He had shouted out, "My *God!"* and awakened shaking, with the terrible sound of his own shout still ringing in his ears. Then Miss Lucy had tapped and called, "Why, *it's* going to be all right," and the horror vanished. He had lain back down, feeling comforted and at home, and now it never annoyed him to hear Miss Lucy's bathrobe dragging.

In the Potters' bedroom the clock struck four, whirring and choking before each clang. James lay tensed, counting the strokes, although he already knew how many there would be. He had slept only in patches all night, and even in his dreams he was searching streets full of people for the thin stooped figure of his brother. In the last dream it had been a year ago—that time they had called from ten miles away to tell him Ansel had been run over, but neglected to add it was only a bicycle that had done it. After that he couldn't sleep at all. He thought of all the things that had happened to Ansel in the past, the really serious things, and all the things that might be happening to him tonight.

When the clock had stopped whirring he found that he was frowning into the darkness so hard that the muscles of his forehead hurt. Then, as if that clock had been some sort of musical introduction, a faraway voice began singing outside:

> *There's sunshine on the mountains,*
> *And spring has come again. . . .*

James sat up and pulled back the curtain. Outside it was pitch black, with a handful of small stars scattered like sand across the blue-black sky. The trees beyond the field were only hulking dark shapes, and not one light glimmered from the town behind them.

> *My true love said she'd meet me,*
> *But forgot to tell me when.*

He climbed out of bed and untwisted the legs of his pajamas. At his bedroom wall there was one sharp tap, questioning (he had learned to read Miss Lucy's thimble language), and he called, "It's all right, Miss Lucy." She resumed her pacing again, with her robe trailing her footsteps like a murmuring companion. James shot out of his room, still buttoning his pajama top, and went downstairs in the dark. The voice was nearer now.

> *I was walking down the track, Lord,*
> *With a letter in my hand,*
> *A-reading how she'd left me*
> *For that sunny Jordan land.*

The front door was open but the screen was hooked shut. James pushed the hook up, jabbing his finger, and swung the screen door open. Then he walked across the porch barefoot, with the cold rough grain of the wooden floorboards stinging the soles of his feet. Around his ankles the cuffs of his pajamas fluttered and ballooned and nearly tripped him (they were Ansel's, and too long); he bent to roll them up. Then he descended the steps, scowling into the dark as he tried to see. He was halfway down the path before he stopped, more by sensing someone in front of him than by seeing him. Ahead of him was a long tall shape, swaying gently, smelling of bourbon. The voice was so close now that James could feel its breath.

> *Oh, there's sunshine on the hills, Lord,*
> *And the grass is all of gold. . . .*

His reedy voice was piercing, but the thinness of it made it seem still far away. James stepped closer. "Ansel," he said.

My love has gone and left me,
And I'll cry until I'm old.

"Ansel," James said again.

"I'm singing, please."

"Come on in."

He took Ansel by the arm. It was stone cold; he could feel the bone underneath. When he pulled Ansel toward the porch Ansel came, but lifelessly and with the shadow that was his face still averted. "People keep asking you in nowadays," he told the dark. "They got a thing about it."

"Careful," said James. "We're coming to the steps."

"The *Potters* downright *lock* you in. Slide little bits of machinery around. You mind if I finish my song?"

"I certainly do."

"I might just finish it anyway. Where you taking me, James?"

"*In*," said James, and half lifted him up the first step. Ansel was as limp as a rag doll. His limpness made James realize suddenly how angry he was at Ansel, after all this worrying and waiting; instead of guiding him so carefully, he felt like giving him a good shove into the house and having done with it. "Get on in," he said, and took his hand away from Ansel's arm. Ansel gave him a deep lopsided bow and entered first.

"Certainly nice of you to ask me," he told James. "Certainly are a *hospitable* man."

"If you're hungry, Ansel—"

"I'm starved."

"Cook up some eggs," said James, and began making his way across the dark living room toward the stairs. Behind him Ansel said, "*Hey, now*—" but James paid no attention. The way he felt, he couldn't even make a cup of coffee for Ansel; he had been worrying for too long, and all he wanted now was sleep. Already he was unbuttoning the tops of his pajamas, preparing to go back to his bed.

"Don't you have food waiting?" Ansel asked.

"Nope."

"Don't you even *care* if I come back?"

"You know how to fry an egg."

"Well, I'll be," said Ansel, and sat down suddenly on something that creaked. "I take it back, James. What's so hospitable about you?"

The stairs were narrow, and James kept stubbing his toes against them. He touched the wall to guide himself, feeling the ripples and bubbles of the wallpaper as he slid his fingers along it. Behind him Ansel said, "You mad at me, James?" but James didn't answer. He could already hear the tapping sound that was coming from upstairs. Miss Lucy must be worried.

"I reckon you're wondering where I was at," Ansel said, and there was another creak when he stood up again. "You always *do* wonder." He banged into something, and then his footsteps wavered uncertainly toward the stairs. "You're taking all my places from me. Once I tell you, I can't go back no more. How long you guess it'll be before I've used up every place there is?" He was climbing the steps behind James now. His voice rang hollowly through the stairwell. For a minute James paused, listening to him coming, and then he continued on up and reached the top, with his hand still on the wall so that he could find his room. "It's all a question of time," Ansel said sadly. "Time and geography."

"If you're coming to sleep in *my* room," James told him, "you'd better shut up that talking."

"Well, I only want to explain."

"I'm sleepy, Ansel."

"I only want to explain."

James kept going, heading in the direction of Miss Lucy's tapping thimble. He could hear Ansel's hands sliding along behind his now on the wall, and then the sliding sound stopped and there was a click as Ansel snapped the hall light on. For a minute the light was blinding. James screwed his eyes up and said, "Oh, Lord—" and Ansel turned the light off again, quickly and guiltily. "I just thought," he said, "as long as we had electricity—"

"It's four a.m., Ansel."

"What're you, wearing my pajamas?"

"Go to hell, will you?"

"I never," said Ansel, but James was past listening. He was in the bedroom now, and on his way to bed he reached out and knocked on Miss Lucy's wall for her to stop that tapping. She did. He eased himself down between the sheets, which were cold already and messy-feeling. When he was lying flat he closed his eyes and wished away the figure of Ansel, standing like a long black stick and swaying in the bedroom doorway.

"I wisht I knew what was wrong with you," Ansel said. "You angry with me, James?"

"Yep."

"I only went out for a walk."

"You usually end up half dead after those walks. It's me that's got to nurse you back."

"Well, wait now," Ansel said. "I can explain. All you need to do is listen."

"How can I listen when I'm asleep?" asked James, and turned over on his side with his face to the window. He could hear Ansel's feet shuffling into the room, and he knew by the soft thumping noise that he had reached the other bed and was sitting on it.

"I tried and I tried," Ansel told him. "I went to the Pikes' first off, but Simon don't like me any more. I went to the Potters', and they locked me in and requested news of my hemoglobin. What could I do? At the tavern I said, 'Charlie,' I said, 'I got a problem.' But all Charlie did was sell me hard liquor under the counter; he didn't listen to no problem."

Ansel's shoes were dropped on the floor, first one and then the other. There was a small whipping sound as he flung his tie around a bedpost. Even with his eyes shut James could picture his brother, how he would be leaning toward James with his shoulders hunched and his hands flung out as he talked, even though he knew he couldn't be seen. "Go to sleep, Ansel," he muttered, but Ansel only sighed and began unbuttoning his shirt with tiny popping sounds.

"This all has to do with Janie Rose," he told James. "Are you listening?"

"No."

"Just about everything has to do with Janie Rose these days. I don't know why. Looks like she just kind of tipped everything over with her passing on. Janie don't like gladioli, James."

James didn't answer. A button flew to the floor and then circled there for an endless length of time, and Ansel stamped one stocking foot over it and shook the whole house. James could feel the floorboards jar beneath his bed. There was a long silence; then Ansel bent, with a small puff of held-in breath, and scrapped his fingers across the floor in search of the button.

"Got it," he said finally. "All today, I was so sick and tired. I had looked at that picture of the Model A too long. I don't know why I do things like that. Then I thought, well, I'll just go up the hill and pay my respects to Janie Rose. I'll go slow, so as not to get overtired. And I did. I stopped a plenty on the way. But when I got close I saw her flowers, how they had got all wilted. I thought: I wisht I'd brought some flowers. I thought: I wisht I'd brought some bluets. You listening, James?"

James gritted his teeth and stayed quiet.

"There's four names for bluets I know of. Bluets, Quaker-ladies, pea-in-the-paths, and wet-the-beds. You can count on Janie Rose; she called them wet-the-beds. Well, she had problems herself in that line. But what I thought was: I wisht I'd brought some bluets. I *didn't* think: I wisht I'd brought some wet-the-beds."

"Oh, Lord," James said tiredly. He turned his pillow to the cool side and lay back down on it.

"Now, bluets are not good funeral flowers. Too teeny. But Janie Rose is not a funeral *person*. Usually it's only the good die young. Consequently I thought: I wisht I'd—"

James raised his head and shouted, "Ansel, will you *hush?*" and on his wall there was the sudden sound of frantic tapping. "I don't want to hear," he told Ansel more quietly, and then lay back down and forced his mind far away.

"I'll just get to the point," Ansel said. "I have to tell you this. James, there are *gladioli* on Janie's grave."

James heard a zipper slide down, and after a minute a pair of trousers was tossed shufflingly across the floor. Then Ansel's socks dropped one after the other beside his bed, in soft crumpled balls, and James heard them fall and winced because his ears seemed raw tonight.

"Janie Rose *despises* gladioli," said Ansel.

James said nothing.

"She hates and despises them. Believes they're witches' wands, all frilled up. She told me so."

James opened his eyes and rolled over. "Funerals are for parents," he said. "Ansel, Janie Rose is dead."

He waited, frowning. Out of the corner of his eye he could see the white blur that was Ansel in his underwear, standing before the bureau with his skinny arms folded across his chest. Finally Ansel said, "I know."

"She's dead."

"I know all about it. Nevertheless, she despises gladioli."

"The funeral is not really for her," James said, and rolled over again to face the wall. "It don't make any difference to her about those gladioli."

"*Oh* now," said Ansel. "*Oh* now." He crossed to his bed, heavily. "It's hard to bury people, Jamie. Harder than digging a hole in the ground."

"Will you go to bed?"

"They keep popping up again, in a manner of speaking."

James dug his head into his pillow.

"I remember Janie Rose's religious period," Ansel went on comfortably. "It was a right short one, wouldn't you know. But she took this tree out back, this scrubby one she was always drawing flattering pictures of. Dedicated it to God, I believe; hung it with tin cans and popcorn strings. Didn't last but a week; then she was on to something new. The birds ate the popcorn. But those tin cans are still rattling at the ends of the branches when a wind passes through, and Mr. Pike sits out back all day staring at them. Thought he had placed every last bit of her in a hole in the ground. Ha."

James reached behind him for the sheet and pulled it up over his head, making a hood of it. The rustling of the sheet drowned out everything else, and then when he was still again the sounds couldn't come through to him so clearly. The creaking of Ansel's bedsprings when he sat down was muffled and distant, and his voice was thin-sounding.

"I ought to studied botany," he was saying. "Don't you think? All I know about flowers, I ought to studied botany."

James lay still, and stared at the dark vines running up the wallpaper until his eyes ached.

"With Mama it was lilies," said Ansel. "Lord, she hated lilies. All she wanted, she said, was just a cross of—"

"We won't go into that," James told the wallpaper.

"We don't go into *nothing*. Getting so the only safe topic around here is the weather. Well, I was saying. Just a cross of white roses, she wanted. No lilies. And you know what they sent? You know what?"

He waited. The silence stretched on and on. James's arm, pressed beneath his body, began to go to sleep, but he didn't switch positions for fear of breaking the silence. He wiggled his fingers gently, without making a sound.

"Well, they sent lilies," Ansel said finally. "I thought you would have guessed. If you'd been there, I wouldn't have to be telling you all this. But I called you. I called you on the phone and said, 'James,' I said, 'will you kindly come to Mama's funeral?' I called you long distance and person-to-person, Caraway to Larksville. But you never answered me. Just hung up the telephone, neat and quiet. If I was the persistent type, I'd be asking still. I'd ask it today: 'James, will you kindly come to Mama's funeral?' Because you never have answered, never once, not once in all these years. I'll ask it now. James, will you kindly—"

"No, I won't," said James.

Across the room there was a little intake of breath, quick and sharp, and over behind the Potters' wall the measured pacing suddenly began again, with the weighted bathrobe sighing behind it. Ansel lay down on his bed.

"There's two kinds of sin," he said after a minute. His voice was directed toward the ceiling now, and sounded dreamy. "There's general sin and there's private sin. General sin there's commandments against, or laws, or rules. Private sin's a individual matter. It's hurting somebody, personally. You hear me? Listen close now; this is essential. What I chose was a general sin, that they'll be a long time forgiving. I did all that drinking, and ran around with that girl that everyone knew was no good. But what you chose was a private sin, that they'll *never* forgive. They got hurt personally by it—you forever running away, and telling them finally what you thought of them and leaving home altogether. Then not coming to the funeral. Think they'll forgive *that*? No, sir. Me they will cry over in church and finally forgive, someday. But not you. I'm a very wise man, every so often."

James didn't say anything. Ansel raised himself up on one elbow to look over at him, but he stayed within his hood of sheets. "James?" Ansel said.

"What."

"You don't care *what* I say, do you?"

"Yes," James said.

"Don't it bother you sometimes? Don't you ever think about it? Here we are. You walked off from them without a backward wave of your hand, and I got thrown out like an old paper bag. Don't it—"

"Got *what?*" James asked.

"What?"

"You got *what?*"

"Got thrown out, I said, like an old—"

"You never got thrown out," said James.

"I did. Daddy said I was an alcoholic; he said I was—"

"He never said that."

"Well, almost he did. He said, 'Leave this house,' he said. 'You and your drinking and that girl in red pedal pushers, I never want to see you again.' That's what he told me."

James raised himself slightly from beneath the hood of the sheet. He peered across the dark room toward Ansel and said, "Don't you give me that, Ansel."

"What?"

"You *left*. You left, I left. Tell it that way."

"Well, what difference does it make? Who cares?"

"I care," said James. "Do *I* make excuses for leaving? Run out on him or don't run, but don't make it easy on yourself; don't tell me he *kicked* you out."

"Well," Ansel said after a minute, "I was drinking all that—"

"You don't even like the taste of it," said James.

"I do too."

James lay back down and pulled his sheet closer over him, and Ansel's voice rose louder. "It has a *won*derful taste," he said. And then, "Well, maybe he didn't exactly throw me out, but anyhow—"

Up on the tin roof, rain began. It started very gently, pattering in little sharp exclamation points that left spaces for Ansel's voice. "James?" Ansel said.

"Hmm."

"There's one thing I don't get, James. It was *you* they liked best. The others weren't nothing special, and I was so runny-nosed. I had a runny nose from the moment I was born, I think, and pinkish eyes. One time I heard Daddy say, 'Well, if there's ever a prize for sheer *sniveliness* given, he'll take it,' and Mama said, 'Hush now. Maybe he'll grow out of it.' They didn't think I heard them, but I did."

"They didn't mean that," said James.

"You know they did. But *you* they liked; why did you leave? Why didn't you come to the funeral? I said, 'Daddy,' I said, 'you want I should ask James to Mama's funeral?' 'Which James is that?' he asks. 'James your *son*,' I tell him. And he says, 'Oh. Oh, why, anything you want to, Ansel.' This was when I was still home and they had hopes I would change my ways; they let me do some things I wanted. I called and said, 'James, will you kindly come to Mama's funeral?' Then he asked what happened. 'Ansel,' he said, 'did you invite that person you had mentioned previously?' And I said no, figuring it was better that way. Daddy said, 'He wouldn't have come. He was born that way,' he said, 'lacking our religion. There was no sense asking him.' "

The rain grew louder. Now it was one steady booming against the sheets of tin, and all of Ansel that could be heard was his words; the quality of his voice was drowned out.

"I'm going back there sometime," he was saying. "They'll forget, and I'll go back. I crave a religious atmosphere." He lay back down and James nodded to himself, thinking maybe he would be sleepy now. "Churches here are somewhat lacking, I think," Ansel went on. "Quiet-like. At home it was better. Mrs. Crowley spoke in tongues. There was things that bound you there. A red glass on the windowsill in the choir loft, with something brown rising above it like the head of a beer. I think now it was wax, and the glass was a sort of candle. But before I thought it was a sort of brown fungus, some kind of mold just growing and growing. Do you remember, James?" He waited a minute. *"James?"* he said, and now his voice rose even above the roaring of the rain.

"No, I don't," James said.

"Sometimes I think your mind is just a clean, clean slate, James."

"I keep it that way," said James.

"You do. I bet when I go back you won't even miss me. I'll go and bring presents. A natural-bristle hairbrush for each sister and a table game for Claude, and a French briar pipe for Daddy. Flowers for the grave and a set of them new, unbreakable dishes to go in the kitchen. A conch shell with the crucifixion inside to make up for that one you dropped, and a crane-necked reading lamp . . ."

The rain roared on, and James listened to that with all his mind. He thought it was the best sound he had heard all day. The heavy feeling was beginning to fade away, and the rain was lulling him to sleep.

". . . a new swing," Ansel was saying, "though none of us would use it now, I reckon. Before, it was a tire we swung on. It was all right and it went high enough, but there wasn't no comfortable way to sit in it. Inside it, your legs got pinched. Straddled above it, you'd be dizzy in no time what with all that spinning. 'Stop!' you'd say, and cling like a monkey on a palm tree while everybody laughed . . ."

8

ON TUESDAY morning, Mr. Pike was the second person awake. He arrived in the kitchen wearing his work clothes and carrying a nylon mesh cap, and when he sat down at the table he sat heavily, stamping his boots together in front of him and scraping the chair across the linoleum. "I'm picking tobacco today," he told Joan. Joan was at the stove, peering into the glass knob on top of the percolator to see what color the coffee was. When her uncle made his announcement she said nothing, because she was thinking of other things, but then she turned and saw him looking at her expectantly.

"I'm sorry?" she said.

"I'm going to pick tobacco," he repeated.

"Oh. All right."

But he still seemed to be waiting for something. He folded his big bony hands on the table and leaned toward her, watching, but Joan couldn't think what was expected of her. She picked the coffeepot off the stove and carried it over to the sink, in order to dump the grounds.

"We need the money," her uncle said.

Joan shook the grounds into the garbage pail, holding the coffee-basket by the tips of her fingers so as not to get burned.

"Well, *some*time I got to start work," he said.

"Of course you do, Uncle Roy."

"Things are getting worse and worse in this house. I thought they'd get better."

"Pretty soon they will."

"I wonder, now."

He watched as Joan set his cup of coffee before him. She handed him the sugar bowl but he just stared at it, as if he'd never seen one before.

"Sugar?" Joan prodded him.

He shook his head, and she set the bowl down at his elbow.

"It's no good sitting in a *room* all my life," he said.

"Drink your coffee," Joan told him. She poured a cup for herself and then sat down opposite him hitching up the knees of her blue jeans. Her eyes were still foggy from sleep and things came through to her blurred, in shining patterns—the blocks of sunlight across the worn linoleum, the graduated circles of Mrs. Pike's saucepan set hanging on the wall, the dark slouched waiting figure of her uncle. When she stirred her coffee with a kitchen knife that was handy, the reflection of the sunshine on the blade flashed across the wall like a fish in a pool and her uncle shifted his eyes to that. He watched like a person hypnotized. She set the knife down and the reflection darted to a point high on the wall near the ceiling, and he stared upward at it.

"You going to want sandwiches?" she asked.

He didn't answer. She took a sip of her coffee, but it was tasteless and heavy and she set the cup down again. "Putting my foot down," her uncle mumbled. Joan drew lines on the tablecloth with her thumbnail. Outside a bird began singing, bringing back all the spots and patches of restless dreams she had had last night, in between long periods of lying awake and turning her pillow over and over to find a cool place. Ever since the rain stopped those birds had been singing. She rubbed her fingers across her eyelids and saw streaks of red and purple behind them.

"In regard to sandwiches," her uncle said suddenly, "I don't want them. I'll come home for lunch."

"All right."

"*Least* I can do."

"All right."

"What's the matter with *you?*" he asked, and reached finally for the sugar bowl. "You mad I'm picking tobacco?"

"No. I think it's the best thing you could do. Don't forget to tell James he won't need to work today."

"I thought you'd do that," said Mr. Pike.

"You can."

"You're not working today; you can spare a minute."

"No, I'd rather you do it."

"*Oh* now," Mr. Pike said suddenly. "You two have a fight?"

Joan took another sip of coffee. It still had no taste. A hummingbird swooped down to the window and just hung there, suspended like a child's bird-on-a-string, its small eyes staring curiously in and its little heart beating so close and fast they could see the pulsing underneath the feathers. Mr. Pike gazed at it absently.

"I never *did* hold with long engagements," he said.

"What?"

"Longer the engagement, the more time for fights. Shouldn't allow it, Joan."

"I'm not engaged," Joan said shortly. "And anyway, it's none of *my* doing." Her uncle looked away from the hummingbird and frowned at her.

"I don't know about that," he said. "And I'll tell you. Some men need a little shove."

"I don't believe in shoving."

"Only way, sometimes. I ever tell you how I came to marry your aunt?"

"I'm not in the mood for that," said Joan.

"I was only going to mention."

"No, I don't want to hear," she said, and pictured suddenly her aunt, no longer young, lying so still upstairs. *"You* go tell James," she said.

"Aw, Joan."

"Someone has to."

"Aw, Joan, you know how it is. I'll go over and there will be Ansel, all talkative and cheerful. Cheerful in the morning—can you feature that?"

"Maybe he's still asleep," Joan said.

"Ansel? No. I heard him come in long after midnight just singing away, and I reckon he sang all night and is singing still. Where's Simon?"

"In bed."

"Been days since I seen that boy. Send *him* over."

"He won't go either."

"Look," said Mr. Pike. He stood up, jarring the table, and the hummingbird flew away without even preparing to go. "I can't see Ansel today," he said. "I don't know why but he gets under my skin nowadays. Will you *please* go?"

"Oh, all right," Joan said.

"All right, that's settled. Thank you very much."

He sat down again, and Joan went back to looking at the patterns in the kitchen. Everything she saw made her homesick, but not for any home she'd ever had. The sunlight on the linoleum reminded her of something long ago and lost; yet she had never lived in a house with a linoleum kitchen, never in all her memory. She kept staring at the design of it, the speckled white floor with bars of red and blocks of blue splashed across it, and the sun lighting up the dents and scrapes made by kitchen chairs. Finally she looked away and into her uncle's frowning, leather-brown face, but her uncle only said, "We need the money," so she looked away again. Her coffee had cooled, and the surface of it was greasy-looking. She drank it anyway.

When her uncle was through with his coffee he pushed the cup toward the center of the table and rose, clamping the mesh cap on the back of his head. "You can take care of things here, I guess," he said.

"Yes."

"I'll be running along, then."

He clomped off toward the front of the house, swinging his boots in that heavy way that Simon always tried to copy. His steps made the whole floor shake. She heard the screen door swing open with a twang of its spring and then slam shut again, rattling on its hinges. Then the clomping continued across the porch, and she waited for the extra-heavy sound of his boots descending the wooden steps to the yard but it didn't come. "Joan?" he called.

"What."

"*Joan!*"

She rose and went out front, wondering why men always had to shout from where they were instead of coming closer. Her uncle was standing on the edge of the porch with his back to the house and his cap off, scratching the back of his head. "What is it?" she asked him, and he turned toward her.

"Well, I already informed your aunt," he said, "but I'm not certain she heard."

"Informed her about what?"

"About my working. But I'm not certain she heard. Will you tell her again?"

"All right," said Joan.

"Say we need the money, tell her. Say I'm sorry."

"All right, Uncle Roy."

"I can't sit looking at *trees* all my life."

"No, I know," said Joan, and reached out to give his shoulder one gentle push so that he would turn and leave. He did, still frowning. Then halfway across the yard he slapped his cap back on his head and thrust his hands in his pockets and began walking more briskly, getting ready to go out into the world again. Joan watched after him till he was out of the yard, and then she went down toward the Greens' end of the porch.

Ansel was in his window, chewing sunflower seeds. He looked very happy. He spit the hulls out on the porch floor and then leaned over, his hands on the windowsill and his elbows jutting behind him like bird wings, and tried to blow the hulls all the way across the porch and into the yard. Joan wished he would fall out. She stood over him with her hands on her hips and waited until he had straightened up again, and then she said, "Ansel."

"Morning, Joan."

"Ansel, will you give James a message?"

"If I can remember it," said Ansel. "My health is poorly this morning. Seems to be growing worse and worse."

"Doesn't look to me you could *get* much worse," Joan said.

"At least you noticed. James just don't even care. He's in a ill mood today."

Joan gave up on him and stepped over to the door and knocked. For a minute Ansel stared out his window at her, puzzling this over; then he shrugged and withdrew. He came to the door and opened it with a flourish.

"Morning, Joan," he said.

"Where's James?"

"Ain't seen you in a long time. James? He's in the back yard, emptying out the garbage."

"Will you tell him he doesn't have to work today? Make up your mind, now. If you're planning to forget I'll just do it myself."

"Oh, I'll tell him," Ansel said. "Come in and set, why don't you. Old James'll be back any minute."

"No, thank you," said Joan.

"Well, suit yourself." He yawned. "Saw your uncle go off to work this morning," he said. "Seems kind of soon for him to be doing that, don't it?"

"No."

"Well, I just thought I'd point it out." He yawned again and fished another sunflower seed from the packet in his hand. The shirt he had on was James's, she saw. It was a dark red plaid and hung too loosely on him. She stared at it a minute and then, without a word, turned and went back up the porch. "Hey!" Ansel called after her, but Joan was inside her own parlor by now, letting the door slam shut behind her.

Upstairs, Simon was sound asleep, with his pajamaed legs sprawled and all his covers kicked loose from the foot of the bed. Joan went over and touched him gently, just on the outflung, curled-in palm of his hand. He stirred a little and then mumbled and turned away from her.

"Get up, Simon," she said.

"I *am* up. I am."

"Come on."

"I'm half dressed already. I got my—"

"Simon."

He opened his eyes. "Oh light," he said, and Joan smiled and sat down on the bed beside him.

"I got something I want to talk over," she told him.

"Okay."

"You listening?"

"I just can't find any clean jeans," he said, and closed his eyes and was asleep again. Joan picked up his hand and shook it, but it hung loose and limp.

"Simon, this is about your mother," she said.

"I'm listening."

"I think your mother should start working today."

He turned over and squinted at her, through foggy brown eyes. "What at?" he asked.

"At her sewing. I want you to stay around and help with the conversation, all right? Missouri says I'm no walking newspaper."

"What?"

"Will you help me out?"

"Oh, why, sure," Simon said, and would have been asleep again if Joan hadn't pulled him to a sitting position. He stayed there, slumped between her hands, with his head drooping to one side. "I was in this boat," he said.

"Come on, Simon."

"Then we started sinking. They told me I was the one that had to swim for it. Do you believe that'll happen someday?"

"No," said Joan, and pulled hard on him till he was standing beside the bed.

"They say everything you dream will happen," Simon told her. "It's true. Last year I dreamed Mama would find out about me smoking and sure enough, that night at supper there was my half-pack of Winstons lying beside my plate and Mama staring at me. It came true."

He bent down to examine a stubbed toe and Joan stood up, preparing to go. "You come down when you're dressed," she said.

"I don't have any clean jeans to wear."

"That's just something you said in your sleep. You have lots of jeans."

"No, really I don't," Simon said. "No one's been doing the laundry."

Joan crossed to his bureau and pulled open his bottom drawer. It was bare except for a pair of bermudas. "Oh, Lord," she said. "I forgot all about the laundry."

"I told you you did."

"Well, wear bermudas till this afternoon, why don't you. By then I'll have you some jeans."

"Have my *knees* show?" Simon asked.

"What's wrong with that?"

"Boys don't *have* their knees out any more. You ought to know that."

"Well, la de da," said Joan, and rumpled the top of his hair. "Wear a pair of *dirty* jeans, then."

"They'd all call me sissy if my knees showed."

"All right. Hurry up, now."

She closed the door behind her and went downstairs. In the parlor she sat down on a faded plush footstool and reached for the telephone, which sat on a table beside her. She hooked the receiver over her shoulder and then opened the telephone book to the very back, where there was space for frequently used numbers. The page was filled to the bottom, and looked messy because of so many different hand-writings. Mr. Pike had listed the names of bowling pals in a careful, downward-slanting script, and Simon had scrawled the names of all his classmates even though he never talked to them by telephone, and Janie Rose had printed names in huge capitals that took two lines, after asking several times how to spell each one—the four little Marsh girls, each listed separately, and the milkman who had once brought her a yellow plastic ring from a chicken's leg, which she had worn every day until she lost it. Mrs. Pike's handwriting was small and pretty, every letter slanting to the same degree, naming off her steady customers one by one with little memos to herself about colors and pattern numbers penciled in lightly beside them. Joan went down the list alphabetically. Mrs. Abbott, who never talked. Mrs. Chrisawn, who was in such a black mood most of the time. Davis, Forsyth, Hammond . . . She stopped there. Connie Hammond was always good to have around during a tragedy. She brought chicken broth whether people wanted it or not, and she knew little things like how to make a bed with someone in it and what to say when no one else could think of anything. As far as Joan was concerned, having a person talk incessantly would be more harm than help; but her aunt felt differently. Her aunt had actually sat up and answered, the last time Connie Hammond came. So Joan smoothed the phone book out on her knees and dialed the Hammonds' number.

Mrs. Hammond was talking to somebody else when she answered. She said, "If that's not the *worst* thing—" and then, into the phone, "Hello?"

"Mrs. Hammond, this is Joan Pike," said Joan.

"Why, Joan, honey, how *are* you?" Mrs. Hammond said, and then softened her shrill voice to ask, "How's your poor aunt?"

"Well, that's what I wanted to talk to you about," said Joan. She spoke at some distance from the receiver, in case Mrs. Hammond should grow shrill again.

"What's that you say?"

"I said, I wanted to *talk* to you about that. Aunt Lou is just miserable."

"Oh, my." There was a rustling sound as Mrs. Hammond cupped her hand over the receiver and turned away. "Lou Pike is just *miserable*," she told someone. Her hand uncupped the receiver again and she returned, breathless, to Joan. "Joan, honey, I told Mr. Hammond, just last night. I said, I haven't ever *seen* someone take on so. Well, of course she has good reason to but the things she *says*, Joan. It wasn't her fault; it was that no account Ned Marsh who did it. How he manages to drive even a *tractor* recklessly is more than I can—"

"Um," Joan said, and Mrs. Hammond stopped speaking and snapped her mouth shut audibly, to show she had been interrupted. "Um, she hasn't even gotten up today. She's still in bed. And Uncle Roy's at the tobacco barns—"

"The where?"

"Tobacco barns. Working tobacco."

"Why, that man," said Mrs. Hammond.

"Well, he can't just sit staring at the *trees* all—"

"He could comfort his wife," Mrs. Hammond said.

"She won't listen. So I was thinking, as long as he's away to-day—"

"Men are like that," Mrs. Hammond said. "Work is all they think about."

"As long as he *is* at work," Joan said firmly, "I think maybe Aunt Lou should start working too."

"Working?"

"Working at sewing. Missouri said—"

"Mrs. *who?*"

"Mrs.—never mind. Wait a minute." Joan switched ears and leaned forward, as if Mrs. Hammond could see her now from where she stood. "Mrs. Hammond," she said, "I know how good you are at helping other people."

"Oh, why, I just—"

"I know you could help Aunt Lou right now, if anybody could. You could bring that dress she was working on, that—was it purple?"

"Lilac," said Mrs. Hammond. "Princess style."

"That's the one."

"Lou said it would add to my height a little, a princess style would."

"That's right," Joan said. "That's the one."

"Especially since it has up-and-down pinstripes."

"Yes. Well, I was thinking. If you could just bring it over and get her to work on it for you, just take her mind off all the—"

"You might be right," said Mrs. Hammond. "Why didn't I think of that? Why, the day before the funeral, when I came—*you* remember— I did feel she was doing wrong to sit so quiet. I said so. I have always believed that baking calms the nerves, so I said to her, 'Lou,' I said, 'why don't you make some rolls?' But she looked at me as if I'd lost my senses. After all, I'd just *brought* two dozen, and a cake besides. Yet I felt she ought to be doing something; that's what I was trying to tell her. You just might be right, Joan."

"Well, then," said Joan, "do you think you could come over sometime today?"

"I'll come over right this minute. I just wouldn't feel at rest until I had. You say your aunt's still in bed?"

"She was a minute ago," Joan said.

"Well, you try and get her up, and I'll be there as fast as I can find the dress. I'll be there, don't you worry."

"All right," Joan said. "It certainly is nice of you to come, Mrs. Hammond."

"Well. Goodbye, now."

"Goodbye."

Joan hung up and sat back to rub her ear, which felt squashed. Now that all that was settled, the next step was to get Simon downstairs. He would have to back her up in this.

Simon was standing in front of his mirror when Joan came in. He was wearing blue jeans but no shirt, and scratching his stomach absently. "Hey," Joan said, and he jumped and looked up at her. "Find yourself a shirt," she told him. "Connie Hammond's coming."

"Aw, gee, Joan. Mrs. *Hammond?*"

"She'll be here any minute. Come on, now. It's a special favor to your mother."

"I bet she'll never notice," Simon said, but he pulled a bureau drawer open. Joan closed the door and went on to her aunt's room.

Mrs. Pike was sitting up against two pillows, fat and soft in a gray nylon nightgown. She had her hands folded across her stomach and was looking vaguely at the two points her feet made underneath the bedspread. "Good morning," Joan said, and Mrs. Pike raised her eyes silently and peered at her as if she were trying to pierce her way through mist. But she never answered. After a minute her eyes passed on to something else, dismissing Joan like the wrong answer to a question she had asked. Joan came to stand at the foot of the bed.

"Aunt Lou," she said, "would you like to get up?"

Her aunt shook her head.

"Mrs. Hammond's coming. Do you want her to find you in bed?"

"No," said Mrs. Pike, but she didn't do anything about it. She settled lower into the pillows, with her eyes worrying at the wallpaper now, and in so much dim clutter she appeared to be sinking, overcome by the objects around her. Under Joan's feet were cast-off clothes, every-where, everything her aunt had been persuaded to put on in the last few days. She had stepped out of them and left them there, returning wearily to her gray nightgown. Mr. Pike, on the other hand, had made some effort at neatness. He had laid his clothes awkwardly on the back of the platform rocker, where they rose in a layered mountain that seemed huge and overwhelming in the half-dark. On the bureau were hairbrushes and bobby pins and old coffee cups with dark rings inside them. The sight of it all made Joan feel caved in and despairing, and she went over to raise the window shade but the light only picked up more clutter. "Aunt Lou," she said, "we just have to get organized here."

"What?"

"We have to start cleaning things up."

Her aunt nodded, without seeming to pay attention, but then she surprised Joan by moving over to the edge of the bed and standing up. She stood in that old woman's way she had just acquired—searching out the floor with anxious feet, rising slowly and heavily. For a minute she stood there, and then she shook her nightgown out around her and faltered toward the bureau. "I'm going to clean up," she told Joan.

"That's it."

But all Mrs. Pike did, once she reached the bureau, was to stare into the mirror. She put both hands on the bureau top and leaned forward, frowning into her own eyes. The alarm clock in front of her ticked loudly, and she reached out without looking to set it farther away. "Some people stop all the clocks when someone dies," she said.

"What're you going to wear, Aunt Lou?"

"If Connie Hammond's coming, why, she'll have to turn around and go off again."

"What *dress* are you going to wear?" Joan asked, and the sharpness of her voice made Mrs. Pike sigh and stand up straight again.

"Any one will do," she said. She pulled out a small plastic box from a half-open drawer and began putting bobby pins into it. One by one she scraped them off the top of the dresser, working like a blind woman with careful fingers while she kept her eyes on the mirror. Joan watched, not moving. Each bobby pin made a little clinking sound against the bottom of the plastic box, and each time the sound came Mrs. Pike winced into the mirror. "My *grand*mother stopped all the clocks," she said. "She would also announce the death to each fruit tree, so that they wouldn't shrivel up. But we don't have no fruit trees." Her fingers slid slowly across the bureau top, and when she found that all the bobby pins were picked up she closed the box and set it down again. Then she went back to bed. She tucked her feet down under the covers and drew the top sheet with great care over her chest.

"No, wait," Joan said.

"I did what I could, Joan."

Joan went over to the closet and pulled out the first thing she touched, a navy blue dress with white polka dots. "Is this all right?" she asked.

"No."

"This, then." And she lifted a brown dress from its hanger and laid it on the bed without waiting for an answer. "It's the prettiest one you've got," she said.

Outside, a car screeched to a halt and sent up a spray of gravel that Joan could hear from where she stood. She looked out and saw Mrs. Hammond's Pontiac swerving backwards into the yard with one sharp turn of the wheel, while Mrs. Hammond herself remained rigidly facing forward. The car came to rest right beside James's pickup, within an inch of running over Simon's bicycle. Then Mrs. Hammond shot out, clutching bits of cloth and tissue paper to her chest and leaving the car door open behind her. All she needed was an ambulance siren. Joan leaned out the window and called, "Mrs. Hammond?" and Mrs. Hammond looked up, with her face startled and worried-looking.

"Just walk on in and come upstairs," Joan told her. "Aunt Lou's in bed still."

"Oh. All right."

She bent her head over her armload of cloth and started running again, and Joan could hear her quick sharp heels along the porch and then inside, across the parlor floor and up the stairs. "Oh, law," she was saying to no one. She sounded out of breath.

But Mrs. Pike didn't say a word to all this. She just lay back against the pillows and folded her arms across her stomach again, her face expressionless. When Mrs. Hammond burst into the room and said, "Why, *Lou!*" as if Mrs. Pike had somehow taken her by surprise, Mrs. Pike only nodded gently and watched the wallpaper. "Lou?" said Mrs. Hammond.

"She was just now getting up," Joan told her.

"Well, I'll help. That's what I came for." She set her load down on the dresser and peered into the mirror a second, pushing back a wisp of hair, and then she came over to sit on the edge of the bed. Every move she made was definite; now that she was here, the room seemed to lose its swampiness. Her face was carefully made up to cover the little lines around her mouth, and she was packed into a nice summery sheath that Mrs. Pike had made two years ago. The sight of so much neatness made Mrs. Pike sit up straighter and pull her stomach in, even though her face stayed blank.

"I was talking about stopping all the clocks," she told Mrs. Hammond.

"*Oh*, no."

"I've about decided to do it."

"Oh, no. I don't think that's necessary."

But Mrs. Pike said, "Yes. I don't know why I didn't think of it before."

"It depends on the type," Mrs. Hammond said. "Ormolu, for instance, or mahogany—that you would stop. But those are the only kind. Isn't that so, Joan?"

Joan hadn't heard that before, but she said, "Well, yes," and Mrs. Hammond beamed at her and rocked gently on the bed.

"Only if it's *ornamental*," she told Mrs. Pike.

"Oh. I didn't know that."

"You wouldn't stop a Baby *Ben* or anything."

"No."

"Do you want to get up?"

"Connie, I just can't," Mrs. Pike said. "I just don't have it in me. You're going to have to go off again."

"Oh, now." Mrs. Hammond shook her head and then began examining the room, as if anything Mrs. Pike said was to be expected and she was just planning to wait till it was over. "This place could use a bit of cleaning," she said. "Also, if I was you I'd add some patches of color to it. You know? I put an orange candlestick in Mr. Hammond's brown den and it just changed the whole atmosphere. He don't like it, but you'd be amazed at the difference it makes."

"I don't care about any of that," Mrs. Pike said distinctly.

"Now, Lou."

"I just want to sleep a while."

"After you make up my lilac dress, I'll let you sleep all you like," said Mrs. Hammond. "I need it for a party."

She stood up and went over to the bureau, where she pulled open the top left drawer as if she knew by instinct where Mrs. Pike kept her underwear. From a stack on the right she took a nylon slip and held it up to the mirror. "Oh, my, how pretty!" she said, and tossed it in the direction of the bed. Mrs. Pike caught it in her lap and stared at it.

From across the hall came the clattering sound of Simon's walk, closer and closer. He had his boots on now. When he reached his mother's door he walked on in without knocking and said, "I'm ready." Then he stood there at the foot of the bed, tilting back and forth in that awkward way he had and keeping his hands jammed tightly in his pockets.

"What're you ready for?" Mrs. Hammond asked interestedly.

"To be sociable at the sewing," Simon told her. "Would you like to know what was the cause of that fight Andy Point's mama and daddy had?"

"In a minute I would," said Mrs. Hammond. "Right now I'm trying to get your mother out of bed."

For the first time, Simon looked at his mother. He looked from under bunched eyebrows, sliding his eyes over slowly and carefully. But she wasn't watching. He kicked at one leg of the brass bed, so that a little jingling sound rose among the springs. Then he said, "Well, I'll be down getting me some breakfast," and sauntered out again. Mrs. Hammond looked after him and shook her head.

"Something is seriously wrong with that boy's hair," she told Mrs. Pike.

"No."

"How long you going to keep on like this, Lou?"

Mrs. Pike looked down at her hands and then shook her head, as if that were her secret. "Are you *sure* not to stop the clocks?" she asked, but Mrs. Hammond didn't answer. She had picked out the rest of Mrs. Pike's underwear, and she tossed it on the bed and then reached out to pull her gently to a sitting position. "That's it," she said. To Joan she said, "You go along and get that boy a decent breakfast. I'll have her down in a minute."

It didn't look to Joan as if they'd *ever* be down, but she was glad to leave the room. She shut the door behind her and descended the stairs quickly, taking two steps at a time, trailing her fingers along the railing. When she reached the kitchen Simon had already taken out the makings for a peanut butter and mayonnaise sandwich. He was running his thumbnail around the edge of the mayonnaise label, making little ripples in it. "Would you like some milk coffee?" she asked him, but he only shook his head. He stopped playing with the label and opened the jar, and Joan handed him a knife.

"From now on, I'm going on no more boats," he said. "I take *stock* in dreams."

"That's kind of silly," said Joan.

"I know when I been warned."

He slapped mayonnaise on top of peanut butter and clamped the two slices of bread together. Then he began to eat, starting with the crust and working his way around until all he had was a small crustless square with scalloped edges. When that point was reached he looked relieved, because he hated crusts. He took a bite out of what was left and began talking with his mouth full.

"Instead of staying here," he said, "I just might go on over to Billy's house. His daddy gave him a chemistry set." He looked up at Joan, but she didn't say anything. "I might do that instead of staying around here talking," he told her.

"Well, suit yourself," said Joan.

"*Mama'd* never notice."

"Sure, she would."

"I bet not."

Joan went over to the cupboard and took down a huge plate, a green glass one that looked like summer and river-water. She began laying out cookies and cakes on it, choosing from boxes that neighbors had brought, while Simon watched her and chewed earnestly through a mouthful of peanut butter. When Joan was finished she stepped back and looked at the cake plate with her eyes squinted a little.

"Aunt Lou does it better," she said.

"Oh, I don't know."

"She puts it in a design, sort of."

"One thing," said Simon, "she don't ever lay out that *much*. Not with just one customer, she don't."

"That's true."

"She uses that little clear sparkly plate."

"Well, it's too late now," Joan said. She picked up the plate and carried it out to the parlor, where she set it on a lampstand by the couch. Then she swung her aunt's sewing machine out into the middle of the room. It was the old kind, run by a treadle, set into a long scarred table. From one of the drawers underneath it she took her aunt's wicker spool box, and while she was doing that she heard the slow careful steps of Mrs. Pike beginning across the upstairs hall. "*That's* it," Mrs. Hammond was saying, "*That's* it." The kitchen door swung open and Simon came out, chewing on the last of his sandwich, to stand at the foot of the stairs and gaze upward. "Mama's coming down," he told Joan.

"I see she is."

"First time she's come before noon. How long have I got to stay here?"

"You don't have to stay at all."

"Well, maybe I will for a minute," said Simon. He swung away from the stairs and went to sit on the couch, and Mrs. Pike's feet began searching their way down the steps. "That's it," Mrs. Hammond kept saying. Joan pulled a chair up to the sewing machine and then stood waiting, with her face turned toward the sound of those heels.

When Mrs. Pike appeared she was dressed more neatly than she had been in days. Her brown dress was freshened up with a flowered handkerchief in the pocket, and her hair was combed by someone who knew how. The only thing wrong was that she had lost some weight, and her belt, which had had its eyelets torn into long slashes from being strained across her stomach, now hung loose and stringy a good two inches below the waist of the dress. Mrs. Hammond was following close behind her to pull the belt up from the back, so that at least it looked right in front, but it kept slipping down again. "Doesn't she look *nice?*" Mrs. Hammond asked, and both Joan and Simon nodded.

In Mrs. Hammond's other hand was the bundle of cloth and tissue paper. She escorted Mrs. Pike to the chair Joan had ready and then she set the bundle down on the sewing table beside her, saying, "There you are," and stepping back to see what Mrs. Pike would do. Mrs. Pike didn't do anything. She looked at the lilac cloth as if she'd never seen it before. "Well, now," said Mrs. Hammond, and began opening out the bundle herself. "If you'll remember, you cut this out back in May, before all that business about Laura's wedding came up, and I haven't tried it on since. Joan honey, do you want to bring your aunt some coffee and a roll?"

"I'm not hungry," said Mrs. Pike.

But Joan escaped to the kitchen anyway, while Mrs. Hammond went on talking. "I've been on a tomato diet for three weeks," she was saying, "all in honor of this princess-style dress. So now, Lou, I want you to pin it on me again. Don't make it an inch too big, because I want to lose five *more* pounds, Lord willing—"

Joan took two cups and saucers down and set them on the tray. Then she poured out the coffee, taking her time because she was in no hurry to get back to the parlor. When the last possible thing had been seen to, she picked up the tray and carried it out.

"The older you get," Mrs. Hammond was saying, "the harder the fat clings." She had patches of lilac pinned on over her regular dress now, but she was more or less doing it herself. Mrs. Pike just kept smoothing down the already pinned-on patches, running her fingers along the cloth with vague fumbling motions. "There's only four pieces," Mrs. Hammond reminded her. "Plus the pocket. Where's the pocket? You remember that's one reason we decided on this. You could whip it up in a morning, you said. Do you remember?"

In the silence that followed the question Joan set the coffee down by the cake plate and passed the two cups over. Her aunt's she put on the table, and Mrs. Hammond's she placed on the chair arm, but neither woman noticed. Mrs. Pike seemed fascinated by the little wheel on her sewing machine. Mrs. Hammond was waiting endlessly, with her hands across her breasts to keep the lilac cloth in place. She seemed to be planning to keep silent forever, if she had to, just so that one question of hers could be answered. But Mrs. Pike might not even have heard.

Then Simon said, "Um, why Andy Point's parents won't *speak* to each other—" and Mrs. Hammond looked up at him. "Why they sit in their parlor in chairs faced back to back," he said, "all dates back to Sunday a week. Least that's what Andy says. But I couldn't hardly believe it, it was such a little thing that set them fighting."

"It's nearly always little things," said Mrs. Hammond. Mrs. Pike nodded and took a packet of pins out of her spool box.

"They were on their way to church, see," Simon said. "Andy was along. They made him come. When suddenly they passed this sign saying, 'Craig Church two miles, visitors welcome,' Mrs. Point she said, 'Why, I never have seen *that* before.' Just being conversational. And *Mr.* Point says, 'Well, I don't know why not. It's been there a year or more,' he says. 'No it ain't,' Mrs. Point says. 'Yes, it has,' Mr. Point says . . .'"

"Well, now, isn't that typical," said Mrs. Hammond. She turned slightly, but Mrs. Pike pulled her back again to pin two pieces of cloth together at the waist. Mrs. Pike's mouth was full of pins, and her eyes were frowning at everything her fingers did.

"So anyway," Simon said, "that was what began it. Andy says he never saw such a thing. He says they've even had to order another newspaper subscription, because they wouldn't share the one between them."

"If that isn't the limit," said Mrs. Hammond. "Ouch, Lou."

"Oh, I'm sorry," said Mrs. Pike. Everyone looked toward her, but she only went on pinning and didn't say any more, so Mrs. Hammond took up where she had left off.

"What doesn't make sense," she told Simon, "is Mary Point's *nature*. She's not the type to bear a grudge."

"Oh, it won't her fault," said Simon. "Andy says she had forgot about it. She just went on into church and never thought a thing about it. But then at dinner, Mr. Point wouldn't eat what she had cooked and made himself a sandwich right after. That's a sign he's mad. Mrs. Point said, 'Andy,' she said, 'I'll be. Is your daddy mad about something?' And Andy said, 'Well, I reckon he's mad you said that sign wasn't there.' So she said, 'Oh, I had forgot all about that,' but then it was too late. Now she's mad at him for being mad, and it don't look like it's ever going to end."

"You haven't lost a pound," Mrs. Pike said. She had finished pinning the pieces together now, and she was shaking her head at how tightly they fit.

"I have too," said Mrs. Hammond. "You allow a good inch for the dress I'm wearing underneath it, Lou." She acted as if it were perfectly natural that Mrs. Pike was speaking, but right on the tail of her words she shot Joan a meaningful glance. Joan nodded, although privately she didn't feel too sure of anything yet. But Simon kept on bravely, with his hands clutching the edge of the couch and his eyes on his mother, even though it was Mrs. Hammond he was speaking to.

"I asked him," he said. "I asked, 'Andy, how you think you're going to *end* it?' And Andy says, 'Same way it started, I reckon. By accident.' "

"Well, no," said Mrs. Pike, and once again everyone's attention was on her alone. She removed the pins from her mouth and laid them on the sewing table, and then she said, "It's not that easy. Why sure, one of them might speak by accident. Mary might. Then Sid might answer, being glad she'd spoken first, but by then Mary would have caught herself. She'd feel silly to speak first, and only snap his head off then. It's not that easy."

"No, you're right," said Mrs. Hammond, and Joan thought she would have agreed no matter what her aunt had said. "You have to think about the—"

The telephone rang. Mrs. Hammond stopped speaking, and Simon leaped over to pick up the receiver. "Hello?" he said. "What?" He was silent a minute. "No, I knew about it. I knew, I just forgot. Well, thank you anyway. Bye." He hung up.

"Who was that?" asked Mrs. Hammond.

"Just that station."

"What?"

"Just that radio station. They got this jackpot on. They call you up and if you don't say, 'Hello,' if you say instead, 'I am listening to WKKJ, the all-day swinging station—' "

"*I've* heard about that," Mrs. Hammond said.

"If he'd just called before, boy. It's not *me* who was prepared for them to—"

Mrs. Pike's spool box went clattering on the floor. All the colors of thread went every which way, rolling out their tails behind them, and Mrs. Hammond said. "Why, Lou," but Mrs. Pike didn't answer. She had crumpled up against her sewing machine, leaning her forehead against the wheel of it and clenching both fists tightly against her stomach. "*Lou!*" Mrs. Hammond said sharply. She looked at Joan and Simon, and they stared back. "Did something happen?"

"I said something," Simon told her.

Mrs. Hammond kept watching him, but he didn't explain any further. Finally she turned back to Mrs. Pike and said, "Sit up, Lou," and pulled her by the shoulders, struggling against the dead weight of her. "What's the matter?" she asked. She looked into Mrs. Pike's face, at her dry wide eyes and the white mark that the sewing-machine wheel had made down the center of her forehead. "What's the matter?" she asked again. But Mrs. Pike only rocked back and forth, and Simon and Joan stared at the floor.

9

ALL TUESDAY morning, Ansel had visitors. The first one was Joan. She mustn't have stayed long because she came and went while James was emptying the garbage, which only took a minute. When he returned Ansel said, "Joan's been here," and then dumped a cupped handful of sunflower hulls into an ashtray and sat down to read the paper.

"What'd she want?" James asked.

"Oh, nothing," said Ansel. He opened the paper out and stayed hidden behind it, with just one tuft of pale hair on the top of his head exposed to view. "You won't have to work tobacco today," he added as an afterthought.

"How's that?"

But Ansel didn't answer. Ever since he had awakened he had been angry; James could tell by his long silences, but he knew there was no point asking what was wrong. So he went on fixing breakfast, and while he was doing that he figured out that Joan must have come to say her uncle was working today. He flipped over a fried egg that was burning and called, "Ansel?"

"Hmmm."

"Is Roy Pike working today?"

But that was another question he never got the answer to. All he heard was the steady thumping of Ansel's foot (Ansel kept time to everything he read, as if it were a poem) and the crackling of newspaper pages. He didn't try asking again.

The second visitor was Maisie Hammond. She came while Ansel was eating breakfast off the Japanese tray, and when she walked in Ansel said, "Um. Maisie," and went on munching on his fried egg. (It was one of those days when James had brought a tray without being asked, simply because it was more comfortable to eat in the kitchen alone. Ansel had said, "*Well.* I see you've taken up cooking again," which hadn't even made sense.) Maisie was wearing a white summer dress with a full skirt, and she stood over his couch like Florence Nightingale and bent down to inspect Ansel's egg. "What's that?" she asked.

"Fried egg, of course."

"It looks kind of funny."

"It's James's," said Ansel.

"Ah." And she turned around, so that now she could see James where he sat eating in the kitchen. "Hey, James," she said.

"Hello, Maisie."

"Taken any pictures lately?"

"No."

That seemed to end the conversation; she turned back to Ansel. "You mind if I sit on your couch?" she asked.

"I'd prefer the armchair."

"Well."

She settled on the very edge of the armchair, spreading her skirt around her. When she bent her head toward Ansel, with the tow-white hair falling over her face, the morning sun seemed to pass right through her hair. She looked like glass. James studied her through the doorway as he munched on a piece of toast, but she didn't look his way again. "I came to ask you to a picnic," she told Ansel.

"Oh, no. Thank you anyway."

"Aunt Connie's giving it."

"Well, it's nice of you to ask," Ansel said.

"Don't you *want* to come?"

"Oh, I can't. James, I'm through with my tray."

"Put it on the table," said James.

"There's too much other stuff there."

James scraped his chair back and went to the living room, still chewing his piece of toast. By the time he reached the couch, Ansel was already preparing to lie down; he held the tray out in one hand, while he swung his feet up onto the couch.

"Ansel won't come to Aunt Connie's picnic," Maisie said.

"That's too bad," said James. He picked the tray up and went back to the kitchen.

"He just won't be reasoned with," Maisie called after him.

"Maybe he don't feel up to it."

"Will you hush?" Ansel asked. "*I'm* not giving any excuses; why should you?"

James made another trip back for the salt and pepper, which were sitting on the arm of the sofa. As he bent to pick them up, Maisie said, "Will you talk to him?"

"Nothing I can say."

"Why doesn't he ever go places?"

"That's *my* secret," Ansel said. They looked at him. He was lying on his back, with his hands crossed over his chest as if he expected to be laid out any minute, and his eyes were staring upwards, wide and blank. But now that he had their attention, all he did was switch his eyes suddenly to the window overhead and say, "Well, now. Yonder goes a jet."

They both waited, still watching him.

"Little white tail behind it," he said finally.

"Are you in some pain?" Maisie asked.

"Well, yes."

She looked across at James. "Ansel's in pain," she told him. But James just sat down on a wooden chair, still holding the salt and pepper, and stretched his legs out comfortably in front of him. If Ansel began an answer by saying, "Well," there was no use believing him.

"What shall I do?" Maisie asked him.

"I don't know."

"Get him a hot water bottle?"

"Hot water bottle on my *feet* won't help," said Ansel.

"Oh. Is it your feet that hurt?"

"I think it is."

"I declare," said Maisie, and then looked at James again, but he didn't offer any suggestions. Finally she said, "Is that why you won't come to the picnic?"

"No."

"It's not till Sunday, you know. You'd be all better by then."

"I just don't want to come," Ansel said. "But thank you anyway."

Maisie couldn't seem to find anything to say to that. She sat there, twisting at the hem of her white skirt, and James began hitting the plastic salt and pepper shakers together until he had worked up to a good rhythm. He was considering starting some more complicated beat when Maisie said, "Will you *stop* that *noise?*"

James stopped. Outside a car suddenly drove up, making a great racket as it skidded to a stop on the gravel road. Maisie stood up and bent forward a little to peer out the window. "It's Aunt Connie," she said.

"Maybe she's come to invite me personally," said Ansel.

"No, she's going toward Mrs. Pike's."

"She won't stay *there* long. Mrs. Pike wants to be by herself."

"Aunt Connie's very cheering," Maisie said.

"Sometimes. *I'm* very cheering, but you know what happened when I—"

"It's Aunt Connie's biggest party of the summer I'm asking you to," Maisie told him. "That's all. The one where she hires the magician and all."

Ansel sighed and looked at the ceiling. After a minute he said, "The actual place it hurts is right behind the anklebones. The pain is awful."

"The anklebones?"

"Last night I walked too much."

"Where'd you walk to?" Maisie asked.

James frowned at Ansel. He didn't want Maisie to hear about last night, not after the scolding she'd given him. But Ansel wasn't looking at James; he went on, placidly.

"I walked just about everywhere," he said. "I thought, 'I got to get out of here. This is no place for me.' I went everywhere I could think of."

"You shouldn't take such strenuous exercise," Maisie said.

"You have no idea how dizzy I was," Ansel told her. "How swimming in the head I was. I couldn't even pack my things. I had to have a little something first to steady my nerves."

"To—oh," Maisie said, and she shot a glance over at James and narrowed her eyes. "Ansel, you *know* what happens. If you get to drinking, you *see* how you feel."

"It was my mood," said Ansel. "I started walking."

James sat forward and said, "There's a pitcher of Kool-Aid in the icebox. Anybody want some?"

"No," Maisie said. "Where were *you* when all this was going on?"

"I was working," said James. He stood up, before she had a chance to say any more. "I've got to go see Dan at the paper. Take him those pictures."

"Well, goodbye," Maisie said, and turned back to Ansel. James was relieved she had let him go that easily.

In the darkroom he got his pictures together—one fire, one family reunion, two ladies' meetings—for this week's paper. Then while he was hunting for a manila envelope he heard a knock on the door. He straightened up and listened (it might be Joan again) but it was only the Potter sisters, dropping in for their biweekly visit to see how Ansel was. He heard their little chirping voices, with Maisie's voice running flatly behind them. "We brought some Jewish grandmother cookies, the kind you like," Miss Lucy said, and Ansel said, "Why, that's real—" "I'll take them," Maisie said. Maisie was always butting in, James thought. He set down his pictures and came out to the living room, just to say hello, and saw that both the Potter sisters were still standing in the doorway while Maisie sat back in her easy chair with a bag of cookies in her lap. "Why don't you sit down?" he asked them, and then the chirping sounds began all over again, and the sisters came toward him with their hands outstretched. They had on those dressy white gloves of theirs with the ruffles around the wrists. Seeing that made him sad—they looked as if they were expecting so much out of the visit, when all they were going to do was sit on the threadbare plush chairs a minute and then go home again. He said, "It's good to see you, Miss Lucy. Miss Faye. Nice of you to bring the cookies."

"We *like* doing it," said Miss Lucy.

"Will you have a seat?"

Miss Faye took the chair he pointed out to her, but Miss Lucy chose to sit by Ansel on his couch. He didn't object. He was sitting upright now, and when she settled down next to him he only smiled at her. "I *heard* you tapping those walls last night," he said.

"Tapping the *what?*" asked Maisie.

Miss Lucy looked very severe suddenly and tucked her head further inside her high collar. She never mentioned her nightwalking during the daytime. "We came to see if you're well," her sister said, "and to remind you that tomorrow's Wednesday. Time for your shots."

"James already told me," Ansel said.

"Last time you forgot *anyway.* You went visiting."

"That's true, I did," said Ansel, and then he sat back and smiled around the room, looking so happy and pleased with himself that everyone else smiled back. The Potters made little ducking smiles down at their gloved hands, and Maisie smiled with narrow eyes straight into Ansel's face. James stood up; now that people were seated and comfortable he could go.

"I have to see Dan Thompson at the paper," he told the Potters. "Sorry to run off."

"Well, now, have a good time," said Miss Faye. "Will you remind him of that announcement about our niece's baby?"

"I sure will. See you later."

He went back to the darkroom. Here it was cool and distant-feeling; the voices in the living room were faded. He put the week's pictures in the envelope and then, to prolong his stay in the coolness, he set that down and began filing away the pictures that Ansel had been looking at a couple of days before—the Model A, Ansel on his couch, Joan in the dust storm. When he came to the picture of Joan he stopped and studied it; he thought it might be the best thing he had ever done. Her figure made a straight, black line through a circle of wavery blurs, and her head was bent forward in that way she had when she walked. He didn't know how many hundreds of times he had seen her like that. And facing that photograph head-on, having a tangible picture of the way he saw her in his mind, made him think about the quarrel again. All last night and all this morning he had been trying not to.

It seemed to him, now that he stopped to consider, that if he wanted things to be smoothed over again it would have to be he who took the first step. Joan wouldn't. She would never change her mind about Ansel or even pretend to, in order to make things easier. He would have to go over and say, "Well, how*ever* we feel, I'm sorry that fight happened," or else she would just stay quietly in her own house, playing games with Simon and occupying herself with little private chores until she died. And all over nothing. He tucked her picture back into the file. Mrs. Pike was always saying, "Someday, boy, that girl is going to walk off and leave you," and he didn't know how right he

was. Last month Joan had packed her things and gone downtown to
catch a bus for home, but then she had decided she might as well go
to a movie first and by the time the movie was over she had changed
her mind and come home again, dragging two big suitcases behind her
and hobbling along on her dressup shoes. She had told James about
it, laughing at herself as she told it, but James hadn't laughed with
her. If she were to go, what would he decide to do about it?

Out in the living room, he could hear Miss Lucy discussing her
nephew, who was a missionary in Japan and a great curiosity there
because of his red hair. "You ought to see him bow," she said. "They
bow all the time, he tells me . . ." James half-listened, drumming his
fingers on the steel file drawer.

If Joan were to go, he had only two choices. That was the way he
saw it. He could let her be, and spend the next forty years remembering
nothing but the way she used to walk across the fields with him from
the tobacco barns and the peppermint smell of her breath when she
kissed him good night. Or he could go after her and say, "Come back.
And will you marry me?" In his *mind* he could say that, but not in
real life. In real life he had Ansel, and would have him always because
he couldn't walk out on that one, final member of his family that he
hadn't yet deserted. And in real life, he could never make Joan and
Ansel like each other.

"I'll take Africa any day," Miss Faye was saying. "Africans *know*
they need a missionary, but these Easterners are eternally surprised."
And Miss Lucy chirped something at the end, but James couldn't hear
what she said.

He stood up and rubbed his knees where they ached from being
bent so long. Then he picked up the pictures for the paper and left
the darkroom. Instead of going out through the front he crossed to the
back door, in order to make his escape as quickly as possible. Outside,
his eyes searched out those daisies he had been meaning to pick,
blowing in the wind and about to be too old. He tucked the pictures
under his arm and went deeper into the field, heading toward the
tallest ones. It always made him feel silly, picking flowers. He didn't
mind doing it (Joan liked daisies far better than bought flowers or any
other kind of present), but he didn't like thinking that anyone might
be watching. In case someone *was*, he picked very offhandedly—yanking
the daisies up nearly by their roots, jumbling them together helter-
skelter without looking at them. But while he was rounding the side
of the house and heading toward the front yard he arranged them
more carefully, and held them up to see if they were all right.

Mrs. Hammond's car was gone; that was one good thing. She must
have left while he was in the darkroom. Now all he wanted was for
Joan to be the one to answer the door. He knocked and waited, frowning
tensely at the screen. For a long time nobody came. Then from some-

where else in the house, Joan called, "Was that a knock?" Her voice echoed; she must have been standing at the head of the stairs.

"It's me," James said.

"Simon, will you let James in?"

Simon came out of the kitchen, dragging his feet. Through the screen, all James saw of him was his silhouette—his spidery arms and legs, his shoulders hunched up as if he were scared of something. Before he reached the door he stopped and said, "You come by yourself?"

"Who would I be bringing?" asked James.

"Oh, no one." And he came the rest of the way to the door and pushed it open. "Joan's upstairs," he said, "putting Mama to bed. She'll be down."

"Your mother got up already?"

"Well, but now she's going back to bed. I said everything all wrong."

"I'll bet you didn't," said James, without being quite sure what he was talking about. He closed the door very softly behind him and went over to a chair. "Is Joan too busy to talk?"

But just then they heard Joan coming downstairs, walking on tiptoe and taking only one step at a time where usually she took two. Simon jerked his thumb toward the sound. "Here she is," he said. When Joan came into view she looked at James blankly a minute, as if she'd forgotten he was here, and then she smiled and said, "Oh. Hello."

"Hello," James said. He stood up and held out the flowers. "I brought you some daisies. I was walking through the field and happened to come across them."

"That was nice," she said, and then frowned at the daisies. James looked at them. They seemed old and draggled now, in a messy little cluster in his hand. "They're not all that special, I guess," he said, but Joan had come out of her thoughts. "I think they're fine," she said. "I'll get a vase."

"Oh, you don't have to get a *vase* for them—"

"Well, of course I do."

She went out into the kitchen, still seeming to walk on tiptoe. Now that James thought of it, there was an uneasy silence about this house. He couldn't tell if it was because of something to do with Mrs. Pike or because Joan was still mad at him, and he didn't know how to ask. He looked across at Simon, who was still standing and staring into space. "Did I come at a bad time?" James asked him.

"Huh?"

Joan came back, carrying a cut-glass vase full of water. He asked her, "Did I come at a bad time?"

"Oh, not really."

"Well, did I or didn't I?"

"It's all right," Joan told him. "Aunt Lou didn't feel well this morning, but she's upstairs now and everything's all right." She took the daisies from him. Her hands when they brushed his were cool and impersonal, and she didn't look at him. "We have to go gradually," she said. "I keep forgetting that. I don't seem to have a *light* touch with anything." Yet her fingers when she arranged the flowers were as light and gentle as butterflies, and the daisies stood up or bent gracefully over the minute she touched them. When she was done they had stopped looking draggled; James was glad now that he had brought them.

"You ought to work for a florist," he told her.

But she set the vase down on a table without even noticing how they looked. She hadn't glanced at them once, all the time she was arranging them. "Mrs. Hammond does," she said. "Have a light touch, I mean. But I'm not sure that's the kind I'm talking about right now."

"I don't know that I follow you," James said.

She shook her head and sat down, as if she had given up on him. "Never mind," she said.

"Mrs. *Hammond* has a light touch?"

"Never mind." She looked suddenly at Simon. "Simon, do you want lunch?" she asked him.

"I just had breakfast."

"Oh."

"*You* have a light touch," James said. "You have the lightest touch of anyone I know."

"Oh, James, *you* don't know."

"Well, I'm trying—" He stopped and glanced toward Simon. It seemed to him Simon looked cold. "Don't you want to sit down?" he asked.

"I'm okay."

"Come on."

Simon shrugged and sat down on the couch. Now that they were all seated here, facing each other and keeping their hands folded in their laps, it seemed more awkward than before. It seemed they should be having a *conversation* of some kind, something that made sense. Not these little jagged bits of words. He tried smiling at Joan but all she did was smile back, using only her mouth while her eyes stayed serious and maybe even angry; he didn't know. "Would you rather I come back another time?" he asked.

"It's all right."

"Well." He sat further forward and looked at his fingernails. "I guess your uncle's working today," he said.

"Didn't Ansel tell you so?"

"In a way he did."

"There's nothing *bad* about it," said Joan.

"Why, no, of course not."

"You have to *do* something. You can't sit around. It's not *fair* to sit around, reminding people all the time—" She stopped, and James looked sideways at her while he kept his head bent over his fingernails.

Her voice was so sharp-sounding it made him uneasy, and he didn't know what he was supposed to say to her. But then she said, "Well. So you don't have to work tobacco any more."

"No," James said.

"That's good."

He waited a minute, and then cleared his throat and said, "It'll be a good season, they say."

"Billy Brandon told me that," Simon said suddenly.

"Barns are nearly full already."

In his shirt pocket he found a plastic comb, with little pieces of lint sticking to it. By running his index finger across its teeth he made a sound like a tiny xylophone, flat and tinny. Joan and Simon both sat watching him. When he saw them watching he stopped and put the comb back in his pocket. "I guess I'll be going," he said helplessly. "I could come some other time."

"All right," said Joan.

"Do you want me to?"

"What?"

"Do you want me to come back?"

"Oh. Yes."

"Okay," he said, but he still wasn't sure. He stood up and went over to the door, with Joan and Simon following solemnly behind. Then he turned around and said, "I could take you to the movies, maybe, Thursday night. The two of you."

"We'll see," Joan said.

"Do you want to come or don't you?"

"I don't know yet if we can," she said.

"Well, I wouldn't ask so far in advance, but tomorrow night I can't go. I'm going to take Ansel playing cribbage. But Thursday—"

"We'll see," said Joan.

"I *know* I wasn't going to chauffeur him around no more, but lately he's been— Well. We don't have to go into that."

"I'm not going into anything," Joan said.

"Yes, you are."

"I wasn't saying a word."

"I could tell the way you were looking."

"I wasn't looking *any* way. I wasn't even *thinking* about it."

She sounded near tears. James stood there, trying to think of what to say next, but he figured anything he came up with would only make things worse. So he waited a minute, and then he said, "I think I'd better leave. Goodbye."

"Goodbye," Simon said.

He was down the porch steps and halfway across the yard when he heard their door close; Joan had never said goodbye. The only sounds now were from Ansel's window—the birdlike sounds of women laughing, all clustered around his brother, their laughter pealing out in clear happy trills that drifted through the window and hung like a curtain across the empty porch.

10

THAT AFTERNOON, Joan had a telephone call from her mother. She was upstairs when it came, getting Mrs. Pike out of bed for the second time and finding it a little easier now than it had been in the morning. "What do you want to wear?" she asked, and her aunt actually answered, with only a slight pause beforehand. "The beige, I guess," she said. She waited while Joan lifted it off the hanger. "Can I wear the abalone pin with that?"

"Of course," Joan said. She would have agreed if her aunt had wanted to wear the kitchen curtains. She picked the pin out of the bureau drawer and laid it beside the dress, and then the phone rang. Both of them stopped to listen.

"Hey, Joan!" Simon called.

"I'm up here."

"Someone wants you on the telephone."

"Well, I'll be back," Joan told her aunt, and she went down the stairs very fast, two steps at a time. She didn't know who she was expecting, but when she heard only the ice-cold, nasal voice of the operator she was disappointed.

"Miss Joan Pike?" the operator asked.

"Yes."

"Are you Miss Joan Pike?"

"Yes."

"Long distance calling."

"All right," Joan said.

There was a pause, and then her mother said, "Is that Joan?", formally, and waited for Joan to go through the whole business of identifying herself again.

"It's me," said Joan. "Hello, Mother."

"Hello," her mother said. "I called to see how Lou was. Your father said to ask."

"She's getting better," said Joan. She heard her mother turn and murmur to her father, probably relaying Joan's answer. In normal speech her mother had a very soft voice, held in as if there was somebody sick in the next room. But when she returned to the phone her tea-party voice came back, louder and more distinct, the voice of a plump woman who stood very straight and placed the points of her shoes outward when she walked.

"Your father feels bad we couldn't make it to the funeral," she was saying. "He says it's only a sniffle he has, but I don't like the sound of it. Is there anything we can do for Lou?"

"Not that I can think of. The flowers were very nice—Uncle Roy said to tell you."

"Well. We weren't quite sure. Some people have a dislike of gladioli."

"No, they were fine," said Joan.

"That's good. How's Simon?"

"He's all right, I guess."

"Tell him hello for us, now. Tell him—"

Her voice had grown almost as soft as it normally was. Joan could picture her, sitting on the edge of that rocker with the needlework seat, with Joan's father standing behind her and bending cautiously forward to hear what was going on. He was a little afraid of telephones himself; he treated them as though they might explode. She saw how her mother would be smoothing down that little crease between her eyebrows with her index finger, and then letting the crease come back the minute she dropped her hand. The thought of that made Joan miss her; she said suddenly, "I'm tired."

"What?"

"I'm just tired. I want to come home. I don't want to stay here any more."

"Why, Joan—" her mother said, and then let her voice trail off. Finally she said, "Don't you think you should be with Lou now?"

"I'm not helping," said Joan. "She just sits. Every place I look, Janie Rose is there, and I don't feel like staying here. Nothing is right."

"Doesn't Simon need you?"

"Well—" Joan said, and then stopped because her father must have asked to know what was going on. The two of them murmured together a while, her mother's voice sounding faintly impatient. Joan's father was growing deaf; he had to be told twice. When her mother finally returned to Joan, she was sighing, and her voice was loud again.

"You know we'd love to have you," she said. "As soon as you can come. When were you planning on?"

"I don't know. A day or two, maybe. By bus."

"Or maybe James could drive you," said her mother. "We'd love to have him."

"He won't be coming."

"Your father's been asking about him."

"He won't be coming," Joan said firmly.

There was another pause, and then her mother said, "Is something wrong?"

"What would be wrong?"

"Well, I don't know. Shall we expect you when we see you, then?"

"All right. Don't go to any trouble."

"It'll be no trouble. Goodbye, now."

"Goodbye. And thank you for calling."

She hung up, but she stayed in the same position, her hand on the receiver. Out of the corner of her eye she caught sight of Simon. He was leaning against the frame of the kitchen door, eating another peanut butter and mayonnaise sandwich. "Hey," she said, but he only bit off a hunk of sandwich and chewed steadily, keeping his eyes on her face. "That was your Aunt Abby," she told him.

"I know."

"She called to see how everyone is."

He straightened up from the doorframe and came over to her, planting his feet very carefully and straight in front of him. When he had reached her he said, "I hear how you're going there," and waited, with the sandwich raised halfway to his mouth.

"We'll see," said Joan.

"You going by bus?"

"I might not go at all. I don't know yet."

"How long would you go for?"

"Look," said Joan. "I don't know that I'm going. I just think it might be good to get away. So don't tell anyone, all right?"

"Well, all right."

"Not even James."

"All *right*," said Simon. He was good at keeping secrets; it was an insult to suggest he might tell somebody. "If you do go—" he said.

"I might not."

"But if you do go, can I go with you?"

"Oh, Simon," Joan began, and stopped there because she didn't know what else to say. "Your parents need you here," she said finally.

"They won't notice."

"Your daddy will. So will your mother, pretty soon."

"No."

"Yes. See, she's coming downstairs now."

He turned and looked toward the stairs. Mrs. Pike was coming down of her own accord, taking each step uncertainly but not asking for help. She had pinned the abalone pin at the neck of her dress, and it was bunching up the material a little. When she reached the bottom of the stairs she looked from Joan to Simon and back again, as if she were expecting them to tell her what to do next. Joan went over to her.

"I could fix you a bite to eat," she said.

"I came to sew."

"To sew?"

"I came to sew Connie's dress together."

"Oh," Joan said. She looked around at the sewing machine, and was glad to see that the dress still lay there. (Mrs. Hammond had gone away all helter-skelter, talking to herself, leaving everything behind her.) "It's all here," Joan told her. "Is there anything else you need?"

"No. I just want to sew."

"Shall we sit here and keep you company?"

"I just want to sew."

"All right," said Joan, but she waited a minute anyway, and so did Simon. Mrs. Pike didn't look their way again. She went over to the chair at the sewing machine and lowered herself stiffly into it, and then she picked up the material and began sewing on it. She did it just that suddenly, without examining what she was about to do first or even looking at it—just jammed two pieces of cloth beneath the needle of the sewing machine and stepped hard on the treadle. Finally Joan turned away, because there was nothing more she could do. "Let's go to the kitchen," she told Simon. She steered him gently by one shoulder and he went, but he kept looking back over his shoulder at his mother. When they reached the kitchen he said, "See?" but she said, "Hush," without even asking what he meant. "Maybe we could go for a walk," she said.

"I found my ball."

"What ball?"

"The one I lost. I found it."

"Well, I'm glad to hear it," said Joan. "Is it all beat up?"

"It's fine. You want to play catch?"

"Not really."

"Aw, come on, Joan."

She frowned at him. "We should have taken you to a barber," she said finally.

"Just for fifteen minutes or so? I won't throw hard."

"Oh, all right," she said.

Simon went over to the door and picked up the baseball that lay beside it. It was grayer than before, and grass-stained, but lying out in the field for two weeks hadn't hurt it any. He began throwing it up in the air and catching it, while he led the way through the kitchen and out the back door.

"If we had a big mowed lawn, we could play roll-a-bat," Joan said.

"Roll-a-bat's a baby game."

They cut through the tall grass behind the house, parting the weeds ahead of them with swimming motions and advancing beyond the garbage cans and the rusted junk to a place where the grass was shorter. Janie Rose had set fire to this spot not a year ago, while trailing through here in her mother's treasured wedding dress and holding a lighted cigarette high in front of her with her little finger stuck out. James and Mr. Pike and Mr. Terry had had to fight the fire with their own shirts, their faces glistening with sweat and their voices hoarse from smoke, while Ansel leaned out the back window calling "Shame! Shame!" and Janie Rose sat perched in the tin can tree, crying and cleaning her glasses with the lace hem of the wedding dress. Now the weeds had grown up again, but they were shorter and sparser, with black scorched earth showing around them. Joan and Simon took up their positions, one at each end of the burned patch, and Simon scraped a standing-place for himself by kicking down the brittle weeds and scuffing at the charred surface of the soil. "Here goes," he said, and wound up his arm so hard that Joan raised both hands in front of her to ward it off before he had even let go of the ball. Simon stopped winding up and pounded the ball into the palm of his other hand.

"Hey, now," he said. "You going to play like a girl?"

"Not if you throw easy like you promised."

He squinted across at her a minute, and then nodded and raised his throwing arm again. This time the ball came without any windup, cutting in a straight clean arc through the blue of the sky. Joan caught it neatly, remembering not to close her eyes, and threw it back to him underhanded.

"Overhand," said Simon.

"Sorry."

Little prickles of sweat came out on her forehead. She tugged her blouse out of her bermudas, so as to make herself cooler, and almost missed the next ball when it whizzed low and straight toward her stomach.

"*Watch it*," Simon said.

"*You* watch it. That one burned my hands."

She threw it overhand this time, and it fell a little short, so that Simon had to run forward to catch it. While he was walking back to his place a screen door slammed behind them, and Joan automatically turned her head and listened to find out what end of the house it had come from. "Coming," said Simon, and just then Joan saw, in the corner of her eye, someone tall in James's plaid shirt, untangling his way through the field and toward Joan. She turned all the way. "*Watch—!*" Simon said, and something slammed into the side of her head and made everything green and smarting. She sat down, not because she had been knocked down but because she was so startled her knees were weak. Beside her, nestled in a clump of grass, was the baseball, looking whiter than she remembered. Her temple began throbbing and she lay all the way down on her back, with the scorched ground underneath her making little crisp brittle sounds. "*Joan!*" Simon was shouting, and whoever wore James's plaid shirt was thudding closer and closer. It was Ansel. She saw that and closed her eyes. In the same moment Simon arrived, with his breath coming fast and loud. He thumped down beside her and said, "*Joan*, oh, *shit*, Joan," which made her suddenly grin, even with her eyes closed and her head aching. She looked up at him and said, "Simon Pike—" and tried to sit up, but someone yanked her back by the shoulders. "*Where* did you—" she began, but then Ansel clapped his hand over her mouth. His hand smelled of Noxzema.

"You lie still," he said. "Don't you sit and don't you talk. I'll call a ambulance."

"An ambulance?" And this time she out and out laughed, and sat up even with Ansel trying to press her back down again. "Ansel," she said, "I *really* don't need an ambulance. I just got surprised."

"I warned you," Simon said. "Oh, Lord, people *break* so easy." He settled back on his haunches, clutching his knees, and for a minute it looked as if he would cry.

"Oh, hey, now," Joan told him. She struggled all the way up, letting Ansel keep hold of one of her elbows, and then reached down to give Simon a hand up. When she stood her head hurt more; it was throbbing. She patted Simon's shoulder. "It was my doing," she said. "I turned to see who was coming."

Ansel kept hanging on to her elbow, too tightly. She tried to pull away but he only tightened his grasp and bent closer over her, looking long and pale and worried with his light eyes blinking anxiously in the strong sunlight. "You're coming inside," he told her. "I'll call a doctor."

"I don't *need* a doctor, Ansel."

"Terrible things can happen."

"Oh, for heaven's sake," she said. "I'm not *about* to die on you."

"You never know. You never can—"

She pulled away from him, this time so hard that he had to let her go, and reached out for Simon's hand instead, in case she got dizzier. Simon accepted her hand like a grave responsibility and led her, soberly and silently, toward the house. Ansel followed, panting from all this unexpected exercise.

"We'll go to my house," he said, "where I have iced tea."

"No, thank you."

"I *want* you to go to my house. I feel responsible. And anyway, I'm lonely. James has gone off to Dan Thompson's."

"Oh, all right," Joan said. It was true that she didn't want to go back to that parlor again. They veered toward the Greens' end of the house, with Ansel parting weeds ahead of them and kicking aside bits of rusted car parts so that Joan could have a clear passage. When they reached the back door he held it open for them and ushered them in with a bow, though neither Simon or Joan paid any attention to him.

"Head on to the front room," he said. "I'll tell you what, Joan: you can lie on my couch."

"Oh, well, Ansel, I don't need—"

"It's not often that I let someone do that."

"All right," she said, and went on toward the couch, feeling too aching to argue. The house smelled like James—a mixture of darkroom chemicals and shaving soap and sunshine—and there was a little of that medicine smell of Ansel's there too. She lay back on the couch and closed her eyes.

Ansel brought iced tea, with the ice cubes tinkling in the glasses and a sprig of fresh mint floating on top. It surprised her, because Ansel was used to being waited on himself. She had thought he wouldn't even know where the glasses were. He set the tray down on the coffee table and handed a glass to both Simon and Joan. Then he picked up his own glass and carried it over to the easy chair, where he sat down a little uncertainly, as if he had never sat there before. Maybe he hadn't. "Cheers," he said, and held his glass up high. "In reference to this doctor business, Joan—"

"I feel *fine*."

"But maybe you should see one anyway," said Simon. "You just don't know *what* might have happened."

"Nothing happened. Will you hush?"

She took a sip of iced tea and closed her eyes. It felt good to be cool again. The room was dim and quiet, and the couch was comfortable, and the heat of outdoors had made her feel relaxed and sleepy.

"What else is good," Ansel was telling Simon, "is to drink iced tea with peppermint candy in it. You ever tried that?" His voice was far away and faint, because Joan was half-asleep. She heard him shift his position in the creaky old chair. "You ever tried it?" he asked again.

"No," said Simon. He was still being cautious with Ansel, although Joan couldn't figure out why.

"You ought to have your mother make it for you," Ansel told him.

"She won't care."

"Sure she will. Sure she will."

"We drink mainly Cokes," said Simon.

"This is better."

There was a long silence. Joan reached over to set her glass on the floor, and then she lay down again and put the back of her hand across her eyes to shut the light out.

"James is at Dan Thompson's," Ansel said.

"You told me that," said Simon.

"He just walked out and left me here, alone."

"I don't care."

"If I drop dead today, he'll forget what name to put on the headstone."

"I don't care."

"Ah, well," Ansel sighed, and there was the sound of his stretching in the chair. "There is a collection, in this world," he said, "of people who could die and be mourned approximately a week. If they're lucky. Then that's the end of it. You think I'm one?"

"I don't know," said Simon. "I'm not listening."

"Oh."

There was another pause, and someone's ice tinkled. Ansel's, probably. Ansel said, "I'm going to go away from here."

"Everyone is," said Simon.

"What?"

"Grown-ups can go and not even let on they're going. I wish I could."

"You can come with me," Ansel said.

"Where's that?"

"This town of mine. This place I come from."

"Is it north?" Simon asked.

"North of what?"

"*North* north. Is it?"

"It's south," said Ansel.

"Oh. I want to go north."

"It's all the same. Who you kidding? This town has got a cop that acts like a night watchman. He goes through the town on foggy nights crying out the hours, singing 'Sunshine on the Mountain' and all other sunny songs, middle of the night. Ain't *that* a thing to wake in the night to, boy."

"Yeah," said Simon.

"To wake up after a nightmare to."

"Yeah."

The throbbing in Joan's head kept time to Ansel's words. She wanted to leave now, and stop listening to that thin voice of his going on and on, but the throbbing made a weight on her head that kept her down. She listened dreamily, without interrupting.

"Lately I've been thinking about home," Ansel said. "It was the funeral that did it, somehow."

"You didn't go to the funeral."

"It did it *anyway*. The only problem is, it's hard to know what way to think about it. No telling how it's changed, and I get no letters from there. James does, from our sisters. He writes them once a month, letters all full of facts, but when he gets an answer he pretends he doesn't. I don't know why. I mean he goes on writing but never mentions what their letters to *him* have said, never comments on them. Why do you think he does that?"

"I don't know," Simon said. "This cop, does he sing every night?"

"*Just* about. And there's a feed store that gives away free hats. Big straw hats, with red plumes curling down like Sir Walter Raleigh's.

Walk down Sedad Street and it's just an acre of people wearing hats, red plumes bobbing up and down. Merchants wearing hats, farmers wearing hats, everyone but little old ladies wearing hats. Old ladies don't like them hats. You go down to Harper's River and find little boys and colored men fishing in leaky boats, wearing red-plumed hats. Why, you can tell when you're coming home again. You look out the bus window into those country fields and find farmers plowing, wearing hats with red plumes, and the mules wearing them too but with holes cut in them for the ears to stick out. That's how you know you're nearing home."

"How about me?" asked Simon.

"How *about* you."

"If I was to ask, would they give me one too?"

"Why, surely."

"I'll ask, then."

"You do that."

More ice tinkled. Joan's hand had stuck to her damp forehead and she took it away, making a tearing sound, and sighed and turned over on her side.

"What exactly is the name of this town?" Simon asked.

"Caraway, N.C."

"Is there buses to it?"

"Six a day."

"Is there people my age?"

"Is there?" Ansel asked, and he laughed suddenly, a chuckle deep in his throat so that he sounded a little like James. "*Is* there, boy. Well, lots. I ought to know. Another thing. This is something I've never seen in any other town, now: the boys wear one gold ring in their ear."

"*Earrings?*"

"Oh, no. No, this is like pirates wear. Pierce their ears and put one gold hoop through. Everyone did it."

"Did you?"

"My family didn't want me to. Well, I wasn't actually in that particular group, anyway. But James was. He had a hoop, but he took it off finally. Only got one because the family told him not to. Eventually *every*one takes them off, when they've grown up and settled down. You'll hear someone say, 'So-and-so's engaged now. He's got a steady job, and there's no more gold in his ear.' But I never had gold in my ear to begin with."

"Does it hurt?" Simon asked.

"Does what hurt?"

"When they pierce your ears."

"Oh, no. At least, I don't think so. Not for long."

"If I went there, would I wear a earring?"

"Sure you would."

"How long is it by bus?"

Joan felt herself drifting off. The house seemed to be spinning around her, making streaky yellow shimmers of sunshine through her eyelids, but when she found that she wasn't even hearing the others' voices now she pulled herself sharply awake. She opened her eyes and found that she was looking at one of Ansel's shoes, tapping lazily on the floor. "Have I been asleep?" she asked. Simon and Ansel looked over at her. "What time is it?"

"Not yet three," said Ansel. "How's your head?"

"It's fine."

"You sure?"

"Yes. Sorry to disappoint you." She sat up and tucked her blouse in. "Simon, we got to get going," she said.

"Aw, I was just hearing something interesting."

"It can wait."

She let him go through the front door first, and then she turned to Ansel and smiled at him. "Thank you for the use of the couch," she said.

"Nothing to it." He poked his head out the door, past Joan, and looked at Simon. "You be making your plans, now," he said.

"All right."

"Plans for what?" Joan asked.

"Nothing," said Simon.

Joan yawned, and followed him down the porch toward home.

11

"THERE'S NOT much difference between one person and the next," Ansel said. "I've found that to be true. Would you agree with me?" He raised himself up from a prone position on the couch to look at James, who was sitting nearby with the paper. "Would you?" he asked.

"Well, more or less," said James, and turned to the sports section.

"Course you do. You have to. Is that the Larksville paper?"

"Larksville paper's not out till tomorrow."

"Oh. I thought today was Wednesday."

"It is," said James. "The paper comes on Thursday."

"Oh."

Ansel lay down again and stared thoughtfully upwards, lacing his fingers across his chest. He had been flat on his back all morning, complaining of dizzy spells, and James had been sitting here keeping him company. It was easier that way. Otherwise Ansel would continually think up reasons to call him into the room and things to ask him for. "James," he would call, "what was the name of that old woman who gave sermons on the street corner?" Or, "Whatever happened to that seersucker suit I used to have?" And in the long run James would have to spend just as much time in this room as if he'd been sitting there all along. He yawned now and turned another page of his newspaper, and Ansel switched his eyes back over to him.

"It's a fact, James," he said. "People don't vary a heck of a lot, one from the other."

"You told me that," said James.

"Well, yes, I did. Because it's true. If you will hark your mind back to that Edwards boy, that bucktoothed one that joined the Army— what was his name?"

"I don't know."

"Oh, sure you know. Sure you know. What was his name?"

"Ansel," said James, "I just don't make a point of *remembering* all these things."

"Well, I wouldn't brag about it. Clarence, that was it. Or Clayton; I don't know which. Now, Clarence, he went almost around the world with that Army outfit of his. Almost everywhere. And you know what he said when he got back? He said that every single country he'd been in, one thing always held true: when mothers and children climb into a car to go visiting, the first act a mother undertakes is spitting on a hanky and scrubbing her children's faces with it. Always. Canada, France, Germany—always. If that doesn't prove my point, what does?"

James ran his eyes down the baseball scores. He frowned over them, absentmindedly making a little *tch* sound under his breath when he came upon a score he didn't like. After a while he became aware of the silence, and he looked up to see Ansel watching him with his eyes wide and hurt. "You weren't even listening," Ansel said, and James sighed and folded his paper up.

"I was listening and reading both," he said.

"No. What's it take to make a man listen?"

"Well, I'm sorry. You can tell it to me over again, if you want."

"No."

Ansel turned slightly, so that his cheek was resting on the sofa cushion, and closed his eyes. "I've noticed more and more," he said, "that no one listens when I talk. I don't know why. Usually I think about a thing before I say it, making sure it's worthwhile. I plan it in my mind, like. When I am dead, what will they remember but the things I talked about? Not the way I looked, or moved; I didn't look like much and I hardly moved at all. But only the things I talked about, and what is that to remember when you never even listened?"

"I listen," said James.

"No. Sometimes in one of those quiet periods after I've said something, when no one's saying anything back because they didn't hear me, I look at myself and think, well, my goodness. Am I *here?* Do I even *exist?*"

"Oh, for heaven's sake," said James. He opened the paper again.

"When I am dead, I wonder what people will miss me. You? Simon? Mrs. Pike will wish she'd brought more hot soup. Joan won't notice I'm gone. Will you miss me?"

James read on. He learned all about a boy named Ralph Combs, who was planning to be Raleigh's contribution to the major leagues. He read Blondie and Dick Tracy and Part 22 of the serialized adventure story, and then he noticed the silence again and he lowered his paper to look at Ansel. Ansel was asleep, with one arm flung over his head and his fingers curling in around the sofa arm. His eyelids were translucent and faintly shining, and over his forehead his hair hung rumpled, making him look the way he had when he was twelve. Seeing him that way made James feel sad. He rose and came over to the couch, standing at Ansel's head and looking down at his long pale face tipped back against the cushions. If he hadn't known better, he would have tapped him on the shoulder and said, "*Now* I'll listen." But then Ansel would wake up and be twenty-six years old again, nervously testing himself for new symptoms, beginning some long monologue that he had begun before, changed forever from that scared small brother who could sit a whole evening without saying a word or raising his eyes from the floor. That twelve-year-old would vanish without a trace, leaving not even an echo of himself in the way Ansel smiled or said a certain word. James moved away from the couch and went over to the window.

Because of the way he felt, the view from the window took on a sad, deserted look. Everything was bowed low under the breeze, straightening up for a second only to bow again. Simon's bicycle lay on its side with a drooping buttercup tangled in its spokes. At the edge of the yard the Potters' insurance man was just climbing out of his Volkswagen. (He came every week, because the Potters had to be constantly reassured that their policy really was all right.) He looked tired and sad. While he was crossing the yard he mopped his face and straightened the plastic carnation in his buttonhole, and then on the first porch step he snapped his head erect and put a bright look on his face. After that James lost sight of him. But he could hear the knocking, and the sound of the Potters' door cautiously opening and the bolts being slid back after the insurance man was taken inside. They slid easily in their little oiled tracks. The quickness of them made James smile, and he could picture Miss Lucy's eager fingers fumbling rapidly at the locks, shutting little Mr. Harding in and the loneliness

out for as long as she and Miss Faye could manage. He stopped smiling
and moved away from the window.

Back in the kitchen it was even worse. There was one daisy on the
counter, a stray one from the field in back, and it was dead and
collapsed against Ansel's untouched lunch tray. ("I'm not eating today,"
Ansel had said. "Do you care?" "Suit yourself," said James.) Out the
back window was the half-mowed field, looking bald and straggly.
Simon Pike was leaning against an incinerator staring at it all, and
while James watched, Simon straightened slowly and began wandering
in small thoughtful circles around the incinerator. With the toes of his
leather boots he kicked at things occasionally, and he had his shoulders
hunched up again so that he looked small and worried. James stuck
his head out the window.

"Hey, Simon," he said. "Why don't you come in?"

Simon raised his head and looked at him. "What for?" he asked.

"Well, you look kind of lonely out there."

"Aw, no."

"Well, anyway," said James, "I want to take a picture of you."

That made Simon think twice. He stood still for a moment to consider
it, with his chin stuck out and his eyes gazing away from James and
across the field. Then he said, "What kind of picture?"

"The kind you like. A portrait."

"Well, then, I reckon I might. I'll come in and think about it."

"*That's* the way," said James.

He let Simon come in his own good time, stopping to kick at a
bootscraper and wasting several minutes examining some blistered paint
on the door. When Simon was troubled about something, this was the
way he acted. He circled all around the kitchen without once looking
at James or speaking to him, and he picked up several things from
counters and turned them over and over in his hands before setting
them down again. Then he jammed his hands into his back pockets
and went to the window. "Mama's hemming a dress," he said.

"That's good."

"She talks a little, too, but not about any concern of mine."

"Well, you got to give her time," said James. "First thing people talk
about is weather and things."

"I know," Simon said. "Daddy is at the fields and Joan too. It's her
tobacco day. Everybody's busy."

"So're you," said James. "You're having your picture taken."

"Yeah, well."

But when James headed toward the darkroom, Simon followed him.
"Where are we going to take it?" he asked.

"Outdoors, if you like."

"I'd rather the living room."

"All right," James said. He opened the door of the darkroom and led the way to where his cameras stood. "You got to be quiet, though, because that's where Ansel's sleeping."

"*Now?*"

"It's one of his dizzy days."

"Oh, cripes," said Simon, and he started walking in circles again. He put the heel of one boot exactly in front of the toe of the other, and keeping his balance that way made him fling both arms out and tilt sideways slightly. "It's a bad day for *every*one," he said. "I declare." He seemed to be walking on an imaginary hoop, suspended high above the ground.

James had seen the kind of portraits that Simon and Janie Rose liked best—the ones taken against a dead white screen, with the faces retouched afterwards. He favored a homier picture, himself. He left the screen behind and brought only a couple of lamps, not the glaring ones, and his favorite old box camera. "We'll put you in the easy chair," he told Simon. He had given the camera to Simon to carry, and Simon was squinting through the view-finder as he walked. "Do you want to be doing anything special?"

"Yes," Simon said. "I want to be smoking a cigar."

"Be serious, now."

"I *am* serious. You asked me what I wanted to be doing. Well, all my life I've been waiting to get my picture took with a cigar. I been counting on it."

"Oh, what the hell," said James. He set his lamps down and went over to the living-room mantelpiece. From the old wooden cigar box that had belonged to his grandfather he took a cigar, the fat black kind that he smoked on special evenings when no one was around to complain. "Here you go," he said. "But don't you light it, now. Just get your picture took with it."

"Well, thank you," said Simon. He crossed to the easy chair, giving Ansel a sideways glance as he passed, but Ansel only stirred and didn't wake up. "He don't know what he's missing," Simon whispered. "Me with a cigar, boy."

"It'll all be recorded for posterity," said James.

While James was setting up the lights, Simon practiced with the cigar. He opened it and slid the paper ring off, and then he sat with his elbow resting on the chair arm and his face in a furious frown every time he took a suck from the unlit cigar. "I'm getting the hang of it," he said, and looked around for an ashtray to practice tapping ashes into. "When do you reckon they'll let me smoke these for real?"

"Never, probably," said James. "Always someone around that objects to the smell."

"Ah, I wouldn't care. I'm going to start as soon as I'm out on my own, boy. Soon as I turn sixteen or so."

James smiled and tilted a lamp closer to Simon. He had been listening to Simon for some years now, and he had a mental list of what he was planning to do at age sixteen. Smoke cigars, take tap-dance lessons, buy his own Woolworth's, and grow sideburns. Janie Rose hadn't even been going to wait *that* long. She asked her mother weekly, "Do you think it's time I should be thinking of getting married?" And then she would smile hopefully, showing two front teeth so new that they still had scalloped edges, and everyone would laugh at her. James could see their point, though—Janie's and Simon's. He couldn't remember that being a child was so much fun. So he nodded at Simon and said, "When you turn sixteen, I'll *buy* you a box," and Simon smiled and settled back in the chair.

"Might not wait till then even," he said. "You never can tell."

"Well, I would," said James. "Tobacco stunts your growth."

"No, I mean to go out on my own. I might go earlier." He stuck out his tongue and flicked an imaginary piece of tobacco off the tip of it. "I been thinking where I could go."

"It's kind of early for that," James said.

"I don't know. You know Caraway, N.C.?"

James stopped fiddling with his camera and looked up. "What about it?" he asked.

"I just thought you could tell me about it. If that's where you are from."

"Nothing to tell," said James.

"Well, there's hats with feathers on them, and them gold earrings the boys all wear. Do you think I might like that town?"

In the view-finder his face was small and pointed, with a worried line between his eyes. He was leaning toward James with the cigar poised forgotten between his thumb and forefinger, and in the second of stillness that followed his question James snapped the picture. "That'll be a good one," he said.

"Will I like Caraway?"

"I don't see how. Do you ever see *me* going to Caraway?"

"Well, the boys wear gold earrings," Simon said again, and he sighed and rubbed the top of his head and James snapped that picture too.

"Sure, the *boys*," he told Simon. "They're the worst in the state, Caraway boys. Got tight little Church of God parents. All they want to do when they grow up is come somewhere like Larksville. What you want to do in Caraway?"

"I could board with your family," Simon said.

James looked up from his camera with his mouth open and then threw back his head and laughed. "*Hoo!*" he said, and Ansel stirred in his sleep at the noise. "I'd like to see that," he went on more quietly. "Would you turn sideways in your chair now, please?"

Simon turned, but he kept his eyes on James. "*Ansel* says—" he began.

"*Ansel* don't know."

"Ain't he *from* there?"

"He don't know."

"Well, anyway," said Simon, "I could go and look it over."

"Your mother would love that. Now, quit watching out of the corner of your eye, Simon. Look at the fireplace."

"Do you think she'd miss me?" Simon asked.

James clicked the picture and stood up, squinting at him sideways to see which way to turn him next.

"I think my mother'd say, '*Who* you say's gone? Oh, *Simon!*' she'd say. 'Him. My goodness. Did you remember to bring the eggs?'" He sat forward again then and frowned at James, twining the cigar over and under the fingers of his left hand. "You see how it'd be," he said.

"You know that ain't so," said James.

He stepped a little to one side and got Simon focused in the camera again, all the while waiting for the argument to continue. But it didn't. In the square of the viewfinder Simon suddenly sighed and slumped down like a little old man, staring abstractedly at the wet end of his cigar. "Ah, hell," he said. "It don't matter."

That made James look up, but he didn't say anything. Instead he snapped the picture and frowned over at the lamps, measuring how much light there was. "Outdoors would've been better," he said finally.

"I also hear," said Simon, "that they sing all night in the dark. And them plumed hats, why, even the mules wear them. With holes cut for ears."

"Look over toward your left," James said.

"There's six buses going there a day, Ansel told me."

James folded his arms across the top of the camera and watched Simon a minute, thinking. Simon stared straight back at him. In the light from the lamps his eyes seemed black, and it was hard to see beyond the flat surface of them. His chin was tilted outward a little, and his lashes with their sunbleached tips gleaming were like curtains over his expression. Who knew what was in his mind? James uncrossed his arms then and said, "Put your cigar, away, now. This last one's for your mother."

"Aw, my mother won't even—"

"She wants a picture she can show to the relatives. What would they think, you with a big fat cigar in your hand?"

"She won't—" Simon began again.

But James said, "You're growing so much, this summer. She wants to get you in a picture before you're too big to *fit* in one."

"She tell you that?" asked Simon.

"Why, sure."

"She ask you out and out for a picture of me?"

"Sure she did," James said. "She said, 'James, if you got time, I wish you'd snap a picture of Simon. We don't have a picture that looks like him no more.' I said I'd try."

"Well, then," said Simon after a minute. He rose and crossed over to the mantelpiece, where he laid down the cigar. When he returned to his chair he settled himself very carefully, tugging his jeans down tight into his boots, running both hands hard through his hair to smooth it back. He looked more posed now; the relaxed expression that he had worn in the other pictures was gone. With both hands placed symmetrically on the arms of the chair, his back very straight and his face drawn tight in the beginnings of a smile, he stared unblinkingly into the lens of the camera. James waited a minute, and then he pressed the button and straightened up. "Thank you," he said formally.

"Oh, that's all right."

"I'll have them for you this afternoon, maybe. Or tomorrow, early. Perle Simpson is coming by for a passport photo and I want to take that before I start developing."

"Okay," said Simon. He stood up, frowningly tucking in his shirt, and then suddenly he looked over at James and gave him a wide, slow smile, so big that the two dents he was always trying to hide showed up in the center of his cheeks. "Well, I'll be seeing you," he said, and sauntered on out, slamming the screen door behind him. When James went to the window to look after him he saw him in the front yard, picking up the bicycle he hadn't ridden for days and twirling the pedal into a position where he could step on it. The buttercup still hung in the spokes, its little yellow head dangling drunkenly from the front wheel and its withered leaves fluttering out like banners when Simon rode slowly off. He rode in the direction of the Terrys' farm; he would be going to see the tobacco pickers, the way he used to do.

When Simon was out of sight, and when James had turned and seen that Ansel was sleeping still, he himself went out the screen door and down the long front porch. The Pikes' window shades were up now. He peered in through the dark screen door and saw Mrs. Pike at her sewing machine, not running it at the minute but sewing by hand on something that was in her lap. "Mrs. Pike," he called gently. She lowered the sewing and looked up at him, her mouth screwed up and lopsided because of the pins in one corner of it. "Mrs. Pike, can I come in a minute?"

"Joan's handing tobacco," she said. Speaking around the pins made her seem like a different woman, like that waitress at the Royal Crown who always had a cigarette in her mouth when she talked. "Did you want to see Joan?"

"Well, no, I just wanted to tell you—" said James. He pulled open the screen door and stepped just inside it, even though he hadn't been asked. "I took a picture of Simon," he said.

"Oh."

"Sitting in an easy chair."

"Well, that's real nice," said Mrs. Pike, and bowed her head to nip a thread off the dress she was sewing.

"Well, I took it for *you*, Mrs. Pike."

"That's real nice of you," she said again. She held the dress up at arm's length and frowned at it. James shifted his weight to his other foot.

"What I actually told him," he said, "was that you *asked* for it. Asked me to take it for you."

She lowered the dress to her lap again and looked over at him, and James thought that surely she would say *some*thing now. But when she did speak, all she said was, "It must be right hard, taking pictures of children"—politely, as if he were a stranger she was trying to make conversation with.

James waited a minute, but she didn't say more. She had lowered her head to her sewing again, fumbling at it with quick, blunt fingers and absentmindedly working the pins from one side of her mouth to the other. So he said, "Well, ma'am, not really," and then turned and quietly let himself out the door again. All the way down to his end of the porch he kept thinking of going back and trying once more, but he knew already it wasn't any use. So he entered his own part of the house and then just stood there a minute, thinking it over, watching Ansel as he slept.

12

THE THINGS Joan Pike owned in this world could be packed in two suitcases, with room to spare. She was putting them there now, one by one, folding the skirts in two and laying them gently on the bottom of the big leather suitcase her father's parents had given him to take to a debating contest fifty years ago. Her own suitcase, newer and shinier, stood waiting on the floor already filled and locked. She had saved out her big straw pocketbook, which was hard to pack and could hold all the things she might need on the bus. It stood on the floor, with one corner of a Greyhound ticket envelope sticking out of it. The ticket she had bought this morning, after spending all of Wednesday night lying in bed rolling up the hem of her top sheet while she thought what to do. She had ridden into town for it on Simon's bicycle, and come back with it hidden inside her white shirt. Nobody knew she was going.

When her closet was empty she cleaned it out carefully, picking up every stray bobby pin and button from the floor and bunching the hangers neatly at one end of the rod with the hooks all pointing the same way. Mainly she wanted to save her aunt the trouble, but also she wanted to go away feeling that she had left a clean sweep behind her—not a thread, not a scrap of hers remaining that she could want to return for. She would like to have it seem as if she had never been here, if that was possible. So she closed the closet door firmly and turned the key in its lock. Then she began on the rest of the room.

She rolled her silver-backed dresser set in sweaters, so that none of the pieces would get scratched. Seeing the set, which her parents had given her on her eighteenth birthday, made her remember that she should be bringing back presents for them, and she frowned into the mirror when she thought about it. Always before, after two weeks at Scout camp even, she had brought back gifts for each of them and formally presented them, and her parents had done the same. But this time she hadn't thought far enough in advance; she would have to come home empty-handed. The idea bothered her, as if this were some basic point of guest etiquette that she, always a guest, had somehow forgotten. She shook her head, and laid the wrapped silver pieces carefully on top of her skirts.

Out in the back yard Simon was running an imaginary machine gun, shouting "ta-ta-ta-ta-tat" in a high voice that cracked and aiming at unknowing wrens who sat in the bushes behind the house. She could see him from her window—his foreshortened, blue denim body, the swirl of hair radiating out from a tiny white point on the back of his head. With luck, he wouldn't see her go. He would stay there in the back yard, and his mother would stay in bed for her afternoon nap, and she could sneak out of the house and across the fields without anyone's seeing her. It might even be supper before they noticed. Mr. Pike would fuss a little, feeling responsible for his brother's child. Mrs. Pike was still too sad to care, but Simon would care. He would ask why she had left without telling him, and how would they answer him? How would *she* even answer him? "Because I don't want to think I'm really going," she would say. It was the first time she had thought that out, in words. She stopped folding a slip and looked down at where Simon sat, with his legs bent under him and the toes of his boots pointing out, sighting along a long straight stick and pulling the trigger. As soon as she got home, she decided, she would telephone to make it all right with him.

Then after supper James would come. "Joan ready?" he'd say. "She's gone," they'd tell him. Then what would he do? She couldn't imagine that, no matter how hard she tried. Maybe he would say, "Well, I'm sorry to hear that," and remain where he was, his face dark and stubborn. Or maybe he would say, "I'll go bring her back." But that was something she didn't expect would ever happen now. A week ago, she might have expected it. She'd thought anything could happen, anyone would change. But now all she felt sure of was that ten years from now, and twenty, James would still be enduring, on and on, in that stuffy little parlor with Ansel in it; and she couldn't endure a minute longer.

She turned away from the window and went back to her suitcase. Everything was in it now. The bureau was left as blank as the bureau in a hotel room; its drawers were empty and smelled of wood again. On the back of the door hung her towel and washcloth, the only things left of her. She plucked them off the rack and carried them out to the laundry hamper in the hall, and then she was finished. No one would ever know she had lived here. When she had locked the second suitcase, and stepped into the high heels that she had taken off so as not to make a noise, she stood in the doorway a minute making sure of the blankness in the room. Then she picked up the two suitcases and the pocketbook and went downstairs.

Carrying it all was harder than she remembered. She kept having to switch the pocketbook strap from one arm to the other, and although the suitcases weren't heavy they were big and bulky and banged against her legs when she walked. Before she was even off the front porch she was breathing hard. Then in the yard, the spikes of her high heels kept sinking into the earth and making things more difficult. If she'd had any sense, she thought, she would have called Mr. Carleton and his taxi service. Except then everybody and his brother would have known she was leaving. She waited until she had crossed the road and was into the field and then she took her first breather, chafing the red palms of her hands and looking anxiously back at the house. No one had seen her yet.

All the evening walks through this field with James or the children had taught her the shortest way to town—the straight line through burrs and bushes, leading apparently to nowhere but more field, emerging suddenly upon Emmett Smith's backyard and from there to Main Street. She walked carefully, to avoid getting runs in her stockings, and kept her eyes strained ahead for the first sight of the Smith house. Around her ears the breeze made a hot, lulling sound, drying the dampness on her forehead to a cold thin sheet. Then another sound arose, like wailing, and she turned and saw Simon running to catch up, his brown hands fluttering to part the weeds in front of his chest and his face desperate. "*Jo*-oan!" he was calling. He made two syllables out of it. Joan set down the suitcases and waited, with her hands crossed over her pocketbook. "Joan, *wait!*" he said, and floundered on. "Oh, Simon," she said, but she kept waiting.

When he came up even with her he was out of breath, and covered with burrs. For a while he just stood there panting, but then his breath came more slowly and he straightened up. "Can I come?" he asked.

"Oh, Simon—"

"I came in to see what you was doing. I couldn't *find* you; I thought—" He stopped, and switched his eyes from her face to the field behind her. "I wouldn't be a bit of trouble," he said softly. She leaned forward, trying to catch his words, and he said it louder: "I wouldn't be a *bit* of—"

"Well, I know that."

"Old James came over with that picture he took yesterday," he said. "You were gone off on my bicycle. He brought it in a special brown envelope like he does to customers. I said, 'Mama, here is that picture you was asking for.' She says, 'What?' I pulled it out to show her. She said, 'Oh,' and then went back to her sewing and didn't look any more. I put it back on James's doorstep."

"Well, now, don't you worry—" said Joan, but she had to stop there, because she wasn't sure what he was talking about. She stood frowning at him, with the wind whipping the hair around her face and her hands clenched white on the pocketbook.

"I won't be a *bit* of trouble," he said again.

She said, "No," and stooped nearer to him. "I can't take you," she said. "I have to go off, Simon. And you have to stay with your family. When they are back to normal, though, you can come and visit."

Simon just stood there, very straight. She didn't know what to do, because he had his head drawn back in that way he had and if she'd hugged him he would have hated her. So she waited a minute, and then she said, "Well, goodbye." He didn't answer. "Goodbye," she said again. She kept on facing him, though, because she couldn't turn first and just leave him there. Then when she was beginning to think they would stand that way forever he swung around and left, and she watched him go. He stumbled through the field in a zig-zagging line, not parting the grass ahead of him but pressing on with his hands at his sides. "Simon?" she called once. But Simon never answered.

When she turned away herself, and bent to pick up her bags again, she was thinking that out of all the bad things she had ever done this might be the one sin. It made her feel suddenly heavy and old; the weight of her sadness dragged behind her through the fields like another suitcase, and she couldn't look up or let herself think about anything but walking, putting one foot ahead of the other.

The Smith house loomed up suddenly, just beyond a little rise in the ground. Inside a wire fence the hens scratched irritably at the dirt, and from the house came the sound of someone's singing. Joan set her suitcases down and looked back, thinking to see some sign of what she had left, but there was only the gentle slope of wild grass stretching as far as she could see. Behind that was James, dark and slow and calm, rocking easily in his chair and never knowing. And that long front porch where she and Simon used to shell peas on summer evenings, while Janie Rose sang "The Murder of James A. Garfield" through the open window. She picked up her suitcases and walked on, with that sudden light, lost feeling that came from walking in a straight line away from people she loved.

The clock in the drugstore where the buses stopped said there were ten minutes to go. Tommy Jones behind the soda fountain checked her bags and handed her the tags, and she said, "Thank you," and smiled at him dazedly without thinking about him.

"Coke while you wait?" he asked.

"No, thank you."

"On the house."

"Oh, no."

Her voice sounded thin and sad. She felt like a stick, very straight and alone, standing upright with nothing to lean against. Surely people should have noticed it, but they didn't; Tommy smiled at her as if this were any normal day, and the two other people in the store went on leafing through their magazines. Dan Thompson's wife came in, wearing one of Dan's baggy printing aprons the way she usually did and carrying a fresh stack of this week's newspapers. The insides of her forearms were smeared with ink from them. When she saw Joan she smiled and came over toward her. "Hi," she said. "You want a paper?"

"I guess so," said Joan. She fished in her purse for the money and handed it over, and Carol gave her a paper off the top of the stack.

"Nothing but the most startling news," she said. "We took it all from the Rockland paper this week. Usually we get it from Clancyville."

"Well, that's all right," Joan said. "I haven't read the Rockland paper either."

"Good. You know what I think sometimes?" She heaved the papers onto a soda fountain stool and began rubbing the muscles of her arm. "Sometimes I think, what if *every* paper gets its news from the other paper? What if this is twenty-year-old news we're reading, just circulating around and around among newspapers?"

"I don't suppose it'd make much difference," Joan said absently.

"Well, maybe not." She picked up the papers again. "You bring James over for supper some night, you hear? We haven't had the two of you together in a long time."

"All right," said Joan. She didn't see much point in telling Carol she was leaving, not if Carol hadn't noticed for herself. And she hadn't. She went off jauntily, with a wave of her hand, and threw the papers on the floor in front of the magazine rack and left the store. Yet there was Joan, all dressed up in her high-heeled shoes. She looked around at the other customers again, but they went on reading their magazines.

When the bus drew up, she was the only person to board it. The driver didn't smile or even look at her; already she was outside the little circle of Larksville, and only another stranger to the people on this bus. She sat in a seat by herself, toward the rear, and smoothed her skirt down and then looked at the other passengers. None of them looked back except a sailor, who stopped chewing his gum and winked, and she quickly looked away again and sat up straighter. The bus started with a jerk and wheezed up to full speed along Main Street, making a sad, going-away noise. Through the green-tinted windows Larksville looked like an old dull photograph, and that made her sad too, but once they had passed the town limits she began to feel better. Some of that light feeling came back. It crossed her mind, as she was pulling on her gloves, that all she was going to was another bedroom, to years spent reading alone in a little house kept by old people, remembering to greet her mother's friends on the street, smiling indulgently at other people's children. But then she shook that thought away, and folded her gloved hands in her lap and began looking out the window again.

It was almost an hour before the bus made its next stop, in a town called Howrell that Joan had always hated. Gangling men stood lined along the street, spitting tobacco juice and commenting on the passengers whose faces appeared in the bus windows. Underneath Joan was the slamming and banging of bags being shoved into the luggage compartment, and then the driver helped a little old lady up the steps and into the bus. She wore a hat made entirely of flowers. From the way she advanced, clutching her pocketbook in both hands, examining the face of each passenger and sniffing a little as she passed them, Joan knew she would sit beside her. Old ladies always did. She stopped next to Joan and said, "This seat taken?" and then slid in, not waiting for an answer. While she was getting settled she huffed and puffed, making little comments under her breath; she would be the talkative kind. "I thought this bus would *never* come," she said. "I thought it had laid down and died on the way." Joan smiled, and turned her face full to the window.

When the bus had started up again, and was rolling through the last of Howrell, Joan checked her watch. It would be nearly suppertime now. If she were in Larksville she would be sitting at the kitchen table cutting up a salad. She pictured herself there, her bare feet curled around the rungs of the chair. In her mind she seemed to be sitting an inch or so above the seat, not resting on anything but air. She ran through other pictures of herself—sitting in her parents' parlor, sitting on the porch with James, even sitting now beside this old lady on a bus rolling west. In all the pictures, she was resting on nothing. She turned her mind back to the firmest seat she knew—James's lap, in the evenings when Ansel had already gone to bed. But even there, there was a good two inches of air beneath her and she seemed to be balanced there precariously, her arms tight around James. She turned away from the window quickly and said to the old lady, "It'll be getting dark soon."

"It certainly will," said the lady. "My daughter will be getting supper on now. The married one. I left them a cold hen, barbecued the way I like to do it."

Joan went back to looking out the window. She stared steadily at the clay banks that rose high and red along the side of the road, and the tall thin tobacco barns from which little strings of brightly dressed women were scattering home for supper. Who would take her place tomorrow at the tobacco table? She stopped watching the barns. All around her in the bus, people were settled firmly in their seats, with their hands relaxed on the arm rests and their heads tipped against the white starched bibs on the backs of the seats. They talked to one another in murmuring voices that mingled with the sound of the motor. A little boy was playing a tonette.

"I'm going to my *other* daughter," the old lady told her. "The one that never married. She has a kidney ailment."

"I'm sorry to hear that," said Joan.

"She's in terrible pain, and there's no one to take care of her."

Out of the corner of her eye Joan saw the Larksville paper she had bought, folded neatly and tucked down between her seat and the wall of the bus. She picked it up quickly and unfolded it, and the old lady turned away again.

There would be nothing interesting in the paper, but she read it anyway. She began with the first page and read through the whole paper methodically, not even skipping the ladies' meeting announcements or the advertisements. There had been one birth in Larksville this week, she saw, and two deaths. The first death was Jones, Laramie D., whom she had never heard of, but she read all about him anyway— the circumstances of his death, the highlights of his life, the list of relatives who had survived him. The second death was Pike, Janie Rose. The name hit into her stomach, as if she hadn't known of the death until this instant. She started to pass over it, but then she went back to it and read it through:

> Pike, Janie Rose. At County Hospital, in her
> sixth year, of internal injuries caused by an ac-
> cident. Beloved daughter of Mr. and Mrs. Roy J.
> Pike, sister of Simon Lockwood Pike. Funeral was
> held from Collins Memorial Home, July 16, in-
> terment in family cemetery.

She read it twice, but it seemed unreal still, something vague and far off. Nothing that bad could happen. When she had finished with it a second time she folded the paper very carefully in half, so that the obituaries were out of sight, and then went on to the rest of the paper. She read very closely now, even moving her lips, so as to shut out all thought of anything she had read before. "Teller-Hokes Wedding Held in First Baptist Church," she read, and although neither name meant anything to her she was careful to find out exactly what the bride wore and who her guests were. Next came the memorial notices, ringed in black like the obituaries. She had never looked at the memorial notices before. She read about someone named Auntie Peg Myers, who had passed away on July 16, 1937, and was dearly remembered by her two nieces. Then she read about Nathan Martin, who had been taken from his wife in 1941. For him there was a quotation. "Too dearly beloved ever to be forgotten," it said. Further down, for other people, there were little poems, but Joan stopped reading. She had a sudden picture of all the years of this century, stretching far back in a chain of newsprint that grew yellower and yellower as the years grew older. 1937 was almost orange, older than she herself was; 1941 was growing brittle at the edges. How would this year look? The print on January was already blurred. And then she pictured how it would be when today was yellowed too, years from now, and the Pikes themselves were buried and Simon an old man. Then on the third week in every July he would print his notice: "In memory of Janie Rose, who passed away just fifty years ago July 13th. Fondly remembered by her brother Simon." He would be remembering her as someone very small with spectacles, who had lived in the tacked-on bedroom in back of the house. But he himself would be a grandfather then, and nobody Janie would recognize. How would Simon look in fifty years? Joan tried to think, but all she saw was Simon as he was today— hunching his shoulders up, tucking his head down in that uncertain way he had.

She looked quickly out the window and saw the town of Graham rolling up, and the bus station with its line of coin machines. "Is this where you get off?" the woman asked her.

"No."

"Oh. You just sat up so sudden—"

"No," said Joan, "but I think I might buy a Coke."

She stood and wormed her way out past the woman's knees, and as soon as she was out the woman slid quickly over to the window. Joan didn't care. She went down the aisle without looking at anyone, and then descended the bus steps. A team of some kind was waiting to board, a group of boys in white satin wind-breakers with numbers on them, and when Joan stepped down among them they remained stolidly in her path, ignoring her. "Excuse me," she said, "excuse me, please," and then when no one noticed she shouted, *"Excuse* me!" For a minute they stopped talking and stared at her; then they moved aside to let her through. She walked very quickly, holding her head up. Out here she felt thinner and more alone than before, with the team of boys all watching her down the long path to the Coke machine. And when she reached the machine she found she didn't even want a Coke. But she put her dime in anyway, and just as she was reaching for the bottle someone said, "Ma'am?"

It was a young man in sunglasses, standing beside her and looking straight at her. She felt scared suddenly, even with all those people around (had he been able to *see* how alone she felt?) and she decided not to answer. Instead she uncapped the Coke bottle and then turned to go.

"Ma'am?" he said again.

She couldn't just leave him there, still asking. "What is it?" she said.

"Can you show me where the restroom is?"

"Why, it's right inside, I guess. Over there."

"Where?"

"Over there."

"I don't see."

"Over *there*."

"I don't see. I'm blind."

"Oh," said Joan, and then she just felt silly, and even sadder than before. "Wait a minute," she told him. She turned around and saw two bus drivers walking toward her, looking kind and cheerful. When they came even with her she tapped the older driver on the arm and said, "Um, excuse me."

"Yes."

"Can you show this man the restroom? He doesn't see."

"Why, surely," said the driver. He smiled at her and then took the blind man by the elbow. "You come with me," he said.

"Thank you, sir. Thank you, ma'am."

"You're welcome," Joan said.

The other driver stayed behind, next to Joan. He said, "Can you imagine traveling blind?" and stared after the two men, frowning a little.

"No, I can't" Joan said. She automatically followed the driver's eyes. Now that she looked, she couldn't think why the blind man had frightened her at first. He wore his clothes obediently, as if someone else had put them on him—the neat dark suit with the handkerchief in the pocket, the shoes tied lovingly in double knots. He reminded her of something. For a minute she couldn't think what, and then she remembered and smiled. That slow, trusting way he let himself be guided forward with his hands folded gently in front of him, was like Simon during the first year she'd lived there, when he was six and still had to be awakened at night and taken to the bathroom so he wouldn't wet his bed. He had gone just that obediently, but with his eyes closed and the shadows of some dream still flickering across his face. (You couldn't stop walking with him for a minute, not in a doorway or going around the bend in the hall, or he would think he had reached the bathroom and proceed to go right then and there.) He had held his elbows in close to his body that way, too, against the coolness of the night. Joan stopped smiling and looked down at her feet.

"You all right?" the driver asked.

"I want to go back."

"Ma'am?"

"I want to go back where I came from. Can I take my bags off my bus and wait for the next one going back?"

"Why, surely," the driver said. "You on that bus over there?"

"Yes. I know this is—"

"Women got a *right* to change their minds," the driver called. He was already heading toward her bus, and Joan followed him with her untouched Coke bottle still in her hands.

"I always do this," she said. "But this time it's—"

"You got the right," said the driver.

"This time it's different. I can't help it, this time; I'm not just—"

But the driver didn't hear her. He was walking up ahead of her and laughing over his shoulder, thinking it was all a joke. She stopped trying to tell him it wasn't.

13

SOMETHING WAS wrong at home. James knew it instantly, the moment he stepped out of the pickup carrying his two bags of groceries. There on the porch stood the Potter sisters and Ansel and Mrs. Pike, all huddling together, and Mr. Pike was a little distance away from them. He was facing toward the road, frowning down at an Indian elephant bell that he held in his hand. When he heard the pickup door slam he looked up and said, "James." The light from the setting sun turned his face strange and orange.

"What's wrong?" said James.

"We can't find Simon."

"Well, where is he?" he asked, and then to cover up the stupidity of that question he said quickly, "He was here at lunchtime."

"We thought you might have him with you," Mr. Pike said.

"No."

They all kept looking at him. Even Ansel. James hoisted his groceries up higher and then said again, "No. No, I've been running errands all afternoon. All by myself."

"Well, then," Mr. Pike said. He sighed and turned back to the others, who still waited. Finally he said, "He's not with James."

"Maybe he's with Joan," James offered.

"No. Joan must have gone off somewhere, but after she left Simon was still around. Lou says so."

James looked over at Mrs. Pike. She was dry-eyed and watchful; her arms were folded firmly across her chest.

"When was the last time you noticed him?" he asked her.

"I don't know."

"Ma'am?"

"I don't *know*," she said, with her voice slightly raised.

"Oh."

"We called the boys he plays with," Mr. Pike said. "And we called the movie-house."

"Did you ask about buses?"

"No. Why?"

"I'd do that," said James. He climbed the steps at his end of the porch and set the groceries on Ansel's chair, and then he straightened up and rubbed the muscles of his arms. "Call the drugstore," he said. "Ask them if he's—"

"Well, I *went* to the drugstore, to see if he'd gone there for a soda. Mary Bennett was on; only been there a half hour or so, but she hadn't seen him."

"Might have gone earlier," said James. "Did you look at the bus schedule?"

"*No* I didn't. What would I want to do that for?"

"Just in case," James said. "Who was there before Mary Bennett?"

"Tommy was, but I can't find him. If it weren't for Lou I'd just sit and *wait* for Simon, but Lou thinks he left with a purpose. Thinks she might have sent him away somehow."

James looked over at Mrs. Pike again. For a minute she stared back at him; then she said, "You believe he's on some bus."

"I didn't say that," said James.

"You think it."

"Now, Lou," Mr. Pike told her.

"I can tell."

"Well, it wouldn't hurt to ask," said James. "I'd track that Tommy down, if I was you."

"*Oh*, now," Mr. Pike said, and accidentally clanged the elephant bell. Everyone jumped. "Sorry," he said. For the first time, Ansel lost his blank tense look; he winced, and leaned back limply against the front of the house. Mr. Pike said, "Sorry, Ansel. But where would he take a bus *to*?"

"There's lots of places," said James.

"Not as many as you'd think," Ansel said. "World's shrinking."

"Hush," James told him. He jingled his keys thoughtfully. "Roy, can I use your telephone?"

"What for?"

"Let him," Mrs. Pike said. The Potter sisters stepped closer to her on either side and patted her shoulders, as if she had suddenly had an outburst of some kind. "You know where it is," she told James.

"Yes, ma'am."

He walked toward the Pikes' end of the porch, with everyone's eyes following him. At the door he stopped and said, "Did he have any money?"

"He gets an allowance," said Mr. Pike. "I don't know if he saved it."

"Did he get some this week?"

He was asking this of Mrs. Pike, but she just shook her head. "I don't know," she said. Finally James turned back again and went on inside.

It was Tommy Jones's mother who answered the telephone. Her voice was breathless, as if she had had to come running from some other part of the house. "Hello?" she said.

"Mrs. Jones, this is James Green. Is Tommy there?"

"No, he's not."

"Do you know where he is?"

"No. Is this about Simon still?"

"Yes, ma'am."

"They haven't found him?"

"No. Do you think Tommy'll be getting back soon?"

"I really don't," she said. "He's off someplace with his girl. Shall I have him call?"

"No, thank you. Sorry to bother you."

"It's no bother."

He hung up and stood thinking a while, and then he went out to the front porch again. In just the short time that the telephone call had taken the color of the evening had shifted, turning from sunset into twilight. The others were standing where he had left them, still looking in his direction as if their eyes had never moved from the spot where he had disappeared. "Tommy's not there," he said.

"Well, *I* could have told you that," Mr. Pike said irritably. He swung his arms down, making the bell clang again, and started toward the front yard. "I'm going to round up a couple others," he called back. "We'll look in all the places where he goes, and ring bells or fire guns if we find him. Want to come, James?"

"I'm not sure that's the way," James said.

"Only thing I can think of. Mind if I use your truck?"

"Well, wait," said James. He came down the steps and crossed over to Mr. Pike. "No, I'd like to take the truck and follow up an idea of my own, I think I—"

"When *I* was a little boy . . ." Ansel announced, and everyone turned around to look at him. He had recovered from that last clang and was standing erect now, placing the tips of his fingers together. "When I was a little boy, I had to tell my mother *every*where I went. It was a rule. And I could never go out of hearing range of this old Army bugle, that my father would stand in the doorway and blow at suppertime—"

"If you could come along," Mr. Pike told James, "and bring a noisemaker of some kind, why, we could start by—"

"I was thinking of Caraway," James said.

"Caraway?"

"I was thinking that was where he might've gone."

"Oh, *Caraway*," Mr. Pike said impatiently. "I been there. No, more likely he went off on some hike or another, and forgot to let us know."

"Well, I'd like to try Caraway anyhow," said James.

"But James, that's a waste of—"

"Let him," said Mrs. Pike, and once again the Potter sisters closed in on her and patted her shoulders. "Hush, hush," they whispered. James pulled out his billfold and checked his money; there was plenty for gas. He turned to Mr. Pike.

"I'm sorry," he said. "I just feel I know where he's at."

"Well, that's all right," said Mr. Pike. "Sure wish I could have the loan of your pickup, though."

"I'll make the trip as fast as I can."

"Well, sure." Mr. Pike sighed, and then he set off wearily across the yard. He carried the elephant bell upside down, with his fingers poked through the inward-curling teeth of it to hold the clapper silent. When he reached the gravel road he turned back and said, "Ansel? You feel up to coming along?"

"Not really," said Ansel. "I just feel miserable about all this."

Mr. Pike nodded several times and then continued down the road in the direction of the Terrys. "Poor man," said Miss Lucy, and then she and Miss Faye began patting Mrs. Pike harder than before.

James said, "Ansel, take in the groceries. And fix yourself something for supper, in case I'm late getting back."

"Well, all right," Ansel said.

"I don't expect you want to come with me."

"No."

James descended the porch steps. In the distance he could see Mr. Pike, far and small already, marching on steadily with his shoulders set. It seemed so clear to James that Simon was in Caraway—where else would he be?—that he felt sorry to see Mr. Pike going to all this trouble. He wanted to call him back, but he knew there was no use. So he just turned around and said, "Ansel—" and bumped squarely into Mrs. Pike, who was standing right behind him. "Oh, excuse me," he said. "I didn't hear you coming." She remained silent, with her arms still folded and her head bowed meekly. "Well," he said. "Ansel, I'm going to call you at the Pikes' number when I get there. To tell you what happens, in case Mrs. Pike is going to be over at the Potters'."

"All right," said Ansel. "Does that mean I can stay at the Pikes' until you call?"

"I don't care, for heaven's sake."

He continued on toward the pickup, and Mrs. Pike kept following after him. When he opened the door on the driver's side she opened the other door, and it was only then that he realized she meant to come along. They stood staring at each other for a minute across the expanse of seat; then Mrs. Pike lowered her eyes and climbed in, and he did the same. He could see that the others on the porch were just as surprised as he was—they came closer together, and turned to look at each other—but Mrs. Pike didn't offer to explain herself. She sat quietly, with her eyes straight ahead and her hands clasped in her lap. Even when he craned his neck around to look out the rear window as he was backing out, she stared ahead. The stoniness of her face gave her a calm, sure look, as sure as James felt inside; she must know where Simon was by instinct.

When they were on the main highway James turned his lights on. Already the opaque white look of early twilight was growing bluer and more transparent, and other cars as they came towards him clicked their own lights on. But he could see around him clearly still: the landmarks of the journey to town slipping by, and then a brief glimpse of Main Street itself before he passed it. It felt funny to keep going straight, instead of turning there. A strange sinking feeling began in his stomach, and he looked into the rear-view mirror and watched the town lights fading away from him. "Don't worry," he said suddenly to Mrs. Pike, but Mrs. Pike wasn't looking worried at all; she only nodded, calmly.

"I'm just waiting," she told him.

"Oh."

"I'll take what I get. Whatever I deserve."

"Yes, ma'am," James said.

He swerved around a little boy riding a bicycle. Where was Simon at this minute? Maybe swaggering down a street alone, trying to look as if he knew where he was going. Searching for some sign—a boy with a ring in his ear or a woman in a red-plumed hat, someone who would expect him the way he had expected them. James frowned. The clomping of Simon's leather boots seemed louder than the sound of the motor; the fuzz down the back of Simon's neck seemed clearer than the road ahead of him.

"It's been a pretty day," he said.

"Yes."

"Where's Joan?"

"I don't know," said Mrs. Pike. She looked out at the road a while, and then she said, "I sewed a dress today."

"Oh, did you?"

"Yes."

"Well, now," James said. He cleared his throat. "I always thought a dress would take *days* to make."

"Anything that happens," said Mrs. Pike, "it's only my fault. My fault."

"Well, now," James said again.

The truck was traveling too fast, he thought. Already the countryside looked like Caraway countryside; not Larksville. In his mind he had added mile upon mile to this trip, stretching the road out long and thin till Caraway might have been in Asia. Yet before they had been on the road half an hour they reached Stevens's Esso Station—the halfway mark—and he braked sharply and turned in. "Need gas," he told Mrs. Pike. She nodded. The meter said the tank was half full, but stopping this way would slow things down a little.

Mr. Stevens himself washed the windshield and filled the tank, with only a brief smile to James because he didn't recognize him. "Three dollars, ten," he said. "Nice evening." He held his hand out flat, palm up, outside James's window, and James counted out the exact change very slowly. When he had paid he said, "This the road to Caraway?" to stretch the stop out even longer.

"Sure is," the man said.

"How much further?"

"Be there in half an hour."

"Thank you," James said. He started the motor and looked over at Mrs. Pike, but she didn't seem surprised at the questions he had asked. She just looked down at her hands and waited for him to drive on.

Almost no one else was on the road now. He drove at a steady pace, and in silence, looking at the country around him whenever they were on a straight stretch of road. At first it was just the occasional, very noticeable things that he recognized—that humped bridge that looked like something off a willowware plate, the funny barbecue house off in the middle of nowhere with pigs chasing each other rapidly in neon lights across the front porch. But after another ten or fifteen minutes, he began to recognize everything. The objects that flashed by were all worn and familiar-looking, as if perhaps without knowing it he had been dreaming of them nightly. Even the new things—the brick ranch houses rising baldly out of fresh red clay, the drive-ins and Dairy

Queens—seemed familiar, and he glanced at them mildly and without surprise. When he reached the town limits it was just beginning to grow really dark, and his headlights glared briefly against the slick white surface of a newly painted sign. "Caraway. Bird Sanctuary," it read. The last time he had been here it had said only "Caraway." And he had looked at it and thought, I'll never see that sign again, not for *any* reason. He hadn't known the Pikes then, nor Joan, nor the Potters; he hadn't foreseen the existence of Simon.

He slowed down as soon as they reached the actual town, and Mrs. Pike straightened up and began looking out the window more intently, perhaps already searching for Simon. James kept his eyes straight ahead until they got to Main Street. Then he pointed to an all-night grill and said, "This is where the buses stop."

"Oh," said Mrs. Pike.

"Do you want to go ask if they've seen him?"

"I guess so," she said, but she was looking at him, obviously expecting that he would be the one to ask. He sighed and swung the truck into a diagonal parking place.

"I'll be right out," he told her.

"All right."

Once on the street, out from behind the shield of the pickup, he felt clumsy and conspicuous. Girls in barebacked dresses waited with their dates in front of the movie theater next door and when he stepped on to the sidewalk they pivoted on their high heels and glanced over at him. He stared back, but there was no one he recognized. And the waitress in the grill was a new one—a fat blond he didn't know. He came up and laid both hands palms down on the counter and said, "Were you here when the last bus from Larksville came?"

"Yes," she said. Her voice was tired, and she seemed hardly able to raise her eyes and look at him.

"Did you see a little boy get off?"

"I wasn't watching," she said.

She began swabbing off the counter with a pink sponge, and James walked out again without thanking her. On the street he looked up and down, hooking his thumbs in his belt and staring over the heads of passersby, but there was no sign of Simon. For the first time he felt uncertain about him, and frightened. He returned to the truck.

"She wasn't watching," he told Mrs. Pike.

"She wasn't," she agreed, and went on looking calmly out the window.

James knew where he was heading, but he was hoping he didn't have to go there. So he drove down Main Street very slowly, looking right and left, peering into the windows of restaurants and soda shops and scanning the faces of people out for evening walks. Several times he saw people he knew. Seen through the truck window, walking in half-dark, six years older and unexpected in new clothes that James had never known, they looked worn and sad to him. He would look after them a minute with a feeling of bewilderment, almost forgetting Simon until Mrs. Pike touched him on the arm. Then he would drive on.

Mrs. Pike didn't ask what he was doing when he turned off Main Street. She seemed to think that this was part of a tour around Caraway that anyone might follow, and she gazed in tourist-like respect at a three-foot high statue of Major John Caraway. ("This is Major Caraway," James's father always explained to them. "He fought in the Big War." Meaning the Civil War, though there'd been others since. "He certainly was a *small* man," said their mother. Their father never answered that.) Even when they turned down Hampden Street, where there were no statues and only private houses, Mrs. Pike said nothing. She kept on searching the sides of the road, poking her nose toward the window so that the skin between her chin and the base of her throat made one slanted line. James drove more and more slowly. He turned left on Winton Lane and then drew to a stop, letting the truck roll into the grass at the side of the road. They were in front of an old gray house with a great many gables, its yard sprinkled with the feather-white skeletons of dandelions. No one was on the porch. For a while James sat silent, tapping the steering wheel with one finger. Then he looked over at Mrs. Pike. She was still searching out the window, almost as if she thought they were still moving. "I'll be back," he told her.

"All right."

He opened the truck door and climbed out stiffly, careful not to make too much noise. But no dog barked. In his mind, he saw now, he had pictured the dog's barking first. He had imagined that everyone would come to the door to investigate, long before he had reached the front steps; he had seen the long rectangle of yellow light from the doorway and the silhouettes of many people, watching as he walked awkwardly through the dandelions. Yet he came to the door in utter silence, with no one noticing. He opened the screen, which creaked, and knocked several times on the weatherbeaten wooden door and waited. For a while no one came. Then there were footsteps, and he stepped back a pace. He fixed his eyes on a point just a little above his own eye level, where he would see that hard white face as soon as the door opened.

But when the door did open, he had to look lower than that. He had to look down to the level of his shoulders, much lower than he had remembered, into the old man's small lined face and his eyes in their pockets of bone. His hair was all white now, gleamingly clean. He wore suspenders, snapped over a frayed white collarless shirt which was only folded shut, without buttons. And his trousers bagged at the knees.

"The dog didn't bark," said James.

"She died," his father said, and stepped back a step to let him into the house.

14

THE FIRST thing Simon said was, "If I'd known *you* were coming, I'd of hitched a ride with you." He was sitting in old Mr. Green's platform rocker, with his elbows resting lightly on the arms of it and his fingers laced in front of him. "Did you just leave home and not tell anyone?" he asked.

"I told *every*one," said James, and looked straight across at the others. They stood in a line behind Simon, the three of them—his father, Claude, and Clara, the one brother and sister still at home. They were standing very still, all three of them in almost exactly the same position, with their eyes on James. When James looked at them Simon turned around and looked too, and just in that one turn of his head, with his chin pointed upwards and the shock of hair falling back off his forehead, he seemed to be *claiming* them somehow, marking them as his own. James's father looked down at him soberly, and Clara smiled, but by then Simon had turned to James again and couldn't see her. "I came on a bus," he said.

"I guessed you had."

"I found them in a telephone book."

Clara said, "James, will you sit down?"

"Oh, I guess not," said James. "Did you call the police?"

"I don't hold with police," his father said.

"I forgot."

"We figured you'd come after him. We didn't call no one."

"I see," James said. He folded his arms and stared down at one shoe. "His mother was wondering where he was."

"Well, now she'll know," said his father. "*Your* mother used to wonder."

"Sir?"

"What did she say?" Simon asked. "Did she see I was gone? What did she say about it?"

Instead of answering, James turned around and looked out the open

door. There was Mrs. Pike, picking her way through the dandelions
and toward that rectangle of light across the porch. She had come
unasked, having waited long enough in the pickup, and because she
didn't know whose house this was or what she was doing here
her face had a puckered, uncertain look. She stumbled a little on the
porch and then came forward, her eyes, squinting against the light.
"James—" she began, and then saw Simon and stopped. "Is that
Simon?" she asked. Her finger began plucking at her skirt, and she
stayed poised there on the porch.

Simon stood up and looked at James, but he didn't say anything.

"Simon, is that you?" his mother asked.

"Yes."

"Where did you go?" She called this into the room from her place
on the porch; she didn't seem able to step inside. "Why did you leave?"

"Oh, well," Simon said uncertainly. He looked over at James's family,
as if they might tell him what was going on here, but they were all
staring at Mrs. Pike. "I just came to see these people," he said.

"Oh," said his mother. She looked down at her skirt. The longer
she stood there the more distant she seemed to become, so that now
James couldn't imagine her *ever* walking in of her own accord. He said,
"Mrs. Pike, will you come in?" and then Clara, who had been gazing
open-mouthed, came to life and said, "Oh. Yes, *please* come in."

Mrs. Pike took a few steps, just enough to get her safely into the
room, without moving her eyes from Simon. "What happened to your
hair?" she asked him.

"What hair?"

"I wish you'd have a seat," Clara said.

"Simon, were you not going to come back?"

"Well, I don't know," said Simon. "I just came away, I guess."

"Oh," Mrs. Pike said. She wet her lips and said, "Will you come
back *now*?"—not looking at Simon any more but at James, as if he
were the one she was asking.

"What for?" Simon asked.

"Why—just to be back."

Whatever Simon was thinking, he didn't show it. He began walking
in those small circles of his, with his eyes on his boots. And James
suddenly thought, what if he *won't* come back? The same idea must
have hit Mrs. Pike. She said, "Don't you *want* to come?"

"Well," Simon said.

"You can't stay *here*."

"How did you happen to come by?" he asked.

"James thought of it."

"I mean, what for? Did you just go off driving?"

Mrs. Pike frowned at him, not understanding. "*James* thought of it,"
she said. "He thought you'd be in Caraway."

"You mean you came specially?"

"Well, *yes*," said Mrs. Pike. "What did you think?"

"*Oh*," Simon said, and the sudden clear look that came across his face made James feel light inside and relieved. It was that simple, he thought; Simon didn't know they had come just for him. "You mean you're here on *account* of my going off," he said.

"Of course we are. Will you let us take you home?"

"Sure, I guess so."

Everyone seemed to loosen up then. James's father said, *"Well*, now," and Mrs. Pike crossed over to Simon and hugged him tightly. He stood straight while she hugged him, looking very stiff and grown up, but there was a little shy, pleased smile pulling at the corners of his mouth. "I came on a bus," he said.

"Wasn't anyone *with* you?"

"No."

"I'm glad I didn't know about it, then. I'm glad I—oh, goodness, Miss, um—"

"Green," James said. "Clara Green, and Claude, and my father. This is Mrs. Pike."

"Your *family*?" said Mrs. Pike. She looked at them more closely. "Well, of *all* things," she said. "I never thought I'd—well. Miss Green, do you have a telephone?"

"In the dining room," said Clara. "I'll show you."

"I want to reach my husband somehow. I hope someone's at the house."

She followed after Clara, with one arm still around Simon, and James watched after them because he didn't know where else to look. Simon walked very straight, holding up the weight of his mother's arm but keeping himself tall and separate from her, and Mrs. Pike moved almost briskly. "They'll be half insane," James heard her say. "Oh, good. Thank you." They were out of sight now. Clara reappeared in the doorway, and James turned away and put his hands in his pockets.

He was standing squarely in front of the fireplace, a small one with a marble mantelpiece. Everything in the room was exactly the way it had been before—the linoleum rug with the roses painted on it, the bead curtains, the turquoise walls made up of tongue-and-groove slats. On the mantelpiece was a Seth Thomas clock that his mother had brought when she came, and a picture of Jesus knocking at the door and a glass plate that looked like lace. At first, not knowing what else to do with himself, James absentmindedly stooped nearer to the fireplace and held out his hands to be warmed. It was only after a minute that he remembered it was summer and the fire unlit. So he had to straighten up again, his hands in his back pockets and his face toward the others. They were all looking at him. Clara had sat down on the footstool, thinner and sharper and with the look of an old maid beginning to set in around her mouth. And Claude was on the couch, twisting a leather lanyard in his hands. He was grown now. The last time James had seen him, Claude was in his early teens and had turned red from the neck up every time he was directly addressed. There had been more of them then. His mother, small and dark, scared of everything, humming hymns under her breath in a tinny monotone as she sewed. His sister Madge, whose one romance they had broken up and who was now in China doing missionary work. And Ansel.

If he had ever imagined coming back here—and it seemed to him now he had, without knowing it—he had not imagined standing like this, wordless. He had thought that of all the mixed-up, many-sided things in the world, his dislike of his father was one complete and pure emotion and that that alone could send words enough swarming to his mouth. Yet his father stood before him like a small, battered bird, the buttonless shirt folded gently over his thin chest and the worn leather slippers searching out the floorboards hesitantly when he walked. He was making his way to the rocker. All the time that Simon had sat there, the old man must have been watching shyly and eagerly, waiting for his chance to reclaim it. (It had always been his property alone, forbidden to the children. On Bible Class nights, when both parents were gone, James would sit in that chair and rock fiercely, and the other children stood around him with wide scared eyes.) Now James's father sat down almost gratefully, feeling behind him first to make sure it was there and then slowly lowering himself into it. When he rocked, the chair complained; it had grown old and sullen with time.

"Yes, the dog died," he said. He surveyed his three children out of eyes the same startling blue as Ansel's, and he smiled a little. "She died."

"I'm sorry to hear that," said James.

"It happens."

"She had cancer," Claude said.

"Can dogs get cancer?"

"Get everything people get," said his father, rocking steadily. "The vet told us so, at the time."

"I never heard that."

There was a silence. Clara sat forward suddenly, throwing her arms around her knees in that swooping way she had and craning her neck up, and everyone looked at her as if they expected her to say something but she didn't. She just smiled at them, with her lips tightly closed.

"You've got your hair a different way," James told her. Clara went on smiling at him and nodded.

"Yes, I do," she said.

"Every thought of every curl is another stroke for the devil," said

her father. "Have you ever thought of that? But *Clara* here don't care;
she *likes* short hair."

"Yes, I do," Clara said again. The tone of her voice was indifferent,
and she included her father in her smile. No one seemed to be as
James remembered.

Out in the dining room, Mrs. Pike said, "Yes? Miss Lucy, I'm glad
you're there. I was hoping you would hear the phone and—"

"You're back," James's father said.

The others looked at him.

"You're back in this house."

"Yes," James said. "Just for—" He stopped.

"Just for a while," his father said. "Just for the boy."

"Yes."

"Ah, well."

Mrs. Pike was talking loudly, apparently trying to break in on something Miss Lucy was saying. "Yes, I know," she said. "I know—Miss
Lucy, will you try and find Roy? First go and shout for him. Yes, I'm
feeling fine, thank you. Then if he's too far away I'll leave a message.
But I'd like to have Simon tell him—"

"The phone is a precarious instrument," said James's father.

"Hush, now," Clara told him. "There's not a machine in this world
you don't say that about."

"A *wavery* thing," said the old man, overriding her. "On a thin line
between what's real and what isn't. Is that person *really* sitting next
to you, the way he sounds? When I called you at your neighbors, three
Christmases ago—"

"Sir?" said James.

"When Clara called three Christmases ago, and Ansel wouldn't talk
to her but stayed in the other room, I happened to be passing near
enough to hear what was going on at the other end. Heard Ansel
shouting how he wouldn't come. And it seemed to me his voice was
trembly-like, unsteady. Is his sickness worse?"

"No," James said. "He's just a little weak sometimes."

"It's the forces from inside that weaken."

"He's all right," James told him.

Simon was on the telephone now. He was talking to Miss Lucy.
"Yes, ma'am," he said. "Then I got on the bus. I figured out the
schedule in the drugstore." James's father rocked sharply forward and
slapped both slippers on the floor.

"That boy is too *young* to travel alone," he said.

"He ran away," said James.

"I realize that. He came to our door and asked to be a lodger. Did
you tell him this family ran a boarding house?"

"No."

"He seemed to think you had."

He rocked on in silence for a minute; the only sound was Simon's voice. Then Clara looked up and, finding her father's eyes on her, gathered her skirts beneath her and spoke. "He likes mayonnaise," she said.

"Who does?" asked James.

"The little boy. He wanted a mayonnaise sandwich."

"Oh." He frowned at her a minute, and then looked over at his father. "What were you going to do with him?" he asked.

"The boy? I figured someone'd come after him."

"What if they hadn't?"

"You *did*," said his father. "Someone *did*. I don't hold with police."

"You could have called the parents."

"I don't speak on telephones."

"His sister just died," said James. "His mother had enough to worry about."

"Most do."

"*More* than enough. Clara could have called."

"I never turn a stranger from my door," his father said. He let his head fall back against the rocker. "Can *you* say that? Did *you* never let a man down?" He looked at James from under white, papery eyelids, waiting for an answer. No one said anything. It seemed to James that his father had raised a banner in the room—the same one as in old days, long and dark and heavy. His lowered eyes were asking "What can you do about it? Can you take my flag down?" and smiling faintly. Yet the lines around those eyes were deep and tired; his children sat limp, not bothering to answer. "Ah me," said the old man, and rolled his head to the other side and then back again and closed his eyes.

"This has nothing to do with me," James said. "It was his *mother* you made worry; it wasn't me."

"Stop it," Clara told him.

"Clara, are *you* against telephones?"

"You could have telephoned here," his father said suddenly. He opened his eyes and looked over at James.

"I was hoping he hadn't got this far," said James.

"I see. Have you got a telephone yet? I didn't think to ask."

"No."

"And money. Have you made a lot of money in your life?"

"No. But I get along."

"Get along, do you." He nodded to himself, several times. "Changed your ways?"

"No."

"No," his father agreed, and relaxed against the back of the rocker again.

Mrs. Pike and Simon came out of the dining room, Mrs. Pike's hand still on Simon's shoulder. She said, "We called collect. I'm sure you're relieved to hear that," and then laughed a little and looked down at Simon. "They're going to relay the message to Simon's daddy," she said.

"Well, I'm glad you got through to them," said Clara. "Will you have a seat?"

"Oh, we couldn't. I'm sorry, I know I haven't said two words to you. Mr. Green, it's nice to see you." She advanced, smiling, heading straight for James's father and holding out one plump hand. He had to rise from his rocker to take it. She said, "You're smaller-boned than James or Ansel. But you've got Ansel's fair skin." The way she spoke of him made him seem like a child being compared to his parents, but he smiled graciously back.

"James gets his skin from his mother," he told her.

"I guessed that."

"He's back in this house now."

Clara said, "Mrs. Pike, I wish you'd sit down and have some lemonade."

"No, we really can't. I have to get Simon home—and I do thank you for taking care of him." She said that directly to Clara, and Clara smiled at her with her narrow, gaunt smile. "He don't *usually* run away, I don't want you thinking—"

"He's too young to be on his own," said Mr. Green.

"He's *not* on his own."

"James used to run away." He sat down in his rocker and looked up at her, staring out from under white arched eyebrows. Mrs. Pike waited, and then when she saw that he wasn't going to continue she turned to the others.

"I thank my Lord we found him," she said. "I feel it's some kind of sign; I've been let off with a warning." She squeezed Simon tight against her, and he smiled at the middle button of her dress and then broke away.

James stood up, preparing to leave, and Mrs. Pike said, "James, I thought we could go back by bus. You probably want to stay on a bit, now you're here."

"No, I'll drive you back," said James. He crossed over to his father and said, "I guess I'll be going."

"We still have your old bed," said his father, but he seemed to know beforehand that James would say no. He rose again from the rocker, very slowly, and shook James's hand while he looked at the floor. It was a small, clean hand, that offered no resistance when James pressed it. To Mrs. Pike, James's father said, "It began when he was four. He ran everywhere."

"What?" asked Mrs. Pike.

"James."

"Oh," she said. "Well, I'm glad to've met you, Mr. Green—" and she shook his hand once more, holding her wrist slightly curved and offering just the tips of her fingers. "I can't thank you enough for all you've done; any time you're in Larksville you just stop in on us."

"We locked doors and tied knots," said Mr. Green. "But he was like Houdini."

Mrs. Pike shook hands with Claude and Clara and made Simon do the same, and James followed behind them. He shook Claude's hand but Clara he kissed, feeling that she would prefer that. Her cheek was bonier than he had expected, and the skin dry. She would probably never get married, he thought. None of them would.

When they went out the door his father followed them, and stood on the porch in his slippers. "Well, goodbye, James," he said. "You'll be back someday, I expect." But his smile when he looked up at James was timid and uncertain, and James smiled back.

"Tell Madge hello for me," he said.

"All right."

They climbed into the pickup at the edge of the yard—Mrs. Pike at the window, and Simon in the middle next to James. Simon said, "Hey, James, can I steer?" but James was starting the engine up and didn't answer. He looked in the rear-view mirror and saw his father still standing on the porch, his arms hugging his chest, his knees bagging, his small white head strained toward the truck. As long as James took getting started, his father remained there, and when he drove away Mr. Green lifted one arm for a goodbye and stayed that way until the truck was out of sight. James drove staring straight ahead for a while, holding that picture of his father in his mind.

When they had turned into the center of Caraway again, Mrs. Pike said, "It's a nice town, isn't it?"

"Some ways," James said.

"Yes." And she settled back, one hand patting the back of Simon's neck. Simon was restless and fidgety after all his adventures. He sat on the edge of the seat, kicking one foot nervously and gritting his jaw in that way he had when he'd had too much excitement. The passing streetlights gleamed briefly on his face and then left it dark again, and his eyes were strained wide against the night.

"Sit back in your seat," James told him.

"I am."

"No, you're not. You'll go through the windshield."

"Yes, Simon," said his mother, and pulled him back. Simon leaned against her side, still kicking that one foot.

"James," he said, "will we ever go back visiting there?"

"I don't know."

"I better tell Ansel."

"Tell him what?"

"I bet New York is better any day."

"Well, maybe so," James said.

"Those earrings were just teeny gold wires, you know? And there *weren't* no feather hats."

"Well, that was just one summer they had those," James said. "Some kind of free sample."

"Why didn't he tell me that?"

"I don't know."

"Why did he say it was all year every year?"

"Go to sleep," said James. "I don't know."

15

JOAN ARRIVED at the Pikes' house in Mr. Carleton's taxi, rattling over the gravel road in pitch dark with the taxi's one headlight making a swerving yellow shaft in front of them. Her suitcases were on the back seat, where they bounced around at every bump in the road, and she sat up front with Mr. Carleton but she didn't talk to him. Twice he tried to begin a conversation. He started off the first time with, "Well, now. Well, now. I didn't know you were even *gone*, Miss Joan." And when she didn't answer that, except for a single motion of her head that might have been a nod, he rode on in silence for a while and then tried again. "Wher*ever* you were," he said, "I sure hope the weather was good." But Joan's face was turned away from him, and she went on looking out the window without even changing expression.

When they turned into the Pikes' yard Joan sat up and opened her straw handbag. She didn't look toward the house. Mr. Carleton said, "Some kind of party?" and then she heard the noises that were floating from Ansel's window. Music, and voices, and someone laughing. The light from that window flooded the yard, fading out the pale yellow of the taxi's headlight. The rest of the house was dark. "I don't know," she said, and reached forward to hand him the money. "Don't worry about my bags; I'll take them in."

"They look pretty heavy for you."

"I can take them."

He climbed out his side of the taxi to drag the bags from the back seat. Somehow the bag that had been her father's had had a strap broken; the strap dangled, looking ridiculous and defeated. When Mr. Carleton handed the bag to her she swayed for a minute, surprised by the weight of it, and then she said, "Okay, I've got it."

"You sure now."

"Sure. Thank you, Mr. Carleton."

"Oh, it's nothing," he said. "Good night." He climbed back into the taxi, slamming the door behind him, and backed out into the road. Joan started for the porch.

The suitcases were hard to get up the steps. She swung them onto the porch one at a time, and then she climbed the steps herself and picked them up again. This all felt so familiar; how many times had she lugged these suitcases into this house? She thought of the first time, coming here in a dust storm, met on the steps by Janie Rose who wore nothing but her underpants and carried one half of a brown rubber sheet that they hadn't been able to get away from her in those days. Now there was no one at all to meet her. When she opened the front door the house was so empty it seemed to echo. She turned on a lamp, and it threw long, black, lonely shadows across the parlor walls.

The first thing she did was put her suitcases back in her bedroom. Whether they had noticed she was gone or not, she didn't want them to come back and find those suitcases. Then she closed her bedroom door and went directly to Simon's room. He wasn't there. The room was black and the door was open, and everything had a strange blank look.

Downstairs, she poured herself a glass of milk from the refrigerator and then wandered through the rooms drinking the milk and switching on every light she came across. Soon all in the house were on, but it didn't seem to change things. When the motor in the refrigerator started up she jumped a little, half frightened for a second. Then she set down the glass of milk and walked very slowly and deliberately out of the house, with that feeling of loneliness prickling the back of her neck as she walked.

The way the music was pouring out, she couldn't identify the voices from Ansel's window. All she heard was words and phrases, and occasional laughter. She stopped at the Potters' window and peered in, but not a single light glimmered there, not even from the very back of the house. They couldn't be far, then. If they planned to be gone for any length of time they turned all the lamps on and sat up a cardboard silhouette of a man reading that was guaranteed to fool burglars. And they couldn't be in bed; it was no later than ten o'clock. She turned away from the window and looked out at the yard, hoping they might come walking up, but they didn't. The only thing left to do was to go on to Ansel's.

No one answered when she knocked. It was too noisy for them to hear her. She opened the screen and knocked once more on the inner door, hard, and then she heard Ansel say, "Wait! Did someone knock?"

"I didn't hear anyone," said Miss Lucy.

Joan knocked again, and Ansel said, "See!" She felt the doorknob twist beneath her hands; then Ansel was standing there, swaying slightly and smiling at her, leaning his cheek against the edge of the door. "Came back, did you," he said.

"What?"

"I saw you go."

"I don't—"

"But I didn't tell," he said, and then swung the door all the way open and threw back one arm to welcome her. "Look what *we* got!" he called to the others. *"Who* we got. See?"

Joan stepped inside and looked around her. The room was full; it looked as if someone had tipped the house endwise so that everyone had slid down to James's parlor. Now they sat in one smiling, rumpled cluster—the Potter sisters, the Pikes, Ansel, and James. When Ansel shouted at them they all turned toward Joan and waved, with their faces calm and friendly. The only one who seemed surprised was Simon. He stood up and said, "Joan!" but she frowned at him. "Hush," she said. The voices rose again, returning to whatever they'd been talking about before. Simon shouted, "What?"

"I said, *'Hush'!"* called Joan.

"Oh, *I* didn't tell. It was like I promised you, I didn't—"

The rest of his words were drowned out, but Joan understood his meaning. Nobody had told. Maybe they thought she'd just been to a movie, or off visiting. Maybe they knew that wherever she'd gone, she'd be back. And now they sat here, cheerful and in a party mood— but what was the party about? Just by looking, she couldn't tell. Miss Lucy and Miss Faye were making a silhouette of James—Miss Lucy holding a lamp up so that James winced in the light of it, and Miss Faye tracing the shadow of his wincing profile on a sheet of paper held against the wall. But that was something they always did; some instinct seemed to push them into making silhouettes at parties, and now everyone in the house had at least one silhouette of everyone else. Nor could she tell anything from Mr. Pike, who seemed to be a little tiddly from some wine he was drinking out of a measuring cup. He sat smiling placidly at something beyond Joan's range of vision, tapping one finger against the cup in time to a jazz version of "Stardust" that the radio was sawing out. And the person who confused her *most* was Mrs. Pike, sitting in a chair in the corner with her hands folded but her eyes alert to everything that was going on. "Fourteen!" she called out; she seemed to be counting the swallows Simon took from his own glass of wine. But her voice was lost among all the other voices, and Joan had to read her lips. She turned to Ansel, to see if he could explain all this. He had lain back on his couch now, like an emperor at a Roman festival, and when he saw her look his way he smiled and waved.

"Have a seat!" he shouted. He pointed vaguely to several chairs that were already occupied. "We're celebrating."

"Oh," Joan said. "Celebrating."

"Simon ran away."

"What?"

Simon smiled at her and nodded. "I went to Caraway on a bus," he said.

"Oh, Simon."

"I saw those gold earrings."

"But how did—"

"James and Mama came and got me. They made a special trip," he said. "We're drinking Miss Faye's cooking wine."

Joan felt behind her for a footstool and sat down on it. "Are you all *right?"* she asked.

"Sure I am."

"Oh, I wish I hadn't gone off and—"

"No, really, I'm all right," said Simon. "Look, they're letting me have wine. They put ice cubes in it to make it watery but I drink it fast before the ice can melt."

"That's nice," Joan said vaguely. She kept looking around at the others. Ansel leaned toward Joan with his own jelly glass of wine and said, *"Drink* up," and thrust it at her, and then lay down again. "Ansel had to find his own supper tonight," Simon told her. "He had one slice of garlic bologna, all dried out. James is going to cook him a steak tomorrow to make up for it."

Joan took a long swallow of cooking wine and looked over at James. He was swiveling his eyes toward the silhouette while he kept his profile straight ahead, so that he seemed cross-eyed. When he felt Joan looking at him he smiled and called something to her that she couldn't hear, and then Miss Faye said, "When you talk your nose moves up and down," and erased the line she had drawn for his nose and left a smudge there. Mr. Pike laughed. He clanged when he laughed; it puzzled Joan for a minute, and then she examined him more closely and found in his lap the elephant bell from Mrs. Pike's mantelpiece. "Why has he got that bell?" she asked Simon.

Simon shrugged, and Ansel answered for him. "He used it while hunting for Simon," he called. "Weird thing, ain't it? Such a funny shape it has. Everything Indians do is backwards, seems to me—"

"Fifteen!" Mrs. Pike said.

"India Indians, of course," said Ansel. "Not American. Hey, James."

Miss Faye's pencil had just hit the bottom of James's neck. She finished off with that same little bump at the base of it that sculptors put on marble busts, and then James stretched and turned toward Ansel.

"What," he said.

"Funny feeling in my feet, James."

James sighed and rose to go over to the couch. "Well, thank you, Miss Faye," he called over his shoulder.

"No trouble at all. Joan, dear, it's your turn."

"How about Simon?" asked Joan.

"They did me first," Simon told her. "I'm the guest of honor."

"Oh." She stood up and went over to the Potters, still carrying her glass of wine. "My hair's not combed," she told them.

"That's all right, we'll just smooth over that part on the paper. Will you have a seat?"

They sat her down firmly, both of them pressing on her shoulders. The lamp glared at her so brightly that it made a circular world that she sat in alone, facing Miss Lucy's steadily breathing bosom while Miss Faye, strange without gloves, skimmed the pencil around a suddenly too-big shadow of Joan. Outside the circle was the noise, and the beating music and the dark, faceless figures of the others. Their conversation seemed to be blurring together now.

"I had a cousin once who did *group* silhouettes," said Miss Faye. "I don't know how. It's a talent I never had—he could make everyone be doing something so like themselves, even in a silhouette of twenty people you could name each person present."

"That was Howard," Miss Lucy said.

"Howard Potter Laskin. I remember him well. If he was only here tonight, why, we could put him right to work. I wish I knew how he did it."

"Where is he now?" Miss Lucy asked.

"I don't know."

Joan looked at her shadow, staring almost sideways the way James had done. "There is a whole *gallery* of silhouettes in this house," she said suddenly.

"Quiet, dear, you've moved."

"Didn't I have this blouse on the last time? There was that same sticking-up frill around my neck."

"Yes," said Miss Faye. She sighed and her pencil moved briefly outside the shadow of the frill. "Simon had the same shirt, too," she said.

"How do you remember?"

"The collar's worn out. Little threads poking up."

Joan looked over at Simon: he nodded and held up the corner of his collar. "This is the shirt I ran away in," he called.

"Didn't you get dressed up to go?"

"You didn't do the laundry yet."

"Oh," said Joan, and she turned back to fit her head into the silhouette. Miss Faye started on the back of her hair, skimming past the shadows of stray wisps the way she had promised.

"The mornings after parties," she said, "Miss Lucy and I cut these out and mount them. Don't we, Lucy? We talk over the parties as we cut."

"I think we should take a picture," said Simon.

"A what?"

"A picture. A photograph. With a camera." He took a swallow of wine.

"Sixteen," said his mother, still counting.

"I *know*. James could take it when you're done with Joan there. Me in my shirt that I ran away in. Everybody else standing around."

"Cameras are all very well," Miss Faye said. "But who can't press a button? If Howard Potter Laskin was here—"

"Howard did *every*thing well," said Miss Lucy.

"I could take you and Miss Lucy drawing silhouettes," James called. He looked up from rubbing Ansel's feet. "Could Howard Potter Laskin do that?"

"Well, now—" Miss Faye said. She lowered her pencil and frowned into space a minute. "A silhouette of a silhouette? I don't know. But Howard could—"

"I'll get my camera, then," said James. He left Ansel's couch and crossed toward the darkroom, stepping carefully through the other people. But the minute he was gone, Miss Faye finished Joan's silhouette with two quick strokes, ending in a point on top of her head that wasn't really there.

"You weren't *supposed* to finish," Joan said. "How will he have you doing a silhouette if there's no more left to do?"

"Oh, now," said Miss Lucy. "People don't *get* photographed making silhouettes. We'll just sit down, I think—maybe on Ansel's couch, if he doesn't object."

They began gather up their pencils and paper. All over the room, people were getting ready for that camera. Simon had buttoned the top button of his shirt, so that he looked as if he would choke, and Ansel was sitting ramrod-straight with his numb feet on the coffee table in front of him. By the time James returned the whole room seemed tense and silent. Even the radio had been turned off. James said, "I don't hardly recognize you all," and everyone laughed a little and then got quiet again. "You're going to have to bunch up now," he said.

They moved closer in, heading toward Ansel who for once allowed someone else to sit on the couch. "Simon can sit on the floor," said James. "That would help. Miss Faye, can you move your silhouettes in?"

"Oh, I don't think—" said Miss Faye, but James cut her off as if he already knew what she would say.

"Sure you can," he said. "*Every*one gets photographed making silhouettes these days." And though Miss Faye smiled, to show she didn't believe him, she brought one of her silhouettes over and set it on the back of the couch against the wall. "That's better," he said. He was carrying his little box camera, and he held it in front of his stomach now and squinted into the viewfinder. "Almost," he said. "Joan, where are you? All I get is your foot."

Joan moved over, squeezing in against Simon on the floor. "Ouch," said Simon. "James, are you going to get in the picture?"

"Not while I'm taking it I'm not," said James.

"You should," Miss Lucy said. "You're the one that went and got him."

"No. I hate being photographed."

"Then what's the use?" Simon said. He looked around at the others. "*James* made that special trip—"

"I'll take it," said Joan. She stood up. "You show me how to aim it, James."

"How to—"

"No, Joan should be in it too," Simon said.

But Mr. Pike came to life suddenly and reached down to touch Simon's shoulder. "Can't have everything, boy," he said. "Come on and get in the picture, James. *Joan* didn't go nowhere; she don't mind."

"No, I don't," Joan told James. "Give it here."

"Well, all right."

He put it in her hands and then he showed her the button. "This is what you press," he told her. "It's not all that hard."

He went over to sit on the arm of the sofa, next to Ansel, and now even James looked self-conscious. When Joan peered at them through the view-finder she saw all of their faces made clear and tiny, with their smiles stretched tight and each person's hand clamped white around a glass of wine. Ansel's feet were bigger than anyone. He still had them propped up, and when Joan raised her head to glare at them he ducked a glance at her and said, "They hurt."

"They're in the way," Joan told him.

"They hurt."

"If you'd get the right size *shoes*—" said James.

Mr. Pike bent forward to stare at Ansel's feet; his elephant bell clanged again and Ansel said suddenly, breaking in on what James was saying, "I had a *cousin* engaged to a India Indian. I ever mention that?"

"No," said Joan. "Your feet, please, Ansel." She lowered her head and stared into the finder again, but Ansel showed no sign of moving his feet.

"I'd nearly forgotten about it," he said. "This particular Indian used to sing a lot. All the time long songs, India Indian songs, without no tune. He'd finish and we'd clap and say, 'Well, wasn't that—' when oops, there he'd go, on to the next line. Got so we were *afraid* to clap. On and on he'd go, on and on."

"Are you *sure* we shouldn't just sit in a chair?" asked Miss Lucy.

"Wednesday came and went," James said. "When will you remember your shots?"

In the finder of the camera Joan could see them moving, each person making his own set of motions. But the glass of the finder seemed to hold them there, like figures in a snowflurry paperweight who would still be in their set positions when the snow settled down again. She thought whole years could pass, they could be born and die, they could leave and return, they could marry or live out their separate lives alone, and nothing in this finder would change. They were going to stay this way, she and all the rest of them, not because of anyone else but because it was what they had chosen, what they would keep a strong tight hold of. James bent over Ansel; Mrs. Pike touched the top of Simon's head, and Mr. Pike sat smiling awkwardly into space. "It starts near the arches," said Ansel, "right about here . . ."

"Be still," said Joan.

She kept her head down and stared at the camera, smiling as if it were she herself being photographed. The others smiled back, each person motionless, each clutching separately his glass of wine.

IF MORNING
EVER COMES

1

WHEN BEN JOE HAWKES left home he gave his sister Susannah one used guitar, six shelves of *National Geographic*, a battered microscope, and a foot-high hourglass. All of these things he began to miss as soon as he hit New York. He considered writing home and asking for them— Susannah probably hadn't even listened when he gave them to her— but he figured she might laugh at him. His family was the kind that thought only children during their first summer at Scout camp should miss anything. So he kept quiet about what he missed and just dropped Susannah a postcard, with a picture on it of the UN building by night, asking if she had learned to play the guitar yet. And six weeks later he got a card back, but not the picture kind, postmarked Sandhill, N.C., and badly rained-on. He turned the card over and learned, from Susannah's jet-black, jerky script, that she had just changed to a job with the Sandhill School Library and was getting rich and could have her hair done every week now. She signed it "So long—S," and then there was a P.S. saying she was going to start learning to play the guitar tomorrow. Ben Joe read this over two or three times, although what she had said was perfectly clear: she had only just now remembered that the guitar existed. Probably she had got up in the midst of doing something else to drag it from his closet and twang the slack strings, but having discovered that she wasn't born knowing how to play and might have to work at it awhile she had dropped it again and drifted on to something else that came to mind. Ben Joe thought about starting up a whole *string* of cards—asking on the next one, for instance, whether the hourglass was still keeping time okay—until she got snappy with him and packed everything up and sent it to New York. But Susannah was flighty, like almost all his sisters, and rarely finished anything she started reading even if it was as short as a postcard; he didn't think she would notice that he might be missing something. So he stopped the postcards and just wrote his regular letters after that, addressed to the family as a whole, asking about the health of his mother and all his sisters and saying he thought of them often.

By then it was November. He had left home late in August, just after his twenty-fifth birthday, to start law school at Columbia, and although he was doing well, even with three years of empty space behind him since college, he didn't like Columbia. On campus the wind up from the river cut clean through him no matter what he wore, and his classmates were all quick and sleek and left him nothing to say to them. They looked like the men who modeled Italian wool jackets in men's magazines; he plodded along beside them, thin and shivering, and tried to think about warm things. Nor did he like law; it was all memory work. The only reason he had chosen it was that it was at least practical, whereas the other ideas he had had were not, and practicality was a good thing when you headed up a family of six women. So all through September, October, and most of November he sat through Columbia's law classes and jiggled one foot across his knee and peeled his fingernails off.

On this particular Thursday the wind was so cold that Ben Joe became personally angry at it. He stepped out of the law building, pulling his collar up over his ears, and the wind suddenly hit him full in the face and left him gasping. That decided him; he changed direction and headed toward the apartment. Lately he had taken to spending the really cold days in bed with a murder mystery, and he was beginning to think he should have done that this morning.

On Broadway he stayed close to the buildings, hoping that there would be less wind there. He passed the brass nameplate on one of the concrete walls and for an instant saw his face reflected there, made yellow by the brass, with his mouth open and his jaw clenched and his teeth gnashed against the cold. If it had been any other day he would have smiled, and maybe stopped to peer into the brass until the passers-by wondered what he was doing, but not today. Today he only hunched his gray topcoat around him more securely and kept going.

His apartment was five blocks from the campus, in a tiny dark old building with unbelievably high, sculptured ceilings. Opening the front door of it took all the strength he had. And all the way up the three flights of stairs he could smell what every family had eaten for the last day and a half—mainly bacon and burnt beans, he gathered. Ordinarily the smells made him feel a little sick, but today they seemed warm and comforting. He climbed more quickly, making each wooden step creak beneath his feet. By the time he was at his own door and digging through his pockets for the keys he was whistling under his breath, even though his face was stiff with cold.

"That you?" his roommate called from the kitchen.

"It's me."

He took the key out of the door and slammed the door shut behind him. Inside it was almost as cold as it was in the street; all it needed was the wind. The living room was taller than it was wide, and very dark, with high-backed stuffed furniture and long, narrow windows that rattled when a gust of wind blew. The mantel and the coffee tables were bare and dusty. There were none of the flower pots and photographs and china doodads that he was used to from the houseful of women in which he had been raised, but a huge clutter of other objects lay around—newspapers, tossed-off jackets, textbooks, playing cards. In the middle of the dark wooden floor was a square scatter rug colored like a chessboard, and ridiculously tiny plastic chess pieces sat upon it in a middle-of-the-game confusion.

Ben Joe stripped his topcoat and his suit jacket off and threw them onto an easy chair. He untied his tie and stuffed it into the pocket of the jacket. From the daybed he picked up a crazy quilt from home and began swaddling himself in it, covering even his head and huddling himself tightly inside it.

"For Pete's sake," his roommate said from the kitchen doorway.

"Well, I'm cold."

He backed up to the daybed and sat down. The bed was a wide one; he worked himself back until he was leaning against the wall and his legs were folded Indian fashion in front of him, and then he frowned.

"Forgot to take off my shoes," he said.

He patiently undid the quilt and untied his shoes. They fell to the floor with two dull thuds. With his cold feet pressed beneath the warmth of his legs, he reached again for the quilt and began pulling it around him.

"Hey, Jeremy," he said, "grab this corner, will you?"

His roommate left the doorway and came over, carrying a cup of coffee in one hand. "I've never seen the like," he said. "You wait till it's really winter. Which one?"

"The one in my left hand. There. Thanks."

He leaned back against the wall again and Jeremy drifted over to the window, slurping up his coffee as he went. He was younger than Ben Joe—twenty-one at the most, and an undergraduate—but Ben Joe liked him better than most of the other people he had met here. Maybe because he didn't have that sleek look either. He was from Maine, and wore sneakers and dungarees and dirty red Brewster jackets to class. His hair was so black it was startling; it gave him a wild look even when he smiled.

"I thought you had *two* classes on Thursdays," Jeremy said.

"I did. But I only went to the one. I got cold."

"Oh, pooh." He sat down on the edge of the window sill and swung one sneaker back and forth. "In Maine," he said, "we'd be swimming in this weather."

"In Sandhill we'd be sending for federal aid."

"Oh, now, don't you give me that."

He stood up and began tugging at the window. It screeched open; a gust of wind blew the newspaper's society section into Ben Joe's lap.

"Will you shut that *window!*" Ben Joe said.

"In a minute, in a minute. I'm trying to see what the thermometer says. Thirty-four. Thirty-four! Not even freezing."

"It's the wind," Ben Joe said.

The window slid shut again, leaving the apartment suddenly silent.

"Want to walk with me to the drugstore, Ben Joe?"

"Not me."

"I got to get a toothbrush."

"Nope."

Jeremy sighed and headed for the bedroom, twirling his empty coffee cup by the handle.

"Last night," he said as he walked, "I figured out the prettiest-sounding word in the English language. I did. And now I can't remember it."

"Hmm," Ben Joe said. He reached behind him to flick on the wall switch and smoothed out the newspaper in his lap. It was last Sunday's, but he hadn't got desperate enough to read the society section till now. It crackled dully on his knees, looking gray and smudgy under the flat light from the ceiling.

"I mean," Jeremy said from the bedroom, "usually you can think of a word that's *one* of the prettiest-sounding. But no, sir, this was *the* word. *Really* the word. I meant to tell this comp professor about it, that I see in the cafeteria. And then I woke up this morning and it was gone. It had an *s* in it, I think. An *s*."

"*That* should narrow it down," Ben Joe said. He grinned and tipped his head back so that it was resting against the wall.

"You want a date tonight, Ben Joe?"

"Who with?"

"This real cute freshman, has red hair and brown eyes, which is my favorite combination, and comes from, um—"

"Too young."

He opened the society section and folded it back, letting his arms emerge partway from the blanket.

"Thank you anyway," he called as an afterthought.

"Oh, that's okay." Jeremy was standing in the doorway now, with one end of a pillow in his teeth. "I've decided to clean the bedroom," he said. The words came out muffled but still intelligible. "I haven't changed my sheets in three weeks." He shook out a pillowcase, held it below the pillow, and opened his mouth to let the pillow drop into the case. Then he tossed the pillow toward his bed and vanished from sight again.

Ben Joe started reading the society section, holding it upside-down in front of him. He had started learning to read when he was three, but his parents wanted him to wait until school age; they made him stand facing them when they read him bedtime stories, so that the book was turned the wrong way around. It wasn't until too late that they realized he was reading upside-down. Usually he read the right way now unless he was bored, and then upside-down words came to his mind more clearly. He held the newspaper at arm's length and frowned, studying an upside-down description of a golden anniversary where the couple had had another wedding performed all over again.

"What's this mess of lima beans doing on the floor of the closet?" Jeremy called.

"Oh, leave them. I'll take care of them."

"I know, but what are they *doing* there?"

"I forget. Hey, Jeremy, if you were having your golden anniversary would you have another wedding performed all over again?"

"Hell, no. I wouldn't have the first one."

On the next page there were ads to run through, detailed little line drawings of silver patterns and china patterns and ring sets. He yawned and then set to picking out a ring set, ending up with a large, oddly shaped diamond and a wedding band that was fine except for a line of dots at each edge that bothered him. Then he chose a silver pattern and a very expensive china pattern, platinum-rimmed, but he was already beginning to be tired of the game and abruptly he turned the paper right-side up, picked out a bride for himself that he considered most likely to meet all his requirements, and, with that finished, pushed the society news to the floor and stood up.

"Where's last Sunday's crossword?" he called.

"I already did it."

"You did it the week before, too."

"Well, I waited till *Wednesday*, for God's sake."

Ben Joe went into the bedroom. Jeremy was sitting on the floor with one of the bureau drawers beside him; he was slowly going through a stack of postcards and throwing some out but keeping most of them. The rest of the room was in chaos; Ben Joe's bed was unmade, Jeremy's was made but covered with the things he had decided to throw out, and there was a heap of dirty sheets on the floor between the two beds.

"Worse than it was before," Ben Joe said.

"I know. That's the trouble with cleaning up."

Ben Joe leaned his elbows on the dresser and looked into the mirror with his chin in his hands. The mirror was wavy and speckled, but he could at least recognize himself: his thin, flat-planed face, which almost never needed shaving and took on a sort of yellow look in the wintertime; his level gray eyes, so narrow that they looked as if he were constantly suspecting people; and his hair, dark yellow and hanging in shocks over his forehead. It was getting shaggy at the back and sides; he looked like an orphan. And walked like one, letting his shoulders hitch forward and burying his hands deeply in his pockets so that his arms could remain stiff and his elbows could dig into his sides. One of his sisters had once told him, meaning it kindly, that he was homely, all right, but *trustworthy*-looking; if people could do what they liked to strangers on the street, they would stop him and reach up to pat the top of his head. He sighed and straightened up and began moving around the room, kicking dust balls with his stockinged feet.

"I thought you were going out for a toothbrush," he said to Jeremy.

"I am. Soon as I finish this drawer. A red one."

"A red what?"

"*Tooth*brush." Jeremy threw a stack of postcards in the direction of the wastebasket. "I always buy a red toothbrush for the wintertime."

"Oh." Ben Joe sat down on the edge of his bed and frowned at the sheets on the floor. After a minute he said, "You ever seen one of those toothbrushes with a bird on the end? The kind that gives a soft little whistle when you blow on it?"

"Sure. That's for kids, to make them want to brush their teeth."

"Well, I know it." He lay back crosswise on the bed and stared at the ceiling. "My sister had one of those once," he said. "My older sister, Joanne. She's away now. But she had a pink toothbrush with a bird on the end, and it wasn't when she was a little girl, either. It was when she was in high school and had taken to wearing red dresses and gold hoop earrings and flinging that black hair of hers around. One night I was writing this philosophy paper. I came out of my room for a drink of water and I felt like hell—my mind all confused and tired but still popping off like a machine gun. And out of the bathroom just then came Joanne, not in red but in a little quilty white bathrobe, and sort of dreamily blowing the bird on her toothbrush. She didn't see me. But it was so damned *comforting*. I went to bed and slept like a rock, no more machine guns in my head."

He lay quiet for a minute, following the sculptured molding around the ceiling with his eyes.

"What was I saying?"

"About toothbrushes."

"Oh. Well, that was all."

He turned and rose up on one elbow to see what Jeremy was doing. Jeremy was reading all the postcards he had saved.

"Hey, Ben Joe," he said.

"Hmm."

"You want to hear something funny?"

"What?"

"It's from this buddy of mine that goes to college out west, with a picture of this gorge, real deep down with a river at the bottom. Says, 'This gorge is habit-forming. Threw a bowling ball down it to hear how it sounded and it sounded so good I moved on to bigger and better things and last night me and some buddies threw a piano down it.' A *piano*. What do you guess it looked like when it hit? Ben Joe?"

Ben Joe looked up.

"Ah, you're not listening," said Jeremy. He put the postcard back in the drawer and moved on to the next one.

Ben Joe sat up, running his fingers through his hair. "What time is it?" he asked.

"I don't know. Eleven or so."

He reached over and pulled open the top drawer of his own bureau. At the right was a stack of letters; he pulled the top one out, looked at it to make sure it had been signed by his sister Jenny (she was the official family letter writer), and then lay back down, holding the letter over his head, right-side up, to read it:

Dear Ben Joe:

We received yours of the 12th. Yes, of course we are well. I don't know why you keep asking us, since you know as well as we do that the last time any of us was in the hospital was five years ago when Susannah had all four wisdom teeth pulled at once. Mama says to tell you you worry too much. We are getting along beautifully & hope you are too.

Financially things are going smoothly. Next month both of the twins are getting raises at the bank, but Lisa is getting $6 more a month than Jane, which make family relationships kind of tense. Tessie is taking drawing lessons after school now for $2 a lesson, which I think we can afford, & the only extra expense this month has been the eaves pipe falling down from the roof outside Tessie's & my window due to Tessie's standing on it. Tessie didn't, tho. Fall, I mean. I'll never know why.

I wish you would write a letter to the family suggesting that we go back to a policy of my doing the grocery shopping. Specially since it was me you left in charge of the money. Gram has been doing it lately & the results are disaster. She gets anything she feels like, minced clams & pickled artichoke hearts & pig's feet & when I ask where are the meat & potatoes she says it's time we had a little change around here. She's ruining us.

Enclosed is next month's check for your expenses, etc. I hope you will remember to send a receipt this time as it makes my bookkeeping neater.

Sincerely,

Enc.   Jennifer.

Ben Joe folded the letter and sat up again. "I wish someone besides Jenny would do the letter writing in my family," he said.

"Why?"

"I don't know." He began walking around the room with his hands in his pockets. "You never know what's going *on*, exactly. Just about the dratted eavespipes and stuff."

"The what?" Jeremy sat back and stared, and when Ben Joe didn't answer, he said, "Oh, now, are you getting started on your family again? What you worried about?"

Ben Joe stopped in front of the window and looked out. There was a venetian blind between him and the outdoors; the buildings across from him were divided into dozens of horizontal strips.

"Someone's lost a red balloon," he said. "They must've lost it out a window, it's flying so high."

"Maybe it's a gas balloon."

"Maybe. What bothers me is, sometimes I think my family doesn't know *when* to get upset—the most amazing things happen and they forget to even tell me. I try to keep quiet, but all the time I'm thinking, 'I wonder what's going on back there. I wonder if maybe I shouldn't just chuck everything and go on back and see for myself, set my mind at rest if nothing . . .' "

He was sitting on Jeremy's bed now, and reaching for the phone.

"You going to call home?" Jeremy asked.

"I reckon."

"You want me to get out?"

"Nah, that's all right— Operator, I want Sandhill, North Carolina, two four oh—"

"You got a Southern accent," she said. She was snappy and cross, with a New York twang to her voice. "I can't tell if you said 'four' or 'five'; you don't—"

"I haven't got one, either. I said 'two, four, oh—' "

"Yes you do. You said 'Ah.' 'Ah haven't got—' "

"I did not. My mother's a Northerner, even."

"Number, please."

"Two four oh, six seven five four. If I had an accent I'd say 'foh.' No 'r.' But I said the 'r.' "

"And *your* number, please."

"Academy four, six five five nine."

"Station to station?"

"Yes'm."

The telephone had a familiar plastic smell; the receiver was warm and already a little damp in his hand. He hated using the telephone. The thought of speaking to someone, and listening to him, without seeing him was as panicky as not being able to breathe. How could he tell anything about a person if he couldn't see him? Sometimes he thought something must be wrong with his ears; what he heard told him almost nothing. And usually he read too much harshness into a voice. He could hang up a telephone receiver and feel hurt and bewildered for days and then find out, weeks later when he asked what he had done to annoy them, that they were just talking above the noise from a TV set. So now, to make it easier for himself, he tried to picture exactly what was going on at the other end. He pictured the house in Sandhill at eleven o'clock on a Thursday morning, with the autumn sun shining palely through the long bay windows in the living room. His sisters would all be at work, he guessed, except for Tessie, who was still in grade school. Or was it her lunch hour? No, too early. That left only his mother, and maybe even she would be gone; she worked part time at a book store. The phone rang twice. He waited, tensed against the pillows.

"Hello?" his mother said. He could tell her from his sisters, although their voices were almost the same, by that way she had of seeming to expect the worst when she answered the telephone.

"Hi," he said.

"I beg your pardon?"

"It's me. Ben Joe."

"Ben Joe! What's wrong?"

"Nothing's wrong. I called to see how you were."

"Didn't you get our last letter?"

"Well, yes. I guess I did. The one about the eavespipe falling down?"

"I think that was it. Did you get it?"

"*Yes,* I got it."

"Oh. I thought maybe you were worried because you hadn't heard from us."

"No, I heard."

"Well, that's nice."

Ben Joe waited, frowning into the receiver, twining the coils of the telephone cord around his index finger. He tried desperately to picture what she looked like right now, but all he came up with was her hair, dust-colored with the curls at the side of her face pressed flat by the receiver. That was no help. Give him anything—eyes, mouth, just a stretch of cheek, even—and he could tell something, but not *hair,* for goodness' sake. He tried again.

"Well," he said, "how *is* everyone?"

"Oh, fine."

"That's good. I'm glad to hear it."

"It's too bad you called while the girls were away. Joanne's the only one here now. They'd have liked to talk to you."

"Susannah, you mean."

"What?"

"You mean, *Susannah's* the only one here."

"No, Susannah's switched to a full-time job now. I thought Jenny told you. She's working at the school library. I don't know why that should be tiring, but apparently it is. She comes home all cross and snappy, and last night she had a date with the Lowry boy and ended up shoving his face into a cone of buttered popcorn at the Royal Crown theater. I forget what movie they were showing."

"Never mind," said Ben Joe. "What I'm asking is, *who* is it that's the only one home but you?"

"Joanne. I told you."

"Joanne?"

"Well, yes."

"Mom," Ben Joe said, "*Joanne's* been gone for seven *years.*"

"Oh. I thought Jenny wrote you about that."

"Wrote me about *what?*" He was up off the bed now; Jeremy looked over at him curiously.

"I think maybe you *didn't* get our last letter," his mother said. "Come to think of it, it was the *next*-to-the-last letter about the eaves pipe falling down. The last one should get there today or so. Have you gotten today's mail yet?"

"No."

"Why, what time is it?"

"Mom," Ben Joe said, "is Joanne home or isn't she?"

"*Yes*, she's home."

"Well, then, why? And when did she get there? Why didn't you—"

"She left," his mother said vaguely.

"Just now? Didn't she know I was on the phone?"

"No, I mean she left Kansas."

"Obviously she left."

"She took the baby and ran away from her husband."

"*What?*"

Ben Joe sat down again on the edge of Jeremy's bed. Jeremy took a sidelong glance at him and then got up and left the room.

"Ben Joe, is there a bad connection on your end? Can't you hear me?"

"I can hear you."

"Well, don't be so dramatic then. What's done *is* done, and it's none of our affair."

Ben Joe closed his eyes, briefly; he wondered how many times in his life he had heard his mother say that.

"Are you there, Ben Joe?"

"Yes'm. How is she?"

"Oh, fine. And the baby's a darling. Very well behaved."

"Has she changed much? Joanne, I mean. What's she like now?"

"Oh, the same as ever."

"Can I talk to her?"

"She's asleep. She stayed up last night to watch the late show."

Ben Joe took a breath, hesitated, and then said, "I'm coming home, Mom."

"Ben Joe—"

"It won't hurt to cut a few classes. I want to just see how everything is."

"Everything's *fine*."

"I know, but I want to set my mind at rest. I've been worrying."

"You're always worrying."

"I'll see you tomorrow, Mom."

"Ben *Joe*—"

Ben Joe hung up, neatly and quietly. There was that giddy feeling in his head that always came from talking for any period of time with his mother, or even sometimes with his sisters; he felt confused and uncertain, as if he and his family were a set of square dancers coming to clap the palms of their hands to each others', only their hands missed by inches and encountered nothing. It was only after he had gone over the conversation in his mind, arranging it in a logical order and trying to convince himself that everything was really all right, that he felt better. He stepped to the door and said, "Jeremy?"

"Yeah, Ben Joe." Jeremy came in, looking quickly at Ben Joe's face. "Trouble?"

"I'm going home for a few days. If the university calls, you tell them I'll be back, will you?"

"Sure."

"I'll take the night train. Be there by morning." He pulled his suitcase out from under the bed and then sat down, staring at it blankly.

"You see what I mean," he said. He spread his arms helplessly, looking up at Jeremy, who was leaning against the wall with his hands in the pockets of his dungarees and his face worried. "You get these cheerful little financial statements, and meanwhile what's going on? Joanne's run away from her husband and come home, after seven years of only phone calls and letters from her—"

"Joanne," Jeremy said. "She the one with the red dress and bangles?"

"Yep. Her. On the way out to get your toothbrush, will you pick up today's mail? I bet they tell about it in a P.S., that's what."

"You going to try and make her go back to her husband?"

"No, just going to see her."

"Well, I'll go get the mail," said Jeremy.

"Okay."

Ben Joe crossed back to his bureau. The drawer was still open; he pulled out a large leather jewelry box and flipped the lid up. Inside were all the odds and ends that he never knew what to do with. He searched through two-cent postage stamps and Canadian nickels and old scraps of addresses and worn-out snapshots and eventually he came across the torn-off flap of an envelope with train times scrawled across it. He picked out the night train to North Carolina. Then, whispering the time to himself as he walked, he went to his closet to choose the clothes he would wear home.

2

His car on the train was only half full; rushing through the darkness it made a hollow, rattling sound. It was cramped and peeling inside, with dirty plush seats and a painted tin roof. At the front hung a huge black-and-white photograph of some people on a beach in Florida, to show that this was the southbound train. Maybe once the photograph had been shiny and exciting, so that passengers gazing at it had counted the hours until they could see the real thing. But now the plastic sheet over it had grown scratched and dull, and the people in it—dozens of tiny people in homely old bathing suits, caught forever in the act of skipping hand in hand toward gray waves or sitting close together under gray-and-white umbrellas—seemed as sad and silent as the flat, still palm trees above them. For a while Ben Joe gave himself up to just staring at it, until the strange feeling it gave him was gone and it was only a photograph again. Then he turned away and looked at the people who shared this car with him.

Mostly they were upright, energetic Negro housewives, sitting like wide shade trees over their clusters of children. Around their feet were diaper bags and paper sacks and picnic baskets; above their heads, in the baggage racks, was an abundance of feathered hats and woolen scarves and sturdy, dark-colored coats. Like Ben Joe, who had a sheepskin-lined jacket folded across his lap, they had come prepared for the time when the hot, stuffy car would suddenly turn too cold for sleeping. They clucked to their children constantly and passed them hot lemonade and pieces of Kleenex, dug up from the bottoms of grocery sacks whenever they heard someone sniff, whether it was their own child or not.

"Here your pacifier, Bertie."

"You let Sadie at the window now; you been at it a sufficient time."

A thin blond man in a pea jacket passed through, carrying a box of toys with "80 cts" printed on it in purple nail polish. He came even with the children just across the aisle from Ben Joe and from the box he pulled out a toy—a rubber donkey with a cord and squeeze-bulb attached to it. The children reached for it, their hands like four little black spiders.

"Want it?" the man asked.

The children looked at their mother. She was a comfortable, smiling woman sitting in the seat ahead of them with a friend. When she heard the man's voice she turned and looked at the children and smiled more broadly, and then frowned and gently shook her head.

"Watch," the man said.

He pressed the bulb and the donkey bucked, tossed his head, kicked up his heels. Then the little rubber knees buckled in the wrong places and the donkey was lying down in the man's hand, limp and ridiculous-looking.

"Only eighty cents," the man said.

The children watched, round-eyed. With one hand the little girl began stroking the back of her mother's head, patting the curls of her hair with soft, tiny pats.

"How much you say?" the mother asked. She turned only halfway, so that she seemed to be asking the woman beside her.

"Eighty cents, ma'am. Eighty little pieces of copper."

"*No* sir," the mother said. She turned to the children and said, "No sir. You wait, chirren, we'll get us something in Efram. In Efram, we'll see."

"Eighty cents," the man said.

"No sir." She reached out to straighten the collar of the smaller child, the girl, and then gave her a soft pat on the shoulder and smiled at her.

"How about you?" the man said to Ben Joe.

"No."

"No kiddies at home?"

"No."

"Ah, well."

The man moved on. At the back of the car it began to be noisier; that was where the men sat. Some of them were apparently the women's husbands, and others—the younger, more carelessly dressed ones, slouching in their seats and tipping hip flasks—belonged to no one. They offered swigs to the married men now and their conversation became gayer and louder. Up front, the women clicked their tongues at each other.

"Lemuel Barnes, I coming back there after you if you don't hush!" one called.

"You watch it now, you men, you watch it!"

That was the woman ahead of Ben Joe, a young, plump woman with a baby whose head rested on its mother's shoulder like a little brown mushroom button. She was sitting alone, but she had been talking steadily ever since she boarded the train, calling to her husband at the rear and soothing her baby and carrying on conversations with the other women passengers. Now she stood up and faced the rear, with the baby still over her shoulder, and shouted in a piercing voice:

"You all going to wake the baby, Brandon, you hear? Going to wake up Clara Sue. You want me come back and check on you?"

She started into the aisle, obviously not meaning to go through with it, and stopped when Brandon shouted back, "Aw, Matilda, this Jackie boy the one. *He* stirring all the trouble up."

The other women chuckled.

"That Jackie, he become a pest afore we even got out of the station."

"Brought him *two* bottles. Say no one bottle'd do him."

"Need a wife to keep him still, that boy."

"*Hoo*, Lord."

Matilda smiled down at them and sat down slowly. "Going to make that Brandon come up *here* he don't behave," she said loudly to the window. "I *mean* it, now."

Ben Joe tried smiling at the children across the aisle, stretching his mouth farther than it wanted to go, but the children stared soberly back at him with little worried frowns. Ahead of them, their mother opened a paper sack and handed back two pieces of fried chicken. The children accepted them automatically, their eyes still fixed on Ben Joe.

"When I get home," their mother said to the woman beside her, "I going to have me a mess of collard greens."

"You got you a good idea there," Matilda called.

The woman turned back and nodded gravely. "They don't feed you right in New York," she said. "Don't know how a person keep himself alive, in New York."

"Ain't *that* the truth."

They were quiet a minute, picturing home. For a minute Ben Joe pictured it with them, knowing almost for a certainty exactly what their homes were like. Who could be that definite about where *he* came from? A hundred years ago, maybe, you could look at a Carolina white man and know what he would have for supper that night, in what kind of house and with what sort of family sitting around him. But not any more—not in his case, at least. He felt suddenly pale and plain, going back to a big pale frame house that no one could tell was his. He looked at his reflection in the black windowpane and frowned, seeing only the flat planes of his cheeks and the worried hollows of his eyes.

"The way they does their chicken in New York," called Matilda, "they puts it in the oven stark nekkid and let it lay awhile. I *seen* it done that way. With a cut-up *frying* chicken I seen it."

"That's so, I know. That's so."

"Ticket, please."

Ben Joe looked up at the conductor, standing stolidly beside him and smiling down over a huge stomach. He handed him his ticket, already a little frayed, and the conductor tore off one section of it.

"Won't have to change," he said. He gave the rest of the ticket back and swayed on to the next passenger.

Someone sat down beside him, so suddenly that Ben Joe was almost frightened for a minute by the jounce in the springs. He turned from the window and found himself no more than three inches from the pointy nose of a curly-haired boy, who was leaning so closely toward him in order to see his face that he was practically lying on his side against Ben Joe.

"*Pardon* me," the boy said. He sat up straight again, folded his coat in his lap, and stared ahead of him at Matilda's baby.

Ben Joe settled back more firmly on his side of the seat and examined the boy's face. He would judge him to be about fifteen, but a New York fifteen; he was very self-assured and his face, except for that one moment of inquisitiveness, was tightly closed and smooth. When he became aware of Ben Joe's stare, he turned toward him again and said, explaining himself, "Just wanted to see what you looked like. See you didn't talk a lot or weren't drunk or nothing."

"I don't talk and I'm not drunk," Ben Joe snapped.

"Okay, okay. But I was sitting with this old man, see, and he was talking all the time. Made me nervous. *All* these guys make me nervous."

"That's *your* problem," Ben Joe said.

"The old man's dying."

Ben Joe looked around, alarmed. "Which one?" he asked.

"White fellow, sitting way back. Can't see him from here."

"Why didn't you tell me before? What—"

"*Relax*. He's only dying slowly, of old age."

"But—"

"He's *okay*, see."

Ben Joe sat back and stared out the window. The rushing sound of the train and the deep blackness outside made everything seem dreamy and unreal. It was hard to believe that the train was going anywhere at all; it was only standing still and swaying slightly, against a moving screen of darkness and the occasional pinpoints of lights. He told himself that he was finally going home, after all that worrying about his family and wanting desperately to see them again. He told himself what was even more real than that: that when he got there he would immediately feel sad and confused again, the way he always did. But no, Joanne was back. Joanne could change things; just by smiling that smile of hers she could make everything seem safe and in its right place. He closed his eyes, picturing home. He pictured his house as another kind of train, lighted also, floating through darkness. But with the sound of his own train in his ears he couldn't hear their voices, he stood outside his family's windows and watched their movements without hearing a single sound.

His mother would be moving rapidly around the house, pursing her lips tight and flouncing her hair because Ben Joe *couldn't* come home, she wouldn't have it, and then going off to put clean sheets on his bed. His grandmother would be standing on a counter in the kitchen to see what Ben Joe might like from her special private stock of food on the top shelf. And in the ruffly, perfumed closed circles of their worlds, his sisters would hear Ben Joe was returning and then forget again until his return was an actuality and they could get briefly excited over it. Joanne would laugh. She would look at her feet, propped bare on their father's leather hassock, and laugh easily for no reason at all.

(Only would she? It was seven years now since he'd seen Joanne; why couldn't he ever realize the happening of a thing? Surely she'd be different now—calmer and more even-tempered. Or did she wear a low-necked, swinging red dress when she took the baby for a stroll? And toss her hair and flash that teasing smile when she ironed her husband's shirt for him?)

"Plate of okra!" Matilda shouted. "That's what *my* mind fixed on!"

"Be right good. I declare if it wouldn't be."

Ben Joe reached into his shirt pocket. From behind a crumpled pack of cigarettes and an old lighter of his mother's he pulled out this morning's letter, already dingy at the creases. He held it up under the tiny bulb that was supposed to be a reading lamp and read, once more:

Dear Ben Joe:

We received yours of the 21st & are glad to hear you are well. It is too bad that the Asian flu shots gave you Asian flu. Also we are sorry to hear that you are cold.

The big news of course is that Joanne is home. She left her husband altho it's not clear why and of course the first thing Mama asked was was he unfaithful, they all are, & Joanne just laughed at her. The baby is as cute as she can be & is going to be spoiled rotten.

Tessie is going to have to have braces, which will be quite an expense. Gram is going to knit you a sweater for the cold but has forgotten the measurement from the tip of your shoulder to your wrist & would like you to tell her. Also what is your favorite color & if it's still purple forget it, because whenever she knits you a purple sweater she gets to seeing polka dots in front of her eyes before she goes to bed at night.

Ben Joe, you did not write telling Gram not to shop any more. Last night we had crabmeat and black olives in our Monday-night casserole. She also thinks I am not handling the money right & so yesterday she went over the bank books and decided the bank had credited us with $112 too much so she quick withdrew it and put it in another bank before they could find out. I had to go & change banks back again this noon.

Let us hear from you & don't worry.

Sincerely,
Jennifer.

Ben Joe put the letter back in his shirt pocket. He pulled the lever under the arm of his chair and pushed against the back of the seat to make it slant more. There was no point in staying awake worrying about things.

Someone sat down in the curly-haired boy's lap. The boy awoke with a start and said, "Hey! What you—" and began fighting, flailing his arms out and heaving his body and hitting mainly Ben Joe. Whoever sat in the boy's lap was big and solid and quiet, in a heavy tweed overcoat, calmly tipping a bottle to his mouth.

"*Brandon!*" Matilda shrieked. She stood up and, with one hand still holding the baby to her shoulder, reached out and grabbed a handful of Brandon's hair and shook him by it, hard. "You no-count you, Brandon—"

"I'm just *set*ting, Matilda," said Brandon.

"You setting on some*body*, Brandon."

Brandon turned around and looked beneath him.

"Oh, hey," he said.

"You are *sitting* on me," said the boy. He was breathing hard, and looked as if he might start crying.

"I surely am sorry, sir. I didn't see you atall, sir, I come to say hey to this yellow-haired gentleman—"

"Get yourself *offen* him, Brandon."

Brandon rose, confused, and bent over Ben Joe's rumpled seatmate. "I surely do hope I didn't hurt you none," he said. "I surely am sorry. I surely am."

"*Forget* it," the boy said. He straightened his jacket and then settled down further in his seat and closed his eyes, determinedly.

"Aren't you *ashamed* of yourself, Brandon."

"Yes'm."

"He ain't *never* like this," she said to Ben Joe. "It's that Jackie egg him on. Brandon has always been a real pillar to me, a real— Come up here and set, Brandon."

"Yes'm, just a minute. I want to speak some with this *yellow-haired*—"

He sat down heavily on the arm of Ben Joe's seat, but taking care not to touch the boy, and leaned across to look at Ben Joe.

"Believe you Ben Joe Hawkes," he said. He switched the bottle to his left hand and shook Ben Joe's hand several times, up and down. His breath smelled of gin, but other than his first mistake he didn't act like a drunken man. His face was sharp and alert, and although he seemed very young there were the beginnings of lines at each corner of his mouth, downward-pulling lines that made him look as if he were in pain. "I'm Brandon Hayes. This here my wife, Matilda. Matilda, this Dr. Hawkes's boy. Dr. *Phillip* Hawkes—him."

"That so?" Matilda said. She turned to Ben Joe, still uncertain, and when Ben Joe nodded, she looked relieved. "Looks like you know a *little*, Brandon, I will say. I remember about him having a boy, though I ain't met you ever." She switched the baby to her other shoulder and sat down again, sideways, so that she could see them over the back of the seat. "Your daddy fixed Brandon here's leg," she said. "Was broke in two places, back when he a boy and me a girl in the same Sunday school class with him. I remember."

"It's true," Brandon said. He settled down more comfortably on the arm of the chair. "Way I saw you, you were in the office with him, wanting him to come home for supper. You mustn't of been but twelve or so but I remembered. I good at faces, yes sir. Been eight years since I even *seen* Sandhill, but there's many I remember though they mightn't remember me. How your daddy now?"

"Well . . ." Ben Joe said, startled. "He, uh, he's dead. Died some six years back."

Brandon looked down at his knees and shook his head, silently. His wife made a sad little cooing sound.

"I do say," Brandon said finally. "Well, I do say. I surely am sorry to hear it. We been gone so long, they don't write the news like they should . . . I surely am sorry."

"How he go?" Matilda asked.

"Heart attack."

"Law, law." She shook her head too, echoing Brandon. "Well, I know it was a dignified passing. Wan't it?"

Ben Joe, taken off guard, didn't answer.

"Oh, I sure it was *very* dignified, Matilda," Brandon said soothingly.

In the cramped space between the wall and the curly-haired boy, Ben Joe carefully crossed his foot over his knee and twisted one shoelace, staring down at it.

"*Well*, now," said Matilda, suddenly becoming very brisk. "How about your mama?"

"Oh, she's fine."

"And there more of you, ain't there? A passle of sisters? I recollect that. How they?"

"Oh, they're fine, too. The oldest one's got a baby of her own now."

"Well, glory. She marry a Sandhill boy?"

"No. She left Sandhill a little before Dad died, and got a job, and then a few years back she called to say she was married to this boy from Georgia. Haven't seen her since, or the boy, either. They live in Kansas. But she's at home now."

"Well, I know you be glad to see her. I bet your mamma went to Kansas when the baby come, hey?"

"No."

"That daddy of yours a fine man," Brandon said. "Fine man."

"Well," said Matilda, "your mama had enough to do with chirren of her own, I reckon. Maybe just couldn't *make* it all the way to Kansas."

"That's a nice-looking baby *you* got," said Ben Joe.

"Well, thank you. Name's Clara Sue. I *knew* it'd be a girl. I got fatter and fatter in the behind all the time I carrying her."

"Now, Matilda, he don't want to hear about that."

"Well, I just mentioning. You want to sleep, Mr. Ben Joe, and I know Brandon he wild to get back to that gin."

"It was good seeing you," Ben Joe said. He and Brandon stood up and shook hands, and then Brandon left and Matilda turned around to face forward again.

When he was settled back in his seat, Ben Joe leaned his head against the windowpane and closed his eyes, trying to ignore the vibration of the pane against his skin. He wished he knew what state they were passing through. The last of New Jersey, maybe. He felt unsure of his age; in New York he was small and free and too young, and in Sandhill he was old and tied down and enormous, but what age was he here?

With his eyes closed, the division between sleeping and waking became blurred and airy. He saw the sunlit front porch of his house in Sandhill floating up toward him through the darkness behind his eyelids. His father came out of the house, humming a tune beneath his breath, and began crossing the yard to the front gate.

"You come pick me up when it's suppertime, Ben Joe," he said, speaking to the empty air. "I'll be in my office."

The sun shone on his lined face, and on the top of his white hair. From somewhere far off, Ben Joe shouted, "But I'm not there! I'm over here!"

His father made a shoulder-patting motion in space. "We'll walk home together," he said.

Ben Joe began running, trying to be beside his father before he reached the gate, but he was too late. When he got there his father was gone, and his mother had come out on the porch holding a glass of lemonade that flashed piercingly in the sun.

"You've been dreaming about your father," she said.

But Ben Joe said, "No. No, I didn't. I never did."

He awoke, and found that the sill of the train window had pressed a wide deep line into his cheekbone.

3

It was still very early in the morning when Ben Joe reached Sandhill. The wooden station house seemed deserted and the parking lot behind it was white and empty, with the pale sunlight glinting on the flecks of mica in the gravel. Beyond that was a thin row of trees and then, after that, Main Street, running parallel to the railroad tracks and lined with the little stores that made up the downtown section of Sandhill. From where Ben Joe was standing, beside the tracks, all he could see of Sandhill was smoking chimneys and white steeples. The town looked small and clean and perfect, as if it were one of those miniature plastic towns sitting beside a child's electric railroad.

The only other passengers to get off at Sandhill were Brandon's family and a tiny old snuff-chewing white man whom Ben Joe had not seen before. They all stood by the tracks in a group, motionless, soaking in the early morning sunshine and listening to the train fading away behind them. When the air was completely silent again Brandon said, "Sure do feel different from New York."

"Sure do," the old man said.

They turned to look at him.

"Softer, I guess," he said. "I don't know."

They nodded and turned away again. Ben Joe felt as if they might almost be a family, the five of them, standing so close together and so watchful. The sleepiness and the sudden silence seemed to have left an odd gentleness, in himself and in the others, that made him reluctant to leave the station.

"Can't see much of a change from *here*," Brandon said. "See they ain't fixed the clock on the Sand-Bottom Baptists' steeple tower yet."

He was holding the baby now, and in his other hand was a large striped cardboard suitcase. Beside him his wife clutched a diaper bag to her stomach. In the sunlight they both looked much younger; Brandon was bundled into a woolly-collared maroon windbreaker that a little boy might wear, and his wife had a thin brown topper on, girlishly awkward and too short-sleeved, and a simple blue dress that had faded a little. Beside them stood the little old man, also faded but still very clean and polished-looking, as if some brisk daughter-in-law had scrubbed him like an apple with a clean white cloth before she packed him on the train. He had a funny way of breathing—short and fast, with a tiny kitten's mew at the end of each intake. Ben Joe wondered if he were the one that the curly-haired boy had said was dying.

"Anyone know where Setdown Street is?" the old man was asking.

"I do," said Ben Joe.

"I want to find it. Be mighty obliged."

"I'll show you."

A dusty black Chevrolet pulled into the parking lot. It seemed stuffed with laughing brown faces, piled three deep, and even before it had come to a complete stop, the doors had popped open and a whole wealth of brightly dressed Negroes had begun pouring out. Brandon gave a joyous hoot of laughter that was almost a shout and said, "*Hey,* man, hey, Matilda, look who *here*!" and the baby woke up and blinked her round berry eyes at Ben Joe.

"You waking Clara Sue," Matilda said.

"It's *all* of them done come, man, all of them!"

"Mr. Ben Joe," said Matilda, turning halfway to him while she seemed still to be looking toward the Chevrolet, "won't your family planning on meeting you? Because we'n take you in the Chevy, you know. That Brandon's brother driving."

"Well, I reckon my family's not even up yet," Ben Joe said. "But the walk'll do me good. Thanks anyway."

"You, sir?" she said to the old man.

"Oh, I'll be going with him. Iffen it's not too far." He looked up at Ben Joe, questioning him, and Ben Joe shook his head.

"Well, good to see you," Matilda said. She turned to catch up with Brandon and her baby. Across the chilly air the voices of their relatives rang cheerfully; they were grinning and standing awkwardly in a cluster now beside their open-doored car, as if they wanted to give Brandon and Matilda time to get used to them again before they descended on them all at once. And Brandon and Matilda seemed in no hurry. They walked slowly and with careful dignity, proud to have such a large turnout for them. Over Brandon's shoulder the baby waved both fists helplessly.

"Might as well start," said the old man.

"I guess."

"Sure it's not far?"

"Sure."

The old man picked up a large, very new suitcase and Ben Joe led the way, with his own lightweight suitcase swinging easily in his hand. "Ought to be just far enough to get you hungry for breakfast," he called back over his shoulder.

"Good to hear that. Been traveling too long for *my* preference."

They cut through the station, through the large, hot waiting room with its rows and rows of naked, dark wooden benches. Ben Joe could never figure out why Sandhill had provided space for so many passengers. The waiting room was divided in two by a slender post, with half the room reserved for white people and the other half for Negroes. Since times had changed, the wooden letters saying "White" and "Colored" had been removed, but the letters had left cleaner places on the wall that spelled out the same words still. A fat, red-haired lady sat in the ticket booth between the two halves of the waiting room; she frowned at the old man and Ben Joe and tapped a pencil against her teeth.

As soon as they were outside, going up the short gravel driveway that cut through the trees onto Main Street, the old man became talkative.

"You shouldn't of mentioned breakfast, boy," he said. "Lord, I'm hungry. Wonder what they'll feed me."

"Who?" Ben Joe asked.

"Oh, them. And you know them colored folks off the same train as us? Know what they're doing now? Setting down to the table with their relations, partaking of buckwheat cakes and hot buttered syrup and them little link sausages. Makes me hungry just thinking of it."

His breath was squeaking more now; the nostrils of his small, bent nose widened and fluttered as he drew in bigger and bigger amounts of air.

"My son got me this suitcase special, just for the trip. It was real expensive. I said, 'Sam,' I said, '*you* don't need to spend all that money on me, son,' but Sam he said, 'It's the least I can do.' 'It's the least I can do,' he tells me. He wanted to come take the trip with me, but I could see he was busy and all. I wouldn't allow it. Law, I am eighty-four years old now and *capable*, it's what I keep telling him. Capable. Though I will admit the train was something bumpy, and I feared that it would jounce all my insides out of place. I got this fear, someday my intestines will get tied in a bow by accident, like shoelaces. You ever thought of that?"

"Not that I can remember," Ben Joe said. He was getting worried now; the old man's voice had become a mere wheezing sound, and he was so out of breath that Ben Joe's own throat grew tight and breathless in sympathy.

"Well, I have. Often I have. I don't know if you ever knew my son Sam. He's a businessman, like on Wall Street, except that he happens to be in Connecticut instead. Got a real nice family, too. Course I think he could of made a better choice in wives, but then Sally's right pretty and I reckon I can see his point in picking her. Just a mite bossy, in all. And then her family's Jehovah's Witnesses. Now, I got no quarrel to pick with *any* religion, excepting maybe a few, but I heard somewheres that Jehovah's Witnesses they turn off all the lights and get under the chairs and tables and look for God. They do. Ain't found Him yet, neither. Course Sally, she's reformed now, but *still* and all, still and all . . ."

On Main Street he became suddenly silent. He walked along almost on tiptoe, looking around him with a white, astonished face. Sometimes he would whisper, "Oh, my, look at that!" and purse his mouth and widen his eyes at some ordinary little store front. Ben Joe couldn't understand him. What was so odd about Sandhill? Main Street was wide and white and almost bare of cars; a few shopkeepers whistled cheerfully as they swept in front of their stores, and a pretty girl Ben Joe had never seen before passed by, smiling. Except for the new hotel, there wasn't a single building over three stories high in the whole town. Above the squat little shops the owners' families lived, and their flowered curtains hung cozily behind narrow dark windows.

At the third block they turned left and started uphill on a small, well-shaded street. Main Street was the only commercial district in the town; as soon as they turned off it they were among large family houses with enormous old pecan trees towering over them. The old man had stopped exclaiming now, but he was still tiptoeing and wide-eyed. Although his baggy coat seemed paper thin and the morning was very cool, the surface of his face was shiny with perspiration. With a small grunt he switched his suitcase to his other hand and it banged against the side of his knee.

"I'll trade you suitcases for a while," Ben Joe said.

"No no. No no. You know, when I was a boy we'd of been plumb through town by now."

"Sir?"

"Town's *grown* some, I said."

"Oh. You mean you've been here before?"

"Born here, I was. But I ain't seen it since I was eighteen years old and that's a fact. Went off to help my uncle make bed linens in Connecticut. Though at the time I never wanted to. I wanted to go to Africa."

"*Africa?*"

"Africa." He stopped and set down his suitcase in order to wipe his

forehead with a carefully folded handkerchief from his breast pocket.
"Wadn't but two streets that was paved then," he said. "Main and
Dower. Dower's *my* name. It was named after my daddy, who moved
out west soon after I went north on account of the humidity here being
bad for my mother's ankle bones. But there wadn't no street called
Setdown then. Got no idea where *that* is."

"Well, it's not far," Ben Joe said. "You got relatives living there?"

"Nope. Nope."

"Where you going?"

"Home for the aged."

"Oh."

Ben Joe stood in silence for a minute, not knowing what to say next.
Finally he cleared his throat and said, "Well, that's where it is, all
right."

"Course it is. Going to die there."

"Well. Well, um, I trust that'll be a long time from now."

"Don't trust too hard," the old man said. He seemed irritated by
Ben Joe's embarrassment; he picked up his suitcase with a jerk and
they continued on up the hill. As they walked, Ben Joe kept looking
over at him sideways.

"Don't you corner your eyes like that," Mr. Dower said. "Not at me
you don't."

"Well, I was just thinking."

"Don't have to corner your eyes just to be thinking, do you?"

"I've been away some time myself," Ben Joe said. "Some time for
me, anyway. Going on four months. It seemed longer, though, and I
sort of left planning not to return."

"Then what you *here* for?" Mr. Dower snapped.

"Well, I don't know," Ben Joe said. "I just can't seem to *get* anywhere.
Nowhere permanent."

"*I* can. Can and did. Went away permanent and now I've come back
to die permanent."

"How can you have gone away permanent if you've come back?"
Ben Joe asked.

"Because what I left ain't here to come back to, that's why. Therefore
my going away can be counted as permanent."

"That's what they all say," said Ben Joe. "But they're fooling themselves."

"Well." Mr. Dower stopped again to wipe his forehead. "How much
farther, boy?"

"Not far. Right at the end of this block."

"Long blocks you've got. Long blocks. This here," the old man said,
pointing to an old stone house, "is where Jonah Barnlott lived, that
married my sister. Like to broke my family's heart doing it, too. He
was a no-count boy, that Jonah. Became a doctor, finally, down in
Georgia, but never had any patients to speak of. Was inflicted with

athlete's foot, he was, and decided shoes were what gave it to him, so he loafed about his office playing patience in a white uniform and pure-T bare feet, which scared all his patients away. My sister left him, finally, and got remarried to a lawyer. Lawyers're better. Not so concerned with bodily matters. So now it's Saul Bowen lives in that house. I reckon you know *him*."

"No, sir."

"Not know Saul Bowen? Fat old guy who goes around town all day eating pudding from a dish?"

"No, sir."

"Well, no," Mr. Dower said after a minute. "I guess not. I guess not."

They were silent for the rest of the block. The old man's shoes made a shuffling, scratchy noise on the sidewalk and the mewing of his breath was loud and unsteady, so that Ben Joe became frightened.

"Sir," he said at the corner, "it's just one block down from here, on the left. But I'd be happy to walk you the rest of the way."

"I can make it. I can make it."

"Well, it's a big yellow house with a sign in front. You sure you're all right?"

"I am *dying*," said the old man. "But otherwise I'm fine and I'd appreciate to walk by myself for a spell."

"Well. Good-by, Mr. Dower."

"Bye, boy."

The old man started down Setdown Street, his suitcase banging his knees at every step. For a minute Ben Joe watched after him, but the shabby little figure was pushing doggedly on with no help from him and there was nothing more he could do. Finally he turned and started walking again, on toward his own home.

The houses in this area were big and comfortable, although most of them were poorly cared-for. On some of the lawns the trees were so old and thick that there was a little whitening of frost on the grass beneath their limbs, even now that most of their leaves were gone. Ben Joe began shivering. He walked more quickly, past the wide, deserted porches and down the echoing sidewalk. Then he was on the corner, and across the street was his own house.

A long, low wire gate stood in front of it, although the fence that went with it had been torn down years ago when the last of the children had left the toddler stage. The lawn behind it had been allowed to grow wild and weedy, half as high as a wheat field and dotted here and there with little wiry shrubs and seedy, late-fall flowers. And the sidewalk from the gate to the front porch was cracked and broken; little clumps of grass grew in it. Towering above such an unkempt expanse of grass, the house took on a half-deserted look in spite of the lace curtains that hung primly in all the windows. It was an enormous white frame house, in need of a little touch-up with a paintbrush, and it could easily be the ugliest house in town. Round stained-glass windows popped up in unexpected places; the front bay window was too tall and narrow, and the little turret, with its ridiculously curlicued weather vane, looked as if it must be stuffed with bats and cobwebs. People said—although Ben Joe never believed them—that the first time his mother had seen the house she had laughed so hard that she got hiccups and a neighbor had had to bring her a glass of peppermint water. And all the while that Ben Joe was growing up, little boys used to ask him jealously if his room was in the turret. He always said yes, although the truth was that nobody lived there; it was just a huge hollow space above the stairwell. The only thing that saved the house from looking haunted was the front porch, big and square and friendly. A shiny green metal glider sat there, and in the summertime the whole porch railing was littered with bathing suits and Coke bottles and the lounging figures of whatever boys his sisters were dating at the time. In front of the door, Ben Joe could just make out a rolled-up newspaper. That brought him to life again; he crossed the yard cheerfully, stopped on the porch to pick up the paper, and opened the front door.

Inside, there was the mossy brown smell that he had been raised with, that seemed to be part and parcel of the house and was a wonderful smell if you were glad to be home and an unbearable smell if you were not. And mingled with it were the more temporary, tangible smells—bacon, coffee, hot radiators, newly ironed dresses, bath powder. He was standing in the narrow hallway and looking into the living room, which was stuffed with durable old ugly furniture that had stood the growing up of seven children. On the walls hung staid oil paintings of ships at sea and summer landscapes. The coffee tables were littered with things that had been there as long as Ben Joe could remember—little china figurines, enameled flower pots, conch shells. Periodically his mother tried to move them, but Gram always put them back again. On the floor was an interrupted Monopoly game, a pair of fluffy slippers, a beer can, and a pink baby sweater that reminded him of Tessie. It must belong to Joanne's baby now. He set down the suitcase and the newspaper and crossed into the living room to pick the sweater up between two fingers. It seemed to him that every girl in the family had worn that. But had it really been that tiny?

In the kitchen a voice said, "I'll tell you what. I'll tell you what, Jane. Every time I even pick *up* a glass of frozen orange juice, it makes me think of vitamin pills. Does it you?"

Someone answered. It could have been any one of them; they all had that low, clear voice of their mother's. And then the first voice again: "I'd rather squeeze oranges in my bare hands than drink my orange juice frozen."

Ben Joe smiled and headed through the hallway toward the voices, with the sweater still in one hand. At the open doorway to the kitchen he stopped and looked in at the five girls sitting around the table. "Anybody home?" he asked.

They all turned at the same moment to look at him, and then their chairs were scraped back and five cheeks were pressed briefly to his and questions hurled around his head.

"What are you doing here, Ben Joe?"

"What you think Mama's going to say?"

"How'd you get *in*, is what I want to know."

"Sure, a burglar could've walked in. We'd never even heard him."

"Would anyone be a burglar before breakfast? And what's to steal?"

"Where's your luggage, Ben Joe?"

He stood smiling, unable to get a word in edgewise. They were circled around him, looking soft and happy in their pastel bathrobes, and if they had been still a minute he would have said he was glad to see them, even if it *would* embarrass them, but they didn't give him a chance. Lisa reached for the baby sweater in his hand and held it up above her head for the others to see and laugh at.

"Why, Ben Joe, you bring us a sweater? Isn't that nice, except I don't reckon it'll *fit* us too well."

"He's been away so long, forgotten how big we'd have grown."

"Aren't you exhausted?"

"I am at that," said Ben Joe. "Feels like my head's come unscrewed at the neck."

"I'll get you some coffee," Jenny said. She was the next-to-youngest— it was only last spring that she'd graduated from high school—but, of all of them, she was the most down-to-earth. She went to the cupboard and took down the huge earthenware mug that Ben Joe always used. "Mama didn't know if you meant it about coming home," she said, "and says she hopes you *didn't*, but she changed your bed, anyway."

"I'm going to it, too, soon as I've had my breakfast. Hello there, Tessie. You're so little still I damn near overlooked you. Maybe it's you this sweater's for."

"Not me it's not," said Tessie. "It's too little for Carol, even."

"Who's Carol?"

"Carol's our *niece*."

"Oh. Where's Joanne?"

"In bed. So's Carol."

"I forgot about her being named Carol," Ben Joe said. "One more girl to remember. Hoo boy." He took off his jacket and turned to hang it on the back of his chair. "Ma gone to work already?"

"Yup. This man's bringing a truckload of books real early."

The mug was set before him, full of steaming coffee. Tessie passed him a plate of cinnamon buns and said, "You notice anything different about me?"

"Well . . ." Ben Joe said. He frowned at her, and she frowned steadily back. Of all the Hawkes children, she and Ben Joe were the only blond ones. The others had dark hair, which they wore short and curly, and their eyes were so black it was hard to tell where they were looking. They were almost round-eyed, too, whereas Ben Joe and Tessie had their father's too-narrow eyes. And there was something tricky about their coloring. At one moment they could seem very pale and at the next their skin would be almost olive-toned. But all of the girls, even Tessie, had little pointed faces and small, careful features, a little too sharp; all of them wore quick, watchful expressions and their oval-nailed hands were thin and restless. People said they were the prettiest girls in town, and the ficklest. Thinking of that, Ben Joe smiled at them, and Tessie tugged at his arm impatiently and said, "Not them, *me*."

"You." He turned back to her. "You've gone and gotten married on us."

"Oh, Ben *Joe*." Her giggle was like Joanne's, light and chuckly. "I'm only ten years *old*," she said. "Don't you see *anything* different?"

"Nope."

"I've had my ears pierced!"

"Aha," said Ben Joe. He took her face in his hands and turned it first one way and then the other, examining the tiny gold rings in her ears. "What for?"

"Oh, just because. Joanne and Susannah and the twins have pierced ears. Why not me?"

"Did it hurt?"

"Yup."

"Did you cry?"

"Nope. Well, tears came out, but I went on smiling."

"Good girl," Ben Joe said. "Better run along and get ready for school, now. You'll be late."

"You'll all be late," Susannah said.

The others got up and left; the pinks and blues of their bathrobes clustered together for a minute at the doorway and then vanished into the hall. Ben Joe could hear their soft slippers padding up the stairs, and somewhere a door slammed. "What about you?" he asked.

"I've got another half-hour."

"Is Gram up?"

"Yes. She's up in her room, making a gun belt for Tessie out of an old leather skirt."

He watched Susannah silently for a while, following her quick little movements around the kitchen. She hadn't changed any; she got the coffee grounds half emptied and fled to the orange-juicer and then to sponge the top of the stove off before she remembered the coffee grounds again.

"Have you talked to Joanne?" he asked.

"Oh, sure."

"What'd she say?"

"What about?"

"About leaving Gary."

"Oh." She tossed the insides of the coffee pot into the sink and went dashing across the kitchen after a cream pitcher. "I don't know," she said. "It never came up."

"Oh, for heaven's sake."

"Well, it's none of *my* business."

"She's your sister, isn't she?"

"That still doesn't make it my business."

"What does, then?" Ben Joe asked.

"*Nothing.*" She lifted up one soapy hand and pushed a piece of hair off her forehead with the back of her wrist. "You're the one that's so worried. Why don't *you* talk to her, if you think you know where she'd be happier."

"It's not that I much want her to go *back* to him," Ben Joe said slowly. "Gary's an awful name. Whatever he's like. It reminds me of a G.I., with a crew cut, and 'Mom' tattooed on his chest, and lots of pin-up pictures on his wall."

"Oh, you," Susannah said. "That's beside the point. Go up and get some sleep, Ben Joe. The house'll be bedlam when Carol wakes up."

"Okay. Have a good day at work."

"Thank you."

He stood watching her for a minute, but Susannah had already forgotten him. She was on her hands and knees under the table now, crawling after one of her slippers, and it was as if Ben Joe had never been there.

4

WHEN HE awoke, his mother was in the doorway watching him. He was not sure whether she had spoken his name or not; in his sleep he seemed to have heard her voice. But maybe all that had awakened him was the feel of her eyes—wide eyes, as dark as her daughters', but with small lines now at the corners. She was the kind of woman who did not become very wrinkled as she aged but instead acquired only a few lines around her mouth and eyes, and those so deep that they were actual crevices even when her face was calm. She was smiling a little, so that the mouth lines curved and deepened even more, and she stood with one hand on her hip and the other on the doorknob and watched Ben Joe.

"Ben Joe Hawkes," she said finally, "what on *earth* are you doing home?"

Ben Joe sat up in the familiar wooden bed and pushed his hair back from his forehead. "I already told you," he said. "I told you the reason on the phone."

"That was no reason." She shook her head. "Of all the things to do . . . What's going to happen to your school work?"

"I don't have to be there every minute."

"If you make good grades you do. If you're going to be any kind of decent lawyer."

Ben Joe shrugged and pulled his pillow up behind him so that he could sit against it. The sheets smelled crisp and newly ironed; his mother had smoothed them tight on the bed herself and turned the covers down for him, and he could hold that thought securely in his mind even when she scolded him for returning. You had to be a sort of detective with his mother; you had to search out the fresh-made bed, the flowers on the bureau, and the dinner table laid matter-of-factly with your favorite supper, and then you forgot her crisp manners. He wondered, watching her, whether his sisters knew that. Or did they even need to know? Maybe it was only Ben Joe, still watching his mother with those detective eyes even though he was a grown man now and should have stopped bothering.

"Have you had breakfast?" his mother was asking.

"Yes'm. Had it with the girls before they went to work."

"Well, I'm home for lunch now. You want a bite to eat?"

"I guess."

She came further into the room and opened his closet door. From the front rack she took a bathrobe and tossed it to him, not watching where it landed, and then crossed to pull the shade up. He saw that she was still wearing those wide walking skirts with the mid-calf hem that had been popular some fifteen years ago. On her, with her bony height and her swinging walk, they still looked up to date. Her hair was a light, dusty color, once as blond as his and Tessie's. It was short and a little too frizzy around the sharp angles of her face, but she still didn't seem like an old woman. He gave up watching her and, pulling the bathrobe around him, stepped barefoot to the floor.

"You're thinner," she said. She had stopped fiddling with the window shade and was taking stock of him now, with her hands deep in the pockets of her skirt. "You've been cooking for yourself, I'll bet."

"Yes'm. What time is it?"

"About twelve."

"Is Joanne up?"

"Oh, yes. She and Carol are in the den, I think."

"Is she okay?"

"Of *course* she's okay. And it's her own business, Ben Joe—nothing we have any right to touch. I don't want to hear about your meddling in it. Hurry up and get dressed, will you? Lunch is nearly ready."

She swung out of the door and vanished, humming something beneath

her breath as she went downstairs. Behind her, Ben Joe sighed and
tied his bathrobe around him. It would be a good time to shave; none
of the older girls came home for lunch.

When he came downstairs he could smell lunch already—all the
varied smells of odds and ends left over in the refrigerator and reheated
now in tiny saucepans. Although he was rested now, his stomach still
felt shaky from the trip and he made a face as the smell of lunch hit
him on the stairs. Gram must be doing the cooking today; she was an
old Southerner and floated all her vegetables in grease.

He pushed open the kitchen door and found his grandmother standing
by the stove just lifting the lid off a steaming saucepan. She was his
father's mother, and close to eighty now, but there was a steely, glinting
endurance to her. Joanne used to say her grandmother reminded her
of piano wires. She was small and bony; she wore men's black gym
shoes that tied around her bare ankles, and her dress, as usual, was a
disgrace—a sort of blue denim coat that was fastened with one string
at the back of the neck and hung open the rest of the way down the
back to expose a black lace slip. (Her underwear was her one luxury;
she had seven different colors in her bureau drawer.) As she stirred
the leftovers she sang, just as she always did, in a deafening roar that
came effortlessly from the bottom of her tiny rib cage:

> *"I ain't gonna knock on your window no more,*
> *Ain't gonna bang on your door . . ."*

"Hello, Gram," Ben Joe said in her ear.

She spun around, just missing him with the saucepan lid. "Ben *Joe!*"
she said. "I hear you came in this morning and didn't even say hey
to me. That true?"

"You were up in the attic making a gun belt," he said.

He hugged her and she hugged him back, so hard that he could feel
her hard, bony chest and the point of her chin just below his shoulder.

"We're having leftovers," she said. "I know what view you hold of
leftovers, but you just wait till tonight. You just *see* what manner of
things we're preparing."

She replaced the saucepan lid and undid her hair. It was her habit
to take three bobby pins from her head, at least twenty times a day,
and let her straight white hair fall almost to her shoulders. Then, with
the bobby pins clamped tightly in her mouth, she deftly wound her
hair around one finger, squashed it on top of her head in a bun, and
nailed it there again with the three bobby pins. All this took less than
a minute. While she was doing it she kept right on talking, shifting
the bobby pins to one corner of her mouth so that they wouldn't
interrupt her speech.

"Turkey we're having," she said, "and giblet dressing, and yams—
Ben Joe, you got to talk to Jenny about her grocery rut. She's got into

a rut about grocery shopping. Buys the same old thing every time. No imagination. Now, Jenny, she is a right good cook and I want to see her get married, real soon. I don't hold with a girl staying and looking after her family and being a little old secretary all her life when she is as home-minded as Jenny is. Got to get a family of her own. But what man'll marry a girl feeds him hamburgers every night? Course she does all *manner* of clever things to dress them up a little, but still and all it's hamburger and the cheap kind of hamburger at that. Ever since you left and put her in charge of the money matters she's been *parsimonious,* is what, taking it too serious. Call people to eat, will you? Your ma's upstairs and the others're in the den."

"Yes'm."

He left the kitchen and headed for the den, which was through the living room and at the other end of the house. It had once been his father's study, and although the medical books on the shelves had long since been disposed of, there was still the extra telephone on the desk, installed when the girls had first become old enough to tie up the lines on the regular house phone. Since their father's death the room was used as a TV room, and now the set was blaring so loudly that Ben Joe could hear it way before he crossed the living room. And once he was inside the den the sound hurt his ears. The shades were down and at first it was too dark to see anything but the silhouettes of the people watching and beyond them the screen, bluish and snow-flecked. A fat man was shouting, "Whaddaya say, kiddies? Huh? Whaddaya say?" and behind his voice was a loud, angry humming from the set itself. Ben Joe blinked and looked around.

All he could see of Joanne was the white line that edged her profile from the light of the TV screen on her face. She had her eyes lowered to something in her lap—a piece of cloth. And she was sewing on it, pushing the needle through and then stretching her arm as far out as it would reach in order to pull the thread tight. Joanne was the type of person who used just one enormous length of thread instead of several short practical lengths. On the cane chair in front of her sat Tessie, also just a silvery profile but with a snatch of yellow over her forehead where the light hit her blond hair. And farthest in front, so that her back was toward Ben Joe, sat a small child in a child's rocking chair. Of her Ben Joe could see nothing, except that she was so small (she would have been two only last June) her feet stuck out in front of her on the chair, and she was rocking violently. He could make out her small hands gripping the chair arms tightly; she flung her head first forward and then back, to make the chair rock. From here he could almost swear her hair was red, although that was improbable. He took another step into the room and said, "Has she got *red* hair?"

Joanne started and looked at him.

"Hi, Joanne," he said.

"Ben Joe, come here! No, wait. Come out into the living room. It's dark as night in here."

She rose and pulled him out into the light and kissed him on both cheeks, hard, and hugged him around the waist. The little dress she was sewing was still in one hand, but the needle had slipped off its thread and was lying on the rug at her feet. It was funny how the tiniest thing Joanne did was exactly like her, even now, even after all these years. Any of the other girls would have stuck her needle into the cloth for safekeeping before she went to kiss her brother. "God, you're thin," she said. She was laughing, and her hair was mussed from hugging him. "I can't believe it's really you. Have you gone back to being a vegetarian?"

"No. Mom says it's eating my own cooking that does it."

"Mm-hm. You're older too. But that's all right. I don't reckon you're *ever* going to get any lines in your face."

"That's from having no character," he said absently. He was trying to decide what was different about her; something was making him feel a little shy, as if she were a stranger. Probably the way she dressed was partly responsible for it. In place of the blazing red dress of the old days was a soft yellow sacklike thing that hung loosely from her shoulders. She was still thin, though, with a face just slightly rounder than her sisters'. Almost immediately he decided what the change in her was; she was pretty much the same, with that same warm chuckly laugh, but she had a different way of showing it. A subtler one, he thought. Yet the bangles were still on her arms, and the twinkling, chin-ducking smile still on her face. He smiled back.

"I see you're not old yet," he said.

"Almost I am. Did you have a good trip?"

"I guess so. I came to call you to lunch, by the way. Gram's dishing up."

"I'll get the children."

She pattered back into the den, barefoot, and came out again with Carol in her arms and Tessie trailing behind her, blinking in the sunlight. The TV had been forgotten; accordion music seesawed out noisily from the empty room.

"You met Carol yet?" Joanne asked.

Ben Joe looked at Carol, checking her hair first because he was curious to see whether it was red or not. It was. It was cut, cup-like, around a small, round face that was still so young it could tell Ben Joe nothing. "Can you talk yet?" he asked her.

She smiled, not telling.

"Only when she's in the mood," Joanne said. "She's got to say a word exactly right or she refuses to say it at all. A perfectionist. I don't know where she gets it."

"What about her red hair?"

"What?"

"Where's she get *that?*"

Joanne frowned. "Where you get any kind of hair," she said finally. "Genes."

"Oh."

"I sure am glad to see you, Ben Joe," she said as they crossed the living room. "I am. You don't know how glad."

Embarrassed, Ben Joe smiled down at her and said nothing. At the stairway he stopped and yelled up, "Mom!" and then continued on into the kitchen, not looking at Joanne or waiting for his mother's answer. But just before they reached the doorway he said, "Well, I'm happy to see *you*."

"That's good," she said cheerfully.

In the kitchen Gram was bustling around, ladling food onto the plates on the table. Joanne pulled the old high chair up and sat Carol in it. "Don't you go wiggling around," she told her. She gave her a little pat on the knee. It made Ben Joe feel strange, watching Joanne with Carol. He never had really thought about the fact that she was a mother now with a child of her own.

"Where's your mama?" Gram asked.

"Coming."

"Well, her meal's getting cold. Sit down, Joanne. Sit down, Ben Joe. Tessie, you got to hurry now. What happened to your napkin?"

"It's on the screen porch."

"Well, it's not supposed to be. No, don't go get it. More important to get your meal down you hot—stave off germs that way. Ben Joe, honey, aren't you tired to pieces?"

"Not any more I'm not."

"Well, you have a big helping of these here beans. Carol just threw her bib on the floor, Joanne."

She put another scoop of beans on Ben Joe's plate, shaking the spoon vigorously. Seeing her hands, so much older than the rest of her, reminded Ben Joe of the old man from the train. He said, "Gram, did you ever know a man named Dower?"

"Dower." She sat down at her own place, smoothing the front of her apron across her lap. "Lord yes, I did. There was a whole heap of Dowers here at one time, though most have died out or moved on. There was the good Dowers and there was the bad Dowers. The good ones were very great friends of the family once. I near about lived at their house when I was a teeny-iney girl. They're all dead now, I reckon. But the bad ones are living here yet. Wouldn't you know. No relation to the good ones, of course. Living off the county and letting chickens in the kitchen. That kind just hangs on and *hangs* on. I don't know why. They're so spindly-legged and pasty-faced, but they keep on long after stronger men's in their graves."

She stopped to take a breath. Ben Joe's mother came into the kitchen and pulled up a chair for herself. Carol threw her bib on the floor again and said, "Carrot."

"We're going to have to tie a double knot in your bib from now on," Ben Joe's mother told her. She took a raw carrot from the plate on the table and handed it to her. "Gram, what are those little things in the dish over there?"

"Smoked oysters. And that child shouldn't have a carrot."

"Smoked *oysters*?"

"That's what I said. Won't have this grocery rut of Jenny's one day longer. My mind's made up. Ellen, take that carrot away from her."

"Why? She's got teeth."

"But it's a big *thick* carrot."

"Well, we can't mollycoddle her. The rest of the girls had carrots at her age."

"Not while I was around," Gram said. "She'll choke on it."

Joanne looked up anxiously and Gram nodded to her.

"On the little pieces of it. She'll choke. I've seen it happen."

"Oh, don't be silly," said Ellen Hawkes.

Joanne reached over and took the carrot away, replacing it with a soda cracker immediately so that Carol didn't have time to start crying. Ben Joe's mother turned back to her meal, resigned. Neither she nor Gram paid much attention to these quibbling arguments of theirs; they were used to them. Gram said Ellen Hawkes was coldhearted and Ellen Hawkes said Gram was soft-cored. The rest of the family was as used to the feud as they were. They went on eating now, cheerfully, and Carol began gnawing at her cracker.

"The reason I asked about the Dowers," Ben Joe said, "is that I met an old man from the train by that name. He said he was born right here in Sandhill."

"That's funny. Good Dower or bad Dower?"

"Well, Gram, I doubt if he'd have said."

"If he was a bad Dower he would have. He would have said he was a good Dower."

Joanne laughed.

"He said there was a street named for his father," Ben Joe said. "I remember that much. He said that when he was here, Main and Dower were the only real streets in town."

Gram looked up, interested now. "That's so," she said. "It's true, that's so."

Carol spilled her milk. It trickled off the high-chair tray and into her lap, and when she felt the coldness of it she squealed.

"I'll get a rag," said Tessie.

She started for the sink, but her mother reached around and grabbed her back by the sash. "You sit right there, young lady. You have to be at school in fifteen minutes."

"It won't take long, Mama."

But Joanne was already up, reaching for paper towels and then lifting Carol out of her high chair to sponge her off. "There, there," she was saying, although Carol was only squealing for the joy of hearing her own voice now and had started pulling out all the bobby pins from Joanne's hair.

"He went off to help his uncle make bed sheets in Connecticut!" Ben Joe shouted above the uproar.

His mother stopped chewing and stared at him.

"Mr. Dower, I'm talking about. And then his family moved away because his mother's ankle bones started hurting—"

"Ben Joe," his mother said, "if all of you children would cast your minds back to when you were small and I told you *never*, on *any* account, to speak to those strange-looking people you seem to keep meeting up with—"

"How old was he when he began in bed sheets?" Gram asked.

"Eighteen, he told me."

"My Lord in heaven!" She laid her fork on the table and stared at him. "Why, that couldn't be anyone but *Jamie* Dower. Jamie Dower, I'll be. My Lord in heaven."

"Was he a good Dower?"

"Good as they come. Shoot, yes. He was six years older'n me, but you'd never believe the crush I had on him. That was the *reason* I practically lived at the Dowers'—following him around all the time. I thought he was Adam, back then."

"*Adam?*" Tessie said. "How was he dressed?"

Her mother pushed her plate closer to her. "Eat your beans, Tessie. Stop that dawdling."

"Where was he going to?" Gram asked.

"Well, um—the home for the aged, is what he told me."

"The home for the aged," she shook her head. "My, my, who'd have believed it? He was a real handsome boy, you know—kind of tall for back then, though nothing to compare with some of those basketball players you see around nowadays. Real fond of stylish clothes, too. What would we have thought, I wonder, had someone told us back then where Jamie Dower would end up?"

"Tessie," said Ellen Hawkes, "I give you to the count of five to drink that milk up. What's that on your front? Beans?"

"Nothing," said Tessie. She finished the last of her milk and wiped the white mustache off her upper lip with the back of her hand.

"That's a funny-looking nothing."

"Well, anyway, I gotta go. Good-by, Mama. Good-by, everybody."

She vanished out the kitchen door, grabbing her jacket as she went. Her mother stared after her and shook her head. "You practically have to *drag* her to school," she said. "Sometimes I think the brains just sort of dribbled away toward the end in this family."

"She's plenty bright," said Gram.

"Well, maybe. But not like Joanne and Ben Joe were—not like them."

"Rubbish," said Gram. She began reaching for the plates and scraping them while she sat at her place. "Too much emphasis on brains in this family. What good's it do? Joanne quit after one year of college and the others, excepting Ben Joe, never went. And Ben Joe—look at him. He just kept trying to figure out what that all-fired mind of his was given him for, and first he thought it was for science and then for art and then for philosophy and now what's he got? Just a mishmash, is all. Just nothing. Won't read a thing now but murder mysteries."

"Neither *one* of you knows what you're talking about," Ben Joe said cheerfully. He had been through all this before; he listened with only half an ear, tipping back in his chair and watching his grandmother scrape plates. "And pooh, what do the girls want to go to college for? I say they're smart choosing not to—"

"Well, sure you do," his mother said. "Sure you do, when all you've got to judge it by is *Sandhill* College. Might as well not have gone at all, as far as I'm concerned—"

"No fault of his," Gram said.

"Well, it's no fault of *mine*."

"If my son'd had his say," Gram said, "Ben Joe'd have gone to Harvard, that's where."

"Your son could've had his say. If he'd come back he could've had his say and welcome *to* it, but what'd he do instead?" She was sitting up straight now, with one hand clasping her fork so tightly that the knuckles were white.

"Who made him like that?" Gram shouted. "Who made his house so cold he chose to go live in another's, tell me that!"

Ben Joe cleared his throat. "Actually," he said, "if I'd made better grades I'd have gotten a scholarship to Harvard. I don't see how it's anyone's fault but my—"

"And who didn't give a hoot when he left?" Gram shouted triumphantly above Ben Joe. "Answer me *that*, now, answer me—"

"That will *do*, Gram," said Ellen Hawkes.

She unclasped her hand from the fork and rose, suddenly calm. "I'll be home by six," she said to Joanne and Ben Joe. They nodded, silently; she pushed her chair in and left. Joanne was staring at the tablecloth as if it were impossible to drag her eyes away from it.

"Cracker," Carol said.

Ben Joe handed her one. She seized it and immediately began crumbling it over her tray.

"I *am* sorry," Gram said after a minute. "There was no call to act like that. I didn't mean to bring it up."

Joanne nodded, still staring at the tablecloth. "I thought you'd have settled that," she said.

"Oh, no. No, just let it slip from being uppermost in my mind, is all. You missed the worst of it. Things went on like before even after you up and left home over it, though you'd think some people might try and change a little. Ah, well, least said soonest . . ."

She sighed and rose to take the stack of dishes to the sink. "Ben Joe, honey," she called over her shoulder, "you reckon Jamie Dower might like a visitor?"

"I don't know why not, Gram."

"You and me'll go, then, sometime this week. I'll start thinking about it."

Joanne rose to help Gram, with her face still pale and too sober. For a while Ben Joe watched them, following their quick, sure movements around the kitchen, but then Carol began blowing cracker crumbs at him and he turned back to her and lifted her out of the high chair.

"Does she get a nap?" he asked Joanne.

"Well, yes. But I'm reading this book that says the same person has got to put her to bed all the time. You better wait and let me do it."

"All right." He headed for the living room, with Carol snuggled in the crook of his arm. "Wouldn't want to make you maladjusted," he told her. She smiled and sucked on a corner of her cracker.

In the living room he sat down in the rocking chair. He pried the soggy mass of cracker from Carol's hand and put it in the ash tray, and then he began absent-mindedly rocking. Carol's head dropped heavily against his chest; her red hair was tickling a point just under his chin. He could feel the small dead weight of her, but he remained unconvinced of her realness and for a long time he just rocked silently, frowning above her head at the faded wallpaper.

5

BY EVENING Ben Joe was beginning to feel the weight of home settling back on him, making him feel heavy and old and tired. He had eaten too much for supper; his stomach ached and he didn't want to admit it to anyone, or to show it by lying down, for fear that his mother and his grandmother would be hurt after all that special cooking. So he wandered aimlessly through the house, searching out something to do or think about. In the den Tessie and Jenny watched television, scowling intently at the screen and not looking up when he came to stand in the doorway. The twins, dressed in different colors now that they were older but still looking exactly the same in every other way, were popping popcorn with their dates in the kitchen, and Susannah and Gram were playing honeymoon bridge. None of them took any notice of him. He went upstairs, hoping to find someone up there who would talk to him, but his mother was using the sewing machine, her mouth full of pins and her eyes narrowed at the sleeve of a dress for Tessie. Joanne was giving Carol a bath. He could hear them even with the door half shut—Carol squealing and splashing, Joanne calming her with low, soothing noises and then occasionally laughing along with her.

"Can I come in?" Ben Joe called.

"Carol, you mind if a man comes to watch your bath?"

Carol made a louder splash, probably with the flat of her hand, and giggled.

"Well, she didn't say no," said Joanne.

Ben Joe pushed the door open and stepped inside. The room was warm and steamy, and cluttered with towels and cast-off clothes. Beside the bathtub knelt Joanne, wearing a terry-cloth bathrobe, with her hair hanging wet and stringy down her neck and her face shiny from her own bath. She had rolled the sleeves of the robe up to her elbows so that she could bathe Carol, who sat in a heap of rubber toys that blocked out almost all sight of bathwater and laughed at Ben Joe.

"Can't be a true Hawkes," said Ben Joe. "No bubble bath."

"Oh, that'll start soon enough."

Ben Joe leaned back against the sink with one foot on a tiny old step stool that read: "For doing some job that's bigger than me." He tested his full weight on the edge of the sink, decided not to risk it, and stood up again.

"I meant to tell you," Joanne said. "Don't feel bad."

"What?"

"Don't you feel bad about what Gram said. About your mind being a mish-mash. It's been in the back of my mind all day to tell you, she didn't mean it. She just said it for the sake of argument."

"I don't feel bad."

"Okay."

She started soaping Carol's hair, expertly, turning the pinkish-red hair dark auburn with her quick, firm fingers. For the first time he noticed that she wasn't wearing a wedding ring. What had she done with it? He pictured her throwing it in Gary's face, but it sounded improbable. Even in her ficklest days, Joanne had never done things that way. No, it would be more like her not even to tell Gary she was going. Or maybe it had been *Gary* who had left *her*; who knew?

"Where's your wedding ring?" he asked.

"In my jewelry box."

"What on earth for?"

"Well, I don't know. I thought maybe I should wear it so I wouldn't look like an unwed mother, but when I got here Mama said there was no point. She never wears *hers*, she said. It would just keep reminding her."

She took Carol by the chin and the back of the neck and ducked her back into the water swiftly. Before Carol could utter more than one sharp squeak she was upright again, with her hair rinsed and streaming.

"Mom's advice is the *last* I would take," Ben Joe said.

"Now, don't go being mean."

"I'm not. She wants you to say, 'Oh, who cares about *him*?' and then your whole problem is solved. You saw what that did for her."

"Mom's not as coldhearted as Gram keeps telling you, Ben Joe. You know that."

"Oh, I know."

"Besides, this isn't the same kind of thing."

"What kind of thing *is* it?" Ben Joe asked.

Joanne picked out a rubber duck and pushed it toward Carol, who ignored it. Carol was raising and lowering one round knee, watching it emerge sleek and gleaming and then lowering it again when the water had drained off to mere drops on her skin. Joanne watched too, thoughtfully, and Ben Joe watched Joanne.

"I always did like first dates," she said after a minute. "I was good at those. I knew what to wear—not so dressy it made them shy and not so sloppy they thought I didn't give a hoot—and how to act and what to say, and by the time I was ready to come in I'd have them all the way in love with me or know the reason why. But the dates after that are different. Once they loved me, what was I supposed to do *then*? Once I've accomplished that, where else is there to go? So I ended up confining myself to first dates. I got so good at them that I could first-date *anyone*—I mean even the people that were on *seventh* dates with me, or even people that weren't dates at all. I could first-date my own *family*, even—just figure out what would make them love me at a certain moment and then do it, easy as that."

She leaned forward suddenly, resting her elbows on the rim of the bathtub and staring into the water at Carol's gleeful face.

"Then I got married," she said.

Ben Joe waited, not pushing her. Joanne stood up and reached for a towel and then just stayed there, holding the towel forgotten in her hands.

"The trouble is," she said, "you have to stop clinking your bracelets and dancing like a maniac after a while. You have to *rest* now and then. Which may have been okay with Gary, but not with me. I didn't know what to do once I had sat down to rest, and so I started being just terrible. Following him around telling him what a awful wife I was. Waking him up in the middle of the night to accuse him of not believing I loved him. He was all sleepy and didn't know *what* was coming off. He'd say sure he believed me and go back to sleep leaving me to lie awake counting the dust specks that floated around in the dark, and making all kinds of plans to get my hair done and have him take me dancing." She frowned at the towel. "Got so I couldn't bear my own self," she said. "I left."

She wrapped the towel around Carol and lifted her out onto the bath mat.

"What'd you come back *here* for?" Ben Joe asked.

She dried Carol silently for a minute. Then she said, "Well, I want Carol to be with some kind of people that know her if I am going to get a job. That's why."

She had finished scrubbing Carol with the towel and now she pulled a white flannel nightgown over the baby's head, saying, "Where's Carol? Oh, I can't find Carol. *Where's* Carol?" until Carol's face poked through the neck of the nightgown, small and round and grinning.

"Besides," Joanne said, tying the ribbon under Carol's chin, "it's not the same place I'm coming back to, really. Not even if I wanted it to be."

"Oh, for God's sake," said Ben Joe.

"What's wrong?"

"You and Mama. You and the girls. And Mr. Dower, even. Of course it's the same place. What would it have gone and changed into? Always pulling up the same silly argument to fool yourselves with—"

"Now, now," said Joanne soothingly. She picked Carol up. "It's *not* the same place really, is it?"

He gave up, helplessly, and followed her out of the bathroom. There was no argument he could give that would convince her; she was too blindly cheerful, giving Carol little pecks on the cheek and talking to her happily as she crossed the hallway. At her mother's door she stopped and looked in. "Gone downstairs," she said. "Come on, Ben Joe. I want to ask you something."

"What?" he asked suspiciously.

"Come *on.*"

He followed her to her own room. It was cluttered with Joanne's odds and ends, and the old white crib had been moved down from the attic to a spot beside Joanne's bed. Other than that, it was almost the same as when she had left it. Huge stuffed animals, won by long-ago boy-friends at state fairs, littered the window seat; perfume bottles and hair ribbons and bobby pins lay scattered on the bureau. She laid Carol carefully in the crib and said, "Where were you when Dad died?"

"Where— Oh, no," Ben Joe said. "No, don't you start that."

"Why not?" She straightened up from kissing Carol good night and turned to face him. "That's not fair, Ben Joe. Nobody'll tell me *anything* about it. I even wrote a letter asking them to tell me. Nobody ever answered."

"Well, you were away," Ben Joe said.

"That doesn't change anything." She spread a blanket over Carol and began tying it down at the corners. "It happened just after Jenny began writing all the family's letters," she said. "Only Jenny didn't write this particular one, I remember. She went through a stage when she wouldn't write or speak the fact that Dad was dead. Susannah told me that. So the twins had to take over the letter writing. Jane and Lisa, they handled everything, although neither one of them will touch a pen ordinarily and you can tell it from their letters. But it was just as well, I guess—their writing the letters, I mean—because I suppose Jenny would just have sent a list of the funeral costs. Or would she, that far back? When did Jenny learn to be so practical? Anyway, there was this note from Lisa saying, 'Dad just passed away last night but felt no pain'—as if anyone could *know* what he felt—and that's all I ever heard. What happened, Ben Joe?"

"What difference does it make?" he asked.

"What?"

"Who won. Mama or that other woman."

"Well, that's the—"

"I know." She turned the lamp around so that it wouldn't shine in Carol's eyes and sat down on the foot of the bed. "It's an awful thing to wonder. And none of my business, anyway. But it's important to know, for all kinds of reasons."

He began searching through his crumpled cigarette pack for the last cigarette, not looking at her.

"Here, take mine," she said.

"Not menthol."

"They won't kill you."

She threw the pack at him; it fell on the floor in front of him and he picked it up and leaned back against the bureau.

"Two weeks before he died," Joanne said, "he was at home. I know he was. Jenny put it just beautifully, in this letter she wrote me. She said, 'You'll be happy to know Daddy has got back from his trip'— 'trip'; that's an interesting choice of words—'and he's living at home now.' Now, where was he when he died? Still at home?"

"At Lili Belle's," Ben Joe said.

"At— Oh." She shook her head. "Lately I've stopped thinking about her by her name," she said. "What with Gram calling her 'Another's House' all the time."

"Well, he didn't *mean* to go and die there," said Ben Joe. "He'd just been drinking a little, is all. Went out to get ice cubes and then forgot which home he was supposed to be going back to. Mom explained that to Lili Belle."

"*Mom* explained it to *Lili* Belle?"

"Well, yes. It was her that Lili Belle called soon as he died. He got to Lili Belle's with a pain in his chest and died a little after. So Lili Belle called Mom, and Mom came to explain how it was our house he'd really intended going back to and not hers; just a mistake. And Lili Belle hadn't really won after all."

"Looks like to me she had."

"But it was by *mistake* he went there."

"Oh, pshaw," Joanne said. She turned to see how Carol was and then faced Ben Joe again. "What about their little boy, his and Lili Belle's? That was named after Daddy? That's more'n *you* were named for. I don't see that *your* name is Phillip. Do you think he would have walked off and left a baby named Phillip for good?"

"That's beside the point. You know, Joanne, sometimes I wonder whose side you're on."

She smiled and ground out her cigarette and stood up. "Don't you lose sleep on it," she said. "Come on, we're keeping Carol awake. I'm going to do my nails and I reckon you have people you'll want to visit."

"I don't know who."

But he straightened up anyway and followed Joanne out of the room. In the hall she gave him a little pat on the arm and then turned toward the bathroom, and he started for the stairs. He stopped at the hall landing, which looked down over the long stairway, and put one hand on the railing.

"You know where the emery boards are?" Joanne called from the bathroom.

He didn't answer; he leaned both elbows on the railing and stared downward, thinking.

"Oh, never mind. I found them."

He was remembering one night six years ago; this spot always reminded him of it. He had been studying in his room and at about ten o'clock he had decided to go downstairs for a beer. With his mind still foggy with facts and dates, he had wandered out into the hallway, had put one hand on the railing and was about to take the first step down, when the noise began. He could hear that noise still, although he always did his best to forget it.

First he thought it sounded like an angry bull wheezing and bellowing in a circle around the house. But it was too reedy and penetrating to be that; he thought then that it must be an auto horn. Kerry Jamison had an auto horn like that. Only Kerry Jamison was a well-bred boy and didn't honk for Ben Joe when he came visiting him. And he certainly didn't drive on the Hawkes's carefully tended lawn.

All over the house the girls had come swarming out of the various room, asking what the racket was. Tessie, who was scarcely more than a baby then and should have been asleep for hours, inched her bedroom door open and peeked out to ask Ben Joe if she could come downstairs with the others, because there was a trumpet blowing outside that wouldn't hush for her. She spoke in a whisper; their mother was reading in bed in the room next to Tessie's and would surely say no if she heard what Tessie was asking. But what neither Ben Joe nor Tessie realized at the time was that their mother was answering the telephone in her room, listening to Lili Belle Mosely tell her her husband was dead. Right then she wouldn't have cared if Tessie never went to bed again, but Tessie couldn't know that and she went on in her whispery voice: "Can I, Ben Joe? Say yes. Can I?"

"*No*," said Ben Joe. "I'll go down and shut it up, whatever it is. Get back in bed, Tessie."

"But it's so *scary*, Ben—"

Their mother's door opened. Tessie popped back into her room just as Ellen Hawkes flew out of hers; they were like the two figures in a weather house. Ellen had on a pair of blue cotton pajamas and her hair was rumpled and she was struggling into a khaki raincoat of her husband's as she ran.

"Your father's dead," she said, and rushed down the stairs.

Ben Joe put both hands on the railing and leaned down. His mother had passed the little landing at the curve of the stairs and now she was directly below him, still running down; he could see the top of her head, and the curls lifting a little as she came down hard on each step. "Your father's dead," she repeated to the girls downstairs. Above her voice came the eerie sound from outside, wheezing and bellowing its way around to the front of the house.

Ben Joe let go of the railing and tore down the stairs after his mother. His shirt was open, and the tails of it flew out behind him as he ran. He had no shoes on. On one of the steps his stockinged foot slipped and he almost fell, but he caught himself and kept on going. The girls were waiting for him at the bottom, with stunned white faces. Tessie had come out to stand on the landing where Ben Joe had stood a minute ago and now she looked down at the others and began to cry without knowing why. She had poked her head through the bars because she was not yet tall enough to see over the railing. Her mother, holding on to the newel post at the bottom of the stairs while she struggled into a pair of Susannah's loafers, looked up at Tessie briefly and said, "She'll have got her head caught in those bars again. Better get her out, somebody."

Tessie's head was a tiny yellow circle on the second floor, outlined against the dark cupola that rose above the stairwell. The house seemed enormous, suddenly. The whole world seemed enormous.

"Where are you going?" Ben Joe asked his mother.

"To your father's friend's house," she said, without expression. "I'll be back. Gram's asleep now. Don't wake her. And try and figure some way of getting Tessie's head free without sawing the bars down again, will you?"

Ben Joe nodded. None of it made sense. Everything was harried and nightmarish and yet the same small practical things were going on at the same time. His mother patted his shoulder and then, abruptly, she was off, out the front door and into the darkness of the moonless, early-autumn night. As she crossed the front porch the eerie, wailing sound from outside became louder; as she descended the steps down to the front walk a soldier came into view playing a bagpipe. He was small and serious, with his eyes fixed only on his instrument, and he walked in a straight line across their front lawn and then around to the other side of the house. He and Ellen crossed paths with only inches between them; neither one of them paused or looked toward the other one.

Jenny, standing with the rest of them on the front porch, said, "It's a *bagpipe.*"

From out in back of the house came the sound of their mother's car starting, rising above the piercing sound of the bagpipes. A minute later the yellow, dust-filled beams of two headlights backed past them out into the street and then swung sharply around and disappeared.

Susannah stopped staring after the car and turned to Jenny, frowning, trying to sort her thoughts and figure what should be done.

"It's no bagpipe *I* ever heard," she said finally. "Bagpipes make tunes. This is only making one note."

"Maybe he can't play," Jenny said. She was only twelve then, a thin, nervous little girl, and she was shivering and seemed to be trying desperately to get a grasp on herself. "I'm sure that's it," she said. "He'll practice this note for a while and then go to the next, and then go—"

"Not in *our* yard he won't," Susannah said. "Run around the back and stop him, Ben Joe."

But there was no need to; the soldier had come around the front again. Apparently he liked having an audience. He emerged from the side of the house at a scurrying little run, with his short legs pumping as fast as they could go, and then as soon as he came into the light from the front porch he slowed to a leisurely stroll in order to parade before them for as long as possible. His chest heaved up and down from the running he had done, and the horrible wailing sound was jerky and breathless now.

"Um . . ." Ben Joe said. He stepped down from the porch and the little soldier stopped. "You think you could do that somewhere else?"

The soldier grinned. He had a small bony face, with the skin stretched tight and shining across it when he smiled. "No, sir," he said. "No sir. Man said no."

"What?"

"Your daddy. 'No,' he says. No."

"I don't—"

"Saw me hitchhiking, your dad did. Told me could I play that thing, I allowed yes I could but not *this* way, with all but one reed gone so there wasn't but one sound. He said anyway, anyway, he said, to play it round his house for a joke and not give up till he come back. When he comes he'll give me a bottle. A free bottle."

He grinned again and put the mouthpiece to his lips, but Ben Joe reached out and took a gentle hold on his arm. "He won't be back," he said. He turned toward Susannah. "Get a bottle of bourbon, Susannah. Bourbon all right with you, friend?"

"Oh yes, oh yes—"

Jenny suddenly came to life. She raced down the front steps and yanked Ben Joe's hand from the soldier's arm. "Leave him be," she said. "You leave him. Let him play." Her face was white and pinched-looking; Ben Joe thought if she shook any harder she would fall down.

"He's getting tired of playing," he told her.

"You leave him."

Susannah came out of the house again, slamming the screen door behind her. "Here," she said.

"Why, thank you, Ma'am. I am much—"

"You play, you," said Jenny to the soldier.

Susannah reached over Jenny's head with the bottle; the soldier held out his hand and Jenny made a grab for the bottle but missed.

"Wait," she said.

"Wouldn't change a thing, making him keep playing," Ben Joe told her gently. "If he played till you had grandchildren, it wouldn't bring back—"

"You wait, you *wait*!"

She was rigid now, not shaking any more but with her hands folded into tense fists and her face wet with tears. When Ben Joe put one hand on her shoulder she spun toward him, not actually fighting him but letting her arm stay rigid, so that her fist swung hard into his stomach and knocked all the wind from him. The soldier clicked his tongue, his eyes round. Ben Joe started coughing and bent over, but he kept hold of Jenny, pinning her arms down at her sides and holding her tight while he and Susannah guided her toward the stairs.

"I told you and *told* you!" she was screaming. "Now you've sent him away and he'll *never* come back—"

The soldier, mistaking her meaning, smiled cheerfully and waved his bottle at her. "*Sure* I'll be back," he called comfortingly. "*Don't* you worry ma'am!"

He set off toward the street, whistling. On the porch, Jane and Lisa took Jenny from Ben Joe while he leaned over the railing and coughed himself hoarse, trying to get his wind again. Susannah whacked him steadily on the back.

"You'll be all right," she said over and over. "You'll be all right. You'll be all right."

She did her best, but she couldn't say it the way Joanne did. And right then he wished for Joanne more than anyone in the world. He thought probably they all did. If she came walking up the steps right now she would fold every single person up close to her and cry, and pat them softly; and they could start crying too and telling her all the secret fears swamping their minds at this minute and then they would realize everything that had happened. If they could only *realize* something, things could start getting better again.

But Joanne didn't come up the steps, and when his coughing fit was through, Ben Joe straightened up and followed Susannah into the house again. Up on the second floor, Tessie was crying.

"You get the twins to give Jenny one of Dad's sleeping pills," Ben Joe told Susannah. "I'll try and get Tessie out of the railings."

Now, six years later, he thought he could still name the two posts where Tessie's head had been caught. All seven children, from Joanne to Tessie, had been stuck in this railing at least once in their lives. But he thought he knew which posts Tessie had been between *that* night, because it was still so clear in his mind. He had soothed Tessie, who had been through this before and was not very frightened, and while he was trying to pull her out he thought about the same thing he always thought when he did this: he must put some screening here, to stop all these ridiculous goings-on. Even if Gram *did* say it would ruin the looks of the railing. Under his hands was the feel of Tessie's head—the thin, soft hair, the tight little bones of her skull. He had turned her face gently, holding her small ears flat against her head, and worked her out from between the bars and scooped her up to carry her back to bed. It was then, standing there with the weight of her against his shoulder, that the first sorrow hit him—just one deep bruise inside that made him catch his breath. He could remember it still. That, and the little flannel nightgown Tessie wore, and the soft sounds of Jenny crying in the room she shared with Tessie . . .

It was so clear still that he could have told Joanne, and by telling her proved that Lili Belle hadn't won. For if his father had *meant* to go to Lili Belle's, he wouldn't have played that bagpipe joke on them. He loved every one of his children; he wouldn't have left them with any unkind tricks. But even though he had thought about telling her, Ben Joe had stopped himself. It was one of those things that wasn't mentioned in this house. Not even he and his other sisters mentioned it.

What else didn't they mention? He looked down the stairs and frowned, wondering what went on behind their cool, bright smiles. What did they think about before they went to sleep at night? He leaned further down, listening. The twins were chattering away in the kitchen; in the living room, someone laughed and Tessie gave a small squeal. He began to feel a sort of admiration for them. It was like watching a man who has been to Africa drink tea in the parlor and make small talk, with all those things known and done behind him that he is not even thinking about. Behind him, Joanne padded back to her bedroom with a pack of emery boards in her hand, but Ben Joe didn't look around. He remained in his own thoughts, with his hand resting absently on the stair railing.

6

WHEN FINALLY he came downstairs he made another tour of the house, just to see if anyone was free to talk to him yet. He started with his mother, who had joined the others in the living room and was taking tiny stitches in a white collar.

"Finish Tessie's dress?" he asked.

"Obviously not, since that's what I'm stitching on."

He stood in the middle of the room, chewing on his thumbnail while he tried to think of another opening.

"Well, how's the book store going?" he asked finally.

"It's all right. What's the matter, Ben Joe, haven't you any plans for tonight?"

"Not offhand."

"You certainly are restless."

He took this as an invitation to sit down and did so at once on the leather hassock beside her. On the couch opposite him Susannah and Gram collected the cards that lay between them and Susannah began shuffling them. The cards made a quick, snapping noise under her fingers.

"Carol sure doesn't look like a Hawkes, does she?" he said.

His mother held the dress up at arm's length and frowned at it. "No, I don't suppose she does," she said finally. She lowered the dress into her lap again and then, feeling that something more seemed to be expected of her, said, "It's really too young to tell yet."

"I wouldn't say that," Gram said. "Has the Hawkes nose, I'll say *that*. Small and pointy. And Joanne's little pointy chin."

There was another silence. Susannah began dealing, slapping down a loud card for Gram and a soft one for herself in a steady rhythm. Ben Joe stood up again and moved aimlessly over to the game.

"I thought we might go see Jamie Dower tonight, Gram," he said. "Car's free."

"Oh, well, I don't think so, Ben Joe. Not tonight."

"Why not?"

"Well . . ." She frowned at the cards in her hand. "I'd rather wait awhile," she said. "He wouldn't have settled his self properly yet."

"What's to settle?"

"Can't be much of a host when you're still feeling like a guest yourself, can you? Give him a couple more days."

"A couple more *days*?" said Ben Joe's mother. "How long are you planning on staying here, Ben Joe?"

"I don't know."

"Well, it seems to me you should be gone by then. Columbia's not going to wait on you forever."

"Oh, well," Ben Joe said. He was wandering back and forth with his hands in his pockets, occasionally kicking gently at a leg of the coffee table as he passed it. "Susannah?" he said.

"Hmm."

"Where's the guitar and the hourglass and all?"

"I'm not sure."

"What you mean, you're not sure?"

She brushed a piece of hair off her forehead with the back of her wrist and then switched a card in her hand from the left end of the fan to the right.

"I asked you if you wanted them," Ben Joe said. "I asked if you would take care of them. 'Yes, Ben Joe. Oh yes, Ben Joe.' " He made his voice into a silly squeak, imitating her. Of all his sisters, Susannah was the only one he was ever rude to—maybe because she was always so cool and brisk that he figured she wouldn't change toward him no matter *what* he did. "I can just see it," he said now. "Bet the whole shebang has just mildewed away to nothing, right?"

"In the *winter*?" Gram said.

"I bid two spades," said Susannah. "Ben Joe, I am sure everything's right where you left it. Except the guitar. The rest of the things I just hadn't assimilated yet."

"Well, where's the guitar, now that you've assimilated that? In the bathtub? Out in the garden holding up a tomato plant?"

"In the *winter*?" Gram said again. "A tomato plant in the winter?"

Ellen Hawkes laughed. When they turned to look at her she stopped and looked down at her sewing again, still smiling.

"I declare," said Gram, "you got no sense of *season*, Ben Joe."

"Where's the guitar?"

"Under the couch in the den."

"Aha, I wasn't far wrong. Right where it belongs."

"Ben Joe," said his mother, "there's no reason to get so excited about a few possessions you've already given away. What's the matter with you tonight?"

"But they're my *favorite* possessions. That I missed all the time I was gone."

"Then you shouldn't have given them away. You're too old to be missing things, anyway. Why don't you stop that pacing and read something?"

He picked the newspaper up from the coffee table and began to read it listlessly as he stood there.

"And *not* upside-*down*!" his mother said.

"Ah, hell."

He threw down the paper and turned toward the den.

"You need someone to take you out walking with a leash around your neck," said Susannah. "Are you going to bid or not, Gram?"

"Pass."

Ben Joe stuck his head inside the doorway of the TV room. "Tessie," he said.

"Sssh."

"Tess, I want to ask you something."

"I'm watching television."

"It's only a cigarette commercial."

"Leave her in peace," said Jenny. "And don't hold that door open, Ben Joe. The noise'll bother the others."

"Don't either one of you want to go to the movies?"

Tessie shook her head, not taking her eyes from the screen. "It's only what it just about always is," she said. *"Phantom of the Opera."*

"Why don't you come in and watch TV?" Jenny asked.

"I don't feel like it. I feel all yellow inside."

"Well, close the door, then."

He closed the door and came back into the living room.

"What happened to all those boys you used to go around with?" his mother asked.

"They went *north*, all of them. A long time ago."

"Do you know any girls any more?"

"Them too," he said.

"What?"

"They went north too."

"Oh."

"Gram," said Susannah, "if you keep holding your hand that way I'm going to have to shut my *eyes* not to see what cards you have."

"What about Shelley Domer?" his mother asked.

"Oh, Mom. She was my *first* girl. Her family went off to Savannah seven years ago."

"Gram, wasn't that Shelley Domer we saw the other day?"

"It was," said Gram. "You have another diamond, Susannah. I know you do."

"I don't either. Want to see my hand?"

"What's she doing *here*?" Ben Joe asked.

"I don't know," said his mother. "Their family kept their house here, I think. Kept planning to come back someday."

"You mean she's living in her old home?"

"She wouldn't have been sweeping the front porch of it if she *wasn't*, would she?"

"I'd go see her if you've nothing better to do," Gram said. "Be something to keep you occupied. And you saw right much of her once upon a time."

"Oh, she was all right."

"That all you can find to say about her? *Spades* are trumps, Susannah.

Keep your mind on your game. Only thing *I* ever had against Shelley
Domer was her family, to be frank."

"What was wrong with her family, for heaven's sake?"

"Well, I'm not saying they didn't have money. Or weren't nice. But
money and niceness neither one isn't all there is. Mrs. Domer still went
grocery shopping in shuffly old slippers with pansies sewn on them,
and that Shelley, well, she was a sweet child and it was no fault of
hers, but many's the time I seen her in a flowered calico skirt and a
plaid blouse *together*, like a tenant farmer's girl would wear, and in
wintertime overalls under her dress, which is a *sure* sign, a sure sign.
As if having those glass-blue, empty-looking eyes like the bad Dowers
have wasn't enough—"

"Well, for one who wears black *gym* shoes to the grocery store—"
Ellen Hawkes began.

"I can afford to. My family is different, and don't have to worry
about being taken for the wrong kind."

Ben Joe's mother bit a thread off the white collar. "Well, I don't see
what slippers have to do with it," she said. "Shelley Domer can't help
her ancestry, that's for sure. No, all I ever had against her was the
way she hung on Ben Joe all the time. None of *my* girls has ever been
a boy chaser, I'll say that for them. They've been raised to have pride,
and—"

"Pride nothing," Gram snapped. "Nicest thing *about* that girl was
her being so sweet on Ben Joe. She used to wait for him every day
after school, I remember. Even in wintertime. Till he'd come ambling
out at whatever hour he chose to say hey to her."

"That's what I'm—"

"Oh, forget it," said Ben Joe. "I'll go and see her now while you
two are arguing." He went to the hall closet and pulled his jacket from
a hanger. "Anyone want anything from outside?"

"No, thank you. Have a nice evening."

"Okay."

Outside it was beginning to get cold. There was a little chill around
his neck where his collar was open, but he just walked more quickly
to make up for it. With his hands in his pockets and his lips pursed
in a silent whistle he headed east, down past rows of medium-sized,
medium-aged houses that jangled faintly with the TV or radio noises
locked inside them. Occasionally he caught glimpses of families moving
around behind lace curtains, but no one was out on the sidewalk. A
dog rushed past, trailing a leash; nobody attempted to follow him. And
at one house an old woman in a man's overcoat rocked on a cold
porch glider.

"Hey," she said.

"Hey," said Ben Joe.

"No moon out tonight."

"No."

He turned up Evers and walked more slowly. None of the walk took any thinking. When he was in high school it had become second nature, like going downstairs in the morning for breakfast and then realizing, once he was down there, that the actual descent had been an utter blank in his memory. The first few times he had come here actually shaking, with his hair slicked down and his face thin from the tension of keeping his teeth from chattering. He would have gone to the bathroom six or seven times in the half-hour before, just from nervousness. But gradually it became just an ordinary thing, this walk. Even when there was no definite date planned he would go, just to sit in the living room with Shelley and talk to her. She wasn't very quick-witted and she didn't entertain him with fast talk and bubbles of laughter the way his sisters entertained their dates, but she did listen. No matter what he talked about she would listen, smiling happily at him all the time, and when he was done she would just hug him or tell him how much she liked the way the barber had cut his hair this week, but he knew she had heard what he had to say, anyway. He smiled into the darkness, thinking about that, and cut through a vacant lot to Holland Street and the Domer house.

The lights were turned on inside. The place was the same as always—big and worn and comfortable, with years of dead leaves piled around it. He would have thought Mr. Domer had raked those up by now; Mr. Domer was a small and tidy man. When Ben Joe crossed the front lawn the leaves roared around his ankles. He climbed the long steps to the front door. Years ago, in the summertime, they would stop at this top step when they came in from a date. They would look up to the open window upstairs and there would be the little triangular-faced, white-nightgowned blur of Shelley's sister Phoebe peering down at them. She must have been about seven, that first year. She had thought, from seeing the cartoons in the *Saturday Evening Post*, that all boys kissed their dates on the girls' doorsteps, and every night she had lain in wait in her bedroom, watching hopefully. How old would she be now? Sixteen or seventeen, he supposed. And gone from that window. There was only the closed glass pane now, and the still white organdy curtains behind it.

He knocked twice. A figure came toward him and peered out the window glass in the door, still only a silhouette behind a mesh curtain. Then she opened the door and let him step in. She seemed stunned for a minute; her mouth was slightly open.

"Ben Joe!" she said. "Is that you?"

"Sure it is. Have I gone and changed all that much?"

"No. No, only it's been such a long . . . Well, hey, anyway."

"Hey."

Shelley stood awkwardly in front of him, beginning to look happy and a little scared. She never had known what to do about greeting people. If she had been one of the girls he had dated after her, she would have come tripping up and shrieked, "For goodness *sake*!" and kissed him loudly on the mouth even if she didn't remember his name. But not Shelley. Shelley stood straight before him, with her hands pleating little bunches of her skirt at the sides, and smiled at him.

"Mom said she saw you sweeping the front porch," he said. "I'm home for a little vacation. I thought I'd stop by and see how you were getting on."

"Oh, well, I'm fine. Just seems funny to see you, I think . . . ."

She moved over almost soundlessly to shut the door behind him, and he turned to watch her. There were little changes in her; he could see that even under the dim light in the hallway. Her hair, which used to hang almost to her shoulders in such straight blond ribbons that it had made him think of corn syrup, was bunched scratchily behind her head now and held there by a few pins, much like Gram's bun. Her face was prettier and more clearly defined, but she still gave the impression of a waifish kind of thinness that made her seem more like fifteen than twenty-five. Partly it was because she was pale and without make-up, and her eyes were such a light blue; partly it was because she was wearing old clothes that must have been her mother's and were far too big for her. The skirt was a dingy pink, accordion-pleated and very long; the sweater was an old bulky maroon one that somehow made her shoulder blades stick out more in back than her breasts did in front. But she still moved the same way—almost frightenedly and without a sound, and always in slow motion. Now she slowly opened her hands at her sides, as if she were consciously telling herself to relax, and looked down at her clothes.

"Now, Ben Joe," she said. "I have to go put another dress on. I didn't know I was about to have company. You wait in the living room, hear? I'll be right—"

"But I'm just going to stay a minute," Ben Joe said. "I only came to say hello."

"Well you just wait."

She turned and darted up the curving stairs, and Ben Joe had to go into the living room alone. He chose a seat at the end of the sofa, nearest the unlit fireplace. The room seemed to him like the huge front room of a long-unused summer house; all the things that were not particularly liked and yet still too good to discard had been left here by the Domers when they moved South. Wicker armchairs and threadbare sofas sat on an absolutely bare wooden floor, and the few decorative items scattered around were worthless—a china spaniel with three puppies chained to her collar by tiny gold chains; a huge framed photograph of a long-ago baseball team; a rosebudded cracked china slipper with earth in it but no plant. Ben Joe shivered. This had been a cheerful room once, back when he was in high school.

He heard Shelley's shoes on the stairs and a minute later she was in the living room, crossing in front of him with a company smile and a white skirt and sweater that fit better than the old ones. She had combed her hair, although he was sorry to see that it was still in a bun, and there was a little lipstick on her mouth.

"I'm going to get you some coffee," she said.

"No, I don't want any."

"It's already made, Ben Joe. You wait here and I'll—"

"No, *please*. I don't want any."

"Well, all right."

She sat down on the edge of a wicker armchair with her hands on her knees.

"Where's Phoebe?" Ben Joe asked.

"Phoebe."

"Phoebe your *sister*."

"Oh," she said. All the breath seemed to have left her; she gasped a little and said, "Phoebe and Mama and Daddy, all of them, they're dead, you mustn't have heard, it only happened a while—"

"Oh, no, I never—"

"They had a wreck."

"I'm sorry," Ben Joe said. He thought of the small white blur in the upstairs window, still almost realer than Shelley herself. He watched Shelley's fingers twisting a pearl button on her sweater. "Nobody told me," he said helplessly.

"I only been back a while now. Not many people know about it."

"Was . . . How old was Phoebe?"

"Seventeen."

"Oh." He fell silent again, and tugged gently at one of the little cotton balls on the sofa upholstery.

"How are *your* sisters?" Shelley asked suddenly.

"They're fine." Almost immediately he felt guilty for that; he thought a minute and then offered: "Joanne's left her husband, though."

"Left him?"

"Yes."

"Well, I declare."

"She's back home now."

"Well."

"Her and her baby."

"I'm going to get you some coffee," Shelley said.

"No, wait. I've got to be—"

"It's *hot* already." She stood up and almost ran to the kitchen, still managing to make it slow motion. Behind her, Ben Joe shifted in his seat uneasily and crossed his legs.

"You're hungry too, I bet," she said when she entered the room again.

"No, I'm all right."

"You look right thin to me, Ben Joe. I got this marble cake from the Piggly-Wiggly. Course it's not real homemade, but anyway—"

"Shelley, I really don't want it."

"Well, all right, Ben Joe."

She was carrying a chipped tin tray with two cups of coffee on it and a sugar bowl and cream pitcher that didn't match. When she set it on the coffee table everything clinked like the too-loud clinking of tea sets in movies.

"You take yourself lots of sugar," she said. "I declare, you *are* thin." She hovered over him, shadowlike, while he took up his coffee cup. He could smell her perfume now—a light, pink-smelling perfume— and when she bent over the table to hand him the sugar bowl, he could even smell perfume in her hair. Then she moved back to her seat, and he relaxed against the sofa cushions.

"Seems like I have got to get used to you all over again, it's been so long," Shelley said. "Are you feeling talky?"

He had forgotten that. She always asked him that question, to give him a chance before she plunged into her own slow, circuitous small talk. This time he remained silent, choosing to have her carry on the conversation, and smiled at her above his coffee cup because he liked her suddenly for remembering. Shelley waited another minute, sitting back easily in her chair. Once the first awkward moments were over, Shelley could be as relaxed as anyone.

"I don't know if I did right or not," she said finally, "coming back here like this. But my family's passing came so sudden. Left me strap-hanging in empty space, like. And I chose to come to Sandhill. I don't know why, except I was helping to run this nursery school for working mothers' children down in Georgia and so *sick* of it, you've got no idea, and saw no way out. I think I got something against Georgia. I really do. Seems like if there is one thing makes me ill, it's those torn-up circus posters on old barns. You know? And Seven-up signs. Well, Georgia's plumb full of those, though one time this girl I worked with told me she thought it was real snotty of me to say a thing like that. That's what our trouble was down there—the trash thought we were snotty and the snotty thought we were trash. Now, my daddy had to work himself up the hard way, but you know how fine he was, and anyway his mama's folks were Montagues, which should have *some* bearing. And there's nothing wrong with Mama's side of the family, either. But anyway I was lonely there. Didn't seem like there was any group we could really say we belonged to. Back in Sandhill it was better. I always have remembered Sandhill. And I still carry your picture."

She smiled happily at Ben Joe.

"That real goofy-looking one," she said, "that we had taken of you in the Snap-Yourself Photo Booth. Mama used to tease me about keeping it—said I might as well throw it out now. Though she always did like you. When you wrote me that letter, after we'd moved, about you starting to date Gloria Herman I thought Mama would cry. She said Gloria was real fast and loud, though it was my opinion that you knew better than Mama who was good for you. And at least you were right honest, telling me. I said that to Mama, too. And then a month later Susan Harpton wrote to tell how Gloria had moved on to someone new and you'd started dating Pat Locker. It got so I couldn't keep up with you any more. But I wasn't mad. Things like that happen when people get separated from each other."

"Well, it was a long time ago," Ben Joe said.

"It was. I know. Well, don't you worry, Ben Joe, I'm dating a real nice boy now. You'd like him. His name is John Horner and he's starting up a construction firm in Sandhill. You know him?"

"Horner." Ben Joe frowned. "Not offhand," he said.

"Well. You'd like him, though. Course we aren't too serious yet—I only been in town a month or so. But he is the *kindest* man. I don't know if I could marry him, yet."

"Has he asked you?"

"No. But I reckon he will one of these days."

The idea of Shelley's marrying someone else surprised him. He looked at her as a stranger suddenly, evaluating her. She smiled back at him.

"Course," she said, "I was surprised he even wanted to *date* me. But I figured if maybe he could just endure through the first few dates, till I got easy with him and not so silly and tongue-tied any more, it'd be all right. And he did. He endured."

"Well, I'm glad to hear it."

She nodded, finished with that piece of news, and then frowned into space a minute as if she were fishing in her mind for the next piece.

"Oh, I know," she said finally. "I know. Ben Joe, I was so sorry to hear about your daddy. I wrote you about it and you never answered. But I hope it was a peaceful passing. He was a sweet man, your daddy."

"Thank you," said Ben Joe.

"Susan Harpton told me about it. And about your going to work at the bank after classes and Joanne getting married and all. She said the whole town missed your daddy."

"I did too," said Ben Joe. "Took to riding trains."

"What?"

"Trains. Riding trains. I rode trains all the time. One time I spent a whole month's salary that way. Mom about had a conniption fit—I was almost the family's only support back then."

"Oh," Shelley said. She frowned; she was on uncertain ground now. "Well, anyway, I just wanted to tell you I missed him. And if he lived a little different from most people, I don't think anybody held it against him. Not your daddy. Remember how when he got to drinking he always wanted someone to sing to him? 'Life Is Like a Mountain Railroad,' that's what he liked. Many's the time I've sung it to him."

"And 'Nobody Knows the Trouble I've Seen,' " said Ben Joe.

"That's right." She smiled into her coffee cup and then looked up

again, with the next subject decided upon. "I hear you're in law school
up north," she said. "Mrs. Murphy told me that. She's the one that's
been keeping an eye on the house all these years. She's nice, though
I found when I came back that she'd looked through the photograph
albums and all Mama's love letters. When your mama and grandma
passed by the porch as I was sweeping I called out 'hey' to them,
meaning to ask about you, but I had trouble making myself heard, as
your grandma was doing some of that singing of hers and your mama
was trying real hard to hush her. When your grandma saw me she
recognized me right off, though. She shouted out to tell me you weren't
married yet, which I already knew, and a minute later your mama
remembered me too. Your mama is a little slow in recognizing folks,
but I don't hold with what Mrs. Murphy says, that she's on *purpose*
slow. This town has always been of the opinion she is coldhearted,
but I think it's because your daddy was their fair-haired boy, and they
didn't want him hurt. Not that I think she *meant* to hurt him. I reckon
she is just a little prideful and thinks pride's the same as dignity
so she doesn't try and change herself. Mrs. Murphy said many's the
time she herself went to your mama to tell her all she had to do was
let herself get to crying and then, as soon as the tears got started good,
go to . . . um, where your father lived at and tell him she wanted
him back, but your mama always just tossed her hair and said who
cared and offered Mrs. Murphy a slice of angel-food cake. It was the
doctor's business and no one else's, she would say, though if it wasn't
the doctor's *wife's* business too, then what did they get married for?

"Well, anyway, I never did get to ask how you were doing up north,
since your mama and grandma were in a hurry. But I know it can be
a lonely place. I went up there once to work for the Presbyterian church
and stayed for a month, rooming with a girl I'd met who turned out
to be a bit touched in the head. Went around in a chiffon gown with
a candle in her hand at four a.m. and talked about craning her swanlike
neck in the rain. I went home again. I always have been a homebody.
I don't know what I'll do without my family. Even Phoebe, and her
so mischievous. The last night that Phoebe was . . . was living, the
last night I ever saw her, she was in the kitchen with her boy-friend
and when—"

"Phoebe had a *boy*-friend?" Ben Joe asked.

"Well, yes, and when I walked in, they were robbing this loose-
change bank of my mama's, shaped like an Indian with a slot in the
top of his head where she puts the money in, for odds and ends-like
that she wants to buy—they were robbing this bank so they could go
to the movies. The boy-friend had just got out his pocketknife to put
through the slot and Phoebe was holding out her hand and saying,
'scalpel,' and that's the last I ever saw of her. I'm awful glad to meet
up with you again, Ben Joe. All these years I been missing you."

"I'm glad to see *you*," said Ben Joe. He smiled at her in silence for a minute and then looked at his watch and stood up. "I've got to go. I was on the train all last night. Need to catch up on my sleep."

"Oh, don't you hurry."

"I've got to."

He picked up his jacket from the couch and put it on as he followed Shelley to the door. Outside it was raining; the sight surprised them both and they stood there looking at it.

"Don't come out with me," Ben Joe said.

"I won't melt."

"No, stay inside."

"I want to see you safely to the street," Shelley said.

Her face was serious, and she looked worried about him. Without knowing why, Ben Joe said, "Um, this Jack Horner—"

"John Horner."

"*John* Horner. Do you think he'd mind if I came back again?"

"I don't know. I don't— You come see me anyway, Ben Joe. You come anyway."

She was smiling now, looking up at him with the porch light shining clear through those sky-blue eyes of hers. Her face was so close he could bend down and kiss her. He had never kissed her on the doorstep before, despite all Phoebe's hopes; he had kissed her in his mother's old Buick, parked somewhere in the darkness, with that pink smell of her perfume circling him and her arms thin and warm around his neck. Her face hovered under his, still close; she looked up at him. But as he was about to bend toward her he thought that maybe this might commit him again; maybe everything would begin all over again, and time would get even more jumbled up in his head than it was already. So he drew back from the pale oblong of her face and said, "Is Sunday evening all right? About nine?"

"Yes."

"Well."

He stood looking at her for a minute longer, and then straightened his shoulders.

"I'll see you then," he said.

"Good night, Ben Joe."

"Good night."

He turned and started down the long steps, being careful not to slip on the soggy layers of leaves beneath his feet. The rain was no more than an unsteady dripping sound now, with an occasional cool drop landing on his face. Once on the street again, he shoved his hands deep into his trouser pockets and walked very slowly, frowning, sorting his thoughts out. But his thoughts wouldn't sort; he felt as if he was never again going to know the reason for anything he did. The puddles on the sidewalk began soaking into his shoes, and he started running toward home.

7

THE NEXT day was Saturday. Ben Joe awoke with a hollow, bored feeling; he dawdled over his breakfast until it was cold and then went back to his room to read a detective novel upside-down on an unmade bed. Halfway through the morning one of the girls knocked on his door and said, "Ben Joe?"

"Mm-hmm."

"It's me. Lisa. Can I come in?"

"I guess so."

She stuck her head in the door and smiled. She was much calmer than her twin; it was the way Ben Joe had first learned to tell them apart. She was wearing a neat blue suit and high heels. "We're going downtown," she said. "Want to come?"

"You have to dress up *that* much just to go downtown?"

"Never can tell who you'll meet." She grinned, and crossed to his bed to hand him a postcard. "Mail," she said. "Who's Jeremy?"

"My roommate. Do you have to read all my mail?"

He looked at the picture on it—the Guggenheim Museum, in an unreal shade of yellowish-white—and then turned the card over and began reading the large, rounded handwriting:

> Dear Ben J.,
>   Hope you are thawing out down there. I borrowed your dinner jacket. That frizzly-haired girl keeps calling wanting to know when you'll be back, and I said Monday or so, right? Pack one of those sisters of yours in a suitcase and bring her along.
>   Jeremy.

"Which one are you going to pack up?" Lisa said.

"What?"

"Which sister?"

"Oh. I don't know. Why—you feel like leaving home?"

"I surely do," Lisa said. She sat down with a little bounce on the foot of the bed and looked at her shoes. "I've used up all the boys in this town, that's what."

"What about those two you and Jane were with last night?"

"I'm getting tired of them. I keep thinking maybe I could start new someplace else, in another town."

"Well, I know the feeling." said Ben Joe. He turned the card over again and looked at it, frowning. "I wonder if I've missed any quizzes.

Jeremy's right—I've got to get started back there pretty quick."

"Well, do you want to come to town or don't you?"

"No. I guess not."

Lisa stood up and left, and Ben Joe looked after her thoughtfully. "Don't you worry," he said when she reached the door. "New boys're always showing up."

"I know. Yell if you change your mind about coming downtown, Ben Joe."

"Okay."

He stared at the closed door for a few minutes and then got up and padded over to his bureau in his stocking feet. The top drawer looked like Jeremy's had in New York—stuffed with postcards and envelopes and canceled checks. He threw the postcard on top of the heap and then idly leafed through what was underneath. At the bottom was a stack of Shelley's letters from Savannah, neatly rubber-banded together. And a few postcards from the times his father had gone to medical conventions. They were dry and formal; his father had trouble saying things in writing. He stacked everything carelessly together again and was about to close the drawer when he saw something pink lying in the right hand corner. It was a unique shade of pink—a deep rose that was almost magenta and never should have been used in writing paper— and it was one that had stuck in his mind for some six years now. Even when he saw something nearly that color in a dress or a magazine ad, even now, it made him wince. He pulled the envelope up and made himself examine it. Large, slanted pencil writing ran in a straight line across it, addressed to his father at his office on Main Street. Only his father had never seen it; Ben Joe had taken it from the box when he had gone to bring his father home for supper one day. He had seen the "L.B.M." on the upper left-hand corner and quietly stuffed it in his pocket. Now he stood staring at it without opening it, letting it lie flat in the palm of his hand. When he had stared at it so long that he could see it with his eyes shut, he suddenly slapped it into his shirt pocket, grabbed up his sneakers from the floor in front of the bureau, and slammed out of his room.

"Lisa!" he called.

His grandmother was on the landing, polishing the stair rail and singing only slightly more softly than usual, because she was intent upon her polishing:

> "When I was *si-ing*le,
> I wandered at my *e-ease*.
> Now that I am *ma-arried*,
> Got a flat-heeled man to
> please . . ."

"Gram," Ben Joe said, "has Lisa gone downtown yet?"

She refolded her cloth and smiled at it, still singing, because she
was at the loudest part and no one could stop her at a loud part:

> "And it's oh, *Lo-o-ord*,
> I wish I was but one lone girl again . . ."

"Oh, hell," Ben Joe said. He galloped on down the stairs, two at a
time, with his sneakers still in his hands. "*Lisa!*"

"What you want, Ben Joe?"

He stepped over Carol, who was sticking toothpicks upright into the
nap in the hall rug. Lisa was in the living room arguing with Jenny
and Joanne over the grocery list.

"If she wants all those outlandish things," Jenny was saying, "she
can darn well go get them herself, that's what *I* think."

Joanne took the list from her and ran her finger down it. "Well,"
she said finally, "I don't reckon it would *hurt* us any to start drinking
burgundy with our meals—"

"But *I'm* the one Ben Joe left in charge of the money. What's the
matter with Gram lately? Ben Joe, I want you to look at this."

Ben Joe sat down on the couch and began putting his sneakers on.
"I've decided to hitch a ride downtown with you," he said.

"*Look*, will you, Ben Joe? Now Gram's making *me* go out and buy
all her silly notions. Burgundy my foot. And her upstairs singing loud
on purpose, been singing all morning without taking breath so that no
one can interrupt and ask her what she wants with burgundy and
oyster crackers and kippered herrings—"

"Oh, she's just tired of the same old things," Ben Joe said. "You
going right away? Because if not, I'll just walk instead of—"

"No, we're coming. Come on, Joanne."

Jenny led the way, looking sensible and businesslike in her open
trenchcoat. At the front door she took the car keys off a hook on the
wall and stuck them in her pocket. "Where's Tessie?" she asked Lisa.

"In the car. Says you and she are going shoe shopping and she's in
a hurry to get started."

"Okay. Close the door behind you, Ben Joe."

They crossed through the weedy grass to the driveway beside the
house where the car was parked. Inside, on the front seat, Tessie
bounced up and down in a short-sleeved plain dress.

"Where's your jacket?" Jenny asked as she opened the door.

"In the house."

"Well, better go get it."

"Aw, Jenny—"

"Jenny, for Pete's sake," Ben Joe said. "I'm in a hurry."

"Well, I can't help that. Run on and get it, Tessie."

Tessie slammed out of the car, and Jenny turned the motor on to
let it warm up. She seemed resigned to all these hindrances; she sat

patiently waiting, while Ben Joe, squeezed between Joanne and Lisa, drummed his fingers on his knees and squirmed about irritably. When Tessie came out of the house, dragging her feet slowly as she worked her way into an old corduroy jacket, Ben Joe leaned forward and shouted, "Come *on*, Tessie!"

"What's the matter with *you?*" Jenny asked. She leaned across to open the door for Tessie. "What you suddenly in such an all-fired hurry for?"

"I've got a lot to get done."

"Ten minutes ago you were going to stay home all day," said Lisa.

"Well, not any more."

"Where you going?"

"Just around." He leaned back with his hands between his knees and stared out the window as the car slipped down the driveway into the street. "Got a couple of things I want to attend to," he said. "And Jeremy's postcard reminded me I don't have all year to do them in."

"Better go see your old music teacher," Lisa said. "And Miss Potter, the one that taught you third grade. She asks about you every time she sees me."

"Okay."

"She wants to know if you're a famous poet yet. Says you wrote your first poem in her class."

"*I* don't remember that."

"Well, she does. Says it went, 'My fish, my cat, my little world,' and she's keeping it still for when you get famous."

"My land," Ben Joe said. "Jenny, how far downtown are you going?"

"Just to the A & P."

"And the shoe store," Tessie reminded her.

"And the shoe store. Why you want to know?"

"Not past that?" asked Ben Joe.

"Well, no. What *is* past that?"

"Where is it you're going, anyway?" Joanne asked him.

He scowled at her and remained silent, and Joanne turned back to the window. They were still among lawns and houses; Jenny drove so slowly that a man walking at a brisk pace could keep up with her. At one point Joanne said, "Was that the Edmonds' house?"

Ben Joe leaned forward to see where she was pointing. Between two houses was a charred space with only a set of cement steps and a yellow brick fireplace left intact.

"It was," he said. "Burned down the year you left."

"Nobody told me about it."

"You used to date their son, I think." He had come upon them kissing in the den one night; Bobby was hugging her and kissing the hollow in her neck, and Ben Joe had left the room again without a sound.

"I'd forgotten that," Joanne said.

Sometimes he thought his sisters had been born senile.

When they reached the A & P on Main Street, Jenny parked the car. "We'll be in here awhile and then to Barton's for Tessie's shoes," she said. "If you're back in the car by then I'll drive you home. Otherwise you can just walk back whenever you're ready. Hurry, Ben Joe, you're holding Lisa up."

Ben Joe was sitting forward but not getting out. Lisa nudged him impatiently. "*Come* on, Ben Joe. I thought you were the one in such a rush."

"Okay, okay."

He climbed slowly out of the car and then just stood on the sidewalk beside Joanne with his hands in his pockets.

"Well," he said.

Joanne looked at him curiously. Jenny and Tessie were already heading toward the A & P, and Lisa was staring at a sweater in the window next door.

"Maybe I'll go wherever you're going," said Joanne.

"No."

"Well, where is it you're going?"

"Um. To call on Miss Potter, for one thing. You go on and do your shopping. Maybe I'll meet you in Stacy's for a cup of coffee later."

"All right."

She stood there still looking at him with that little half-smile. He wished she weren't so nosy. The others didn't know the meaning of privacy, they were continually bursting into his room unannounced or reading his postcards, but at least they didn't go ferreting around to see what he was thinking about, the way Joanne did. Sometimes he thought she had even *succeeded* in her ferreting—like today, when she remained absolutely motionless and smiled her knowing smile. He scowled back at her.

"So long," he said.

"So long."

When she still stood there, he whirled around abruptly and headed for the drugstore at a businesslike pace. Once inside, he peered out the glass door and saw that her back was to him now; she was calmly waiting for a car to pass before she crossed the street.

The drugstore smelled like his house did when all the girls were getting ready to go out on dates at once. It was spicy and perfumey, with several different kinds of scents that were mingled together and made him want to sneeze. He headed toward the back, where the toilet articles were kept. From the rack on top of the counter he chose a pack of razor blades, taking a long time to compare prices and brand names, and then he turned to the magazine counter and picked out a crossword-puzzle book that was made of dull comic-booklike paper which would depress him before he finished the first puzzle. These he paid for at the cash register; he counted out the exact change to pay a white-haired man he had not seen before.

"Don't bother about a bag," he said.

He dropped the razor blades into his shirt pocket, next to the pink envelope and his cigarettes. The crossword-puzzle book he rolled up carelessly and stuck into his back trouser pocket. Then he looked out toward the street again. This time there was not a sister of his in sight. He smiled good-by to the man at the cash register and headed outside.

Beyond the A & P, which was the last real store on Main Street, the millworkers' houses again. At first they were the big old houses that had been built by well-to-do families but had turned gray and peeling with "Room for Rent" signs on them. Their side yards, once grassy and shaded with oak trees, were now cement squares where Esso stations sat. And beyond these were smaller, grayer houses, most of them duplexes. Dirty-faced children played on the porches in skimpy sweaters; the yards were heaped with old tires and rusty scrap metal. Behind the houses, barely visible above the tar-paper roofs, were the tall smoking chimneys of the textile factory where all these people worked. They made blue denim, day in and day out. It was toward these chimneys that Ben Joe headed. He crossed a vacant lot, knee-high with weeds and brambles, and stumbled over a rusted-out pot-bellied stove that lay smack in the middle of the field. Then he was on the gravel road that ran down to the muddy little river where the factory was. Opposite the factory was Lili Belle Mosely's house.

He had been here before, many times. The first time was when his father was still alive, living at Lili Belle's as if it were his home and having his patients call him there in the night if they needed him. He had first rented a room there; people said that one night he had finished mending a millworker's arm and was setting out for home when it suddenly hit him that he couldn't bear to go home again, so he had stopped here and rented a room. His wife, hearing about it, clamped her mouth shut and said that was *his* lookout, nothing she could do about it. She said the same when she heard that he had taken to sharing a room with the landlady's daughter; and the same when she heard about little Phillip's being born. But Ben Joe, who never could resign himself to the fact that it was his father's lookout alone, had come to see his father at Lili Belle's one night with his heart pounding and his eyes wide with embarrassment. They had fed him supper— green beans cooked with fat back, hashbrown potatoes in a puddle of Mazola, pork chops coated with grease that turned white when he let the chops cool on his plate. Everyone laughed a lot and his father ate more than Ben Joe had seen him eat in years. And Ben Joe had not been able to say a word to his father about coming home. He hadn't tried.

As he stood now, facing the long, squat house with its dingy front porch, he could almost see how he must have looked coming out of it. His head down, his face puzzled, his feet dragging. Not just once, but many times, because he had gone back again and again. First he had gone to see his father. Then his father died and left a request that Lili Belle and her son get a little money each month, which Ben Joe's mother could have contested but didn't; she said it wasn't worth her bother. So Ben Joe took Lili Belle her money in person once each month. And once each month his mother said, "Ben Joe, have you mailed off all our bills for this month?" and Ben Joe said, "Yes'm," not ever letting on he had taken it in person. Every month he had taken it, up until he had left for New York and turned the money matters over to Jenny. Now Jenny mailed the money, as she was supposed to, in a business envelope. She wouldn't have that feeling Ben Joe always had, looking at his mother with pure guilt on his face and wondering why he kept on lying to her and visiting a woman whose name was never mentioned in the house. He couldn't have given a reason. When he was a senior in high school, his father came home for an hour one day (after he'd been gone a year) to say that all his life he had been saving the money for Ben Joe to go to Harvard and now there was enough. Ellen Hawkes said that unless he came home she wouldn't take a penny, and he said, well, he didn't see that it would really matter to her if he never came home again. Ellen Hawkes didn't answer that. So Ben Joe went to Sandhill College. But even so, even knowing that Lili Belle was the reason he had to go there, he still came to sit in Lili Belle's house and talk to her about the weather and he still threw little Phillip up in the air and caught him again, laughing.

He crossed the scrubby little yard and climbed up to the porch. The wooden floor boards made a hollow sound under his shoes. At the door he knocked and waited, and then knocked again. One corner of the chintz curtain rose slowly. The door swung open.

"Lili Belle?" he said.

"It's *me*, boy."

It was her old mother standing in the shadows behind the door. Ben Joe had seldom seen her before. She was fat and puffing but very dignified, and she had kept out of sight for sheer shame ever since the day her daughter's baby had been born. Now she closed the door sharply behind him and said, "What you want, anyway?"

"I want to see Lili Belle."

"Hmm." She crossed her fat arms under the shelf-like bosom of her black crepe dress. "Lilian Belle is very tired, Benjamin," she said. "Got troubles of her own. What you wanting to see her for?"

"Mrs. Mosely, I won't stay long. I just wanted to see her a minute. It's important."

"Well, I'll tell her. But I don't know, I don't know."

"Thank you, ma'am."

He followed her across the small, mousy-smelling hallway into the almost totally dark sitting room. Against the shaded window he could make out the outline of an unlit lamp, double-globed and beaded. Mrs. Mosely stood like a mountain barring the rest of the view; she called into the room, "Back."

Lili Belle was in the shadows, sitting on a cane chair. She stirred a little and said, "You say something, Mama?"

"Back again to pester us."

"Who?"

"Him." She jerked a thumb behind her. "Ben Joe."

"Oh, my goodness. Benjy, honey, come *in*!" She stood up and ran to the windows to raise the shades. In her right hand was a bowl of soup, which she shifted awkwardly to her left hand when she tried to maneuver the shade. The room was suddenly light again. With the light a feeling of relief came to Ben Joe; this wasn't going to be as hard as he thought. He always forgot how easy Lili Belle made him feel the minute he saw her.

"It's okay, Mama," she was saying now. "You can go on now. Come on in, Benjy honey. I do apologize for sitting in the dark like this, but my eyes is strained."

"It's okay," Ben Joe said.

He looked at her closely, noticing how tired she looked. It was hard to tell how old she was. Nine years ago, when his father had first met her, she had been about twenty. Now she could be any age. Her face seemed never to have resolved itself but stayed as vague and unformed as when she had been a girl. Her hair was straggly and colorless, and she was never anything but homely, but she had an enormous, bony frame that made people look a second time when they passed her on the street. There was not an ounce of fat on her. When she walked, her bones seemed to swing loosely, and she never hit hard upon the earth or seemed, for all her boniness, to have any sharp corners to her. Yet he could see the strain lines beginning around her eyes and mouth, and the way the skin of her face had grown white and dry.

"You sit yourself," she was saying now. "Wait a minute . . ." She looked around among the straight-backed chairs, searching for the most comfortable. When she found it she pushed the bowl of soup into Ben Joe's hands and ran to pull it up. "If we'd of known," she said, "I'd of cleaned up house a little. How come they've not told us you were back?"

"Well, I only got here yesterday."

"Sit, now. Oh my, let me take that soup bowl off your hands. What you think of New York?"

"I like it all right." He sat down on the chair and stretched his feet out in front of him. On the table under the window, among the doilies and flower pots and bronzed baby shoes, sat a photograph of his father. It was taken when he still had his mustache, long before he had ever

met Lili Belle, but he looked much the same as he had when he died—
rumpled hair, black then with only the first touches of white, and
crinkling gray eyes and a broad, easy smile. Except for Gram's bedroom,
where Ben Joe's mother never set foot, this was probably the only
place in the world that still had a picture of Phillip Hawkes. Ben Joe
reached out and turned it a little in his direction, looking at it thoughtfully.

"You have to excuse Mama's being so rude," Lili Belle was saying.
"She has gotten like that more and more. The other day this lodger
of ours, he stopped to talk to me on account of wanting to know where
the clean towels were kept, and Mama clunked him in the chest with
the griddle-cake-flipper. Didn't hurt him none, but I had a whole heap
of explaining to do."

"Was she right about your having some kind of trouble?" Ben Joe
asked.

"I'd say she was. That's why I was sitting in the dark like a spook.
Little Phillip is in the hospital with pneumonia and I was resting my
eyes from sitting up with him so much. I don't know where he got it.
Folks tell me I take *too* good care of him, so it can't of been that he
got too cold. Though he is right much of a puddle-wader, that could've
done it. I told him and told him. When it was serious and I had reason
to be worried I was just *possessed* by the thought of those puddles. I
had it in mind, in this dream I had one night, to take me a vacuum
cleaner and go vacuum all the puddles up. But the worrying part is
over now. Doctor says another ten days or two weeks and he'll be
out."

"How long's he been in?" Ben Joe asked.

"Two weeks."

"How're you managing the bills?"

"I plan to make it up gradual. I been working at the mill part time
since little Phil started school, but not a full day, because I like to be
home when he needs me. Oh, Mama would take care of him—says
she's ashamed he was ever born, but I notice she's right fond of him.
But I'd rather it be me. I'll work full time till the bill's paid off and
then go back half-days again."

"We've got some money in the savings account," Ben Joe said.

"No, honey, I don't want it."

"But we never even touch it. It's the money Dad saved up and Mama
won't use it no matter what—says it's only for emergencies. You're
right, you shouldn't work when little Phillip's at home."

"I wouldn't take it, Benjy. It bothers me to take what we *do* take
offen you all. Your sister Jenny's been bringing it real regular."

"Been what?"

"*You* know—the once-a-month money. She's not missed a time."

"But I thought— Doesn't she mail it?"

"Why, no." Lili Belle stopped playing with the folds of her skirt and looked up at him. "Neither *one* of you's ever *mailed* it," she said. "What she said the first time she came was, she would bring it the same as you'd always done."

"For Pete's sake." Ben Joe sat forward in his chair with his elbows on his knees. "I wonder how she knew."

"Oh, girls're smarter than you think." She laughed, and then became quiet again and looked at her hands. "She's a real nice little girl," she said. "First time she came I was just merely polite, you know, figuring that what's your mama's is your mama's and I didn't want to seem to be trying to make friends of your mama's own daughter. But she was so friendly—came in and taught little Phil how to play this game about scissors cutting rock and rock covering paper, or something. Real good with children, she is."

"She is," Ben Joe said. He sat quietly for a minute, and then he cleared his throat and said, "Lili Belle?"

"Hmm?"

"I've got something I want to talk to you about."

"Well, I'm listening."

"I thought I should get it said, in case I don't come back to Sandhill for a good while again. I figured . . ."

He was silent.

"I'm right here listening," she said. Her face was gentle and interested; Ben Joe wondered if it would become angry by the time he was through talking. Did Lili Belle ever get angry?

"I've got this letter," he said miserably.

"This . . . ?"

"Letter. Letter." He touched his pocket, where the rim of the pink envelope showed. "This, um—"

"*Oh*, yes."

"Ma'am?"

"Letter."

"Yes. And I wanted, wanted to show it to you because—"

"Well, I seen it before, Benjy honey."

"I know you have. That's what I'm trying to—"

"No, I mean I seen it on *you* before." She laughed gently, startling him. "Sure. First time you came after your daddy died, I seen it. Little piece of pink in your pocket, just like now. You'd not been to see me for two whole months, and then you came by but never said nothing about the letter. I figured you had found it in your daddy's office and read it, all about how I was asking him to come back to me and little Phillip. I was afraid you'd come to taunt me with it."

"Why to *taunt* you?"

"Account of the spelling, of course."

"The what?"

"The spelling. I never spelled too good."

"Oh," he said. He could think of nothing else to say; he was too surprised. For a moment he sat staring at her blankly and then he had to smile back at her.

"When you never did mention it," she was saying, "I figured you had just brought it along that one time to show me you had it safe. To show me you had took it from his office after he died so that no one else could see it. That why you brought it, Ben Joe?"

"No, ma'am," he said.

"No?"

"No, I took that letter *before* he ever died. What I came to tell you is, I took it before he even *saw* it."

He was afraid to look up at her. When he finally did, when she had been silent so long that he *had* to look, he saw that she didn't seem shocked or angry but was just absorbing the news still, shaking her head a little and trying to fit all this in with what she already knew.

"Lili Belle, I am awfully sorry," he said. "It's bothered me for so long I couldn't see any way to get rid of it now but to tell you, and say how sorry I am."

"Well, that's all right, Ben Joe." She licked her lips nervously, still frowning off into space. "That's all right—it didn't make no difference, did it? Everything would've happened the same, I reckon, letter or no letter."

"But I—"

"You didn't do nothing *wrong*, Benjy. Why, it seems to me your family is kind of queer-like sometimes. Meaning no offense. It's not *natural* to come see me and all, not even to speak to me on the street, but you do, and I reckon it's even a little relief, maybe, having you do something on your mother's side like most would do."

"Well—" Ben Joe stopped, not certain what to say. "What bothered me," he said, "is that maybe Dad would have gone back to you soon as he got your letter. And then, who knows, not had that heart attack a week later. Old Gram, she's blamed herself forever for forgetting to refill the ice-cube trays. Says that's why he died—going downtown to get ice. Though Mom says he could have stepped next door if he'd been sober enough to think of it. But sometimes when Gram gets on those ice-cube trays I'm almost tempted to show her the pink envelope, to prove it's not she that's to blame."

"Well, it surely ain't *you*," Lili Belle said. She bent forward to rub her eyes, tiredly, and then leaned her head back again and smiled at him. "I don't guess my letter would of made any change in him one way or the other. If your mother'd said one *word* he'd have stayed with her, always would have. He was just wanting her to ask him. But she didn't. He waited two weeks, and I guess he would have waited that long if I'd sent *fourteen* letters, even. Then he came back to me, not even planning to but just drunk and tired, and I took him in."

"But you can't say for sure," Ben Joe said.

"What?"

"You can't say for sure your letter wouldn't have made him come back earlier, you can't say—"

"Benjy honey, don't you worry. Can't say *nothing* for sure, if it comes to that. Don't you worry."

Both of them were silent for a minute, Lili Belle rocking steadily in her chair and filling the silence with slow creaks. Then she sat up straight again and said, *"Well*, how long you going to be here?"

"I don't know yet. Not too much longer, I guess."

"I heard your older sister's in town."

"That's right."

"Well, it'll work out. Her husband'll come and get her, you just watch. She's a right pretty girl—I seen her downtown before—and *he'll* come claim her. You just wait."

"Well, maybe so."

"Uh, you know my brother? Freeman? Well, Freeman he—"

"I thought his name was Donald."

"No, he changed it. That's what I was about to tell you. He said he was sick of this town and sick of blue denim and wanted to be free, so he changed his name to Freeman and went to work in a diner in New York. He likes it right much, I hear. Sent us this picture postcard saying, 'This here New York is a right swinging town.' That's what he said, 'a right swinging town.' You being in New York reminded me of it."

Her head was against the back of her chair again, lolling wearily. There was no telling how many nights she had sat up with little Phillip.

"You're tired," Ben Joe said. "I'll be going, Lili Belle. Here's the letter."

He pulled out the pink envelope and put it in one of her hands. She took it listlessly, stopping her rocking to frown down at it.

"Oh, land," she said. "Land."

She didn't go on speaking, though Ben Joe waited. She dropped the letter in her lap and went on rocking.

"I'll find my own way out," he said finally. "And I'm going to take care of that hospital bill, Lili Belle. Soon as I get it from the bank."

"No, Benjy, I don't—"

She was up on her feet now, wanting to protest, but he pulled on his jacket and left hurriedly. "You tell little Phil hey!" he called back.

"Well—"

He ran down the porch steps and into the yard. The sky above the river had grown churned and dark, and a cold wind was rising. As he walked he stuck his hands deep into his trouser pockets and hunched up his shoulders against the cold.

8

WHEN HE had finished what he had to do at the bank, Ben Joe headed toward Stacy's. It was a small, grim-looking café, but he and his friends had almost lived there once, back when they were in high school. They could meet up with almost anyone they wanted to see there if they waited long enough. Now, looking at the dirty gray front of the building while he waited for the traffic light to change, Ben Joe wondered why they had ever liked it. The picture window was dark and smudged, cluttered with neon beer signs and hand-lettered pizza posters. In front of it two weird-looking high school boys slouched, watching the people who passed by. When Ben Joe crossed the street and came closer to them, he stopped looking in their direction and stared steadfastly at Stacy's doorknob in order to avoid those amused eyes of theirs. But once inside it was no better; clustered in the dimness, lit briefly by the twirling rainbow from the jukebox, were more slouching boys and more leather jackets. Occasionally he caught a glimpse of a girl or two, with her hair piled in a fantastic frizzed mountain on her head and her skirt well above her knees. It was only after he had blinked a couple of times and strained his eyes into the farthest corners that he found Joanne.

She was sitting at a booth with her red coat thrown back behind her and a cup of coffee sitting on the table in front of her. But the coffee was going unnoticed; Joanne stared out at the empty dance floor with her mouth partly open and her eyes thoughtful.

"Hi," Ben Joe said.

She started a little and looked up at him. "Oh, hi," she said. She turned toward the cash register and called, "Stacy!"

Stacy was a fat blond woman who hated everyone under forty. No one knew why it was to her place that all the high school kids came. She bumbled toward them down the aisle, muttering something under her breath and slapping her round feet hard upon the floor at every step.

"*What*," she said.

"Ben Joe's here now."

"Hmm!" She stared at him blankly, with her eyes narrowed. "What you want?"

"Coffee. With double cream."

"With *what*?"

"Double cream."

"Double cream, hey. Double cream. My soul, double cream." She stamped off again, still muttering.

"Seven years gone by and she hasn't changed a mite," Joanne said. "How long's it been since you've come here, Ben Joe?"

"Oh, I don't know. Couple of years. Why?"

"I just wondered. Seems to me it used to be more lively."

"Mmm."

"Doesn't it to you? Seem that way?"

"I guess."

"On one of these tables there's a monument carved," she said. "It says, 'Memorial to Joanne, for her spirit.' Buddy Holler did that the day I walked out of chemistry class because it was boring."

Ben Joe smiled across the table at her. He wasn't listening to what she said; he was just glad to be having that cheerful voice of hers babble on. Before he had been walking too thin a line, losing sight of the division between Lili Belle's world and his mother's. Now there was Joanne to help. She was talking in an everyday voice about matter-of-fact things, and she was from home and reminding him that that was where he was from, too.

"Joanne," he said, "how well would you say you know Jenny?"

"Jenny our sister, you mean?"

"Yes."

She frowned. "Oh, I don't know. How old was she when I left— only eleven. Just barely getting a good start in life."

"You don't figure you know her very well?"

"No, not very well."

"Well, how about— What does she say in her letters to you?"

"Oh, *you* know." She grinned suddenly. "Just facts and figures— gotten much worse since you turned the money over to her."

"Does she say how she spends the money?"

"Sure."

"No, I mean does she tell you what bills she mails and what bills she takes in person? I mean . . ."

His coffee was set before him. He looked above the steam of it to Joanne's puzzled face.

"I'm not following," she said. "What do—"

"Well, does she say how the money is partitioned *up*, for instance? A certain amount to groceries, a certain amount for savings, and so on. Has she ever told you that?"

"Not even *Jenny* gets *that* specific," said Joanne. "What's the matter, Ben Joe?"

"Nothing. No, I just . . ."

He picked up his coffee and began drinking it, not meeting Joanne's eyes. She was giving him that amused little knowing smile again; he'd never find out how much she knew. Either she didn't know a thing or she was determined not to tell what she *did* know, and he'd never be able to find out which it was.

"I don't understand a soul in this world," he said.

"What makes you think you should? Especially girls. Think what a— Oh, hey, speaking of girls. Is that Shelley Domer?"

Ben Joe turned. Shelley was just coming in the door, dressed all in blue and carrying a coat over her arm. Behind her came a man Ben Joe didn't know.

"Who's he?" Joanne asked.

"I don't know."

"Sure looks familiar."

"Well, it might be Jack Horner. Shelley said the other night—"

"*John* Horner," Joanne said. "I remember all about him. Used to live just outside Sandhill, went to Murphy High School."

She put her chin in her hand and examined John Horner. So did Ben Joe, although he tried to look as if he were watching something else. He was surprised to see that Horner was a nice enough looking man, with a broad face and a mop of brown hair. For some reason, Ben Joe had pictured him as thin and sinister; he couldn't say why. Shelley was smiling up at him with that small, formal smile she always put on when she felt awkward, and when she saw Ben Joe she looked pleased and her smile broadened. Immediately she came over to their table, letting Horner follow if he wanted to.

"Hey, Ben Joe," she said. "Hey, Joanne. It's good to see you again."

"It's good to see *you*. Why don't you sit down?"

"Well, all right."

Shelley looked back and forth, first at the seat beside Joanne and then at the seat beside Ben Joe, and finally she chose the one beside Ben Joe and slid shyly into it. Opposite her, John Horner sat down by Joanne and began talking to her immediately, not waiting for an introduction to Ben Joe.

"You look kind of glum," Shelley said to Ben Joe.

"I do?"

"What you been doing that makes you look so glum?"

"Well, I don't know. What've *you* been doing?"

"Looking for a job. I didn't find one, though."

"Where'd you look?"

"Sesame Printery." She smiled, unexplainably, at her fingernails. "I worked there one summer proofreading, remember? And they're so low on work that Mr. Crown—that's the boss—he's just thinking *up* things to keep the typesetters busy. This morning they turned out five hundred labels reading 'Strawberry Jam,' one hundred labels reading 'Pickled Pigs' Feet,' though Mrs. Crown hates them and won't pickle any no matter *what* inducement Mr. Crown offers, and seven schoolbook covers saying 'All cats look gray in the dark,' because that's little Sonny Crown's favorite quotation. This afternoon they'll print the Crowns' stationery. So I don't reckon they need any help."

Across the table, Horner was laughing at something Joanne had said. Shelley looked over at them and said, "I'd introduce you to John if he wasn't talking just now. But anyway, that's the John Horner I was telling you about. You like him?"

"Well, what I see of him I do," Ben Joe said.

"He and I are going roller-skating this afternoon. I just know I'll break my neck."

"Has he asked you yet?"

"Asked me what?"

"About marrying him."

"No, not yet."

"What you going to say?"

"Oh . . ."

"Come on, now," he said. He was teasing her, but she turned suddenly serious and began pleating the paper napkin beside his saucer. "Haven't decided yet?" he asked her more gently.

She shook her head.

"You couldn't *drag* me in this place again," Joanne was saying to John. "It's all taken over by hoods, looks like. Used to be a real happy place, everybody dancing together—"

"Remember Barney Pocket?" John asked. "Remember how he used to make up dances all by himself? Lord, he was a funny guy. Put himself through college later, calculating how soon people would die and then borrowing money from them. It worked, too."

"He walked to Newfoundland one summer," Joanne said. "On a dare."

Ben Joe cleared his throat. "Joanne," he said, "I think Gram expects us home for lunch."

"Okay, Ben Joe."

Shelley and John stood up to let them out. While Ben Joe was struggling into his jacket, Shelley edged closer and said, "You coming tomorrow?"

"Sure," Ben Joe said. "I'll be by at—"

"Hush!" She frowned toward where John was standing talking with Joanne and then turned back to Ben Joe. "Will you *hush?*"

The urge to tease came over him again. He grinned down at her and said, "Don't tell me he doesn't *know* I'm coming! Why, Shelley Domer, that amounts to outright two-timing. I swear if you're not—"

"I *mean* it, now!" Her face was white and miserable; Ben Joe immediately felt sorry. "He *is* a steady boyfriend, after all," she said. "I don't want to—"

"Okay, okay."

He reached around to help her with her coat, and then raised one hand in Horner's direction.

"See you," he said.

"So long."

When they were outside, Joanne stopped to button up her coat. "It's getting kind of chilly," she said. "Shelley hasn't changed much, has she?"

"I don't know."

"I mean, she's still sort of quiet and drifty. You always did alternate between two extremes, come to think of it—first a dreamy, drifty girl and then a shrieky, dancing one."

"Well."

"That all you got to say?"

He watched the traffic light patiently, not hearing her.

"What you got on your mind, Ben Joe?"

"I don't know. Joanne?"

"What?"

"Would you say about ten dollars a day is enough to pay for a stay in a hospital?"

"That depends on the circumstances."

"Well, I don't know the circumstances, really. It's just this friend of mine. I'm worried about how much money he'd need."

"Light's changed."

She pulled him impatiently into the street, but once they had crossed she walked more slowly, studying the question.

"It sounds like a fair guess," she said. "Yes, I'd say so."

"Well, I don't know," said Ben Joe. "I keep thinking it should be more, somehow."

"That's *your* problem," said Joanne.

9

OVERNIGHT THE weather turned much colder. The wind howled and rattled at the bones of the house, and dry leaves scraped along the sidewalk. In the evening, when Ben Joe began dressing for his date with Shelley, his whole family pounced on him out of sheer boredom and wanted to know where he was going.

"Just out," he said.

He was in the living room, buttoning up the shirt Jenny had just ironed.

"I thought you might take me to see Jamie Dower tonight," Gram said.

"In *this* weather?"

"Well . . . it's Sunday. Good visiting time."

"I'll take you tomorrow," he said. "I don't know why we can't get synchronized on this Jamie Dower thing. If I'm ready to go you've got an iron-bound excuse *not* to, and now that I'm busy you're almost out in the car honking for me. Where's Susannah? I bet you anything she took my cuff links."

"She's in the attic," said Tessie. "Hunting squirrels."

"Oh."

"She took the only gun of mine that really shoots and she's been up there since suppertime. Got a whole soup can full of B-B's beside her."

"Funny way for a grown woman to spend her time. You notice if she's wearing my cuff links?"

"The squirrels have been nesting there," his mother said. *"Someone* had to get rid of them. Besides, your shirt has button cuffs."

"Oh. Well, then, it's the wrong shirt. I asked for the one with the French cuffs on it."

Jenny, sitting on the rug with a book, looked up and made a face at him. "Serve you right if I'd made you iron it yourself," she said.

"That one looks just as nice, Ben Joe."

"Okay, okay. How can she hunt squirrels in the dark?"

"She's got the extension lamp," Tessie said. "She's really mad at them."

"She'll never shoot one."

"Ben Joe, your shirt tail is out."

"I know it."

He jammed it into his trousers and went to the hall mirror to put his tie on. In the wavy glass he saw his face, sullen and heavy with the boredom of a long day at home. Behind him a part of his family was reflected, looking just as bored as he did. His mother sat in the rocking chair, absently glancing through a newspaper; her neck was made funny and crooked by a flaw in the mirror. Beside her sat Tessie, doing nothing at all but looking admiringly at her new shoes and occasionally wetting one finger and bending down to wipe at an imaginary scuff. The shoes were not reflected, but he had been asked to give an opinion of them so many times in the last day and a half that he thought he would be seeing them in his sleep forever—clumsy, too-white oxfords that were still new enough to look enormous on her feet. Also, in the mirror were Jenny's legs, but not the rest of her. He thought even her legs looked bored.

He finished knotting his tie, made a ferocious face in the mirror to see if his teeth needed brushing, and went back into the living room for his jacket.

"I'm going," he said.

"Are you going to be anywhere near the drugstore?"

"Or the newsstand?"

"Nope," he said. "Not going anywhere near anything."

"Well, it's hard to believe when you're dressed up so handsome," Gram said. "Come kiss me good night."

He bent down and kissed her cheekbone, and then kissed the tops of Tessie's and his mother's heads for good measure.

"I won't be late," he said.

"All right, Ben Joe."

At the doorway he turned to look at them again. He was in one of those faraway moods when everything he saw seemed to be inside a shining goldfish bowl, and he suddenly saw how closed-off his family looked. They went peacefully on with what they were doing; Ben Joe, having vanished, might as well not exist. When he stepped outside he gave the door an enormous slam, just to make himself exist a minute longer.

The wind bit at his face and his bare hands. It was very dark, without a moon, but he could see the white clouds swimming rapidly past the house tops. And before he had even reached the front gate, the cold had begun to seep in all over. He didn't care. He was glad to get out in the fresh air after the long, stuffy day, and he was glad to be going to Shelley's, although he couldn't say why. There were times when even Shelley's shyness and her slowness seemed to be exactly what he needed. And he would like the way she greeted him at the door, with her face so formal.

He hurried on, making his arms hang loosely instead of huddling them close to his body, because the cold air still felt good. A twig from one of the trees along the sidewalk stung across his face. He ducked and then turned in, whistling now, to climb the long steps to Shelley's house.

She answered almost as soon as he knocked. He saw the outline of her behind the mesh curtain, running in order to let him in quickly. The minute the door was open she tugged at his arm with both hands and said, "Get in, Ben Joe, aren't you *frozen?*"

He nodded, smiling at her, and stepped inside so that she could shut the door behind him.

"Come on in," she said, "come in. I declare, I think you're just frozen stiff and silent. Take off your coat, now. That's right."

She took the coat from him and smiled into his eyes. It had been a long time since he had seen her looking so pretty. Her hair was down, the way she had worn it when she was in high school, and it was well brushed and shining. There was something besides lipstick on her face—rouge, he thought—that made her look excited and bright-eyed, and she was watching him with that half-scared expression.

"I sure am glad to see *you*," he said suddenly.

"Well, thank the Lord you've said something. I thought maybe you were going to be speechless all evening."

She took a hanger from the closet for his coat, and Ben Joe went into the living room. A fire had been lit in the fireplace, a tall fire that roared out and glinted on the bare wood floor. The thought of having to go out again, away from all this warmth, was depressing. But as soon as Shelley came into the living room he turned and said, "Do you want to go somewhere?"

"Oh, I don't care. What do you want to do?"

"Well, anything you want to."

"No, you say."

He spread his hands helplessly. *"You* say," he said.

"I really don't have a preference in this world, Ben Joe."

"You must have."

"Oh . . ." She put her hands together and stared into the fire. "I hate to be the one to say," she said finally.

The fire light kept moving and flickering on her face. And her hair just brushed the top of her collar. Something about her—the expectant way she stood, the dress-up navy dress with its spotless white collar— reminded him of a night he thought he had forgotten, back when his sisters were still very young. Joanne had thrown a barbecue party, with what seemed like millions of couples, and had suggested offhandedly that anyone in the family could have some barbecue with them if they wanted to. At the time Jenny was no more than eleven, but she was just beginning to notice boys and had started reading beauty magazines. The night of the barbecue the whole house reeked of some heavy-scented bath oil and no one knew why; but then down the stairs came Jenny, wearing a white puff-sleeved dress, with her hair perfectly combed and a thick envelope of perfume encircling her wherever she moved. She had come down and sat quietly on the lawn with the older couples, who were in sloppy Bermudas and T shirts, and she hadn't spoken unless spoken to, but all evening she watched the party with that same happy, frightened look. He had wanted to cry for her, without knowing why—or at least hug her. He wanted to hug Shelley now, but she had awakened from her staring into the fire and was watching him.

"What're you thinking about?" she asked.

"I don't know."

"Well, I tell you. One thing I do know about New York is that when they have dates they like as not never set *foot* in a movie house or a skating rink. The girls just serve them cocktails in their apartments. So I have bought some bourbon, in case that's what you're used to doing. Is that all right?"

"It's a wonderful idea," Ben Joe said.

She ran out to the kitchen immediately; for some reason she didn't seem to be in slow motion tonight. Ben Joe sat down on the couch and relaxed happily against the cushions. The fire was slowly drawing the cold out of him, leaving him warm and comfortable. He could hear glasses tinkling in the kitchen.

"I've put you some ice and a little water," Shelley said when she came in again.

"That's perfect."

She had brought the bottle in on a tray, and next to it stood their two glasses, her own very pale. When Ben Joe picked his glass up, she watched his face carefully to see if he liked it, and smiled when he nodded to her.

"Just right," he said.

"I'm glad."

She picked up her own glass and, after turning over in her mind the problem of where to sit, chose a spot next to Ben Joe on the couch, settling there so delicately that her drink hardly wavered in its glass.

"Is it you that's going to talk?" she asked.

"Well, I don't know."

"I think it is."

"Why?"

"Oh . . ." She took a sip of her drink and began turning her glass around, smiling into it. "When you come in slow and smiling, likely something is on your mind. Also if you're too much the other way. And then me, I'm not in a real talky mood myself. So I figured it would be you to talk."

"Maybe so." He slid down, so that his feet were under the coffee table and his weight was upon the small of his back, and scratched the top of his head. "I'm thinking about it," he explained when she laughed.

"Well, tell me what you did with your day."

"My day. Lord. Nothing to speak of. It was Sunday. We all got the Sunday blues. Got them so bad that Susannah's up in the attic hunting squirrels with a B-B gun now. Nobody went out. Me, I slept and then I read the funny papers twice through, and then I finished a murder mystery and peeled potatoes for Gram. It's been a God-awful day, considering."

He sat up straighter and took a swallow of his drink.

"You know," he said, "except for an occasional Sunday, they don't make days like they used to. I mean, they don't make them *whole* any more. You noticed?"

He looked over at Shelley, but she only shook her head, puzzled.

"Oh, well, what I mean is, the days seem to come in pieces now. They used to be in blocks—all one solid color to them. Sometimes whole *weeks* would be in blocks. Someone could say, 'What's this week been like?' and right off the bat you could say, 'Oh, lousy. My father won't let me have the car because he caught me scratching off in front of Stacy's café the other day.' Or it would be a great week, for another reason just that clear-cut. It's not that way any more."

"Well . . ." Shelley said. She was trying, but in the end she gave up and said, "I reckon I never did notice that, Ben Joe."

"No, I guess not."

"You tell me about the pieces, then."

"All right."

He settled back again and thought a minute. "What I'm mainly wondering," he said, "is whether Mom ever looks at the bank records.

I've never actually seen her do it. She's real funny that way. Sometimes I think Jenny is the one who manages the family now, as if Mom weren't there. Jenny tells her what's going on but only to keep her informed, not to ask her for any decisions. So maybe she doesn't know anything about the bank books."

"What difference does it make if she does?" Shelley asked.

"Well, I took some money out when I shouldn't have. I don't know what she'd do if she knew. I'm worried about it."

He drained the last of his drink and then balanced the glass on his knee. It made a cold, dark ring in the fabric of his trousers. "I don't know why it's always so hard deciding which side I'm on," he said.

"Let me pour you another drink, Ben Joe."

"Also, I found out Joanne's asking for a divorce," Ben Joe said. He watched Shelley's hands as she poured his bourbon; they were long, thin hands that seemed uncertain about what they were touching. "She says she just *left* Gary, not even telling him about it. The lawyer's getting in touch with him now. Sometimes I'm hoping Gary'll say no, she can't have the divorce, and Joanne will leave Sandhill and go back and be happy in Kansas again. But most times I'm hoping she'll get divorced and stay with us. That Gary, I don't know whether I like him or not. Well, hell, I've never even *seen* him. Except in this blurred snapshot Joanne sent us of him holding Carol when she was just newborn. There was all kinds of excitement when Carol was born. The girls went around calling each other 'Aunt'—even Tessie—and Mom was 'Grandma' for I don't know how long. Then they forgot about it. But Gary sent out these birth announcements that say there's a new product on the market, giving the name of the manufacturers—that's the parents—and all."

"I think that's *nice*," Shelley said.

"Well. It just seems funny in our particular family, is all. Like that sentimental kind of letter he wrote us after Joanne called to say they were married. It began, 'Dear Mom,' in this unreadable handwriting, and Mom looked at the greeting and then at the closing to see what stranger was calling her Mom and she said, 'Who's Gary?' It wasn't till she'd read the letter that she figured it out. No, that's a nice idea but it doesn't fit, somehow, and I kind of hope he'll give Joanne the divorce." He sat up straight again and stared into the fire. "Why can't they all just let *me* take care of them? My sisters are so separate. I'd be happy to take care of them."

"I know," Shelley said comfortingly.

He smiled at her. She was sitting very straight and still, almost touching him, and listening completely to what he said. Anyone else he knew would be getting restless by now.

"*You* talk," he said.

"I got nothing to say, Ben Joe."

"Neither do I, seems like." He bent to untie his shoelaces and slip the shoes off. Then he swung his legs up and settled his feet on the coffee table. "Tomorrow we're going to see Jamie Dower," he said. "He's eighty-four. How do you reckon it would feel to be eighty-four? Do you think you'd *realize* you were that old? I don't realize I'm twenty-five. I keep thinking I'm about eighteen or so. I don't even know if Gram realizes how old *she* is. Somehow I think not, or she wouldn't still be making a fuss about bygone things. Still keeping up the old war with Mom. She never did like her much. Grandpa, now, he thought Mom was wonderful. Said she had backbone. First time she came to visit here before she and Dad got married, she came down to breakfast saying she was thirsty and Grandpa poured her a glass of water. Only it turned out not to be water but moonshine, that clear kind that comes out of a Mason jar. Mom was right surprised but she drank it anyway, without coughing, and Grandpa said, 'Honey, *you're* no Yankee,' and loved her like a daughter ever since. But Gram, she said all it proved was that she was no lady. Oh, hell, I'm getting off the subject. Whatever the subject was."

"It's all right," Shelley said. "Don't you worry, Ben Joe."

"Me? I'm not worried."

"Well. Anyway, it's all right."

She looked sad, and Ben Joe didn't know why. He didn't know what to do about it. He put one arm along the back of the couch behind her, not actually touching her but just protecting her, and looked at her face to see what was bothering her. There were lots of things he *might* do; he might say something funny and make her laugh, for instance. But for some reason he didn't. He pulled his hand in tighter, around the curve of her shoulder, and then leaned forward and kissed her cheek.

"Nothing's worrying me," he said.

She turned her face full toward him, and he put his other arm around her and kissed her mouth that was as familiar as if he had been kissing her only last night instead of almost seven years ago. Even the taste of her lipstick was the same—like strawberries. And she had the same way of hugging him; the minute she hugged him she stopped seeming scared and became soft and warm, first kissing him and then gently laying her cheek against his as if he were a child to be comforted. For a minute he relaxed against her, but then he began to feel a crick in his neck. He sat up straight again and cleared his throat.

"Um . . ." he said. He leaned forward a little, with his elbows on his knees. "I forgot about Horner," he said.

"What?"

"Horner. I forgot about him."

"Oh."

He lit a cigarette and puffed on it a few times before he looked at her again. "Have you got an ash tray?" he asked her.

"I'll get you one." She stood up and crossed to the desk. She was the kind of person who rumpled easily; her hair was fluffed now and her lipstick was a little blurred. When she came back with the ash tray she said, "We're not *engaged*, after all. I just go out with him some."

"Well, still."

"Of course, I *like* him and all . . ."

"Oh, sure. Sure, he looked like a nice person."

"He is. He's real nice, he really is."

"Where did you meet up with him?" he asked.

"At my aunt's house. She used to know his family."

"That's right. Joanne said he was from around Sandhill. I don't know where *she* met up with him."

"At a basketball game," said Shelley, "when Joanne was still in high school."

"How you know that?"

"Oh, John's told me *all* about his past." She settled back against the cushions, smiling a little now.

"His *past*? Does that include just meeting a girl at a basketball game? He must have been pretty thorough."

"Oh, no, he dated her a while. But he felt—" She stopped, and looked into her half-empty glass.

"He felt what?"

"Oh, now I've forgotten what I was going to say."

"Come on, Shelley."

She kept on staring at her drink, pressing the corners of her mouth down. Finally she said, "Well, I suppose he just met her at . . . at one of those ages when girls are in a sort of, um, wild stage. I mean, rebellious. That's what I mean. *Rebellious* stage."

Ben Joe sat up straighter.

"Now, Ben Joe, I'm sure he didn't mean to—"

"Who does he think he—"

"Ben Joe, I *know* he didn't mean to carry tales. He wouldn't do that."

"Oh, never mind." He sat back again. "She *was* kind of a *flirt* in high school," he said. "The way she dressed and all. I suppose if you just met her a couple of times you'd think she really *was* wild."

"But—" Shelley looked down in her drink again. "Well, yes, Ben Joe, I'm sure that's what he meant. You want another drink?"

"No."

"There's lots more."

"No. People who just look at them on the surface, *they've* got no right to say what my sisters are like."

"I know that."

"Okay."

She was still watching him, trying to tell if he was feeling better. He looked back at her blankly.

"Ben Joe," she said finally, "have you got a girl in New York?"

"Why?"

"Because I want to know."

"Not one steady girl. No."

She nodded, satisfied. "Anyway," she said, "I'm sorry I told you what I just did. I wouldn't have you worried for anything."

"I'm *not worried!*" ·

"All right."

She put her hands on his shoulders and he settled down next to her again, fitting his head beneath her chin. Against his back he could feel her hands patting him softly, so lightly he could hardly feel it.

"The trouble is," he said into her collarbone, "I'm reversible."

The words were muffled. She pulled back a little and looked down at him and said, "What?"

"I don't guess you're hardly *alive* if you're as reversible as I am. But the irreversible people, they get someplace. Good or bad. Murder is irreversible, for that matter. Even if it's bad, you can tell you're getting somewhere definite. But me, I am reversible."

"You silly," Shelley said. "You talk like you're some kind of raincoat, Ben Joe. Don't get upset, now."

He was pulled in next to her again, and soothed with the same small pats. Gradually he closed his eyes and let the full weight of his head rest against her chest.

He heard Shelley's voice beginning above him, far-away and soft, saying, "You were the first person I ever wanted to ask me out. There'd been two other boys asked me out before, but I didn't like them and I've forgotten now where we ever went or what we did. One was that fat little Junior Gerby, who was shorter than me, and the other was Kenny Burke, who was so greasy and hoody back in those days. Though later on he changed. His mama says he's right nice now. She was always afraid he'd end up in Alcatraz. But when I started thinking about you asking me out, now that you weren't just a little boy to play roll-a-bat with any more, I'd pray every night for you to ask me. I'd say, 'Please, God, you let Ben Joe Hawkes ask me out and I will never ask for anything more as long as I live.' Though I knew at the time it was next to impossible. There were three other girls after you and all of them prettier than me, though you never noticed and were always playing baseball and fiddling with your microscope. I took to shoplifting lipsticks, even if I *did* have plenty allowance, and trying on all manner of different shades in front of the mirror. Then I figured God was mad at me for it and I buried all my lipsticks in the backyard, where they are to this day."

He moved his head a little, and she let him settle down again and then began stroking his hair with her hand. Above him the voice went on; he barely listened to the words but just concentrated on the sound, slow and murmuring above him.

"And then they announced how the Future Homemakers were going to have a supper at the Parnells' Restaurant out by the college and we could ask dates, and I asked you, although I was shaking so hard I had to lean against the wall while I was talking to you. When you said yes I got all happy, but then when it came time to go I was terrified and wished I'd never asked you. I was afraid I'd vomit at the dinner table. And I didn't know what to order. I could order spaghetti and get a big, long, endless strand of it and have to keep sucking it up from the plate just indefinitely. Or pizza, and misjudge how soon it had cooled, the way I always did, and take a hot bite and have to spit it out. Or chicken, and have it slide from under my knife and fork right across the table into somebody else's plate, like it had done once before."

"What did you order?" Ben Joe asked sleepily.

"A roast-beef sandwich. Only the meat was tough, and when I took a bite the whole slab of beef came out of the sandwich and hung from my teeth."

She was quiet a minute. Ben Joe stirred again, sitting up straighter so that his face was level with Shelley's.

"I love you, Ben Joe," she said.

This time when he kissed her her mouth was softer, with that first stickiness of her lipstick gone, and he didn't care whether there was a crick in his neck or not now. He wanted to say he loved her back, but he couldn't because her mouth was in the way, and then when she drew back to nestle down next to his shoulder, he felt too warm and comfortable to say anything at all. He just sat still, letting her nuzzle a little place for her face between his neck and his shoulder. It was only when he knew that they were about to fall asleep that he spoke again, and then in the softest whisper, as if her family was still alive and gently watchful in other parts of the house.

"Shelley."

"What?"

"I better go home."

"It's early still."

"I know, but anyway."

"Well, all right."

They both stood up, Shelley patting her hair down as she rose. The minute Ben Joe was up he was awake again and felt almost sorry that he had mentioned going home. But he took the coat when she handed it to him and kissed the top of her head and said, "When can I come back?"

"Tuesday. You going to?"

"Yes."

She pulled the door open and a blast of cold air came in, taking both their breaths away.

"You hurry, now," she said. "You're going to freeze, Ben Joe!"

"Good night," he said.

"Night."

Then the door closed behind him, and all he could hear was the shrieking of the wind.

10

OUTSIDE IT was sheer blackness, rolling in around him with the wind. He walked down Shelley's steps slowly, pausing when he reached the street to button up the collar of his coat. But walking was too quiet; he wanted to run. And if no one had been within earshot he would have started singing, too, or laughing at nothing, because he felt happy and easy. But it was the hour just before bedtime, when everyone had something to do outdoors—walk the dog, or set out the milk bottles, or simply take a breath of fresh air in the yard before they shut themselves up in their houses for the night. So he ran silently; he doubled up his fists and tore down the sidewalk with the leaves rattling behind him and people occasionally pausing on their porches to turn and watch him run.

Someone came down a front walk and set a cat down outside the gate. It was a small cat of some nameless color, with its sling-eyes glowing, and when its owner turned to go inside, the cat hunched sullenly on the sidewalk as if it resented being put out for the night. It stared unblinkingly at Ben Joe. Ben Joe stooped down to pat it.

"There, there, cat," he said. His hand reached out for the cat almost blindly, aiming only for a blurred patch of darkness against the lighter background of the sidewalk. When he felt the cat's head under his hand he stroked it gently. "I'll take care of you," he said.

The cat was used to people; it began purring instantly and pressing its little head against Ben Joe's hand. Ben Joe picked it up and began walking again, hugging the cat next to his chest to keep it warm. He was afraid to run, for fear the cat would become frightened, but he was tired, anyway, and contented himself with walking fast.

Some of the houses were already dark; most of them still had soft yellow lights in the windows. He could see people moving around upstairs, pulling down shades or simply walking about their rooms in bathrobes. In one house a woman stood brushing her hair, and Ben Joe stopped to watch the dreamlike rhythm of it. Then the little cat stirred restlessly, and Ben Joe went on. The sky above the lights of the houses was a deep blue-black, but when he stepped out into the street and kept his eyes away from the lights it was pale and glowing, and stretched almost white behind the black skeletons of trees. He was almost running again, and the cat began mewing softly and squirming in his arms.

"Now, don't you worry, cat," Ben Joe said. "No call to worry."

He laughed, for no reason he could name. Laughing made his teeth cold. He closed his mouth and his teeth felt cold and dry against the inside of his lips.

"That you, Ben Joe?" someone called.

He turned; a dark figure was standing on the sidewalk.

"It's me," he said. "Who's that?"

"Jenny."

"Oh. What *you* doing out?"

"Nothing." She stepped off the sidewalk and walked over to him. "I went to bed early and just got myself all wound up in the bed sheets," she said. "Thought I'd have a walk and hot milk and then try going to bed all over again. What's that you got?"

"A cat. There's something I meant to talk to you about."

"Where'd you get him?" She bent forward to see the cat, and then touched it. All he could see of her was a pale face and the dark hollows where her eyes were. "Doesn't like being carried," she said.

"I'm keeping it warm. I wanted to ask you—"

"It doesn't *want* to be kept warm."

"It does too. Jenny, there's a sort of money matter I'd like to—"

"You better put it *down*, Ben Joe."

"He *likes* me, I tell you."

"Got his own little overcoat sewn right on him, doesn't he? What's he want to be kept warm for? No, when they squirm like that, Ben Joe . . ."

He gave in, knowing she was right, and bent to let the cat hop down and run away.

"It's much happier now," she said.

"*Jenny!*"

"Well, I'm listening."

He smiled suddenly, without knowing why. "Oh, never mind," he said. "Oh, what the hell, what the hell . . ."

"Well, good night, Ben Joe."

"Night."

He was off again, tearing along the cracked pavement and leaving Jenny far behind. He swung three times around the tree on his corner, the way he had always done for good luck when he was small. Then he clattered through the wire gate and up the walk to the porch. The bark from the tree had left his palm gritty: he rubbed his hand against the side of his coat as he climbed the steps. At the front door, dark now with only the softest yellow light glimmering through the round stained-glass window, he bumped smack into a girl and boy.

"Excuse me, excuse me," he said, and found himself smiling again. "I didn't see you. Funny house this is—they just never think of leaving the light on for you. They forget all about you, the minute you—"

He opened the screen door with a flourish, almost bumping into the couple, and with his hand on the knob of the inside door he turned back again.

"Excuse me," he said.

John Horner and Joanne were looking at him, their faces serious and lit very dimly by the pale-yellow light. Joanne's hand was clasped in John's, against John's chest, but it was forgotten now as they both stared at him.

"*Quite* all right," said John Horner.

The heat inside the house burned Ben Joe's cold face. As soon as he had slammed the door behind him he ripped off his overcoat and threw it on a chair in the hallway and began undoing his collar as he climbed the stairs.

"That you, Ben Joe?" his mother called.

"Yup."

"Come on into the living room and say hello, why don't you?"

"I can't," Ben Joe said.

He stopped on the stairs, hearing his mother's footsteps in the hallway, and turned to look down at her.

"Why can't you?" she said.

"I just can't. I just can't. I can't be bothered with that right now."

"You can't be—"

He climbed the rest of the stairs at a steady, slow pace. His tie trailed by one hand. It wasn't until he was in the upstairs hallway that he let the actual picture of the couple on the porch come back to him, and then all he did was stop and stare tiredly at the wallpaper. After a minute he turned and started doggedly down the hall toward his room.

11

"BEN JOE," Gram said, "a promise is a promise. If you didn't want to see Jamie Dower you shouldn't have told me he was here."

Ben Joe pushed a rubbery piece of scrambled egg around his plate.

"You hear me, Ben Joe?"

"Yes'm."

"Well, you going to take me there or aren't you?"

"All I'm doing is being honest about it," he said. "I just honestly don't *feel* like going to the home, Gram. Never have liked going. That time I went to see Mrs. Gray with you I couldn't get it out of my mind again."

His grandmother poured him a second cup of coffee and then slammed the pot back on the stove. "Liking's got nothing to do with it," she said. "What's the matter with it, anyway? No, I don't enjoy thinking of my friends in an old folks' home, but this I *will* say: homes are a lot more cheerful nowadays. They don't *depress* the tar out of you."

"I don't care if they depress me. I just get confused in homes. I walk out of there all confused and I never can tell what time it is."

"What difference is the time of day? What difference does it make?"

"Well, the time of *day* doesn't make *any* difference, Gram. That's not what I'm talking about."

"You." She flounced into the chair opposite him and began pulling out her three bobby pins. "Now, it's got to be this morning that we go, Ben Joe, because I got to take Tessie to her drawing lesson this afternoon. Your mother's too busy. *Busy.*" She jabbed one of the bobby pins back in.

"What you need me along for? To go to the home, I mean. What good'll I do? You tell me a good reason, I'll be glad to come."

"I just want someone with me. Besides."

"What."

"Besides, I want you to remember how I tagged around after Jamie Dower when I was little. Then you'll see how it might seem a little forward for me to be going there alone today."

"I don't see why," Ben Joe said. "You're seventy-eight years old now, Gram."

"That's not too old to do things ladylike."

"All right, I'll go." He knew it was no use arguing; he shrugged resignedly and speared another piece of egg.

"You promise?"

"I promise. Give me a minute to finish my breakfast."

"Well, do you think I look all right?"

He looked at her carefully for the first time that morning. She was wearing a huge black turtleneck sweater, knitted in haste, and a wrap-around denim skirt, and on her feet were the usual black gym shoes. But there were a few small changes that he hadn't noticed: her face looked feverish with its dabs of rouge and the careful line of orange lipstick that ordinarily she never wore; and next to the worn little wedding band on her finger was a huge diamond engagement ring that was used only for church-going.

"You look fine," he said.

"I bet he won't recognize me."

"I bet he won't."

"Last time he saw me I was a little roly-poly fat girl with lollypop juice down my front. I bet he won't know what name to call me by, even."

"No, I bet he won't."

"Come *on*, Ben Joe."

He gulped down the last of his coffee and stood up. "Where are the keys?" he asked.

"On the wall, where they belong. Put your dishes in the sink, now. Jenny was raising the roosters about how you don't do your share of picking up around here."

"Oh, pick up, pick up." He stacked the dishes helter-skelter in the sink and then knelt to tie his shoe. "*Joanne* never picks up. I had to scrape pablum off the damn *toaster* this morning."

"That was Jane that fed Carol. Joanne's still in bed."

"No wonder," he said.

"No wonder what?"

"No wonder she's still in bed. Get your coat, Gram."

"I've got it right here." She picked up one of his father's old lab coats from the back of a chair and began putting it on. It came down almost to the top of her gym shoes, but she looked at it proudly and stuck her hands in the pockets.

"You going to be warm enough in that?" he asked.

"Course I am."

"Well, it's your lookout."

He followed her across the living room, which was still cluttered with all the things the family had been doing the night before. His heel crushed something; it was the flatiron from the Monopoly set. He scraped it off his shoe and kept going.

Outside it was bright and still. The wind was gone but it was still cold, and in shady places there was something that was either very heavy frost or light patches of snow. He turned on the windshield wipers in the car to get rid of the thin covering of frost.

"Now, I want you to be very polite to Jamie," his grandmother said.

"Am I ever *not* polite?"

"Sometimes. Sometimes. Or at least, absentminded. So you watch it, Ben Joe. Jamie Dower is older even than I am. I used to think maybe someday he'd save my life."

"How would he do that?"

"Oh you know. Pull me out of the water or something. I'm just saying that to show how *much* older he is. Old enough to be kind of looked up to and admired, so's the only way he'd really notice me would be for me to die or something."

"All right," Ben Joe said. "I'll be polite."

She settled back, satisfied. But when they had pulled out into the street and were drawing closer to the home, the anxious expression came back to her face and she crossed her legs and began picking at the white rubber circle at the ankle of her gym shoes, a sure sign she was worrying.

"Maybe I should've brought him something," she said.

"I thought you were going to."

"No. No, ordinarily I would, would have brought something to pretty up his room or tempt his appetite. But Jamie never liked that kind of thing. When I was little I would walk to his house every day and bring him my dessert from lunchtime, but he never wanted it."

"Well, that was nearly seventy years ago. You want to stop at a florist's?"

"No thank you, Ben Joe."

She settled back again, still frowning. When they drew up in front of the home, which looked like just a larger sort of yellow brick family house, she remained in her seat and looked at it through the window pane without changing her expression or giving any sign that she was about to go in.

"Would you rather not go?" Ben Joe asked gently. "I could bring you back another time, if you want."

"No, no. I was just thinking, oughtn't to ever put brownish curtains in a yellow house. It's ugly." She swung her door open and got out, grunting a little as her feet hit the ground. "Don't know what they could have been thinking of," she said.

"We'll get inside where we don't have to look at it."

But she kept standing there, looking up at the home.

"You're going to stay right by me, aren't you, Benjy?" she asked.

"Course I am."

"They say," she said, beginning to walk slowly across the yard, "they say when people get old they take to reading the obituary column to see if their names're in it. Well, I'm not to that yet, but one thing I have noticed: I do hate going to the home for the aged, for fear I can't get out again. They might mistake me, you know. When I said I wasn't a patient, they might think I was just planning to escape."

Ben Joe took her by the elbow and began walking with her. "I'll watch out for you," he said. "Besides, they must have a sort of roll book here. And your name's not on it. They couldn't keep you here."

"Oh, don't be so *reasonable*, Ben Joe." She made an exasperated face and pinched the arm that she was hanging onto. "You're just like your mother. So reasonable. Just like her."

"I am not."

"Well, no, but you surely are an annoyance."

"If you're not more polite I'm going to leave you here," Ben Joe said. "And sneak up and put your name on the roll book just to make sure you stay." He gave her a small pat on the back.

The front door of the home was huge and heavy. Ben Joe pulled it open and they stepped inside, into suffocating heat and the smell of furniture polish. The flowered brown rug they stood on was deep and made everything seem too quiet; it stretched for what seemed like miles across a huge sort of social room. There were easy chairs arranged next to the walls, and in them sat a few old people talking or playing

checkers or staring into space. In the center of the room hung a great
tarnished chandelier that Ben Joe could almost have reached on tiptoe.
He stared past it at the old people, but his grandmother looked fixedly
at the chandelier, never letting her eyes move from it.

"Can I help you?" a nurse said. She had come up soundlessly on
her thick-soled shoes, and now she faced them with her arms folded
across the cardboard white of her uniform and her face strangely young
and cheerful.

"We've come to visit a Mr. Dower," Ben Joe said.

"Algernon Hector James Dower the Third," said his grandmother,
still looking intently at the chandelier.

"You members of his family?"

"Raised together."

"Well, he's not feeling too good. He's a bed patient. If you'll only
stay a few minutes . . ."

"We'll be quiet," said Ben Joe.

"Follow me, then."

She led them through the social room, toward an elevator around
the corner. As they passed the other patients there was a whispering
and a stirring, and everyone stared at them. "Mr. Dower," the nurse
told them. They nodded and kept staring. The nurse turned back to
Ben Joe and his grandmother and gave them a sudden, reassuring smile;
when she smiled, her nose wrinkled like a child's and the spattering
of freckles stood out in a little brown band across her face.

"If you'll just step in here," she said.

The elevator smelled dark and soapy. It was so small that it made
Ben Joe nervous, and he could see that his grandmother was beginning
to get that lost look on her face and was twisting her engagement ring.
He smiled at her, and she cleared her throat and smiled back.

"Here we are," the nurse said cheerfully.

The door slid open. Gram bounded out like a young goat, with a
surprising little kick of her heels, and looked back at the nurse.

"My, I wish *our* people were as spry as *you* are!" the nurse said.
Gram smiled.

"Are those—those are very, um, sensible shoes you're wearing," the
nurse went on pleasantly. "They must be—"

"I get them at Pearson's Sport Shop," Gram said.

"Ah, I see. Down this corridor, please."

The corridor was very long and silent. It was hard to imagine that
such an average-looking house could hold it all. The walls were covered
with a heavy brown paper that had columns of palm leaves up and
down it, and the doors were of some dark wood. At the next to the
last door, which was slightly open, the nurse stopped and tapped lightly
with her fingernails.

"Mr. Dower?" she called.

She peeked in, all smiles, and said, "We have company, Mr. Dower."

Then she looked backed at Ben Joe and Gram and said, "You can come in. Don't stay long, now. I'll be out here when you want to go down again."

They tiptoed in, Gram ahead of Ben Joe. Jamie Dower was lying in a spotless white iron bed, with his white hair fluffed out around his polished little face. His eyes were as alert as when Ben Joe had first seen him, but his breathing was worse; even when he was lying flat now, there was that squeaky kittenish sound that had been there when he'd climbed the hill.

"Oh, young man," he said, recognizing Ben Joe.

"Hello, Mr. Dower."

"Who is—"

Gram stepped forward. She had her hands folded primly in front of her and she looked very small and uncertain. For a long time she looked at Jamie Dower, taking in every change she must have seen in him. Then she dropped her hands and became brisk and lively, the way she always did at a sickbed. "I look familiar?" she asked him. She flounced over to sit on the edge of the chair beside his bed and smiled brightly at him. "I look like anyone you know, Jamie Dower?"

"A doctor—"

"Oh, no, no." She twisted out of the white lab coat impatiently and flung it behind her. "Now?" she asked.

"Well, ma'am . . ."

"*I'm* Bethany Jane *Chrisawn!*" she caroled out loudly. The nurse came swiftly to the doorway and put one finger to her lips, but Gram was watching only Jamie Dower. "*Now* you remember?"

"Bethany . . ." He raised himself up on one elbow and stared at Gram puzzledly. For a minute Ben Joe held his breath; then the old man's face slowly cleared and he said, "Bethany! Bethy Jay *Chrisawn,* that's who!"

Ben Joe breathed again, and Gram nodded smugly.

"Bethy *Jay!*" the old man roared.

"Mr. Dower, *please,*" the nurse said.

"Well, I'll be," said Jamie Dower. He lay back down and shook his head as he stared at her. "Bethy," he said, "you surely have changed some."

Gram turned around and beamed at Ben Joe. "I told you," she said. "Didn't I? Before we even left the house I said to Ben Joe, I said, 'I bet he won't recognize me.' This is Ben Joe Hawkes, Jamie. My grandson. He's the one told me you were here."

"I'm going," the nurse called across to Ben Joe, barely mouthing the words. She trilled the fingers of one hand at him, gave him a warning look, and vanished.

"Never thought you'd still be alive," Jamie said.

"Why, I'll be! I'm younger'n *you* are."

"Well, I know that. I know."

He tried to sit up higher, and Gram reached behind him to pull the pillows up.

"You're looking good, Jamie," she said.

"That's funny. View of the fact that I'm dying."

"Oh, now, *you're* not dying."

"Don't argue, Bethy Jay. Your word against the doctor's and I'll take the doctor's any day. Yes sir, I'm dying and I come to die where I was born at, like any good man should. Not that I'd *recognize* the damn place."

"Language, Jamie. You're right, town has changed some."

"Sure has. This your grandson, hey? You got married?"

"Well, of *course* I got married. What'd you think?" She sat up straighter and glared at him. "I married Lemuel Hawkes, that's who."

"Lemuel *Hawkes?*"

"Why, sure."

"That kind of chubby guy whose voice wasn't changed?"

"Well, by the time I *married* him it was changed," Gram said. "Good *heavens*, Jamie."

"When I knew, when I knew—" He laughed, and the laugh ended in a wheezy little cough. "When I knew him he was sending away for all kinds of creams and secret remedies, that's what. He had this kind of black syrup made by the Indians, you're supposed to put it on your throat and lie out in the moonlight with it, and it was guaranteed to give a manly vibrance to your voice. A 'manly vibrance,' that's the exact words. Only his mother found him lying under the clothesline and all she could see was something dark and wet all over his neck, oh, God—" He choked and choked again and still laughed, with his little wheezing breaths pulling him almost to a sitting position.

"When *I* knew him," Gram said firmly, "he sang bass in the Baptist choir. Had his own business, and—"

"Did he have a little sort of pot above his belt? With his navel sitting on it like a button on a mountain? Oh, God—" and he was off again, laughing delicately this time so as not to choke.

"*And,*" Gram said, "I married him and had four girls and a boy and all of them healthy. Lemuel he died after the children were grown on account of having influenza, but the children are all alive to this day excepting Phillip, who passed on due to a combination of circumstances. And he left behind him seven children, Joanne Ben Joe Susannah Lisa Jane Jenny and Tessie and a wife and a granddaughter Carol who is just as—"

"Let me say mine," the old man said. He struggled up higher against the pillows and folded his hands across the sheet. "While making bed linens in New Jersey I married my secretary though of good family and not just an every*day* secretary, mind you, and to my grief she died having Samuel our son—"

"You're not married any more?"

"Don't interrupt me. You always were one to interrupt me. I raised him honest and respectful and first he kept books—"

"A *bookie?*"

"A book*keeper,* for our company and gradually rose to an even higher position than I ever had. He has now got a wife and six healthy children Donald Sandra Mara Alex Abigail and uh, uh, Suzanne and one of them—"

"*I* got a grandchild named Susannah," Gram said.

"*One* of them, I say—"

"How's she spell it?"

"*One* of them went to *Europe!*" the old man shouted joyfully.

"Is that so!"

"Summer before last, she went."

"*My* Susannah is spelled kind of like 'Savannah,' Georgia," said Gram. "Only it's *Susannah.*"

"Well, mine's not. It was Sandra that went to Europe. She got to see the Pope."

"The Pope!" Gram's mouth fell open. "Why, Jamie Dower, you haven't gone and become a—"

"Oh, no. Oh, no. But she went with this touring group, her and her aunt, and the itinerary said they could have an audience with the Pope. The family came to me and asked what I thought of it; they ask me about everything important. And I said, 'Sandra, honey,' I said, 'I'll tell you what do. You go visit the Pope and then right after that, the very same day, you go see a *Protestant* minister too. And encourage him in his work and all.' Only it turned out the touring group had to move on before she could track down a Protestant. She was heart*broken* about not keeping her promise."

"Did she sell the clothes the Pope blessed her in?" Gram asked.

"Oh, yes. Excepting her shoes. I think it's good to keep *something* he blessed her in, just in case, you know."

"Ma'am," the nurse said, "remember what I said about keeping it short, now. If you could be thinking about drawing your visit to a close . . ."

She was standing in the doorway with her hands pressed neatly together in front of her, and when they looked up she smiled. Ben Joe, leaning silently upon the window sill, nodded at her. When she was gone he turned back to look out at the view, but Gram and Jamie kept on staring blankly at the place where she had been. Their faces seemed crushed and pale. Finally Gram forced her bright smile again and began anxiously working her dry little hands together.

"Um, Jamie," she said. "Do you remember the time your cousin Otis bought a wild horse?"

"Horse?"

"I was thinking about it while watching a Western the other night. He bought this wild horse that couldn't *nobody* tame and rode off on it practically upside-down, the horse was bucking so bad, but he was waving his scarf and shouting all the same, with your mother and your aunt on the porch watching after him and crying and wringing their hands. And after dark he came back safe and sound and singing, with the horse so polite, and dismounted into the sunken garden and broke his leg in two places. Oh, law, I reckon I never *will* forget—"

"You know," said Jamie, "I just can't recall it."

"Well, it came to me out of the blue, sort of."

He nodded, and for a minute there were only the kitten squeaks of his breathing.

"Then I reckon you remember Grandfather Dower getting religion," he said finally.

"Not offhand I don't."

"Sure you do. Along came this revivalist by the name of Hezekiah Jacob Lee, preaching how nothing material is real and things of the spirit is all that counts. He only stayed for some three days of preaching, but Grandfather Dower, he latched right on. Gave up his swaggering ways and his collecting of old American saloon songs and went around acting unfit to live with. And one day, after Hezekiah Jacob Lee had been gone about a month, Great-Aunt Kazi got stung by a bee on the wrist knob and naturally she went to Grandfather, him being a doctor, and he stamped his foot and shouted, 'Don't bother *me* with your material matters; put mud on it, woman!' when suddenly he frowned and his eyes kind of opened and he said to her, 'Why,' he says, '*why* do you reckon Hezekiah Jacob Lee went off and left me holding the bag this way?' And what a party there was *that* night, with alcohol floating on the garden path—"

"I declare," Gram said, "it rings a bell, sort of. I just vaguely do remember."

They were quiet again, thinking. Jamie Dower drew the edge of his sheet between his small, brittle fingers.

"About all that's left now is Arabella," said Gram.

"Arabella."

"Your cousin, the fat one. Auntie Adams's little girl."

"Oh, her."

"I don't see her much," Gram said. "She was always kind of a prissy girl."

"She was. She was at that. She went to study in Virginia, I remember, before I'd even left home. We heard from her regular but stopped reading her letters."

"It was on account of her mother, I believe," Gram said. "She was the same way. Told Arabella to watch out for germs in public places. Every letter Arabella sent us after that sounded like something from a health inspector. All these long detail-ly descriptions of every—you remember that? Auntie Adams finally wrote back and said she would take Arabella's word for it, but I don't recall that Arabella paid her any mind."

"How about her brother Willie?" Jamie asked.

"Oh, he was prissy too. That whole *section* of the family was prissy."

"No, I mean, what is he doing now?"

"Oh. Well, he's dead. He died about a year ago."

"I didn't know that."

"And of course Auntie Adams is dead. She died."

"I remember someone telling me."

"All that's left now," said Gram, "is Arabella."

They both stared at a place in Jamie's blanket. Behind them the door cracked open softly and the nurse poked her head in and said, "About time to be saying our good-bys now."

"Do you remember," Jamie said suddenly, "do you remember that funny old L-shaped bench that sat on your front porch?"

"What color was it?"

"Green. Dark green. Forest green, I think they call it. Us kids used to sit all together on it in the summer afternoons and eat fresh peaches out of a baskety box. Remember?"

"Well, no."

"I do. I do. You-all were having Hulda Ballew as your maid then, and it was she that set the peaches out for us to dice up small with sharp kitchen knives and eat in little bitty bites, the boys to poke a bite on the tip of a knife to some girl they liked and she to bite it off, dainty like, on summer afternoons. You got to remember that."

"Well, I don't," Gram said. "I remember Hulda Ballew, but no green bench comes to mind."

"You got to remember."

"Ma'am," the nurse said.

Something in her voice made Gram know it was time to give up. Her shoulders sagged and she fell silent, but she kept staring at the blanket.

"Say bye to our guests, Mr. Dower."

"I'm coming," said Gram. "We'll come back, Jamie Dower. If you want us."

"That'll be right nice, Beth. Funny thing," he said, looking at her suddenly. "You were such a *fat* little girl."

Gram patted his hand on the sheet and then stood up and left the room, so suddenly that she took all of them by surprise.

"Well, good-by," said Ben Joe.

"Good-by, young man."

"You take a nice little nap now," the nurse said. She pulled the venetian blinds shut and then tip-toed out of the room behind Ben Joe, closing the door behind her. "He's not well at all," she whispered as they walked down the hall. "I don't know how he lasted this long, or managed to get here all by himself."

"Hush," Ben Joe said. They were approaching Gram, who stood waiting by the elevator. The nurse nodded without surprise and clamped her mouth shut.

When they were out in the car again Ben Joe said, "Put on your coat, Gram, you'll catch cold."

"All right, Ben Joe."

"You want me to turn the heat on?"

"Oh, no."

He started the motor but let it idle while he watched her, trying to think whether there was something to say or whether there was even any need for anything to be said. Her face, with its clown's coating of rouge, told him nothing. When he kept on watching her, she folded her arms across her chest and turned away, so that she was looking out of the window toward the home. Ben Joe let the car roll out into the street again.

"That house," Gram said, looking back at the home, "wasn't even *here* when Jamie Dower was born."

"I know."

"It wasn't even here when we were growing up, did you know *that?* They hadn't laid the first brick yet. They hadn't even dug the foundation yet. There were only trees here, trees and brambly bushes with those little seedy blackberries on them that aren't fit for pies, even—"

"I know. I know."

She grew silent. He didn't know what her face looked like now. And he didn't try to find out, either. He just looked straight ahead at the road they drove on, and kept quiet.

12

ON THE wall behind the silverware drawer in the kitchen was a combination blackboard and bulletin board, frayed at the edges now from so many years of use. Ben Joe stood leaning against the refrigerator with a tomato in his hand and studied the board very carefully, narrowing his eyes. First the blackboard part. Jenny's great swooping handwriting took up half the board:

> Eggs
> Lavoris
> Contact lense fluid

Who in this family wore contact lenses? He frowned and shook his head; he felt like a stranger. Under Jenny's list his grandmother had written, in straight little angry letters:

> Chewing gum

And then came Tessie's writing, round and grade-schoolish, filling up the rest of the board right down to the bottom:

> What shall we do about it?
> I will think of somthing.
> What I want to know is,
> how do you think?

He switched the tomato to his left hand and picked up the piece of chalk that hung by a string from the board. With his mouth clamped tight from concentrating, he bent forward, inserted an "e" in "something," and then stepped back to look at it. After a minute he underlined the "e" twice and then dropped the chalk and reread the whole message. Something about it still confused him.

His eyes moved over to the bulletin-board part. In the old days it had been crowded with the children's drawings, ranging from kindergarten-level pictures of houses with smoking chimneys up to the tiny complicated landscapes Ben Joe had done in upper grade school. Now only one of them was left—a drawing done by Jenny, when she was six, of a circle superimposed on a furry cylinder, which she had said was the Lone Ranger and Silver seen from above. Other than that, there were only two yellowed scraps of paper. The first was one of the few reminders of his father that had been allowed to remain; it was a note written by Susannah, back when her writing was as uncertain as Tessie's, saying:

> Mama, the last five times that Gram has gone to a church supper and you've gone to a Legal Women Voters' supper both at the same time Daddy has fed us as follows:
> (1) popcorn
> (2) grilled cheese sandwiches
> (3) fudge
> (4) popcorn
> (5) ice cream, please talk to him.

Ben Joe frowned again, considered changing the comma to a semicolon, but eventually let it go for some reason and turned to the next piece of paper. This was his own, in crooked, preschool capitals, and he could not remember when or for what reason he had written it. It said:

> SONG *by*
> *Benjamin Josiah Hawkes*
>
> *What shall we do with the trunk-ed sailor*
> *Is a matter worth disgusting.*
> *Everybody's pinto is agoing to heaven*
> *Heaven, in the morning.*

It had a tune, his mother had told him, something like the scissors-mender's chant, all on one note, except that the last word in each line was several notes lower. They said he used to sing it at the beach, but he had no memory of it now.

He looked down at his tomato. There was a bite in it, although he hadn't noticed he had taken one. He considered storming into the den and accusing Tessie of spit-backing, which was a habit she had developed after biting into chocolates that turned out to be caramel-filled; but on second thought he decided he might have taken a bite after all. There was no telling. He had been confused and absent-minded all day; he attributed it to the visit at the home for the aged, but just knowing the reason didn't help him any. All he could think of that might help was to isolate himself in the kitchen for a while after supper and stare at the bulletin board, where years arranged themselves one on top of the other in layers before his eyes. Sometimes that helped. Sometimes it didn't, too. He sighed, took another bite from his tomato, and began rereading the blackboard.

> Eggs
> Lavoris . . .

"What are *you* doing here?" Jenny asked.

"Why?"

"I thought you were just going out to get a snack. You missed the last half of the program."

"Oh. Okay."

He moved aside to let her get into the refrigerator.

"Ben Joe . . ."

"*What*," he said. Every time she interrupted him he had to go back to the very top of the blackboard and begin reading all over again.

"Never mind," she said.

"Well, go *on*, now that you've interrupted me."

"I just wanted to know where the ice water is. I'm getting some for Gram. What's the matter with you tonight?"

"I don't know. I went with Gram to the old folks' home." He jammed his hands into his pockets and with the toe of his sneaker he began tracing patterns in the linoleum. There was no sense in going back to reading the blackboard until Jenny was out of the room again.

She had found the ice water. She poured it into an orange-juice glass and put the jar back in the refrigerator.

"Hey, I wonder . . ." she said suddenly.

But Ben Joe, off on another track now, interrupted her. "Who in this family wears contact lenses?" he asked.

"Contact— Oh, you're talking about the list. Susannah does."

"How come I didn't know?"

"You weren't here," Jenny said.

"Oh."

"She got them with her first pay check from the library, after she switched jobs."

"I never heard about it."

"You weren't *here*, I said." She picked up the glass of water and started out again. At the door she stopped. "What I was just wondering," she said, "was it this morning you went to the home? With Gram?"

"Yes."

"Well, why don't you come out into the living room? Gram just heard an old friend of hers died. She says she only saw him this morning, so that must be who it is. That Mr. Dower."

"He's dead?"

"That's what she said."

"But he can't be. We only saw him this morning."

"Doesn't stop him from being dead, does it? Why do people always—"

"Ah, no," said Ben Joe. He shook his head gently and turned his back to the bulletin board. (What good would it do him now?) There was no reason for him to feel so sad, but he did, anyway, and he just kept staring at a corner of the kitchen cabinet while Jenny watched him curiously.

"Why don't you come talk to Gram?" she asked him.

"Well . . ."

"Come on."

She backed against the door to open it and let Ben Joe pass through ahead of her. "All I ever know to do is get people water," she said, "I know when *I'm* sad *I* don't want water, and I don't guess others do, either, but it's all I know to do."

"Well, I'm sure she'd like it," Ben Joe said.

"Maybe so."

In the living room he found his grandmother upright on the couch, sitting very stiffly with her hands in her lap and her eyes dry. Around her was clustered most of the family, some sitting next to her and some on chairs around the room.

"Only this morning," she was saying. "Only this morning." She caught sight of Ben Joe and called out, "Wasn't it, Ben Joe? Wasn't it only this morning?"

"Yes," said Ben Joe.

"There. Ben Joe can tell you." She turned to nod at the others and then, realizing that Ben Joe hadn't yet heard the whole story, she looked his way again. "I called the home," she said. "I wanted to tell him about something I'd forgotten. This evening I was just hunting under the bed for Carol's hair brush and suddenly it came to me, so clear: Jamie's mustache cup."

"His what?" Ben Joe asked.

"Mustache cup. Mustache cup. You know, Jamie Dower was the only

man I ever knew who really did use a mustache cup. That was something
wonderful, when I was twelve. He got it just the last year he was
home, on account of this lovely mustache he was growing. He was
kind of a dandy, Jamie Dower. *Always* was. But it was a beautiful
mustache, I have to say. Ben *Joe* knows. You tell them, Ben Joe."

"Well . . ." Ben Joe said. The picture of Jamie's face was before
him, small and white and clean-shaven.

"Ben Joe knows," Gram said to the rest of them. She smiled down
at her hands. "I know it's a small thing, but I suddenly thought of
that mustache cup, white with pink rosebuds, it was, and I just had
to tell him about it. So I called the home, and after a right long spell
of hemming and hawing they told me. They said he had passed on
just an hour ago. I didn't let on how it hit me. I just said I hoped
he'd had a peaceful passing, and hung up." Her mouth shook for a
minute, and the first tear slid down the dry paper of her cheek. "But
it was only this *morning* . . ." she said.

A glass of water was poked suddenly under her chin. Gram drew
back and blinked at it through her tears. Her eyes traveled slowly from
the glass itself to the poker-stiff arm that held it and above that to
Jenny's face, sober and embarrassed.

"Why, thank you," she said. She took the glass, looked at it a minute,
and then smiled at Jenny and drank until the glass was empty. "There
is nothing like clear water," she told Jenny formally.

Ben Joe looked around at the rest of the family. His mother was in
the easy chair, looking worried; Tessie was on the arm of the chair,
and the twins and Susannah were sitting around their grandmother on
the couch. All of them were unusually quiet. When the silence had
gone unbroken for at least a full minute, his mother cleared her throat
and said, "We'll have to send a nice wreath of flowers, Gram."

"He wouldn't like it," Gram said. "Used to get angry when I brought
him my dessert."

"Your— Well, anyway. It'd be a nice gesture to send a small wreath,
just to show—"

"I will *not* send him *flowers*!" Gram said.

Ellen Hawkes was quiet a moment, figuring this out. Finally she said,
"Well, some people prefer the money to go to a worthy cause instead.
Maybe to the missionary league of his church, if he has one—"

"I tell you, no, Ellen. He never could accept a gift graciously. My
mother said accepting gifts graciously is the true test of a gentleman,
but I don't go along with that. Jamie Dower was a gentleman all the
way through. He just didn't like gifts, is all."

"But that was some seventy *years* ago, Gram—"

"No point discussing it," said Ben Joe. "We don't send flowers."

Gram began crying again. The girls fluttered and crowded in around
her and Jenny backed toward the door, in case she had to get more
ice water. Ellen Hawkes clicked her tongue.

"What's going on?" Joanne said.

She was standing in the doorway dressed to go out and carrying a coat over her arm. Everyone looked up except Gram, who had just been handed Ben Joe's handkerchief and was now blowing her nose in it.

"Gram's lost an old friend," Susannah said.

"Oh, no." She came quickly over to the couch and knelt down in front of her grandmother. "Who was it?"

"Jamie Dower," said Gram, "and I can't send him flowers."

"Well, of course you can. What's the matter with this family? Mom, since when have we got so poor we can't send—"

"My God," her mother said. She stood up and left the room, not sharply but with a slow kind of weariness.

"It's not the money," Ben Joe said. "It's that Jamie never could accept a gift graciously."

"Oh, I see." She nodded and began gently stroking Gram's shoulder.

"If you see," her mother said from the doorway, "will you please explain it to *me*?"

"Well, it makes sense."

"Not to me it doesn't. Does it to you, Ben Joe?"

"Well, yes," said Ben Joe.

His mother vanished into the hallway.

"What *doesn't* make sense," Ben Joe said, "is why it makes you unhappy not sending him flowers. If you know he'd be happier not getting them."

"Because I *want* to send them, that's why," his grandmother said. "I always did want to give him flowers."

She began crying into her handkerchief, and the other girls moved over so that Joanne could sit beside her and hug her. "I know, I know," she said soothingly. "Now, I tell you what do, Gram. You just buy some flowers and give them to someone you like. Prettiest flowers you can find. And then you tell yourself you wouldn't have done it if Jamie Dower hadn't died. That way you solve the whole thing, right?"

"Well, maybe," Gram said.

The doorbell rang. Joanne gave Gram a brisk pat on the shoulder and stood up. "Don't bother," she told Ben Joe. "I'll get it. It's my date."

"What?"

But she didn't answer; she was already out of the room. Gram refolded the handkerchief to a dry place and then suddenly, in the middle of the process, stopped and looked up at Ben Joe. "What'd she say?" she asked.

"She said it was her date."

"Did she mean her appointment? Or did she mean her date?"

"Her date, is what she said."

All of them fell silent, listening. A young man laughed in the front hallway. Ben Joe could read in Gram's face the slow transition from grief to indignation.

"Why *she* can't do that!" she said. "Joanne?"

The two voices ran on, ignoring her.

"*Joanne!*" Gram said.

Joanne reappeared, still carrying her coat over her arm.

"Who's that you got with you?" Gram asked.

"John Horner, Gram. Come on in, John."

John Horner appeared next to her, soundlessly. He still had his broad, open smile and he didn't seem to think it strange to be greeted by a whole silent, staring family grouped around a weeping old woman. He nodded to all of them in general and lifted a hand toward Ben Joe, whom he recognized.

"This is my grandmother," said Joanne. "And Ben Joe, and Susannah, and Jane, Lisa, Jenny, and Tessie. This is John Horner."

"How do you do?" John Horner said. He was addressing mainly Gram, as the oldest member of the family, but Gram just sat up straighter and stared narrowly at him.

"I wish I'd of married Jamie Dower," she said.

"Ma'am?"

"Gram has just heard that a friend passed away," Joanne began. Her voice was the old high-school Joanne's, soft and bubbling. She stood very close to John Horner while she talked to him. Under cover of Joanne's voice Gram went on muttering to the others.

"If I'd of married Jamie," she said, "I would of had a different family. On account of different genes mingling. They wouldn't all have gone and done queer things, or acted so—"

"Hush, Gram," Susannah said.

"Ben Joe?" Joanne called.

"What."

"John was asking you something."

"Excuse me?"

"I was just asking," said John, "aren't you the one that's at Columbia?"

"That's right."

"I was there for a while. Took a business course. Mrs. Hawkes, ma'am, I'm sorry to hear about your friend's passing."

Gram frowned. "Well," she said ungraciously. She thought a minute and then added, "Troubles always descend lots at a time, seems like."

"They do," said John. He came further into the room to sit on the arm of the rocker, and Joanne moved over to stand beside him. "My old man had a saying. My old man used to say, 'It never rains but it—' "

"Who is your daddy?" Gram asked suddenly.

"Jacob Hart Horner, ma'am."

"Jacob Hart Horner. That so."

"Yes'm."

"Oh. I know him."

"Do you really?" He smiled politely.

"*Yes,* I know him."

"Ah."

Gram nodded a while, considering.

"What you think he'd say if he saw you here?" she asked.

The silence before her question had been long enough so that John was just beginning to consider the conversation over. He froze now, in the act of turning toward Joanne, and looked back at Gram blankly.

"Ma'am?" he said. "What's that?"

"If he saw you here. If Jacob Hart Horner saw you here. What you think he'd say?"

"If he saw me *here?*"

"*Yes,* here."

"I don't—"

"Saw you taking Joanne out. Joanne Hawkes *Bentley* out. What you think he'd say?"

"Well, nothing, I don't guess."

"Nothing." She nodded again, with her eyes fixed veiled and thoughtful upon the floor. "No, I don't guess he would," she said finally. "*I* remember Jacob Hart Horner. Remember him well. Came here in his teens, he did, and took up with my boy Phillip. He was supposed to be working, but he didn't do much of *that.* Lived off little Sylvester Grant and my boy Phillip. I never *will* forget, one time he called his folks long distance from this very house and me sitting in the same room listening to him. I reckon they wanted to know had he got a steady job and he said yes, he was working in the chicken cannery. There was a chicken cannery then, down by the river near the blue-denim factory, but I never saw *him* near it. And I reckon they wanted to know what he did there, because he started talking about carrying grain—said that was his job. Now, I don't know what his folks were like and I don't *want* to know, but let me just ask you this: what kind of intelligence do you suppose they had, to believe a body could get a job carrying grain in a factory that deals with dead chickens?"

"Well, now, I don't know," John Horner said. He was laughing, and didn't seem to be insulted.

"There's bad blood there," Gram said. She looked at him a while, at the friendly face with the dark eyes made slits by laughter, and then she blew her nose and looked down into her lap. "I am getting old," she said.

The room grew silent. John looked over at Joanne soberly, and she clutched her coat more tightly to her and started toward the door.

"Gram," she said, "I hope you feel better."

"Well. New things come up. A minute ago Jamie Dower slipped from my mind altogether for a second."

"Sure. It's always that way. You'll—"

"What I was meaning to bring up a minute ago," Gram began, "what I wanted to say . . ."

She stopped and looked over at Ben Joe.

"Um," he said. He took his hands out of his pockets and walked over to where John was standing beside Joanne.

"What's the matter?" Joanne asked.

"Well, I was just wondering." He looked at her face, with its blank brown eyes, and then changed his mind and directed the question toward John. "What I think Gram was trying to say," he said, ". . . well, hell with it, what *I'm* trying to say is, it doesn't look to me like a good idea for you to be going out, Joanne." But he was still facing John; it was to John's more open eyes that he said it.

"Why *not*," John said, turning it into a challenge instead of a question.

"Well, it's a small town. That's one reason."

"Small town, what's *that* got to do with it? Listen, boy, you and your family got to stop hanging on to your sister this way. Got to start—"

"But she's still *married*, damn it!"

His mother, coming in on the tail end of the sentence, stopped in the doorway and looked at Ben Joe.

"What?" she said.

Ben Joe turned to her. "Mom, I'm asking you, now. Do you think Joanne ought to go out on a date?"

His mother frowned. "Well," she said finally, "I don't know. If it's just an old friend of hers, I don't see the harm in her getting out of the house for a while. It's up to Joanne, after all. None of *our* business."

"But he's *not* just an old *friend!*"

"What is he, then?"

There was a silence. Everyone looked at him.

"Frankly," John said finally, "I don't see how—"

"No, listen. Please *listen!*"

"We're listening, Ben Joe," said his mother.

"No, you're not. You never are. Look, I was just worrying if people would *talk*."

"What would they talk about?"

He sat down, realized immediately the disadvantage at which this put him when everyone else was standing, and stood up again.

"Joanne," he said, "don't you see my point?"

"No," Joanne said.

"John? *You* do."

"I'm sorry, I don't," said John.

"*You* talk, don't you?" Ben Joe said. He took a step closer to him. "Don't you?"

John blinked his eyes at him.

"Look," Ben Joe said. He was facing all of them now, with his arms straight by his sides and his fists clenched. "All I'm trying to do is stop one more of those amazing damned things that go on in this family and everyone takes for granted, pretends things are still all right and the world's still right-side up. The most amazing things go on in this family, the most *amazing* things, that no one *else* would *allow*, and this family just keeps on—"

"Just what sort of amazing things are you talking about?" his mother asked. She was looking at him straight on and sternly, with her eyes just slits. "This family's just like any other family, Ben Joe. There's nothing going on here that—"

"Oh, *no?*"

"No."

He slitted his eyes back at her.

"Just to give you a for-instance," he said, "I don't know if you all can dredge far enough back in your memories or not, but I can recall a time when Dad and the sheriff were out all one night in their pajamas—"

"That is *enough*," his mother said.

"—pajamas, chasing down to Dillon, South Carolina, because Joanne had run off with a total stranger that came here selling clear plastic raincoats one autumn afternoon, run off to get married as soon as he asked her, which as near as we could figure it was three seconds after she had opened the front door to his ringing, and Dad was frantically chasing down every highway to Dillon and finally found them at seven-thirty in the morning waiting to fill out a marriage license. And he brought her back and everyone just said, 'Well, let her sleep.'"

"It's true!" Gram said. "It's true. I remember it all!"

"What else could we have done?" his mother asked the clock.

"Which was fine, except didn't they wonder even what *led* to it, or *why*, or try to do something to help her? No, and at supper they all told jokes and passed the biscuits and there was Joanne with a new trick, a piece of plastic that looked just exactly like vomit—she'd bought it at the magic store—and she was retching and then throwing the plastic on the floor, and she squealed, 'Ooh, wouldn't my vomit go good on the living room *rug!*' and you all laughed and ran with her to the living room and life went on, and on, while—"

Joanne stepped up, and for a minute he thought she was going to hit him, but instead she pushed her coat in his face, choking him with the force of it, leaving him in a forest-green darkness that smelled of wool and spice perfume. He could feel the bones of her hands pressing through the wool to his face, and above the uproar John Horner was shouting, "Stop it, *stop* it!" but the coat was still being pushed against his face.

"Anybody home?" someone called.

There was a long, deep silence.

The coat fell away from Ben Joe's face and hung, crumpled, around his shoulders. He blinked his eyes several times. Everyone in the room was looking toward the door, with their faces blank, staring at the tallest man Ben Joe had ever seen. He was bony and freckled with a long, friendly face, and though his overcoat hung on him badly, there was something very easy and graceful about the way he was standing.

"I would have called," he said cheerfully, "but then if I had, you probably would be gone when I got here. And I would have waited for you to answer the door, but a man can't wait forever. Can he?" he asked, and grinned at Ben Joe.

People were coming out of their surprise now, opening their mouths to speak, but the stranger had moved rapidly into the center of the room with his hands still in his pockets and he said, "I knew the house. Know it anywhere. Though that glider has *got* to be new. I didn't know that. You people are—" he looked around at them, still cheerfully—"Gram, Ben Joe, Mom, uh . . . Jenny? and a man I don't know with, of course, Joanne—"

"You go away," Joanne said softly.

"But I only just got here."

"I'm telling you, Gary . . ."

But before the name was out of her mouth, Ben Joe knew. He suddenly recognized the hair, flaming red and pushed carelessly back from his forehead exactly like Carol's, and the familiar-looking eyes that had stared out of the dim snapshot. He stood gaping at the three of them—Joanne and Gary and John—in a brightly tensed, three-cornered group in the center of the room.

"I'm leaving," he said.

"Ben Joe!" his mother called.

"I don't care, I don't care, I'm *leaving!*"

And he shoved the coat back in Joanne's face. It fell to the floor, but she let it stay there and didn't look his way. Jenny was in his path; he pushed her aside without even knowing it and flew through the hallway and out the door. Then he was outside. He was in the dark wind, with the cold already slapping at his face.

13

SHELLEY'S FACE was small and white; her hair was a mass of sausage-shaped curlers, shrouded under a heavy black net. She stood behind her screen door and looked out to where Ben Joe stood on the porch, under the yellow outside light, and to Ben Joe it seemed as if she was suddenly considering every detail of him, weighing him in the back of her faraway mind. With one hand she reached up vaguely to touch her curlers, obeying that part of her that wondered always, no matter what, whether she was fit to be seen. But it was only the most absent-minded gesture. Her eyes were still fixed on him, and she frowned a little and bent forward to see him more clearly.

"It's me," Ben Joe said.

"I know."

She kept watching him. The two of them seemed to be standing between the two ticks of a clock, in a dead silence of time where there was no need to hurry about anything; as long as she stayed silent and watchful they were frozen stock-still between that clock's ticking. Then she gave up, not finished with whatever it was she was trying to do but just giving up in the middle of it, and, clutching her quilted bathrobe more tightly about her, opened the door for him.

"I've been walking for hours," he said.

She nodded. Nothing seemed to surprise her. When he stepped inside she held up both hands, in a gesture like a doll's in a toy-shop window, to take the light sweater he was wearing, and he shucked it off and handed it to her.

"I know you weren't expecting company," he told her as she turned to hang up his sweater. "You can go on and do whatever you were doing before. I won't mind."

She didn't answer. The hangers in the closet tinkled flatly as she rummaged among them, and when she lifted one from the rod another fell with it, making a blurred explosive sound as it landed on a floor full of old rubbers and high-heeled galoshes. She ignored it; her eyes concentrated upon what suddenly seemed, to Ben Joe, the impossibly complicated task of getting his sweater upon the hanger. What was wrong with Shelley? Her fingers fumbled tightly at the collar of the sweater, taking hours to make it lie straight around the hook of the hanger. If it had been any other night, Ben Joe would have gone on in, would have left her in the hallway and headed for the living-room sofa. But tonight he felt uneasy. He wanted to tread as delicately as possible so that she would turn out to be glad he came. So he stood clenching his cold aching hands together and waiting hopefully for Shelley to finish this interminable business of getting his sweater up, and he never even looked toward the living room.

"I reckon you'll want some bourbon," she said.

"No."

"It'll do you good, if you're cold."

She headed toward the kitchen, making only the softest whispering noise across the floor in her bare feet. After a minute Ben Joe followed her. If she took so long to hang a sweater up, how long would she spend making a drink? And he really didn't want one; he felt awkward and foolish stumbling in here like this, and he didn't want to make it worse by accepting anything.

"I'm sorry I came without warning," he said.

"It's all right."

"I should have called first."

"It's all *right*, Ben Joe."

She stood on tiptoe to reach a liquor bottle from the cupboard, and Ben Joe leaned against the kitchen sink. He was surprised at how messy everything was; ordinarily Shelley was almost old-maidishly tidy. He could remember her spreading peanut butter on a piece of bread and then washing the knife and putting it and the peanut butter away even before she finished making the sandwich. And she had some sort of phobia about seeing that all the cannisters were neatly aligned along the counter and all the measuring spoons hung in order on the wall according to their sizes. But tonight the place was in chaos. Dishes and leftovers littered the counter; a recently washed sweater was baled up in the dish drainer and a shower cap was flung over the towel rack. He looked around at Shelley, trying to figure out what sort of mood she must be in. In her pale flowered bathrobe, a little too small for her, she looked wire-thin and brittle. But the shyness was gone, so much forgotten that she seemed not at all embarrassed at being caught in her bathrobe. In place of the shyness was a sort of heavy sullenness that he hadn't often seen in her before, that made her face look fuller and the lower lines of her cheeks sag. Her eyebrows had lost the high, uncertain arch they usually had and sat straight over blank eyes, and she was poking out her mouth in a way that made it seem like a pouting child's mouth. When she poured the drink she did it heavily, with finality.

"Have you got something on your mind?" Ben Joe asked.

She stopped, looked at the bottle, and then reached for another glass and poured a drink for herself.

"If you do," he said, "I wish you'd tell me. I hate this ferreting things out of people. I ask what's wrong and they say nothing, and then I say *please* to tell me and they say no, really, it's nothing, and I say well, I can just *feel* something's wrong. And by then we both hate each other. I keep thinking of everything bad I've done in the last ten years, things you wouldn't even begin to know, but somehow I start thinking maybe you've found out—"

"Oh, Ben Joe," Shelley said tiredly.

She handed him his drink and then picked up her own and headed for the living room. Behind her Ben Joe walked slowly, dragging his feet and watching the back of Shelley's head. The curlers bobbed up and down cheerfully, but her shoulders were slumped and careless. When they entered the living room, Shelley chose a seat in the wicker chair by the fireplace and Ben Joe had to sit alone on the couch opposite her. He felt exposed and defenseless, with all that bare expanse of couch at either side of him.

"I would do anything to help," he said. "But I don't know what's wrong."

Shelley raised her eyebrows slightly, as if what he was saying was a curious little toy he had handed her and she wanted to act polite about it. He had forgotten that she could be this way. He had seen her angry only a few times in his life—once or twice when he had dated other girls, and then one memorable time when she had taken three months to knit him a sweater in high school and then found he had grown two inches while she was busy knitting. Each time that she had been angry, the change in her had surprised him all over again. She became suddenly cool and haughty, and she left him feeling bewildered. Tonight no matter how hard he looked at her, no matter how patiently he waited for her to speak, she was unchangingly cool and blank-faced, sitting aloof in her solitary wicker chair. He sighed and took a long drink of the straight warm bourbon. He thought about the bourbon winding slowly to his stomach; with his head cocked, he seemed to be listening to it, noting carefully which part of him it was burning now. Shelley was turned into a carefully shut-out inanimate object on the other side of the room. A tune began in his head, hummed nonchalantly by that sexless, anonymous voice that lived inside him and always spoke words as he read them and thoughts as he thought them.

"So I guess I won't be coming tomorrow night," he said absently. Shelley's fingernail, tapping rhythmically against her glass, was suddenly stilled. "I've got to go back to New York."

The fingernail resumed its tapping. Ben Joe watched a specific place on the coffee table, a corner where the dust had gathered between the table top and the raised rim of it in a tiny triangle. He suddenly thought, without meaning to or wanting to, that tomorrow night when he was rattling northward on the rickety little train, this table corner would be exactly the same, would exist solid and untouched no matter where he was. Shelley would wash and neatly stack her dishes, and Gram would roar songs at the top of her lungs while she polished the silver, and everything—the solid little coffee table, the narrow polished windows, the hundreds of curtained front doors, all this still, unchanging world of women—would stay the same while he rushed on through darkness across the garishly lit industrial plains of New Jersey and into the early-morning stillness of New York. He leaned forward, resting his chin on his hand, and stared at the floor.

"Every place I go," he said, "I miss another place."

Shelley was silent.

"I don't know why," he said, just as if she'd asked. "When I am away from Sandhill, sometimes the picture of it comes drifting toward me—just the picture of it, like some sunny little island I have got to get back to. And there's my family. Most of the time I seem to see them sort of like a bunch of picnickers in a nineteenth-century painting, sitting around in the grass with their picnic baskets and their pretty dresses and parasols, and floating past on that island. I think, I've got to get back. I think, they need me there and I have got to get back to them. But when I go back, they laugh at me and rumple my hair and ask why I'm such a worrier. And I can't tell them why. There's nothing I can tell them. Pretty soon I leave again, on account of seeing myself so weak and speechless and worried. I get to thinking about something I just miss like hell in *another* town, like this tree on a street in Atlanta that has a real electric socket in it, right in the trunk, or the trolley cars in Philadelphia making that faraway lonesome sound as they pass down an empty street in the rain, through old torn-down slum buildings with nothing but a wallpapered sheet of brick and a set of stone steps left standing . . ."

Shelley was staring at him now, with her forehead wrinkled, trying to understand and not succeeding. When he saw that he wasn't making sense he stopped, and spread his hands helplessly.

"Oh, well," he said.

"No, I'm listening."

"Well." He paused, trying to arrange his words better, but finally he gave up. "Nothing," he said. "So you *go* to Atlanta, and you *see* the damn electric socket, and you *go* to Philadelphia and you *see* the damn trolley cars. So what? They only turn out to be an electric socket and a trolley car, in the long run. Nothing to keep you occupied longer than five minutes, either one of them. Then, in the middle of being loose and strong and on my own, wherever I am, along through my mind floats this island of a town with my family on it, still smiling on the lawn beside their picnic baskets . . ."

Shelley nodded several times slowly, as if she understood. He couldn't tell if she really did or not. He thought probably she didn't, but what mattered more than that right now was whether she was still in that black mood of hers and whether she would tell him why. He looked across at her steadily; her face returned to its original blankness and she stared back at him.

"So you're going back to New York," she said.

"I guess."

She was silent again. He began twirling the bourbon around in his glass, watching it slosh up and leave its oily trail along the sides.

"So you just come," she said, "and then you leave."

"Well, that's what I've just been explaining to—"

"You're not fair, Ben Joe Hawkes."

He looked up; Shelley's eyes were narrowed at him and she was angry. As soon as he looked at her she reached one hand up to her curlers again and then began pulling them down, with hasty, fumbling fingers, ripping them out and tossing them into her lap, where her other hand was clenched so hard that the knuckles were white. In spite of all his worries, in spite of being concerned at her anger and sad at the way this whole night had been, a part of Ben Joe wondered detachedly why she was taking her curlers out and why she was choosing this moment to do it. He watched, fascinated. Her hair without the curlers remained still in little sausage shapes around her head, and since she had no comb handy, she began raking her fingers through the curls in order to loosen them. But all the while her face seemed unaware of what was going on, as if this business with her hair was just a nervous habit.

"You come and then you leave," she repeated, "just like that. You're not fair. The trouble with you, Ben Joe Hawkes, is you don't *think*. You're a kind enough person when you think about it, but that's not often, and most of the time you—"

"Don't think about what?" he asked.

"Your coming and your going."

"Shelley, for God's sake."

"And then on *top* of all that, there's your sister."

He stopped in the middle of putting his drink on the table and looked up. There was something nightmarish about this. It was like one of those dreams in which he was playing the leading role in a play on opening night and had no idea what the play was.

"My sister," he said.

"*Yes*, your sister."

"Which one?"

"Benjamin Hawkes, don't you joke with me."

"Well, but what *sister*?"

"What sister my foot. How can you—"

"I have six," Ben Joe said patiently. He took another breath to go on and then suddenly, realizing what she meant, let his breath out again and sank back. Once more John Horner and Joanne stood looking at him on the porch steps, stood defensively close together in the Hawkes's living room, and Ben Joe shook his head at his own stupidity. There was something about Joanne; the minute she met a man, that man seemed to belong to her. Even John Horner, whom Shelley had so definitely identified as her own, was associated in Ben Joe's mind only with Joanne now that he had seen the two of them together. He had seen them first, after all, the night that Shelley had seemed to forget about John Horner completely. It was too confusing; he shook his head and said, "Lord, I'm stupid."

"Why?" Shelley asked curiously. She seemed to have expected more of a fight, and now she was temporarily taken aback.

"Joanne, you meant."

"Well, of course." She put both hands together in her lap and stared down at them. "Mrs. Murphy told me," she said. "Well, if it hadn't of been her, it'd been someone else. This town knows everything. I know she's your sister, Ben Joe, but I tell you she's just wild. With a husband and a baby, even, she's wild. She's wild and no-count and after anyone who'll pay a little attention to her. Anyone can tell you that. Doesn't take a detective to figure it out. It's just you that won't listen. You don't hear facts too good if it's your own precious sister they concern."

"I hear them," Ben Joe said. He sat there, not looking at her, twisting his hands aimlessly between his knees.

"Oh, I didn't mean to go mud-slinging . . ." Shelley said suddenly. For the first time that evening Ben Joe saw the beginnings of tears in her eyes. She looked up shinily, with her mouth blurred and shaky, and stared hard at a point just above his head to keep from blinking the tears onto her cheeks. Shelley was the kind of girl who cried often, and from years of experience he had learned that with her the best thing was to be cheerful and brisk and to pay as little attention to the tears as possible. The little anonymous voice in his head picked up the tune again and went cheerfully da-da-deeing along. He kept his eyes upon an empty knickknack shelf in the corner behind Shelley's chair.

"Anyway," he said finally. He kept his voice pleasant and reasonable. "At least we've got to why you're angry with me."

"Why?" Shelley asked, and bit her lip hard and went on staring above him.

"Well, you were with me and therefore John went out with Joanne. It was black magic. Once in college I was in love with a coquette. She had a cute little pony tail that bobbed on the back of her head every time she took a step, and I thought she was wonderful. I would go for whole weeks without even looking at other girls, not even looking at one that I just saw on the campus somewhere, because I thought that then she wouldn't look at another boy. Sometimes it amazes me how superstitious I am. In the end, of course, she ran away and got married to this tuba player from Ditch 29, Arkansas—"

"You are just as lighthearted as a bird," Shelley said. "I declare, every time a body gets sad, it's a fact that someone'll come along all cheerful and tell them *their* problems, which aren't a bit more related—"

"I'm sorry," Ben Joe said. "I thought it was related. I'm sorry."

He began twisting his hands between his knees again, still not looking at her. When it seemed safe to start speaking again, when he was fairly sure that he hadn't sent her off into a real crying fit, he said, "All I meant was, that's why I'm to blame. Because it was me you were with. If you're superstitious too, of course. But I surely didn't mean to send John Horner off to my sister. God knows I—"

One of Shelley's tears must have escaped. She was too far away and the room was too dim for him to tell for sure, but he saw her hand flicker up to her cheek and then back to her lap again.

"Oh, well," he said, "you're probably not superstitious at all. It's probably nothing to do with that. But I'm trying to think what I've done and I can't come *up* with anything—"

"Oh, you silly," Shelley said. She hunched forward and began crying in earnest now, without trying to hide it any more, burying her face in her brittle white hands.

"Well," Ben Joe said for no reason. He searched hurriedly through his pockets, but there wasn't a handkerchief. On the mantel he spied a purse, a black leather clutch purse with a clasp, that always reminded him of old ladies. He rose and went to it just at the moment when the tune started up in his head again, but this time not even the little voice could drown out the whispery choking sounds behind him. He rushed through the contents of the purse—glasses, keys, coin purse, lipstick, arranged neatly inside—and found beneath them an unused Kleenex. Shaking the folds out of it as he went, he crossed over to Shelley and stuck the Kleenex in her hand.

"The way you talk," she said in a thick voice as she took the Kleenex, "you haven't done a thing in the world and are just asking what you did wrong to humor me, like. Well, I'll tell you what you've done." She blew her nose lightly. Ben Joe, standing over her, felt as if she might be Tessie or Carol. He wanted to say, "Come on now, blow hard. You'll never breathe again if you blow *that* way," but he resisted the urge and only waited silently for her to continue. "You just come to me when you want comforting," she said, "without ever thinking, without giving it any thought. My own mama told me that, although she thought the world of you. Like when things got bad at home you would drop over to get comforted and then leave, bam, no thought to it, and when it came time for the Pom-Pom prom you asked Dare Georges, who I *will* say was as *flighty* as the day is long, her and that little majorette suit she wore everywhere but church—"

"Oh, Shelley," Ben Joe said wearily, "try and stick to the subject, will you?"

She blew her nose and nodded at the floor. When Shelley cried she became almost ugly, with that translucent skin of hers suddenly mottled and blurred. As if she were thinking of this now, she passed one hand across her face and through her uncombed hair, and she sat up straighter.

"It's worse this time," she said. "Worse than the times before, I mean. Because this time I had a steady boyfriend, who was getting serious, and then along you came and superstition *nothing*, it's plain fact I had to tell John Sunday night was out because of you. Well, I know it's my fault going out with you. And I know I shouldn't be crying if I turned him down for you, but he's *someone*, isn't he? Someone that'll stay, and think about me sometimes, and let me have a kitchen with pots and pans?"

She had worked herself up to a good crying session again. Her voice was shaky and her chin wobbled. Sometimes Ben Joe thought girls must actually enjoy crying, the way they kept dwelling on what made them sad. He reached down for her drink, which stood almost untouched beside her chair, and bent over her with it.

"Take a good drink," he said.

"No."

"Come on."

He held it to her mouth and she took a swallow and tried to smile. Her face was puffy, with her eyes sleepy little slits, like a child's, and her mouth smooth and swollen. He thought there must be something about tonight that made it right for crying. First Gram, and then Shelley, and in a way even he felt like crying now.

"One more drink," he said.

She drank obediently.

"You want a cigarette?"

She pressed her lips together stubbornly and shook her head. "No, thank you," she said. "They give me halitosis."

"Oh. Okay."

He took one for himself and lit it. It was the first he had had all day and it tasted bad, but he kept puffing hard and not looking at her.

"Well, it's really me to blame," Shelley said, as if they were in the middle of an unfinished conversation. "It's me. For years, now, I haven't let anyone sweep under my feet."

"Under your—"

"So that I wouldn't be an old maid. I worry too much about having someone to settle down with, but I can't help it. Back home, when my family was alive, I would come in from work every day at the same time and climb the front steps of where we all lived thinking, 'It's five-ten just like it was yesterday and the day before, and just like then I am climbing these steps with no one but the family to greet me and the family to spend my evening with playing parcheesi and no man to care if I *ever* get home.' And I'd come in and head up the stairs toward my room and Mama would call from the parlor, she'd say, 'That you, Shelley?' and I'd say, 'It's me.' I'd climb the rest of the stairs and go toward my room and then out of Phoebe's room Phoebe would call, 'That you, Shelley?' and I'd say, 'It's me—' "

"Shelley, I don't think we're really getting anywhere with this," Ben Joe said.

"I'm explaining something, Ben Joe. I'm explaining. I'd go to my room and change to my house clothes, and I'd hang up my work dress neatly and I'd take my stockings to the bathroom and wash them out and hang them over the shower rail. Then I'd go back to my room and rearrange my underwear drawer, which I'd rearranged the week before, or I'd mend something or work a double crostic. At suppertime there'd be two questions for me. Daddy always said, 'You have a good day, Shelley?' and I said, 'Yes, Daddy,' and Mama'd say, 'You going to be doing anything special tonight?' and I'd say, 'I don't guess so, Mama.' Which was true and which went on and on, so sometimes I think I could have just sent a tape recording home from work with my same old answers on it and done as well—"

"Well, what are you telling me for?"

"I'm explaining why I'm mad at you."

"You're still mad?" he asked.

"Course I am."

"Oh, look now. Look, *don't* be mad at me."

"You come, you go," she said doggedly.

"I don't either."

"You don't?"

"Well, I won't," he said. He had a desperate, sinking feeling; there swam into his mind again the picture of himself on the train and Shelley behind in Sandhill calmly washing dishes as if he'd never been there.

"I don't believe you *ever* change, Ben Joe," she said.

"Shelley, I won't come and go. I won't go on not thinking. Look, you come with me. You come to New York."

"Oh, now, wouldn't *that* give people—"

"No, I mean it. We could . . . hell, get married. You hear? Come on, Shelley."

She stopped looking at her hands and stared at him. "I beg your pardon?" she said.

"We could . . ." The words in his mouth sounded absurd, like another line from the unknown play in his nightmare. He hesitated, and then went on. "Get married," he said.

"Why, Ben Joe, *that* wasn't what I was after. I wasn't asking—"

"No, I mean it, Shelley. I mean it. Don't be mad any more. You come with me on the train tomorrow and we'll be married in New York when we get there. You want to? Just pack a bag, and Jeremy will be our best man . . ."

She was beginning to believe him. She was sitting up in the chair with her mouth a little open and her face half excited and half doubtful still, trying to search underneath his words to see how much he meant them.

"Sure," he said. "Oh, hell, who wants to go away and leave you with the dishes—"

"The what?"

"And come back like, I don't know, Jamie Dower maybe, with no one to recognize him but a girl, and even she went on and married someone else—"

"Ben Joe," Shelley said, "I'm not following you too well, but if you mean what you say—"

"Of course I do," Ben Joe said. And he did; he was becoming excited now, watching her face eagerly to see that she was convinced and not angry any more. "Do you want to, Shelley? I'll meet you at the station for the early-evening train tomorrow. Do you want to?"

"Well, I reckon so," Shelley said slowly. "I just don't know . . ." For the first time that evening she really smiled, even with her eyes, and she rose and crossed over to where he stood. "You won't be sorry?"

"No, I won't be sorry."

"All right," she said.

"Will *you*? Be sorry, I mean. Will you?"

"Oh, no. Didn't I always tell you that, even back in high school?"

"I guess so," he said.

"Seems like you are always loving the people that fly away from you, Ben Joe, and flying away from the people that love you. But if you've decided, this once, to do something the other way, I'll be happy to agree. I'll meet you at the station, then."

She reached up and kissed him and he smiled down at her, relieved.

"What time is it?" he asked.

"About one."

"Lord. Shelley, if it's all right with you, I want to sleep on your couch. I can't face going home right yet, and I'll be out of here before morning."

She looked a little doubtful, but then after a minute she nodded. "Won't do any harm, I guess," she said. "But it's bumpy."

"That's all right."

"Phoebe used to sleep there sometimes. She was a little bit sway-backed, and she said there was a poking-up spring on that couch that would support the curve in her back."

She gave his cheek a pat and then turned and went quickly over to the hall closet. From the top shelf she took a crazy quilt, permanently dingy from years of use.

"This ought to keep you warm," she said as she walked back to the couch. "You just hold this end, now, and I'll wrap you up in it. That's warmer than just having it over the top of you. Here."

He kicked off his shoes and then took the end of the quilt she handed him. Shelley walked around him in a circle, winding the blanket about him like a cocoon. When she was done she stood looking him over and then nodded to herself.

"You'll be fine in that," she said. "The lamp's above your head, and if you need anything you just call. Good night, Ben Joe."

"Goodnight."

He stood there by the couch, wrapped tightly in his quilt, until she had smiled for the last time and climbed the stairs to her room. When her bare feet padded gently across the floor above his head he laboriously unwound himself again and tucked the quilt around the foot of the couch. Then he took one of the throw cushions and placed it at the head for a pillow. He did these things with the special businesslike air that he always adopted when he didn't want to be bothered with thinking; if he let himself think tonight he would never get to sleep at all. So he sat on the couch and worked his feet down under the quilt methodically, concentrating solely upon the mechanical business of getting settled. And once he was in bed he made his mind into nothing but a blank, faceless blackboard, bare of everything that might remind him of the restless puzzling at the back of his mind.

14

IT WAS not yet morning when Ben Joe passed through the gate in front of his house again. The night was at the stage when the air seemed to be made up of millions of teeming dust specks, and although he could see everything, the outlines were fuzzy and the objects were flat and dim, like a barely tinted photograph. Ahead of him his house loomed, blank-faced. If he were passing by in a car at this hour, he would look at the house for a second and envy the people inside it, picturing them gently asleep in silent darkness. Even now he envied them, in a way. His eyes were gritty from a bad night and he thought of his sisters in their clean white beds beneath neatly curtained windows, most probably sound asleep and dreamless. But because he was no mere stranger passing by, he paused at the gate, and stared harder at the house than any stranger would have. It was such a locked-looking house, and so importantly secretive. In the daylight, especially in summer daylight, the house passed off those secrets carelessly and took on an open, joyous look; the screen door banged innumerable times and the girls in pastel dresses passed out lemonade to the young men lounging on the porch railing, and bumblebees buzzed among the overgrown hollyhocks beside the steps. But now, with those voices stilled and the porch deserted and all the windows black and closed against the winter darkness, who knew how many secrets lay inside? Who knew, from that self-important, tightly shut front door, what had gone on tonight and what new decisions his sleeping sisters had arrived at? He hesitated with his hand upon the gate and found himself swinging between loving that house and hating it, between rushing into the sleepy darkness of it and turning away and shrugging off its claim on him forever. Then the gate squeaked a little, and he pushed harder against it and walked on up the sidewalk to the front steps.

His feet on the cement made a gritty, too-clear sound; except for a few aimless chirpings in the trees around the house it was the only sound he heard. When he began climbing the steps his footsteps seemed dogged and heavy, and he thought again of how unreasonaby tired he was. He had awakened often during the night, always with a sense of having forgotten something or left something undone, and even his sleep had been restless and strewn with brightly colored fragments of dreams. Now his head swam with just the effort of climbing the porch steps. Instead of going directly into the house, he turned toward the porch glider and let himself sink slowly down on it, to rest a minute and look out across the yard.

The cold of the metal glider soaked sharply through his trousers. He shivered and hugged his arms across his chest, and after a while his body became used to the cold and relaxed once more. The glider whined back and forth, making a lonesome, sleepy sound that sank into him as clearly as the sound of his footsteps had. If he were asleep now, safe inside his house in a warm deep bed, and it were someone else upon this glider, those slow, gentle creaks would lull him into a deeper and deeper sleep. He would turn a little on his pillow and pull the blankets up closer around his ears, and the sound of the glider penetrating into his dreams would gradually build pictures in his mind of warm summer evenings and soft radio music drifting across green lawns . . .

He stood up sharply, feeling his eyes begin to mist over with sleep. If he were found asleep here in the morning, wouldn't they laugh then? Neighbors on their way to work would stop and look over the gate at him and smile. One sister would find him and would call the others delightedly, and they would all come out and laugh to see funny old Ben Joe torturing himself on a cold tin glider. Ben Joe the worrier. He would wake up to come in and have a sheepish breakfast among their little jokes, or he could sit huffishly out here and be even funnier. No, he didn't want to take a chance on falling asleep in the glider.

He sighed and crossed the wooden floor toward the front door. The backs of his legs were cold and stiff, like metal themselves, and there was a sore place in his side where Phoebe's favorite couch spring had poked him. As he was turning the key in the door he decided the only thing to do was go to his own bed. Tomorrow—or today—was going to be hectic enough and he might as well get rested up for it. The lock clicked open and he went through the complicated process of getting inside the house, ordinarily an automatic one but now, in his dreamlike state, as sharp in his mind as a slow-motion movie: press down the thumb latch, pull back hard on the door until it clicked, then abruptly press downward and inward upon the door until it gave and swung open, creaking a little and brushing across the hall carpet with a soft *sssh*. He stepped inside, pushing the front door shut behind him. There was a close, dusty smell in the hallway that rushed to meet him instantly, and for a minute he paused to adjust to the sudden darkness and warmth. He could see almost nothing. A pale flash on the wall identified the mirror; that was all. There was a deeper silence here than outdoors, but also there was the feeling that people were in the area. He no longer felt that he was by himself, even though there was no definite sound to prove it.

He headed blindly across the hall toward the stairs. As he passed the living room he looked through the wide archway of it and saw that the room was lighter, lit gray-white by the long bay windows. On the couch was a long, dark shape that stirred slightly as Ben Joe watched, and to satisfy his own curiosity, he changed direction and headed toward the couch. At his feet there was a sharp *ping;* a saucepan full of what looked like popcorn had been in his path. But the figure on the couch didn't move again, and after holding his breath for a minute, Ben Joe went on. He stopped at the head of the couch and stooped over, squinting his eyes in the attempt to see through the dusty dimness. It looked like Gary. His expression was hard to see, but Ben Joe could make out his pale face emerging from the depths of two feather pillows. His mouth was open but he was not snoring, only breathing gently and regularly in little even sighs. And his hair, drained of all its flaming color by the night, stuck out in sharp spikes against his pillows. Ben Joe watched him for a minute, considering the blandness of people asleep. Not even dreams or fits of restlessness seemed to bother Gary; he was peaceful and relaxed. Ben Joe shook his head and then, after putting away the thought of waking Gary up and asking him what had happened that evening, he turned back toward the hallway again.

Halfway up the stairs a sudden picture crossed his mind. He saw millions of houses, viewed from an airplane, and every couch in every tiny house was occupied by someone from yet another house. Everyone was shuffled around helter-skelter—Ben Joe on Shelley's couch, Gary on Ben Joe's couch, and God knew who on Gary's couch. The picture came to him sharply and without his willing it, and before it faded, it had nearly made him smile.

The upstairs hall was almost black; no windows opened onto it. He felt his way past the circle of tall white doors, all of them them closed and with only the murmuring sounds of sleep behind them. Then he was in his own room, where his bed was a welcoming white blur with the covers turned neatly down and waiting for him. From the bedside stand he picked up his alarm clock and tilted it toward the light from the window, frowning as he tried to see where the hands stood. Five-thirty. That gave him at least another hour, and maybe more if only the girls would rise quietly for a change. The shade on his window was raised and a square of pale white shone through it onto the rug; he pulled the shade down to the sill so that the sun wouldn't waken him. Then he undressed, doing it slowly and methodically and hanging his clothes neatly in the closet so that he could go to sleep with the feeling that everything had been attended to in an orderly fashion. His socks he put in the small laundry hamper behind the door, making sure to lower the lid again without a sound. All his sisters slept lightly—

downright night birds they were, and prone to wandering around at all hours—and right now there wasn't a one of them he wanted to see. He tiptoed to his bed and lay down, still in his underwear, and reached for his blankets gingerly so as not to creak the springs. The top sheet against his skin was cold and smooth and he felt immediately protected, and more ready for sleep than he had been under the rough, mothball-smelling quilt at Shelley's. He pulled the sheet up under his chin and closed his eyes, feeling them burn beneath the lids.

Wanting to be quiet kept him from changing his position. Gradually he grew stiff and tense, and his face muscles wouldn't loosen up, but he was afraid to move around. Why hadn't he got into bed on his stomach? He *knew* he couldn't sleep on his back. Carefully he turned on his side, trying to make his body light on the mattress and tightening his jaw with the effort. Now he was facing the center of the room, away from the wall. He could see all the dim objects he had grown up with and a white rim of pillow case besides (his right eye was half hidden in the pillow), and he couldn't *not see* them because his eyes wouldn't close. They kept springing open again. They looked around the room continually and searched out the smallest thing to stare at, while the rest of his body ached with tiredness and a headache began just above the back of his neck.

His room seemed to be made up of layers, the more recent layers never completely obliterating the earlier ones. Of the first layer only the peeling decals on the closet door remained—rabbits and ducks in polka-dotted clothes, left over from that time when he had been a small child. Then the layer from his early boyhood: a small red shoe bag, still in use, with a different symbol of the Wild West on each pocket, a dusty collection of horse books on the bottom shelf of the bookcase. And after that his later boyhood, most in evidence: a striped masculine wallpaper pattern, brown curtains, a microscope, the *National Geographics*. He tried closing his eyes again and thought about how each layer had become less distinct progressively; the top layer was flat and impersonal, consisting only of a grownup's clothes in the closet and a grownup's alarm clock on the stand, while the bottom layers were bright and vivid and always made him remember things, in striking detail, that had happened years and years before. He turned to the other side, grimacing at a creak in the springs, and faced the one picture on the wall: a black-and-white photograph of himself and Joanne on tricycles, in look-alike playsuits, with a younger, out-of-date mother between them in a mannish shoulder-padded suit and black lipstick. There had been another picture, with the cleaner square on the wall left to prove it, of his father in slacks on the mowed lawn with his hand on a teenaged Ben Joe's shoulder; but during the bad years Ben Joe had burned it, not knowing what else he was supposed to do.

He pushed his eyes shut; they popped open again. He turned on his back and looked at the ceiling and switched the room upside-down, picturing the furniture hanging from the ceiling and the light fixture sticking straight up from a bare and peeling plaster floor. To go out of the room, he must reach up an unusual height to the white china doorknob, and when the door was opened he must step over a two-foot threshold of striped wallpaper onto the chandeliered floor of the hallway . . .

The door opened. The crack of black at one side of it widened and widened until a girl's face appeared in it, a small oval that could have been any of them except that a sort of space helmet of lace above it identified the face as Jenny's. She didn't speak out but crept very stealthily toward his bed without so much was creaking the floor. To Ben Joe, lying there watching her from under heavy, aching eyelids, she seemed very funny all of a sudden—cautious and bent forward like a nearsighted old woman.

"Ben Joe?" she whispered.

He didn't answer.

"Ben *Joe*."

Her whisper was piercing; she must have seen the slits of his half-open eyes. Ben Joe stirred slowly and then muttered something, making his voice purposely sleepy-sounding.

"Come on," she said patiently. "*You're* not asleep."

She came to the foot of his bed, hugging her bathrobe around her, and sat down with a bounce that he was sure would wake the whole household. He sighed and drew his knees up.

"I'm *almost* asleep," he said.

"You're not."

She settled herself down more securely, tucking her feet up under her to keep them warm. Her face was lively and wide awake.

"How come you're up?" he asked.

"I don't know. Well, for one thing, I was wondering where you were."

"I'm all right," he said.

"Well, I was just wondering."

He lowered his knees and swung his feet to the other side of the bed so she would be more comfortable, and smiled at her, but all he could think of to say was "I'm all right" again.

"I know." She rested her chin in one hand and looked at him seriously. "Where'd you go?"

"Just out."

"Oh."

He paused a minute, and then finally gave in and said, "What happened to Gary?"

"He's sleeping on the couch."

"I know, but what happened to him? To him and Joanne?"

"Nothing, I guess." She began stirring around restlessly and after a minute she rose and pulled the window shade up. "Joanne said she was committed to a date and was darn well going to keep her commitments," she said. She was leaning her elbows on the window sill now; her whisper came back cool and sharp, resounding off the pane. "And even though that Horner guy said he thought it'd be better to take a rain check, she said no and went out real quick, leaving Gary kind of empty-handed-looking and Gram crying into the sofa cushions and wishing she'd married Jamie Dower—"

"What happened when she got back?" Ben Joe broke in.

"Joanne? I don't know. I don't think her date came inside with her when he brought her home again—"

"Thank God for small gifts," he said.

"Well, but she and Gary didn't talk too much. She just went on to bed after a few minutes. I reckon she's counting on getting it settled in the morning. While she was on her date, Gary stayed home and taught us how to make a French omelet. You take—"

"Jenny, I'm getting awful sleepy."

Jenny went on looking out the window, her face cheerful and her mouth pursed silently to whistle. "You should see Lisa," she said after a minute. "She's out walking under the clothesline. Can't get to sleep, I guess."

"Oh, Lord."

"Well, it's no wonder she had to go all the way outside, considering she shares a room with Jane. Can't make a sound in there. Step on a dust ball in your bare feet and Jane's wide awake wanting to know what that crunching sound was."

"Well, tell Lisa to come in," Ben Joe said. "Makes me nervous."

"You'd be more nervous if she did come in."

"No, I wouldn't."

"Oh, she'll come soon of her own accord, anyway. Don't worry about it."

"Well, all right," said Ben Joe. But he frowned and picked at the tufts on his bed spread. He never could have the feeling that the whole family was under one roof and taken care of; one always had to be out wandering around somewhere beyond his jurisdiction.

"You try and get some sleep, now," Jenny was saying. She straightened up and left the window, heading toward the door and tying the sash of her bathrobe as she walked. When she reached the hallway she turned back and said, "Night."

"Night."

"See you in the morning."

She smiled suddenly and closed the door on him with a gentle click. Ben Joe turned over on his side, facing the wall. He closed his eyes and found that this time they stayed closed, although the muscles of his face were still drawn tight. Against his cheek the pillow was cool and slightly rough. Every time he breathed, the pillow brushed his skin with a soft, crisp sound and it made itself into a rhythm, plunging him farther and farther down until he found himself in the black, teetering world of half-sleep.

His father was sitting at the sunlit breakfast table. His mustache was gone and his face was as lined and leathery as it had been the day he died, although Ben Joe himself was only a small boy sitting at the table beside him. Why wasn't he dreaming the ages correctly? Either his father should be a mustached, smooth-faced young man or Ben Joe should be at least old enough for high school. He pulled his mind up from the deep water of his dream and opened his eyes. He must get all this arranged right. No, he thought about flat, green things—leaves, chalk boards, lawns seen from a distance—to make his mind blank again. The face of his father stayed in one corner, twinkling and deeply lined.

He closed his eyes and gave in, sinking back into the stream of the dream. His father, frozen in one position at the breakfast table, became animated again, like a movie that has been stopped and then started at the same place. He was telling a story, one that they all knew by heart. Only he told it in that anonymous voice inside Ben Joe's head instead of his own deep booming one; Ben Joe's mind, searching frantically, was unable to recapture even the vaguest semblance of his father's voice. But the story came to him perfectly, word for word:

"When I was young, and liked to go places, my Uncle Jed said he'd take me to the Farmers' Market in Raleigh. *You* remember Uncle Jed. He was the one could walk barefoot on broken glass without feeling it and went on farming even after the family got their money. Well, sir, this was back in the days when the farmers went to market the night before and all slept on the ground in blankets so as to be up at five. And that's how I saw my first silly-minded boy.

"Not that I haven't seen plenty since.

"Big as an ox, he was, and kind of round-eyed, and hung his head like he knew he was silly and was damned ashamed of it, too. And well he might be. For soon's we all got to bed this boy began saying, 'What time's it, Pa?'

"And his pa would say, growly-like, ' 'Bout ten o'clock, Quality.'

"Quality Jones, that's what his name was.

"Name like that would make anybody silly-minded.

"And then Quality would say, 'What time's it *now*, Pa?'

"And his pa'd say, 'Little after ten, Quality.'

"Well, sir, this went on for maybe two hours. Farmers are patient men. They got to be. Got to see those seeds come up week by week, fraction by fraction, and sweat it out for some days not knowing yet is it weeds or vegetables making all that greeny look. So they kept quiet—just sort of muttered around a little. And when Quality started snoring, there was this little relaxing kind of sigh, like a breeze through a cornfield, all over the Farmers' Market.

"What good's a clock to a man in bed? What good?

"But that wasn't the half of it. For soon's Quality started snoring, his pa raised up on one elbow and looked over at him and he says, 'Quality, son?'

" 'Huh, Pa?' says Quality, all sleepy-like.

" 'You all right?' his pa asks.

"And Quality says, 'Yes, Pa.'

"That's the way it was all night. A fellow didn't have time to get his eyes shut properly before it'd be, 'You want to pee, son?', 'You want a drink of water, Quality?' Lord, I never will forget.

"After about two hours of this, my Uncle Jed he stood up and grabbed his army blanket and he shouted, to the whole market place he shouted, 'Folks,' he says, 'if morning ever comes, I hope you get to meet this Quality!'

"And everyone laughed, but Uncle Jed paid them no mind. He grabbed my blanket right up from under me and said, 'Come on, boy, we're going home,' and that sure enough is where we went.

"I never went back to that market place. Folks say it is still going, only modern now, but every time I think about it, it seems like the only way I can see it is at nighttime still, with Quality still on his crazy quilt, and all those men still waiting, waiting still, for morning to be coming. Yes, sir. Yes sir."

His father smiled, and leaned back to look around at his family. In his sleep Ben Joe smiled too. (He was proud of himself; he'd dreamed it all correctly from beginning to end.) And there was the contented murmuring of the family settling back in their chairs in the sunlight. It was their favorite story. It belonged to them; their father always told it after a night like this one, when he said the women in this family thought night was only a darker kind of daytime, just as good as any time for wandering and for talking. Ben Joe leaned back in his chair exactly the way his father did, and looked around and smiled at his family smiling.

His mother said, "The *least* you could do is try to keep it a secret from the *children*."

(How had that got in? That was from another time; that was from years later.)

A man said, "Feel the calluses on my hand."

Ben Joe sat on an unfamiliar porch beside his mother. His mother was very angry. He looked down at the old man, way below him on the ground, reaching his hand to Ben Joe.

"Feel the *calluses*," the old man said. "I've worked and worked."

"Don't do it," his mother said.

He looked at his mother and then at the old man. He bent down toward the man's upturned, lined face and then he touched the man's hand, and quick as a wink the hand gripped his, vice-like, and hauled him off the porch and down to blackness.

"*Mother!*" he screamed.

But his mother's hand, reaching for him, gripped him harder, yanked him until his shoulder snapped. He was torn from the blackness back toward the porch but too far, and too hard, and now he was in greenness and falling even faster.

"Wake up," a voice said.

He awoke and he was on the glider, only it was the wrong color. In front of him stood his mother, looking out thoughtfully across the lawn with her arms folded. When he opened his eyes the eyelids creaked and groaned and scraped like the heavy tops of old attic trunks, and at the sound his mother turned and glanced down at him.

"You've been dreaming about your father," she said.

"I haven't," said Ben Joe.

"Ben Joe, *please*. Wake *up*."

He opened his eyes for the second time; this time he knew without a doubt that he was really awake. At the foot of his bed stood his mother, with a faded corduroy bathrobe tossed hastily around her. She was bent over a little the way Jenny had been earlier, and she was watching him with kind, worried eyes.

"What?" he said.

"You had a bad dream, I guess," she said. "You screamed 'Mother!' I thought—Where's your pillow?"

"Oh . . . on the floor," said Ben Joe. He watched dazedly as she reached down to pick it up for him.

"Is something wrong?" she asked. She had stepped closer now, and he could see the deep lines around her mouth and the anxious twisting motion of her hands upon the cord of her bathrobe.

"I'm all right," he said. "You go back to bed now. I'll be fine."

"If you'd like for me to sit with you awhile—"

"No, no. You go back to bed. Please."

She stayed another minute, looking down at him anxiously, but he made his face smooth and cheerful and eventually she sighed and straightened up again.

"Well, all right," she said. "But if there's anything I can get you, now—"

"Good night, Mom."

"Good night."

He thought she would never leave. Finally she turned and went absently to the door, and after looking back at him one more time she was gone. He tried to unstiffen his muscles. His legs were rigid and cold, and he couldn't relax them for more than a second before they stiffened again. But gradually, as the dream faded piece by piece and image by image from his memory, his body relaxed again. All that was left was a faintly sad feeling because he was afraid he had been rude to his mother. In this house there was only one recognized cure for nightmares; you rushed to the dreamer's room and offered him Postum and pleasant conversation. Only with Ben Joe that always seemed to make it worse. Probably that was what his mother was telling the others now. He could hear her voice in the hall, murmuring along against a background of other voices, low and questioning. When was night going to end?

He lay back tensely, and with great determination he began naming all the places he had ever been. Even one-night stays in hotels. He pictured every single place (though the hotels tended to merge into a single dreary prototype) in his mind's eye, exactly as it would look at this very hour. His New York apartment, with Jeremy curled up like a bear in the pale light from the dirty window. The camp cabin he had slept in when he was ten, with half-finished lanyards dangling from all the nails on the wall. The boat he had stayed on one summer in Maine with his uncle, where the sunlight came to pick up the colors in the Hudson Bay blankets at something like five o'clock in the morning. Only no, it was winter now. He'd forgotten. Maine would be icy and gray with only the bleak Nova Scotia lobster boats moored in the tiny harbor. Maybe not even they would be there; he'd never seen it in the winter.

He reached back, turned his pillow over to the other side, and let his head fall back into the coolness of it. At the back of his mind the little voice began prodding him, pushing him into the next subject. Shelley. He frowned at the ceiling, turning the idea of Shelley every possible way and trying to think how all this had come about. He pictured himself walking to the train station and meeting Shelley, taking her to New York and surprising the daylights out of Jeremy and the few other friends he had. Writing home and announcing he was married. It sounded to him like one of those wild little what-if thoughts that was always wandering through his head—nothing logical or concrete but only a little tale to pass the time. But when he forced himself to believe it, when he went over all the plain facts of it like actually buying Shelley's ticket, he began to believe it. He sat up straighter now, tenser than ever. He caught himself in the act of sitting up and tried to lie back down, but his eyes were doing their springing-open act again; it was no use.

The clock said 6:45. He stood up and stumbled toward the closet, not caring now *how* much racket he made. From the hangers he pulled down a white shirt and an old pair of slacks and piled himself into them hurriedly. He didn't want to stay in this room another minute.

Again the door opened. He heard the creak.

"What now?" he said, with his back to the door. He threaded his belt through the loops.

"Ben Joe?" Tessie said.

"Yes."

She padded over in her bare feet to stand beside him. In her too-long bathrobe and rumpled hair, she looked no older than Carol, and so cross and sleepy that Ben Joe felt sorry for her.

"Ben Joe," she said "is it time to get up yet?"

"I think we could say so."

"I'm so *glad*," she said.

She turned around and walked out again. Out in the hallway Gram started singing, just a little more softly than usual, as she came down the stairs from her attic room:

> "If you don't love me, love whom you please.
> Throw your arms round me, give my heart ease . . ."

The shower in the bathroom was turned on. One of the twins opened the door of their bedroom and shouted out, "Susannah, does milk chocolate remind you of Chicago?"

"Of what?" Susannah said. It sounded as if she were in her closet.

" 'Chicago,' I said."

"I've never *been* to Chicago."

"I've been thinking about it all night," said the twin. "Milk chocolate reminds me of Chicago."

"You've never been to Chicago either."

"Well."

Someone downstairs started playing the piano. Ben Joe got down on his hands and knees beside his bed and began fishing under it for his shoes with an unstrung tennis racket.

15

"GARY," Ben Joe said. "Hey, Gary. Wake up, will you?"

He hated to wake people up. His grandmother had told him after breakfast that it wasn't good for people to sleep late and especially not in the middle of the living room, and that it was his job to see that Gary got up, but Ben Joe had put it off all morning. Now it was almost eleven; he had spent the last half-hour whistling very loudly in other parts of the house and kicking the furniture in the hallway, but Gary was still peacefully asleep with his mouth open.

"You're worse than Joanne," Ben Joe said to the freckled face. "*Gary?*"

Gary opened his eyes, opaquely blue, and stared up at Ben Joe. "Hmm?" he said.

Ben Joe was instantly embarrassed, caught peering at the privacy of a man's face asleep.

"Uh, would you like some breakfast?"

"That wouldn't be half bad," Gary said. It was amazing how quickly he came alive. He sat straight up and swung his incredibly long, pajamaed legs off the couch and scratched his head.

"What time is it?" he asked.

"About eleven."

"Oh, Lord."

He reached for the faded blue bathrobe at the foot of the couch and stood up to put it on. "It's a disgrace," he said, grinning happily. "I should've been up hours ago. What goes *on* in this house at night? All night long it sounded like mice above my head, just scurrying around as busy as you please. They went to bed so early and I thought it was a peace-loving family. And then I find out they didn't go to bed at all, seems like, just adjourned upstairs to carry on where they'd left off before, slamming doors and visiting back and forth. Me, I've always thought sleep was a wonderful invention. Not that being awake isn't nice too, of course. But when I get up in the morning I think, boy, only fourteen more hours and I can be back to sleep again. I like to see the covers turned down and waiting and the pillows puffed up so I can hop right in. And I never dream, because it distracts my mind from pure sleeping, so to speak . . ."

He was dipping his arms into his robe and tying it and then folding up the bed clothes as he talked, stopping every now and then to gesture widely with one arm. There was something fascinating about that constant flow of speech. He was the way he had been the night before—big and graceful and always in the center of the room, chattering happily away in a steady stream that left his listeners virtually speechless. Even Ben Joe, who had been an incurable talker as a small boy and had once lost a family bet that he could keep totally silent for fifteen minutes straight, could find no place to break in.

"Not that I'm complaining," Gary was saying. "I just think it's worth commenting on, is all. For years now I've been wondering at Joanne, wondering where she got her habits. You'll have to admit they're kind of odd. She's the only mother I know of that used to keep waking the *baby* all the time, instead of the baby waking her. And making milk shakes in the Waring blender at two a.m. Now, where, I'd think, as I'd wake up and hear her whistling and the blender going and the dishes clattering, *where* did she learn to live like that? Well, I'm mighty glad to meet your family, Ben Joe. It's good to see you."

He stuck out one long, bony hand and Ben Joe, taken off guard, stared at it a minute and then shook it.

"Uh, how about that breakfast?" he asked.

"Sure thing."

"I'll get it."

Ben Joe fled. He was glad to get out to the kitchen; Gary was much better than he had pictured him, but at the same time he felt inadequate around him. He couldn't welcome him or say he was glad to see him or make one small response to all that puppy-dog friendliness because Gary was too busy talking to hear. Where had Joanne ever met him? He dropped an egg in the frying pan and stared out the window, trying to remember, but it seemed to him that Joanne had never said. She had simply announced that she was married. Well, Joanne never *was* one to tell much of her personal life. Her letters were full of things like how much wool cost in Kansas nowadays and what movies they had seen and how crabby Carol's pediatrician was. Everyone in the family wrote like that when they were away; it was probably because of Jenny's being the official letter writer. What *else* could you answer to a letter of Jenny's except the price of wool in Kansas? Still, he wondered where Joanne had met Gary. He cracked the second egg into the frying pan and went to the refrigerator for orange juice.

Gary appeared the instant his breakfast was ready, rubbing his hands together. He was dressed in a plaid shirt that clashed with his hair and a pair of corduroy slacks and he looked exuberant.

"Boy oh boy," he said, "I just love a big breakfast. They tell you what we had before bed last night? Pizza. A great big pizza with all *kinds* of stuff on— You seen Joanne?"

"She went out," Ben Joe said. "Downtown, I think." He cleared his throat. "I was just wondering where you and Joanne ever met up with each other."

"Oh, she was dating a buddy of mine. This was when I was in the Marines, back east. She was one of those gals that flits around a lot. Danced with practically everyone at this dance and I was one of them. Keeping her *with* me, now, that was harder than just dancing one dance with her. And she didn't like it that in civilian life I'm a salesman. Said salesmen always smiled even when they didn't want to, so how could she trust me. That's what she kept harping on, how could she trust me. And, besides, she thought I had no manners. You ever seen Joanne's feet?"

"What?"

"Her feet. You ever seen them?"

"Well, of course," Ben Joe said. "She's always barefoot."

Gary nodded and shoveled half a fried egg in his mouth. "That's why," he said with his mouth full. "Why they look like they do, I mean. The rest of her is kind of slim, but her feet are wide and smooth and brown like a gypsy's maybe, or a peasant's. You see her barefoot and *you'll* know what I mean. I always liked her feet. First time she ever met my mother she had little bare sandals on and her hair piled high and I was so proud of her I said, 'Mama, this is Joanne Hawkes. See her peasant feet?'

"And after we were alone again, you should have seen the row. She kept saying, 'I've never been so embarrassed in my life before; see my peasant feet, see my peasant feet?' and kicked me in the shin with one of them peasant feet so hard I can still feel it if I think on it awhile.

That's why she said I was bad-mannered. That and this door-opening business. I believe in opening a car door for a girl when she gets *in*, mind you. But when she gets *out*, well, she just sits and sits all useless in the car while you get out and plod all the way around to the other side . . ."

He held his hand out toward the cream pitcher and Ben Joe, mesmerized, placed it in his hand while he kept staring at Gary's face.

"*So*," Gary said, "I went off on a fishing boat named the *Sagacity* one weekend with a fellow from Norfolk. Figured there wasn't any use staying around right then. Joanne said she didn't trust me far as she could throw a tractor and then went and accepted five dates for that weekend. *Five*, mind you. There was this about Joanne back then: seems she liked drawing people to her. Once she got them, she sort of forgot what she was planning to do with them, like. But if you drew *away*, she'd be out to draw you to her again. So when she heard I had left she got them to radio the *Sagacity* to come in again. Saturday, it was. They kept calling the *Sagacity* but the catch was this: it was a borrowed boat and me and my buddy, who was the captain, thought its name was the *Saga City*. We didn't connect them, you see. Makes a difference. So the man told Joanne there wasn't any answer and he didn't know what could be the trouble, and she started crying and all, and by the time the mess was straightened out we were on dry land again and Joanne had her arms around my neck and said she'd marry me. That was quite some day," he said.

Ben Joe nodded, with his mouth open. Gary laid his fork down and rocked back easily on the kitchen chair.

"So we got married and all, and of course Carol came along. You get to see that first picture we took of her?"

"It's somewhere around the house right now," Ben Joe said.

"Well, I'm glad. It's a real good picture, I think. I was hoping you all thought so too. I always wondered why your mama didn't come when Carol was born, or one of your sisters maybe. Almost a custom, you might say. But no one came."

"Well, anyway, we were glad to hear about it," Ben Joe said.

"That so?" Gary looked happy.

"Um . . ." said Ben Joe. He bent forward to lean his elbows on the table. There was a long string of questions he wanted to ask, like why was Joanne here now and why was Gary himself here, but he would hate to see that happy face of Gary's get a closed, offended look. In the tiny silence he heard the front door open and a pair of high heels walk in, with little, soft baby steps beside them. He looked up at Gary to see if he had heard too, but Gary was musing along on some path of his own. The high heels climbed the stairs, and Ben Joe in his mind followed their journey to Joanne's bedroom.

"I'd like to have a lot more children," Gary said unexpectedly. "Dozens. I like kids. Joanne takes too good care of just the one. She needs a whole group of them. She's always saying how Carol's got to be secure-feeling, got to have no wonders about being loved or not. But this way she just makes Carol nervous—follows her around reading psychology books. Wants to know what her nightmares are about. I say let her alone—kids grow up all right. But that's just *like* Joanne. She got in this Little Theater play once back in Kansas and had a whole bunch of lines to learn and got all worried about it. So did she just take a deep breath and start learning them? No sir. The night before the play opened I asked her did she know her lines and she said no not yet but she *had* got almost all the way through this book called *How to Develop a Super-Power Memory*. If that isn't just like her . . ."

He smiled into his plate and then clasped both hands behind his neck and stared at the ceiling.

"She was like that about *me* once," he said. "Followed me around reading books about marriage. But when Carol came along she got sidetracked, sort of. It happens. So if she was too busy with Carol I'd just go bowling with the boys or watch TV maybe. And Joanne'd start feeling bad—say it was her fault and she was making the house cold for me. First time she said that was in a heat wave. You couldn't hardly see for the little squiggly lines of heat in the air. 'Cold?' I says. 'Cold?' Honey, you make this house cold and I'll love you forever for it," but Joanne, she didn't think it was funny. Carol was crawling across the table in rubber pants and Joanne picked her up and spanked her for no reason and then started crying and saying history was repeating itself. Huh. You believe in history repeating itself, Ben Joe?"

"Well, not exactly," Ben Joe said.

"No, I mean it, now. Do you?"

"No," said Ben Joe. "I can't believe history's going anywhere at all, much less repeating itself."

Gary lit a slightly bent Chesterfield that he had pulled from his shirt pocket. He was enjoying himself now—as wrapped up in his story as if he were watching it unfold right there on the kitchen ceiling, he never even looked at Ben Joe.

"Course she meant *you*-all's history," he said, "which is so confusing I never *have* got it straight and don't intend to. Hardly worth it at this late date. But whatever it was, it's got no bearing on us and Joanne's house wasn't a cold one, no. But Joanne, she gets *i*-deas. And up and left one day. Well, I don't know why. But here I am, come to get her. I always say," he said, looking suddenly at Ben Joe, "no sense acting like you don't miss a person if you do. Never get 'em back pretending you wouldn't have them if they crawled."

"I hope you do," Ben Joe said suddenly. "Get her back, I mean."

"Thank you, sir. Thank you. It's a right nice house you have here. You born in this house?"

"Yes."

"I figured so. I always have wanted to come visit you all. Joanne, she sometimes talks about this place when she's rested and just sort of letting her mind drift. Tells about all the things that go on here just in one day. It's right fascinating to listen to. Tells about your daddy, and how his one aim in life was to go to Nashville, Tennessee, and watch real country-music singers, the way some people want to go to Paris, only he never did get there—"

"I'd forgotten that," Ben Joe said.

"Oh, Joanne didn't. She was full of things. I know about the time when your mamma and daddy were just married, and he bet her that she'd drop out first on a fifteen-mile hike to, to . . ."

"Burniston," said Ben Joe.

"Burniston, that's it. Only neither one of them dropped out, they both made it, but what really got your daddy peeved was that the whole town of Sandhill followed behind them for curiosity's sake, and none of *them* dropped out, either . . . O, ho . . ." He threw his head back, with his mouth wide and smiling for pure joy, so that Ben Joe had to smile back at him. "And how you are the only boy in Sandhill that they made a special town law for, forbidding you to whistle in the residential sections because it was so awful-sounding. And Susannah's cracker sandwiches, made with two pieces of bread and then a cracker in between—"

"Joanne told you all *that?*"

"She did."

Ben Joe was quiet for a minute. For the first time he actually pictured Joanne married, telling a person what she had noticed in a lifetime and giving someone bits of her mind that none of them had even known she had. What bits, he wondered, would he give Shelley (if there were any to give)? And how did one go about it? Would he just lie back and say what came into his mind the minute it came, removing that filter that was always there and that strained the useless thoughts and the secret thoughts from being made known? But how could *that* be any gift to her? He frowned, and marked the tablecloth over and over with his thumbnail.

"I'll do the dishes," Gary said.

There were some things Ben Joe didn't want to tell; he didn't care if she *was* his wife. He wouldn't want to tell all about his family, for instance, the way Joanne had done. Or about the little aimless curled-in-on-themselves things he was always wondering, like if you were an ant, how big would the rust on a frying pan look and could you actually see the molecules going around; and why was it that a sunlit train going through a tunnel did not retain the sunlight for a minute, the way the world did just at twilight, so that it was a little trainful of sunshine speeding through the dark like a lit-up aquarium—useless things that a child might think and that Ben Joe had never seemed to grow out of. What would Shelley say to him if she knew all that?

"Did you hear me?" Gary said. "I said, I'll do the dishes."

Ben Joe pulled his thoughts together. "No," he said, "Gram gets mad if we do them. She says that the only thinking time she has is when she's doing the dishes."

"You sure?"

"Sure."

"Well, then . . ."

For the first time that Ben Joe knew of, someone managed to interrupt Gary. It was Gram, bellowing from somewhere near the front of the house:

"Soft as the *voices of a-angels* . . ."

"What on earth," Gary said.

He scraped his chair back and stood up to head for the sound, with Ben Joe trailing aimlessly after him. They found Gram in the den, standing in the middle of the floor with her head thrown back and her arms spread like a scarecrow's, roaring at the top of her lungs:

"*Whispering* ho-o-ope
Da da *da* da da . . ."

In front of her, Carol sat in her rocking chair and rocked like mad. Her little feet stuck out in front of her; her head was ducked so that she could throw her weight forward.

"You're not *listening*," Gram told her. She dropped her arms and beamed at Gary and Ben Joe. "I'm teaching her 'Whispering Hope.'"

"What for?" asked Ben Joe.

"What *for*? *Every* little girl should know something like that. So she can stand up in a lacy little pinafore like the one she's got on now— that's what reminded me of it—and perform before refreshments are served on Sunday afternoons when callers come. All your *sisters* know how to do it. Joanne used to recite Longfellow's 'My Lost Youth' and then Susannah would sing 'Whispering—'"

"*I* don't remember that," Ben Joe said.

"Well, we never actually did it in front of guests. Your mother wouldn't allow it. But we had our own private tea parties, sort of."

"Well, I'm leaving," Ben Joe said.

But behind him, as he left, Gary was saying, "That's a *great* idea. Do you know 'My Heart Belongs to Daddy'? I'd like—"

Ben Joe climbed the stairs two at a time and crossed the hall to Joanne's door.

"Joanne?" he called.

"Who is it? That you, Ben Joe?"

"Yes. Can I come in?"

"Sure, I guess so."

He opened the door. Joanne was at the door of her closet, looking at herself in the full-length mirror that hung there. She had on one of the gypsy-red dresses that she used to wear in high school and that had been left behind in her closet because it had faded at the seams. Faded or not, it was still a brighter shade of red than Ben Joe had been used to seeing lately. He blinked his eyes, and Joanne laughed and turned around to face him.

"I found it hanging here," she said. "I'd forgotten I had it. Do you remember when I used to wear this?"

"Of course I do," Ben Joe said. "You wore it up till the time you left home."

"I'd forgotten all about it."

She spun once more in front of the mirror and then stopped smiling and sat down abruptly on the bed with her shoulders sagging.

"Did you want something?" she asked.

"Well . . . no."

"Is Gary up?"

"Yes."

He took his hands out of his pockets and crossed to sit in the platform rocker opposite her.

"How do you like him?" she asked.

"Oh, fine."

There seemed to be no words that would fill in the silence. He got up again and wandered aimlessly around the room. At the bureau he stopped and began looking through a silver catch-all tray under the mirror, full of odds and ends like rolled-up postage stamps and paper clips and pieces of lint.

"Hey," he said, "here's my nail clippers."

"Take them."

"I can prove they're mine. See this little license tag on the chain? I got it from a cereal company when I was about twelve. It has the year on it and the—"

"*Take* it, for *goodness'* sakes."

She lit a Salem and threw the match in the direction of the window. With the nail clippers in his pocket Ben Joe wandered back to his seat, still with nothing to say.

"I've been looking all over for them," he said finally. "Also there's a dent in the file part, where Jenny bit it when she was only—"

"Ben *Joe!*"

"What?"

"Nothing," she said after a minute.

"Well, what'd you say 'Ben Joe' for?"

"No reason."

"It seems kind of funny," he said, "just to scream 'Ben Joe!' at the top of your lungs as a way of making small talk. Why, I could think of a better topic than *that* if I—"

"Are you *trying* to irritate me?"

"Well, maybe so." He examined his fingernails. "Yes," he said after a minute, "I liked him fine. I did. Gary, I mean."

"You did?"

"Yes."

He looked up, saw that she was waiting for him to go on, and went back to frowning at his fingernails. "Came all the way here for you," he said finally. "That's something."

Joanne blew out an enormous cloud of smoke and nodded. She seemed still to be waiting for him to say more, but there was nothing else he could think of to say. When she saw that he was through speaking, she went over and sat down at her dressing table, still not speaking. She put her cigarette in the groove of a glass ash tray and began unpinning her knot of hair.

"If I could just get *organized*," she said. "I never have believed in going backwards instead of forwards."

Ben Joe looked up at her. He knew suddenly, without her telling him, what she had decided she was going to do about Gary. He could tell by her face, half happy and half embarrassed at having to announce that she was as reversible as anyone. He could almost read what she was thinking, and how she was trying to figure out the best way to say it gracefully.

Her hair fell to her neck in a little puff. She put the bobby pins in a china coaster, and picked up a comb and began pulling it through her hair. The red dress made her different, Ben Joe thought. It turned her into exactly the same old Joanne, right down to the swinging hair that she tossed with a little teasing movement of her neck. And this could be any day seven years ago: Ben Joe in the chair watching her get ready to go out, funny old fussy Ben Joe telling her she really should start coming in earlier; and Joanne thin and quick and vaguely dissatisfied in front of her oval mirror. Any minute one of the children would come in (they were still called "the children" back then, not "the girls") to watch, too. Going out was something exciting and mysterious then, something only Ben Joe and Joanne and Susannah were allowed to do; and the others always liked coming to watch the preparations. He felt suddenly sad, thinking about them—as if instead of merely growing up and still being right here they had died, and he was only now realizing it. He pictured all the children in a circle on the floor, newly bathed and ready for bed (it would have to be evening, then), all looking in the mirror to see the miraculous things Joanne did to her face. Joanne would be talking rapidly, teasing the children behind her and giving that saucy smile as she stared at her mascara in the glass—"Oh, it's only old Kim Laurence I'm going out with. I think I'll just stay home and let the baby go instead. You hear that, Tessie?" She would turn around and make a little face at Tessie, only three years old and already half asleep in the lap of a twin. "And won't

Kim Laurence be surprised when his date comes rolling toward him in a baby carriage?" Or: "I'll tell you who I'm seeing tonight—it's Quality Jones. Quality Jones, and he's taking me to a New York night club and he's such a *fascinating* conversationalist. All he says is, 'What time is it, Joanne?' and I say, 'If morning ever comes, Quality, I'll be happy to tell you.' "

The image of the real Joanne, seven years older, glimmered in the mirror. Ben Joe bent his head and laid his index fingers across his eyelids, just lightly enough to cool them, but the muscles of his throat stayed hot and aching with all those tears held back, pressing forward for no reason he could name.

"Headache?" the face in the mirror asked.

Ben Joe nodded silently.

"I'll get you an aspirin." She stood up and started for the door. When she was directly in front of him she stopped there—looking down at him, he guessed—but she didn't say anything and after a minute she went on out.

She was gone long enough for him to be sitting up straight and whistling a little tune under his breath before she entered again.

Soft as the voices of *a-angels* . . .

he whistled. Downstairs Gram's voice, coming loudly and only a little indistinctly through three closed doors, tramped along with him.

"Here," Joanne said. She handed him an aspirin and a glass of water.

"Thank you," he said cheerfully.

He swallowed the pill with one gulp of water and set the glass down on the floor beside his chair. There was a frown on his face now; he sat with his hands clasped tightly together and tried to think of a way to help Joanne say what she wanted to.

"Um, if by any chance you changed your mind about leaving Kansas . . ." he said.

He paused, waiting without realizing it for Joanne to interrupt, but she didn't.

"If just by chance you did," he said finally, "I don't know that I would call it going backwards instead of forwards. Sometimes it's not the same place when a person goes back to it, or not the same . . ."

That little inner mind of his, always scrutinizing him as if it were a separate individual from him, winced. Ben Joe nodded and tipped his hat to it; the separate mind returned his bow and withdrew.

"Not the same person," he finished.

"Oh," Joanne said. She was looking down at her hands, acting as if this were a brand-new idea that would have to be given time to soak in.

"I don't know," she said finally. Her voice was relieved, and light-hearted. "That is something to think about, I guess . . ."

Ben Joe stood up. "Thank you for the aspirin," he said.

"That's all right. Bye."

"Good-by."

He bowed again, this time for real, and left, clicking the door gently shut behind him.

16

BEN JOE came downstairs as slowly and quietly as possible; his feet instinctively veered away from the centers of the steps, where the slightest pressure always brought forth a creaking noise. In his left hand was his suitcase, held high and away from his body so that it wouldn't bang against anything. His right hand was on the polished stair railing. His whole face seemed to be concentrated on the sleek wood of it and the thin film of wax that clung a little to his skin. He lifted his hand and rubbed his thumb and fingers together, frowning down, and then abruptly dropped his hand to his side and descended to the next step. As yet he had not made a single sound. He could go all the way downstairs and out the front door without anyone's ever knowing it if he wanted to. But he wasn't sure he wanted to. If he left without saying good-by, could he really feel he had left for good? He switched the suitcase to his other hand and began descending more rapidly, still frowning at how silly he would feel to announce so suddenly that he was leaving. In the back of his mind he knew he would never leave the house without telling anyone; yet his feet still moved cautiously and he still held the suitcase carefully away from the railing.

Once in the downstairs hall, he moved quickly across the half-lit area between the stairs and the front door. There was a square of warm yellow light on the rug, cast through the wide archway of the living room, and the murmuring voices of his sisters were as clear as if they were out in the hall also, but nobody noticed when he crossed the yellow square. At the front door he stopped, setting his suitcase by his feet, and stood there a minute and then turned back and entered the yellow square again.

"Mom?" he said at the living-room doorway.

"Mmm." She didn't look up. She was sitting on the couch, sipping her after-supper Tom Collins and leafing through a *Ladies' Home Journal*. Beside her Gram was reading Carol a chapter out of *Winnie-the-Pooh*, although Carol wasn't listening, and on the other side of the room Jenny and Tessie and the twins were arguing over a game of gin rummy. The other two were out somewhere—Susannah with the school phys-ed instructor and Joanne with Gary, showing him her home town before they went back to Kansas in the morning. But those who were still at home looked so calm and cheerful, sitting in their lamp-lit room, that Ben Joe almost wished he could stay with them and forget the suitcase at the front door.

"Hey, Mom," he said.

"What is it?" She looked up, holding one finger in the magazine to mark her place. "Oh, Ben Joe. Why don't you come on in?"

" 'Many happy returns of Eeyore's birthday,' " Gram was saying in her bright, reading-aloud voice. Carol sniffed and bent down to touch the bunny ears on one of her slippers, and Gram glared at her. "I said, 'Many happy returns of—' "

"I'm going back to school," Ben Joe said.

" 'Eeyore's birthday,' " Gram went on, no longer looking at the book but just finishing the sentence automatically. "Where you say you're going, Ben Joe?"

"To school," he said.

"You mean, *tonight* you're going?"

"Yes'm."

His mother folded the page over and then closed the magazine. "Well, I don't see—" she began.

"I just suddenly remembered this test I've got, Mom. I really have to go. I'm going to catch that early train . . ."

His sisters turned around from their card game and looked at him.

"Where's your suitcase?" Jane asked.

"Out in the hall. I just stopped in to say good-by."

"Well, I should hope *so*," said his mother. "Why didn't you tell us earlier? Now I don't know what to do about those shirts of yours that are still in the laundry—"

"Don't worry about it. You can send them to me later." He felt awkward, just as he knew he would, standing empty-handed in the doorway with everyone staring at him. His grandmother was the first one to stand up. She came toward him briskly, her arms outstretched to hug him good-by, and he smiled at her and went to meet her halfway.

"If you'd only told us, I could've made some cookies," she said.

"No, I don't need—"

"Or at least some sandwiches. You want me to whip you up some sandwiches, Ben Joe?"

"I haven't got time," he said.

The rest of the family was clustered around him now; Carol had her arms about one of his knees as if he were a tree she was about to climb. Behind his sisters stood his mother, with her face no longer surprised but back to its practical, thoughtful expression.

"I suppose it's about time," she said. "Looked as if you'd *forgotten* school."

"We'll drive you to the station," said Lisa.

"No, thank you, I've got plenty of time."

"But you just said you *didn't* have—"

"No, really. I feel like walking. Come kiss me good-by, everyone."

There was a succession of soft, cool cheeks laid against his. His grandmother held Carol up and she kissed him loudly on the chin, leaving a little wet place that he wiped off absent-mindedly with the cuff of his sleeve.

"Look, Mom," he said, when his mother stepped forward to hug him, "you tell Joanne good-by for me, okay? And Susannah. Tell Joanne I'm sorry to leave without—"

"Of course I will," she said automatically. "Try to get some sleep on the train, Ben Joe."

Gram kissed him again, with her usual angry vigor, and said, "Don't buy a thing on the train if you can help it, Benjy. You never know how much they're going to upcharge. Me, now, I have some idea, because I used to be a good friend of Simon McCarroll that sold cigarettes and Baby Ruths on the train from here to Raleigh some twenty years back. He used to say to me, 'Bethy Jay,' he says, 'you'll never know how they upcharge on these here trains,' and I'd answer back, I'd say—" She stopped, staring off into space. It was her habit, when saying good-by's, to lead the conversation in another direction and ignore the fact that anyone was leaving. Taking advantage of her pause, Ben Joe's mother patted him on the shoulder and became brisk and cheerful, just as she always did at such times.

"I know you'll have a good trip, Ben Joe," she said.

"You got enough money?" Jenny asked.

"I think so. Jenny, you tell Susannah to take good care of my guitar, will you?"

"I will. Bye, Ben Joe."

"Good-by."

His sisters smiled and began turning back to their gin-rummy game. His mother led the way to the front door.

"You'll tell her too, won't you?" he said to her. "Tell her it's a good guitar, and a good hourglass and all. Don't let her go forgetting—"

"Oh, Ben Joe." She laughed and pulled the door open for him. "Everything'll take care of itself."

"Maybe."

"Everything works out on its own, with no effects from what anyone does . . ."

He bent to pick up his suitcase and smiled at her. "Good-by, Mom," he said.

"Good-by, Ben Joe. I want you to do well on that test."

He started out across the porch, and the door closed behind him.

When he was across the street from his house he turned and looked back at it. It sat silently in the twilight, with the bay windows lit yellow by the lamps inside and the irregular little stained-glass and rose windows glowing here and there against the vague white clapboards. When he was far away from home, and picturing what it looked like, this wasn't the way he saw it at all. He saw it as it had been when he was small—a giant of a place, with children playing on the sunlit lawn and yellow flowers growing in two straight lines along the walk. Now, as he looked at the house, he tried to make the real picture stay in his memory. If he remembered it only as it looked right now, would he miss it as much? He couldn't tell. He stood there for maybe five minutes, but he couldn't make the house register on his mind at all. It might be any other house on the block; it might be anyone's.

He turned again and set off for the station. The night was growing rapidly darker, and his eyes seemed wide and cool in his head from straining to see. Occasionally he met people going alone or in two's on after-supper errands, and because it was not really pitch-dark yet, almost all of them spoke cheerfully or at least nodded to Ben Joe whether they knew him or not. Ben Joe smiled back at them. To the older women, walking their dogs or talking to friends on front walks, he gave a deep nod that was almost a bow, just as his father had done before him. Two children playing hopscotch on white-chalked lines that they could barely see stepped aside to let him pass. He walked between the lines gingerly so as not to mess them up, and didn't speak until the smaller one, the boy, said hello.

"Hello," said Ben Joe.

"Hello," the little boy said again.

"Hello," Ben Joe called back.

"Hello—"

"You *hush* now," his sister whispered.

"Oh," the little boy said sadly. Ben Joe turned right on Main Street, smiling.

People were gathering sparsely around the glittering little movie house, and he could see dressed-up couples eating opposite each other in the small restaurant he passed. Just before he crossed to head down the gravel road to the station, a huge, red-faced old man in earmuffs stopped beside him and said, "You Dr. Hawkes's son?"

"Yes," Ben Joe said.

"Going away?"

"Yes."

"Funny thing," the man said, shaking his head. "I outlived my doctor. I outlived my doctor, whaddaya know."

It was what he always said. Ben Joe smiled, and when the light changed, he crossed the street.

The gravel road was just a path of grayish-white under his feet, but he could see well enough to walk without difficulty. Even so, he went very slowly. He stared ahead, to where the station house, with its orange windows, sat beside the railroad tracks. The tracks were mere silver ribbons now, gleaming under tall, curved lamps. All around there was nothing but darkness, marked occasionally by the dark, shining back of some parked car. Ben Joe shivered. He suddenly plunked his suitcase at his feet and after a minute sat on it, folding his arms, staring at the station house and still shivering so hard that he had to clamp his teeth together. He didn't know what he wanted; he didn't know whether he wanted Shelley to meet him there or never to show up at all. If she was there, what would he say? Would he be glad to see her? If she wasn't there, he would climb on the train and leave and then it would be *he* who was the injured party; something would at last be clearly settled and he could turn his back on it forever. He looked at the blank orange windows, still far away, as if they could by some sign to let him know if she was there and tell him what to do about it. No sign appeared. A new idea came: he could wait a while, till after his train had left, and then surreptitiously catch a local to Raleigh and take the later train from there. But what good would that do? The picture arose in his mind of chains of future wakeful nights spent wondering whether he should have gone into the station or not. He rose, picked up his suitcase again, and continued on down the hill.

It was warm and bright inside, and the waiting room smelled of cigar smoke and pulp magazines. Nearest Ben Joe was a group of business-men, all very noisy and active, who mulled around in a tight little circle calling out nicknames and switching their brief cases to their left hands as they leaned forward to greet someone.

"Excuse me," Ben Joe said.

They remained cheerfully in his path, too solid and fat to be sidled past. He changed directions, veering to the right of them and continuing down the next aisle. A small Negro man and his family stood there; the man, dressed stiffly and correctly for the trip north, was counting a small pile of wrinkled dollar bills. His wife and children strained forward, watching anxiously; the man wet his lips and fumbled through the bills.

"Excuse me," Ben Joe said.

The husband moved aside, still counting. With his suitcase held high and tight to his body so as not to bump anyone, Ben Joe edged past them and came into the center of the waiting room. He looked around quickly, for the first time since he had entered the station. His eyes skimmed over two sailors and a group of soldiers and an old woman with a lumber jacket on; then he saw Shelley.

She was sitting in the far corner, next to the door that led out to the tracks. At her feet were two suitcases and a red net grocery bag. Ben Joe let out his breath, not realizing until then that he had been holding it, but he didn't go over to her right away. He just stood there, holding onto the handle of his suitcase with both hands in front of him as if he were a child with a book satchel. He suddenly *felt* like a child, like a tiny, long-ago Ben Joe poised outside a crowded living room, knowing that sooner or later he must take that one step to the inside of the room and meet the people there, but hanging back anyway. He shifted the suitcase to one side. At that moment Shelley looked up at him, away from the tips of her new high-heeled shoes and toward the center of the waiting room, where she found, purely by accident, the silent, watchful face of Ben Joe. Ben Joe forced himself to life again. He crossed the floor, his face heavy and self-conscious under Shelley's grave stare.

"Hello," he said when he reached her.

"Hello."

Her dress was one he had not seen before—a waistless, pleated beige thing—and she had a round feathered hat and gloves the same color. So much beige, with her dark blond hair and her pale face, made her look all of one piece, like a tan statue carved from a single rock. Her face seemed tighter and more strained than usual, and her eyes were squinched up from the bright lights.

"Ben Joe?" she asked.

He sat down quickly in the seat opposite her and said, "What?"

For a minute she was silent, concentrating on lining up the pointed toes of her shoes exactly even with each other. In the space of her silence Ben Joe heard the whispery sound of the train, rushing now across the bridge at Dublin Cat River and drawing nearer every second. Men outside ran back and forth calling orders; a boy pushed a baggage cart through the door and drenched them for a second in the cold, sharp air from outside. Ben Joe hunched forward and said, "What is it, Shelley? What've you got to tell me?"

"I came by taxi," she said after a moment.

"What?"

"I said, taxi. I came by taxi."

"Oh. Taxi."

He stood up, with his hands in his pockets. Outside the whistle blew, louder and closer this time. The two sailors had risen by now and were moving toward the door.

"I got my ticket," Shelley said. "And I've got, wait a minute . . ." She dug through the beige pocketbook beside her and came up with a navy-blue checkbook. "Travelers' checks," she said. "I don't want my money stolen. We didn't talk about it, but, Ben Joe, I want you to know I am going to get a job and all, so money won't be any—"

The train was roaring in now. It had a steamy, streamlined sound and it clattered to a stop so noisily that Shelley's words were lost. All Ben Joe could hear was the steaming and the shouts and above all that the garbled, rasping voice of the loud-speaker. Shelley was looking up at him with her eyes glass-clear and waiting, and he knew by her face she must have asked a question.

"What'd you say?" he asked when the train had stopped.

"I said, I wondered, do you still want me to come?"

She started lining up the toes of her shoes again. All he could see of her face were her pale lashes, lying in two semicircles against her cheeks, and the tip of her nose. When the shoes were as exactly even as they could get she looked up again, and it seemed to him suddenly that he could see himself through her eyes for a minute—Ben Joe Hawkes, pacing in front of her with his hands in his pockets, setting out in pure thoughtlessness toward his own narrow world while she looked hopefully up at him.

"Course I still want you," he said finally.

She smiled and at once began bustling around, checking in her purse for her ticket, leaping up to push all her baggage out into the middle of the floor and then stand frowning at it.

"We'll *never* get it all in," she said. "I tried to take just necessities and save the rest to be shipped, but—"

"Come on." He grabbed her two suitcases and left her to carry the grocery bag, which seemed to be filled with hair curlers and Kleenex, and his own, lighter suitcase. When she had picked them up, he held the door open for her, and they followed the straggling soldiers out into the cold night air, across the platform and up the clanging steps to the railroad car.

"Passengers to New York and Boston take the car to the right!" the conductor sang out cheerfully. He put one hand under Shelley's elbow to boost her up the steps. "Watch it there, lady, watch it—"

A thin white cloud of steam came out of Ben Joe's mouth every time he breathed. Ahead of them the soldiers paused, looking over the seats in the car, and Ben Joe was left half inside and half out, with his arms rigidly close to his body to keep himself warm. He looked at the back of Shelley's head. A few wisps of blond hair were straggling out from under her felt hat, and he couldn't stop staring at them. They looked so real; he could see each tiny hair. In that moment he almost threw down the suitcases and turned around to run, but then the soldiers found their seats and they could go on down the aisle.

The car was full of smoke and much too hot. They maneuvered their baggage past dusty seats where all they could see of the passengers were the tops of their heads, and then toward the end the car became more empty. Shelley ducked into the first vacant seat, but Ben Joe touched her shoulder.

"Keep going," he said. "There're two seats facing each other at the back."

She nodded, and got up again and continued down the aisle ahead of him. It seemed strangely silent here after the noise outside. All he could hear were the rustlings of newspapers and their own footsteps, and his voice sounded too loud in his ears.

At the last seat they stopped. Ben Joe put their luggage up on the rack, and then he took Shelley's coat and folded it carefully and put it on top of the luggage.

"Sit down," he told her.

She sat, obediently, and moved over to the window. When Ben Joe had put his own coat away he sat down opposite her, rubbing the backs of his hands against his knees to get them warm again.

"Are you comfortable?" he asked.

Shelley nodded. Her face had lost that strained look, and she seemed serene and unworried now. With one gloved finger she wiped the steam from the window and began staring out, watching the scattered people who stood in the lamplight outside.

"Mrs. Fogarty is seeing someone off," she said after a minute. "*You* remember Mrs. Fogarty; she's got that husband in the nursing home in Parten and every year she gives him a birthday party, with nothing but wild rice and birthday cake to eat because that's the only two things he likes. She mustn't of seen us. If she had she wouldn't still be here; she'd be running off to tell—"

She stopped and turned back to him, placing the palms of her hands together. "What did your family say?" she asked.

"I didn't tell them."

"Well, when *will* you tell them?"

"I don't know."

She frowned. "Won't it bother you, having to tell them we did this so sneaky-like?"

"They won't care," he said.

"Well. I still can't believe we're really going through this, somehow."

Ben Joe stopped rubbing his hands. "You mean more than usual you can't?" he asked.

"What?"

"You mean it's harder to believe than it usually is?"

"I don't follow your meaning," she said. "It's not usual for me to get married."

"Well, I know, but . . ." He gave up and settled back in his seat again, but Shelley was still watching him puzzledly. "What I meant," he said, "is it harder for you to believe a thing now than it was a week ago?"

"Well, no."

He nodded, not entirely satisfied. What if marrying Shelley meant that she would end up just like him, unable to realize a thing's happening or a moment's passing? What if it were like a contagious disease, so that soon she would be wandering around in a daze and incapable of putting her finger on any given thing and saying, that is that? He looked over at her, frightened now. Shelley smiled at him. Her lipstick was soft and worn away, with only the outlines of her lips a bright pink still, and her lashes were white at the tips. He smiled back, and relaxed against the cushions.

"When we get there," he said, "we'll look for an apartment to settle down in."

She smiled happily. "I tell you one thing," she said. "I always have read a lot of homemaking magazines and I have picked up all kinds of advice from them. You take a piece of driftwood, for instance, and you spray it with gold-colored—"

The train started up. It gave a little jerk and then hummed slowly out of the station and into the dark, and the tiny lights of the town began flickering past the black window.

"I bought me a white dress," Shelley was saying. "I know it's silly but I wanted to. Do you think it's silly?"

"No. No, I think it's fine."

"Even if we just go to a J.P., I wanted to wear white. And it won't *bother* me about going to a J.P. . . ."

The Petersoll barbecue house, flashing its neon-lit, curly-tailed pig, swam across the windowpane. In its place came the drive-in movie screen, where Ava Gardner loomed so close to the camera that only her purple, smiling mouth and half-closed eyes fitted on the screen. Then she vanished too. Across from Ben Joe, in her corner between the wall and the back of her seat, Shelley yawned and closed her eyes.

"Trains always make me sleepy," she said.

Ben Joe put his feet up on the seat beside her and leaned back, watching her face. Her skin seemed paper-thin and too white. Every now and then her blue-veined eyelids fluttered a little, not quite opening, and the corner of her mouth twitched. He watched her intently, even though his own eyes were growing heavy with the sleepy rhythm of the train. What was she thinking, back behind the darkness of her eyelids?

Behind his own eyelids the future rolled out like a long, deep rug, as real as the past or the present ever was. He knew for a certainty the exact look of amazement on Jeremy's face, the exact look of anxiety that would be in Shelley's eyes when they reached New York. And the flustered wedding that would embarrass him to pieces, and the careful little apartment where Shelley would always be waiting for him, like his own little piece of Sandhill transplanted, and asking what was wrong if he acted different from the husbands in the homemaking magazines but loving him anyway, in spite of all that. And then years on top of years, with Shelley growing older and smaller, looking the way her mother had, knowing by then all his habits and all his smallest secrets and at night, when his nightmares came, waking him and crooning to him until he drifted back to sleep, away from the thin, warm arms. And they might even have a baby, a boy with round blue eyes and small, struggling feet that she would cover in the night, crooning to him too. Ben Joe would watch, as he watched tonight, keeping guard and making up for all the hurried unthinking things that he had ever done. He shifted in his seat then, frowning; what future was ever a certainty? Who knew how many other people, myriads of people that he had met and loved before, might lie beneath the surface of the single smooth-faced person he loved now?

"Ticket, please," the conductor said.

Ben Joe handed him his ticket and then reached forward and gently took Shelley's ticket from her purse. The conductor tore one section off each, swaying above Ben Joe.

"Won't have to change," he said.

Ben Joe took his suit jacket off and folded it up on the seat beside him. He put his feet back on the opposite seat and slouched down as low as he could get, with his hands across his stomach, so that he could rest without going all the way to sleep. But his eyes kept wanting to sleep; he opened them wide and shook his mind awake. Shelley turned to face the aisle, and he fastened his eyes determinedly upon her, still keeping guard. His eyes drooped shut, and his head swayed back against the seat.

In that instant before sleep, with his mind loose and spinning, he saw Shelley and his son like two white dancing figures at the far end of his mind. They were suspended a minute, still and obedient, before his watching eyes and then they danced off again and he let them go; he knew he had to let them. One part of them was faraway and closed to him, as unreachable as his own sisters, as blank-faced as the white house he was born in. Even his wife and son were that way. Even Ben Joe Hawkes.

His head tipped sideways as he slept, with the yellow of his hair fluffed against the dusty plush. The conductor walked through, whistling, and the train went rattling along its tracks.